THE GAP INTO MADNESS

CHAOS AND ORDER

STEPHEN R. DONALDSON

BANTAM BOOKS

NEW YORK • TORONTO • LONDON • SYDNEY • AUCKLAND

THE GAP INTO MADNESS
CHAOS AND ORDER
A Bantam Book / July 1994

SPECTRA and the portrayal of a boxed "s" are trademarks of Bantam Books, a division of Bantam Doubleday Dell Publishing Group, Inc.

Book design by Diane Stevenson, Snap-Haus Graphics.

Library of Congress Cataloging-in-Publication Data
Donaldson, Stephen R.
The gap into madness : chaos and order / Stephen R. Donaldson.
p. cm.
ISBN 0-553-07179-3
I. Title.
PS3554.0469G34 1994
813'.54—dc20 94-5850
CIP

Published simultaneously in the United States and Canada

Bantam Books are published by Bantam Books, a division of Bantam Doubleday Dell Publishing Group, Inc. Its trademark, consisting of the words "Bantam Books" and the portrayal of a rooster, is Registered in U.S. Patent and Trademark Office and in other countries. Marca Registrada. Bantam Books, 1540 Broadway, New York, New York 10036.

PRINTED IN THE UNITED STATES OF AMERICA
BVG 0 9 8 7 6 5 4 3 2 1

TO

HOWARD MORHAIM:

a good friend,

a great agent,

and a hell of a Ping-Pong player.

MIN

Battered, weary to the bone, and profoundly baffled, Min Donner joined *Punisher* shortly after Warden Dios returned to UMCPHQ from Holt Fasner's Home Office. She hadn't slept since the day before her visit to Sixten Vertigus, hadn't eaten since her ride back to UMCPHQ from Suka Bator. A headache like a threat of concussion throbbed in her forehead. Occasionally her hearing buzzed like neural feedback.

She felt that her whole life was being rewritten around her; reinterpreted to mean something she hadn't chosen and couldn't understand.

Why was she *here*?

In some sense, Warden had answered that question. The last time she'd spoken to him, he'd told her, to her utter astonishment, *I have reason to think Morn Hyland may survive—* Even though he'd convinced her long ago that Morn was being abandoned, that he'd sold her body and soul, he'd said, *If she does, I want someone to make sure she stays alive, someone I can trust. That means you.* For that reason—apparently—he was sending Min away from her duties at UMCPHQ.

Nevertheless his reply explained nothing. All she really knew was that she was here now because he'd lied to her earlier; lied to her systematically and incessantly for months.

What in God's name was going on?

His signal of farewell reached her as she rode her personal shuttle out toward the gap range where *Punisher* had already turned and started preparations for an outbound acceleration; but she didn't answer it. She had nothing more to say to him. Instead of returning some vacant acknowledgment or salute, she replied to the questions of her crew by shaking her head. Let Warden Dios take her on faith, as she was required to take him. He'd left her no other way to express her galling confusion—or her blind, baffled hope.

With as much of her accustomed grim determination as she could muster, she put kazes and assassinations, treachery and intrigue behind her, and concentrated instead on the job ahead.

Her orders were superficially simple. She was instructed to take command of the first available UMCP warship—in this case, *Punisher*—and go immediately to the Com-Mine asteroid belt. Under cover of the belt, she was supposed to "watch for and respond to developments" from the direction of Thanatos Minor. In other words, to observe and presumably deal with the outcome of Angus Thermopyle's covert attack on Billingate.

That was plain enough. But why was it necessary? After all, at Fasner's orders human space along the Amnion frontier—especially in the broad vicinity of Com-Mine Station and the belt—was being webbed with the most intensive communications network ever deployed. Any decipherable information from the direction of Thanatos Minor would reach UMCPHQ in a matter of hours, whether she was present in the belt or not.

What kind of "developments" did Warden expect? Angus Thermopyle—Joshua—would either succeed or not. If he succeeded, Nick Succorso and the danger he represented would be finished. Min's suspicions of Milos Taverner would come to nothing. And Morn might—conceivably—survive. On the other hand, if Angus failed, everyone and everything would be lost. Morn would be just one more casualty.

Either way, there would be nothing for Min to do, except possibly pick up survivors—or warn off an Amnion pursuit. Com-Mine Station could have done that. *Punisher* herself, despite her battle-worn and depleted condition, could have done it. Min Donner was the UMCP Enforcement Division director: she belonged elsewhere. Back at UMCPHQ, rooting out kazes and traitors. Or even down on Suka Bator, helping Captain Vertigus prepare and present his Bill of Severance. She had no reason to be *here*.

No reason, that is, apart from Warden's desire to get her out of the way—to dissociate her from the fatal game he played with or against Holt Fasner. And his unexpected assertion that Morn might *get away alive*.

If she does, I want someone to make sure she stays alive—

Was that the truth? Or had Warden said it simply to ensure that she obeyed him?

She didn't know; couldn't know. But in the end, his orders were enough. She obeyed because she had sworn that she would.

Nevertheless she couldn't shake the dark feeling that she was doomed; that between them Warden Dios and Holt Fasner were about to cost her everything she had ever believed in or trusted.

At last her shuttle thunked against the docking port in *Punisher*'s side; grapples jerked home. Min nodded to her crew and stepped into the shuttle's airlock as if she didn't care whether she ever returned.

The bosun commanding the honor guard which greeted her inside the ship's personnel bay looked as worn-out and abused as she felt. Min winced inwardly at the sight: she hated seeing her people in such bad shape. However, she kept her chagrin and anger to herself while she returned the bosun's salute.

"Captain's apologies, Director Donner," he said. He sounded even worse than he looked—a young officer who had been under too much pressure for far too long. "He can't leave the bridge. We weren't expecting to head out—he hasn't had time to get ready—" The bosun caught himself, flushed like a boy. "You already know that. I'm sorry.

"Captain will see you whenever you want. I can take you to your quarters first."

Min had scanned *Punisher*'s reports before leaving UMCPHQ. The cruiser had just come home from a bitter struggle with fifteen or twenty illegal ships which had turned Valdor Industrial's distant binary solar system into a virtual war zone.

Because of the kind of mining, processing, and heavy manufacturing carried on by the station, Valdor and the traffic it serviced were rich with prizes. And like most binary systems this one was a maze of orbits—masses of rock revolving around each other in patterns so complex that they defied mapping by anything less than a megaCPU. The pirates were entrenched among the almost innumerable planets, planetoids, and moons cycling around the twinned stars called Greater and Lesser Massif-5.

Over a period of six months, the Scalpel-class cruiser had engaged in dozens of pitched battles, weeks of pursuit. And all to little avail. Two pirates had been destroyed, one captured. The rest had fought back with such concerted ferocity, or had fled with such intimate knowledge of the system's hiding places, that no mere cruiser could have hoped to deal with them all.

No wonder the bosun was exhausted. No wonder the faces of the honor guard ached with despair at the prospect of another mission. *Punisher* needed rest, *deserved* rest. The UMCP were spread too thin; would always be spread too thin, simply because the gap drive made available more space than any police force could control. Not for the first time, Min thought that as long as the threat of the Amnion endured—as long as forbidden space offered wealth in exchange for stolen resources—her people were doomed to fail.

As usual, she kept that idea to herself. Instead she told the bosun, "I'll go to the bridge." Then, before he could give any orders himself, she dismissed the honor guard. In general she disliked the formalities of her position; and in this particular case she actively hated wasting the energy of these weary men and women on ceremonial duties.

Momentarily flustered, the bosun began, "Director, Captain ordered—" But an instant later he swallowed his discomfiture. With a salute, he let the guard go. "This way, Director."

Min knew the way. On any ship the UMCP had commissioned, she could have found the bridge blindfolded. She let the bosun guide her, however. She'd already undercut him enough by dismissing his honor guard.

By the time she left the first lift and headed forward through the ship's core, she knew *Punisher* was in trouble. Because of the recent damage to her eardrums, she still couldn't hear clearly enough to pick up the cruiser's characteristic hums and whines. But she could feel centrifugal g through the soles of her boots; she could sense vibrations with the nerves of her skin. Subtle stresses reached her like undamped harmonics.

"You've got internal spin displacement," she commented to the bosun. "Bearings are grinding somewhere."

He gaped at her sidelong. "How—?" She was the ED director, however: he wasn't supposed to question her. With an effort, he mastered himself. "Forward," he answered. "We took a hit that knocked the whole core off true. But that's not all. We've got micro-leaks in some of the hydraulic systems. Several doors stick until the pressure rectifies. Half a dozen bulkheads don't quite seal. And we've been holed twice. We've kept integrity, but we lost the conduit to one of the sensor banks. Captain has men outside right now, trying to jury-rig leads before we go into tach. For the rest—

"Director, we haven't had time to trace those leaks or patch those holes. We've been at battle-stations for most of the past six months. And only a shipyard can fix internal spin."

The young officer sounded so raw that Min frowned to herself. "No criticism intended, bosun," she told him quietly. "It was just an observation."

He swallowed hard. "Thank you, Director." Until he blinked them clear, his eyes were perilously moist.

Punisher was desperate for rest.

Full of outraged protectiveness toward her people, Min thought harshly, Fuck you, Warden Dios, and the horse you rode in on. You had goddamn better know what you're doing.

The ship was a swarm of activity. Men and women hurried in all directions, rushing to and from the hundreds of duties required by a new mission. The few who recognized Min Donner paused to salute; but most of them were concentrating too hard—focused by fatigue and urgency—to notice her. Scalpel-class cruisers carried a crew of sixty-plus, but *Punisher* didn't have that many to work with. Her reports had cited four dead and eleven confined to their quarters or sickbay by injuries or battle-shock: fifteen crewmembers lost across the four watches. As soon as Min had received Warden's orders, she'd dispatched a provisioning shuttle to meet the cruiser; but in the time available *Punisher* couldn't be adequately resupplied. No wonder the captain was too busy to leave the bridge. Damaged, shorthanded, and ill equipped, his command was a poor candidate for any important assignment. *Punisher*'s best hope was that this mission proved to be as trivial as Min feared.

With one palm she stroked the butt of her handgun to steady herself as she accompanied the bosun forward.

Aside from weight, armament, and crew, one of the differences between a cruiser like *Punisher* and a destroyer like *Starmaster* was that *Punisher*'s bridge occupied a command module which could be detached from the main ship to function separately. If Captain Davies Hyland had had a vessel like this, he might well have survived *Starmaster*'s destruction; survived to keep his daughter out of Angus Thermopyle's hands. That was another detail for which Min blamed herself uselessly, despite the fact that she herself had approved *Starmaster*'s construction and had selected Davies Hyland as captain.

None of that showed on her face, however, as she went with the bosun—ahead of him now—through the aperture which linked the rest of the ship to the command module. She encountered *Punisher*'s captain and bridge crew with her features set in characteristic lines, stern and unreadable.

Almost instantly all movement on the bridge stopped: techs working on the screens and boards froze; the bridge crew—helm, targ, data and damage control, communications, engineering, scan—hesitated momentarily, their hands poised on their stations, their faces tense.

Their attention made her feel that she deserved her reputation as Warden Dios' executioner.

But then the captain, Dolph Ubikwe, broke the pause by swinging his g-seat toward Min. In a granite rumble, he said stolidly, "Director Donner. Welcome aboard."

At once the bridge crew rose to salute. The techs moved out of Min's way as if they believed—or wanted to believe—that they were beneath her notice.

There was no welcome in Captain Ubikwe's voice, however. It seemed to pulse from his chest like the cut of a subsonic drill. Even if Min had been deaf, she might have been able to hear him through the bones of her skull. Ensigns under his command often said that his voice could strip paint at twenty paces.

He was a large man—almost too large to pass the UMCP physicals—with a heavy mass of muscle hidden under his fat. Too much strain and too few showers caused his black skin to gleam in the featureless light. Red rimmed his bloodshot eyes; they appeared to bulge in their sockets. Fists as heavy as cudgels rested on the arms of his seat.

"Thank you, Captain." Min didn't expect welcome. "At ease," she told the bridge crew without shifting her gaze from Dolph Ubikwe. As they resumed their g-seats, she asked him, "How soon can you go into tach?"

His fists tightened slightly. "Depends on whether that's a request or an order. You order it and we're gone. All we need to know is where. But if it's a request"—he lifted his heavy shoulders—"we can probably be ready in three or four months."

In another place, at another time, Min might have smiled. She knew this man well. He had first come to her attention in the Academy ten years ago, when his air of insubordination and his poor grades had threatened to deny him a commission. She had overruled the Academy commander in person to make Dolph Ubikwe an ensign. Despite his resistance to discipline, which had showed in his sloppy classroom work as well as his excess weight, she had sensed a fettered emotional power in him, a charisma similar to Warden's. It might make him an effective leader—if he ever learned how and when to unleash it. Since then, he had vindicated her judgment by rising swiftly to the command of his own vessel. Under other circumstances, she would have had no qualms about using him to carry out Warden Dios' orders.

"If it were a request," she replied to his tight stare, "I wouldn't be here."

His mouth twisted. "Then perhaps the Enforcement Division director would condescend to tell us where we're going. It does make a difference, you know—heading, velocity, all those troublesome little gap details."

Now she did smile—a smile as humorless and bleak as an arctic wind. Instead of reacting to his sarcasm, she said simply, "The Com-Mine belt. Close to forbidden space."

At once a new tension crackled across the bridge. The data officer breathed, "Oh, Jesus," and the man on targ muttered, "Shit!" as if he thought Min wouldn't be able to hear him.

A muscle at the corner of Captain Ubikwe's mouth twitched like a flinch. "Now why in hell," he asked Min, "would we want to do a thing like that?"

She didn't snap at him. She also didn't drop his gaze. She could have made *Punisher* obey her blind—she could require unquestioning compliance from any ship in the fleet—but she had no intention of doing so. For one thing, she owed this ship an explanation. And for another, she knew that Dolph Ubikwe would serve her better if she let him be himself.

"Because," she answered, "there's been a covert UMCP attack on Thanatos Minor's bootleg shipyard. As I'm sure you remember, that planetoid is in forbidden space relatively near the Com-Mine belt. For the better part of a decade, illegals have been using the belt to cover them on their way to Thanatos Minor. The Amnion tolerate encroachment from that direction, if not from anywhere else.

"While we're standing here, the shipyard is under attack. I'm not prepared to discuss the nature of the operation here, except to repeat that it's covert. For now, the important point is this. There's going to be fallout.

"I have no idea what kind of fallout. I can't know. There may be survivors." *Morn Hyland may survive*— "Our people, or illegals on the run. Or there may be a full-scale Amnion retaliation."

Borrowing Warden's conviction because she had so little to spare of her own, Min concluded, "Whatever it is, we're going out there to deal with it."

The bridge crew stared at her. They had all turned their stations toward her. From their g-seats—command and communications in front of her, engineering and data off to the sides, scan and helm and targ apparently hanging upside down over her head—they studied her in fear or anger or despair or plain numb weariness, as if she had just instructed them to commit suicide.

For a moment Dolph lowered his eyes. When he raised them again, they seemed oddly naked, as if he had set aside some of his defenses. "Permission to speak frankly."

Just for an instant Min wondered whether she should refuse. Then she decided against it. By some standards, disagreements—not to mention hostility—between commanders was bad for discipline. On the other hand, *Punisher* was his ship: the tone which either inspired or dismayed his people was his to set, no matter what she did. She was willing to trust his instincts.

She nodded once. "Please."

He shifted his posture as if to launch his voice at her from a more stable platform. "Then let me just ask you, Director Donner," he said in a tone of raw outrage, "if you are out of your incorrigible mind. Don't you *read* reports anymore? Haven't you got a clue what we've just been through? Or maybe you think dodging matter cannon fire and asteroids alone for six months is some kind of holiday. You sent us out to Valdor to do a job which would have been too much for five cruisers. We're lucky to get home limping instead of just plain dead.

"We're shorthanded here. *That* was in the reports, too. Some of my people are drifting around Massif-5 in *caskets*. We've got holes and hydraulic leaks and a scan bank with no wiring. But never mind that. After what we've been through, we can stand a few minor inconveniences. We've got worse problems."

His voice was harsh enough to hurt Min's ears, but she knew from experience that he still had plenty of volume in reserve. For the sake of her personal comfort, she hoped that he didn't use it.

"Have you *listened* to this ship yet, Director Donner? Or have you forgotten what internal spin displacement sounds like? Have you forgotten what that kind of displacement can do to a warship? In case you've been spending too much time behind your desk and not enough on the firing line, let me remind you. If the bearings go and internal spin freezes before we can shut it down, centrifugal inertia is transferred to the whole ship. The whole ship starts to spin—which is a nightmare for scan and helm, never mind targ. *Punisher* isn't made for that kind of maneuver. And if we start to spin like that in the belt—or in combat—then you can kiss your hard ass good-bye along with all the rest of us.

"This is all crazy, Director Donner. How many warships have we got now? Fifty? Fifty cruisers, destroyers, gunboats, and full battlewagons? Do you expect me to believe they're *all* unavailable for this job? That not one of them is in reach?

"If that's true, let Com-Mine Station do it, whatever it turns out to be. Hell on ice, Director, they've got enough in-system firepower to slag *three* ships like this. Let them police their own goddamn belt for a few more hours.

"*We* are in no shape for this."

For reasons which she had never tried to explain to herself, Min often liked her officers best when they were angry at her. Perhaps because she understood Captain Ubikwe's indignation and approved of it, or perhaps because she was so angry herself that his ire formed a strange bond between them, she smiled back at his protest with something like affection.

"Are you done?"

"No." Her reaction disconcerted him, but he obviously didn't want to show it. "I'm going to say it all again, and this time I'm going to say it *loud*."

"That won't be necessary," she drawled. "You've made your point."

Captain Ubikwe studied her hard. After a moment he asked more quietly, "Then why do I get the impression you're not going to let us off the hook?"

"I'm not," she replied. "You *are* the only ship available. You're *here*. Sure, I could pull your replacement away from Valdor. I could signal a battlewagon from Betelgeuse Primary, or take a destroyer off frontier patrol. I could try Com-Mine and hope they do a good job.

"But none of them can get *me* out there."

The bridge received this in surprise, dull shock, or dread. The man on scan let a thin whistle through his teeth like an effort to ward away spooks. From above Min, the targ officer muttered again, "Shit."

Dolph flashed a look upward. "Glessen," he rasped at targ, as throaty as a combustion engine, "if you say that again in front of Director Donner, I'm going to take you out in the woodshed and cane you." None of his people laughed: they knew better. "In case you weren't paying attention, the director of the entire UMCP Enforcement Division, which we so proudly serve, has just announced that she's putting her life in our hands. She isn't sending us out to the belt to see what we're made of—she's going with us. Where I came from, we called that 'putting your money where your mouth is' "—abruptly he pounded a fist on his board—"and we *respected* it."

Suddenly everyone on the bridge seemed busy with one task or another. No one glanced at the Glessen as he murmured, "Aye, sir."

Glowering excessively, Captain Ubikwe returned his gaze to Min.

She suspected that he was swallowing a grin. His tone was grave, however, as he asked, "Are you telling me ED has a stake in this covert attack? I thought only DA did work like that."

Min didn't want to mention Morn Hyland. She wasn't ready to open that door into her own heart. Instead she said what she thought Warden Dios would have wanted her to say.

"No. I'm telling you the UMCP has a stake in it. Humankind has a stake in it."

The captain sighed. For a moment or two he peered at his hands while he considered the situation. Then he dropped his palms onto his thighs. "In that case—" With a heave, he rose from his g-seat and stepped aside. "As Enforcement Division director and the highest-ranking UMCP officer aboard, the bridge is yours. Take the command station. I'll evict targ—I can work from there until we're ready to go into tach."

Min made a quick gesture of refusal. "She's your ship, Captain. We're better off with you in command. And I need rest." In fact, she hadn't slept for two days; hadn't eaten in twelve hours. "If you'll detail someone to show me my quarters, I'll get out of your way."

A touch of gratitude softened Dolph's face as he sat down again, but he didn't thank her. Automatically he hit keys on his board, checked his readouts. "Bosun will take you." The young man still stood by the aperture. "If you've got more orders for us, better spell them out. We were busy before you came aboard, but we're a hell of a lot busier now."

Min didn't hesitate. "I want to be on the other side of the gap in two hours," she answered promptly, "and in the belt in three. That means you'll have to cut it fine."

She knew the risks. If internal spin froze in the gap, *Punisher* might resume tard half a hundred or half a million kilometers off course, tossed askew by the interplay between inertia and hysteresis—almost certainly a fatal problem near an asteroid belt. And if spin froze while *Punisher* navigated the belt, some kind of collision would be inevitable. To protect herself the ship would be forced to do almost everything without g. And she hadn't been designed for that. Her people weren't used to it.

But whatever Angus Thermopyle did or failed to do was out of Min's control, beyond her knowledge. Somewhere in the vicinity of Thanatos Minor, the chronometer was running on a deadline which she didn't know how to meet. That fact gave her a greater sense of urgency than Warden's actual orders did.

"As soon as we hit normal space," she continued, "I want communications on maximum gain across all bandwidths. If it's out there, I want us to hear it.

"Assuming we don't encounter any surprises, take us into the belt over on the far side—say, ten thousand k from the border—and find some rock we can hide behind, anything with enough magnetic resonance to confuse opposing scan. Wake me up when something happens or when we're in position, whichever comes first. I'll go into more detail then."

Captain Ubikwe lifted his head and bared his teeth, dismissing her. "Consider it done."

Softly but distinctly, so that everyone could hear her, she pronounced, "I do. Otherwise I would have taken command."

To spare him the distraction of answering her, she turned away and let the bosun guide her through the aperture back into the main body of the ship.

On the way to her assigned quarters, she made a mental note to consider transferring Dolph's targ officer to her personal staff. She wanted people around her who were willing to raise objections.

If Warden had let Min raise enough objections, she might not be here now, dragging a damaged ship with a battered crew across the gap on a mission which would turn out to be either so useless or so critical that it should have been given to someone else.

HASHI

Hashi Lebwohl was not a dishonest man. It was more accurate to say that he was a-honest. He liked facts; but truth had no moral imperatives for him, no positive—or negative—valuation. It had its uses, just as facts had theirs: it was a tool, more subtle than some, cruder than others.

It was a fact of his position as the UMCP director of Data Acquisition that he was expected to satisfy certain requirements. Warden Dios himself liked—indeed demanded—facts. For that reason among others, Hashi respected his director. Warden Dios made no effort to play fast and loose with reality, as the late and unlamented Godsen Frik had done endemically; or as even Min Donner did, in ways which she characteristically failed to recognize. Warden lived in the world of the real. Under no circumstances would Hashi Lebwohl have hesitated to do his job by supplying Warden with facts. And he was seldom reluctant to share his understanding of the way in which facts linked with each other to form more complex, less tangible realities.

On the other hand, he felt no obligation whatsoever to tell Warden Dios—or anyone else—the truth.

He received his first hints of what had happened on Thanatos Minor long before anyone else; quite some time before any other information reached UMCPHQ. Yet he withheld the facts for nearly an hour. And he kept the truth entirely to himself.

The hints went to him, first, because they were coded exclusively for his use, and second, because no one in UMCPHQ Communications knew that they had anything to do with Billingate or Joshua. They were nothing more or less than flares from DA operatives, and such messages were always routed straight to the DA director the moment they came in.

The earlier of these two signals was a cryptic transmission from Nick Succorso aboard *Captain's Fancy*. Initially Hashi didn't mention it because it contained no useful information. Later, however, he suppressed its contents because they disturbed him.

If you can get her, you bastard, Nick had sent, *you can have her. I don't care what happens to you. You need me, but you blew it. You deserve her.* Then, for no apparent reason, Nick had added, *Kazes are such fun, don't you think?*

A pox upon him, Hashi thought in bemusement. Curse his black soul. Her? Who? *You can have her.* Was he talking about Morn Hyland? Was he deranged enough to think that Joshua had been sent to Billingate to rescue her?

No. His reference to kazes contradicted that inference. Clearly he meant to warn or threaten Hashi concerning some woman who was involved with kazes. Yet that, too, made no sense. What could Nick possibly know about events here? How could he be aware that UMCPHQ and the GCES had suffered terrorist attacks?

Perhaps the "her" he referred to was *Captain's Fancy* herself? Perhaps he meant to suggest that if Hashi or the UMCP made any attempt to interfere with *Captain's Fancy* the frigate would become a kaze aimed at UMCPHQ?

You deserve her.

"Deserve" her?

You need me, but you blew it.

Apparently Nick Succorso had lost his mind.

At last Hashi put that flare aside. He found himself unable to divine Nick's intentions. And that troubled him. He disliked his sense of incomprehension.

The later signal was another matter.

No one outside his domain, and perhaps no more than three people within it, knew that Angus Thermopyle, Milos Taverner, and Nick Succorso were not the only men he'd helped send to Thanatos Minor; or that the fourth had been dispatched for precisely this reason, to observe events and report on them.

The transmission was from a purportedly legal merchanter called *Free Lunch*; "purportedly" because Hashi had equipped her with false id and records so that she could travel freely in human space while she nurtured her private reputation—also more putative than real—as an illegal. According to her captain, Darrin Scroyle, he and his ship had escaped the vicinity of Thanatos Minor just ahead of the shock wave of the planetoid's destruction.

So Joshua had succeeded. That was good, as far as it went. But Captain Scroyle's message conveyed other facts as well, the implications of which inspired Hashi's decision not to pass his information along to Warden Dios immediately. He needed time to consider the situation in the light shed by Captain Scroyle's revelations.

Under Hashi Lebwohl's absolute supervision, Data Acquisition employed agents and operatives of all kinds. Some were free-lance rogues, like Nick Succorso. Others were spies in the more traditional sense, hunting secrets under deep cover among the tenuous spiderweb societies of humankind's illegals.

And others were pure mercenaries. Unlike the rogues, they were men and women of peculiar honor, who gave their loyalty and their blood to anyone who paid their price. They could be trusted to do a specific job for a specific price, to question nothing, to complain about nothing—and to say nothing about what they'd done when the job was finished.

The only disadvantage to such an arrangement, from Hashi's point of view, was that the next job any given mercenary accepted might well be for some other employer; perhaps for one of humankind's enemies. As much as he could, he avoided this embarrassment by keeping his mercenaries busy—and by outbidding other employers.

Darrin Scroyle was a mercenary. He and *Free Lunch* were among the best of the breed: daring, heavily armed, and fast; capable of both recklessness and caution, as occasion warranted; willing for violence on almost any scale, and yet able to act with subtlety and discretion.

When *Free Lunch* reached human space and passed her message through a listening post by means of a gap courier drone to UMCPHQ, Hashi gave Captain Scroyle's report his full credence.

The gist was this. *Free Lunch* had left Billingate as soon as Captain Scroyle had become convinced that events were near their crisis. That was as Hashi had ordered: he didn't want *Free Lunch* caught up in whatever explosion resulted from Joshua's mission. But during her departure from Billingate's control space, *Free Lunch* had scanned the planetoid and its embattled ships with every instrument she had, and had observed several significant developments.

A team in EVA suits had emerged from docked *Trumpet* in order to sabotage Billingate communications. After that they had broken into the Amnion sector—and then escaped.

Captain's Fancy had destroyed *Tranquil Hegemony*, not by matter cannon or lasers, but by ramming—apparently to prevent the Amnion warship from killing the EVA team.

A shuttle had left the Amnion sector to be picked up by *Soar*.

And *Free Lunch* had seen *Calm Horizons* moving to intercept *Trumpet*'s escape, supported by a small flotilla of illegals sent out by Billingate.

That was bad enough; full of surprises and unexplained possibilities. But there was worse.

Before their departure, Captain Scroyle and his people had spent as much time as they could around the installation, studying scan and communications, listening to rumors, looking for information. They had witnessed *Captain's Fancy*'s arrival from the direction of Enablement Station, harried by warships. They had seen Captain Succorso's ship launch an ejection pod which had veered away from *Tranquil Hegemony* in order to be intercepted by *Soar*. And they had heard stories—

The story that the Amnion had revoked Captain Succorso's credit on Billingate.

The story that he, the Amnion, and the Bill were locked in a three-way conflict over the contents of the ejection pod.

The story that Captain Succorso had spent time together in a bar with Captain Thermopyle and his second from *Trumpet*.

The story that the Bill's guards had been attacked and the contents of the pod stolen.

The story that *Soar*'s captain, a woman named Sorus Chatelaine, had a mutagen immunity drug for sale.

The story that Captain Succorso had bartered one of his own people, a woman, to the Amnion in order to obtain—so the rumor went—*Captain's Fancy*'s freedom to leave Billingate.

Taken all at once, such information might have given Godsen Frik the vapors with a vengeance—the worst case of collywobbles in his adult life. It had a different effect on Hashi Lebwohl, however. In a sense, he lived for such crises: oblique events with disturbing implications which called for all the cunning, misdirection, and initiative he could supply. The fact that he took nearly an hour to consider the situation before sharing what he knew—or some of what he knew—didn't mean that he was frightened. It simply meant that he wanted to give his best attention to this particular conundrum.

Soar and *Captain's Fancy*. *Trumpet* and *Calm Horizons*. *Tranquil Hegemony* and an Amnion shuttle.

Joshua, Nick Succorso, the Bill, Milos Taverner, Sorus Chatelaine, the Amnion. Not to mention Morn Hyland, who must have played some crucial part in Nick's decision to visit Enablement, and who therefore simply could not be irrelevant to Nick's conflict with the Amnion—or with the Bill.

If you can get her, you bastard, you can have her.

Morn?

No: not possible.

There were too many players; too many pieces moving across the game board. In particular Hashi wanted to know more about this Captain Chatelaine and her ship. Was she Nick's "her"? Could the rumors about her conceivably be true? If they were, where could she have obtained a mutagen immunity drug, except from Nick himself? Then why would he have given it to her?

But even while he accessed his personal board to call up whatever information Data Storage had on Sorus Chatelaine and *Soar*, Hashi considered deeper possibilities.

He was by no means an unintuitive man. And he knew himself well. He recognized from experience that the issues which first focused his attention when he studied a problem often proved to be of secondary importance. Those issues frequently served as mere distractions for his conscious mind so that other parts of him could work more efficiently. Therefore he didn't waste his time wondering why Nick's message continued to nag at him, suggesting doubts he could hardly name. Nor did he worry about how many of Nick's intentions were contained or concealed in the rumors Darrin Scroyle reported. Instead he concentrated deliberately on gleaning data; deflecting himself from the questions he most needed to answer.

Unfortunately that took time. Under the circumstances, he wasn't sure he could afford it.

Well, he required the time. Therefore he would afford it as best he could.

You deserve her.

While Data Storage spun retrieval routines over its mountains of information, he keyed his intercom and told DA Processing—which was what he called his center of operations—that he wanted to see Lane Harbinger. "At once," he added laconically. "Right now. Five minutes ago."

A tech replied, "Yes, sir," and went to work.

Lane was the granddaughter of the famous explorer/scientist Malcolm Harbinger, but that meant nothing to Hashi. Its only significance was that she'd come by her meticulousness honestly. He wanted to see her because she was the hardware tech he'd assigned to help ED Chief of Security Mandich investigate Godsen's murder.

He could not have said what connection he imagined or hoped to find between Captain Scroyle's report and Godsen's murder. He was simply distracting himself; allowing his intuition the time and privacy it needed in order to function. Preserving himself in that fertile state of mind in which the least likely connections might be discovered.

Lane Harbinger responded to his summons promptly enough. When his intercom chimed to announce her, he adjusted his glasses by sliding them even farther down his thin nose, rumpled his hair, and verified that his lab coat hung crookedly from his shoulders. Then he told the data tech who served as his receptionist to let Lane in.

She was a small, hyperactive woman who might have appeared frail if she'd ever slowed down. Like any number of other people who worked for Data Acquisitions, she was addicted to nic, hype, caffeine, and several other common stimulants; but as far as Hashi could tell these drugs had a calming effect on her organic tension. He assumed that her meticulousness was yet another kind of drug; a way of compensating for internal pressures which would have made her useless otherwise.

Presumably she was also a woman who talked incessantly. She knew better than to do that with him, however.

"You wanted to see me," she said at once as if the words were the merest snippet of a diatribe which had already been going on inside her for some time.

Hashi gazed over his glasses at her and smiled kindly. "Yes, Lane. Thank you for coming." He didn't ask her to sit down: he knew that she needed movement in order to concentrate. Even her most precise labwork was done to the accompaniment of a whole host of extraneous tics and gestures, as well as through a cloud of smoke. So he let her light a nic and pace back and forth in front of his desk while she waited for him to go on.

"I wanted to know," he said, peering at her through the haze she generated, "how your investigation is going. Have you learned anything about the kaze who brought about our Godsen's untimely demise?"

"Too soon to be sure," she retorted like a rushing stream caught behind a check-dam of will.

"Don't worry about being sure," he countered amiably. "Just tell me where you are right now."

"Fine. Right now." She didn't look at him as she paced. Her eyes roamed his walls as if they were the limits, not of this office, but of her knowledge. "It's a good thing you sent me over there. ED Security is motivated as all hell, and careful as they know how, but they don't understand what 'careful' really means. Let them stick to shooting people. They shouldn't be involved in this kind of investigation. Five minutes without me, and they would have made the job impossible.

"It could have been impossible anyway. That wasn't a big bomb, they never are, there's only so much space you can spare inside a torso, even if you only expect your kaze to be able to function for a few hours, but it was high brisance, I mean *high*. No particular reason why it shouldn't have reduced his id tag and credentials to particles so small even we couldn't find them, never mind the embedded chips themselves.

"But Frik's secretary knows more than she thinks she knows." In full spate the tech's tone became less hostile; or perhaps simply less brittle. "Ask her the right questions, and you find out that after she did her"—Lane sneered the words as if they were beneath contempt—" 'routine verification' on this kaze, he didn't put his id tag back around his neck. He didn't clip his communications credentials back onto his breast pocket, which is so normal around here we don't even notice it anymore, hell, I'm doing it myself"—she glanced down at the DA card clipped to her labsuit—"you're the only one who gets away without doing it. But he didn't do that.

"He shoved them both into his thigh pocket, the right one, according to Frik's secretary. Which is not the kind of thing you do if you're trying to plant evidence when you blow yourself up, because the bomb is still going to reduce everything to smears and scrap. But it *is* the kind of thing you do if you're new at this and you know you're going to die and acting normal in secure areas isn't second nature. So his id tag and credentials were just that much farther away from the center of the blast.

"I found part of one of the chips."

Hashi blinked his interest and approval without interrupting.

"You know how we do this kind of search." As soon as she finished her first nic, she lit a second. "Vacuum-seal the room and go over it with a resonating laser. Map the resonance and generate a computer simulation, which helps narrow the search. When we chart the expansion vectors, we can tell where the kaze's residue is most likely to be. Those areas we study one micron at a time with fluorochromatography. When you're operating on that scale, even a small part of a SOD-CMOS chip emits like a star."

He did indeed know all this; but he let Lane talk. She was distracting him nicely.

"As I say, I got one. Two, actually, but one was driven into the floor so hard it crumbled when I tried to extract it. Even I can't work with that kind of molecular powder. So there's just one.

"I don't know much about it yet. We can assume its data is still intact, that's exactly what this kind of chip is good for, but I haven't found a way to extract it yet. SOD-CMOS chips add state when power is applied to the source and drain. They read back by reversing the current. But to do that you have to *have* a source and drain. This particular piece of chip doesn't include those conveniences."

Another nic.

"But I can tell you one thing about it. It's ours."

Fascinated as much by her manner as by her explanation, Hashi asked, "How do you know?"

"By its particular production quality. Legally, nobody but us is allowed to make them, that's part of the datacore law. Of course, we don't actually manufacture them ourselves, the law simply gives us the power to license their manufacture, but we've only granted one license, Anodyne Systems"—she didn't need to mention that Anodyne Systems was a wholly owned subsidiary of the UMC—"and they supply us exclusively. In fact, everybody in Anodyne Systems actually works for us. The whole company is really just a fiction, a way for the UMC to keep a hand in what we're doing, and for us to get SOD-CMOS chips without having to find room for an entire production plant in our budget.

"There's only one way to make a SOD-CMOS chip. On paper, they should all be identical, no matter who produces them. But it doesn't work that way in practice. Quality varies inversely with scale. The more you make, the more impurities creep in—human error, if not plain entropy. The less you make, the fewer the impurities. Unless you're incompetent, in which case I wouldn't expect the chip to work anyway."

"So if a chip were manufactured illegally," Hashi put in, "you would expect it to be purer than ours."

Lane nodded without breaking stride. "*This* chip came from Anodyne Systems. It's indistinguishable from the chips in our most recent consignment, which we picked up and brought here six days ago."

"In other words," he concluded for her, "we have a traitor on our hands."

She corrected him. "A traitor or a black market. Or simple bribery. Here or in Anodyne Systems."

"Quite right. Thank you." He beamed his appreciation. Meticulousness was a rare and treasurable quality. "A traitor, a black market, or bribery. Here or over there." After a moment, he added, "It fits, you know."

She paused in her pacing long enough to look momentarily breakable. "Fits?"

"It's consistent," he explained casually, "with the fact that our kaze arrived on the shuttle from Suka Bator. He had already been cleared by GCES Security. That detail enabled him to succeed here. If he had come from any other port, the estimable Min Donner's people would have scrutinized him more closely—and then he might not have been allowed to pass."

Lane had resumed moving. "But I still don't see—"

"It is quite simple," Hashi replied without impatience. He enjoyed his own explanations. "Min Donner's people were not negligent. They had reason to rely on GCES Security. Routine precautions around Suka Bator are as stringent as ours at the best of times. And at present, so soon after a similar attack on Captain Sixten Vertigus in his own office, those precautions were at their tightest. Surely no threat would be allowed to pass. Our kaze would have presented little danger if he had not already been verified —in a sense, legitimized—by GCES Security.

"But how was that legitimacy achieved? Was GCES Security negligent? Under these circumstances, I think not. Therefore our kaze's various credentials must have been impeccable."

The smoking tech couldn't keep silent. "All right, I get it. Whoever sent the kaze didn't just have access to our SOD-CMOS chips. He also had access to GCES Security codes, not to mention ours. So he must be GCES personnel. Or UMCP."

"Or UMC," Hashi added. "They own Anodyne Systems."

"Or UMC," she agreed.

"But we can dismiss the GCES," he continued. "Unlike the United Mining Companies and the United Mining Companies Police, our illustrious Council has no access to Anodyne Systems.

"Conversely, of course, the Dragon in his den holds enough votes to obtain whatever he desires from the GCES."

Lane considered this for a moment, then nodded through a gust of smoke. When Hashi didn't go on, she asked, "So where does that leave us?"

"My dear Lane"—he spread his hands—"it leaves us precisely where we are. You have gleaned a certain fact. Each fact is a step, and enough steps make a road. We are one step farther along our road.

"I am eager to see if you will be able to provide us with another fact, or perhaps two."

She didn't hesitate. "I'm on it," she announced brusquely as she turned for the door.

"I am sure you are," Hashi said to her departing back. "Thank you."

For a useful distraction, he added while the door closed. And for some intriguing possibilities.

Sitting nearly motionless at his desk, he considered them.

If the list of suspects in Godsen's premature effacement included only those men and women directly or indirectly involved in the manufacture and transshipment of SOD-CMOS chips, that was daunting enough. The prospect became actively appalling if the list were expanded to name every minion who might have been able to draw on Holt Fasner's clout with the GCES.

Hashi was neither daunted nor appalled, however. Such lists were self-winnowing, in his experience. Each new fact uncovered by Lane Harbinger, or by ED Security, would narrow the range of suspects. No, his thoughts ran in other channels.

What, he wondered, would be the Dragon's reaction to the provocative information that Nick Succorso had brought some sort of cargo or prize back from Enablement Station? Hashi could hardly guess what it might have been—but he could estimate its value. It was so precious that the Bill and the Amnion were willing to fight over it; so precious that Captain Succorso was willing to sell one of his own people in order to buy it back. So precious that someone would risk stealing it from such formidable adversaries.

The Dragon, Hashi concluded, would want that cargo or prize for himself.

Hints and possibilities. He needed more than that.

Kazes are such fun, don't you think?

If you can get her, you bastard, you can have her. You deserve her.

What was the malign and unreliable Captain Succorso talking about?

For a moment he scrutinized his covert mind, probing it for answers. But the intuitive side of his intelligence wasn't yet ready to speak. Perhaps it still lacked sufficient data.

He consulted his chronometer; he considered the hazards involved in contacting Warden Dios and saying, I have received some information concerning events on Thanatos Minor, but I decided to withhold it from you temporarily. Then he shrugged. Some processes could not be rushed.

Whistling tunelessly through his bad teeth, he keyed his intercom again and issued another summons.

This time he was less peremptory; more subtle. He meant to speak to Koina Hannish, but he had no wish to betray the nature of his connection with her. So he instructed Processing to seed Protocol's routine data stream with an update on one innocuous subject or another—an update which would catch her eye because it contained a preagreed combination of words. Then he set himself to wait.

Unfortunately waiting didn't constitute distraction.

You deserve her? he inquired. Was it possible that Nick meant Morn Hyland?

How could that be? Hadn't Warden Dios explicitly refused—over Min Donner's and Godsen Frik's strenuous objections—to allow any provision for her rescue to be written into Joshua's programming? Whatever Joshua did to Thanatos Minor—and, not incidentally, to Nick Succorso—his actions would not include any effort to procure Ensign Hyland's survival. Therefore she was dead. She wasn't aboard *Trumpet*, and only *Trumpet* could hope to escape the destruction of Billingate.

It followed impeccably that Morn Hyland was irrelevant.

Yet the DA director found that he couldn't let the matter rest there. It reminded him of other questions which he hadn't been able to answer.

You need me, but you blew it.

One was this: Why had Warden Dios decided to sacrifice Ensign Hyland? The UMCP director had no history of such decisions. Indeed, he had often displayed a distressing resemblance to Min Donner in situations involving loyalty toward his subordinate personnel. Hashi had presented arguments which he considered convincing; but he was under no illusions about Warden's ability to ignore those reasons, if he chose. So why had the director made such an atypical decision?

Had he acceded to Hashi's reasons because he had already met similar arguments from Holt Fasner—or perhaps even been given direct orders?

Certainly a living Morn Hyland represented a palpable threat to the UMC CEO. To that extent, she might conceivably constitute a kaze of a peculiar kind. Within her she carried information which was undeniably explosive.

As Hashi had determined during his interrogation of Angus Thermopyle, she could testify that Com-Mine Security bore no fault for *Starmaster*'s death. And she could testify that Angus was guiltless of the crime for which he'd been arrested and convicted. However, the still-recent passage of the Preempt Act had been founded squarely on those two accusations: that Com-Mine Security had performed or permitted sabotage against *Starmaster;* and that Security had conspired with Captain Thermopyle to steal Station supplies.

The Preempt Act was the capstone of Holt Fasner's ambitions for the UMCP. If the perceived reasons for the Act's passage were revealed as inaccurate, or if DA's hand in the fabrication of those reasons were exposed, the Act itself might be reconsidered. The web of power which Fasner had so carefully woven for his personal cops might begin to unravel.

Hashi didn't doubt that Holt Fasner wanted Morn Hyland dead.

So was Warden Dios simply following the Dragon's instructions? Or was he playing some deeper game?

This brought Hashi to another question which had troubled him for some time.

Why had Warden Dios insisted on "briefing" Joshua alone immediately prior to *Trumpet*'s departure? Joshua was nothing more than a welded cyborg: a piece of equipment in human form. Since when did the director of the United Mining Companies Police waste his time "briefing" pieces of equipment?

I don't care what happens to you.

Hashi couldn't persuade himself to stop worrying about Nick Succorso's flare.

His chronometer continued to tick threateningly onward. The longer he waited, the harder-pressed he would be to account for his delay. And that in turn conveyed other dangers. Under pressure he might find it necessary to admit his dealings with Captain Scroyle and *Free Lunch*. If those dealings became, in a manner of speaking, "public" between him and his director, he might find his freedom to offer Captain Scroyle new contracts restricted. In addition every passing minute increased the chance that *Free Lunch* might be forced to move beyond reach of the nearest listening post, which would prevent her from receiving any new offers—at least temporarily. Hashi would lose his opportunity to put Captain Scroyle back to work.

He permitted himself an intimate sigh of relief when his intercom chimed to inform him that Koina Hannish wished to see him.

He didn't admit her right away, however. Instead he took a moment to calm himself so that he could be sure none of his private urgency showed. Only when he was certain that he would give nothing away did he tell his receptionist to let the new UMCP Director of Protocol in.

As befitted a PR director, Koina Hannish lived on the opposite end of the emotive spectrum from Lane Harbinger. Where Lane emitted tension like a shout, Koina breathed an air of quiet confidence. Immaculately tailored and tended, she conveyed almost by reflex the impression that every word she spoke must be true, by virtue of the simple fact that it came from her mouth. Hashi supposed that most men would have called her beautiful. Under any circumstances he could imagine, she would make a better PR director than fulsome, false Godsen Frik ever had. She would have risen to her present position long ago if Godsen hadn't held the job on Holt Fasner's authority.

"I don't like this, Director," she said frankly as soon as the office door was closed and sealed. "It doesn't feel right."

Hashi smiled benignly. "Director yourself, Koina Hannish. I will not waste your time by thanking you for this visit. You are desperately busy, I know. What is it that 'doesn't feel right' to you?"

She settled herself upright in a chair across the desk from him before she answered, "Seeing you like this. Talking to you. Working for you."

"My dear Koina—" As an affectation, Hashi pushed his glasses up on his nose. They were nearly opaque with smears and scratches: he knew from careful study that they made him look like he was going blind. But he didn't need them; his vision was fine without refractive help. He had trained himself long ago to see past them. "We have worked together for years. You have never expressed disaffection for our relationship before."

"I know." A small frown tightened her brows over the bridge of her nose. "I've never felt this way before—not until I got your summons. I've been asking myself why. I think it's because until today my nominal boss was Godsen Frik. Just between us, I always considered him 'slime,' to use one of his words. He symbolized everything that's wrong with this organization—by which I mean Holt Fasner. Working for you seemed—well, more honorable than working for him. Even though I was stuck in Protocol, I was able to help the real job of the UMCP go ahead with as little interference from him as possible.

"But I began to have my doubts after I saw the tapes of the director's video conference with the GCES—was it just yesterday? You did most of the talking, Godsen wasn't on camera at all, but I thought I heard his voice every time you opened your mouth." A timbre of anger which Koina made no effort to conceal roughened her tone. "Hearing you explain how you sold that ensign, Morn Hyland, so your Nick Succorso could use her any way he wanted to, I felt like I was witnessing the collapse of everything we're supposed to stand for.

"When the director offered me this job, I wanted to turn it down.

"But that was before he talked to me," she went on quickly. "I'd never had a private conversation with him before. Until then, I hadn't felt how much"—she groped for the right word—"how much *conviction* he conveys. And he gave me the cleanest mandate I've ever had. Cleaner than anything Godsen Frik ever touched, cleaner than working for you. If you can believe him, he wants me to do my job *right*."

She made a small, vexed gesture, as if she were frustrated by the inadequacies of her account. "I can't explain it any better than that. All of a sudden," she concluded straight into Hashi's gaze, "reporting to you behind his back seems—disloyal."

"That is his great gift," the DA director responded equably, "his ability to inspire loyalty. If you fear that you alone are vulnerable to such suasion, only look at Min Donner." He was engaged in a test of suasion himself; a challenge he relished. "But permit me to offer another consideration which you may have missed, and to tell you a fact which you could not have known.

"The consideration is this. I, too, have felt the force of Warden Dios' charisma. I, too, find myself drawn to loyalty." This was not a notably honest assertion. Nevertheless it contained an adequate level of factual accuracy. "I ask you to serve me in Protocol, not to undermine my director in any way, but to help me ensure that my own service is as apt as possible.

"As for the fact," he continued so that she wouldn't question what he'd just said, "it is simply that our disloyal Godsen was present when the director and I addressed the GCES. If you had seen his face, you would, I believe, have found his consternation delicious. I hardly need inform you that he had no scruples concerning the use made of Ensign Hyland. In his master's name, however, he had every conceivable scruple concerning the revelation of that use. In no other way could the director have so plainly declared his independence of the great worm."

There Hashi stopped. He didn't need to add, And I with him. Koina had already demonstrated her grasp on the importance of Hashi Lebwohl's role in the director's video conference.

"I see." Her frown seemed to turn inward as she scrutinized this information. "Thanks for pointing that out. I should have caught the distinction myself. But I was so horrified by what I was hearing, I didn't explore all the implications."

Still smiling, Hashi let his glasses slide down to their more familiar position on his nose. If he'd been a man who kept score, he would have added several points to his column.

With a small shake and a deliberate smoothing of her forehead, Koina brought herself back to the present. "Why did you send for me?" Only a hint of reserve in her tone suggested that she still held any doubts about her relationship with the DA director. "Is there something you want me to do?"

Hashi spread his hands like a man whose soul was as open as his palms. "I seek only information. My appetite for facts is bottomless, as you know. I am something of a dragon myself in that regard." He enjoyed joking about the truth. "One of my questions you have already answered. I wished to know the nature of your 'mandate' as Director of Protocol. All well and good. I approve unqualifiedly. I hope only that you are willing to tell me what transpires in your department.

"What actions has the GCES taken? What requests have been made of Protocol? What are the most pressing matters awaiting your attention?" Deliberately he spoke to her, not as his agent, but as his equal. "Will you tell me?"

She held his gaze. "If you'll tell me why you're asking. I mean, aside from your 'bottomless appetite for facts.' "

On the spur of the moment, Hashi decided that he'd been amiable long enough. He permitted himself a sigh. With the air of a man whose patience was running out, he replied, "Koina, you disappoint me. Have you forgotten that Godsen was murdered, or that the venerable Captain Sixten Vertigus has been attacked? On whom do you think the primary responsibility for the investigation of these crimes devolves? Oh, on Enforcement Division Security, naturally. But Min Donner's otherwise admirable cadres are as ham-fisted as they are diligent. The true work of investigation must be done by Data Acquisition." The natural wheeze of his voice took on a waspish buzz. "I seek *clues*, Director Hannish. For that reason, your own labors, like any other activity here or on Suka Bator, are of signal interest to me.

"If you doubt me, ask Chief of Security Mandich what he has learned concerning Godsen's murder which my people did not uncover for him."

As he spoke, a slight flush came and went on her cheekbones. "I'm sorry," she murmured. "I take your point. I think I do know something that you might find useful."

More briskly, she continued, "You can guess most of what I've been dealing with. Maxim Igensard has been burning the channels with demands. So have Sigurd Carsin and Vest Martingale. Every five minutes I get another abject appeal from Abrim Len.

"I can't answer any of them right now. I want to tell them the truth, and I don't know what that is, any more than I did yesterday. But Data

Storage is working on it. In a few hours, I should have every file that isn't locked away under the director's personal clearance on my desk."

Her gaze said clearly, Even yours, Director Lebwohl.

This didn't trouble Hashi, however. He'd always been chary of trusting his work to Data Storage. Most of it was still held by Processing—and so walled around with clearance protocols and access routines that it was well-nigh unreachable.

"On top of that," Koina said, "Chief Mandich wants me to deal with Suka Bator for him. Ever since they let that second kaze through, he and GCES Security can't seem to talk to each other without yelling.

"But there is"—she slowed thoughtfully—"one other matter. I've received a flare from Captain Vertigus. Personal and urgent. He wanted to warn me"—she swallowed a moment of discomfort—"that I might be next."

Almost involuntarily, Hashi raised his eyebrows. " 'Next'?"

Koina didn't hesitate. "Next to be attacked."

"Ah." The DA director felt suddenly that he had stepped off the surface of reality into the near-infinite realm of subatomic possibilities. "And how does he account for his apprehension?"

"He says," she answered with admirable firmness, "that the next time the GCES meets—which should be in about thirty-six hours, unless President Len panics again—he's going to introduce a Bill of Severance to take the UMCP away from the UMC. He wants to make us a branch of the Council. He thinks he was attacked to try to stop him. And he thinks Godsen was killed because whoever sent those kazes assumed PR must be working with him. Which makes me a logical target. If he's right.

"He probably shouldn't have told me," Koina admitted. "I don't know what our position is going to be, but I'm afraid the director will have to fight him. Holt Fasner won't let us act like we want to be out from under his thumb. So Captain Vertigus," she remarked dryly, "has handed me an interesting problem in ethics. Do I tell the director? How much do I tell him?

"But the captain knows all that," she concluded. "He simply can't stand to let me be a target without warning me."

Hashi blinked at her as if he were stunned.

A Bill of Severance. Attacked to try to stop him.

Kazes are such fun, don't you think?

The thought gave him the sensation that he was caught in a swirl of quarks and mesons; bits of logic so minuscule that they could scarcely be detected, and yet so necessary that palpable facts were meaningless without them. The coreolus filled him with a sense of exhilaration that was indistinguishable from terror—an emotional mix which he found more stimulating, desirable, and addictive than pseudoendorphins or raw cat.

A Bill of Severance, forsooth! Now, where did venerable, no, antique, *ancient* Captain Sixten Vertigus come by the sheer audacity to propose an idea like that? The man was barely sapient.

No matter. Treasuring his excitement, Hashi kept it to himself.

"How extraordinarily conscientious of him," he replied to Koina's questioning gaze. "I understand his dilemma—and yours, my dear Koina. If I were to presume to advise you, I would suggest that this matter should be put before the director immediately. Sooner." Which might serve to distract Warden Dios from Hashi's delay on other subjects. And the outcome might prove entirely fascinating. What would Warden do when he learned of Captain Vertigus' intentions? "His response may surprise you."

Koina studied the DA director, frowning as if she couldn't quite believe what she heard. Then, abruptly, she rose from her seat. Putting him to the test before he could change his mind, she said, "Thank you, Director Lebwohl. I'll do that."

Without waiting for an answer, she set her hand on the door and signaled the tech outside to unseal it.

Hashi was in a hurry now. To complete her departure, he protested, "No, Director Hannish. *I* thank *you*."

But his attention was already elsewhere; on his hands as they worked his board, nimbly running commands to call up the results of his retrieval request from Data Storage.

You deserve her.

Nick Succorso, he half sang, half whistled through his teeth. Where are you? What are you doing? What do you *mean*?

He was as happy as he'd ever been.

Which was more plausible? That Nick had access to knowledge concerning events on Earth? Or that he'd gained an understanding of Morn's usefulness as an informational kaze aimed at the UMCP? The latter, obviously. Yet Hashi found the idea difficult to credit. He couldn't imagine how Nick—or Morn herself—might have become aware that what she knew was explosive.

Surely the most plausible interpretation available was that when Nick said "her" he meant Sorus Chatelaine.

What is the *connection*?

Data Storage supplied it—although Hashi couldn't have said precisely what "it" was. A coincidence; a hint, perhaps; the cornerstone of a fact: nothing more. Nevertheless he treasured it as if it were essential to his exhilaration.

Hard information on *Soar* and her captain, Sorus Chatelaine, was scant. Like most illegals, she was purportedly a freighter—in her case, a gap-capable orehauler. Ship id showed that she'd been built and registered legally out of Betelgeuse Primary; armed heavily enough to defend herself, but not enough to make her an effective pirate. Except for her recent appearance at Thanatos Minor, no positive evidence indicated that she was illegal. The marks against her were negative in kind.

According to Data Storage, *Soar* had done virtually no logged and certified work in the past five years. Before that, she'd been steadily employed by various mining concerns and stations: after that, nothing. And she'd been identified in the vicinity of one or two raids under circumstances which made it unclear whether or not she'd been involved.

Data on Sorus Chatelaine was even thinner. After graduating with a master's license from the space academy on Aleph Green, she'd served aboard several different gap ships for a few years; then she'd disappeared when her vessel was apparently destroyed by an illegal. Missing and presumed dead: no confirmation. That was the last entry in her id file.

But it wasn't the last entry to appear on Hashi's readout.

Somewhere in the bowels of Data Storage, an enterprising tech had engaged in some imaginative cross-referencing, and had appended the results to *Soar*'s file.

As a starting point, the tech noted that *Soar*'s emission signature and scan profile as recorded by ships sighting her during the past five years diverged significantly from the characteristics defined by the shipyard which built her. Indeed, both signature and profile bore a much closer resemblance to those of one particular illegal vessel which had been presumed lost nearly ten years ago. Not a definitive resemblance, but an intriguing one. Enough of a resemblance to suggest that the illegal vessel, after a five-year hiatus, had regained her freedom to travel in human space by attacking the original *Soar* and taking on her identity—in essence, by stealing her datacore.

The name of that illegal vessel had been *Gutbuster*.

And *Gutbuster*'s file held a mine of potential connections.

For example, Hashi read, *Gutbuster* was the vessel which had killed the original *Captain's Fancy*, leaving only one survivor aboard, her cabin boy, Nick Succorso.

And she was the vessel which had once damaged the UMCP cruiser

Intransigent, commanded by Captain Davies Hyland. His wife, Bryony Hyland, Morn's mother, had died in the fight.

According to *Intransigent*'s records, *Gutbuster* carried super-light proton cannon. That was almost unprecedented for an illegal vessel: the expense of such guns, both in credit and in power consumption, was prohibitive.

On the other hand, she had no gap capability.

Which explained her five-year hiatus from action. In order to survive, she'd limped to a bootleg shipyard—or perhaps into forbidden space—to retrofit a gap drive.

That, in turn, accounted for the subtle, but unquestionable discrepancies between *Gutbuster*'s known and *Soar*'s recorded emission signatures and scan profiles.

Hashi was tempted to postpone other, more urgent matters for a while: just long enough to issue a commendation for the tech who'd compiled this report. He had no time for such luxuries, however. Strange and unquantifiable ideas spun through his head as if they could hardly be contained by the mere bones of his skull or the walls of his office. If the facts and suggestions he'd gleaned were as evanescent as quarks—microevents with little more than a theoretical reality—they nevertheless partook of subatomic energies potent enough to produce thermonuclear detonations and core meltdowns.

Caught in a whirl of exhilaration and terror, he snatched off his glasses and covered his eyes with his hands, not to prevent vision from entering in, but rather to keep an electron storm of potentialities from escaping.

Kazes had attacked the GCES and UMCPHQ, using legitimate id made from UMCP SOD-CMOS chips.

Kazes are such fun, don't you think?

Captain Vertigus proposed to introduce a Bill of Severance. He feared threats against the UMCP Director of Protocol.

Morn Hyland and Nick Succorso had in common a connection with *Soar* née *Gutbuster*—a vessel which just happened to be present at Thanatos Minor when both they and Joshua arrived there. A vessel which Morn had good reason to hate, but to which Nick might be linked by bonds of another kind.

And Hashi was under no illusions about the nature of the relationship between Nick and Morn. Whatever she may have felt toward him, he was capable of nothing but exploitation.

You deserve her.

But that wasn't all. Certainly not.

Darrin Scroyle's people had heard rumors of an antimutagen for sale from *Soar*'s captain, Sorus Chatelaine.

Nick was presumably the only man in that quadrant of space with a mutagen immunity drug in his possession—the only man from whom Sorus Chatelaine might have obtained an antimutagen.

He'd been seen talking to Joshua and Milos Taverner.

And he'd brought a cargo of some kind from Enablement Station: a cargo which he'd sent by ejection pod to Billingate to prevent the Amnion from reclaiming it: a cargo which someone had subsequently stolen.

Later Nick was rumored to have sold one of his people to the alien sector on Thanatos Minor. Then that sector had been raided by an EVA team from *Trumpet*. *Captain's Fancy* had rammed an Amnion warship and died in order to keep the raiding team alive.

Nick no longer had a ship. Yet he must have rescued *something*. Something more valuable to him than his frigate.

If you can get her, you bastard, you can have her.

Reality itself seemed to be in flux as Hashi Lebwohl rode coriolus forces around and around inside his head. Micro-events remapped the macro-world. If he'd been under less pressure, he might have paused to notice that he enjoyed this sensation; that he felt more alive at moments like this than at any other time.

The pressure to act was real, however; ineluctable despite the uncertainty of its cartography. Yet action was impossible until some manner of readable map, no matter how intuitive or speculative, had been obtained.

He needed to *understand*.

Very well, he told himself. Construct a hypothesis and explore its implications. Theoretical reality is better than no reality at all.

Clamping his hands harder over his eyes, he began.

He wasn't prepared to guess who'd sent kazes against Sixten Vertigus and Godsen Frik. That ground was too dangerous: he didn't mean to walk it until he was sure of each step. But he was quite ready to hazard other speculations—

When he did so, his thin heart nearly stopped.

Kazes are such fun, don't you think?

Suppose for the moment that Nick Succorso and Sorus Chatelaine were working together; that they'd conceived a plan to bring themselves almost limitless wealth. And suppose, further, that Morn Hyland had opposed them, inspired by her old enmity toward *Gutbuster*, if not by loyalty to the UMCP. Suppose that they'd decided to rid themselves of her, and to greatly increase their opportunities for wealth, by producing and then selling the DA immunity drug under circumstances designed to terrify the population of human space.

According to this hypothesis, Nick had taken Morn to Enablement so that the Amnion could make use of her—perhaps by transforming her into some manner of genetic kaze aimed at UMCPHQ itself. After that everything he, Sorus, and the Amnion did had been part of an elaborate charade.

Hashi reconstructed the charade in his mind, even though it made him tremble.

The Amnion had pursued *Captain's Fancy* to Billingate in order to create the illusion that they wished to stop Nick and Morn. To confirm that impression, Nick had sent her to the Bill in an ejection pod. From Joshua and Milos Taverner, Nick had learned what had brought a UMCP cyborg to Thanatos Minor. Then he and his partner, Captain Chatelaine, had begun the rumors that she possessed an antimutagen.

To demonstrate the efficacy of her drug, as well as to reinforce the impression that he was bargaining in order to save his own life, he'd given Morn back to the Amnion. With their connivance, he'd retrieved her again. After that, he'd tricked his way aboard *Trumpet,* perhaps with Milos Taverner's aid.

Hashi's pulse pounded in his head; in his eyes. He rode a mad swirl of phosphenes and alarm. His hypothesis was self-consistent. It fit the available data. It could be true.

If Nick succeeded at putting her aboard the gap scout, Morn would survive to wreak mutagenic ruin on the UMCP. And the knowledge that Sorus Chatelaine had obtained an immunity drug would spread. It was spreading even now. Genetic kazes were the stuff of nightmare—the worst horror visceral human DNA could imagine. Driven by panic, humankind would offer her every kind and scale of riches in self-defense.

You deserve her.

Nick had sent his message to Hashi as a taunt, trusting that no cop would be able to guess the dark truth. Of course, his plan would fail if the UMCP themselves made the drug available. But they could hardly do so when a genetic kaze had gone off in their faces—when they were being torn apart by self-replicating alien nucleotides.

Shivering in an ague of speculation, Hashi strove to fault his hypothesis.

I don't care what happens to you.

Was it possible? That was the essential question: every other concern faded to vapor by comparison. Could Joshua be tricked or maneuvered into keeping Morn alive?

He had no orders to preserve her life. Quite the reverse. On the other hand, she was UMCP personnel. Therefore he couldn't kill her himself: his programming protected all UMCP personnel from direct violence. What if she were forced on him in some way?—for example, if her survival was the price he had to pay for the success of his mission? What then?

Under those conditions, Hashi acknowledged feverishly, Joshua's datacore would not preclude her rescue.

And the information she carried within her was as destructive as any mutagen. Quite apart from other possibilities, it could ruin Warden Dios and all his senior personnel; perhaps end their lives; quite conceivably destroy the UMCP itself.

Supposition proved nothing. Nevertheless Hashi suddenly found it not only possible but credible to think that Morn Hyland might still be alive.

Lethal! his covert mind shouted at him. Deadly! Such a development would be *fatal*—entirely fatal.

You need me, but you blew it.

Perhaps he'd misjudged the depth of Nick Succorso's malice.

Abruptly he dropped his hands from his face to his board. Their pressure against his eyeballs left his vision blurred; but he didn't need clear sight to hit the keys he wanted.

Perhaps he'd been more honest with Koina Hannish than he wished to admit when he'd spoken of loyalty. Whatever the reason, he didn't question his decision once it was made. He'd been passive too long. Instead of hesitating further, he prepared a new contract for Captain Scroyle and flared it out to the same listening post which *Free Lunch* had used to contact him.

It was the richest contract he'd ever offered a mercenary; a king's ransom in exchange for *Trumpet*'s destruction and the death of everyone aboard.

The mere act of coding that message filled him with an inexpressible sense of conscious alarm and intuitive relief. The risk he took was extreme. Nevertheless, directly or indirectly, he'd created the threat Nick represented. He'd hired Nick. More than once. He was responsible for the danger.

As soon as his transmission was on its way, Hashi Lebwohl left his office and went looking for Warden Dios. The walk would allow him a chance to recover his composure. And he wanted to report in person so that he could more easily give his director an edited version of what he'd learned.

What followed then would enable him to refine his speculations. In addition, it would reinforce or undermine his impression of Warden Dios as a man who lived in the world of the real.

ANCILLARY DOCUMENTATION

GAP TRAVEL

The "Juanita Estevez Mass Transmission Field Generator," almost exclusively known as the "gap drive," was a revolutionary discovery. It virtually re-created the future of humankind. The frontiers of human space were immediately and profoundly altered. Access to desperately needed new resources, combined with the simultaneous wealth and hazard of commerce with the Amnion, ended a prolonged period of economic deterioration. Instead of being constricted by poverty and the sun's gravity well, the horizons were now limited only by the velocity of human ships, the power of human gap field generators, and the scope of human imaginations. In a sense, the entire galaxy of the Milky Way now lay within reach.

However, some of the gap drive's effects were more subtle. For example, it produced an insidious distortion in the perception of real space. The ability to travel imponderable distances almost instantly created the pervasive illusion that those distances were indeed effectively small. *The entire galaxy of the Milky Way now lay within reach.* The implications of such a statement were at once mind-numbing and misleading. In the crude spiral of the Milky Way, Earth's approximate distance from galactic center was 26.1×10^{16} kilometers: 2,610,000,000,000,000,000 k. A ship traveling at a velocity of .5c would take roughly fifty-five thousand years to reach galactic center. At the speed of light, the trip would still take 27,500 years. Taken at an arbitrary average, human ships could cross ten light-years with every gap crossing. Even at that rate, 2,750 crossings would be required to cover the distance.

Being what they were, however, human beings found 2,750 a conceivable number. Therefore the space between Earth and the center of the Milky Way became conceivable.

The fallacy in all this was so subtle that most people failed to notice it.

In real time, effective time, the light-years crossed by the gap drive didn't exist. A ship with a gap drive didn't travel those light-years: it bypassed them through dimensional translocation. But when the crossing was done, the ship returned to normal space—and normal space was so vast that its scale was *not* truly conceivable.

Most people thought, So what? The gap drive did exist. The only real time involved in travel was taken up by acceleration to attain the necessary velocity and then by deceleration at the other end. Amnion space was just a few days away at the best of times.

True: Amnion space was just a few days away in a gap ship. And communication was equally fast: messages conveyed by ship could arrive centuries or millennia ahead of any speed-of-light transmission. But neither space nor time had meaning in the strange physics of the dimensional gap. Ships didn't encounter each other there: they didn't communicate or exchange shipments; they didn't do battle or give chase. Every action of any kind, human or Amnion, took place in normal space, at space-normal speeds. And at space-normal speeds even the nearest stars were pragmatically out of reach.

In other words, the discovery of the Juanita Estevez Mass Transmission Field Generator had a transforming effect on humankind's relationship with vast distances—and no effect at all on humankind's place in normal space.

The dilemma of piracy was a case in point.

Why was piracy such a virulent problem? How had it attained such power in human space? Ships could cross the gap in a matter of instants. If a pirate raided, say, Terminus, the information could be transmitted to Earth by gap courier drone, and within hours UMCPHQ could send out a cruiser to support the station. How could any illegal flourish under these conditions?

Quite simply, piracy flourished because it took place in normal space. Like the UMCP, illegals often had gap ships. Nevertheless their every action took place in normal space. Gap ships could change the sector of space in which they acted with incredible ease; but the actions themselves still consumed real time and involved real distances. A UMCP cruiser might well chase a pirate vessel across the entire galaxy—and yet every effort the cruiser made to give battle occurred in normal space, where simply hunting through a solar system for telltale emissions was a job that might take months.

These hindrances were vastly increased by the fact that gap travel itself was not as precise as it appeared on paper. Both course and distance for any crossing were susceptible to several forms of inaccuracy. Minuscule fractions of a degree in course became hundreds of thousands of kilometers when those fractions were multiplied by light-years. And the calibration of distance was even more complex. The distance a ship traveled through the gap varied according to a number of factors, including speed, rate of acceleration, and the ratio between her mass and both the actual and potential power of her gap drive.

In addition the interaction of those elements was ruled by the gap drive's hysteresis transducer, which controlled the extent to which the drive's effect lagged behind its cause: too much lag, and the ship never went into tach; too little, and the ship never resumed tard. As a result, tiny fluctuations in power or hysteresis, or minute miscalculations of mass, became large shortfalls or overshots. Superhuman precision was required to make any ship resume tard right where her captain intended when he went into tach.

For that reason—and because ships came out of the gap with all the velocity their crossing demanded—Earth required the solar system's massive non-UMCP traffic to use a gap range beyond the orbit of the last planet; and ships approaching any station were expected to resume tard well outside the sphere of that station's control space.

Here again the sheer scale of space subtly undermined humankind's apparent mastery of inconceivable distances. Being a pirate was easier—and fighting piracy was harder—than most people understood.

SORUS

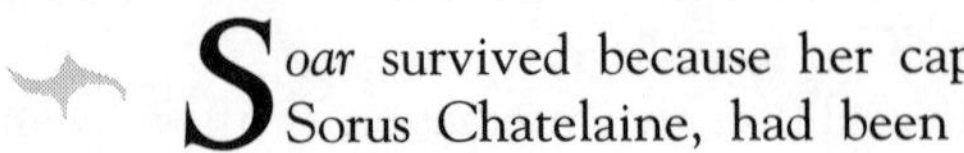

Soar survived because her captain, Sorus Chatelaine, had been forewarned.

The Amnion shuttle's passengers had warned her, of course. She'd saved the small craft after it was thrown off course and out of control by the repercussions of her brief, one-sided fight with *Captain's Fancy*. The shuttle's passengers were aboard now: they stood in front of her on *Soar*'s bridge, talking to her—and to *Calm Horizons*—constantly. They told her what they could about the attack on the Amnion sector; about the rescue of Morn Hyland; about the powers and exigencies which had come into conflict on the planetoid.

But that information might not have been enough to preserve *Soar*. It arrived perilously late. Fortunately Sorus had been forewarned in other ways. The damage to Billingate communications showed her that the installation was in trouble—and she knew how to jump to the kinds of conclusions which kept ships and illegals alive.

Captain's Fancy should have been under *Calm Horizons*' control. The Amnion had Nick Succorso's priority-codes—and Succorso himself wasn't aboard his ship to countermand them. The Amnion should have been able to take effective command of the frigate. In fact, his ship had given every sign that she was indeed responding to those codes; submitting to *Calm Horizons*' instructions. Nevertheless her subsequent, suicidal attack on *Tranquil Hegemony* demonstrated that her submission had been a ruse.

The codes were false. Perhaps they'd never been true. Or perhaps they'd been changed recently. In either case, it was clear that *Captain's*

Fancy had feigned helplessness, not in order to prepare an attack on *Soar*—as Sorus had assumed—but rather to defend the raiding party from *Trumpet* which had entered the Amnion sector.

In other words, events weren't moving as the Amnion wanted—or predicted. The understandings which they'd shared with her prior to the arrival of the shuttle's passengers were inaccurate. And *Trumpet* was behaving no more predictably than *Captain's Fancy*.

Such things forewarned Sorus before Milos Taverner told her what he knew of the danger. By the time *Calm Horizons* ordered her to the warship's support against *Trumpet,* she'd already rigged her ship for battle or collision, and had begun putting distance between herself and Thanatos Minor.

Her preparations and those extra k proved critical. When Thanatos Minor exploded, *Soar* had every gun trained, not on *Trumpet,* but on the dark rock; had every force screen and mass deflector on that side at full power. And Sorus had reoriented her ship to present the stone barrage with the smallest possible profile.

Soar endured the mad, hurtling onslaught of debris by blasting stone to powder before it hit; by deflecting some impacts and absorbing others. The shock wave tossed her toward oblivion as if she'd received a direct hit from *Calm Horizons'* super-light proton cannon; but then the concussion ran on past her, leaving her battered and reeling, but whole.

And *Calm Horizons* survived in much the same way. The warship's profile was larger, of course. On the other hand, she was considerably farther from the center of the blast. And her guns—not to mention her targ—were superior to *Soar*'s: able to destroy more of the careening rock before it hit.

After the explosion, Thanatos Minor was gone.

Only two ships remained—the two which had received Milos Taverner's warning. Every other vessel in this quadrant of space had been torn apart and scattered along the subatomic winds of the dark. *Soar*'s receivers could pick up the blind fallout of the blast, the enharmonic squalling of the debris, the thunderous distortion of the aftershock, but no voices.

Sorus clutched at the arms of her g-seat, fighting acceleration stress and nausea. The wave front had flung her against her restraints as easily as if she were an empty shipsuit: she felt like she'd been hit with a stun-prod. She wasn't young anymore, couldn't suffer this kind of abuse without paying for it. The clamor of shouts and the yowl of klaxons across the bridge told her that she was still alive, that her ship was still alive—but not for how long.

A blast like that could have broken *Soar*'s back, or torn the ship's core open to hard vacuum; could have snapped conduits like twigs, cracked drive housings, crumpled vanes and antennae, ruptured fuel cells—

The displays in front of her had gone crazy or blind; g pulled at her stomach, partly because of the blast, partly because she'd shut down internal spin to improve *Soar*'s maneuverability. Despite the racket of pain in her head, the pressure like hemorrhage in her lungs, she hauled herself upright by main strength and struggled to clear her vision.

"Damage report!" she barked through the clamor. "Ship's status!"

Her command seemed to open a space for itself through the noise and confusion. "We've been hit!" her data first shouted back, "three times, no, four!" giving her information as fast as it came to his readouts. "Deflectors and screens couldn't hold.

"One hit along the prow, glancing blow, no penetration, no structural damage. One five-meter dent in the outer hull amidships, leaks at the seams, automatic systems have it under control," pumping plexulose plasma sealant into the gap between the hulls. "One took out a midship deflector vane."

"Captain!" called the communications first. "*Calm Horizons* wants—"

Sorus cut off the interruption with a slash of her hand. She didn't want to hear anything else until she knew the condition of her ship.

The data first hadn't stopped. "—must be why the last one hit so hard. Breached a cargo bay. Interior bulkheads show green, no leakage. But we can't seal a hole that size. Damn rock's still in there, along with what's left of the cargo."

Sorus snatched a breath into her sore lungs. "Injury report."

The data first hit more keys. "Four so far, five, six—that's all so far. Impact stress, mostly—contusions, breaks, whiplash. No casualties."

"Captain—" communications demanded again.

"I'm fucking blind," the scan first protested to no one in particular. "Can't see a fucking thing." She flapped her hands as if she were trying to clear away smoke. "All this fucking distortion!"

Sorus ignored them both; she ignored Milos Taverner's bulk almost directly in front of her. "Helm?"

The man at the helm station shrugged. "We're still riding blast inertia. Away from Thanatos Minor. If there's anything left of it. But I can't tell you where we actually are until we get scan back."

"Or who else survived," scan put in harshly.

Sorus felt that fear herself—the cold, visceral dread of running blind down the black gullet of the void—but there was nothing she could do about it.

Another voice cut at her attention.

"Captain. *Calm Horizons* must be answered. It is imperative."

That was the other half-mutated human, Marc Vestabule. He stood at the communications station. Like Milos Taverner in front of Sorus, he'd planted himself there by clamping his hands to the sides of the board; he seemed immune to the receding g of the concussion, immovable. Before the blast had reduced reception to gibberish, he'd been talking to *Calm Horizons*, presumably giving the Amnion warship the same information Milos Taverner had given her—and asking the same questions.

"Then do it," she snapped back at him. "Just don't bother me."

Apparently calm, Marc Vestabule released one hand to take a receiver from the communications board and jack it into his ear. Then he accepted a pickup from the communications first. At once—but without any discernible urgency—he began to make alien noises into the pickup.

That was the thing Sorus Chatelaine distrusted or loathed or feared most about the Amnion. None of them ever showed any urgency; any ordinary mortal dread or desperation. The pilot and guard which had accompanied Vestabule and Taverner aboard the shuttle still stood by the bridge doors, bracing themselves there as quietly as if nothing had happened. As for Taverner himself—

In almost every way, he looked as human as she was. Perhaps more so: his pudgy face and besmirched scalp, his nic-stained fingers and pallid skin, conveyed an impression of flaws, frailties. Only anger could have given his face dignity. On his features any other emotion would have looked like self-pity.

Nevertheless she knew that he was an Amnioni—as single-minded and unshakable as Marc Vestabule; as the shuttle's pilot and guard; as every member of the crew which served *Calm Horizons*. The signs were unmistakable.

His eyes betrayed the working of the mutagens which had taken away his identity. They were an acrid yellow color, lidless, with deformed irises like slits; they made his physical softness and his unnatural calm seem somehow demonic, like a glimpse of damnation. Genetic transformation had altered everything about him except his appearance: rearranged his DNA strings, restructured the fundamental, definitive encryption of his nucleotides, until only a detached and sometimes imprecise memory-pool remained of the former deputy chief of Com-Mine Station Security.

Sorus was familiar with the process. She'd known Marc Vestabule for years.

Irritated at the way Taverner watched her as if nothing she did could surprise him, she snapped past him, "Scan, I want a *report*!"

"I told you, Captain, I'm blind," the scan first answered defensively. "There's too much fucking distortion all across the spectrum, the instruments can't—"

"Then *fix* it," Sorus retorted. "Filter it somehow. Tell the computer what happened so it can compensate. I want to know what's *out* there."

"Captain." Vestabule turned his bifurcated gaze at her, one eye human, the other Amnion. "*Calm Horizons* reports no other surviving vessels. The planetoid Thanatos Minor no longer exists. You are in no danger. Distortion should recede to the tolerances of your equipment in four minutes. *Calm Horizons* has identified your position. Coordinates will be transmitted to your helm."

Sorus nodded sharply. The helm and communications officers hit keys to route information between their stations.

"More data follows when you are ready to receive it," Vestabule added.

"Not yet," she told him. "I've got other priorities.

"Data, give me damage assessment on that holed cargo bay. And a repair estimate for the deflector vane."

With her thumb, she punched open a ship-wide intercom channel. "All hands secure for g. I'm going to reengage internal spin. Get to sickbay if you need it. The rest of us have work to do. Damage control says we're still true, but I don't trust it. We were hit too hard. Report *anything* that makes you think we've got displacement."

Glaring back at Taverner's soft calm, Sorus thumbed off the intercom and began to run commands on her board.

Before she could activate internal spin, Marc Vestabule said, "Haste is required, Captain Chatelaine." He sounded as inexorable as an iron bar.

Pain made her feel her years—and the pull of time made her angry. "Haste for what?" she retorted. "Where are we going? You just told me everybody else is dead. Gone, blown to scrap." The thought left a cold place in the pit of her stomach. Even the Bill was gone. He'd been as untrustworthy as any man she'd ever known, but he'd met some of her needs and supplied others—sometimes without knowing it. She couldn't imagine how she would replace him. Without what he'd given her, how would she bear her indentured servitude to the Amnion? "If we're in no danger, what's the hurry?"

"Decisions have been made," Vestabule replied in a tone like rust. "Action must be taken. *Calm Horizons* instructs acceleration along an interception course. The proximity of vessels will facilitate preparation."

Perhaps he felt the urgency of events after all: as he relayed *Calm Horizons*' orders, he sounded more inhuman than usual.

Sorus faced him while apprehension throbbed in her temples and the aftereffects of g-stress ached in her nerves. Decisions? Action? Maybe as many as ten thousand people just died here. How much more *action* do you need?

"If you want me to take this seriously," she said through her teeth, "you'd better explain it."

Vestabule appeared to consult the alien coding of his genes for a moment before he answered, "Scan data suggests that *Trumpet* was not destroyed."

Incuriously Taverner turned his head to look at his fellow Amnioni.

Hunched over her readouts, the scan first muttered, "I'm starting to get something. One ship—yes, that's *Calm Horizons*. Can't be sure of anything else yet."

Sorus swallowed a curse. She believed Vestabule the instant he spoke: the Amnion didn't often make mistakes in matters of factual accuracy. But if *Trumpet* was still alive somewhere, still out there with Morn and Davies Hyland, Angus Thermopyle and Nick Succorso, aboard—

Sick with premonitions, as if she knew what was coming, she drawled sourly, "But you told me we're the only ships here. 'No other surviving vessels,' you said. So if *Trumpet* isn't here and wasn't destroyed—"

She let the implication hang.

"As the wave front struck," Vestabule said, "*Calm Horizons* detected the emissions of *Trumpet*'s gap drive."

"So she's gone," Sorus cut in harshly. "You lost her. All this plotting and maneuvering, all this destruction, and you *lost* her." She made no effort to contain her anger. She knew from experience that the Amnion didn't understand such emotions—and didn't fear them. "Billingate and all those ships, destroyed for nothing, wasted. I thought you didn't like waste.

"Goddamn it, didn't you tell *Calm Horizons* who was aboard that ship? Didn't you tell them what Angus Thermopyle is—what he came here to do? Why did they let *Trumpet* get away? Why didn't they use that damn cannon—cut their losses, solve this problem once and for all? Don't you understand how dangerous those people are?"

Because she knew what was coming, she struggled against it. "Angus

Thermopyle is a cyborg. The cops sent him to destroy Billingate. That's bad enough—letting him get away is bad enough. But there's worse.

"Nick Succorso's priority-codes didn't work on *Captain's Fancy*. Haven't you figured out yet what that means?"

"What does it mean, Captain Chatelaine?" Taverner asked steadily.

Sorus kept her glare on Marc Vestabule. She'd known him longer, distrusted him less; she feared that if she looked at Taverner, she might not be able to control her desire to punch in his fat face.

"It means one of two things.

"*Either*," she articulated harshly, holding up one finger like an accusation, "those codes were never good in the first place. Morn Hyland and Nick Succorso planned the whole thing together, carried it out together. Their visit to Enablement was a trick, a ruse—probably one of Hashi Lebwohl's covert operations. They got something from you, learned something, set you up for something, I don't know what it was. All I know is, it worked. It paralyzed you long enough to let them get away.

"*Or*"—she raised a second finger beside the first—"Hyland told Succorso she'd given you his priority-codes *before* he turned her over to you. So he had time to rewrite them. But that still means Hyland and Succorso must be working together. Why else would she let him in on a secret like that, when he was about to sacrifice her? And why else is she still human, if she didn't get some kind of immunity drug from him?"

Now Sorus began to see what lay behind Nick Succorso's rumor that she herself had access to such a drug. If Billingate hadn't been destroyed, neither the Bill nor anyone else would have left her alone—or let her live. The consequences of Nick's lie would have driven her out into space, where he could attack her.

"So the whole thing was still a ruse," she concluded. "I don't know what they were trying to get from you, but they as sure as hell got *away* with it.

"What possessed *Calm Horizons* to let them do that? Why didn't she blast *Trumpet* while she had the chance?"

Milos Taverner confronted her now as if he and she were alone on the bridge. The force of his attention seemed to pull her eyes to his. "You ask an important question, Captain Chatelaine." His vocal cords, less mutated than Vestabule's, nonetheless made his voice sound alien: more spectral than human. "It suggests another, which is for you to answer.

"When the ruse was revealed—when *Captain's Fancy* began to act contrary to Amnion instructions—why did you not 'blast' the vessel? It was within your power to spare *Tranquil Hegemony*, yet you did not do so. You question our inaction. Will we not also question yours?"

Sorus felt the threat: it was palpable and ominous, like static building in the air. Abruptly she let go of her anger. She couldn't afford it here. Instead she hid her fear behind a mask of sardonic confidence—the mask she'd always worn when she was with the Bill.

Covering herself while she marshaled her resources, she dropped her gaze to her board and completed the sequence of commands that reengaged internal spin. At once the almost subliminal whine of servos and motors filled the bridge as the floor eased into motion under her. As smooth as oil, *Soar* began to generate centrifugal inertia. A familiar sense of her own weight settled in her muscles. Both Vestabule and Taverner were able to relax their clamped postures.

"All green," data reported. "Sensors aren't picking up any rubs or vibrations. Looks like we're spinning true."

"Confirmation?" Sorus asked scan.

"No," the scan first said. "Not yet. I'm sure we're the only ships here. That whole fucking rock is gone, and everything else with it. But I can't see far enough yet to get an exact fix on anything. We might have instrument tremor, or we might not."

Sorus kept her relief to herself. With a trenchant snort which was as close as she could come to outright mockery, she answered Taverner, "I didn't have a choice. You know that. I couldn't attack *Captain's Fancy* because I was busy rescuing you.

"I hit her once, hard enough to be sure she wasn't going to live much longer. After that I had my hands full trying to take hold of your shuttle without reducing you to so much g-flattened meat. I had to grab you *carefully*. If I hadn't done that—or if I'd left you to concentrate on *Captain's Fancy*—you would probably be dead right now."

Smiling into his eyes, she thought, Argue with that and be damned.

"Precisely, Captain Chatelaine." Taverner retained enough of his human resources to smile back. "You comprehend the essential concept. Confronted with two conflicting requirements, you found that one outweighed the other, despite the fact that both tended toward consequences which were uncertain. Perhaps we"—he made a stilted gesture that included Vestabule, the shuttle pilot, and the guard—"would have died. Perhaps not. Perhaps *Captain's Fancy* would fail to inflict serious damage on *Tranquil Hegemony*. Again, perhaps not. It is at the intersection of perhaps and perhaps not that decisiveness exercises itself. You chose rightly to rescue us. Was it not conceivable that *Tranquil Hegemony* might successfully defend herself?

"*Calm Horizons* chose not to fire on *Trumpet* because it was conceivable that *Trumpet* might be captured. Perhaps the destruction of Thanatos Minor would fail altogether. Perhaps it would be delayed. Perhaps *Trumpet* would come within range of a laser which would cripple her drives without killing the humans aboard. Confronted with conflicting requirements—to capture *Trumpet* and to prevent her escape—*Calm Horizons* found that one outweighed the other. To capture *Trumpet* would prevent her escape, but to prevent her escape might preclude her capture."

"The Amnion understand," Marc Vestabule inserted in a crusted tone, "that what you name 'a ruse' has been practiced against us. Indeed, events suggest that humans have dealt falsely with us in several ways, or in one way with several implications. Milos Taverner has spoken of his perception that the actions of this 'cyborg' were directed against us as well as against Billingate in ways which we do not yet comprehend."

His stance conveyed no impatience, no tension; but his human eye blinked frantically, as if the last of his human emotions had no other outlet.

"Yet the fact that a ruse was at work has been known to us from the first. On a previous occasion prior to his union with the Amnion, Milos Taverner informed us of Captain Nick Succorso's false dealings on behalf of the United Mining Companies Police. He informed us of Morn Hyland's identity as a United Mining Companies Police ensign. For that reason we sought to retain her body. The tissues of a UMCP ensign would have yielded much.

"We have always presumed that their dealings were designed for our harm. We have allowed their ruse to proceed so that we may learn its meaning, and so that we may turn it to our own purposes.

"But this is not an intersection of perhaps and perhaps not, Captain Chatelaine. This is an incidence of *must*. Action is essential. You are required to initiate the course and acceleration which *Calm Horizons* has instructed."

Beyond question Sorus knew what was coming. But she'd just lost the only place she might have called home, the only people she might have called friends; her ship was damaged; and her enemies were gathering—enemies who turned out to have allies in unexpected places. She had no intention of letting mutated monstrosities like Marc Vestabule and Milos Taverner make her do their work for them. Under these circumstances she would have refused a direct order from the Mind/Union which was the highest source of "decisiveness" she knew of in Amnion space.

"You still haven't answered my original question," she countered stubbornly. "Why are we in a hurry? *Trumpet* is gone. We can't stop her now. What do we need haste for?"

Vestabule's human eyelid fluttered like a signal flag, but his gaze held hers firmly. "Amnion scan has not yet been restored to full function," he said. "Therefore data is imprecise. However, it will be made precise in a short time. At present the characteristic residue of 'going into tach' "—that human phrase sounded awkward on his tongue—"is discernible, despite the bombardment which clouds your instruments. As distortion fades, *Calm Horizons* will be able to determine *Trumpet*'s gap vector. Her velocity and acceleration may be calculated from previous data. What is known of the gap drive parameters of such vessels will enable us to extrapolate both direction and distance.

"The results will be approximate," he finished, "but pursuit will be possible."

There it was. Pursuit. She'd known it was coming, but she still hated hearing it said aloud. Pursue a UMCP ship on UMCP business into human space, where no doubt there were half a dozen warships waiting to keep trouble off her tail.

"What, us and *Calm Horizons*?" she protested acidly, not because she expected Vestabule or Taverner to heed her, but simply because she needed to acknowledge the weight of mortality hanging from her bones. "Have you considered the possibility that the pure and righteous UMCP just might consider that an act of war? Have you considered the possibility that maybe you have more to gain from this kind of peace than they do, and if you break it you might have to pay more?"

Taverner shook his head slowly, as if the movement were one which he'd memorized but didn't understand. However, it was Vestabule who answered.

"Once again you speak of an intersection of perhaps and perhaps not. We have not yet reached that intersection. *Calm Horizons* will remain in Amnion space. You will pursue *Trumpet*. You will capture her and her people, if that goal is attainable. Otherwise you will destroy them.

"But *Calm Horizons* will come to your support, if it is required. At that intersection, we will accept the hazard of war rather than permit *Trumpet* to gain safety."

Nausea twisted through her stomach as he spoke. An act of war—and

Soar right in the middle of it. She was too old for this; she was born too old for it.

"Damn it," she objected, knowing that objection was hopeless, "you're days away from getting a message to the Mind/Union. How can you take a risk like this on your own? How do you know the Mind/Union will approve?"

The decision he'd announced had a human sound, a sound of desperation. Was it possible, she wondered, that the origins of creatures like Vestabule and Taverner could affect Amnion decision-making processes; inject an element of terror which their kind couldn't recognize?

Whether that was true or not, Vestabule had no trouble answering her. "We are Amnion," he replied flatly. "And we must act. That is required. The perils of inaction now outweigh those of action.

"To 'approve,' " he added, "is not a concept which has meaning in relation to the Mind/Union."

Facing Sorus directly, he continued, "You also must act. I will not speak of this again. You are required to approach *Calm Horizons* at the course and velocity you have been given."

No flicker or variation of his tone betrayed the threat. Nevertheless she saw it in his eyes. This was a test of wills, of loyalty: his inexorable Amnion exigencies against her human familiarity with fear.

A test—but no contest. Since the day when she'd fallen under the power of his kind, she'd belonged to them body and soul. At the core of herself she'd been overtaken by a darkness which didn't bear close examination.

"Do it," she told the helm first bitterly. "Course and thrust according to *Calm Horizons'* instructions. Initiate immediately."

A moment later she heard the muted hull-roar of thrust, felt the complex g of acceleration conflicting with internal spin and the shock wave's vector. Her stomach rebelled briefly, then settled back down.

Swiveling her station so that she could look away from the Amnion, she went on, "Targ, this would be a good time to run every test you can think of on your systems."

"Aye, Captain," targ responded in a clenched voice. He went to work without raising his head.

"Scan, give me status."

"Almost clear," scan replied as if she were accustomed to hearing her captain and the Amnion argue over *Soar*'s fate. "I still can't confirm instrument stability, but we can see well enough to verify what *Calm Hori-*

zons is telling us. Except I can't pick up any emission trace for a ship going into tach."

Sorus dismissed that concern: Amnion scan was better than hers. If *Calm Horizons* reported gap emission, she believed it.

She wasn't done with Vestabule and Taverner yet, however. She would obey as she always did; but she meant to know the truth when she did it.

Simply because he'd been human more recently and might remember more, she directed her glower at Milos.

"Listen to me," she breathed, clenching her teeth. "It's easy for you to say 'the perils of inaction now outweigh those of action,' but I'm the one who has to do something about it. I need to understand what's at stake here. I'm human, my ship is human, we'll be in human space—that's why you're sending us instead of going after *Trumpet* yourself. But in human space the rules are different. There might be more than one kind of action I can take. I won't be able to make the right choices unless I understand what's at stake."

In response, Taverner attempted a smile; but beneath his alien eyes the stretching of his mouth resembled a rictus. "You do not need to understand. I will accompany you. I will be invested with decisiveness for this pursuit."

Sorus swallowed an impulse to shout at him. Still softly, she countered, "That's not good enough. You aren't human. You don't even talk human—your grasp on how humans think and act is already starting to fray. You *need* me to understand."

For reasons which weren't clear to her, Taverner glanced at Vestabule. Nothing she could discern passed between them—nothing more than the erratic blink of Vestabule's eye—but when Taverner faced her again, a decision had been reached.

"Very well. I will explain.

"The Amnion have much to gain by *Trumpet*'s capture, and much to lose by her escape."

"That much I guessed," she muttered darkly.

He was unperturbed. "The matter of gain," he said, "centers on Morn Hyland and Davies Hyland. Her importance is simple. She is a United Mining Companies Police ensign. With her capture all of her knowledge comes into our possession. This is significant, but not critical.

"In addition, she is a human female protected by zone implants. Her capture would enable us to acquire other knowledge. For example, if she

were bred with an Amnion male, such as I am, what would result? Again this is significant, but not critical."

Bred? Sorus thought in cold horror. Oh, shit. But she didn't interrupt.

"Her offspring," Taverner continued as if the subject were purely abstract, devoid of personal necessity, "represents opportunities which are indeed critical.

"The techniques which you call 'force-growing' and 'transfer of mind' are old and common among us. Our ability to bring human genetic material—your language supplies no adequate means to convey these concepts, the word 'mutate' is quite insufficient—into mind/union with the Amnion is also old and common. More recent research has enabled us"—he may have shrugged—"to mutate human genetic material with diminishing discrepancies of appearance. Still we have failed to produce Amnion which may pass as human.

"Doubtless this is because genetic manipulation cannot replicate patterns of thought, expression, or behavior, the learned content of being human. Hence the importance of transfer of mind and Davies Hyland."

Sorus listened hard; but at the same time she tried not to hear what he was saying. She'd left her links with humanity behind so long ago that she couldn't pretend to be concerned for her kind now—and yet the implications of Taverner's explanation chilled her from the surface of her skin to the center of her embittered heart.

"To enable one of us to pass as human," he was saying, "we must provide a human mind. Among ourselves, Amnioni to Amnioni, such transference presents no difficulties. Yet when we work from human source to human target, we are able to produce a successful target only at the cost of a ruined source. We speculate that human fear causes the source to be effectively erased during transference. And when we work from human to Amnioni, both source and target are ruined. The fear of the source is replicated upon a genetically incompatible target.

"We improve, but we do not progress.

"However, the successful transfer of mind between Davies Hyland and his source demonstrates that our techniques may indeed operate effectively on human genetic material. If a human female with a zone implant can endure a transfer of mind to a force-grown offspring without loss of reason or function—and if the condition of that offspring is also truly functional—then the same procedure may prove viable between human and Amnioni.

"In that case, we will become able to produce Amnion with access to learned human thoughts and behaviors. If those Amnion are grown in human shapes, they will be undetectable to humans. Then human space could be seeded with hosts of Amnion, and the overthrow of Earth-bred life could be accomplished at one stroke.

"Thus the capture of Davies Hyland is critical. A study of his physical and mental integrity can supply the information we require. His value is only increased by the fact that he also possesses the mind of a United Mining Companies Police ensign."

Sorus' brain reeled involuntarily at the idea. He was talking about genetic kazes: undetectable terrorists who could plant mutagens wherever and whenever they wished—

Taverner wasn't done, however. "The matter of loss," he continued inexorably, "centers on the cyborg Angus Thermopyle and Captain Nick Succorso.

"The cyborg has done us severe harm in destroying Billingate, and must not be permitted to return to the United Mining Companies Police victorious. We must demonstrate our capacity to counter his actions. This is significant, but not critical. In addition we have cause to suspect that the harm for which he was designed is not yet complete. Therefore also he must be stopped. Finally we wish to study him so that we may learn the techniques of his construction. These considerations as well are significant, but not critical.

"Captain Nick Succorso is critical. He possesses a drug which renders him immune to us. This would be a grave threat even if we did not have cause to suspect that the United Mining Companies Police are involved in the uses he has made of that drug. It is imperative that he is not permitted to disseminate his immunity in human space. If humans can be preserved from mutation, they will be able to wage warfare of a kind which must defeat us. In a raw test of technological resources, we will fail. Our means of production are too precise, time-consuming, and costly to compete with yours.

"Yet that is not the sum of the threat which Captain Succorso represents. By some means which we do not understand—perhaps by what you term 'intuition'—he has acquired knowledge of our researches into the use of uniquely designed gap drives to produce space-normal velocities which very nearly approximate the speed of light. If our defensives could attain those velocities, our prospects in warfare would be greatly improved."

With an effort, Sorus kept her expression blank; but inwardly she gave a groan of surprise. "Greatly improved" was a stunning understatement. If a battlewagon like *Calm Horizons* could be accelerated to .9c or more, no human station could stand against her. Even Earth might have no adequate defense.

Without pausing, Taverner concluded, "Captain Succorso must not be permitted to convey his knowledge to the United Mining Companies Police. We fear that human space would have no choice but to engage us in warfare immediately, if only to prevent us from completing our researches.

"Do you understand now, Captain Chatelaine?"

She nodded slowly, dumbly. Oh, she understood, all right. She hated her role, but she understood it. If she'd been the "decisive" of *Calm Horizons*—or even the Mind/Union itself—she would have made the same choice. The stakes were high enough to justify risks on almost any scale.

Yet she couldn't let the question rest there. Some streak of stubbornness in her, some mute, unsubjugated piece of her genetic inheritance, pushed her to raise one more objection.

"I understand fine, but I'm not sure you do. You can talk all you want, but you've already missed your chance to take the only action that would have made a difference. You let *Trumpet* get away. And since then too much time has passed. What good will it do to send me after her now?

"The cops'll be waiting for her to come back—with a whole fleet, if they think they need it. Even if I could catch her before she reaches them—which I can't—I couldn't stop her from transmitting any messages she wants. And if you're right that Succorso is working for the cops, they already know about his immunity drug. They probably gave it to him. Nothing I do can possibly prevent them from spreading that information.

"Sending me into human space to get shot by a fleet of damn cops is going to accomplish zip."

The human side of Vestabule's face frowned as if he were unsure of her slang. Again he and Taverner glanced expressionlessly at each other before Taverner replied.

"The question of Captain Succorso's immunity is not a simple one. I"—for a minute he hung fire, as if his memory had slipped—"I have been the deputy chief of Com-Mine Station Security. If an immunity drug were known anywhere in human space, that knowledge would surely have come to me. Assume that this immunity is a devising of the United Mining Companies Police, and that Captain Succorso received it from them. Still it has not been disseminated. In my"—again he faltered briefly—"my experience, no knowledge or record of such an immunity exists. Therefore we must also assume that the United Mining Companies Police have chosen to suppress this immunity.

"I—" Taverner stopped. To her surprise, Sorus saw that he was in distress. The effort of thinking like a human drew sweat from his pores, turned his pale skin the color of bone.

"I speculate," he resumed in a thin, slightly hurried tone, "that some intraspecies betrayal which I find difficult to comprehend is taking place. One faction has developed this immunity, and now holds it secret from the other in order to gain advantage. I find the concept abhorrent, but I remember that such explanations are plausible among humans."

"We do not understand human behavior in this matter," Vestabule put in roughly. "We wish to understand it. But for the present understanding is not critical. Rather it is critical that knowledge of this immunity has not yet been disseminated in human space, and presumably will not be disseminated unless Captain Succorso takes that action upon himself.

"As for your concern that *Trumpet* has fled to the haven of 'a fleet of damn cops,' consider this.

"Our analysis of *Trumpet*'s departure emissions is complete. We have determined her gap vector, calculated her velocity and acceleration, and estimated her gap drive parameters. Here are the results."

Without waiting for permission, he reached forward and began tapping keys on the communications board. Almost immediately one of the main screens in front of Sorus flashed to life.

Vestabule had called up a 3-D coordinates schematic for this quadrant of space. Phosphors marked the spot where Thanatos Minor had once occupied the vacuum. *Soar*'s position blinked green; *Calm Horizons*' showed amber.

Swiftly a red line traced *Trumpet*'s course in normal space: numbers along the line indicated exact changes in thrust and vector. Then a small crimson cross indicated her leap into the gap.

Based on *Calm Horizons*' calculations, straight blue pointed the direction of *Trumpet*'s crossing. The Amnion warship could only speculate as to how far *Trumpet* had gone, but she was able to define the gap scout's course precisely.

That blue line didn't run anywhere near human space.

Sorus had used up her objections. Now she had nothing left except obedience—and darkness.

Deliberately she thumbed the ship-wide intercom.

"Stand by," she told her crew. "We've got our work cut out for us. First we'll rendezvous with *Calm Horizons*. Then we're going hunting."

Wherever Angus Thermopyle and his people were headed, it wasn't back to the UMCP.

ANGUS

Trumpet came out of the gap with Nick Succorso at the helm and Angus Thermopyle handling everything else scarcely 500,000 kilometers from Thanatos Minor—still within easy scan range.

Proximity alarms echoed the warnings of Angus' datacore and the raw squalling of his own instincts. *Trumpet*'s thrust drive still burned, piling on acceleration. Nevertheless the instantaneous disappearance of brisance from the planetoid's destruction affected the ship like braking; slammed him and Nick forward helplessly against their restraints. From a hand's width away, he gaped at his command readouts, but his eyes couldn't absorb their information rapidly enough.

His own calculations were quicker.

Trumpet wasn't moving fast enough to outrun Thanatos Minor's debris.

"Too close!" he rasped urgently. "Hit it again, Nick! You cut it too close!"

Nick sprawled across the second's station. His eyes were glazed; his hands fumbled for a grip they couldn't find on the sides of his board. He'd been hurt too much: Angus had punched him in the forehead hard enough to crack his skull; Ciro had jolted him with stun; his ship and most of his crew were dead. Lashed by g, he'd gone limp—too limp to react.

Angus' brain and his computer ran decisions at microprocessor speeds, but on separate tracks. Driven by preprogrammed exigencies, his fingers punched keys like scattershot, routing helm control back to his station, adjusting thrust for more power than Nick had known *Trumpet* possessed, defining gap parameters for human space. At the same time, his brain scrambled to identify his exact location, gauge it against the possibility of pursuit. According to his most recent data—only seconds old—neither *Soar* nor *Calm Horizons* had picked up enough velocity to attempt a gap crossing. And certainly not in this direction. But *Stonemason* and some of the other ships from Billingate were another matter. Milos must have told the Amnion why Angus had been sent to Thanatos Minor. If the Amnion had told the Bill somehow—if the Bill had flared out a warning—

They would know where to look for the gap scout.

Cued by his urgency, perhaps, or by some other in-built latitude, his datacore let Angus reset the gap parameters and throw *Trumpet* into another brutal course shift.

Klaxons wailed like the damned. Millions of tons of shattered rock hurtled closer, hot on the heels of the wave front. The displays plotted both brisance and stone as they scoured the void like furies: the ragged teeth of nightmares.

For half a dozen seconds, the gap scout hauled herself to the side so hard that only his zone implants kept Angus from passing out.

Nick collapsed against his restraints, unconscious. But welded reinforcements gave Angus the strength to endure. *Trumpet* was still turning—still broadside to the storm of Thanatos Minor's ruin—when he reached out against a weight of six or more g's and tapped the key which sent the gap scout into tach.

The violence which had riven the planetoid didn't touch her.

Instead, with a disorienting lack of transition, she found herself perilously far down the gravity well of a red giant nearly three light-years deep in Amnion space.

Moving too quickly for caution, Angus hadn't consulted astrogation—except by an almost autonomic reference to his internal databases—or made any attempt at precision; he'd simply pointed *Trumpet* at the nearest loud star he knew of and kicked her into the gap.

Luck and a near-miraculous synergy between his organic mind and his machine reflexes brought him close without killing him.

A red giant was exactly what he wanted: relatively low in mass, so that he could get nearer to it than to a heavier star; and relatively high in luminosity as well as other radiation, so that it might cover *Trumpet*'s trail. He hoped that brisance and debris would confuse the traces of his maneuvering near Thanatos Minor, prevent other ships from seeing where he'd gone. And if that didn't work, he hoped that a star as loud as this one would make *Trumpet* impossible to detect.

The gap scout was still accelerating at full burn, ramming herself down the gravity well at a frightening rate. Minutes away, immolation loomed ahead of her. Despite his zone implants and enhanced strength, Angus was giddy with g-stress. Phosphors seemed to dance across his board, disabling the readouts; the tidal pressure of his pulse in his ears made the new alarms which the ship flung at him sound muffled and imprecise, vaguely meaningless.

But now his visceral fear and his computer's programming worked together. One centimeter at a time, they forced his hand forward until his fingers found the keys which would ease *Trumpet*'s thrust and turn her aside from danger in a long curve across the pull of the well.

Then he was able to breathe again.

Sweet oxygen filled his lungs as the pressing weight of his body lifted. Relief spread a brief red haze across his vision, then wiped it clear. At the first touch of acceleration, automatic systems had locked the bridge in its thrust attitude, retracted the companionway. Now, as Angus stabilized *Trumpet*'s position in the red giant's well, the orientation bearings unlocked, allowing the bridge to revolve within its hulls to accommodate the star's gravity. His back and legs settled more comfortably into his g-seat.

Nick folded slowly over his belts and remained limp, breathing through his mouth.

A few more helm adjustments, and Angus would be able to relax. His computer ran calculations: his hands ran commands. When he was done, *Trumpet* had attained an elliptical orbit which would carry her around the star, absorbing gravity as momentum, and then enable her to slingshot herself back in the direction of human space at several times her present velocity. Fast enough for a gap crossing which would take her three or four light-years past the Amnion frontier.

There. Angus sucked air deep enough to distend his belly and held it until the CO_2 balance in his lungs had slowed his heart rate a few beats. God, he was thirsty! Thanks to Milos' abuse, and to the dehydration he'd suffered in his EVA suit, his mouth and throat felt like they'd been scoured with abrasives. A grainy sensation afflicted his eyeballs, as if they turned in grit. He was hungry and tired, and there was nothing he wanted right then more than a chance to check on Morn, find out if she was all right; touch her as if she still belonged to him.

His datacore had already allowed or coerced him to do several things he hadn't expected. Maybe it would permit that as well.

Except that she had her zone implant control now. Or rather Davies did: it came to the same thing. Neither of them was likely to let him within ten meters of her. Not without force—and Angus didn't believe for a second that his datacore would let him force himself on Morn Hyland. Warden Dios hadn't gone to all this trouble to rescue her—and to keep it a secret, for God's sake—just so that Angus could ease the dark ache in the pit of his heart.

Slowly he stretched out the muscles in his back and arms, then returned his attention to his board.

Trumpet's course was stable. The red giant spat out so much radiation that he could hardly scan her trace himself, even though he knew where to look. And within an hour the star's tremendous bulk would eclipse her from the direction of Thanatos Minor: she would be safe from pursuit or detection until she rounded the giant's far side.

If he couldn't approach Morn, he could at least drink several liters of fluid and get himself something to eat. Nick could be left where he was. He appeared to be asleep, overcome by the combined pressure of loss and g. And if he woke up, he couldn't do any harm. It was a simple matter for Angus to disable both bridge stations with his own priority-codes, which would effectively frustrate any tampering or interference.

He'd unstrapped his restraints and started to his feet before he realized that he didn't understand what he'd just done.

Wait a minute. He sat down again in shock. Wait a fucking minute. What the hell are we doing *here*?

At that moment Nick stirred. Twitching, his hands found the edges of the second's station; he braced his arms there to push himself upright. His eyes were dull with stupor. He blinked them deliberately, trying to clear them. His mouth hung open. Through the grime on his cheeks, his scars showed like small strips of bone.

By degrees a frown tightened his face as he blinked at his readouts.

He checked the screens in front of him, considered his readouts again. Unsteadily he tapped two or three keys. Then he turned his stunned gaze toward Angus.

As if he and Angus had the same thoughts for the same reasons, he asked, "What the hell are we doing *here*?"

"Hiding," Angus retorted. "What does it look like?" He had no idea what the truth was. Appalled by chagrin and incomprehension, he couldn't think. In a few instants of gap travel, a few minutes of mad flight, everything had changed. Suddenly his predicament was profoundly altered, as profoundly as it had been by his datacore's unexpected decision to rescue Morn, or by hearing Warden Dios say, *It's got to stop;* by his discovery of Morn herself aboard *Starmaster*, or by UMCPDA's req. Once again nothing made any sense, he had to start learning the rules and guessing the limits from the beginning—

" 'Hiding.' " Nick made an obvious effort to sound sarcastic, but he couldn't raise his voice above a thin mutter. "Who the fuck are we hiding *from*? I didn't bring us here. I must have passed out—you took the helm. Christ! Angus, we're three fucking light-years inside Amnion space. If you could generate that kind of gap crossing, why didn't you head the other way? Solve all your problems at once, let fucking Hashi Lebwohl welcome you with open fucking arms. What kind of shit *is* this?"

Good question. Angus would have said that aloud, if his programming had permitted it. UMCPDA had welded him precisely and explicitly for this mission. Either Hashi Lebwohl or Warden Dios had made every crucial decision. So what was Angus doing *here*? Why had his datacore led him to take this course, when it could have, should have, forced him to leap for human space?

"*Calm Horizons* was after us," he suggested weakly.

"And you thought she would follow us past the frontier?" Nick did his best to sneer. "Commit an act of war right in the cops' face? So what? She couldn't have caught us. We had momentum on her, we had a vector she couldn't match. And we've got"—he clicked keys, peered at a readout for confirmation, then hissed softly through his teeth in surprise—"shit, Angus, this ship has a thrust-to-mass ratio a lumbering tub like that can't compete with. Once she gets going, she can probably keep up with us in tach, but she can't match us in normal space.

"Don't tell me you came here to hide from *her*." Despite the dullness in his eyes and the pallor of his scars, he was recovering some of his energy. "I couldn't believe that even if I used both hands."

Angus couldn't believe it himself. And yet it was the truth. He himself, Angus Thermopyle—not his datacore, not Dios or Lebwohl—had made the decision to come here because *Calm Horizons* and *Soar* and maybe some of the Bill's ships were after him.

Echoing Nick involuntarily, he protested in dismay, What kind of shit *is* this?

Then, like another echo, he remembered the last time his programming had spoken to him directly. When Milos had attempted to take control of him in the Amnion sector of Billingate, a soundless voice in his head had countermanded Milos' orders.

You are no longer Joshua.

Jerico priority has been superseded.

You are Isaac. That is your name. It is also your access-code. Your priority-code is Gabriel.

"Shut up," he told Nick. Let me think. "I don't care whether you believe it or not. If I wanted you to know what my reasons are, I would have explained them already."

Access-code Isaac, he told the gap in his brain which served as a datalink. Why did you let me come here? Why didn't I have to head straight for UMCPHQ?

His datacore replied with a silence so complete that it seemed to resonate in his skull.

That fit. Although his computer had supplied him with vast impersonal bodies of information on such subjects as astrogation, *Trumpet*'s design, and fusion generators, it'd never revealed anything about itself. Dios had promised him, *Your programming will tell you what you need as you go along*. However, no one had ever offered him any kind of explanation.

The intercom chimed. "Angus, what's happening?" Davies' voice sounded ragged with g and helplessness. "Where are we? Can I wake up Morn yet? Is it safe?"

More vehemently than he realized, Angus hit commands on his board to disable all the ship's intercoms.

He couldn't suffer more distractions: he needed to *understand*.

Had Warden Dios or Hashi Lebwohl finally lost him? Had he somehow passed beyond the limits of his programming; broken free?

Or were his tormentors simply playing a deeper game than he could imagine?

God, was it possible that he'd *broken free*?

"Fine," Nick drawled. "Keep it to yourself." He studied Angus curiously. "Are you going to do that with your precious Morn, too? How do you think she and her self-righteous brat will react when they find themselves three light-years deep in Amnion space, and you refuse to explain why? My people I don't know about—I guess they've lost their minds. But Morn and Davies are going to go ape-shit."

"Shut *up*." The intensity of Angus' concentration congested his voice in his throat. He could hardly force out words. "I'm trying to think."

Frantic for answers, he cried his access-code in the silence of his head, used it to open a window on his databases. That worked: he hadn't lost his computer—or the information it contained. But did it still control him? Could he ignore its unspoken requirements?

A test: he needed a test. Some way to confirm quickly whether or not his datacore still ruled him. Some way to determine how far his ability to make his own decisions extended.

At once his heart tightened like a fist. Nick was here: the perfect choice. He was protected by his links to UMCPDA—and Angus hated him. If he spoke now, ignored or taunted Angus in any way, Angus would hit him again; hit him hard enough to splinter his skull, drive shards of bone into his brain, *kill* him by tearing his cerebral synapses to shreds—

"It's a little late for that," Nick remarked. Angus' distraction appeared to intrigue him. "We're *here*. And you can't pretend there won't be any consequences. My God, Angus, what is Hashi going to think of you? Or Min Donner?

"Sooner or later you'll have to start telling us the truth. You won't have any choice."

Now. Test it.

Gathering the strength of his shoulders, tensing his arms, Angus rose from his g-seat, readied himself to strike—

—and stopped. All the muscles he needed froze. At that instant he couldn't have swung his fist to save his sanity. Even the effort of closing the distance between himself and the second's station was beyond him.

He knew the sensation too well. It was intimately familiar: as brutal as a rape; and so compulsory that he would never be able to fight it. The emissions of his zone implants were stronger than will and hope.

Confusion swirled through him, as complex as a masque; his breathing felt caged in his chest. Damn you! he raged uselessly. Damn you to hell! His programming refused to let him pound his fists on the command board, so he ground them against his thighs. You bastards, why don't you tell *me* the truth once in a while? What would it cost you to let me know what you want?

But he couldn't afford to fall into the abyss of his fury: not now, with *Trumpet* three light-years deep in Amnion space, and Morn aboard.

Savagely he hauled himself back from despair.

All right. Don't give up. *Understand* it. His datacore still held him. He couldn't break past his programming. Nevertheless *some*thing had changed. Neither Dios nor Lebwohl could have known that he would try to bring *Trumpet* here—and yet his programming had allowed him to do it.

"Tell you what," Nick offered casually. "You sit there and think. Think until you burst a seal." He undid his belts, shifted to his feet. "I'll go tell your people and mine they can take a break from their cabins. Treacherous little shits, they'll like that. I'm sure they want to talk to you. They'll love hearing you refuse to explain why we're here—or, for that matter, how you and Milos managed to snatch Davies right out from under the Bill's nose, or what makes Morn so fucking important.

"Along the way I'll bring you something to eat and drink. You look like you could use it."

He paused, waiting for some acknowledgment.

Angus waved a hand to dismiss Nick; ignored Nick's departure from the bridge. He wanted hope, wanted desperately to let himself hope. Nevertheless all his instincts screamed against it.

It didn't make sense that the fucking cops would turn him loose. Someone—Dios or Lebwohl—had simply decided to pull a different set of strings. Strings and more strings, manipulating him like a puppet.

And yet the impulse to hope refused to let go of his heart.

Understand, God damn it!

Surely even his programming had limits. The more he did, the farther he traveled from UMCPDA's surgical wing, the more likely it became that cracks would appear in the blank wall of his mental prison. That motherfucking Lebwohl couldn't foresee *every*thing.

But of course the cops knew that. They must have made some provision for it. Otherwise the cumulative inadequacies of his instruction-set might let him be captured; or let him escape.

What could they do?

They could kill him themselves. Hardwire some kind of self-destruct into his datacore. But if they did that they would lose *Trumpet* and everyone aboard. They would lose Morn. And they obviously did not want to lose Morn. If they decided to kill him, they wouldn't do it until they learned what had happened to Thanatos Minor; until they got their hands on Morn.

Or they could put someone in a position to control him. That had been Milos' job. But Milos had betrayed the cops—and clearly Lebwohl or Dios had seen that coming; had planned for it. And there were no other candidates: not now; not while *Trumpet* remained out of contact with UMCPHQ. No one aboard knew the codes to command him.

Angus couldn't think of any other alternatives. Only one option remained.

Simply to keep him alive, the cops would have to let him make some of his own choices. Until they were able to put another of their stooges in Milos' place.

But if they did that, they would have to let him make decisions more and more often as time passed. And the gap between what he did and his original programming would widen. Eventually it might widen enough to let him slip through.

His brain seemed to burst with possibilities as a pain as bright as the detonation of Billingate's fusion generator exploded in the back of his head.

He'd already undone his restraints. The force of the blow slammed him facedown on his board, blind with agony: the impact split the skin of his left temple and cheekbone. Then his own recoil toppled him off the command station.

Another blow struck like impact fire below his right shoulder blade; drove him headlong to the deck. He skidded across a small splash of blood.

In microseconds a window opened like a screen in his head; damage assessments scrolled past his awareness. The shielding for his computer and power supply had absorbed most of the power of the second blow: his back was bruised but not broken. But the first concussion had pulped his scalp, spread a fretwork of stress fractures through his occipital lobe, compressed his brain. Another strike like that might kill him.

The sheer scale of the pain was going to kill him right now, every neuron in his body misfired anguish across his senses, he couldn't see or feel anything except the hurt in his skull.

He'd been hit from behind, his computer explained. His attacker was moving around the g-seat to get at him; moving fast—

Instantly his zone implants switched off the pain. They galvanized his muscles like an electric charge. His senses cleared.

He flipped over onto his back in time to see Nick plunging at him like *Captain's Fancy* out of the void toward *Tranquil Hegemony*, as full of ruin as a mine-hammer.

Loss and wild rage twisted Nick's face into a mask of savagery. His scars seemed to stream from his eyes like streaks of dark tears; a soundless howl stretched his mouth. As he dropped toward Angus, his right fist swung a C-spanner in a fatal arc for Angus' head. He must have found it in one of *Trumpet*'s emergency toolkits. Its head was stained with blood and hair from Angus' skull.

"Fucking sonofabitch!" Nick snarled as the spanner fell. "You did this to me!"

Savage himself, Angus snatched up his hand and caught the spanner centimeters away from his forehead.

One hand was all he needed. Despite Nick's force and weight, the blow stopped as if it had struck a bulkhead. He was stronger than Nick in any case. And welded struts reinforced his joints, improved his leverage; his reflexes ran at microprocessor speeds. He caught and held the spanner so solidly that Nick lost his grip and tumbled forward, throwing himself onto Angus.

With a twitch of his shoulder and a flick of his wrist, Angus clapped the spanner against Nick's temple and ear. Nick fell to the side, slapped his length along the deck.

At once he tried to crawl away. But he was too weak with shock and damage to move effectively. His hands seemed unable to find the surface under him: his elbows couldn't hold his weight. He collapsed onto his face; struggled up and collapsed again.

Angus rolled onto his feet and stood over Nick.

His hands and face were full of murder: violence steamed like vitriol in his veins. He *wanted* to kill Nick, would have given anything he could think of to take Nick's neck between his strong fingers and snap it like a stick.

His zone implants didn't permit that: they held him, trembling with fury and numb pain, where he stood.

"You dumb shit." Words were the only outlet he was allowed. Most of them came out in a clenched growl; some shouted like klaxons against the walls. "That was *stupid*. Do you think you can survive without me? Do you think you or Mikka or Morn or *any of you*"—his vehemence spattered blood from his temple and cheek—"can survive without me? I've already locked the bridge with priority-codes you don't know and can't break. You're three *light-years* deep in Amnion space. Without me you're going to drift here until you *rot*!"

Nick found the deck, pushed himself up onto his hands and feet. "I know," he murmured as if he were talking in his sleep. With a tortuous effort, he forced one leg under him, then the other, and staggered upright. "I know it was stupid. I just don't know why."

Wobbling on unsteady knees, he turned to face Angus.

"Why you're able to do things like that." Stupefied by his griefs and hurts, he couldn't keep what he was thinking to himself. "Why you can do things like that, but what you do with it doesn't make any sense."

Angus' programming prevented him from murder. On the other hand, it did grant him certain kinds of latitude. As smooth and swift as a snake, he reached forward and grabbed Nick by the front of his shipsuit, twisted the fabric into a knot. Shifting his weight, he lifted Nick into the air.

Eyes closed and neck limp, Nick dangled from Angus' grasp. Slowly the pressure of the knot at his throat began to strangle him; yet he didn't resist. Blood mounted in his face; his face swelled; spasms of anoxia ran reflexively along his arms. Nevertheless he didn't lift a hand to defend himself.

Good. The disasters which had overwhelmed him ever since he'd taken Morn aboard his ship may have driven him out of his mind, but he was still capable of learning—if the lessons were loud and hard enough.

"Can you think of *any* reason," Angus rasped harshly, "why I should explain myself to you? Why I should tell you *anything* except what I want you to do when I want you to do it?"

Retching for breath, Nick shook his head; mouthed, No.

"That's better."

With a silent curse of regret, Angus opened his hand and let Nick crumple to the deck. After one hoarse whoop for air, Nick sprawled flat and lay still.

Abruptly Angus' heart began to pound, and his own breathing caught in his throat. The window in his head had started to impinge directly on his optic nerves, flashing alarms across his vision to get his attention. The damage to his skull was serious. If his zone implants had let him feel it, the pain would have overwhelmed him like a tidal wave. He needed to get to sickbay.

Swallowing a rush of panic, he turned back to the command station.

Fortunately his computer kept his hands steady, his manner even. He typed a quick series of codes to reenable *Trumpet*'s intercoms, then thumbed a toggle to open channels to all the cabins. He didn't know who had taken which cabin, and didn't care: it didn't matter.

"All right, listen," he pronounced roughly. "For the next eight hours or so we should be about as safe as we're likely to get. Mikka, Davies, I want you on the bridge to keep an eye on Nick. He just tried to kill me. If he hadn't fucked it up, you would all be as good as dead."

Why didn't he bind and gag Nick, lock the bastard in a cabin? Because his programming declined to permit that. Even now, Nick was protected by his association with UMCPDA.

"I don't care what the rest of you do," Angus added. "Just leave me alone for a while."

He started to silence the intercom, then changed his mind. "Davies," he went on more quietly, "wake Morn up if you want to. Otherwise let her sleep. She looks like she can use it."

He could only guess what she'd been through aboard *Captain's Fancy*

—not to mention in the Amnion sector of Billingate—but it was obvious that she needed more than sleep to heal what Nick had done to her.

He wanted to heal her. She'd belonged to him once—been totally in his power, to use or abuse or adore as much as he desired. That made her part of his heart. He hoped—

No. Cursing again, he stopped himself. Hope was dangerous. He'd known that all his life; but in the confusion of his welding and mission he'd let himself forget it. Now it came back to him, however, as vivid as the warnings from his datacore. Nick wouldn't have been able to sneak up on him, hurt him like this, if he hadn't been distracted by his hunger for hope. Fear kept him alive. Heroes were all dead men: only cowards survived.

Carrying the damage to his skull as if it were the reason for his fear—as if it had nothing to do with his hope—he climbed the companionway and headed for *Trumpet*'s sickbay.

DAVIES

When Angus finally answered him over the intercom, Davies began to burn like hard thrust.

In a sense, he was always on fire. The endocrine intensity which his body had learned to accept as normal in Morn's womb kept his nerves hungry, his heart hot. He lived on the edge of combustion. Yet when he heard Angus' voice the flame in him leaped higher.

Sometime earlier, perhaps only half an hour ago, he'd taken Morn from the bridge into the first cabin he could find. It might have been Angus': it might once have been used by Milos Taverner, for all he knew. He didn't care. It had what he needed—two bunks equipped with g-seal webbing and sheaths to protect their occupants during high acceleration. As more and more of her memories came back to him, he found that he knew how to use her black box. If he'd trusted himself, he could have put his fingers on the right buttons with his eyes closed. When he was sure that she was deeply asleep, he'd secured her in one of the bunks, then done the same for himself. After that he'd waited for *Trumpet* to live or die.

More helplessness; more waiting.

He'd already lost track of how long he'd been alive. He'd spent too many of his few hours just like this, waiting in one kind of prison or another while other people somewhere else decided his survival. He couldn't distinguish this day or this moment from their predecessors. In a sense, Morn's past was more precise than his own; more distinct, as if it were more recent. Nevertheless, when g came slamming through *Trumpet*'s hull, he'd been grateful—briefly—for the restraints which kept him from being beaten to pulp against the cabin walls.

Once the ship appeared to have settled on a stable course, however, with clear gravity under her and no pressure from the thrust drive, larger questions had loomed. He'd waited as long as he could stand; then he'd risked leaving his bunk in order to reach the intercom and ask Angus what was happening.

The fact that Angus hadn't answered—that the intercom had gone dead under his thumb—made this prison no different than any of the others; as comfortless as his cell aboard *Captain's Fancy*, or his constricted ride in the ejection pod, or his room in Billingate. Because he wanted to live, he'd returned to his bunk, resealed the g-sheath and webbing. He could make that choice; but no others were allowed to him.

Then the intercom chimed, and Angus spoke at last.

"All right, listen." His voice was guttural with stress or pain. "For the next eight hours or so we should be about as safe as we're likely to get. Mikka, Davies, I want you on the bridge to keep an eye on Nick. He just tried to kill me. If he hadn't fucked it up, you would all be as good as dead.

"I don't care what the rest of you do. Just leave me alone for a while."

Angus paused. More quietly he finished, "Davies, wake Morn up if you want to. Otherwise let her sleep. She looks like she can use it."

Davies' heart responded like a magnesium flare. Without transition the questions became larger with a vengeance.

He flung himself out of his bunk. He needed movement; freedom from restraint. *As safe as we're likely to get.* How safe was that? *For the next eight hours or so.* Where were they—where had Angus taken them? *He just tried to kill me.* How safe could any of them be with Nick aboard?

But when he turned to consider Morn, he stopped; froze.

All the essential questions of his life were there in her abused face and imposed sleep.

She didn't look like she could "use" sleep: mere slumber was too fleeting to meet the scale of her need. She looked like she required the solace of physicians and psy-techs and utter peace, months of rest and healing.

She hadn't had time to lose much more weight since he'd first seen her in the Amnion birthing environment where he'd been force-grown. Nevertheless she seemed frailer, more emaciated, as if strain and zone implant addiction caused her to consume her own flesh for fuel. Her eyes had sunk deep into her skull; the sockets were as dark as wounds. Grime and unlove clogged her hair, but couldn't conceal the fact that patches of her scalp had been pulled bare: she might have just been through a failed course of chemotherapy. Despite the insulation of her g-sheath, her slack lips quivered as if she were freezing—or as if even the coercive emissions of her zone implant couldn't protect her from dreams of terror and loss.

She'd been a beautiful woman once. Now she looked spectral and condemned, stricken by mortality.

She was his mother. And she was virtually everything he knew about himself. His past and all his passions were hers.

The sight reminded him that she looked like this because she wanted him to live; that she'd exposed herself to Amnion mutagens and Nick's brutality—that she'd taken on all of *Captain's Fancy* alone and risked putting herself back in Angus Thermopyle's power—for him.

And he, Davies Hyland, held the black box which ruled her.

He didn't have time to stand over her, absorbing her pain—not if he wanted to help Mikka handle Nick—and yet he couldn't do anything else until this was done.

A sound like a palm slapped the cabin door. Muffled by bulkheads, Mikka Vasaczk called out, "Come on, Davies! If we don't stop that bastard, nobody else will."

Frustration and fire rose like a conflagration in Davies' chest until he heard Sib Mackern's voice.

"Take care of Morn, Davies. I can help Mikka. I've still got the handgun."

A rush of relief deflected the pressure. "I'll be there in a minute," Davies answered. He didn't know whether Mikka and Sib could hear him.

Gripping the zone implant control, he turned back to Morn.

She'd committed a crime.

Angus had done this to her. His violence and the sickness of his lust came back to Davies easily. Whenever he let himself remember them, they filled him with so much visceral loathing and disgust that he wanted to puke. Angus had put the electrode in her head, initiated her addiction.

But then he'd handed her the black box. She'd struck a deal with him, and he'd given her this small tool which made her simultaneously so much more and less than human. Instead of turning herself over to Com-Mine Security and the UMCP so that they could help her, she'd sold her soul to obtain Angus' power over her.

Davies remembered how she'd felt and what she'd thought well enough to understand her. Nevertheless he didn't share her addiction—or rather he was unaware of the nature of his own dependencies, his developmentally programmed appetite for levels of noradrenaline, serotonin, and endorphins which might have killed an ordinary man. He couldn't stop thinking like a UMCP ensign.

You're a cop, she'd told him for Nick's sake. *From now on, I'm going to be a cop myself. We don't do things like that.*

He should pick her up, carry her to sickbay; program the cybernetic systems to remove the electrode from her brain. Then he could help her face the consequences of her addiction. Surely he knew her well enough to get her through any crisis, even one that massive and personal.

Or else he should turn her over to the UMCP. They wouldn't punish her; they would acknowledge the circumstances which extenuated her crime. But they would be able to give her the kind of rehabilitation she deserved as well as needed.

Then he should arrest Angus. Nick had told him that Angus worked for the cops. *He doesn't want to, of course, but they've got his neck in a noose. He's doing this little job for them to keep them from snapping his spine.* And Angus had confirmed it, at least indirectly, by admitting that his former second, Milos Taverner, was a bugger for the UMCP. But that justified nothing. If for no other reason than to make them account for the fact that they'd chosen a rapist and butcher to do their work for them, Davies should deliver Angus to the police.

Yet Morn's lips still quivered as if she struggled to say his name through a veil of dreams and weeping. The fine muscles around her sore and sunken eyes twitched as if her dreams were full of pleading.

While he looked at her, he realized that he couldn't do any of the things he should. Could not. Not because Angus controlled the ship, controlled the lives of everyone aboard, but for entirely different reasons.

Morn was his mother; she was his mind; she'd performed miracles and suffered torments in his name. As far as he was concerned, she'd earned the right to choose her own fate. And Angus was his father. Angus had rescued him from the Bill—fought Nick for him—done everything possible to keep him safe. Regardless of what the cops or the law said about it, Davies was in Angus' debt.

Without warning, the intercom chimed. "Davies," Mikka said tightly, "you'd better get down here. You won't believe this if I just tell it to you. You need to see it for yourself."

That was true, he thought, looking at Morn. He needed to let her and Angus determine their own dooms. See for himself what they would do.

A strange sadness filled him as he touched the button which canceled the zone implant's emissions; but he didn't let it stop him. Gently he eased one of Morn's arms out of the g-sheath. The marks on her forearm appeared to be healing. As if the act were a caress, he folded the black box in her fingers and slid her hand back into shelter. For a minute grief clogged his throat; then he swallowed it down and moved toward the door.

"Davies."

She woke up more quickly than he would have believed possible. Exhaustion and prolonged dread turned his name into a croak.

Caught by sorrow—and by a touch of his father's unreasoning fear—he wheeled to face her.

With an effort, she blinked her dull gaze into focus. Slowly she forced her mouth to shape words. "Where are we?"

"I don't know." Like a kid, he wanted to go to her, comfort her; let her comfort him. "I'm going to find out."

Shaking with strain, she propped herself up on her elbow. "Take me with you," she breathed in a hoarse whisper.

"You need rest," he protested. "You've been through hell. I think we're done with heavy g, but you still need sleep. Wherever this is, we're probably going to be here for a while. You can afford—"

She shook her head. For a moment her head went on wobbling on her neck as if she lacked the strength to stop it. "I don't know what Angus thinks he's doing," she said like the rustle of hardcopy. "I don't trust him. I can't"—she faltered and closed her eyes as if she were praying, then forced them open again—"can't let him make all the decisions."

Weakly she began to pry herself out of the g-sheath.

Davies started forward to help her, then stopped. Her weakness was painful to see: maybe if he let her struggle alone she would exhaust her little energy and drop back to sleep.

But when she got her hands out of the sheath, she found the zone implant control in her grasp.

"Oh, Davies."

Sudden tears spilled down her cheeks. Hugging the black box, she huddled into herself as if she were about to break.

He couldn't bear it. A brief flash of killing rage at Angus and Nick and all men like them burned through him. Then he strode to the side of the bunk and took her in his arms. While she clung to her control, he unsealed the g-sheath and webbing, and lifted her out. After that he held her upright until she could remember how to stand.

He expected her to activate the black box, but she didn't. She hugged it to her chest for a minute or two, then lowered her arms and pushed the control into one of her pockets.

"Oh, Davies," she repeated through her tears, "what did he do to you?"

She was his mind: he understood her perfectly. Fighting the constriction in his throat, he answered thickly, "Nothing. I remembered, that's all. Seeing him made me remember. It was hard, but he didn't do it."

Loyalty required him to say this, despite the crimes Angus had committed against her.

"He rescued me. From the Bill. I still don't know how." Angus had said, *I can hide us visually, but I can't block sound. Not without distorting every bugeye in range*— How was that possible? "He brought me to the ship. He protected me from Nick. And he made Nick and the others"—Mikka and Ciro, Sib and Vector—"help us rescue you. I don't know what he thinks he's doing either. But he hasn't done anything to me."

One of her hands clutched at his arm; the other tried to rub tears out of her eyes. "I'm glad," she murmured as if the words were a cry from so far away that it was barely audible. "I don't understand, but I'm glad."

The intercom chimed again. This time Sib spoke.

"Davies, Vector is here. Nick isn't trying anything, but Vector can hold the gun on him. And Pup still has that stun-prod. If you want, I'll stay with Morn so you can come to the bridge."

Davies looked a question at Morn. She nodded; took more of her weight on her legs. When he was sure that she could stand, he went to the intercom and toggled the switch.

"She's awake. We're both coming down."

"Good," Mikka put in abruptly. "We need to talk."

Davies silenced the intercom without answering.

"You ready?"

Morn's bruised gaze hung on his face as she took one unsteady step toward him; another. Fearing she would fall, he put out his arms. But she stayed on her feet until she reached him.

Shaking weakly, her hands rose to touch the sore places on his cheekbones and along his jaw where Nick had hit him.

"I couldn't," she said, nearly choking, "couldn't believe you were safe. They told me you were, but I didn't dare believe it until I heard your voice— Then you took off your helmet, and I saw you'd been beaten up. I thought Angus did it, but you say he didn't."

Obliquely Davies remembered that at one time she hadn't been able to say Angus' name. Somewhere in the course of her imprisonment and rescue, her own perceptions of his father had undergone a subtle shift.

"Who was it?"

"Nick," he answered roughly. Then, because he owed her the truth, he added, "I started it. I had to keep him from leaving the ship. I knew he was cheating, but Angus didn't. He didn't know Nick had already sold you to the Amnion."

Morn bit her lip, gave him another loose nod. "I understand. And you remember what he did to me. You remember it all. That's why you wanted to lock him out of the ship.

"But there was something else. After you took off your suit, when you headed for the bridge, there was something—" Her gaze dropped, then came back up to his like an appeal. "You looked proud.

"I can't"—her throat closed convulsively—"can't remember what that feels like. What were you proud of? What did you do?"

Proud? Davies thought. The moment had been so brief, and what followed after it had been so urgent, that he had difficulty recollecting it. Proud?

Then it came back to him.

"It's hard to explain. The Bill had me. He talked to me a couple of times, questioned me—he was trying to find out what I knew so he could decide who to sell me to. But I didn't know anything. Except that I was finished as soon as he made up his mind. So I told him lies. I invented stories—about you and Nick—to make him unsure of himself."

Davies shrugged uncomfortably. "It worked. I didn't know the truth, but I made up lies that were so close to it he couldn't ignore them. And if I hadn't done that, I would have been out of reach. The Bill would have sold me, and Angus might never have been able to rescue me. Somehow I saved myself.

"When I finally learned the truth—when I saw why my lies worked—it felt good."

That wasn't the whole truth, however. He didn't go on to say, And I'm proud of Angus. When I don't think about you, about his crimes, about who he is, the things he does make me proud. He's my father—and he's superhuman.

That emotion seemed so odd and unjustifiable that Davies couldn't bring himself to admit it aloud.

Morn blinked as if she were fighting fresh tears. "What lies?"

Those memories were no more painful than any of the others. "The first time," he answered, "I told him you and Nick were working together. For the cops. I wanted to keep him from handing me back to Nick. And I wanted to make him think I was valuable—give him a reason to hold on to me, instead of turning me over to the Amnion."

So what you're saying, the Bill had replied later, *is that our Captain Nick had the colossal and imponderable gall to cheat the Amnion on one of their own stations.*

Then the woman with him—Davies guessed now that she was Sorus Chatelaine—had said, *It's more than that. He's saying Succorso had something so valuable to offer them that they were willing to trade force-growing for it. And then he cheated by not giving it to them.*

"The second time was more complicated. I had to make him think the stakes were so high that he couldn't afford to let go of me."

The Bill had countered by revealing that Nick had just turned Morn over to the Amnion. And Davies had replied with his best lie; his masterstroke.

"I told him you and Nick had a mutagen immunity drug."

Morn's eyes widened. "You were *guessing?*"

Davies nodded mutely.

After a moment a fragile smile eased her appearance. "You're good at it. I'm proud of you myself."

He smiled in return. Her approval released him from at least one of his fears.

She closed her eyes briefly; she might have been basking in the simplicity of his reaction. When she looked at him again, her smile was gone. Nevertheless some of the dullness had left her gaze. Her own questions had begun to clarify themselves.

"I guess I'm as ready as I'll ever be," she murmured. "Let's go. I want to know where we are."

Davies also felt ready; readier now than just a few moments ago. He offered her his arm. She accepted it, leaned on him gratefully while he keyed the door.

DAVIES

Together they went out to the companionway and started down to the bridge.

Davies saw at a glance that everyone except Angus was there. Nick lay on the deck below one of the display screens with his head braced on his hand as if he couldn't be bothered to stand. A red welt swelled along his temple and ear; in a few hours it would match the livid bruise on his forehead.

Two or three meters out of his reach, a C-spanner rested against the bulkhead. Its head was crusted with dried blood.

More blood marked the left side of the command console. There was blood on the deck.

Mikka sat in Angus' g-seat. Sib had taken the second's station: he used the board to support his forearms so that he could keep his handgun trained on Nick without tiring. Both Vector Shaheed and Ciro, Mikka's young brother, were on their feet. The engineer peered at an auxiliary command board which he'd located off to one side of the screens. Apparently Ciro had already accepted his new role as *Trumpet*'s cabin boy: he was passing around a tray laden with sandwiches, coffee, and hype.

They all turned when they heard Davies and Morn on the companionway. Concern filled Sib's face, but Vector grinned with sudden pleasure. Mikka's ingrained glower loosened without releasing its grip on her features. Only Nick kept his attention to himself. Except for the way he chewed the inside of his scars, he looked relaxed and self-absorbed, as if he were alone.

"Morn, you shouldn't be up," Sib protested. "You need—"

Mikka cut him off brusquely. "Worry about something else, Sib. She knows what she's doing."

With unexpected precision, Davies remembered the exact moment at which Morn had told Mikka about her zone implant. He could taste the specific loneliness which had inspired her to take that risk.

As she and Davies finished their descent, she demurred thinly, "I wouldn't go that far." Then she let go of her son's arm and gestured toward Ciro. "But I know I need food."

Eager to help, Ciro hurried to offer her his tray.

"Thanks." She took a hype capsule—affectionately known as "industrial-strength caffeine"—then helped herself to a sandwich and a mug of coffee.

Everyone but Nick watched her while she swallowed the capsule, bit into the sandwich, sipped the coffee; they all waited to hear what she would say, see what she would do.

Between bites, she asked impersonally, "Where's Angus?"

Mikka answered in a tone as harsh as her glare. "He didn't say where he was going. He just told us to leave him alone. 'For a while,' he said."

"Sickbay, probably," Nick supplied for no apparent reason. A grin jerked like a spasm across his teeth and then faded. "He's got one hell of a dent in his skull."

"Nick, I don't understand you," Mikka retorted with elaborate patience. "Don't you ever *think* about what you're doing?" Behind her patience, exasperation seethed like acid. "He's the *captain* of this ship. If he's like you, he's got everything locked away with priority-codes we can't touch."

"I'll vouch for that." Vector pointed at the board he'd been studying. "I've been trying to look at his records, just to see what this ship can do, how she does it. But I can't get access. I can't even call up engineering diagnostics. Scan and astrogation are available—nothing else. Not even communications.

"Unless he let you in on any of his secrets." He cocked an eyebrow at Davies.

Davies shook his head. He had no idea what codes Angus might have invoked in the past hour.

"You kill Angus," Mikka finished, "and we might as well cut our throats. We'll be helpless."

"You mean," Nick sneered back at her, "you don't already feel like you've had your throat cut?"

"Nick—" Mikka began hotly.

"That's enough, Mikka." Although Morn's tone was quiet, it stopped Nick's former second like a command. She seemed to take over the bridge just by being there, despite her weakness. She was only an ensign, had never commanded a vessel before; yet she might have been *Trumpet*'s true captain, regardless of who held the priority-codes. "Don't waste your time on him. He's just dangerous—he isn't important anymore."

Mikka glared at Nick while anger clenched and unclenched on his face. Sib tightened his fist around the gun. But Nick didn't move; didn't glance at Morn or Mikka. After a moment Mikka breathed, "Right," and turned back to Morn.

"Do you want to sit down?" As if in recognition of Morn's position, Mikka offered her the command station. She sounded perplexed as she added, "You don't look strong."

No doubt she'd assumed that Morn was using her zone implant to keep herself on her feet.

"Thanks." As Mikka stood, Morn moved to the g-seat and lowered herself like a sigh into her place. For a moment she closed her eyes and bowed her head, as if she were waiting for hype or coffee to take effect. Then she emptied her mug and clipped it into a holder on the side of the armrest.

"We've got a lot to talk about," she announced softly. "We should probably do it before Angus comes back.

"If you can access scan and astrogation, I assume you know where we are."

Mikka glanced at Vector. In response, he hit keys on the auxiliary board, and at once a schematic starchart gleamed to life on one of the screens. More keys: a blip marked *Trumpet*'s position on the chart.

"Oh, shit." Davies didn't need anyone to tell him what the coordinates along the sides of the display meant. Morn's years in the UMCP Academy were fresh in his mind; he knew what she knew about astrogation. "What are we doing *here?*"

Trumpet rode a tight elliptical orbit around a red giant in Amnion space. She was roughly three light-years from the frontier of human territory.

Mikka shrugged tightly. "I guess that's why Angus says we're safe for a while. *Calm Horizons* probably won't think to look for us in this direction. And that's a loud star—it's roaring like a smelter all across the spectrum. So it provides a lot of cover."

"But that's not the good news," Vector put in calmly. "The good news is that this orbit gives us acceleration. We can slingshot off the far side fast enough for a gap crossing twice the size of the one we took to get here. If," he added, "that's what Angus has in mind."

"So it makes sense." Davies was taken aback by the sharpness of his desire to trust Angus. "Coming here makes sense."

Mikka didn't hesitate to contradict him. "Only if you assume it makes sense not to head in the opposite direction." Her stance—the way she cocked her hips and held her arms—was unselfconsciously assertive. "Instead of coming here, we could have crossed three light-years into human space. Maybe this is safe. *That* would have been safer. Especially if you believe what we've heard about Angus working for the cops. In that case, they probably have an entire fleet waiting to protect us."

"Which means?" Vector asked, not as if he didn't understand, but rather as if he wanted everything to be explicit.

"Either he isn't working for the cops," Mikka finished, "or we haven't even begun to understand what this is all about."

Nick snorted contemptuously, but didn't speak.

"But that's crazy," Sib protested. "He *must* be working for the cops. How else did he get his hands on a ship like this? How else did he manage to arrive just when we needed him?" Forgetting Nick in his anxiety, he turned toward Morn and Davies. "Why did he rescue you? This is Angus Thermopyle we're talking about. Maybe he didn't commit the crime we framed him for, but he's a rapist and a murderer, we all know that. None of it makes sense unless he made a deal so the cops wouldn't execute him."

"Sib," Mikka warned, "pay attention."

With a gulp of chagrin, Sib swung back to face Nick.

Nick hadn't moved.

Morn studied the display for a moment longer, then looked away. "That doesn't matter," she pronounced finally. "Maybe he made a deal and then decided to break it. Maybe he and—what was his name, Milos Taverner?—really did steal the ship and come here on the run." She glanced at Mikka, at Vector, at Davies. "Maybe the UMCP is engaged in something corrupt, like taking Intertech's mutagen research to keep it secret." Anger echoed in her voice, but it didn't distract her. "None of that matters.

"We're *here*. We have to face the situation as it *is*. And if we're going to do that, we'd better figure out what we want. We'd better agree on it. There are too many of us. If we don't stick together, we'll all be useless.

"Let's talk about *that*. Let Angus take care of himself."

A sudden silence took the bridge. For a moment there was nothing to hear except muffled breathing and the faint electronic hum of *Trumpet*'s equipment.

Davies understood Morn's condition clearly: what looked like assurance in her was really exhaustion and a sense of absolute necessity. Her willingness to take so much on herself amazed him.

He yearned to believe that he could do the same.

Then Nick muttered sardonically, "You think you're going to be able to make him do what you want? Good luck."

At once Sib spoke as if he'd been stung. "You decide," he told Morn. "Leave me out of it. I got what I wanted when we ended up here, instead of dead on *Captain's Fancy*, or trapped on Billingate." Half apologetically, he explained to Mikka, "I never really belonged with him." He indicated Nick. "I never liked what we were doing—even before he started selling people to the Amnion. After that I guess all I wanted was for somebody to make me brave enough to go against him. Maybe that's all I've ever wanted." Addressing Morn again, he concluded, "As long as he's not in command, I'll go along with whatever the rest of you decide."

Mikka snorted in response, but her disdain wasn't directed at Sib. "You know, it's funny," she mused. "For the longest time it never occurred to me to want anything except what he wanted. I never questioned what he did—or why he did it. I even got you into this," she told Ciro, "because I couldn't think of an alternative. I couldn't imagine there were any alternatives. There are worse ways to live"—she glared straight at Morn—"than being illegal.

"But you broke it. Whatever it was I thought I was doing, whatever it was that kept me in my blind little world and didn't let me think, you broke it. You were better-looking than me, more capable, stronger. And you sure as hell must have fucked better than I did. Once you came aboard, there was no chance Nick was ever going to take me seriously again. And that broke it. I started thinking about the consequences—for Ciro, if not for me. I don't mind playing games with the cops, but I started thinking about what it means when you play games with the Amnion. Especially when the stakes are so high.

"I guess I'm like Sib. All I want is to not be aboard *Captain's Fancy*—not take any more orders from Nick. And maybe give Ciro a chance for something better. I haven't had time to come up with anything else yet."

Her brother shifted his feet self-consciously whenever she referred to him; but when she was done, he nodded several times, as if he thought she needed his support. "I want to be an engineer," he said in a rush so that his embarrassment wouldn't stop him. "Vector's teaching me. Maybe Angus can teach me." He faltered for a second, then went on with a kid's abashed dignity, "Engineers don't kill people. They don't betray their own crew."

Nick raised his head, brandished a snarl. "I couldn't betray you, Pup. You aren't real enough. There's nothing there to betray."

"I imagine Vector feels the same way," Mikka put in to cover Nick's malice. "So it's up to you and Davies."

"Actually, no," Vector remarked promptly. "I don't feel that way. But I would rather not talk about it"—he faced Morn steadily with his blue gaze and his calm smile—"until I hear what you and Davies have to say."

Mikka frowned her surprise, but didn't object.

Davies studied the damaged patches on the back of Morn's head while she regarded Vector. When she spoke, he seemed to know what she was about to say before he heard it.

"What about you, Davies? What do you want?"

I want to be you, he answered silently. I want to be Angus. I want to make something good out of all this.

But he didn't say that aloud.

"I'll tell you what I think we should do," he replied instead. "I think we should turn this whole mess over to the UMCP. Mikka's right—when the stakes are this high, we have to consider the consequences. The Amnion know an immunity to mutagens is possible. Nick made that obvious —you confirmed it. The UMCP need to know about that. It changes the whole dilemma of dealing with forbidden space.

"And they need to know about me. I mean they need to know why the Amnion are after me. If we—if humankind is in danger of being infiltrated by Amnion who look just like us, we've got to warn them. That's the only defense." The thought of being used to help create more effective versions of Marc Vestabule filled Davies with a nausea which had nothing to do with his stomach.

"That's right," Sib put in, suddenly urgent. "And there's something else. I just remembered. Nick said he figured out why the Amnion gave us those gap components—the ones that nearly killed us. If he's right, it was an experiment. They're testing a way to reach near-C velocities by using a special kind of gap drive. When Vector saved us, we came out of tach at almost 270,000 kps. Nick thinks that's exactly what those components are for."

Nick nodded to himself. He still lay on the floor; yet he conveyed the impression that everything on the bridge revolved around him.

"We know it works," Sib hurried on. "If they can make it work—if they can do what we did without slagging their drives—then ships like

Calm Horizons can hit human space at .9C. Ships with super-light proton cannon.

"There's no defense against something like that."

At once new apprehensions burned along Davies' nerves. Sib was right: there was no defense— A much slower vessel with super-light proton cannon, a lumbering tub called *Gutbuster*, had killed his—no, Morn's—mother; had nearly killed her father's entire command.

His nerves cracking with adrenaline, he insisted, "That's another reason why we should turn this mess over to the UMCP. They need to know."

Morn, they *need* to know.

"I know you think they're corrupt," he argued even though she hadn't contradicted him; hadn't said anything at all. The mute steadiness of her gaze made him feel that he had to justify himself—that if he couldn't persuade her something precious would be lost. "Nick's immunity drug proves it. But keeping our mouths shut isn't the answer. We've got to tell them what's going on so they can defend against it. And we can force them to account for themselves if we make what they've done public."

He stopped hard, almost held his breath while he waited for her reaction.

She didn't need to think before she answered. Her ordeals had taught her to be sure. With the strength of hype and caffeine rather than of zone implant emissions, she said, "I gave them more than confirmation. They took samples of my blood when I still had the drug in my system. I don't know if those samples survived. If they were on the shuttle—if *Soar* or *Calm Horizons* got them—then it's only a matter of time before they're taken to a lab where they can be analyzed. Then the Amnion can start redesigning their mutagens."

Before Davies could say anything, she went on, "But you mentioned consequences. Have you thought about what happens to Mikka, or Sib, or Vector?

"You say you want to 'turn this whole mess over to the UMCP.' Suppose Angus lets us do that. Or suppose we take the ship away from him, so he doesn't have any say in the matter. What happens to Mikka and Sib and Vector? They're *illegals*, Davies. And they saved our lives. Do you want them arrested? Do you want them executed? Ciro might get leniency—he's still young. But Mikka and Sib and Vector could be executed.

"I told you we're cops, but I think you know what I meant. I wasn't talking about the kind of cops who suppress antimutagens so that men like

Nick can play with them. I was talking about my mother and father—your grandparents. You remember them as well as I do. What do you think they would have done?"

Her grave eyes searched Davies; her question touched him as profoundly as her refusal to let him lock Nick out of the ship. Shortly after he was born, she'd said to him, *As far as I'm concerned, you're the second most important thing in the galaxy. You're my* **son.** *But the* **first,** *the* **most** *important thing is to not betray my humanity.*

He recognized her there. As if they'd reached a place where he could be her, where they were the same, he said quietly, "They would have fought for what they believe in until it killed them."

Her smile was small and fragile, as naked as glass; nevertheless to him it looked like dawn.

Turning her station toward Nick, she said, "That leaves you." Her tone was impersonal, as if she no longer felt threatened by him—or as if her loathing for him had become so vast that it could no longer be expressed. "What do you want?"

Ciro looked at her in surprise. "Morn!" Sib objected immediately; and Mikka growled, "Morn—" But Vector nodded his approval; his smile conveyed a suggestion of relief.

Because he recognized her, Davies didn't protest.

Morn didn't react to Sib or Mikka; Nick ignored them. For a moment he continued to lie still, as if he hadn't heard Morn. But then, smoothly, like a hunting cat, he rose into a sitting position with his legs crossed in front of him and his back against the bulkhead.

"I want Sorus." A mad grin clutched his mouth. He held up one fist with the knuckles white, as tight as a vise. "I want her heart."

"Fine." A tinge of acid gave Morn's voice bite. "She's yours. On the other hand, that isn't very useful. You aren't likely to get a chance at her anytime soon. I can't help thinking there must be other things you *want*." She seemed to stress the word deliberately. "What were you after before you recognized Captain Chatelaine? I presume you were going to sell your immunity drug to the Bill so you could pay for repairs. Isn't that still what you want?

"You don't need repairs anymore, but you could use leverage. Otherwise your future doesn't look good. You might not live long enough to have a chance at Sorus Chatelaine. Aren't you scheming right now? If you could find the right buyer, you might be able to hire enough help to take on all the rest of us. Even Angus."

Now Mikka understood what Morn was after. "Sure," she rasped, "he must be. Whatever else we do, we'd better tell Angus to keep him away from communications. He can't find buyers if he can't access communications."

Nick didn't glance at Morn or Mikka. For a minute or two, he studied his hard fist and white knuckles as if he might be able to read his fate there. Then, slowly, he lowered his arm.

"There's only one thing I want from you, Morn," he said distantly. She might not have been present; he might have been talking to himself. "Take off that shipsuit—let me fuck you right here in front of your kid and your friends.

"You liked it the last time. Nothing's changed since then—nothing significant. You haven't suddenly become honest. The only difference is that you needed *me* then. *Now* you need Sib and Vector and Mikka and your asshole of a son. You even need *Pup*, you poor bitch. You need *Angus*. One way or another, you're going to have to let them all fuck you.

"You're better off with me."

Davies couldn't stop himself: he had too much of his father in him. And he knew Nick too well: he could remember every detail of the anguish Morn had suffered at Nick's hands. Snarling between his teeth, he sprang past the command station.

Morn snapped his name. Mikka followed him a step, then stopped. Ciro jerked himself out of the way. Sib jumped from his g-seat, trying to keep a clean line of fire on Nick.

Davies didn't have Angus' bulk or experience, but he'd inherited Angus' strength. With his fists knotted in Nick's shipsuit, he hauled Nick to his feet and punched him at the bulkhead. Centimeters from Nick's face, he spat, "Are you *finished?*"

Nick didn't resist. He hardly bothered to focus his gaze on Davies. Nevertheless his scars stretched like sneers across his cheeks as he countered softly, "Are you?"

"Davies!" Morn commanded. "Leave him alone. I don't care what he says. He can't hurt me."

Neurotransmitters crackled like fire along Davies' synapses; a conflagration hungry for violence. Morn had been trained to fight in the Academy. With one swift smash of his forehead, he could hammer Nick's skull against the bulkhead, crush his nose, maybe drive splinters of bone into his brain.

But Nick made no effort to protect himself. Morn's response to a passive or helpless opponent had also been trained into her; into her son. Davies could imagine the strike which would turn Nick's face to pulp and perhaps kill him. That was as far as his mother's convictions and reactions allowed him to go.

"You're lucky," he muttered to her as he opened his fists and pushed away from Nick. "He hurts *me* just by being here."

Then for a second he thought that so much restraint was more than he could bear. Every nerve in his body had been bred to passion and fury and bloodshed: he couldn't simply turn his back and leave Nick untouched.

Wheeling like a blow, he raged, "You sonofabitch, you never gave her a *chance*! You didn't want honesty—you didn't give a *shit* whether she was honest! You just didn't like being so fucking *mortal*. You wanted her to make you feel like *God*!"

A spasm like a flinch pulled at Nick's face, but he didn't retort.

Davies swung his anger toward Morn. Balked by her forbearance, by the part of her which reined him, he demanded harshly, "It's *your* turn. You've asked all the rest of us. Now tell us what *you* want."

Shadows of pain moved in the depths of her eyes. For a moment exhaustion filled her face, and her shoulders slumped as if mere hype and caffeine weren't enough to sustain her assurance. He could see that she'd told him the truth, as far as she knew it: Nick had lost the power to hurt her. But her son was another matter. He could inflict pains which reached her core.

"It's not that simple," she murmured weakly. "What I want isn't what counts. We need to face the bigger issues—"

From the head of the companionway, Angus rasped, "This is *my* ship." His harshness was like Davies', but deeper, more organic. "You're all here because I *allow* it. You're all under my command.

"Don't any of you care what *I* want?"

Davies clenched his fists at his sides and froze as if he were caught between his own desire to welcome Angus' arrival and Morn's impulse to fling herself at Angus' throat.

DAVIES

Morn stiffened in her seat. Mikka muttered a curse under her breath; instinctively protective, she held out a hand to draw her brother toward her. Shrugging to himself, Vector keyed off the auxiliary board and retracted it into its slot in the engineering panel. Sib flinched; pulled his handgun around to cover Angus, then forced himself to turn the weapon back on Nick. Nick stood leaning on one of the display screens as if he didn't want to waste his strength holding himself upright.

Scowling a sneer at Sib, Angus came down the treads to confront Morn and Davies.

He'd removed his EVA suit, put on a nondescript shipsuit; perhaps so that sickbay could treat him more easily. A bandage which reeked with the characteristic oily smell of tissue plasm was plastered to the back of his head; a small welt on his forearm marked the place where the sickbay had injected him with analgesics, antibiotics, metabolins. Another bandage covered a wound high on his cheekbone. Nevertheless he didn't move like a man who'd been injured. He looked rested, strong—and untouchable. His porcine eyes were yellow with malice.

"I'm disappointed," he rasped sourly. "Doesn't *any*body care what I want?"

After a last glance around the bridge, he fixed his attention exclusively on Morn.

Abruptly Davies forgot why he'd wanted to welcome Angus. Morn's memories stung his heart. As if it were happening in front of him, he could see Angus' fist on the black box—

Angus reached into one of the compartments along the bulkhead, selected a scalpel, and handed it toward her. "Take it."

Anguish she couldn't utter had filled her like wailing.

The zone implant control demanded a smile; she smiled. It told her to kneel in front of Angus: she knelt.

Grimly Davies stepped between her and Angus, braced one hand like a refusal on Angus' chest. "I'm warning you—" His voice caught in his throat; he couldn't go on.

Angus didn't look at his son: he faced Morn as if the two of them were alone on the bridge.

"All right, I'll ask," she said tightly. "What do you want?" She might have been fighting down a desire to scream.

His brows knotted in a scowl that shrouded his eyes. His tone was a strange mixture of truculence and terror.

"I want you."

Davies looked over his shoulder at Morn, hoping that she would give him permission to hit Angus.

"Angus, listen to me." Deep within Morn, Angus' words seemed to find a place of anger and loathing. Her fatigue and pain sloughed away as if she'd forgotten them; as if she'd used her zone implant control to switch them off. From her pocket she pulled out the black box and held it up against him like a weapon. "I swear to you that if you touch me—if you try to put one finger on me—I'm going to hit all the buttons at once and fry my brains. I would rather turn myself into a lump of dead meat than let you have any piece of me."

Her eyes held his, daring him to doubt her.

Davies swallowed the constriction in his throat. "And I'll kill you."

"One of us will," Mikka promised severely. "We'll find a way somehow. We're alive because of you, and I'm grateful. But I won't let you have her."

Sib nodded as if his commitment to Morn affected him like panic.

"Oh, get out of the way, Mikka," Nick taunted. "Let him have her, if that's what he wants. You're illegal. Like me. You've done worse than sacrificing the occasional reluctant slut, when you had something to gain by it. You've helped me do worse. Don't try to be so goddamn righteous now. It isn't credible."

Angus didn't glance at Nick. No one else reacted to his gibe. The tension between Angus and Morn ruled the bridge: Nick couldn't penetrate it.

As if he were relieved—and infuriated by it—Angus retorted, "Why am I not surprised?"

Without warning he aimed his anger at Davies. "Get your hand off me. I'm not going to touch her."

Davies did his best to match Angus' scowl. He leaned his weight into his palm, hoping to make Angus feel at least that much of his strength; trying to tell his father what he'd learned from Morn's memories. He wouldn't let himself be cowed: he couldn't afford it.

Then he stepped back.

It's because of men like you I became a cop.

If Angus had received any part of his son's message, however, he didn't show it. Already he'd shifted his attention back to Morn. The strain on his face was impossible to interpret: it might have been rage conflicted with intimate grief. Or perhaps the sickbay systems simply hadn't given him enough analgesics to contain the pain in his head.

"I've got something for you."

With a negligent flick of one hand, he tossed an object toward her as if it were trivial.

Flinching in surprise, she nearly dropped it. But her fingers caught on the chain.

Her eyes widened as she recognized her id tag. "Where—?"

She stopped, unable to finish the question.

"Nick gave it to me," Angus replied in a tone as troubled as his expression. "He wasn't being generous. We made a deal. I was supposed to snatch Davies and give him to Nick. Nick was supposed to let me have you. He gave me your id tag to show he was serious." He shrugged tightly. "He didn't bother to mention that Davies is my kid. Or that he'd already handed you over to the Amnion." Sardonically Angus concluded, "Must have slipped his mind."

Morn ducked her head as if she were trying to hide tears. Relief or chagrin twisted her mouth. Past the screen of her dirty hair, she breathed, "At least he didn't sell it."

The Amnion would have paid well for the id tag of a UMCP ensign.

"If he had, it wouldn't have made any difference," Angus retorted. He seemed to find an obscure satisfaction in pointing out Nick's treacheries. "The Amnion already knew about you. They must have known you were a cop when you went to Enablement."

Morn's head jerked up; dismay filled her bruised eyes.

Angus answered her silent question. "It turns out Milos Taverner—that motherfucker who used to be my second—was a bugger for just about everybody, Com-Mine Security, the cops, Nick, the Amnion. Anything he knew he sold. He must have sold what he knew about you long before you ever went into forbidden space.

"The Amnion understood the stakes. Better than Nick did. That's why they were willing to keep on making deals with him when he'd already cheated them so often."

"Then why did they let me go?" she asked in a tense whisper.

"I've got a better question," Nick put in.

Morn glared at Nick as if he'd insulted her. Davies nearly told Nick to shut up, but he swallowed the impulse. In a situation like this, hungry to reestablish some sense of his own importance, Nick was likely to say something crucial.

Nick grinned with a hint of his old savagery. "Why did they let *me* go? Milos told them I did work for Hashi fucking Lebwohl. They had reason to be suspicious."

Angus turned his scowl on Nick. "Somehow I just know you're going to tell us the answer. Otherwise we might forget how smart and cunning you are."

"Because," Nick explained to Morn as if he hadn't heard Angus; as if Angus and Davies were irrelevant, like Mikka and Sib, Ciro and Vector, "they didn't know *you* were 'Morn Hyland' until you took over my ship. None of us actually said your whole name before that. And even then they probably needed time to run it through their computers."

"Is any of this true?" Angus asked Morn sharply.

"I think so." Her eyes were dull with doubt and the effort to remember. "I wasn't in good shape at the time."

Unselfconsciously Davies nodded in agreement. He could recollect hearing Nick call her simply a "human female" when he spoke to the Amnion.

"Besides," Nick went on, "they made a deal with me—and they live by deals. They needed a reason to break it, and they didn't know I was cheating until after they tested my blood. By that time they already knew they wanted Davies. And then they realized who you were.

"Using us to test those gap drive components must have seemed like a stroke of genius. They couldn't lose. If the acceleration experiment succeeded, we would still be in forbidden space when we resumed tard. They could get the confirmation they wanted, and still catch you and Davies. And me. And if the experiment failed, we were all dead. They got rid of several threats at once, and they learned those components weren't ready to use on their own ships."

"And it would have worked," Davies cut in, "if Angus hadn't come along. You're pretty good at figuring these things out after the fact, but you weren't able to handle them at the time."

Nick twitched one shoulder in a small shrug, but didn't respond.

For a moment the bridge was silent. Mikka chewed the private bitterness of her thoughts; Vector watched Morn and Angus as if he were waiting for something; Ciro concentrated hard, like a kid fighting not to drown in waters over his head. Absentmindedly Sib scratched his thin mustache with the muzzle of his handgun; then he remembered to level the gun at Nick again.

Slowly Angus turned away from Nick. He stood facing Morn like a recognition that she was in command.

She made a palpable effort to recover the assurance—the desperate clarity—which had sustained her earlier. With undisguised hunger she looked at her zone implant control; then, as if she were punishing herself, she pushed it back into her pocket. Grimly she dragged her hair away from the sides of her face, tucked it behind her ears.

At last she met Angus' gaze.

Confronting him with her wounded eyes, she said, "That brings us back to what we were talking about before. It all went wrong for the Amnion when you intervened. So now they have even more reason to want to stop us." She paused, holding his stare, summoning her courage. Then she asked bluntly, "What are we doing here, Angus?"

Angus' expression was unreadable. Davies could see the small muscles around his eyes tug and release as if they were signaling, but their message was coded; indecipherable.

After a moment Angus answered, "Hiding."

"Shit," Nick sneered. "I've already told you what I think of that explanation."

Mikka glanced at Nick dourly, then said to Angus, "He's right. That's bullshit. Why do we need to hide? Why didn't we head straight for human space as soon as we got clear of Thanatos Minor's debris? Who're we supposed to be hiding from?"

"We're three light-years deep in Amnion territory," Morn added. Her tone grew steadier as she spoke. "We're safe for now, but we've given them time. Time to react. Time to hunt for us. Time to organize a blockade—or a chase.

"Why did you do that, Angus?"

When he didn't respond, she tightened her jaw. Carefully she articulated her real question. "Who are you working for?"

The muscles around his eyes tightened and released like little spasms of pain; the corners of his mouth knotted. Suddenly Davies thought he knew the truth. He'd seen Angus look like that once before—or rather Morn had.

After Nick had crippled *Bright Beauty*, Morn had regained consciousness in time to see Angus sitting like a battered toad in his g-seat. She'd checked her readouts, learned what had happened. Then she'd said to him, *"You're beaten. He beat you."*

He'd turned a face gray with despair toward her. As if he were trying to be angry, he'd retorted, *"Proud of him, aren't you.* **Beat** *me."*

"Angus." She'd never used his name before. "I can save you. I'll testify for you. When you go back to Com-Mine, I'll support you. I've still got my id tag.

"Just give me the control. The zone implant control."

Her desperation had been that profound. Angus had broken her in ways he hadn't anticipated.

To her dismay, she saw tears in his eyes.

"I'll lose my ship."

"You can't save it," she shot back. "I can handle Station Security. And the UMCP. But **nothing** *can save your ship."*

Softly, he said, "And give up my ship. That's the deal, isn't it. You'll save me. If I let you have the control. But I have to give up my ship."

She nodded. After a moment, she replied, "What else have you got to bargain with?"

There, right then, he'd looked the way he did now—trapped and helpless, more bitter than he could bear. In some fashion that Davies couldn't understand, Angus was trapped again; caught by needs and exigencies he could neither avoid nor satisfy.

When he replied, his tone was casual and false.

"Hashi Lebwohl."

Ciro opened his mouth in surprise; Mikka gaped like her brother. Disappointment clouded Vector's blue eyes, and his habitual calm smile drooped.

Like a crackle of static, Nick laughed. "I knew it. It had to be the cops." He shook his head scornfully. "You miserable bastard, if they can make *you* do their dirty work, we're all doomed."

Morn held Angus' gaze and remained still as if she didn't dare betray any reaction. Nevertheless Davies believed he knew what she was thinking. He could hear Vector telling her, *The UMCP is the most corrupt organization there is. It makes piracy look like philanthropy.* He could feel her anguish. *We had the raw materials for a defense, we had all the rungs. And they took it, they* **suppressed** *it. Forbidden space is their excuse for power.*

For some reason Davies didn't feel that same distress. His confusion toward his father produced a different response.

"This is one of his operations," Angus explained as if he were lying—or using pieces of the truth to hide a lie. "He set it all up. He broke me and Milos out of UMCPHQ, got us this ship, sent us to Billingate. I had two jobs. Blow up Billingate's fusion generator." He hesitated like a man swallowing panic, then finished, "And rescue you.

"But it's all covert," he continued harshly. "We can't just sail back into human space like we're expecting a goddamn hero's welcome. That would ruin our cover."

" 'Cover'?" Mikka snapped. "What do we need cover for?"

Angus ignored her. "We're supposed to go on looking like illegals. Like rogues. Lebwohl doesn't want to be accountable. So there's no fleet waiting for us. If the Amnion decide we're worth breaking the frontier treaty for, we're on our own. Until I get new orders." A complex and ambiguous rage vibrated in his voice. "We can make our own decisions for a while."

Morn frowned. Davies felt the strain in her; the arduous struggle to concentrate despite her exhaustion and dismay. "Don't you have to report?" she asked with difficulty. "Surely DA wants to know what you've done—what you're doing?"

A small, strange convulsion like a crisis seemed to come over Angus. All his muscles knotted; his eyes bulged. He might have been on the verge of an infarction. Yet his tension passed almost instantly, as if he'd taken a massive dose of cat. When he answered, he sounded unexpectedly simple. His conflict had disappeared—or been vanquished.

"Of course he wants a fucking report. This is Hashi Lebwohl we're talking about. But I can't exactly send him one from here, can I?" The question was rhetorical. "It would take three years to get there—*if* I could send it, which I can't." He slapped a gesture at the schematic on the display screen. "We're already occluded by that star."

Abruptly Vector left the engineering panel. Frowning to contain his eagerness, he moved to the command station; gripped the edges of the console as if he needed to brace his hands so that they wouldn't shake. Close to Morn, he faced Angus.

"Where will you go?"

Angus chewed his answer for a moment before replying, "I haven't decided."

"Back to human space?" Vector offered.

Angus shrugged bitterly. "We're safer here. With any luck at all, we could skip around Amnion territory for years without getting caught. They can't chase us if they can't find our trace. They can't pick our emissions out of all this noise, even if they have some way to know we were here.

"But then," he rasped, "I wouldn't be able to report, would I?"

"Then let me make a suggestion," Vector said quickly. "Let me tell you what *I* want."

Morn looked at him in surprise. She was too tired to jump to the kinds of conclusions which leaped through Davies.

Angus considered the engineer. "Why not?" he sneered. "Hell, let's *all* make suggestions. We've got eight hours before we have to decide anything."

Vector's blue gaze was impervious to scorn. "Angus," he said intently, "Morn knows things about me you don't. We had time to talk aboard *Captain's Fancy*." Nick rolled his eyes in contempt, but didn't bother to speak. "I think that's the first time she'd ever heard there might be such a thing as a mutagen immunity drug."

Unselfconsciously Morn and Davies nodded in unison.

"*I* know about that drug because I helped develop it. Before I"—Vector grimaced in self-mockery—"went into this line of work, I was a geneticist for Intertech. I was on the project to develop an antimutagen until the UMCP shut it down. Not the United Mining Companies, Angus—the United Mining Companies *Police*. We were so close to an answer I could taste it, and they took it away from us.

"Obviously DA must have finished our research. Otherwise Nick wouldn't be able to go visiting in places like Enablement Station. And"—he glanced at Morn—"you wouldn't still be human. The Amnion must have given you mutagens when they had the chance. They would have changed you, if you hadn't taken the drug."

Morn nodded again, watching him closely.

"Angus," Vector went on, "we've got the drug. And I know how to work on it. Hell, I've already *done* most of the work." Still supporting himself on the command console, but holding his head up so that he could face Angus straight, he announced, "I want a lab."

Passion made his voice carry and ring as if he were shouting, even though he spoke quietly. "I want a place where I can analyze that drug—discover the formula, learn how to make it."

The blaze of hope in Morn's eyes was so radiant that Davies suddenly felt like crowing. Ciro and Sib stared at Vector in astonishment. However,

Mikka aimed her black scowl at Angus as if she could already hear his refusal.

"And then?" Angus demanded as if Vector couldn't sway him; as if no human passion were precious or compelling enough to touch him.

"And then I want to *tell* people," the engineer answered urgently. "I want to broadcast it like a proclamation. I want to put it on the public news channels.

"I don't trust the cops, Angus. They've already suppressed this too long. And humankind *needs* it. Hell, we need it ourselves. We could go to some station that isn't owned by the UMC, Terminus maybe, and let them process and distribute it. Or we could just transmit the formula ourselves everywhere we go, make it so public that it *can't* be suppressed.

"I don't care how we do it. I just want to *do* it. This is my chance"—distaste twisted his mouth—"my chance to redeem everything I've done since I left Intertech."

Sib had forgotten Nick completely. Carried along by Vector's emotion and his own fears, he put in, "And it's a chance to fight the Amnion. I mean, really fight them, do something effective—not just talk about it, like the cops. Not just shoot a few illegals so the UMC can have more trade and get richer."

"Yes," Davies breathed. He still found the concept of UMCP corruption difficult to accommodate, but nothing prevented him from recognizing the power of Vector's idea, and affirming it.

"Wait a minute," Mikka protested. "You're getting ahead of yourselves." With an intuitive leap, Davies saw that her anger was the distrust of a woman who had learned at considerable cost the danger of hoping for the wrong things at the wrong time. "You can dream all you want, but it's worthless if you don't figure out how to make it work. Where do you propose to *find* a lab? And how do you plan to get access to it once you find it?"

"Oh, that part's easy." Nick's smug grin suggested that he was taunting Angus, daring him to take Vector seriously. "Any illegal lab in human space will let you in, if you tell them what you're doing—and offer to share the results. As long as you convince them you're illegal, too.

"*Finding* a lab, on the other hand—that could be tricky."

Angus glared at Morn while her eyes shone as if he'd already given his approval. Without shifting his gaze, he responded to Mikka, "You seem to be the only one here with any sense. Why don't you tell these bleeding hearts why this idea stinks? *Explain* to them that we can't go find a lab because we don't know where to *look*."

Mikka opened her mouth to speak; but her brother was faster. Impulsively he blurted out, "Valdor."

She closed her lips and stared at him as if he'd had the temerity to slap her.

"That's where—" he began. "Valdor Industrial. We lived there. It's—" But he couldn't go on; whatever he was about to say seemed to stick in his throat, caught by Mikka's shock and Sib's amazement and Vector's broad grin.

Flushing with embarrassment, Ciro ducked his head.

"He's right," Morn whispered.

Davies knew that as well as she did. Lectures, reports, even rumors that she'd heard in the Academy tumbled through his mind. The system where Valdor Industrial revolved around the binary star Massif-5 was a staggering conglomeration of moons and planetoids, asteroids and planets; a morass of orbital masses so complex that navigational errors were nearly as lethal as piracy. Valdor was located there because of the rich availability of the resources it needed for its enterprises, primarily smelting and heavy industry. An enormous traffic carried the station's output to Earth. And for exactly that reason the whole system swarmed with illegals. By reputation none of the individual bootleg shipyards or other illegal operations hidden in that maze of g and rock could compare with Billingate for size and diversification. Taken together, however, they served many more ships, processed more plunder, concealed more facilities. Illegals who disliked proximity with the Amnion had always preferred Massif-5, with its wealth and hiding places.

Incomprehension tightened Angus' face. His lost ship, *Bright Beauty*, hadn't had a gap drive: in all likelihood, he was entirely ignorant of the Massif-5 system. But his confusion lasted no more than a second. As if he'd somehow instantaneously accessed one of *Trumpet*'s computers, called up a database on Valdor Industrial, and absorbed its contents, his expression cleared.

"Can you locate a lab there?" he asked Mikka.

Morn fought visibly to control herself as Mikka considered the question. When Mikka finally muttered grudgingly, "I think so," a relief as poignant as sorrow came over Morn's features, and she had to grind her palms into her eyes to hold back tears.

"Shit," Nick growled to no one in particular. "Now we're going to let a *kid* tell us what to do."

Angus studied Morn intently. He had to swallow several times before he could find his voice.

Darkly he murmured, "It's probably better than hanging around here. I hate forbidden space anyway." The malign yellow in his eyes made him look like a man who hated everything. "Even the vacuum smells like Amnion."

Unable to stop himself, Davies touched Angus' arm in thanks.

Instantly furious, Angus jerked his arm away; snapped at Davies like a lash, "Fuck *you*, too. If you think *I've* turned into some kind of bleeding heart, you're using your asshole for brains."

"You wish." Because he was his father's son, Davies met Angus' anger with a hard grin. "On the other hand, *you're* using your gonads. Fortunately that's the only part of you I trust."

Nick chuckled appreciatively.

"Then there's just one more thing," Vector interposed. Eagerness still glinted in his gaze, but he'd recovered his air of calm. "I need the drug."

Morn didn't speak. Maybe she couldn't. Nevertheless she lowered her hands, lifted her raw gaze. After digging in her pocket for a moment, she brought up three small gray capsules in her palm and offered them to Vector.

He accepted them almost reverently, as if he knew what they meant to her.

"But you didn't take them all," he commented quietly. "If you did, Nick would have noticed they were gone. He would have figured out you had them. Nick—"

"Nick must have the rest," Davies finished for him.

Abruptly Sib remembered to aim his handgun at Nick.

Everyone on the bridge looked at Nick. He scrutinized the deck in front of him, ignoring their eyes.

"Hand them over, Nick," Angus ordered.

Nick ignored that as well.

Davies started forward, but Angus was already ahead of him. Two quick strides put Angus directly in front of Nick.

"I'm not going to warn you," Angus rasped. "If you need warning by this time, you're too stupid to live."

Nick peered at the deck as if he were bemused by the way the plates were welded together. He put up no resistance—didn't react at all—as Angus shoved his fingers into one pocket after another until he found Nick's vial of capsules.

"Good boy." Angus tossed the vial to Vector. "Tomorrow I'll teach you to roll over."

Vector opened the vial, checked the contents, then put Morn's capsules with the others. "I don't know if that's all of them," he said, "but it should be enough." His smile had a rueful tinge, as if he could taste the years he'd lost. "If I can't crack the formula from a sample like this, I'd better go back to engineering."

Nick's scars had turned the color of cold ash; a tic pulled at the edge of his cheek. Nevertheless he didn't raise his eyes from the deck.

Watching him, Davies felt sure that Nick was contemplating murder.

ANGUS

Angus wanted to sit down on the deck and hold his head. Only his zone implants kept him on his feet, preserved the appearance that he was in control of himself. If they hadn't automatically stepped up their emissions midway through the ordeal of facing Morn, he would have fallen apart already.

He couldn't *believe* what was happening.

Had he just agreed to take Vector Shaheed to a lab in the VI system? He'd never been there before; knew nothing about it except what his databases told him. And was it all for the sake of some shit-foolish humanitarian gesture? This wasn't what he did to bleeding hearts. This wasn't how he manipulated them—or reacted to them. He had a long and feral history of making such bastards *pay* for their moral superiority.

In fact, he'd achieved his greatest victory that way. He'd hijacked a ship called *Viable Dreams* virtually intact and sold her crew to the Amnion in exchange for the knowledge that enabled him to edit datacores; and he'd accomplished it with a fake distress call and a few dead bodies to prove he was in trouble—in other words, by appealing to her captain's bleeding heart.

What was *wrong* with him?

It must be his programming: Dios or Lebwohl was pulling his strings again; embedded commands in his datacore had taken over again. Never mind that it didn't make any sense. Either Dios or Lebwohl wanted him to act like a fucking philanthropist.

And yet he hadn't felt the coercion—

Not that sort of coercion, at any rate. Electronic impulses forced him to appear self-contained, decided for him what he could and couldn't reveal, finally stifled any outward sign of his inner torment. But those emissions hadn't forced him to say the words which accepted Vector's proposal; the command hadn't reached him through his datalink.

No, the coercion was of another kind.

It came from Morn.

With her ravaged beauty and her raw gaze, her plain weakness and her strange strength, she compelled him. She was as precious as *Bright Beauty*, and as vulnerable: so vulnerable that she seemed to make him vulnerable in her place, as if he wanted to protect her, sacrifice himself for her; as if *he*, Angus Thermopyle, had it in him to want anything from her except to possess her.

He'd agreed to Vector's suggestion because she desired it.

The thought filled him with so much helpless rage that he stormed and howled like a beast inside the mute cage of his skull. *It's probably better than hanging around here*. He had to assume that whatever he accepted or decided here didn't mean anything. His programming was simply biding its time, waiting for someone to invoke the codes which would return him to UMCPHQ. At that point he would effectively betray Vector and Ciro, Mikka and Sib.

And Davies.

And Morn.

When Davies had put a hand on his arm, he'd said, *Fuck* you, *too*. But he hadn't been talking to his son.

As for Morn, he'd made a deal with her. She'd given him his life: he'd promised not to betray her. That promise still held him, even though he was powerless to do anything about it.

Because he couldn't collapse on the deck and wail like his torn heart, he looked around the bridge and nodded grimly as if everything was settled; as if every important question had been answered. "All right," he told the wonder and anguish on Morn's face, the hot passion in Davies' eyes, "that's enough. You need rest. Shit, we all do.

"We've got"—he consulted his computer—"roughly seven and a half hours until we're in position to head for human space." He indicated Davies. "You and Sib take Captain Sheepfucker and lock him in one of the cabins. After that you can put yourselves to bed. As long as he can't hurt anything except himself, the rest of us are probably safe."

Clutching his gun, Sib stood up from the second's station. Davies studied Angus for a moment, flicked a glance like a question toward Morn, then shrugged and moved to join Sib. An opportunity to treat Nick as Nick had formerly treated him was one he couldn't refuse.

Nick's cheek ticked urgently, but he didn't protest. While Sib aimed the handgun at the small of his back, he crossed the bridge and climbed the companionway ahead of Sib and Davies.

Addressing Vector and Ciro, Angus went on, "You two get off the bridge. If you think you don't need sleep, think again."

Ciro turned toward Mikka, asking silently whether he should stay with her; but Vector took his arm and drew him after Davies and Sib.

As he passed the command station, Vector paused to say, "Thank you."

He was speaking to Morn, not Angus.

Angus knew exactly how the engineer felt.

With a private snort of bitterness, he faced Mikka.

"You're my second now. I need somebody with the right kind of experience." Somebody who thought like an illegal, not a cop. "Also somebody who knows the Valdor system. Captain Sheepfucker already had his chance. But I don't need you until we're ready to leave here. If you don't rest now, you'll have to stay tired for a long time. Come back in six and a half hours so you'll have time to get used to your board. Stay away until then."

Mikka nodded slowly. Her black scowl had been replaced by something more complex and speculative; almost a look of bafflement. For a moment she glanced back and forth between Angus and Morn like a woman trying to measure her options; then she grimaced uncomfortably.

"None of this makes sense," she said to Angus. "You know that." There was no challenge in her tone. "I feel like somebody changed all the rules behind my back. When did you turn into a man who cares whether humankind has an immunity drug? You say you're working for Hashi Lebwohl. When did *he* turn into a man like that?

"You rescued Davies and Morn. You rescued us. I want to trust you. I just don't know how."

Angus growled deep in his throat, but didn't answer.

"Do you mind being left with him?" Mikka asked Morn.

Morn's eyes flared with anger or panic; she looked like she wanted to say, Are you crazy? Of course I *mind*. For some reason, however, she shook her head. "If he wants me dead," she murmured, "all he has to do is touch me. In the meantime, I need to talk to him."

Mikka may have thought Morn was crazy. Nevertheless she shrugged.

"I'm going to leave my door open," she remarked as she headed for the companionway. "If you shout, I'll hear you."

Morn watched Mikka go as if she were taking all the courage off the bridge with her.

Angus ached at the sight of her visceral distress. At one time he'd loved seeing her like this; loved her horror and revulsion because they confirmed his possession of her. Or he'd believed he loved it; tricked himself into believing it. Now that emotion was gone; lost. He'd suffered too much of her helplessness. His own head had become a crib as cruel and inescapable as the one in which *his mother filled him with pain*— The gap between his needs and anyone else's was as great now as it had been then. For that reason Morn's fear and hatred affected him like *Bright Beauty*'s wounds: they confirmed nothing except the fact that he'd failed.

Choosing to be alone with him here must have been one of the hardest things she'd ever done.

Savage to avoid the anguish he'd once craved from the bottom of his heart, he rasped harshly, "Get out of my seat."

She didn't move. When Mikka reached the head of the companionway and passed out of view, Morn brought her gaze slowly to his, let him see the nakedness of her abhorrence. Yet she didn't do what he told her. She might not have heard him.

"Mikka's right," she said stiffly, as if she were fighting for calm. Nevertheless she kept her voice low. "None of this makes sense. *You* don't make sense. But I'm not going to ask you to explain it. I don't care what your reasons are. I'm not even going to *try* to trust you.

"I just care what you do."

"Thank you." In despair Angus mocked Vector's more tolerable gratitude.

Morn studied him with the same cold and bloody determination her father must have felt when *Starmaster* went after *Bright Beauty;* when he fixed his targ on *Bright Beauty* and ordered Angus' destruction. Her tone and her loathing seemed as steady as steel.

"Are you really going to send a report when we reach human space?"

Angus glowered, not at her, but at the contents of his datacore. "Yes."

"What are you going to say?"

He didn't know the answer—or he wasn't allowed to reveal it. "What do you want me to say?" he countered.

"Tell them about Davies," she answered promptly. Perhaps there was no hesitation left in her. She may have had no remaining scruples except the ones on which her definition of herself rested. "Tell them why the Amnion want him. Tell them the Amnion may have gotten a sample of the drug from my blood.

"And be sure to tell them the Amnion are experimenting with gap components to reach near-C acceleration."

"Yes, sir, Captain Hyland, sir," Angus sneered. What else could he do? She surpassed him in every dimension. And he was helpless to turn off his anger and grief. "Anything else?"

She shook her head.

"What?" he pursued sarcastically. "No mention of zone implants? No mention of Captain Sheepfucker's adventures in creative treachery?"

Morn held his gaze. She might have been daring him to outface her. "You can do that if you want. But I hope you won't."

"In that case—" He leaned toward her threateningly. His prewritten instructions permitted that: they didn't care how badly he scared her. "Get out of my seat."

He couldn't break her, however; not this way; maybe never again. She complied by rising from the command station and stepping out of his way; but she didn't drop her eyes—or the focused demand of her hate.

He could play that game. The terror bred in his bones was as good as hate. And his programming gave him an oblique support: it steadied him reflexively when he was afraid. But he found he didn't want to fight her on those terms. He'd lost his appetite for seeing her lose. So he used the motions of sitting in his g-seat and looking at the information on the command readouts as excuses to turn away from her; let her go.

Warden Dios had said, *It's got to stop.* Angus couldn't imagine what the UMCP director meant, but he had his own answer.

This. This has got to stop.

Morn regarded him in silence for a moment or two. When she spoke, her tone had changed. It was softer, more open; it ached quietly. Like her bruised eyes, it reminded him that her abhorrence was based on pain.

"How do you feel about having a son?" she asked. "About having Davies for a son?"

Angus' heart clenched in a grimace which didn't show on his face, a spasm which didn't touch his body. In more ways than he could bear to examine, Davies was him—another abused child. *Afterward she used to comfort him as if it were him she loved, and not the sight of his red and swollen anguish or the strangled sound of his cries.* The crib and the torture were different: the cost was the same. If Davies made something more out of it than his father had, that was due to Morn—to her presence in her son's mind; to the fact that she surpassed his father.

Angus couldn't bring himself to look up at her. His answer was like a cry from the core of his being.

"How do *you* feel," he retorted, "about having gap-sickness—about needing a zone implant so you won't go ape-shit and try to kill everyone when we hit hard g?"

She sighed to herself. "That bad?" The words might have expressed recognition or rejection: he couldn't tell the difference. And yet he seemed to hear a smile in her voice as she added, "Then I guess we're both in pretty poor shape."

With his peripheral vision, he saw her turn away. But he didn't watch as she put her hands on the rails of the companionway and left the bridge. It was already too late.

How do you feel about having a son?

She shouldn't have asked him that; shouldn't have opened that door. He could feel the slats of the crib closing around him, sealing him to his terror. He'd spent his whole life running away from this, headlong across space and time. Every act of violence, every atrocity, every instance of destruction, had been a form of flight: an attempt to hold his own fear at bay by inflicting it on other people; an effort to stave off his past by consuming others in the present. And now Morn had translated it across the gap of years and crimes to reach him.

As soon as it caught up with him, he was finished.

Stop! he cried out voicelessly. *It's got to stop!*

But Warden Dios' unexplained convictions and ambiguous intentions were irrelevant here. For all its exigencies and compulsions, Angus' computer was no help to him. His zone implants replied to the physiological symptoms of panic by calming him. Thus unwittingly they contributed to the erosion of the defenses he needed most.

Caught inside *Trumpet*'s hulls and his own skull, he lay *in the crib*
with his scrawny wrists and ankles tied to the slats
while his mother filled him with pain—

She'd been a lost woman, as lost as Angus himself. Like her son, she'd thought that she had no choice about the things that were done to her, or the things she did.

She'd been born by accident to a couple of guttergang kids in one of Earth's dying urban centers. They had no love for her, of course; and like kids they made her know that from the day she was born. But they found that she had a couple of uses. She was a lever with their own parents, a means to extort support or credit—or a place to hide. And she was another kind of lever with the crumbling social infrastructures which still struggled —as misguided and stubborn as most other bureaucracies—to provide some kind of welfare for the destitute. She wasn't a child: she was just a tool. Her parents, and later the entire guttergang, treated her like a tool. They picked her up when they needed her, and tossed her aside when they didn't.

This remained true until she was old enough to have other, more recreational uses. Then she was picked up more often, tossed aside less. But this was not an improvement. She grew up illiterate; functionally retarded; dirty and diseased. By the time she was twelve, she was of no use to herself.

And then the guttergang to which her parents belonged was slaughtered in a struggle with a rival power.

Like other women in other corrupt wars, she became plunder.

As plunder she was introduced to an experience which society had once called a "gang bang" and now referred to as "freefall." After all, a gang bang might be considered a one-sided orgy. Over time "orgy" became "oh-gee" and then "zero g": hence "freefall." At the hands of the guttergang which had supplanted her own, she tasted freefall any number of times.

This might have killed her; perhaps should have killed her. But it didn't. The gang kept her alive because of her connection to the welfare infrastructure. And the welfare infrastructure kept her alive because it was still trying to do its job. After a certain amount of freefall, she naturally became pregnant, which increased the scale of support she received. As an act of conscience initiated by men and women long since dead, for reasons long since forgotten, welfare provided her with a small room to live in, a bit of food, some baby furniture. But the bureaucracy supplied no hope: all its other benefits were taken by the guttergang.

Somewhere in the process she went privately and irretrievably mad.

Little Angus was all that belonged to her.

He was also her only outlet.

Alone with him in her room, waiting for freefall and death, she began experimenting with the cycle of abuse and solace which he identified as *the crib*.

In a strange way, her impulse to comfort him after she tortured him was sincere. His small body seemed to have an almost limitless capacity for pain; his wild squalls and his red-faced agony gave her an acute frisson of pleasure, at once guilty and addictive. And the way she cuddled him in her arms and cooed over him and eased his hurts *as if it were him she loved* felt like the care she herself needed from the bottom of her heart and had never received.

The effect on him was quite different, however.

Its consequences were everywhere, no matter how he fled. His dread of EVA, like his abhorrence of confinement, came from that source. Yet the more he tried to escape, the more he carried with him the things from which he ran. Ever since he'd escaped her and the guttergang, he'd striven with a kind of bleak and absolute stubbornness—as unselfconscious and self-destructive as the damned—to replicate on someone else his mother's look of degraded desperation. As long as he fought to turn the tables on her, he remained her victim.

Now at last the logic of his life seemed to have reached its blind conclusion, its ineluctable cul-de-sac. His victimization was complete. Just when prewritten requirements and machine compulsion eased their grip on him, he found that Morn had the power to put him back *in the crib*. His efforts to change roles with her had failed: she surpassed him. And there was nothing he could do about it. He couldn't even keep his promises to her. The men who'd programmed him would never let him keep them.

Access-code Isaac! he cried into the void of his datalink. Priority-code Gabriel! Tell me it's going to stop! Tell me what I'm going to do. Let me at least warn her. Don't make me be the one who betrays her!

The silence which answered him felt like his mother's abject, ravenous laughter.

Alone on the bridge, Angus Thermopyle bowed his sore head over his board and waited for Warden Dios or Hashi Lebwohl to destroy him.

Naturally they didn't do it by killing him; or by letting him die. Their malice was too profound—and too oblique—for that. They went about their purposes in other ways.

His datacore kept his future to itself: it allowed him access to new information only when it pertained to his immediate present. For that reason he couldn't see the several ways in which his masters prepared his ruin until each one took effect.

However, none of them had become apparent by the time *Trumpet* reached her window on human space. His zone implants had interrupted his despair with a few hours of sleep, a trip to the galley for food; after that he'd coded his report to UMCPHQ. In addition to describing the outcome of his mission—and of Milos Taverner's treachery—he'd included the information Morn desired. And he'd left out the things she didn't want mentioned. His message was ready to be transmitted as soon as *Trumpet* passed within range of a listening post.

As the gap scout rounded the occlusion of the red giant and approached her window, Mikka Vasaczk chimed him to say that she was on her way to the bridge. He responded with an intraship broadcast forbidding anyone else from joining him. In particular he didn't want Nick loose on the ship. Or Morn: he ordered Davies to stay with her so that he could take care of her if *Trumpet* encountered circumstances which required hard maneuvers on the other side of the gap. If he hadn't needed Mikka, he would have told her to stay away, too. Whatever Lebwohl or Dios were about to make him do, he didn't want witnesses.

She arrived with two g-flasks of coffee. She handed one to him, then seated herself at the second's station and belted herself down. Some of the knots in her expression had loosened. She didn't smile, but she no longer looked like a woman for whom smiling was impossible. Apparently she was glad of a chance to be useful.

After studying her board for a moment or two, she asked, "What do you want me to handle?"

"Targ," Angus answered brusquely. He'd already eased a certain number of his coded restrictions on her board. "We're linked on scan, data, and astrogation. As long as we don't run into trouble, I want you to calculate headings and distances for the Valdor system—put a course up on the main screen. Update it as often as you can. I'm counting on you to keep us away from Station itself, or the shipping lanes. We're looking for a bootleg lab, not a dogfight with some paranoid orehauler."

Mikka nodded. Slowly at first, then with more confidence, she began to run commands. In moments a macro-plot began to form on the screen, displaying a purely hypothetical direct line between the red giant and Massif-5. Distances accumulated as the plot completed itself; but the line was only hypothetical because it took no account of gravity wells, intervening bodies, or *Trumpet*'s gap capabilities.

Angus had already pushed those numbers through his own computer, verified them against his databases. He wanted Mikka to run them herself simply to show him that she was competent.

This was her first opportunity to look at what the gap scout could do. She already had enough information to guess how far the ship could go in tach; like Nick, however, she was surprised by *Trumpet*'s thrust-to-mass ratio. Moving more quickly now, she returned to her course projection.

The macro-plot was replaced by a more proximate line. Without lifting her head from her board, she told Angus, "We've got a window on that heading in twenty-seven minutes. At this velocity, we can cover 6.2 light-years every time we go into tach. That's good—we won't have to go anywhere near Com-Mine or the belt."

Then she looked up at Angus. "But we can do better. I've never seen a small ship with this much thrust. Hell, we're as fast as *Captain's Fancy*. And a lot more agile. If we burn"—she punched in more numbers, scanned the results—"for the next twenty minutes, we can hit almost .3C. We might be able to cross as much as seven light-years. If we accelerate enough after we hit human space, we can probably do tach in ten light-year hunks. That'll save us a lot of time between here and Valdor."

Angus dismissed the suggestion. "In the meantime, Morn goes crazy every time we hit hard g. Someday gap-sickness is going to take hold of her and not let go. I don't want to push her luck.

"Anyway," he added, "we're not in that goddamn much of a hurry. Nobody knows where we're going. We don't have to act desperate about getting there."

Mikka opened her mouth to argue; closed it again. The falseness of his answer was hidden from her. After staring at him for a moment, she shook her head and turned back to her board.

He drank coffee and watched her while he waited for his ruin to commence.

Shortly before *Trumpet* hit the window, he chimed the cabins to announce, "Zero g in five minutes. Make sure you're secure. Except you, Nick. Bouncing off the bulkheads'll be good for you.

"Davies, is Morn all right?"

"I'm fine," Morn replied promptly. "I've given Davies the control. He'll turn me back on"—the bridge speaker made her sound little and distant—"when you tell him it's safe."

Stifling a snarl, Angus toggled off the intercom.

He waited until the last minute before laying in his tach parameters.

As his datacore gave them to him, he recognized them: the first small, subtle step in his imposed self-destruction.

Mikka recognized them, too, in different terms. Suddenly frightened, she swung her station to face him. "Angus!" she snapped, "what the hell are you doing?"

He replied with a blank glare.

"That's the Com-Mine belt!" she protested. "We can go farther than that—you're cutting our gap crossing short. God damn it, Angus, we're going to resume tard right on the edge of the belt. Where Com-Mine Security and any number of miners and maybe the whole goddamn UMCP will have a chance at us!"

"You think I don't know that?" he snorted. She couldn't override him: her board had no access to the helm. "But I'm supposed to send a fucking message. Hashi Asshole wants a report. And Morn wants me to do it. Well, *that's* the nearest listening post—right there on the goddamn edge of the goddamn belt."

The facts were true. Only the explanation was a lie.

Bitterly he concluded, "You think I can afford to ignore it?"

"I think," she rasped back, "if you were in such a hurry to report, you wouldn't have come here in the first place. You would have gone straight for human space and saved about nine hours."

"Think what you want," he retorted. "I don't give a shit."

Before she could protest further, he keyed commands which flung *Trumpet* into the center of his tach window.

As Com-Mine Security had discovered when they arrested him and took *Bright Beauty*'s datacore, his many illegalities hadn't made him rich. In all his crimes, he'd never accumulated enough credit to buy or retrofit a gap drive. So he'd never actually piloted a vessel into tach until Warden Dios put him aboard *Trumpet*. Nevertheless his welded resources gave him the knowledge of an expert. And he already had the instincts.

Despite his mounting dread and helpless anger, his hands were as steady as servos as he engaged the gap field generator; slipped *Trumpet* into the gap and out again without discernible transition, as if nothing significant had happened.

The change was dramatic, however. The red giant's mass and emissions vanished; inevitably the ship slewed off course, pulled aside by stored inertia as centrifugal and gravitic forces vanished. Angus' weight sawed him against his belts while *Trumpet*'s automatic systems used navigational thrust to absorb the new vectors. In the same instant scan broke into a mad jumble of dissociated impulses: the instruments were struggling to see a starfield which was no longer present; to filter out radiant distortion which had been left three light-years behind.

The computers had already extrapolated a template from the gap drive parameters, however. Otherwise they would have had to spend long minutes running SAC programs on the astrogation databases in order to identify the ship's position. Still *Trumpet* was deaf and blind for five seconds before she could begin to interpret the new readings accurately.

Then the displays and readouts sprang back into coherence; and Mikka cried out, "Christ!"

At the same instant the ship's proximity alarms went off like banshees, wailing of destruction.

Angus' instincts were good; as precise in their way as the calculations of his microprocessor. Together instinct and calculation handled the crossing correctly. Despite the inertial course displacement, *Trumpet* hit human space within five thousand k of her intended re-entry target.

Unfortunately the error occurred toward the belt rather than away from it. *Trumpet* resumed tard at more than seventy thousand kps on a collision course for an asteroid the size of an Amnion warship.

Years with Nick had trained Mikka well. She brought up targ and slammed charge into the ship's forward lasers almost instantly; too quickly to notice that Angus could deal with the emergency on his own.

In a splinter of time too small for his synapses to measure, his zone implants split him into pieces. He began multitasking like a megaCPU.

At machine speeds the helm computations were trivial: distance and velocity; the amount of thrust necessary to pull *Trumpet* away from collision; the scale of raw g human tissue—not to mention the ship herself—might conceivably endure. Then compromise, trade off one factor against the others: *that* much g was needed; *this* much was available; *so* much could be survived.

Angus had one hand on the helm keys as soon as he recognized the emergency.

But his datacore also required other, simultaneous actions which necessitated more complex calculations. The listening post was *there*, roughly three light-seconds away. In order to tight-beam a transmission, *Trumpet*'s main dish had to be focused *there*—and programmed to retain orientation while the ship maneuvered.

Angus' free hand fired commands like lightning at the communications keys. His datacore assigned his report to Warden Dios a priority as high as survival. If *Trumpet* hit the asteroid and died, his report would die with her. Therefore he wasn't allowed to wait until he'd resolved the danger of collision.

At the same time he had one more job to do; one more small step to take toward his own ruin.

This was his best chance. Mikka couldn't see what he did: she was too busy, too desperate. In seconds the lasers would be ready. In a few seconds more the ship would either live or die.

Prewritten exigencies jumped at the opportunity. Screaming inside while his zone implants compelled him, Angus activated a homing signal; a constant transmission of navigational data and gap drive parameters, updated at every change. It was a dedicated UMCP signal: no one else would be able to interpret it. But it would enable any cop to follow him wherever he went.

Hashi Lebwohl or Warden Dios wanted to be sure they were able to get their hands on him.

Betrayal—

Angus had let Morn think he was taking her to a bootleg lab near VI. But a homing signal denied that; made him a liar. Once the cops caught up with *Trumpet*, they could invoke Angus' priority-codes. Put someone else in Milos' position over him; some earnest or corrupt cop who didn't give a shit about Morn's hopes—or Angus' promises. Mikka and Ciro, Vector and Sib would be arrested. Morn would be silenced. Angus himself might be dismantled. And Nick—

Nick would probably be given a fucking medal.

Everything would be lost.

But Angus didn't have time to curse his tormentors. Mikka hammered at her board; her fists seemed to fling bolts of crimson fire toward the looming hunk of stone. And in the same heartbeat all of his disparate actions took effect.

The communications readout showed the transmission dish revolving into alignment. An impersonal blip on the bottom of the screen indicated that the signal was active.

And lateral thrust—rapid brisance thrust of a kind usually reserved for cruisers and destroyers—began to blare through *Trumpet*'s hull, driving Mikka and even Angus almost instantaneously to the edge of blackout. No ordinary gap scout could have burned hard enough to avoid that collision. If she hadn't been rebuilt specifically for this mission—as full of secrets as Angus himself—she would have died.

Mikka's hands fell from the targ keys as acceleration compressed her like putty in the corner of her g-seat.

The pieces into which Angus had been divided reassembled themselves there, on the boundary of unconsciousness. While darkness piled up inside his head as if it leaked in from the vast outer void, he had room for one bitter instant of gratitude.

Mikka hadn't seen what he was doing. She couldn't have.

He had at least that much reason to believe there were no witnesses to this one act of treachery.

If he could have held himself out of the roaring dark for just a few more seconds, however, *Trumpet*'s scan would have told him that he was wrong.

MIN

"Director Donner."

The intercom seemed to reach her asleep on the bottom of a deep sea of exhaustion. Dreams as viscid and impenetrable as the depths of an ocean held her down, despite the metallic demand of the speaker.

"Director, can you hear me?"

No, she couldn't hear him. Even Dolph Ubikwe's voice didn't have the power to plumb her fatigue. Concealed by the depths, bombs and shame pressed her down. Morn Hyland had been abandoned: betrayed and then abandoned. Sold to Nick Succorso as if she were nothing more than a credit-jack; not even worth picking up off the floor after he discarded her. Godsen Frik was dead, and Sixten Vertigus had nearly died, and Warden Dios had sent Min here to witness the outcome of Morn's abandonment; of Holt Fasner's manipulations and his own crimes. Trapped in mortification, she would never hear the intercom.

"Director, this is the bridge. We've got traffic."

Nevertheless she did hear. She was Min Donner: she rose to such demands, no matter what they cost. And Warden had *reason to think Morn Hyland may survive*— He'd told her so. The game he played was deeper than dreams.

Somehow her hands found the seals on the g-sheath and webbing which secured her in her bunk; her legs swung out. As soon as her boots touched the deck, she reached for the intercom.

Swallowing shame and abandonment, she called, "Bridge. Captain Ubikwe." Unselfconsciously she rubbed the butt of her handgun to reassure herself that it was still in its holster. She'd slept fully dressed and armed so that she would be ready for this moment. "What traffic?"

"There's two of them," Dolph Ubikwe answered promptly, "but we haven't got id yet."

His bass rumble made her notice that a few hours of rest had improved her hearing. Her eardrums felt acutely sensitive, but they no longer reported voices as if they were caught in a feedback loop.

"They haven't announced themselves," he went on. He sounded tired himself, despite the intercom's inflectionless speaker. "On the other hand, we haven't asked. And we aren't broadcasting, so why should they?"

Don't get cute with me, Dolph, she wanted to snap at him. Her dreams had made her bitter. I asked a straight question—give me a straight answer. But she controlled the impulse. He didn't need her sarcasm. *Punisher* was already in enough trouble.

Instead she replied quietly, "Keep it simple, Captain. I'm still half-asleep. Where are we?"

"At the moment"—the intercom couldn't do justice to his subterranean growl—"we're thirty thousand k off forbidden space on the far side of the belt from Com-Mine. We would have been in position an hour and a half ago, but I haven't been able to find a hiding place that suits me." His tone suggested a humorless grin. "We're just dodging asteroids and trying to look inconspicuous until we locate the right kind of magnetic resonance."

Now Min had to clench her teeth to hold down a whiplash of anger. A glance at her cabin chronometer told her that she'd been asleep for at least four hours—and she'd ordered Captain Ubikwe to have *Punisher* positioned in three.

God *damn* it, you sonofabitch, I told you to wake me up!

He'd been procrastinating; putting off what came next as long as he could—

With an effort, she swallowed that irritation as well. If she weren't willing to tolerate his insubordinate approach to authority, she shouldn't have left him in command.

"Don't hail them yet," she ordered. "Just keep listening. I'm on my way."

Roughly she thumbed off the intercom.

God damn and *damn* it, she needed time. Time to rest; time to make sense of Warden's orders; time to talk to Dolph privately so that he would understand what was at stake. But *Punisher* had already encountered traffic *out here*, where there shouldn't be any ships. That was why Angus had been programmed to bring *Trumpet* here at his own pace, in the event that some act of treachery by Milos Taverner had caused Joshua's computer to supersede its priority-codes. Even illegal prospectors with no brains weren't likely to be in this sector of the belt, this close to forbidden space and trouble, of their own free will.

The odds that those two ships had arrived here now by chance had to be calculated in negative numbers.

Because she needed the discipline, Min forced herself to use the san and wash her face before leaving her cabin; and to walk all the way to the aperture and the bridge.

Along the way, her feet and now her ears received the impression that *Punisher*'s spin displacement was getting worse. The sensation affected her like nausea; but she couldn't do anything about it, so she schooled herself to ignore it.

When she gained the bridge, she saw immediately that Captain Ubikwe himself was the only one who remained of the dozen or so people who'd been here four hours earlier. The techs were gone, along with the rest of the watch which had been on duty when she boarded; new men and women occupied the bridge stations. So presumably Dolph should also have gone off duty.

He needed rest, that was obvious. His bulk seemed to slump on his bones, as if he were melting into his g-seat; fatigue jaundiced his eyes. The sheen on his skin made him look sick.

Now she permitted herself to snap at him. "Captain, haven't you ever heard of duty rotation?" The fact that he'd made exactly the same decision she would have made in his place didn't deter her. "In case you haven't noticed, you're as human as the rest of your crew. Don't you have at least one command officer who can be trusted to follow a few simple orders?"

He gave her a yellow glare; a snarl showed his gums, pink against his black lips. "With respect, Director"—his tone was like a grimly muted trumpet—"I guess you *don't* bother to read reports. If you did, you might have observed that my second was one of our casualties. And my *third* lost most of her left arm. She got caught by a vacuum seal the second time we were holed—confined to quarters for medical reasons. *Fortunately* Command Fourth Hargin Stoval has about as much respect for 'duty rotations' as I do. Between the two of us, we've been trying to avoid pushing duty on officers who are even *tireder* than we are."

Min stopped as if she'd run into a wall of chagrin. Only determination and training kept her distress off her face. Good, Min. Nice work. *You* feel like shit, so you take it out on the first innocent bystander you see.

And then you get it wrong. Keep this up. Maybe you'll come out of it with a fucking *commendation*.

"My apologies, Captain," she pronounced distinctly. "I did read your report. And I didn't assign fresh personnel. I assumed you would prefer to work with people you already knew."

Dolph relaxed almost immediately; he didn't have the energy to stay angry. Slumping deeper into his seat, he growled, "You were right. I don't want new officers—this isn't the time or the place for them." Taking a deep breath, he went on, "As it happens, my fourth has the constitution of an ox. He can stand the extra watches. And I'm"—he fluttered a hand to dismiss his weariness—"usually tougher than this.

"What really made me tired," he continued before she had time to respond, "was seeing those ships. If I could think of a better expletive, I wouldn't have to ask what the fuck they're doing out here."

Min was accustomed to setting her own emotions aside. The exercise was difficult: nevertheless it often came as a relief. Instinctively she moved closer to the command station so that she could consider the bridge and *Punisher*'s situation from Dolph's perspective.

"First things first," she told him. "Where *are* they?"

Captain Ubikwe relayed her question. "Porson?"

"Aye, sir," the scan officer responded. "They're right on the edge of our range. I mean, one of them is." He pointed at one of the displays. Scan plots showed the trajectories of the rocks and asteroids around *Punisher*'s course. Beyond them, at the fringes of the image, an insistent red blip indicated another ship. "She's still in forbidden space, but she's heading this way. Not fast—she's probably studying us too hard to hurry." He paused, then added, "If she'd been on that course for a while, she came from the vicinity of Thanatos Minor."

"Illegal," Dolph put in unnecessarily. "She wants to get away from whatever's happening behind her, but she doesn't want to face us. I expect she'll change course before she gets much closer. We won't find out who she is unless we go after her."

Min nodded, concentrating on the screen. A small, combative tingle itched in her palms. "What about the other one?"

The scan officer, Porson, appeared to consider her question a reprimand. "Sorry, sir." In a rush he explained, "I said she's on the edge of our range. I meant our effective range." He highlighted a second scan blip. "She's a lot closer, but she's behind us in the belt. If she were any deeper, we wouldn't be able to pick her out from the rubble."

Min studied him closely. He was an older man, but he had the same worn, uncertain look she'd seen on the bosun's face. Fatigue had eroded his confidence until inquiries sounded like criticisms.

In fact, none of the bridge officers appeared any more rested than the watch they'd replaced. *Punisher*'s exhaustion was so severe that mere hours of sleep couldn't soften it. The whole crew needed an extended leave.

Min had to admit that Dolph was right. He had to do as much of the ship's work himself as he could. His people were in no shape to take on more duties.

Turning her attention back to the screen, she asked Porson, "Is she moving?"

He shook his head. "Drifting, sir. With the rock."

"Hiding?"

"Could be, sir," he answered. "But I don't think so. Data reports one of our listening posts at those coordinates. She's sitting right on top of it."

Min cocked an eyebrow in surprise. *Trumpet?* Is she here already?

Suppressing her impulse to jump to conclusions, she asked, "You still haven't got id on her?"

Porson shook his head like a flinch. "No, sir. She isn't broadcasting. And she's drifting, so there isn't much emission data to work with." Again he sighed, "I'm sorry, sir."

Pained by the scan officer's apology, she looked at Captain Ubikwe. "Are we close enough to access that post?"

She caught him with his eyes closed. Without opening them, he rumbled, "Cray?"

"Affirmative, sir," the young woman at the communications station responded. "We've already adjusted course to keep a window open. Three-second lag there and back."

Min nodded her approval. Leaving Dolph's side, she walked the curve of the bridge to the communications station.

Cray watched her expectantly as if she could guess what Min had in mind. Perhaps because she was younger, she didn't look as worn down as Porson or the rest of the watch.

"What's its status?" Min asked her.

At once Cray began running commands. "Checking now, sir."

Three seconds there and back, Min thought. 450,000 k.

For reasons she couldn't name, premonitions of disaster burned in her palms.

"It's on standby, sir," Cray reported. "According to the log"—she had to swallow her own surprise—"it flared a drone to UMCPHQ a little more than eight hours ago. Now it's just receiving. Waiting."

Trumpet? Is it really *Trumpet?*

"That ship sent us a message," Dolph remarked to no one in particular. "Now she's waiting for an answer." His tone conveyed a shrug. "She must not have known we would be out here."

Would Angus Thermopyle wait there, drifting like that—as helpless as a sacrifice? Min dredged her memory for details of his programming; the ones Hashi had bothered to reveal. If Milos had betrayed Joshua, his priority-codes would be automatically superseded. But under those circumstances, on the assumption that Milos' treachery would entail secondary risks for everyone associated with the cyborg, Angus' instruction-set had been written to preclude his return to UMCPHQ—or Earth.

How had Hashi explained it? It was pragmatically impossible for any advance programming to cover every conceivable eventuality. Discrepancies between what Angus could do and what he needed to do were bound to arise. And as time and events accumulated, the risk of such discrepancies increased exponentially. The likelihood grew that programming inaccuracies might force Angus into some perverse form of suicide just when his mission neared success.

For that reason, among others, he needed a companion who could control him; impose necessary adjustments to his instruction-set. But if Milos had betrayed him, Angus was in a sense out of control.

In the name of his own survival, and of the success of his mission, he needed significantly greater latitude to choose his own actions. And yet any latitude made him dangerous.

Therefore, in the event that his priority-codes were superseded, his datacore required him to report; to stay away from UMCPHQ and Earth; and to do whatever he chose to keep himself and his ship alive until his new priority-codes could be invoked by someone who was in a position to control him.

"Copy that transmission," Min ordered harshly. Her mouth was full of bile. "I want to know what it said."

"Aye, sir." Cray complied with a rush of keys.

Four seconds later her readouts gave her an answer that turned her cheeks pale.

"Access denied," she reported in a thin voice. "It's coded exclusively for Data Acquisition. For Director Lebwohl."

Dammit, Hashi! Min swore. What're you playing at now?

"Good old Hashi," Dolph muttered sardonically. "I always liked him."

After years of experience, Min had become adept at typing upside down. She hit a quick flurry of keys, then stepped back from the board. "Use those codes," she told the communications officer. "Override the access restrictions. Override every damn instruction-set in the log, if you have to. I want to know what that ship told UMCPHQ."

Fine sweat beaded on Cray's lip as she worked. When the answer came back, she groaned involuntarily, flicked a look of chagrin at Min, then tried again, stabbing urgently at her board. Every passing second seemed to cost her more of her resilience.

"Negative, sir," she breathed without raising her head. "Access denied. I can't crack it." Like Porson, she murmured, "I'm sorry, sir."

"Never mind, Cray," Dolph put in at once. "It's not your problem. That's why Director Donner is here. We'll let *her* worry about it."

Min gripped her handgun, clamped the butt into her palm to retrain her anger. "He's right," she told Cray, doing what she could to ease the sense of inadequacy she appeared to inspire. "You can't play if they don't tell you the rules."

From the communications station she faced Captain Ubikwe.

His eyes were open now. Summoning new sources of energy from somewhere under his fat, he'd hauled himself more upright in his g-seat. As soon as Min looked at him, he said almost cheerfully, "I'm glad you're here, Director. We've already got two surprises on our hands—and with our luck there're more on the way. *I* don't want to make this decision." He may have been enjoying the sight of her clenched ire. "What do *you* want to do about them?"

She didn't hesitate: she knew her job. "Keep track of that ship in forbidden space. Let me know if she does anything—shifts course, decelerates, starts transmitting, anything. Other than that, forget her. We'll concentrate on Hashi's bugger."

She used the word "bugger" deliberately. How *dare* the DA director keep anything as vital as information which came from this part of the belt to himself?

"Hail her, Captain," she instructed grimly. "Announce yourself, tell her to do the same. Then ask her what the hell she's doing parked on top of one of our listening posts."

Dolph also didn't hesitate. His instinct for insubordination didn't apply in situations like this. That was one of several reasons why she trusted him. "Cray, give me a channel," he ordered promptly. "Porson, I want coordinates."

"Aye, sir," they answered.

"Targ," he went on, "recharge one of the matter cannon. I know, they're already charged. But I want that ship to scan us and *see* we're getting ready to hit her."

The targ officer responded, "Aye, sir," and turned to his board.

Dolph toggled the command station pickup. In his most authoritative bass, he pronounced, "Unidentified vessel at"—he quoted coordinates off one of his readouts—"this is United Mining Companies Police cruiser *Punisher*, Captain Dolph Ubikwe commanding. Identify yourself." A smile settled on his face as he spoke. "You are in the path of a hostile action. We will consider you hostile until you respond."

Three seconds passed. Six. Min wrapped her impatience around her handgun and waited.

Abruptly the bridge speakers crackled to life.

"*Punisher*, this is contract merchanter *Free Lunch*. I'm Captain Darrin Scroyle. Ship id follows."

Not *Trumpet*. Something inside Min slumped at the information: relief or disappointment, she didn't know which.

The data officer didn't wait for orders: he pounced on the code-string as soon as it came in. "Got it, sir," he said quickly. Tapping databases, he reported, "*Free Lunch*, port of registry Betelgeuse Primary, owner and captain Darrin Scroyle. Listed for general cargo, long-range hauling. Current contract UMC. More when you want it."

He broke off because the speakers were crackling again.

"What hostile action?" the voice out of the belt asked. "No, don't tell me—I don't want to know. Just tell me which direction to run, and I'm gone."

Dolph swiveled to face the data station. "List every contract that ship's had since the day she left the shipyard. Summarize it for me fast."

"Aye, sir." The data officer began typing; and almost immediately names, dates, and consignment-codes scrolled across one of the screens. "It's all general cargo, sir," he reported. "About half independent contracts, the rest UMC. Usually between Betelgeuse Primary, Valdor Industrial, and Terminus, but she's been to Com-Mine a couple of times. Betelgeuse to Com-Mine is the most recent."

"In other words," Dolph snorted, "she's innocent, and this is all a coincidence. Unless"—he glanced at Min—"the director of Data Acquisition in his infinite wisdom has seen fit to supply that ship with fake id."

Min shrugged bitterly. "It happens. Most of what DA does is covert. Director Lebwohl has to give his operatives cover, whether I like it or not." Through her teeth, she added, "There's no law that says he has to keep me informed."

She was thinking, But he has to keep Warden informed.

She didn't believe in *Free Lunch*'s innocence for a moment.

Dolph hit his pickup with a heavy thumb. "Captain Scroyle," he grated, "don't bullshit me. I haven't got time for it. And I'm not likely to believe you're drifting right on top of a UMCP listening post by accident. In any case, the UMC doesn't pay ships to drift around this far out in the belt. I've got you on targ, and I'm in no mood to be polite.

"What're you doing here?"

Three seconds there and back; one and a half seconds each way. Captain Scroyle didn't take any time at all to consider his answer.

"Captain Ubikwe," he replied out of the void, "the last contract you have on record for us is a consignment from Betelgeuse Primary to Com-Mine Station. We finished that four days ago. We took some time off to enjoy the profits—then I got a message by gap courier drone, offering us this job. The records haven't had time to reach UMCPHQ from Com-Mine.

"The message was from Cleatus Fane, First Executive Assistant, United Mining Companies." Unnecessarily he added, "He works directly for Holt Fasner." Both Min and Dolph, like everyone else aboard *Punisher*, knew Cleatus Fane's name and reputation. "He gave me the coordinates of this listening post," Captain Scroyle went on, "and offered me a contract to use it.

"He said—let me quote this right—he said he was 'expecting events in forbidden space to spill over into the belt during the next few days,' and he wanted a witness. Someone to watch and report—and stay the hell out of the way.

"That's what we're doing."

Min considered toggling the communications station pickup in order to shout at *Free Lunch* herself, then rejected the idea. She didn't want anyone else to know she was here. And she was sure that Dolph could handle the situation.

In fact he was in his element: he had the personality as well as the voice for what he was doing.

"That's it?" he cracked at the merchanter like a mine-hammer. "He didn't tell you what you're supposed to watch for, what kind of 'events' he's expecting?" The simple pleasure of wielding sarcasm and authority seemed to refresh his stores of energy moment by moment. "Do you usually take on jobs that don't make sense without asking any questions?"

Again Captain Scroyle didn't need to think before he responded.

"I do when they pay as well as this one does."

"Well, don't keep me in suspense," Dolph retorted. "What have you seen? What did you report?"

This time the reply arrived more slowly. Three heartbeats, four, five passed before Captain Scroyle's voice returned from the speakers.

"Captain Ubikwe, what's wrong?" He sounded suddenly grim—and perhaps just a bit unsure of himself. "You already know the answer. Our scan saw you talking to the post. What else do you want me to think you were doing, if you weren't copying the post log to read our transmissions?"

Now Dolph let his voice drip acid. "We *can't* copy the post log. Your codes deny us access. And they weren't UMC codes, I'll tell you *that* out of the goodness of my heart.

"What's going on here, Captain Scroyle? I don't think you're being honest with me. This is a UMCP *cruiser* talking, and I want answers."

Three seconds; no more.

"It's the truth, Captain Ubikwe, I swear it." The speakers carried a note of urgency. "Cleatus Fane gave me those codes. I don't know what the hell they are—I just used them. Of course I know this is a UMCP post. I assume Fane wanted me to use it because the UMC doesn't have one in a better location. So I also assume any message we sent him would be routed through UMCPHQ. Don't you and the UMC do that kind of thing all the time? *I* don't know why you can't access the post log."

Dolph silenced his pickup. "Sure, bozo," he muttered. "And I'm the Flying Dutchman. Nobody's *that* naive." Then he looked at Min. "What do you want me to do? I can tell him to copy his report to us—but if you believe what he sends us, you'll believe anything. Or I can demand a datacore readout under Emergency Powers. Then we'll get the truth—but we won't be able to charge him with anything afterward." Delicately he sneered, "*That's* against the rules."

Min started to say, Get me that readout. The words boiled up in her, hot with anger. But before she could speak, Porson let out a croak from the scan station.

"More traffic, Captain!"

"Shit," someone growled; Min didn't see who it was. She and Dolph snapped around in unison to face the scan officer.

Without transition Dolph dropped his harsh manner. Calmly he drawled, "Tell me about it, Porson."

"She just resumed tard"—unsteady on the keys, Porson ran commands, clarifying and interpreting sensor data—"God, that was close! Captain, she came out of the gap only five thousand k off our stern. Heading the other way, away from forbidden space. Velocity .2C." His voice cracked. "*Into the belt*, she's heading into the belt, she's going to *hit*—"

Min left scan to Dolph. Fire ached in her palms as she gripped the edges of the communications board and pulled her face down to Cray's, demanded Cray's attention. "That ship is transmitting," she whispered intensely, as if she knew the truth; as if she were sure. "She's here to use that listening post. *Catch* it, Cray. Whatever she transmits, catch it! I want that message."

"She's firing!" Porson blurted. "Laser fire, trying to cut that asteroid out of her way, she's not going to make it!"

"Keep track of her," Dolph ordered, deliberately nonchalant. "When you get a moment, check on that ship in forbidden space. And watch *Free Lunch*. I don't want to let her off the hook."

"Aye, sir."

Compelled by Min's intensity, Cray flung her hands at her console, fought to reorient *Punisher*'s dishes. An instant later she looked back up at Min, her face stricken with chagrin. "Missed it, sir. She must have started flaring right after she resumed tard."

Must have known exactly where the post is.

Must have known that flaring the post was more important than survival.

"She's turning!" Porson cried. "That's impossible, nobody can take that much g-stress! They must all be unconscious. Or dead. But she's clear! Veering out of the belt."

"Then get it from the post log," Min rasped. "Every ship in the goddamn galaxy can't have codes to deny us access."

"Aye, sir." Cray hurried to obey.

A blip from her board snagged her attention. She gaped at her readouts, typed quickly, received verification.

"Sir," she breathed, "that ship—the one that just passed us— She's broadcasting a homing signal. A Class-1 UMCP homing signal, trace-and-follow, emergency priority. She's—"

"I know." Min felt that her heart had stopped beating. "Needle-class UMCP gap scout *Trumpet*." Angus was still alive; his mission was still alive. "Worry about her later. I want her flare."

Swallowing urgency, Cray went back to work.

Five seconds later she reported, "Got it, sir." Her eyes were wide with relief.

Abruptly Porson jerked out, "Captain, the ship in forbidden space just started to burn! And she's shifting course. Now on the same heading as that gap scout."

"*Trumpet*," Dolph remarked in a comforting rumble. "Director Donner knows her. What about *Free Lunch*?"

"Still drifting, sir. No effort to evade us. And she doesn't want a fight —she hasn't charged her guns."

Min ignored everything around her. As if *Trumpet*'s message were all that mattered, all that existed, she focused on it. With one hand she indicated a communications readout: the other turned the station so that she could read over Cray's shoulder.

Cray copied *Trumpet*'s transmission to the readout and stared at it with Min.

Min saw at once that the flare was coded for Warden Dios.

Not Hashi Lebwohl.

No matter what Hashi thought he was doing, Angus still reported to Warden.

Grimly she concentrated on the message. With the ease of long practice, she sorted through the codes and id, the transmission and routing data, to the body of Angus' report.

It said, *Isaac to Warden Dios, personal and* **urgent.**

Mission to Thanatos Minor successful.

Gabriel priority activated. Milos Taverner has gone over to the Amnion.

Personnel aboard include survivors from Captain's Fancy: *Morn Hyland, Davies Hyland, Nick Succorso, Mikka Vasaczk, Ciro Vasaczk, Vector Shaheed.*

Amnion vessels in pursuit.

Morn? Only years of training and harsh experience enabled Min to contain herself when she saw Morn's name. Morn was *alive*!

I have reason to think Morn Hyland may survive what's happened to her.

Warden had told the truth. He hadn't abandoned Morn. Risked her, yes: let her suffer. But not abandoned her. Apparently he'd never meant to abandon her.

I want someone to make sure she stays alive— That means you.

He was playing a deeper game—

Clutching Cray's g-seat for support, Min followed Angus' message as it scrolled down the readout.

Urgent, he insisted. *The Amnion know about the mutagen immunity drug in Nick Succorso's possession. It is possible that they have obtained a sample of the drug from Morn Hyland's blood.*

Morn must have fallen into the hands of the Amnion somehow. Who rescued her? And why was she still human? Did *Nick*, Nick *Succorso*, give her the drug?

Hashi, you moron! Didn't you have the brains to see this coming as soon as you trusted a man like him?

Urgent. Bright with phosphors, Angus' message moved relentlessly across the small screen. *Davies Hyland is Morn Hyland's son, force-grown on Enablement Station. The Amnion want him. They believe he represents the knowledge necessary to mutate Amnion indistinguishable from humans.*

Min ignored Cray's small gasp of fear. She clung to the readout, unwilling to be deflected.

Urgent, Angus continued as if he feared no one would listen to him. *The Amnion are experimenting with specialized gap drives to achieve near-C velocities for their warships. Nick Succorso and his people have direct knowledge of this.*

We will try to survive until new programming is received.

Message ends. Isaac.

"Director," Dolph interrupted with a touch of asperity, "what do you want us to do? *Free Lunch* won't wait around indefinitely. We've got an unidentified vessel burning toward us from forbidden space. And for some reason"—he smiled like a grimace—"*Trumpet* left us a homing signal to follow. Let's make up our minds, shall we? One way or another, we need to do some burning of our own."

Min hardly heard him. Morn Hyland. Alive because Warden had saved her. Morn with a zone implant and a force-grown son. And Amnion in pursuit. Presumably the ship from forbidden space was Amnion: the stakes were high enough for that.

And she was stuck on a fleeing gap scout with the two men who'd hurt her most; the two men she had most cause to fear.

I want someone to make sure she stays alive—

It was time: time for Min to prove herself; time to show that Warden had chosen well when he selected her.

She held up one stiff hand to silence Dolph. With all her authority in her eyes, she faced the communications officer.

"How many courier drones have you got left?"

Cray didn't need to check: she knew her job. "Three, sir."

"Use one," Min ordered. "This can't wait for regular service—not out here. That could take hours. Send a message to UMCPHQ. Code it for Director Dios. Give him a copy of *Trumpet*'s transmission. Dump in everything that's happened since we reached this sector, he can sort it out. And include all the data you get from that homing signal—velocity, heading, gap parameters, whatever comes in before you launch the drone.

"Tell him"—at last she looked across the bridge at Dolph, met his questioning gaze with a glare like a promise—"we're going after Isaac.

"Do it now."

Instinctively Cray glanced at Captain Ubikwe for confirmation.

The muscles under his fat were strained tight; his eyes bulged with anger or doubt. Nevertheless he replied with a short nod, and she went to work.

He held Min's eyes as if he wanted to shout at her. "Let me be clear about this, Director," he said in a voice full of raw harmonics. "We're going after this 'Isaac,' whoever he is. You want me to turn my back on a possible Amnion incursion into human space, even though it might constitute an act of war. And you want me to turn my back on *Free Lunch* and her dubious contract with UMC First Executive Assistant Cleatus Fane, even though that might constitute an act of treason. Instead you want me to concentrate on what's really important, which is a Needle-class gap scout crewed by people so crazy or stupid they can't maintain a safe distance from an asteroid belt.

"Does that about sum it up?"

"No," Min snorted. She understood his need to express his frustration —both for his own sake and for the sake of his crew. But she was near the end of her tolerance. "She came in so close because flaring that post was more important than staying alive."

"Sure. That's clear." Cocking his head at scan, Dolph asked, "Porson, can you tell where *Trumpet* came from?"

"Just the general direction, sir." Under the pressure of his duties, Porson didn't have time to feel defensive. "Somewhere in forbidden space. But if you're asking if she came from Thanatos Minor, the answer is, no. Her heading was all wrong."

"Oh, well"—Dolph made a show of throwing up his hands—"that's all right, then. As long as *nothing* makes sense, I'm satisfied.

"You heard the director," he told his helm officer. "Bring us around on a pursuit heading. Triangulate from her homing data. As soon as we're secure for hard g, give us as much acceleration as we can stand without falling out of our seats.

"Director Donner," he finished dourly, "you'd better find a place to strap yourself down. This is going to be rough. We need a hell of a lot of thrust to match *Trumpet*'s velocity."

Min nodded sharply. Her heart was full of yelling, but none of it was aimed at Captain Ubikwe or *Punisher*. Morn was one of *her people*. She'd been raped and tortured, she'd had a zone implant forced into her head, at least two murdering illegals did whatever they wanted to her for months, the Amnion had her for a while—and the UMCP had *set her up* for it. The organization Min served had *sold* Morn when she most needed help.

Now Warden wanted her back. Wasn't he done with her *yet*? How much more did he think she could endure?

"I'll be in my cabin," Min answered Dolph. "I want regular reports. If I make the mistake of falling asleep, wake me up. I want to know what's going on."

Captain Ubikwe opened his mouth to retort, but something in her face stopped him. Instead he murmured, "Yes, sir," then turned his attention to the helm station and the display screens.

The helm officer had already opened a ship-wide intercom channel. "All personnel secure for g," he announced. "We're going to burn. Watch officers report when ready."

He hit the acceleration warnings, and klaxons like distant cries went off everywhere.

As Min left the bridge, the entire ship seemed to echo with g-alarms and urgency.

ANCILLARY DOCUMENTATION

GAP COURIER DRONES

Gap courier drones were marvelous devices, in their way. They conveyed information—news, records, and messages, contracts, financial transactions, and corporate debates, data reqs, id files, and cries for help—from one part of human space to another in a matter of hours; seldom in more than a standard day. Considering that the distances involved were measured in dozens or hundreds of light-years, communication within hours was an amazing achievement.

In essence, a gap courier drone was all power. Aside from its fuel cells, the negligible bulk of its miniaturized transmitter and receiver, and the virtually nonexistent weight of its SOD-CMOS chips—which carried astrogational data as well as messages and other information—it had no mass except that of its drives. Therefore it could be given thrust-to-mass ratios and hysteresis parameters which no manned vessel might hope to emulate. It could accelerate faster, attain higher velocities, and perform longer gap crossings than a manned vessel.

Indeed, gap courier drones might have performed their function in minutes instead of hours, if they hadn't been required to execute maneuvers in real space: acceleration and deceleration; course shifts to avoid obstacles, or to correct the inevitable inaccuracies of gap crossing.

Under normal circumstances, a gap courier drone never arrived in physical contact with the transmitters and receivers it serviced. The instant it resumed tard within range of its programmed target, it fired off its cargo of data in intense microwave bursts, then immediately began deceleration. By the time the target was ready to transmit new informational cargo, the drone was positioned to commence acceleration back in the direction from which it had come. Thus the drone could shuttle between its targets with no time lost waiting. It was only required to stop moving when it needed maintenance, or when its fuel cells had to be recharged.

Gap courier drones were a familiar feature of humankind's interstellar life. Only their cost prevented them from being truly common. For most ordinary purposes, however, individuals, corporations, and governments found it less expensive to commit their informational cargo to manned vessels which happened to be going in the desired direction anyway. This method of communication compensated for its relative inefficiency by being far cheaper. And the inefficiency was only relative: normal commercial traffic was regularly able to deliver informational cargo to its intended recipient in a few days, a week at most. Naturally most individuals, corporations, and governments chose to accept the delays of commercial traffic rather than to invest in gap courier drones.

For that reason, the United Mining Companies Police was much the largest single user of drones, although the UMC and the GCES as well as humankind's distant stations kept them available for emergencies; and the UMCP used them primarily to service the listening posts which watched the frontiers of Amnion space.

Still gap courier drones *were* familiar, as common to public knowledge—if not to public use—as the gap drive itself. They were assumed to be steadily at work everywhere, helping the GCES to govern, and the UMCP to defend, the species' interstellar territory.

As much as any other single human exercise in self-delusion, they contributed to the irrational perception that vast space was small enough for men and women to manage.

WARDEN

Warden Dios was as scared as he'd ever been in his life.

He'd planned for this occasion, prepared for it. In some sense it was almost predictable. Surely by now he ought to be ready. If he weren't, he never would be.

Nevertheless he was scared to the bone; so frightened he wanted to beat his fists together and yell.

Unfortunately he couldn't.

He'd just received *Punisher*'s—Min Donner's—report. It scrolled remorselessly down the phosphors of a readout on his desk in one of his secure offices. But he couldn't study it now because Koina Hannish, his new director of Protocol, sat across the desk from him, talking intently about matters which had consumed her attention since he'd appointed her. He had to finish with her, get rid of her, before he could absorb Min's report.

He was scared because Min hadn't used his exclusive priority codes. She'd allowed *Punisher* to code and route her message through normal UMCPHQ channels.

He had no reason to think anyone outside UMCPHQ Communications could read her transmission. Still "normal channels" meant that its arrival was common knowledge in both Communications and Center. In other words, the fact of the report's existence had already been included in the routine data-sharing which occurred constantly between UMCPHQ and Holt Fasner's Home Office.

The Dragon would hear about Min's report soon—if he hadn't already.

That was predictable: entirely in character for Min Donner, as well as for the relationship between UMCPHQ and Fasner. And Warden had schemed hard to bring it about.

Yet now that it'd happened, it appalled him.

He didn't know what was in Min's message; what it entailed; what it cost. The consequences of his acts were about to bear fruit he couldn't control and might not be able to imagine.

Here the contest between him and his master began in earnest. From now on he would have no leeway to make ambiguous decisions, no opportunity for misdirection. If he couldn't carry his old fight into the open and win, everything he'd striven for himself, as well as everything he'd asked of his people, would be wasted.

He needed to know what was in that message.

His fear wasn't Koina's problem, however. She hadn't caused it, and couldn't cure it. In fact, he had no one but himself to blame for it. He hadn't warned Min Donner to be secretive; hadn't ordered her to conduct *Punisher*'s operations as if they were in any way different than any other UMCPED action. Instead he'd left her free to contact him in a way which would inevitably come to the Dragon's attention.

By an act of will, he let nothing of what he felt show on his face in front of the PR director. Years of planning and searching to recover his compromised integrity had taught him at least that much self-abnegation.

Immaculate and self-possessed, she watched him expectantly while he tapped a key to pause the scrolling of his readout. If she'd had a IR scanner like his prosthesis, she could have seen his turmoil; but of course she wasn't afflicted with artificial devices and perceptions—or with artificial loyalties like the ones which had doomed Godsen Frik. Warden saw her clearly enough to know that she brought nothing into his office except her honesty; her commitment to her job.

Nevertheless she was tense; emanations of strain colored her aura. If she was honest, she wasn't done.

Indicating his readout, he told her, "This is urgent. I need to deal with it. Is there anything else we should talk about before I let you go?"

He'd been so difficult to track down, so preoccupied by the subtle and dangerous implications of the information he'd been given by Hashi Lebwohl, that by the time he'd granted Koina a private conference, she'd accumulated a substantial list of matters for discussion. But he'd already covered a number of items with her, primarily Special Counsel Maxim Igensard's demands for data and explanation, similar requests from such GCES Members as Vest Martingale and Sigurd Carsin, and generalized appeals for cooperation and pacification from Abrim Len. For the most part, he'd simply reassured her that he did indeed want her to carry out her duties as she thought right. In particular he'd reaffirmed the importance of "full disclosure" to the GCES—although he hadn't offered to fill in any of the gaps which prevented her "disclosure" from being truly "full."

Yet while they'd talked his heart had ached, as it ached more and more these days. God! why did he have to *say* these things? Was he so wholly compromised that his own people found him impossible to trust?

What was left?

Which parts of his complex and hermetic plotting had begun to spring leaks?

"Just one more," she assured him. Her manner remained calm despite the sudden increase in her tension; as loud to his prosthetic eye as a shout. "I took it to Director Lebwohl first because, frankly, I wasn't sure *what* to do. But he urged me to bring it to you, which was what I preferred in any case."

Hashi, Warden thought. Again. First the DA director received information about events on Thanatos Minor from a source Warden didn't know about—provocative information, ominous information. And now Warden learned that he acted as the Director of Protocol's confidant and counselor. What was going on? Was Warden's old shame making him jump at shadows, or was *everybody* trying to manipulate him?

"Director"—for a fraction of an instant Koina nearly faltered—"I've received a personal flare from Captain Sixten Vertigus. The United Western Bloc Senior Member," she added unnecessarily. "He feared that he was taking a serious risk by contacting me, but he felt—well, he said"—she quoted Captain Vertigus easily—" 'I wouldn't be able to look at myself in the mirror on those few occasions when I wake up if I didn't warn you.' "

" 'Warn you'?" Warden put in more abruptly than he intended. He was in a *hurry*.

Koina faced him firmly. "Director, he told me that as soon as the GCES reconvenes—which will probably be within the next twenty-four hours—he intends to introduce a Bill of Severance which will separate us from the UMC."

She paused, allowing Warden a moment to absorb this revelation. Then she continued.

"He believes that's the reason he was attacked, to stop him. And he believes Godsen was killed on the assumption that Protocol must have been working with him. For the same reason, he believes I might be next." She shrugged slightly. "He felt he had to warn me, despite the risk."

Warden was too full of impatience: he couldn't stifle all of it. Cursing the raw edge in his voice, he demanded, "What risk is that?"

In response she lowered her gaze. Min wouldn't have done that; but in other ways Koina reminded him of the DA director in the old days—before he'd begun to inspire so much outrage.

"The risk that we might tell the Dragon," she answered. "The risk that warning me might give the UMC and the UMCP time to work against him together."

Damn! Damn it to *hell*! Unable to contain himself any longer, Warden rose to his feet as if he were dismissing the PR director. Her qualms filled him with an acid chagrin, corrosive and bitter.

He watched her stand opposite him. Then he pronounced harshly, "Hashi was wrong. We shouldn't be talking about this. We shouldn't know about it at all. As of right now, we *don't* know about it. You've forgotten everything Captain Vertigus said on the subject, and if you made any record of your conversation, I hope you believe in an afterlife, because I won't take pity on you in this one.

"If and when the question of a Bill of Severance comes to your attention through normal, *public* channels, our position is one of strict and absolute neutrality. We have no opinion, for or against. Our only legal authority for what we do comes from the GCES, and it is the proper business of the GCES to make decisions about that authority. We accept those decisions, whatever they might be. We are the police, not the government. We have neither the competence nor the wisdom to sway the Council concerning a Bill of Severance.

"Have I made myself clear?"

"Not completely." Koina didn't hesitate to use her beauty, when she needed it. Her eyes were limpid and kind, and her mouth smiled with an endearing quirk; even her tone suggested affection. Only her words themselves conveyed a challenge. "Are we going to take the same position with Holt Fasner?"

However, Warden was in no mood for her defenses—or her challenge. His shoulders hunched in a clench of disgust, which he deflected into a shrug. "Koina, do I look like a man who has the time to stand here lying to you?" Making a virtue of necessity, he let his exasperation show in his voice. "Of *course* we're going to take the same position. It's the right position." Then he admitted frankly, "It's also the only one we can afford."

At once—and smoothly, as if the transition were easy—she became all brisk professionalism. "Thank you, Director." Already she'd turned for the door. "I'll get out of your way now and let you do some real work."

Without his IR sight, he would have had no way of knowing that she'd been touched by his answer, or that she accepted it.

Muttering imprecations at his lack of self-command, he stopped her. Before he keyed the door—before he opened the security envelope which kept their conversation private—he told her quietly, "By the way, I don't think you're in any danger."

She raised a delicate eyebrow, smiling as if she considered the question purely academic. "Why not?"

"Because Captain Vertigus is wrong. That's not what this is about."

"I see." She considered his answer for a moment, then asked, "What is it about?"

He had no intention of telling her that; her or anyone else. "Watch the next GCES session," he returned. "It might give you some ideas."

To keep her from saying anything else, he keyed the door and waved her through it.

The instant she was gone he sat down and faced Min's message.

A tremor of anxiety he didn't bother to control afflicted his hands as he tapped his console. He could afford to be cryptic with Koina Hannish, but with himself he needed facts and accuracy. Without them he would never be ready to face the Dragon.

How much time did he have left before Holt summoned him to demand an accounting? Would he be left alone long enough to make his own decisions and act on them, or would everything that followed from this moment be directed and shaped by Holt Fasner's purposes?

How soon would the Dragon learn the truth about him?

Growling softly through his teeth, he forced his one human eye into focus on the readout.

He noted the time-stamp and origination coordinates—Min's message had taken roughly seven hours to reach him by gap courier drone from the far side of the Com-Mine belt—but ignored all the rest of the secondary codes and data. He wanted the substance of the transmission.

When he found it, however, his heart lurched; missed a beat.

The report began with a copy of a flare from *Trumpet* to UMCPHQ.

No doubt the original of that message was still in transit, being carried Earthward by the listening post's regular drone service. Min had used one of *Punisher*'s few courier drones because she felt her information couldn't wait that long.

Warden shut down his recognition of his unsteady pulse and trembling hands; shut down his fear; shut down his awareness of ticking time; and read.

Isaac to Warden Dios, personal and **urgent,** the flare from Angus began. *Mission to Thanatos Minor successful.*

Gabriel priority activated. Milos Taverner has gone over to the Amnion.

Personnel aboard include survivors from Captain's Fancy: *Morn Hyland, Davies Hyland, Nick Succorso, Mikka Vasaczk, Ciro Vasaczk, Vector Shaheed.*

Amnion vessels in pursuit.

Urgent. *The Amnion know about the mutagen immunity drug in Nick Succorso's possession. It is possible that they have obtained a sample of the drug from Morn Hyland's blood.*

Urgent. *Davies Hyland is Morn Hyland's son, force-grown on Enablement Station. The Amnion want him. They believe he represents the knowledge necessary to mutate Amnion indistinguishable from humans.*

Urgent. *The Amnion are experimenting with specialized gap drives to achieve near-C velocities for their warships. Nick Succorso and his people have direct knowledge of this.*

We will try to survive until new programming is received.

Message ends. Isaac.

Warden could have stopped then; wanted to stop so that he could take all this in and find space for it among his complex priorities. He needed an opportunity to connect it to what he'd learned from Hashi; needed a chance to celebrate and worry. Morn was alive! Angus had gained that much for him, whatever else happened. But Min's report went on at much greater length, and he had to know it all.

What followed after *Trumpet*'s flare was a literal extract from *Punisher*'s datacore, beginning when the cruiser had reached her position near forbidden space on the far side of the Com-Mine belt. Typical of Min: the data was unedited; devoid of commentary or interpretation. She refused either to do Warden's work for him or to risk slanting his perceptions. He had to consider every detail in order to pan out the nuggets.

The nuggets were there, however. He identified them without trying to evaluate them yet.

Angus' programming still held: *Trumpet* had reached human space, flared a report, and activated her homing signal exactly according to his prewritten instructions. A ship from forbidden space—presumably an Amnioni herself, or an Amnion proxy—was heading across the frontier very much as if she were in pursuit of *Trumpet*. For that reason among others, *Punisher* was leaving the belt to chase the gap scout.

And then there was the matter of *Free Lunch*, owner and captain Darrin Scroyle, an apparently legal merchanter drifting right on top of the listening post Angus had risked his ship and his life to reach. *Free Lunch* claimed that she had some kind of contract with Cleatus Fane—in other words, with Holt Fasner—to observe and report events from forbidden space. Warden didn't dismiss that explanation, but he jumped to another of his own. *Free Lunch* was Hashi's unexplained source for his knowledge of events on Thanatos Minor. This Warden deduced from the strange fact that Darrin Scroyle—or Cleatus Fane—had seen fit to route *Free Lunch*'s transmission through UMCPDA.

It all looked like chaos; but Warden couldn't afford to think like that, couldn't let his conflicting emotions overwhelm him now. He'd put most of this in motion himself; perhaps all of it. If he lost his composure, if he failed to haul events into the kind of order he needed, then real chaos would result—pure, brutal, self-destructive anarchy.

Morn was *alive*. And Angus would keep her alive as long as he survived himself. That victory lifted Warden's heart when he considered it.

Milos' treachery didn't dismay him. From the first he'd planned to lose the former deputy chief of Com-Mine Security. Making it possible for Milos and his headful of knowledge to go "over to the Amnion" was the most insidious attack on them Warden could devise; a crucial gambit in his efforts to protect human space while he betrayed Holt Fasner's trust.

Put baldly, his intent with Milos—as well as one of his several purposes for Morn and Angus—was to lure the Amnion to commit an act of war which he would be able to crush, thereby driving them into a psychological retreat just at the time when humankind was most vulnerable to assault.

Therefore he wasn't daunted by the prospect of an Amnioni in pursuit of *Trumpet*. His gamble with Milos was starting to pay off.

At the same time, however, he tasted a tentative alarm at the idea that Morn Hyland had a son; a son the Amnion would risk much to recapture. *Force-grown on Enablement*. To some extent that explained Nick Succorso's unauthorized foray into forbidden space. And it gave the Amnion more reason to risk an incursion. But how was it possible that the boy had any mind at all, not to mention a mind that *represents the knowledge necessary to mutate Amnion indistinguishable from humans*? By what conceivable method were the Amnion able to "force-grow" a functional human consciousness?

The image of *Amnion indistinguishable from humans* made his skin crawl. Genetic kazes of one form or another were the stuff of nightmare. Yet that idea was less immediately appalling than the bare thought that the Amnion might have gained the means to achieve near-C velocities. If that were true, his efforts to protect his species had already begun to go wrong with a vengeance. No quadrant of human space would ever be safe again.

As for Hashi's dealings with *Free Lunch*—

Just for a moment Warden gave in to an incendiary and betrayed rage. What was Hashi *doing*? Working with the Dragon? Had he gone over to Holt's side behind Warden's back? Was it possible that Warden had been *that* wrong about him?

You sonofabitch, I know you don't even know what the truth *is*, but I *trusted* you! I *need* you!

He couldn't afford that, however, absolutely could not afford to submit to fury; not *now*. Too much was at stake. His hopes, even his survival, depended on his ability to keep his head *right now*, to understand what was going on and make accurate decisions about it. He'd set himself up for this; set Holt Fasner up, and most of humankind as well. If he faltered or failed, he might as well go over to the Amnion himself: the harm he did would be incalculable.

He brought his torn passions under control just as what he called the "disaster light" on his console began flashing at him.

When he was in one of his secure offices, he officially ceased to exist. In theory no one could find him; no one could reach him. But in practice that was unworkable—not to mention irresponsible. His duties required that he could be contacted in the event of an emergency. UMCPHQ Center accomplished this by activating a signal in all his offices simultaneously.

It was too soon—but then everything was always too soon when so much hung in the balance. At least he'd been given time to read *Punisher*'s report. He could think about it on the way.

Already he could see possibilities—

Faced with a crisis, he mastered himself. His hands were as steady as stones as he toggled his intercom.

"Dios." He announced himself as if he were immune to panic. "What's going on?"

"Director," a young voice from Center answered quickly. "Sorry for the intrusion, sir. I didn't know what else to do." Too young: the officer on duty sounded like a kid. "Holt Fasner's been yelling at us. No disrespect, but I thought he was going to burst something. He said—" The officer stumbled momentarily on the words. "Sorry, sir. He said if you don't get your ass over there in five minutes, he's going to feed your balls to his mother." In chagrin the officer repeated, "Sorry, sir."

Five minutes. Well, *that* was impossible, at any rate. No matter what the Dragon wanted, he would have to give Warden more time than that.

"Don't worry about it," he told the duty officer. "If I thought you were accountable for what the Dragon says, I would order you to wash his mouth out.

"Get my shuttle ready. Tell the crew I'm on my way. Then send CEO Fasner an ETA."

Warden clicked off the intercom and rose to his feet. If Holt could count, he would know that his UMCP director had responded to his summons immediately. Even a great worm—the term was Hashi's—couldn't demand more than that.

Now more than ever it was vital for Warden Dios to look like a dutiful subordinate.

UMC Home Security delivered him to the same office where he'd last faced his master. Nothing had changed physically, either in the room itself or in Holt Fasner. Aside from a utilitarian desk and a few chairs, the office contained no furniture: the remaining space was thick with data terminals, display screens, and communications systems. And the Dragon wasn't discernibly older. He wore his one hundred fifty years as if they were sixty or seventy; his heart still beat strongly; the working of his brain had lost none of its legendary fierceness. His true age showed only in the odd ruddiness splashed like stains across his cheeks, the rapid blinking of his eyes, and the way his hands sometimes shook.

Warden was mildly surprised to see that Holt wasn't angry. The Dragon's IR aura conveyed a mortality which wasn't obvious to normal sight: it was shot with acrid hues and fluctuations which Warden associated with hunger, distrust, connivance; an old and undifferentiated hate. None of that was new, however. Holt had roared at UMCPHQ Center with a vehemence he apparently didn't feel—or no longer felt.

Warden didn't wait for a greeting. He didn't sit down; didn't approach the desk. As soon as the door closed behind him, sealing the room with security screens and baffles, he said harshly, "I hope you had a good reason for yelling at my people. They don't need that, and I don't like it."

Holt fluttered a hand as if he were waving away the needs—or the reality—of Warden's people. "Sit down, sit down." His tone was calm, but it held no welcome. "Your 'people,' as you so naively call them, are more interested in protecting you than in doing their jobs. I had to get their attention."

"Why?" Warden countered. "I don't ignore you when you summon me. And I don't keep you waiting."

Holt leaned forward; strange hungers pulsed in his aura. "This is urgent. You know that as well as I do. You received a report from the Com-Mine belt—a report on what happened to Billingate. I want to know what it said."

Warden made no effort to disguise his bitterness. "I thought you already knew."

Holt reacted by jerking up his head. His eyes widened; for a moment they stopped blinking.

"Now how in hell would I know that?"

Quickly Warden studied the Dragon's emanations, searching them for signs of falsehood. Routine data sharing between Home Office and UMCPHQ would have included only the fact of the report's arrival, not its content. But if Hashi had gone behind Warden's back to Holt—

"There's a ship out in the belt," Warden pronounced, "*Free Lunch*, Captain Darrin Scroyle. He says he's working for you."

"Then he's a liar," Holt snapped. "I turned all UMC communications resources over to *you*. I haven't had either the time or the facilities to set up another net of my own.

"I'll have this"—he spat the name—"this Captain *Scroyle's* license revoked and his ship decommissioned by the time you get back to UMCPHQ."

"Fine," Warden growled. "You do that." Holt's disgust and indignation were plain; honest as far as they went. His aura didn't suggest calculation. He was trying to evaluate Warden, not conceal subterfuge from him.

So Hashi had not gone behind Warden's back. The DA director was playing a different kind of game.

Warden found no comfort in that.

It was certainly plausible that *Free Lunch* had lied to protect herself from *Punisher*. Having no conscience about the truth himself, Hashi liked working with people who dissembled well. He seemed to find a specialized pleasure, almost a kind of exaltation, in the challenge of defining and profiting from other people's falsehoods.

"But in the meantime," Warden went on without pausing, "maybe you'll explain why you assume I wasn't going to send you a copy of that report?"

"Because," Holt retorted, "you don't look good to me right now. Your dependability is, shall we say, starting to fray around the edges?

"My sweet old mother, bless her malicious soul, thinks you're getting me in trouble. I always pay close attention when she tells me such things." Threats and distrust whetted his tone. "And you went out of your way to confirm her judgment in that appalling video conference with the GCES. But you didn't stop there—not you, in spite of your elevated reputation for good sense. You appointed this—this Koina Hannish—to replace Godsen without consulting me. And you sent Joshua against Thanatos Minor under the control of the most accomplished double-dealing bugger you could find.

"I don't want to wait around until you think the time is right to let me know what's going on. I prefer hearing the truth in person."

Grimly Warden stifled an impulse to rasp back, Fine. Let's *both* tell the truth. I'll tell you why I really sent Angus to Billingate. You tell me what you gain from this goddamn hostile peace with the Amnion. Tell me why you work so hard to make sure that nothing we do to protect ourselves is ever quite good enough. Tell me what's so absolutely important that you have to misuse and manipulate me to get it.

He couldn't say that: he knew the Dragon too well. And yet in some sense he *had* to tell the truth. There was no choice about it. Holt had too many other sources of information. As matters stood, he owned the UMCP. And he'd built Warden's domain to suit his own purposes. Data-sharing with UMCPHQ Center wasn't his only mechanism for gathering knowledge. If other means failed, he probably had a dozen strategically placed buggers he could rely on.

"All right." To cover himself while he controlled his yearning for honesty, Warden took a chair and sat down opposite Holt; folded his heavy forearms over his chest. "You need to know this in any case. Some of it's out of my province." Carefully he prepared himself to offer the bait which he hoped would lure Holt into a mistake; the one mistake he needed. "And some of it's just too damn scary to keep to myself."

He wanted Holt to let Morn live. But the Dragon would never do that unless he were given something that he thought was worth the risk.

Desperation or providence had supplied Warden with something that might suffice—

"The report came from Director Donner," he explained, "but she got it directly from *Trumpet* and flared it to us. It isn't remotely complete. You have to understand that Joshua is running for his life. He was betrayed by Milos Taverner, and he's got Amnion after him."

Holt's gaze became a hard glare.

"I know you don't like the chances I took," Warden went on, "but Director Lebwohl and I haven't been stupid about this. We knew Milos couldn't be trusted. And we knew we couldn't foresee everything that might happen to Joshua. If we tried to write instruction-sets to control him completely in every situation, then any problem we hadn't foreseen might paralyze or kill him. So we gave him alternate priority-codes—codes Milos didn't know about—and programmed them to take effect automatically if Milos betrayed him.

"But if those codes went into effect, it meant the situation was worse than we thought it would be. Treachery adds dangers we couldn't predict. And without Milos to control him, Joshua might make decisions that multiplied the hazards. Under those circumstances, we knew we couldn't afford to let him come back here on his own. We wouldn't have any idea what kind of trouble he was bringing with him until it arrived.

"Director Lebwohl and I compensated by writing protections into his datacore. If he was betrayed, his programming requires him to send in a report, activate a homing signal so we can find him—and then go on the run. Keep himself alive until we decide what to do about him. That way we're covered. We can find out what's going on before we have to commit ourselves.

"Well, it all happened. Milos did betray him. His new priority-codes are in effect. His homing signal and his report confirm that. Now he's on the run because that's how we programmed him. And he's got Amnion after him because we sent him into a mess that was worse than we thought it would be."

Personnel aboard include—

Warden paused to tighten the grip of his arms. He'd planned for this crisis, prayed for it; readied himself— Now he had to see it through.

He'd promised Holt that Morn Hyland would die. But Warden himself wanted her alive.

Deliberately he added, "Joshua has quite a few people with him."

" 'People'?" Holt interrupted. "What 'people'?" Hints of IR fire licked through his aura. "This wasn't supposed to be a goddamn passenger run."

Now, Warden thought, gripping himself harder. This is it.

As if he weren't staring ruin in the face, he answered calmly, "Nick

Succorso. Four of his crew—Mikka and Ciro Vasaczk, Sib Mackern, Vector Shaheed."

He almost hoped Holt would recognize Shaheed's name. The fallout would be awkward; but at least Holt would be distracted.

Unfortunately the Dragon was concentrating too hard to call on his encyclopedic knowledge of his enemies.

"Joshua, of course," Warden continued as if he'd only paused to swallow. "Morn Hyland. And a kid named Davies Hyland."

The bait.

Fasner may not have heard that last piece of information. He was already on his feet, already yelling.

"Morn *Hyland?*" His fists punched the air at Warden's face; an apoplectic flush mottled his cheeks. "You God damn sonofabitch! You sent Joshua out there to rescue *Morn Hyland?*"

"No, I didn't," Warden said stolidly; falsely.

"Are you saying he broke his programming?" Holt roared. "He's a *cyborg*! You told me it's impossible for him to do anything he wasn't programmed for! And you *specifically* told me he wasn't programmed to rescue her!"

"He wasn't." Holt's fury made it easier for Warden to retain his poise. Nevertheless he didn't bother to conceal his own anger. He hated lying, even to the man he considered humankind's worst betrayer. "But he also wasn't programmed to kill her. If that was what you wanted, you should have said so. I assume Joshua needed Nick for something, and taking Morn along was Nick's price."

Nearly screaming, Holt fired back, "Then why aren't they dead now? Have you gone stupid, or is this treason? Morn Hyland is alive! *What's the matter with you?* I *ordered* you to kill that ship, kill everybody aboard, if anything went wrong! Don't you call *this* wrong? Why didn't your fucking Min Donner carry out my orders?"

" 'Treason,' " Warden snorted with a glower. "I like that. You haven't even heard my report yet, and you accuse me of treason. Do you really want to miss the point *now*? Wouldn't you rather wait until I'm finished?"

Unaccustomed to men who disobeyed him—or, worse, men who acted like they knew better than he did—Holt gaped back at the UMCP director. Above his open mouth, his eyes blinked like cries.

"Then sit down and stop shouting," Warden commanded as if he'd gained what he wanted. Trying to undermine Holt's indignation, he added, "You're giving yourself an infarction." Holt knew what Warden's prosthetic sight was good for. "None of this is simple. I need you to pay attention."

The Dragon closed his mouth. He sat down. For a moment his emissions turned pale with uncertainty. Unaware of what he did, he raised a trembling hand to his chest as if he wanted to rub his heart. He was a discerning judge of his own symptoms, however, his own condition. Almost immediately he came back into focus like a beast emerging from a lair, ready for battle.

To prevent him from speaking, Warden said acidly, "Director Donner didn't just send us that report. She read it. She has enough sense to see what it means. She didn't kill *Trumpet* because she knew I would flay her skin off if she did. We need that ship alive, Holt—we need everybody aboard *alive*."

Smell the *bait*, you heartless bastard! Give me a chance.

Holt hawked an obscenity. "Ward, you're hanging by your balls here. You had better do an *extraordinary* job of convincing me. Otherwise you're gone. Your commission won't last long enough to get you back on your own shuttle. And I promise you this. The next UMCP director will know how to make that bitch of yours follow orders."

"Fine." Warden kept his arms locked to his chest, but he wielded his voice like a lash. "I'm trying to save your entire kingdom for you, not to mention your personal ass. If you can't think of anything more useful to do than threaten me, I'll quit now and let the 'next UMCP director' make sense out of all this."

Without a blink or a flicker, Holt held Warden's glare. His aura yowled of furies that didn't show on his face. This was the Holt Fasner who scared Warden down to his bones: the man who used rage and hate and hunger as forms of concentration, to make himself invulnerable.

Warden also knew how to concentrate. But his emotions were of another kind. Slumping slightly, as if he were able to relax with the Dragon's glower fixed on him, he resumed his report.

"Don't ask me to explain all the details. I only know what was in *Trumpet*'s flare. But here's the way it looks, as far as I can put it together.

"Nick Succorso and Morn Hyland went to Enablement Station because she was pregnant. I don't know why either of them cared, or why they thought going there was a good idea. All I know is, they went there, and she had them 'force-grow' her a son, whom she named 'Davies Hyland'—after her father, I suppose. Then they got in trouble.

"Apparently the Amnion decided they want Davies. They think he holds the secret to mutating Amnion so that they'll be indistinguishable from human beings." Are you listening, Holt? Do you hear what I'm really saying? "Which means they could infiltrate our space without being detected. They could destroy us without a shot being fired, and we wouldn't even know it was happening until we were already doomed."

Can you smell it?

Holt's aura roiled with agitation and a clenched, acidic lust, but his features revealed nothing. Only his eyes blinked and blinked.

"So *Captain's Fancy* ran," Warden rasped, "and the Amnion sent warships after her. She must have lost her gap drive—instead of trying to reach human space, she headed for Billingate, the nearest port with a shipyard.

"That's crucial. She's a tach ship. What happened to her gap drive? And how did she get there and back so fast at space-normal speeds? A trip like that should have taken years.

"Joshua's message said, 'The Amnion are experimenting with specialized gap drives to achieve near-C velocities for their warships. Nick Succorso and his people have direct knowledge of this.' Here's what I think happened.

"Nick blew out his gap drive getting to Enablement, and he couldn't fix it, so he traded for repairs. I don't know what he had to trade *with*, but he must have had something, or else he wouldn't have been able to pay to get Morn's son force-grown. Maybe the Amnion thought it was valuable enough to cover repairs. Or maybe it was an experiment—they used *Captain's Fancy* to test their 'specialized gap drives.' I can't imagine how else Nick and his crew would know about it."

"You're wasting my time," Holt snarled impatiently. His ability to contain his furies seemed to be weakening. "I don't care about weapons systems. That's your worry. If you can't figure out what to do about this, I'll find someone who can."

Warden nodded. "Fair enough. I'll do my job. But that's only a piece of the story.

"Whatever happened after *Captain's Fancy* left Enablement, the warships cut her off before she reached Billingate. They *wanted* Davies." That was as close as Warden dared go to waving his bait under Holt's nose. "Trying to protect himself, I guess, Nick put Davies in an ejection pod and fired him to Billingate." Warden had arrived at this conclusion by an intuitive leap based on the combination of *Punisher*'s and *Free Lunch*'s transmissions. "Now *Captain's Fancy* was allowed to dock. I'm assuming the Amnion didn't want to alienate Billingate, so they didn't take Davies by force. Instead they ordered Nick to get him back and hand him over or face the consequences of cheating them.

"Apparently Nick gave them Morn. He must have been trying to buy time." However Hashi had come by it, his information was invaluable. "But she wasn't the one they wanted. As far as he was concerned, it was Davies or nothing. But before he let him have her—this is crucial, too—he gave her some of DA's mutagen immunity drug. Joshua says it's possible they know about the drug because they may have found it in her blood."

Trying to make Morn's survival more palatable, Warden offered Holt vindication as well as bait. The Dragon's every instinct had rebelled against Vector Shaheed's antimutagen research for Intertech. Warden had persuaded the UMC CEO to give the research to DA against his better judgment. Perhaps being proved right would soften Holt's outrage.

He kept his reaction to himself, however. His emissions boiled and spat; but they articulated his emotions in colors and patterns, not in words.

Fear tugged at Warden's guts. He could feel failure gathering in the room around him.

"That's when *Trumpet* arrived," he went on stiffly. "What happened next isn't clear yet. Joshua and Milos got together with Nick. Then Milos went over to the Amnion. He may have been trying to warn them." He refrained from mentioning that this detail was crucial as well. "And someone stole Davies from Billingate. Someone—Nick and a few of his people—raided the Amnion to get Morn back.

"Somehow they all ended up aboard *Trumpet*—Nick, four of his crew, Davies, Morn, and Joshua. *Captain's Fancy* went down attacking one of the warships so that *Trumpet* could get out of dock. But Joshua did his job. When Billingate's fusion generator blew, he escaped by riding the confusion."

Warden lifted his shoulders as if he were consigning his fate to the Dragon's whim. "That's the report. Director Donner added the information that there's a ship, presumably Amnioni, heading out of forbidden space after *Trumpet*. And she told me about *Free Lunch*'s alleged contract with you. Then she went after *Trumpet* herself"—he did his best to spare Min the consequences of Holt's anger—"to keep the Amnion off Joshua's back until we decide what we want to do with him."

"Fine." Holt's emissions suggested mockery. "You make it all sound wonderfully tidy and successful. In fact, you almost make it sound reasonable.

"What do you propose to do now? *Trumpet* is back in human space.

Presumably you can protect her. If I give you enough rope so you can go ahead and hang yourself, what decisions will you make?"

Warden was ready for this. He was prepared to tell one more lie—a lie which was close enough to the truth to be plausible.

Leaning forward in his seat as if he'd come to the heart of his intentions, he said with quiet intensity, "I know you don't want Morn back, Holt, but I think we're damn lucky we got her. We're damn lucky we got all those other people. We need them."

Holt's emanations looked as hot as a solar eruption, although he didn't interrupt.

Softly Warden insisted, "We need what Nick and his people know about those near-C experiments. We need Joshua because he's too valuable to throw away. We need Morn because of what she can tell us about the Amnion—and because she gives us a way to check whatever Nick says, which probably won't be the truth unless he knows we'll catch a lie. And we need Davies so we can learn what the Amnion hope to get out of him.

"This is our chance. We can put Director Donner aboard *Trumpet.* Once she gets close enough to transmit a message, she can invoke Joshua's new codes. Then he'll take her orders. With her in command and *Punisher* as escort, she can take them all to someplace safe—a place where the Amnion won't find them and nobody else will get in our way. We can learn everything they know at our own pace, and we won't have to let events rush us.

"And there's another benefit," he hurried to add before Holt ran out of patience. "Special Counsel Maxim Igensard wants blood. If we don't contain him"—deliberately Warden spoke of *we* as if there were no distinction between himself and his master—"he won't stop until he finds something that makes us look dirty. So dirty he can dictate his own terms to the GCES.

"But if we produce survivors from Billingate, these specific survivors, most of his case against us will collapse. We'll be able to prove that what we've gained justifies the risks we took. We'll even be able to give him an explanation he can't refute for what we did with Intertech's mutagen immunity research. And not abandoning Morn Hyland will do wonders for our credibility."

Faced with the Dragon's seething concentration, Warden asked tightly, "Are you listening to me, Holt? When you look like that, I feel like I'm talking to a wall.

"This is an opportunity we can't afford to miss."

Abruptly Holt snorted. As if he were emerging from a trance, he shook his arms and shoulders, rubbed his hands over his cheeks. His eyes blinked rapidly to clear his vision.

"You probably believe that, you blind idiot," he growled. "Ward Dios, the fucking idealist." His anger was so vivid that it left afterimages on Warden's IR sight. "You almost make me regret choosing you for this job. After all these years you still don't know what you're *for*—what the whole goddamn UMCP is *for*. You still think I invented you because I wanted *cops*. If this weren't a terrible time to change directors, I would throw you out on your ass and find somebody with better brains.

"Well, *you*, listen to *me*, Ward. This is your last chance.

"Do you really think I've missed the point?"

A pang twisted Warden's heart; but he tightened his arms so that the pain didn't show. "When you start yelling," he retorted trenchantly, "I don't know what to think."

"In that case," Holt said like a breath of flame, "I'll keep my voice down. I don't want to give you any excuse for making a mistake. These are orders, and *you*"—with the knuckles of one hand, he rapped every word onto his desktop—"are going to carry them out.

"If the Amnion want this Davies Hyland, so do I. I want him delivered here, to me, in person."

Warden tried not to let himself hope; he couldn't afford it in front of the Dragon. Holt was taking the bait.

"Why?"

"If you can't figure that out," Holt rasped, "you don't deserve an answer.

"But it does mean *Trumpet* has to be kept alive. I don't like anything else you've done here—and you as sure as shit haven't convinced me I can trust you—but I'll give you that one. *Trumpet* has to be kept alive.

"Since I don't trust you, I'll tell you how to do it. I'm not going to put up with arguments or insubordination or delays. If you give me any grief, I'll jerk you out of UMCPHQ so fast your vital organs'll be left behind."

Warden braced himself behind his arms and waited for the ax to fall.

Rapping the desktop again, Holt said, "I want you to contact *Trumpet*. Make 'Director Donner' do it," he sneered harshly. "You're so busy protecting her, I want her to get her hands dirty. I want you to *make* her get her hands dirty."

Go on, say it. Warden clasped his chest until he could hardly breathe. *Say* it and get it over with.

Holt's aura shone with cruelty and relish. "Tell her to give Joshua's new priority-codes to Nick Succorso."

In spite of his grip on himself, Warden flinched. For an instant time seemed to stop. Behind his rigid expression and his flat stare, he went into shock.

Tell her to give Joshua's new priority-codes to Nick Succorso.

A magnesium flare took fire in his guts. This was worse than anything he'd feared, anything he could answer. Holt had beaten him. In his most costly nightmares he hadn't dreamed that his master would go so far.

—to Nick Succorso.

"We'll let Succorso take Taverner's place," the Dragon explained as if he were licking his chops. "That way we can make sure Joshua doesn't spring any more surprises on us. Succorso can force him to follow my orders when I'm ready."

Joshua's new priority-codes—

Whom had he betrayed most, Angus or Morn? They were the offspring of his most secret desires: he'd stripped them of everything they needed or owned in the name of passions they hadn't asked for and couldn't share. And those passions had just died as if Holt had driven a stake through Warden's heart.

"Once Succorso takes command of Joshua and *Trumpet*—and gives us confirmation so I know I'm safe—we'll give him the rest of my orders."

Tell her—

Oh, Min, you are going to hate me for this.

Without Morn's testimony the Bill of Severance would never pass. Not now. And certainly not later, when Holt would be more vulnerable.

But Warden couldn't collapse now; couldn't bear to let Holt unman him entirely. He still had work to do. Damage-control: his last duty when everything had gone wrong, and the Dragon's rapacity swallowed human space. Shame if nothing else required him to stand up; face the consequences of his arrogance and folly; save what last small things might still be preserved. He refused to fail under the burden until he'd paid for everything.

From somewhere, as if he were digging it out of a grave, he found the strength to ask, "Which are?"

Holt grinned. His aura reeked of pleasure. "Kill everybody aboard except Davies Hyland. Have him bring Davies to me. Let him keep one or two of his people, if he needs them. Make him kill the rest. *Especially* Morn Hyland and Vector Shaheed. You and those two bastards have done enough harm."

Through a storm of chagrin, Warden realized that Holt had recognized Shaheed's name after all.

In a bleak tone, like one of the damned, he murmured, "How am I supposed to make him do all that? *He* doesn't have any priority-codes."

Holt positively gleamed with ferocity. "By offering him something he wants. We'll let him keep *Trumpet* and Joshua. He'll jump at it. He can't refuse a ship like that—or the chance to have a welded cyborg for crew."

Angus, oh, Angus, it was all for nothing, I did it to you for nothing. I told you it's got to stop, but instead of stopping anything I committed a crime against you that you'll have to live with until Nick does you enough harm to kill you.

And Morn as well. Nick might agree to kill her, but until the end she would be his to torment and degrade as much as he wished.

Past his arms and his lacerated heart, Warden sighed. "I'm sure you're right. Nick Succorso is exactly the kind of man who'll jump at an offer like that."

Holt leaned forward; pouncing. Sharp with relish, he hissed, "You sonofabitch, you're mine, *mine*. I invented the *cops*—I invented *you*. You're as welded as any cyborg, and you've had your last chance at getting me in trouble. From now on you're going to do *what* I tell you, *when* I tell you, *how* I tell you. And you're going to *thank* your pitiful ass you aren't dead.

"Do you *really* think I've missed the point?"

Warden shook his head. Slowly he unclamped his arms. Every muscle in his chest and legs ached with cramps: he felt as stiff and unsteady as a cripple. Nevertheless he climbed to his feet. Holt didn't need to dismiss him: he knew he was finished. Fighting knots and strain, he limped toward the door.

"Follow orders," Holt said after him. "I'm watching—and you know I can do it. That's what all those listening posts are for. If you mess with me, I'll find out. Then you're dead."

Warden nodded as if he were beaten.

When Holt unsealed the door, however, Warden didn't open it. Instead he turned back to the Dragon.

Holt had surprised him with an act of imaginative malice he hadn't expected and couldn't match. There were other things he could do, however. He understood power and manipulation; he could still fight. With his hand on the door and no hope left, he replied to his doom with an imaginative act of his own.

"Speaking of your mother," he said distantly, "I haven't seen her for a long time. Do you mind if I visit her before I go? It should only take a few minutes. And I can spare the time. We have more than an hour before our best window on the next listening post *Punisher* is likely to pass."

"My mother?" Holt was surprised: his face showed it as plainly as his emissions. "Norna? What in hell do you want to visit *her* for?"

The UMCP director shrugged awkwardly; falsely. "She's become something of a legend over the years—like an oracle, you might say. I want to ask her what makes her think I've been trying to get you in trouble."

Holt scrutinized Warden hard. The uncertainty of his aura suggested that he felt the threat in Warden's request, but couldn't identify it. After only a moment, however, his expression cleared, and he laughed acidly.

"You poor, misguided lump of shit, you're still trying to play games with me. Go ahead"—he fluttered his hands—"visit her. *Enjoy* it if you can. You two deserve each other. And there's a good chance you're going to end up just like her."

As Warden opened the door and closed it behind him, Holt was speaking into an intercom, instructing HS to conduct the UMCP director to Norna Fasner and let him talk to her for ten minutes before escorting him to his shuttle.

"Privately," Warden told the two guards who came to his sides. As soon as he left Holt's sight, his manner became authoritative and sure: he sounded as steady as a rock. "I want to talk to her alone. Check with him if you don't trust me."

"Yes, sir." As far as Home Security knew, Warden Dios was still the second most powerful man in human space. "This way."

Walking briskly to work the cramps out of his legs, Warden followed the guards. Holt had said, *You are mine*, but he was wrong. Warden may have lost everything else, but he was still himself.

While any piece of him remained, he intended to go on fighting.

WARDEN

He was at his best when he was ashamed.

He could not have explained that: he was hardly aware of it. Yet it was true. The tension between his unyielding passion for standards of integrity, commitment, and efficacy so untrammeled that they could never be attained and his sense of mortal chagrin when he fell below those standards was fruitful for him. It taught him strengths he might never have known he possessed.

Shame and idealism were the means by which Holt Fasner had manipulated him into becoming what he was: the director of the UMCP, guilty as charged; the man most directly responsible for the corruption of the cops. Holt had focused his idealism—his essential belief that it was the honorable and necessary function of the police *to serve and protect* humanity—to position him where he would be vulnerable; then had exercised his shame to push him farther and farther from those ideals.

In a sense Warden had accepted this. Presumably he could have refused at any time—could have preserved the man he wished to be by letting Holt fire him. At the worst Holt might have had him killed. So what? Warden knew to his cost that there were many worse fates than death.

Yet he hadn't refused. At every crisis he'd resisted the Dragon's cunning up to a certain point; then he'd let it carry him along.

In a sense, the reason he did this was simple.

All his life, he'd considered himself inadequate to his dreams; unequal to the task of making them live. Certainly he'd been too flawed to see Holt

Fasner accurately when the Dragon had first hired him to work for SMI Security. Stupid with naïveté, he'd believed that he was being given a chance to do good, valuable work for a good, valuable man. And Holt had encouraged that illusion with every trick at his command. Hungry with dreams and shame, Warden had learned to define himself in terms of law enforcement at its noblest: service and protection for those who needed it most—and could afford it least.

By the time he'd realized that Holt used the cops for no purposes but his own, and that those purposes had nothing to do with idealism, Warden had already acquired a taste for the nourishment his sore heart craved: the food of lawful power.

So who could hope to stop the Dragon, if not an officer of the law? Whose job was it? And to whom did that job properly belong, if not to the man who had helped make the Dragon powerful by allowing his own hopes to blind him?

Precisely because he considered himself culpable, Warden Dios had sworn to take any risk and pay any price which might help him undo the harm he'd caused by supporting Holt Fasner's ambitions.

Of course he couldn't undo that harm if he weren't a cop. The authority of his position as director of the UMCP was all that enabled him to act. He couldn't afford to sacrifice that authority in the name of personal honor.

Therefore he swallowed the compromises and betrayals necessary to keep his job, earn the Dragon's trust. When he wasn't engaged in some dirty business of Holt's, he developed and ran the UMCP as if his organization were indeed as incorruptible as it should be. And in the dark corners of his mind, through the gaps between his other commitments, he set about the complex, secret task of arranging Holt's downfall.

Inevitably the Dragon caught glimpses of this. He knew better than to trust his UMCP director too much. So he strove to bind Warden closer to him with new acts of complicity and shame. But there he erred. He misunderstood the true nature of Warden's dreams. Each new piece of extorted cynicism drove Warden farther away; drove him to imagine more, dare more, suffer more in the name of his real passion.

Shame *pushed* him.

He was no longer the man he'd once been: he'd transcended himself long ago. By will and mortification he'd become more than he or Holt Fasner or anyone else realized.

When Holt outplayed him, demanded that he sacrifice Morn and Angus as well as everything they represented, Warden was left stripped of his hopes; naked with chagrin at all the harm he'd done—and done for nothing.

Intertech's antimutagen had been denied to humankind—but not to the Amnion. Vector Shaheed, the one free man with the knowledge to replicate Intertech's work, was about to be killed. Morn Hyland had endured Angus Thermopyle and Nick Succorso, rape and zone implants, for *months*. Now she would be discarded like a piece of scrap. Angus himself, who carried the core of Warden's desperation in his welded resources and secret programming, would become Nick's plaything and tool; the perfect illegal, violent and dehumanized.

What was left, except shame and the price of failure?

Warden Dios was at his best when he asked to see Norna Fasner.

He didn't try to explain the request to himself. It was purely intuitive—a small gesture to counterbalance what he'd lost—and he accepted the consequences of acting on it. Yet it seemed to make him stronger with every passing moment. As HS guided him into the secure depths of Holt's headquarters, his heart grew steady and his respiration calmed. Neither his stride nor his composure gave his guards any hint that the Dragon had found a way to deprive him of what he loved most.

There was always something left.

Perhaps that was why he wanted to consult an oracle.

So he followed his escort until the two men delivered him to the specialized cave of life-support systems and video screens where Norna Fasner lived. At the door he dismissed them. They had no orders to accompany him in. And surely the Dragon could eavesdrop on his mother whenever he wished.

Warden entered her sickchamber alone and closed the door.

The lights were off in the high, sterile room; but he could see by the phosphorescent glow of the video screens which filled the wall in front of Norna's bed and equipment. That wall was all she had, her whole world: the bed held her rigid, as if it were a traction frame, so that her equipment could do the delicate and obscene work of keeping life in her immured carcass. Only her eyes and mouth could move—and her fingers, allowing her to control the illumination and screens. In the flat, heartless light, she looked spectral and bereaved. The medical advances which sustained her son had come too late to do anything more than impose existence on her. Mortality stained her shriveled skin so that it seemed filthy against the clean linen of her bed.

Her equipment gave off so many IR emissions that Warden's prosthetic sight was effectively useless. As far as he could see, she had no aura;

perhaps no emotions; possibly no mind. Yet Holt had told him over the years that she remained conscious—not only sentient but sharp. On one occasion Holt had said, "I keep her alive, you know. I don't mean my doctors or my orders—I mean me personally. *I* keep her alive. She would go out like a candle if she didn't hate me too much to die. She lives for the hope that she'll get to see me destroyed. And maybe, just maybe, that she'll be able to see it coming."

The Dragon had laughed as he said this. Apparently he considered it funny.

Warden was of a different opinion.

He kept it to himself, however, now as much as then. He wasn't here to feel sorry for the woman who had taught Holt his hungers. And he had only ten minutes. If Norna couldn't answer him in that time, the risk of visiting her would be wasted.

Nevertheless he stopped just inside the door, momentarily paralyzed. Holt had told him about the video screens; but he hadn't realized how daunting they could be: twenty or more of them, all alive, all projecting their images simultaneously, all gabbling at once; and all dead because they had no human IR emissions and therefore contained no life. As inert as Norna herself, newscasts and sex shows vied with comedies, sports programs, and dramas to dominate his attention; voices conflicted with background music and sound effects up and down the audible spectrum. The effect was at once hypnotic and disturbing, like a white-noise rumble which felt soothing, but which presaged some kind of tectonic cataclysm. It created the strange illusion that all but one of the screens offered gibberish as a way of concealing the sole exception; that the exception displayed instead a soothsayer's version of pure, cold truth; and that it changed places constantly with all the others, so that only the most savage and unremitting concentration could hope to glimpse its wisdom as it passed from screen to screen.

Warden stifled an impulse to curse the Dragon. He didn't have time for that.

Steadying himself on urgency, he forced his legs to carry him away from the door toward the screens until he entered Norna's field of view. There he turned; put his back to the video wall and faced her.

"Hello, Norna."

In the phosphor gleam her eyes looked empty, transfixed by death. They made no apparent effort to track individual images: perhaps she'd learned how to focus on all the programs at the same time. Or perhaps she'd merely forgotten what she was looking for. Her lips and gums chewed constantly, as if she were trying to remember the taste of food. Saliva she couldn't control drooled into the wrinkles across her chin.

Just for an instant, however, her gaze flicked toward him. Then it returned to the screens.

"Ward." Her voice barely reached him through the ambient mutter. "Warden Dios. It's about time."

He cocked an eyebrow in surprise. "You were expecting me," he remarked because he didn't know what else to say.

"Of course I've been expecting you," she muttered like the voices of her world. "Who else can you talk to?

"Move. You're in my way."

Warden glanced behind him, saw that he was indeed obstructing one edge of her view of the wall. Shrugging an apology, he took a step to the side. "Is that better?"

" 'Better'?" Something in the twist of her bloodless lips gave the impression that she was laughing. "If you think anything around here ever gets 'better,' you've wasted a visit. We don't have anything to talk about."

He frowned. He was in no mood for verbal sparring. Nevertheless he kept his response casual. "Forgive my choice of words. I certainly haven't seen anything get better."

Her toothless gums continued chewing. "No. And you won't. Not until you finish him."

Well, Holt had warned him that she was sharp; almost presciently cognizant of the world beyond her screens—the world she couldn't see. Still her bluntness took him aback.

" 'Finish him'?"

"Isn't that why you're here?" Although she appeared to focus on nothing, follow nothing, her gaze never left the restless movement of images. "Don't you want me to tell you what you need to know to finish him?"

A frisson of alarm ran down Warden's back, settled in his lower abdomen. How much could Holt hear? Softly, trusting her to pick his voice out of the gabble—trying to warn her—he asked, "Norna, does he listen in when you have visitors?"

He couldn't tell whether she heard him or not. For a moment she was silent. Then her mouth gave another twist that might have been laughter.

"How should I know? I never have visitors."

He made another attempt. "Should you be careful what you say?"

This time she didn't pause or hesitate. "Why? There's nothing left he can do to me. And if you were worried about yourself, you wouldn't be here."

Her blank concentration on her screens was eerie, almost ghoulish. Like a woman inured to death and corruption, she watched them as if they showed maggots feasting on corpses—one scene repeated from different angles on all the screens.

"Of course," she went on, "he doesn't realize how much I know. He has no idea what I might tell you. That could be dangerous. But I think you're safe enough."

Safe? The mere concept startled him. He raised a hand to interrupt her, ask her indulgence.

"Norna, forgive me. I guess I'm slow today—I'm not keeping up with you. What makes you think I'm safe here?"

Her face in the cold light looked so hollow and doomed that he half expected her to intone like a sibyl, Everyone who comes here is safe. This is the cave of death, where no other harm enters. As long as you remain, you are beyond hurt.

Her actual reply was more prosaic, however. "After all the trouble you've caused, he needs you. He can't afford to punish you now."

Baffled as much by the way she spoke as by what she said, he countered, "He's Holt Fasner, CEO of the entire created universe. What can he possibly need *me* for?"

Again that twist like laughter. Apparently she liked his sarcasm. Almost soundlessly her lips shaped her answer.

"A scapegoat."

Ah, Warden sighed to himself. Someone to blame. That made sense. He felt suddenly that he'd been freed from the confusion of the screens and the mystification of her manner. Now he knew how to talk to her.

"Thank you," he said more confidently. "I think I understand.

"As I'm sure you can guess, I've just come from talking to him. You mentioned all the 'trouble' I've 'caused.' And he told me you warned him I was getting him in trouble. Does he know what kind of trouble it is?"

"Shame on you, Ward." Through the interference of other voices she sounded like a disappointed schoolmarm. "That's not the right question. You know better."

Before he could absorb this criticism, she asked, "What did you talk to him about?"

He swallowed a rush of impatience. He was running out of time. Yet he had nothing to gain by trying to hurry her. Trusting that she didn't need long explanations, he answered, "I told him that Joshua's mission to Thanatos Minor was a success. But it was also a surprise. Joshua has come back into human space with some unexpected survivors."

"Such as?" she inquired quickly.

He had no business discussing such things with her. On the other hand, why had he bothered to come here, if he weren't willing to face the hazards involved?

Shrugging to himself, he let her have her way.

"Nick Succorso. Some of his crew—including a man named Vector Shaheed who used to work for Intertech back in the days when Intertech was doing antimutagen research. Morn Hyland." He did his best to mention Morn as if she had no special significance. "And somehow she has a son—a full-grown kid, apparently. She calls him Davies Hyland."

Norna considered this information for a moment.

"What does he want you to do about it?"

Warden felt that he was exposing his heart as he replied stiffly, "Deliver Davies to him." Like Norna he didn't need to refer to the Dragon by name. "Give Nick control over Joshua. Kill everybody else aboard."

Her empty gaze didn't shift. Chewing incessantly, her jaws leaked a small sheen of saliva into the smear on her chin. Only her lips reacted, twisting from side to side like a grimace.

Now he couldn't tell whether she was laughing or crying.

He waited until her grimace eased and her cheeks fell slack. Then in a low whisper he repeated his question.

"Norna, does he know?"

"I told him," she answered, invoked by mirth or grief. "But he doesn't understand. He fears death too much. It distorts his thinking."

"Most of us fear death," Warden countered, still whispering. "Most of the time we're able to ignore it."

She let out a hiss of impatience or vexation. "This is no ordinary fear of death. Have you suffered under him so long without figuring that out? If I called it 'mortal terror,' that would be an understatement.

"He wants to live forever." Bitterly she nodded to herself. "Yes, forever. Haven't I seen it? Why do you think he keeps me damned here? I've spent fifty years paying for what I see.

"He thinks the Amnion are the answer. Genetic magic. He thinks they know how to rescue his body before it fails. Or maybe they can grow him a new one.

"He can't make peace with them. Humankind wouldn't let him get away with it. Human beings are stupid"—she referred to her screens—"but nobody is that stupid. But if he lets you go to war, he'll lose everything he wants from the Amnion. So he needs this hostile truce."

As if she were still on the same subject, she demanded, "What makes Davies Hyland so precious?"

Warden had asked himself that question half a dozen times already. Now under the pressure of Norna's insight and his own needs, he forced himself to consider it again.

Thinking aloud, he murmured, "The Amnion used a technique called 'force-growing.' I've been hearing for years that they have the means to mature bodies rapidly. And it must work. Otherwise Morn would still be pregnant. She wouldn't have a son yet, never mind a full-grown kid.

"But how can he have a mind?" That was the crucial question, the fatal unknown. "How did the Amnion compensate for all the years of learning and experience he didn't get?"

Norna's stare never left her wall of images, yet it forced Warden to go on.

"They must have some way to create minds artificially." The human organism was inherently functionless without acquired training and information. "Or copy them.

"Copying sounds more plausible. But what did they use for an original?

"Did they impose one of their own on him? Then he would be an Amnioni—and Joshua would kill him, if Morn didn't." Panic and possibilities ran through him, riding a burst of intuition like high-brisance thrust. "They must have copied some human mind into his head."

He didn't need to finish the thought; didn't need to say, If they could do that for Davies, they could do it for Holt. Norna was already nodding. Her mummified lips chewed saliva and silence as if that were her oracular secret; the meaning of life.

Is that really *it*? He manipulates the GCES, suppresses the immunity drug, handcuffs my people and me, keeps this undeclared war alive, betrays humanity, just so he can fucking live *forever*?

Dear God, he's got to be stopped!

Fine. How?

Whose mind did Davies have?

"Director Dios?"

Warden had been concentrating on Norna so hard that he hadn't heard the door open, or seen the guard stick his head into the room.

"Time's up, sir," the man announced carefully. "Your shuttle's waiting."

Full of alarm, Warden turned his attention on the guard.

Almost immediately his prosthetic eye gave him one small piece of reassurance. The man's aura spoke of impatience, boredom, weariness, but no unusual anxiety or strain. Therefore HS wasn't preparing an ambush: Holt hadn't changed his mind about letting Warden return to UMCPHQ. No doubt he was determined not to spare Warden the burden of betraying Angus and Morn.

"I'm coming," he told the guard.

At the edge of Norna's sight, however, he paused to bow and murmur softly, "Thank you. I'll do what I can."

Her parting words harried him out of the sickchamber like furies, naming his anguish and loss.

"That's not good enough, Warden Dios."

The guards looked questions at him, involuntarily curious—or perhaps only cautious. *Not good enough.* He answered them with a shrug and an impersonal frown.

Neither of them pursued the matter. He was the UMCP director—and they apparently hadn't been ordered to challenge him. Instead they simply guided him back to his shuttle, letting him keep his shame to himself.

He knew as well as Norna did that merely doing what he could wasn't *good enough.* He just didn't have any better ideas.

Battering his brain for inspiration all the way back to UMCPHQ left him in a foul mood. Holt's orders galled him absolutely; they ate at his sore heart like an injection of vitriol. If he were the kind of man who threw up when he felt nauseous, he would have puked his guts out, trying to rid himself of his despair.

Angus and Morn were the children of his best passion, his deepest need. He could sacrifice Vector Shaheed and the rest of Nick's people if he had to; could give *Trumpet* up and let Nick go: he'd done worse. Davies would live—and Warden could at least pray that something would happen to spare the boy from what Holt had in mind. But to give Nick power over Morn and Angus, to hand them over to degradation and death after what they'd already suffered in Warden's name—

That was completely and utterly *not good enough.*

Fulminating uselessly as his shuttle approached dock, he told his crew to flare Hashi Lebwohl, order the DA director to meet him in one of his private offices in ten minutes. He may have failed to be *good enough* for

Angus and Morn, but he was by God going to get the truth out of Hashi. He needed all his tolerance and more to endure the distress inside his own skull: he had none to spare for Hashi's games.

The evidence suggested that Hashi was pulling strings behind Warden's back, interposing his own decisions between the UMCP director and events. That could be called malfeasance; it could even be called treason. On the other hand, Hashi apparently wasn't pulling strings for the Dragon. His game was his own, for good or ill.

Warden had half an hour left until his window opened on the best available listening post. He could wait that long before he coded and sent his orders to Min Donner—before he made his own treachery irrevocable. In that time, he intended to find out how much harm Hashi had done.

Naturally, inevitably, the post itself belonged to the UMC: it was part of the vast communications network which Holt Fasner had put in place. In a hundred fifty years of hunger and aggrandizement, the Dragon had learned to plan ahead.

He would be able to obtain copies of Warden's orders to *Punisher*.

That thought made Warden want to tear Hashi's head off.

His anguish had nowhere else to go.

Ignoring the salutes of dock security and the urgent requests for his attention from Center's communications techs—these days Center considered everything urgent—he strode through the corridors of his domain until he reached the office he'd specified in his message to Hashi Lebwohl.

The DA director was already there, waiting. His face wore a bleary, amiable smile, as if he'd just exchanged some pleasantry with the guards outside the office. In contrast, their expressions were nonplussed, uncomfortable: their relief as they saluted Warden was plain to his IR sight. Apparently they didn't know how to take Hashi's sense of humor.

"Director Dios."

Hashi's glasses, antique and uncared for, seemed to refract his blue gaze, confusing whatever he saw—or perhaps only whatever he allowed other people to see. Characteristically his lab coat looked like he'd found it in a waste-disposal bin—and then slept in it for weeks. The laces of his old-fashioned shoes trailed at his heels: it was a wonder that he could walk without tripping himself.

"Inside," Warden snapped brusquely as he thrust the door open. Without waiting for Hashi to precede him, he stalked into the room, rounded the desk, and sat down in his chair.

Hashi didn't dally. He entered the office behind Warden, closed the door. As Warden keyed the door seals and security shields, Hashi came forward to stand in front of the desk. Despite his air of assurance and his disreputable-professor's appearance, something in the twitching of his long fingers or the smudged glitter of his glasses conveyed the impression that he knew he was in trouble.

"From the origination of your flare," he began as if he wanted to defuse Warden's anger, "I deduce that you have just returned from bearding the Dragon in his lair. UMCPHQ scuttlebutt confirms this. And from the darkness of your glance I deduce that the encounter did not go well." As if he were quoting, he intoned, " 'The great worm's in his heaven, all's wrong with the world.' My condolences."

Warden let a snarl bare his teeth. "No jokes, Hashi," he warned. "Spare me your usual line of claptrap. Yes, I've just come from a meeting with my boss. No, it didn't go well. Now I intend to find out why."

Hashi permitted himself a bemused frown. Gesturing toward a chair, he asked, "In that case, may I sit?"

"No."

Behind his lenses, Hashi's eyes widened slightly. "I see. Apparently you consider me the reason your meeting with Holt Fasner did not go well. May I inquire how that is possible?"

"You tell me."

Holding Warden's glare, Hashi lifted his shoulders in a small, helpless shrug. "How can I? I have no idea what subject you wish to discuss."

"I'll give you a hint." Warden clenched his hands into fists on the desktop. "Tell me about *Free Lunch*."

Hashi blinked opaquely. Hints of tension sharpened his aura, but he may have been simply baffled. "What is 'free lunch'? Conventional wisdom asserts that no such thing exists."

Warden swallowed a curse. Softly, *softly*, so that he wouldn't rage, he articulated, "Hashi, listen to me. This has gone on long enough. Where did you get that information about events on Billingate you reported to me a few hours ago?"

"As I told you at the time, sir"—apparently the DA director had decided to respond by acting huffy—"it arrived by routine drone service from a listening post in the Com-Mine Station asteroid belt. It was routed to me precisely because it was routine, and as a matter of routine I have assigned a high priority to any data or transmission which makes reference to Thanatos Minor.

"The listening post overheard a broadcast from a ship that did not identify herself—therefore, presumably, an illegal." The more he talked, the more Hashi's pose of indignant virtue began to sound like a disguise for more complex emotions. "The broadcast was just that, broad cast, not tight-beamed to the listening post. I have no evidence that this ship knew of the listening post's existence. She was simply trying to warn other vessels—presumably other illegals—of developments on Thanatos Minor, to the extent that she had witnessed them.

"Some of the details she cited—I mentioned this at the time also, sir" —he stressed the word *sir*—"were not ones which I would have expected to find included in such a broadcast. For that reason I distrust both the content and the motives of her transmission. However, I delivered the information to you because of its obvious importance."

Subtly sarcastic, Hashi concluded, "In what way has my conduct in this matter contributed to the disagreeable outcome of your discussion with our revered CEO?"

As if he'd made his point, proved his innocence, he allowed himself to fold down into the nearest chair.

"Liar!"

Leaning forward, Warden hammered the desktop with his fists so hard that Hashi jumped out of his seat as if he'd been struck. His glasses slumped to the end of his nose: he stared at Warden over them in plain astonishment.

"You've betrayed me, and I won't *have it.*" Warden pronounced each word like an act of violence. "You're finished. I want your resignation *here*"—he thumped the desk again—"in less than an hour."

Hashi's mouth hung open; he seemed to have difficulty swallowing. "You?" he gaped. "Betrayed *you*? Personally? What does this have to do with you?"

Warden gestured his disgust. "All right—I'll say it differently. You've betrayed your trust. You've betrayed your *job.*"

Hashi's reaction was instantaneous. His eyes flashed blue lightning as he retorted, "No. Never."

His IR emissions said that he was telling the truth—if the word "truth" had any meaning where he was concerned.

"Then, God damn it, tell me about *Free Lunch*!" Warden let himself yell. If he didn't, Hashi's bland chicanery was going to drive him mad. "Min found her parked right on *top* of that listening post! She'd used the post to send a message, but Min couldn't crack it because the codes were too goddamn *secure.* When she was challenged, she told Min she was working for the UMC—for Cleatus by God Fane himself! But *Holt* says that's a lie—and *he* doesn't lie was well as you do."

Abruptly Warden dropped back in his seat. He took a deep breath, held it while he mastered himself, then let it out in a hard sigh. "So tell me the truth, Hashi, while you still can. What kind of shit is this?"

During Warden's outburst, Hashi's eyebrows crawled like insects on his forehead. Slow sweat beaded on his temples; a small flush, incongruously round and precise, appeared in the center of each cheek. Blinking furiously, his blue eyes seemed to send out flares of stark panic and absolute glee, as if for him they came to the same thing.

"In that case, Warden," he murmured, "perhaps you'll permit me to amend my earlier report."

"Please."

"*Free Lunch*," Hashi said quickly. "Captain Darrin Scroyle. If Captain Scroyle told the estimable director of Enforcement Division that he was in the employ of the United Mining Companies, either in the person of Cleatus Fane or through some other agency, he was"—Hashi made a palpable effort to restrain his instinct for rhetorical camouflage—"lying to protect his dealings with me."

Warden scowled; but in other ways he kept his reactions to himself.

"Captain Scroyle is a mercenary," Hashi explained. "I employ such individuals as occasion warrants. And I demand security for my operations. In addition, much of Captain Scroyle's value to me rests on his ability to pass as illegal. For these reasons, he misled Director Donner.

"On this occasion I had employed him several weeks ago to visit Thanatos Minor as my surrogate—what you might call a mobile listening post. I am not a complacent man, Warden. I trust the work I have done with Joshua, and I stand by it, but I do not care to rely on it exclusively. Therefore I employed Captain Scroyle to do exactly what he has done—to provide an early report on the outcome of Joshua's mission.

"Have I acted unwisely?" he concluded. "Has Captain Scroyle's information not already shown its value?"

Warden dismissed the value of Captain Scroyle's information with a snort. "That's not the real question, and you know it." In fact that information was priceless. Yet it wasn't as critical as his ability to trust the DA director. "The question is why you didn't tell me all this. I'm the goddamn *director* of the UMCP. What made you think you should lie to *me*?

"You are in charge of Data *Acquisition*. It's your *job* to give me facts, not bullshit."

Hashi Lebwohl was the only man Warden knew who could prevaricate without showing it. A calm face and confident manner were easy; so were any number of disguises and distortions. But to inhibit the body's autonomic response to stress was normally impossible. And the specific anxiety of falsehood had an IR signature which Warden had learned to recognize—in every case except Hashi's. By this more than any other evidence, he knew that Hashi made no essential distinction between truth and lies. He showed no stress because he felt none.

He felt it now, however. His aura squirmed with it; his pulse labored under its weight. Warden's demand touched a vulnerability in him which may have had nothing to do with truth or falsehood.

Shrugging uncomfortably, he replied, "I knew that you would be required to share any information you received with CEO Fasner, and I did not wish to compromise Captain Scroyle by making his usefulness known to men I distrust. In addition, I believed that your position with CEO Fasner would be stronger if he were denied knowledge of all the resources at my command—therefore at your disposal. On the other hand, it would be plainly fatal if you withheld information from your superior and were detected doing so. I chose to spare you that hazard."

More bullshit, Warden thought. He could hear it as well as see it; he could practically smell it. On impulse, however, he decided not to challenge it. He wanted to see how deep Hashi's dishonesty ran.

Glowering his impatience, he rasped, "That's not good enough. How am I supposed to trust you now? How much do you think I can afford to tell you?"

Hashi didn't need to study the question. He had an answer ready. "Our positions are dissimilar. You must report to the GCES, as well as to CEO Fasner. I report only to you. Neither great worms nor councils of indecision have power over me. Anything which you withhold from me can only damage my effectiveness." Almost pleading, he said softly, "I cannot do my *job*, Warden, if facts are kept from me."

Warden restrained an impulse to pound the desk again. He'd mastered his anger: it was cold and hard, and he used it to focus his scrutiny of the DA director. While all his hopes unraveled, and his chronometer ticked away the lives of the people he needed most, he concentrated on surprising, coercing, or perhaps earning one critical piece of accuracy from Hashi Lebwohl.

"All right. I'll copy Min's report to DA. You can study it in your spare time. But I'll give you the real highlights.

"*Trumpet* is alive. She came out of forbidden space while Min was arguing with your Captain Scroyle, flared a transmission to that listening post, and headed on.

"According to her message, she succeeded. Billingate is gone. That's the good news. The bad news is that Jerico priority has been superseded.

Milos went over to the Amnion. That would have been a disaster if it hadn't been so damn predictable. So Angus isn't coming anywhere near here until we position someone to invoke his new codes."

Hashi nodded to himself. His smile was impersonal, but it hinted at a certain complacency. His work with Joshua was being vindicated.

"He has quite a passenger list," Warden went on. "If *Trumpet* were any smaller, they would be sleeping in the drive spaces." He spoke in a drawl like a sneer, preparing the blow he meant to strike at Hashi—the first of several, if he needed them. "Nick is there. He brought four of his people with him—Mikka Vasaczk, Ciro Vasaczk, Sib Mackern, and—by some truly monumental coincidence—Vector Shaheed, whose name I'm sure you'll recognize."

"How could I forget it?" Hashi radiated confidence and falseness. "I lament for him whenever I go to my rest, although only my pillow hears me. To take his work from him before he could complete it was necessary, but unfortunate—grievous to a man of his abilities. Under better circumstances he would have been nurtured for his achievements rather than discarded."

The DA director was stalling, Warden observed; filling the air with words to cover him while his mind raced to examine the implications of Shaheed's presence aboard *Trumpet*.

Warden didn't give Hashi time to think. After only a short pause, he announced harshly, "In addition there's Morn Hyland."

"Aboard *Trumpet?*" Hashi croaked. "Aboard *Trumpet?*"

Warden nodded. "With Nick and Angus."

The information didn't stagger Hashi. He sat down reflexively, as if his legs had been cut out from under him; yet his IR aura betrayed no shock. Instead it flared like an eager sun; sent out crackling flares of excitement and apprehension.

"So it is true," he breathed. "I considered the eventuality that she might survive. I believed it—yet I feared to believe it. Why is it not impossible?"

Brutally dishonest, driven by shame, Warden demanded, "Do you still stand by the work you did with Joshua?"

Aren't you to blame for this?

Of course he wasn't. Warden had done it himself: he had no one else to accuse. But Hashi didn't know that. And Warden intended to hit him as hard as necessary to learn the truth.

Hashi seemed not to have heard him, however; not to have felt the veiled accusation. His aura surged with emissions which would have indicated terror in anyone else, but which in him appeared to imply exultation.

"Director," he murmured softly, "there is treason here. Treachery and betrayal. Nick Succorso is—"

But then he stopped himself. "No, I will not judge this rashly." The smears on his lenses refracted his blue gaze into streaks of hope and apprehension. "Joshua's mission has become a great and terrible thing. To master it, we must also be great and terrible."

Hashi's concentration had turned entirely inward. Trying to drag it outward—break past Hashi's defenses—Warden rasped through his teeth, "There's one other highlight you should know about. Apparently she has a son."

Hashi didn't react. He might not have heard Warden.

"She calls him Davies Hyland. Nick's kid—or Angus'." The thought twisted Warden's heart. "It turns out the reason—the only reason we have so far—they went to Enablement was so she could have this boy force-grown. Do you know anything about that? Do you know how the Amnion supply minds to kids whose bodies mature in hours instead of years?"

Whose mind has Davies got?

Hashi shook his head. His emissions wrapped around him in coils of self-absorption.

"Director, I must understand this," he said from the center of his private thoughts. "Do you wish me to credit that Joshua has broken his programming?"

"What else?" Warden snapped.

Hashi blinked behind his glasses. At last he shifted his attention to Warden. "Can you think of no other explanation for Morn Hyland's unlooked-for survival?" he countered. "Then why does he still act as we have instructed him, reporting his own freedom when surely escape is what he desires most?

"In some sense," he concluded, "his essential instruction sets hold. He remains ours."

"All right." Warden conceded the point. "You tell me. Why is she still alive?"

What treason are you talking about?

Hashi pulled IR flares and flails into focus.

"Is it not possible," he asked, "that her survival represents a bargain of some kind? Perhaps Joshua encountered situations, dilemmas, complexities on Thanatos Minor which we did not foresee. Perhaps the presence of Amnion warships—or Milos Taverner's treachery—challenged him beyond his limits. Or perhaps Milos saw fit to adjust one or another of his priorities. Under those conditions, he may have recognized the need for aid.

"And to whom would he turn, if not to another of our affiliated operatives—to Nick Succorso? If Captain Succorso demanded Morn Hyland's life as the price for his assistance, Joshua's programming would not have precluded acceptance."

"Fine," Warden growled. He'd offered the same argument to Holt Fasner. It was false, and he knew it. "Why in hell would Succorso do such a thing?"

What's this treason you're afraid of? Are you talking about yourself?

Hashi straightened in his seat. As if he didn't notice what he was doing, his hands made incongruous, tentative attempts to smooth his rumpled lab coat. For a moment he seemed unwilling to meet Warden's gaze. Then he faced Warden squarely.

"Director, what I must tell you will anger you." A wheeze of pressure made his voice raw. "Yet I believe I have acted with almost prescient wisdom."

Warden folded his arms over his chest; waited grimly, hoping that he would hear the truth.

"You are angry," Hashi began, "because I have not been wholly open with you. In terms our redoubtable Governing Council would employ, I have not practiced 'full disclosure.' For that you will censure or value me, as you deem fit.

"But I must say plainly," he added with a defensive buzz, "that I do not consider 'full disclosure' germane to my duties. I have never failed to reveal my acquired data when it was needed. And it is clear that disclosure is necessary now."

He adjusted his glasses to confuse or clarify what Warden saw.

"Captain Scroyle's report is not the only transmission I have received concerning events on or around Thanatos Minor. There has also been a flare from Captain Succorso. The implications of his message explain my reluctance to reveal my data fully, as well as the actions I have taken in response."

There is treason here. Treachery and betrayal. Nick Succorso is—

Warden bit down on the back of his tongue to contain his impatience. What treason? What *actions*?

"I will quote Captain Succorso exactly." The strain in Hashi's tone made him sound unusually formal. "He said, 'If you can get her, you bastard, you can have her. I don't care what happens to you. You need me, but you blew it. You deserve her. Kazes are such fun, don't you think?' "

Startled out of his self-control, Warden echoed involuntarily, " 'Kazes are such fun.' He said *that*?"

Hashi nodded. He may have been gratified by Warden's surprise. "You see the difficulties. Superficially he appears to possess an implausible knowledge of our recent adventures. And his taunting references to 'she' and 'her' are obscure.

"I considered it my job, Director Dios, to draw conclusions from Captain Succorso's transmission—and from Captain Scroyle's. To account for the plain threat in Captain Succorso's words, as well as to explain the suggestive details of Captain Scroyle's report, I have constructed a scenario which appalls me."

He didn't look appalled. The smeared gleam of his eyes suggested pride.

Kazes are such fun. Fun?

"One more item of background," Hashi continued pedantically, "and then I will proceed. As you know, Captain Scroyle makes mention of *Soar*, a vessel captained by a certain Sorus Chatelaine. Data Processing has presented me with the hypothesis that *Soar* is a retrofitted avatar of a former illegal by the name of *Gutbuster*. Perhaps coincidentally—and perhaps not—*Gutbuster* was responsible for the death of Morn Hyland's mother. And *Gutbuster* also killed the original *Captain's Fancy*, leaving only the boy Nick Succorso aboard alive."

Warden tightened his arms, clamping himself in his stolid pose. Get to the point! he wanted to yell. What *actions*?

But Hashi's love of his own explanations was inexorable. He plodded on.

"Nick Succorso, Morn Hyland, and Sorus Chatelaine are linked to each other by bonds of bloodshed. It may be, however, that those bonds are of opposing kinds. The natural assumption is that Morn Hyland loathes *Gutbuster*'s memory. In contrast, Nick Succorso's survival aboard *Captain's Fancy* may have been a gift from Sorus Chatelaine."

Warden snarled in the pit of his stomach. "What's the relevance of all this? I'm running out of time. I need facts, not moonshine."

I need the truth.

Hashi flapped his hands as if he could wave away urgency. "Grant that it may be so." His aura suggested more than pride; it hinted at righteousness; vindication. "Consider what follows.

"Morn Hyland and Nick Succorso are natural enemies, if for no other reason than because he must have used her zone implant against her. Being who he is, he could hardly do otherwise. And he and Sorus Chatelaine may be allies. Why would a man such as Nick Succorso risk visiting Enablement Station simply so that a natural enemy could have a son? And why would rumors of an antimutagen surround a possible ally on Thanatos Minor?

"Here, briefly, is my scenario."

Warden took a deep breath against the weight of his arms.

"Nick Succorso and Sorus Chatelaine propose to make themselves unimaginably wealthy." Hashi spoke with his head tilted back, as if he were addressing the ceiling. Despite the abstraction of his delivery, he sounded almost smug. "At the same time they mean to punish us for our failures to give him support when he demanded it. Morn Hyland was taken to Enablement with the connivance of the Amnion so that she could be transformed into some manner of genetic kaze aimed at us."

By an act of will, Warden showed no reaction. Yet his head seemed to reel as if it were full of ghouls. Autonomic terror squeezed sweat like blood from the bones of his forehead. A genetic kaze? Horrific idea: anyone but Hashi would have been appalled by it; dismayed to the quick. And it was *possible*. Warden had prepared or planned nothing which might have prevented it. And Angus would accept her in that condition, as long as he failed to detect any sign of genetic tampering.

Christ, it could work! Treason was too small a word for it. If Hashi's view of the connection between Nick and this Sorus Chatelaine was accurate, Warden could think of no reason to dismiss the DA director's interpretation.

Oh, Morn! What have I done to you?

Hashi hadn't stopped, however. Still regarding the ceiling, he explained, "All subsequent conflict between Nick Succorso and the Amnion was mere chicanery, designed to conceal the truth. Morn was sent to the Bill by ejection pod as a pretense. Then she was reacquired, presumably with Amnion aid.

"For her part, Sorus Chatelaine began spreading the gossip that a mutagen immunity drug exists—and exists in her possession. The crewmember delivered to and then retrieved from the Amnion by Captain Succorso was a ploy to demonstrate the efficacy of the drug. That done, Captain Succorso positioned himself—perhaps by means of his past association with Milos Taverner—so that he and Morn Hyland would be preserved with *Trumpet*.

"What results? Apparently harmless, Morn is brought to us. UMCPHQ falls to genetic assault, terrorizing all of humankind. And where does the species turn for hope? Why, to Nick Succorso and Sorus Chatelaine, who possess a proven antimutagen."

Finally Hashi lowered his gaze to Warden's. "Does this not sound like our Captain Succorso? He becomes as rich as the stars. At the same time" —Hashi smiled bleakly—"we are discomfited. Hence his flare. He dares to taunt us because he believes that we cannot penetrate his deception—and he cannot resist displaying his superiority."

Warden swallowed harshly. "That's it?" He couldn't force himself to stop sweating; but he kept his voice under rigid control. "That's your scenario?"

Hashi nodded. Pride stained his aura like a malignancy.

"And you believe it?" Warden demanded.

" 'Believe it'?" Hashi waved away the question airily. "I neither believe it nor disbelieve it. It is a hypothesis, nothing more. I consider it plausible. Therefore it may be accurate. Belief or doubt are moot."

"But it doesn't scare you," Warden pursued.

" 'Scare' me? No, I am not scared. As a conception, I find it appalling. In practice I see nothing to fear."

Warden released his arms in order to clench his fists on the desktop. He wanted Hashi to see his anger—and his restraint.

"It doesn't scare you," he rasped, "because you've already done something about it. You've already 'acted with almost prescient wisdom,' as you call it." Done something *great and terrible*. "Don't stop now. That's the part I've been waiting to hear."

Hashi's mouth twisted primly. He adjusted his glasses, crossed one thin leg over the other.

"Director, I did not speak of this earlier because I did not trust the time. You will tell me whether I have judged aptly.

"When *Punisher* encountered *Free Lunch* and Captain Scroyle, he had relayed his transmission to me and was awaiting orders. In response I offered him a new contract."

Warden was suddenly sure that he was about to hear the truth. "What contract? What was it for?"

Hashi faced his director like a blue sky. "In my judgment action was urgently required. Therefore Captain Scroyle has been handsomely remunerated to destroy *Trumpet* and everyone aboard."

Warden nearly cried out; nearly broke into a yell—or a wail. His fists hit the desktop. Destroy *Trumpet*? Kill Angus and Morn just when Warden himself had almost literally moved heaven and Earth to keep them alive?

Hashi, you bastard! You unconscionable *bastard*.

But his surprise and shock pulled him in so many different directions at once that they held him mute; hurt him in so many different ways that he couldn't utter any of them.

Destroy—?

This of course *of course* was the real reason Hashi had concealed his dealings with *Free Lunch*. He hadn't wanted to admit what he'd done. Left alone, he might have taken his involvement in the ruin of what he saw as Nick's treason to his grave.

Warden didn't know how he kept from howling. His fists pounded the desktop so that he wouldn't hit himself.

Hashi's gambit dismayed him to the bone. But at the same time, oh, shit, *at the same time* it offered him a way to subvert Holt Fasner's orders; a seductive answer to the treachery Holt demanded. Let *Trumpet* be killed by *Free Lunch*. Morn and Angus would be granted a clean death, if no mercy; Nick would die as well; and Davies would be kept away from the Dragon. Warden's own hopes and needs would die with them; but he could claim with at least superficial honesty that his hands were clean.

Didn't that make sense? If Morn was a genetic kaze?

No, he swore with all his heart. No. I *will* not.

He was ashamed to the pit of his stomach, the core of his heart; his blood burned with shame in his veins. He was beside himself with fury at the DA director—yet Hashi wasn't to blame. This would never have happened if Warden's own plotting and subterfuge, his complicity with the Dragon and his covert efforts to be free of it, hadn't created an environment which permitted, encouraged, even necessitated manipulation and secrets for the people around him.

He was the director of the United Mining Companies Police; no one else. *He* was responsible.

And he was Warden Dios. Shame made him strong.

Grimly he unclosed his fists. He couldn't swallow his anguish and rage, but he allowed himself no recrimination.

"There's only one problem," he retorted through his teeth. "It's all bullshit. Your scenario may be plausible, but it's not true. That's not why Morn is alive."

Hashi opened his mouth; closed it again. Streaks of apprehension ached across his aura. As if he didn't notice what he was doing, he put down his hands to support himself on the sides of his chair.

"She's alive," Warden grated, "because I told Angus to rescue her. I changed his programming—I swapped out his datacore before he and Milos left. You're trying to kill her"—the words broke from him like a cry—"*and I need her alive.*"

Hashi's heart staggered; missed several beats. The blood drained from his face as if he were being sucked dry. Nevertheless he didn't flinch; didn't protest; didn't refuse to hear or believe. The blow was hard, but he strove to bear it.

"You changed his programming." He spoke like a sigh. "You need her alive." His hands shook slightly as he raised them to his face and removed his glasses; folded the stems carefully; tucked the glasses into the breast pocket of his lab coat. Without them his face seemed oddly vulnerable, as if he wore them to conceal a weakness. "You are a challenge to me, Warden. Your game is deeper than I imagined.

"Only now does it occur to me that you might profit from Morn Hyland's life."

Warden hugged his pain and remained silent, giving Hashi time to think.

"In one sense," Hashi went on, "she threatens us all. But in another—" His voice cracked; his emanations cried out with chagrin. More than anyone Warden had ever known, Hashi relied on his own mind. Now he was being told that his intelligence and skills had failed him. "Ah, your game is indeed deep. Now that the opportunity has passed, I ask myself how you might better demonstrate your honor and usefulness to our esteemed Council in these troubled times than by rescuing the very woman who has suffered most for your decisions.

"And the benefit is only increased by the threat she represents." He seemed to be sinking in his chair; shrinking in his own estimation. "If she is a kaze, we are forewarned. We will be able to guard against her. But your honor and effectiveness—your survival—would inevitably be enhanced by the rescue of a woman who has such tales to tell at the Dragon's expense."

He may have been able to lie to the whole world, but apparently he couldn't lie to himself.

"Please accept my regrets, Director. I have done you a singular disservice."

True. But the contract had already been sent. It was beyond recall. Unless—

Wearily Warden asked, "I don't suppose there's any way you can contact Captain Scroyle?"

"Alas, no." Hashi frowned in regret. "I cannot know where he has gone, except in pursuit of *Trumpet*. And he will not expect contact from me. Therefore he will not look for it."

No, of course not. That would have been too easy.

"In that case"—bracing his palms on the desktop, Warden pushed to his feet—"you can go back to work. I'm out of time. Like everybody else around here, I've got orders to carry out."

You don't have to resign, Hashi. I still need you.

Hashi rose from his chair. Fumbling in his pockets, he found his glasses and put them back on his nose. He made no pretense of looking through them, however.

"Forgive me if I appear slow," he wheezed. "I simply wish matters to be clear so that I will make no more mistakes. Do you have orders for me?"

"Yes." Warden didn't hesitate. "You have no more responsibility for *Trumpet* or Joshua. Leave them to me. If any more information about Billingate, the Amnion, *Trumpet*, Joshua, *Free Lunch*, or even Min happens to be routed your way, you will make sure I see it immediately."

No more games, Hashi.

The DA director nodded. "I understand."

"Instead," Warden continued, "I'm leaving the investigation of Godsen's murder to you."

Hashi cocked an eyebrow, but Warden couldn't tell whether he was surprised or relieved.

"Min isn't here, and her chief of Security is out of his depth. If you can't uncover the truth"—Warden used the word deliberately—"about those kazes, no one can.

"But there's one fact you may not know. Shortly before that kaze reached him, Godsen got a call from Holt Fasner. Holt wanted Godsen to go see him immediately. Godsen refused because I'd restricted him to UMCPHQ."

After only a slight pause, Warden finished, "Before he died, Godsen called me to tell me what he'd done."

Now Hashi's surprise was unmistakable. He pursed his lips, hissed softly between his teeth. "So our Godsen discovered loyalty before he died. I would not have believed it."

"That's why he was killed," Warden pronounced harshly. "Because he discovered that particular loyalty."

Are you listening, Hashi? Do you hear me?

"I see," Hashi murmured while he considered the implications. "Then perhaps he deserves to be lamented."

Warden forced himself to make his point more clearly. "Hashi, don't let it happen to you."

The DA director replied with a smile that left his blue gaze cold. "I am not afraid. His position and mine are dissimilar. No one but you has ever had reason to question my loyalty."

He gave Warden a small bow, then moved to the door and waited for Warden to unlock it.

As the bolts and seals opened, however, he turned back to his director. "It occurs to me," he said in a musing tone, "that the Amnion cannot force-grow a mind."

Warden was running late. And he still had decisions to make—decisions on which any number of lives depended, including his own. "I jumped to the same conclusion," he retorted brusquely.

Hashi didn't stop. "It seems consistent with what we know of their methods in other areas, however, that they are able to copy one. Therefore, if young Davies Hyland has a mind, it must have been imprinted from someone else."

"Fine," Warden growled. "From whom? Nick Succorso?"

"I think not." Hashi was still chewing on the question; but his emanations were calm, and his voice sounded confident. "Can you imagine that Captain Succorso would submit to such a process? Surely the Amnion could have offered him no certainty that his own mind would remain intact when it was copied.

"Indeed, it seems unlikely that any ordinary human being would have valued Davies Hyland enough to accept the hazards of such a process."

Hashi flashed a speculative glance at Warden, but didn't wait for a response. He reached for the door, opened it; in a moment he was gone.

Yet he'd left behind the hint Warden needed; left it in the air and silence after he closed the door as if he were trying to make amends.

Hashi Lebwohl, you God damn sonofabitch, you're a genius.

Davies Hyland must have a mind, a human mind. Otherwise the Amnion wouldn't want him back—not badly enough to risk an act of war by chasing *Trumpet*. That was the whole point. If his mind was Amnion, they wouldn't have lost him in the first place.

So where did he get it? *Whose* mind did he have?

Who would consider him precious enough to be worth the risk of madness or even a complete breakdown? What kind of person would do such a thing?

Only Morn.

Davies Hyland had his mother's mind.

Warden couldn't afford to think about it. He was perilously close to losing his window to contact Min Donner; to carry out Holt's orders. And if he paused long enough to hope, he might be so shaken by it—or so paralyzed by doubt—that he would fail to grasp this one slim opportunity.

Slim? It wasn't *slim:* it was by God *emaciated.* Slender to the point of invisibility.

Nevertheless he took the risk. It was all he had.

Dropping into his seat, he leaned over the desktop console and began writing Holt Fasner's orders—as well as his own—for transmission to Min Donner and *Punisher*.

SIXTEN

Captain Sixten Vertigus was old.

He was old when he got up in the morning, and the face that greeted him in his mirror was as wrinkled and used as a sheet of crumpled tissue. What was left of his hair clung to his scalp in wisps so fine that they responded to any kind of static. When he shaved—an atavistic habit which he had no inclination to give up—his hands shook as if the exercise was strenuous; and the skin of his hands was translucent enough to let him see his veins and tendons. He couldn't dress himself without fumbling.

He was old when he went to his rooms in the Members' Offices wing of the GCES Complex, or to the Council chamber, and if he happened to forget his age, everyone he met from the lowliest data clerk to Abrim Len himself reminded him of it by treating him as if he were an invalid, temporarily risen from the bed in which he was long overdue to die.

He was old while his aides shuffled documents back and forth across his desk; while his colleagues feigned including him in their discussions because he was too much a legend to be ignored; while the other Members and their aides, and President Len and *his* aides, droned on and on about the endless, mindless, necessary details of governing human space. Sometimes when he stared at people he was actually asleep; and even when he was at his most alert, his eyes were so pale that he looked blind: he might have been a man to whom sight no longer meant anything.

On top of that, his whole body still hurt. The aftereffects of the explosion which had killed Marthe, and which had very nearly done the same to Sixten himself, lingered in his fragile bones and tired head, his sore chest and unsteady stomach.

On some occasions—but especially this one—he felt more than old; he felt like an antique, a relic. The former hero of *Deep Star* and humankind's first contact with the Amnion was abysmally and irretrievably ancient.

His condition was not untreatable, of course. As the GCES Senior Member for the United Western Bloc, he could easily have obtained the same rejuvenation techniques which had prolonged Holt Fasner's life. But he didn't do it; didn't even consider it. He didn't want to live long enough to see whatever future the Dragon made.

He was far too old to tackle the job of trying to bring Holt Fasner down.

If he could have thought of one other Member who might be trusted to take the chance and face the consequences, just one, he would have handed over the responsibility without hesitation. But to the best of his knowledge, there were no other candidates. The people on Suka Bator who might have been willing to accept the risk—Special Counsel Maxim Igensard came to mind because he was due to arrive in Sixten's office at any moment—were tainted by motives which Sixten considered wrongheaded at best, fatal at worst. And everybody else—the Members even more than their aides—was too easily scared.

So eventually he considered that maybe it was good to be old. After all, what did he have to lose? There wasn't much time left to him in any case. He'd never had any significant amount of power. His position as the hero of *Deep Star* and the UWB Senior Member, not to mention as a symbol of probity for such groups as the Native Earthers, was largely ceremonial; and he only endured it because it gave him an occasional opportunity to act on his convictions. And his self-esteem was in no real danger. For years he'd been about as effectual as the figurehead of an ancient sailing vessel. Failure now wouldn't make him feel any more useless.

Still he had to ask himself whether he could truly bear to fail again.

That was the wrong question, however.

Could he truly bear not to make the attempt?

He'd told Min Donner that his "mission" on the Council had always been *to oppose Holt Fasner in all his ambitions*. He'd only had personal encounters with the UMC CEO twice, once before *Deep Star* was sent to establish contact with the Amnion, once afterward. Yet those experiences had determined the course of his life—*to study what he did and how he did it until I could learn the facts which might persuade other people to oppose him with me*—until, inspired by age and foolishness, he'd entrusted his research to his subordinates, and so lost it all.

In his own mind nothing larger than himself exists. In his own person he considers himself bigger than the United Mining Companies, bigger than the Governing Council for Earth and Space, perhaps bigger than all humankind.

In a sense, Sixten told himself now, his years and his old failures were irrelevant. Even the possibility that he might be killed was irrelevant. Instead of worrying over such things, he should be grateful that Min Donner had brought him this one last chance. If he failed again, nothing new would be lost. And if he succeeded, something of inestimable value would be gained.

In any case—whether he failed or succeeded, lived or died—he would know that he was still man enough, still *person* enough, to act on his beliefs.

He tried to feel gratitude while he waited for Special Counsel Igensard.

Unfortunately his years refused to take pity on him. Time didn't care whether he was a hero or a coward. He intended to finish his work on Min Donner's Bill of Severance; but instead he was sound asleep in his chair when Marthe's replacement chimed his intercom to inform him that the Special Counsel had arrived.

His eyes felt as dry as stones: he'd nodded off with them open. Blinking painfully, he fumbled for the intercom toggle. When he finally located it, he heard Igensard's voice in the background. "Is he sleeping in there?"

Sixten hated the note of humorless complacency in the Special Counsel's tone; the veiled contempt.

"Of course I was sleeping," he told his pickup. He also hated the high, thin quaver of his own voice, but there was nothing he could do about it. "Do you think being this old is easy? Send him in."

By the time Igensard opened the door and entered, Sixten had straightened his clothes, rubbed some of the blur off his gaze, and made sure that his private intercom was active.

Maintenance had done an efficient job restoring both his office and the outer hall where his aides had their desks and cubicles. The ceiling had been repaired; the walls, patched. The carpeting and even his crystallized Formica desktop had been replaced. There was no visible evidence that a kaze had ever attacked him.

Nevertheless Maxim Igensard came into the room as if he expected to smell high explosives and blood.

He was a gray man who cultivated an air of diffidence which had the effect of making him appear smaller than he was. His hair capped itself to his head as if it didn't want to attract attention. He wore tidy, gray bureaucratic garments with impersonal lines and no distinguishing features: his suit could have been worn by anybody. Because it hadn't been cut to fit him, however, it failed to conceal the unexpected bulge of his belly. As a result, his stomach contrasted incongruously with his lean face and limbs. Except for his abdomen, he looked like a man who didn't eat often enough to become fat.

"Special Counsel." Sixten didn't trouble to stand; he had enough years and status to get away with sitting in almost anyone's presence. "It's easy to catch a man like me sleeping, even if you get plenty of rest yourself. But you look like you haven't been to bed for days."

This wasn't actually true: Maxim looked neither more tired nor less alert than usual, and his clothes were fresh. But Sixten preferred to credit the Special Counsel with frailties which didn't show. The uncomfortable alternative was to think that Maxim might indeed be as devoid of weaknesses as he appeared.

"You'd better sit down," Sixten concluded, nodding at the nearest chair.

From there Igensard wouldn't be able to see the small LED on Sixten's private intercom which indicated an open channel.

"Not at all, Captain Vertigus." Igensard's tone was as gray and unassuming as his demeanor—and as unamused. "Of course, there's a great deal of work to be done. But I have a capable staff. And a number of the other Members are eager to give me every assistance."

He didn't decline to sit, however.

By some perceptual trick, his air of being smaller than he was made him appear more solid when he sat; denser, perhaps more powerful as well, as if he contained a nuclear core which was shrinking to critical mass.

"Your concern is misplaced," he continued, "if only because *I* have not recently become the target of assassins." Deftly he redirected Sixten's attempt to take control of the conversation. "Are you sure you're all right? President Len assures me you weren't injured, but I find that hard to believe. You were so close to the blast—"

Sixten cut him off brusquely. "My apologies, Special Counsel." He had no intention of discussing the kaze's attack with this man. "Just for a minute there, I thought you looked tired. Must be my eyes—Lord knows at my age I can't get away with blaming it on the light.

"Shall we get right to the point? You asked to see me. My time is yours, as much as you need. But I know you're busy. The best staff in the world can't cure that for a man in your position. What can I do for you?"

Maxim was impervious to such delicate sarcasm. He smiled in a way that left his face smooth and didn't soften his diffident, untouchable gaze.

"I hope you'll call me Maxim, Captain Vertigus," he replied. "We hardly know each other, but I would like you to be as open as a friend with me. I'm certainly prepared to be open with you. I'll keep this conversation as confidential as you like, but I think it would be extremely valuable if we could be entirely frank with each other."

"Maxim." Sixten pursed his lips—an expression which in his opinion made him look like a desiccated prune, but which he employed deliberately because it used so many facial muscles that it didn't betray such emotions as surprise, consternation, or despair. "I appreciate the courtesy, naturally. Still I must confess—in the spirit of openness—that you've taken me somewhat aback. What are you prepared to be open with me about?"

"Sixten—" the Special Counsel began, then paused to ask, "May I call you Sixten?"

Sixten kept his mouth tight to disguise his relish. "I prefer Captain Vertigus." To avoid the impression of rudeness, however, he added, "It's an honorable title, and I earned it."

Maxim shrugged noncommittally. "Captain Vertigus, then. I'll answer any questions you want to ask—any questions at all—about my investigation of Warden Dios and the UMCP."

"I see." Sixten stifled a grimace with difficulty. The ineffectuality of his admittedly subtle efforts to ruffle Igensard reminded him of other, more profound failures. Once again he found himself in the presence of a man with power and secrets—and he had no idea what to do about it. "And what exactly do you want *me* to be open about?"

"I would like to ask you a couple of questions," Maxim replied promptly. His tone suggested that he knew he was being presumptuous, but felt he had no choice. His duty was exigent. "The more honestly—and the more fully—you answer them, the more I'll benefit. I don't mean personally, of course, but as the Special Counsel charged with this investigation by the GCES."

"I see," Sixten repeated. He took a moment to examine his conscience, and found that he was in no mood for bullshit. "It's an interesting proposal. Forgive me if I don't fall out of my chair hurrying to take you up on it. Frankly, I can't think of anything you could tell me that I might want or need to know.

"You know where I stand—I've been holding my ground alone for decades. I support the UMCP. I oppose the UMC. And my position doesn't depend on such functional details as honor or malfeasance. Convince me Holt Fasner is as pure as the heavens—show me the Number of the Beast etched on Warden Dios' forehead—and I'll say the same. Humankind needs the UMCP. Humankind needs to be rid of the UMC. We should be discussing matters of structure, not function. But structure, as I understand it, is outside the mandate of your investigation."

Then he shrugged. "However, that doesn't mean I'm unwilling to answer questions. I'm just a crotchety old man, not an obstructionist. What do you want to know?"

What are you after, Special Counsel? What are you trying to get out of me?

While Sixten spoke, Maxim waited without moving a muscle. He seemed to have an inexhaustible supply of patience. Nevertheless in some way he appeared to be shrinking into himself, becoming at once more compact and more dangerous. Sixten received the disturbing impression that if Maxim ever exploded, the detonation would be indistinguishable from madness.

"You're an interesting man, Captain Vertigus," Igensard observed deferentially when Sixten stopped. "It occurs to me that you should be director of the UMCP."

Sixten flapped his hands. "Flattery—" he began.

"After a few decades of Warden Dios," Maxim continued as if he couldn't be interrupted, "what humankind really needs is probity, integrity. Men like Dios and Lebwohl specialize in moral legerdemain, and we've had as much of that as we can stand. We won't survive much more. You, on the other hand—you could do the job in your sleep."

"—is a waste of time," Sixten finished abruptly. "I do everything in my sleep. That doesn't make me a fit UMCP director. It makes me *old*.

"Go ahead—ask your questions. When I hear what they are, I'll decide whether I want to answer them."

"Certainly." Igensard complied with an air of smugness, as if he'd gained the point he wanted most. "Captain Vertigus, is there any truth to the rumor that you once made it your business to investigate Holt Fasner and the UMC?"

Surprised past his defenses, Sixten nodded mutely.

"Forgive me for asking," Maxim went on to avoid any impression of discourtesy. "You understand that anything you did years ago was before my time. I know nothing about it. You aren't accountable for rumors, of course. But I couldn't think of any way to learn the truth except by coming to you directly.

"Would you be willing to share what you discovered with me? I mean, with me and my staff?"

Sixten tried to purse his mouth again and found that he'd left it hanging open. *Learn the truth*. He was out of his depth. *Share what you discovered—?* Age had left him stupid as well as frail. What was going on here?

"Why?" His throat caught on the words. "Why do you care?"

As he faced Sixten—without moving, without expression—Maxim's diffidence began to look more and more like arrogance. Or cunning.

"I'm perfectly aware," he said easily, "that CEO Fasner and his various enterprises are outside the mandate of my own investigation. But I'm looking for hints, if you will—patterns of conduct or implication—which will help me put Director Dios' actions in context. That *is* within my mandate. I'm sure you'll agree that it is unquestionably germane to inquire whether his rather high-handed style of law enforcement was ever condoned or encouraged, by CEO Fasner if not by the GCES. If it was, his excesses become more understandable"—Maxim seemed to think that this would console Sixten—"perhaps more excusable.

"The more I know about his background, the more intelligently I can carry out my commission."

Now Sixten grasped the truth. The possibility that someone might value or need the work he'd done—and lost—years ago frayed and faded like a old man's brief dreams. Igensard would only pretend to be disappointed if Sixten told him what had happened to his research: the question itself was only bait.

Sixten pressed his hands flat on the desktop to steady them. "You're still trying to flatter me." For a moment anger made his voice hard enough to sound firm. "Why don't you just cut all this crap and tell me what you really want? Ask an honest question. Trust me to give you an honest answer."

"You misunderstand me," Maxim countered disingenuously. "How could I presume to flatter you? I asked the question for exactly the reasons I've stated.

"But for some reason you're suspicious of my motives. I won't try to persuade you otherwise. If the fact that I've come to you in pursuit of my duty as the Special Counsel charged with this investigation, rather than as a private individual with an ax to grind, doesn't make me trustworthy in your eyes, nothing I can say is likely to change your mind. And if the fact that you've recently become the target of assassins for your beliefs doesn't convince you that the issues we face now are serious, my words won't make a difference."

Sixten wanted to retort loudly, but he stifled the impulse. He knew from experience that his voice sounded weaker when he raised it. Instead he did his best to produce a sharp rasp.

"You're trying my patience, Special Counsel. Anybody who wants me dead for my beliefs has had years to work on it. If I'm suddenly a target now, something must have changed, and it isn't me." Grimly he risked saying, "Maybe it's your investigation."

Maxim remained unruffled; unmoved. "I don't see how that can be true," he mused. "If it is, however, I would expect you to be eager to cooperate with me. You're in danger until whatever lies behind that attack is exposed. My investigation is your best hope."

"Bullshit," Sixten snorted. He was too vexed to choose his words carefully. "You forget who you're talking to. I *support* the UMCP. I *oppose* the UMC."

If anything threatens me, you smug egomaniac, your investigation is as good a candidate as any.

That reached the Special Counsel. His brows went up; a small flush tinged his cheeks. He continued to sit still, as if he were relaxed, but his voice hardened.

"I reject the inference, Captain Vertigus. It's insulting, and I don't deserve it."

Then a look of calculation came into his eyes. "Unless you're trying to tell me without quite saying so that your involvement with the UMCP goes beyond mere support. That you are engaged with Warden Dios in dealings which have earned you enemies who want you dead."

Sixten was so pleased by this near miss that he wanted to laugh. "What? Me and Godsen Frik? That isn't just wrongheaded, Special Counsel—it's silly."

Maxim replied with a tense frown. "I see you're determined to play games with me." His irritation—the fact that he could be irritated—made him seem both physically larger and emotionally less dangerous. "Clearly there is little to be gained by continuing this conversation."

But he didn't rise from his chair.

"I would be derelict, however," he went on in the same tone, "if I didn't ask one more question. Out of respect for your years and experience, if not for your views, I wouldn't trouble you. But this is too crucial to be dismissed, Captain Vertigus."

Sixten held his breath while he waited for Igensard to finally get to the point.

"President Len informs me that you have legislation which you wish to introduce at the next Council session"—he didn't need to consult a chronometer—"in eighteen hours. He says that you've claimed Senior Member's privilege to place your legislation first on the agenda, that other matters will have to be postponed until your bill has been presented, and that you decline to reveal the nature or even the general subject of your bill.

"Captain Vertigus, I must ask you to tell me what kind of legislation you propose to introduce."

Ah. Sixten let his breath out with a sigh. The truth at last. For this Maxim had flattered him; offered to share the results of his own investigation; reminded him that his life was in danger. Sixten had suspected as soon as Maxim Igensard asked to see him that the conversation would come to this. That was why he sat here with a channel open on his private intercom.

He should have pretended surprise; but he didn't bother.

"Forgive me, Special Counsel. I don't mean to be rude. But that's none of your goddamn business."

"You disappoint me, Captain Vertigus." Maxim didn't sound disappointed. He was shrinking again, consolidating himself around his hot core. "In that case, I must ask—no, I must demand—that you yield your privilege to Eastern Union Senior Member Sen Abdullah. Or, if you consider that undignified, yield to your own Junior Member, Sigurd Carsin.

"This is not a trivial matter, and I don't insist on it lightly. But the safety of human space hangs in the balance. As long as Warden Dios remains Director of the United Mining Companies Police, we are effectively defenseless.

"You must yield, Captain Vertigus. My business with the Council must take precedence."

Sixten took pride in holding Igensard's gaze squarely.

"No."

For a moment the Special Counsel seemed to think that he would gain what he wanted if he simply met Sixten's stare without blinking; that Sixten would fold under that small pressure. But Sixten had an equally simple defense against such tactics: with his eyes open and his face calm, he took a short nap.

When he awakened a few heartbeats later, he found that Maxim had risen to his feet in exasperation.

"You're a fool, Captain Vertigus—an old fool." Hints of brutality lay behind his cold tone. "You're implicated in Dios' malfeasance, and when he falls, you'll fall with him."

He reached for the door without saying good-bye.

Pleased by his own equanimity, Sixten drawled, "I can think of worse fates."

At that the Special Counsel turned back. His eyes glittered like chips of mica, and his features were dense with anger.

"I'll tell you something I've learned," he said softly, ominously. "You haven't asked—you aren't interested in 'functional details'—but I'll tell you anyway.

"Angus Thermopyle was arrested for stealing supplies from Com-Mine Station. There didn't seem to be any other explanation, so he was presumed to have an accomplice in Com-Mine Security. That 'functional detail' broke the opposition to the Preempt Act. It gave Dios the last piece of authority he needed to become the only effective power in human space.

"But who was Thermopyle's accomplice?" Although Maxim kept his voice quiet, he wielded it like a bludgeon. "Who did he pay off? Hashi Lebwohl tells us it was Deputy Chief Milos Taverner—the same man who somehow managed to help Thermopyle escape from UMCPHQ right under Dios' nose. That sounds plausible, doesn't it?—if you assume UMCPHQ Security is lax enough to let something like that happen. And it's consistent with the fact that Taverner did a great deal of off-Station banking. His records are still sealed—I don't have authorization to open them—but for a mere deputy chief he had an enormous number of transactions.

"He sounds like a traitor, doesn't he?"

Sixten stared back at Igensard as if the Special Counsel were a kaze who might go off at any moment.

"But here's the interesting part, Captain Vertigus—the part that should make you rethink your intransigence. If Milos Taverner was receiving illicit payments, they didn't come from Angus Thermopyle. He had no money. The evidence of his datacore is irrefutable on this point. *He had no money*. Despite his legendary reputation, he wasn't even able to accumulate enough credit to repair his ship.

"We're left with a fascinating question, Captain Vertigus. Who paid Taverner to help Thermopyle?" Maxim nearly spat the words. "Who *benefited*?

"When I get Council authorization to req the UMCP's financial records—especially Hashi Lebwohl's—I believe I'll learn the answer.

"Think about 'functional details,' Captain Vertigus. Think about 'worse fates.' Call me if you change your mind."

As if he were a juggernaut, massive and unstoppable, Igensard hauled open the door and left.

Sixten continued to stare at the door after his visitor was gone. At the moment he couldn't imagine—or perhaps merely couldn't remember—what he'd hoped to gain by frustrating the Special Counsel. Who benefited? He didn't want to know. All he wanted was sleep. Everything else was muffled by the precipitous drowsiness of the old.

Warden Dios, what are you *doing*?

With an effort, he remained awake long enough to lean over his private intercom and mutter, "You might as well come out of hiding. He's gone."

A voice replied promptly, "I'm on my way."

She's paying attention, he observed to no one in particular. That's good. One of us ought to.

Consoling himself with that thought, he let himself fall into the dark without Maxim Igensard's provocation.

Once again the sound of his intercom pulled him out of dreams he couldn't recollect and didn't care about.

"Captain Vertigus?" Marthe's replacement was barely thirty—only a kid. To his ears, confused by sleep, she sounded like she'd just crawled out of her crib. "UMCP Director of Protocol Koina Hannish is here to see you."

He sighed. "Send her in."

Warden Dios had paid Milos Taverner to frame Angus Thermopyle. So that the Preempt Act would pass.

"Where does Personnel get these damn children?" he muttered to himself while he straightened his clothes. Does she think I don't know who Koina Hannish is?

For a moment or two he missed Marthe so acutely that tears came to his eyes. She'd been his aide—executive assistant and personal secretary in one—for as long as he'd sat on the GCES; and for at least the last fifteen years, ever since his wife died, she'd been his only real companion. The knowledge that she could be blown to bits just because someone somewhere with access to kazes and no heart had taken it into his head to wish death on an old man made Sixten feel bitter and brittle.

My position doesn't depend on such functional details as honor or malfeasance. Show me the Number of the Beast etched on Warden Dios' forehead, and I'll say the same.

Bullshit.

Koina Hannish came into his office while he was still trying to rub the tears off his cheeks.

She stopped when she saw him. "I'm sorry," she murmured quickly, "I'm intruding. I'll wait outside."

He made a gesture of denial. "Don't bother." Then he beckoned her in, flapped one hand to tell her to close the door. "Take my advice," he growled thinly while he blinked his eyes clear. "Don't get old. It makes you soppy."

Koina did him the courtesy of taking him at his word. Radiating kindness despite her immaculate professional manner, she shut the door, crossed to the chair Igensard had recently vacated, and sat down.

"Captain Vertigus, you can be as soppy as you want with me," she said softly. "I don't mind. In fact, I like being reminded that there are still people in the world who can be touched."

Sixten didn't want to discuss old grief—or more present despair. Given the choice, he found his failures easier to contemplate. To deflect Koina's attention, he muttered, "I take it you didn't get the impression that Special Counsel Maxim Igensard can be touched?"

He didn't intend the change of subject as a reproach, however, so he was glad to see that she didn't appear to take it as such. In any case she made the adjustment smoothly.

"Not really." Her smile was detached; comradely in an impersonal way. "He seems too driven for that." Then she shrugged. "He's doing his job. These questions have to be raised. For that matter, they have to be answered." She hesitated briefly before remarking, "I'm still not sure I understand why you wanted me to overhear your conversation."

Tears continued burning at the backs of Sixten's eyes as he faced her. He wanted to ask nakedly, Is it true? You work there—is it true? Did Warden Dios pay Milos Taverner to betray Com-Mine Security so the Preempt Act would pass? But he wasn't sure that he could bear her response. She might say something that would do his courage—not to mention his convictions—more damage than he could sustain.

Instead he did his best to concentrate on her own uncertainty. "Is there a problem?"

"Well"—she considered the situation as she spoke—"it does put me in a rather compromising position. I know something I shouldn't about the Special Counsel's investigation. And Warden Dios is my boss. Do I tell him what I've heard, or do I keep it to myself? If he's corrupt, he should be caught and stopped. But if he's honorable, he deserves a chance to defend himself."

Do you believe he's honorable? Sixten wondered. But he didn't challenge her because she might not have an answer. She was new to her job, if not to PR: she might very well not know whether the UMCP director was malign or honest.

"I can't help you with that," he replied more brusquely than he intended: pain and time left him too fragile to match her kindness. "You'll have to trust your conscience.

"But I wasn't trying to cause you trouble," he went on with better composure. "I didn't know what Igensard was going to say. As I've already told you, I'm afraid you're in danger. It can't be an accident that both Godsen Frik and I were attacked on the same day. Men like Godsen and me have been safe for decades. His association with Holt Fasner protected him. And I—" He spread his hands weakly. "I've been safe because I don't represent any danger.

"I have to ask myself what's changed. And I can only come up with two answers. One is the Special Counsel's investigation. I don't know how or why. Frankly, I can't imagine how either of us is relevant. But that's no worse than the other answer, which is that someone wants to stop me from introducing this Bill of Severance. Again, I don't know how or why. And it doesn't make sense in any case. Nobody—except you, now—has any idea what I'm about to do."

Except Min Donner, he added to himself. If she set me up, she's crazy, and we're all doomed.

"I wish I could think of some other explanation," he told Koina thinly. "I've tried, and I can't. But under the circumstances I can't ignore the possibility that you're next."

She frowned as if she were thinking hard. "I appreciate your concern," she replied slowly, "more than I can easily explain. I'm new to my position. And until Director Dios promoted me, I served under Godsen Frik." She shrugged delicately. "That taught me a rather jaundiced view of Protocol. In fact, I was reluctant to be promoted. The prospect of being asked to do the same kind of job Director Frik did was"—her mouth twisted—"unpleasant. However, since Director Dios persuaded me to accept the assignment, I've begun to feel differently.

"Your concern for me—your willingness to take the risk that your efforts might be opposed because you spoke to me—has given me an interesting litmus test for the people I serve. My 'conscience,' as you call it, required me to tell Director Dios of your concern."

Trying to conceal a sudden pang, Sixten assumed his prunelike expression. Oh, God, what have I done? How many of us have I betrayed?

"His response," she went on intently, "was just what I was praying for. He told me—I wish I could quote him as convincingly as he spoke—he said, 'We shouldn't be talking about this. We shouldn't know about it at all. If and when the question of a Bill of Severance comes to your attention through normal, *public* channels, our position is one of strict and absolute neutrality. Our only legal authority for what we do comes from the GCES, and it is the proper business of the GCES to make decisions about that authority. We accept those decisions, whatever they might be.' "

Sixten twitched uncomfortably. "I'm still worried. It's easy to say things like that. If you have the voice for it, it's easy to say them with conviction. I know you were doing what you thought was right, Director Hannish, and I don't blame you." Warden Dios had paid Milos Taverner to frame Angus Thermopyle. So that the Preempt Act would pass. "But I'm afraid you've given him time to figure out how to stop me."

She shook her head. A complex conviction of her own showed in her eyes. "He also told me I'm in no danger. He was quite clear about it. He assured me that the attacks on you and Director Frik had nothing to do with your bill."

Sixten forgot to keep his mouth pursed. He stared at her, too full of astonishment or horror to be careful. "You mean he knows what's really going on?"

Koina held his gaze firmly. "He didn't say that in so many words, but the implication was unmistakable. And he told me that the next GCES session might shed some light on it."

Sixten could hardly contain himself. His high voice sounded like a yelp. "You mean he even knows what's going to happen in the next session?"

She nodded. After a moment's hesitation, she added, "That's when I realized I believed him."

"Even if Igensard is right?" he protested. Even if Dios bribed Milos Taverner to frame Angus Thermopyle?

She didn't falter. "Even then." Her eyes were as clear as gems. "Somehow I don't think the Special Counsel has the whole story."

Afraid that he might start to weep again, Sixten raised his hands to his face and ground the heels of his palms into his eyes. What did it *mean*? For God's sake, what was Dios *doing*? The UWB Senior Member was old; *too* old; he'd lost whatever capacity he may once have had for dealing with conspiracies and crises. Min Donner had—

Abruptly his heart stopped. In a blaze of inspiration or paranoia he imagined what it would be like if a kaze went off in the Council hall while the GCES was in session. With a vividness which appalled him, he felt the carnage; saw bodies sprawling like scrap among the wrecked furniture; heard the slow, bitter dripping of blood from the walls.

After which naturally Warden Dios would have no choice but to declare martial law, take over the government of all human space himself; answerable only to Holt Fasner.

That was exactly the crisis a Bill of Severance would prevent. If it passed.

Sixten's pulse began racing to catch up with his fear. He found himself in a cold sweat, shivering feverishly while perspiration turned to ice on his forehead and ran down the sides of his jaw.

Min Donner had set him up. She'd put his life on the line in an attempt to stave off a future which Warden Dios—if no one else—could see coming.

"Captain Vertigus?" Koina murmured anxiously. "Are you all right?"

No, Sixten insisted to himself, groping for sanity. It was too much. Too blatant; too brutal. No one would go that far. Even Holt Fasner the megalomaniac wouldn't go that far—

"Are you all right?" Koina repeated more urgently.

—unless he was provoked.

Unless Igensard's investigation threatened the Dragon in ways Sixten couldn't imagine.

Then he might do anything.

With an effort, Sixten faced the PR director. "Take my advice." His voice shook; he couldn't control it. "Don't get old. It gives you nightmares even when you're awake."

"Captain Vertigus," she breathed, "Sixten, is there anything I can do? Can I get you anything. What do you need?"

I need. I need. He could hardly think of an answer. I need to make up my goddamn mind. I need to just *face it* and take the consequences.

Or yield to Igensard. Start running and never stop until this pitiful excuse for a heart cracks open and lets me go.

CHAOS AND ORDER

Barely able to form words past the pressure in his chest, he croaked, "Who do you trust?"

"Trust?" She stared at him in confusion.

"I mean besides Dios. Somebody you know—somebody in UMCPHQ. Who do you trust?"

Koina replied with a perplexed frown. She may have thought he'd lost his mind: she looked like she was about to stand up and leave; dissociate herself from him before he started raving. But after a moment she reached a different decision.

Carefully she replied, "Director Lebwohl."

Grimly Sixten fought down the sight of bodies and blood. Get a grip on yourself, you old fool. He was the first human being who'd ever seen an Amnioni. He'd gone to the Amnion vessel alone, against Holt Fasner's direct orders, so that he could meet the unknown, the future, and believe that he was able to face it. Surely he could do the same now.

Still shaking, he addressed Koina. "Tell Director Lebwohl I'm afraid there's going to be another attack. During the next session. Tell him if he's ever been a real cop—if he cares at all about the integrity of the UMCP, or the rule of law in human space—or even if he just wants to clear his reputation—he's got to keep kazes away from the hall."

Her eyes widened: he'd taken her by surprise. However, her reaction wasn't what he'd expected.

"I'll tell him," she promised. "I'll tell him your exact words. And I think he'll listen. He'll take you seriously.

"But in the meantime—"

She paused as if she had to choose her words.

"You haven't heard—it hasn't been announced yet. Some rather difficult negotiations have been going on between GCES Security and UMCPHQ. You could say that they've been fighting over 'turf'—jurisdiction. I think I've finally worked out an agreement. In fact, President Len has already signed it. And Director Dios has given his authorization.

"Within the next four hours, we're going to double the number of security personnel on Suka Bator. Every precaution you can think of will be in effect. The UMCPHQ Chief of Security will be in command. He's one of Director Donner's people," she added as if she hoped that would allay some of Sixten's fears.

He didn't know what to say to this, so he concentrated on keeping his mouth shut; controlling his panic.

"I don't ask you to be content with that," Koina continued. "You've already been attacked once—you can't be expected to trust ordinary security. And there's no reason why we shouldn't both ask Director Lebwohl to take additional steps. He might very well think of something UMCPHQ Security has missed."

Come on, he adjured himself. Pull yourself together. Don't leave her hanging.

"Thank you." He thought that was the best he could manage; but his voice sounded so pitiful in his own ears that he forced himself to try again. "Maybe some things are worth dying for."

Clearly she didn't understand him. How could she? Resuming her professional manner, she said, "Let's hope it doesn't come to that."

The Bill of Severance was Min Donner's idea. She'd given it to Sixten.

And Warden Dios had paid Milos Taverner to frame Angus Thermopyle.

Koina started to rise, then lowered herself back to the edge of her seat. "I need to go," she said with a hint of anxiety, "but before I do, I think I should tell you that I'm going to let Director Dios know about your conversation with Special Counsel Igensard. If I really believe in him, I'd better act like it."

Sixten's shrug felt less unconcerned and more helpless than he liked.

She leaned forward. "I don't mean to hover over you, but I have to ask. Are you all right? Are you really all right?"

To his relief he found that his fright was receding. He may have actually reached a decision. Or perhaps he was merely sleepy. Whatever the explanation, he was able to respond in a more normal tone.

"My dear young lady, at my age it's almost impossible to make a useful distinction between being and not being 'all right.' Please don't worry about it. At a guess, I would say that I'm not quite ready to collapse."

If he'd been a decade or two less ancient, her smile might have warmed his heart. "In that case," she said as she stood, "I'll go catch my shuttle."

He didn't get to his feet—he didn't think he had the strength—but from his chair he gave her a formal bow when she reached the door and turned to say good-bye.

As she left, he realized that he'd already gone too far to change his mind. Whether he lived or died, he was going to stand by his beliefs.

ANCILLARY DOCUMENTATION

MATTER CANNON

Like the relationship between order and chaos, the relationship between matter and energy is easily stated. However, the application of that relationship on which the peculiar effectiveness of matter cannon depends is less easily explained.

Simply put, matter is nothing more than energy in a more condensed or concentrated form. Matter is "frozen" energy, just as order is frozen or rigid chaos. Conversely energy may be understood as "liquid" matter in the same way that chaos appears to be liquid order, order in flux.

Nonetheless to discuss matter/energy in terms of order/chaos may appear disingenuous. Energy, of course, is not random or unpredictable in any useful sense. However, the analogy between matter and order is plain. And the common understanding of chaos as "randomness" or "unpredictability" is imprecise.

It is axiomatic in chaos theory that the concepts of randomness and unpredictability have meaning only within themselves—inside their own arenas of operation. Just as energy is defined or structured by fields (electromagnetism, gravity, large and small nuclear forces), chaos is defined or structured—in other words, limited—by the means and principles by which it is set in motion, as well as by the scale on which it is deployed.

Although the effects of entropy on complex systems cause them to mutate or degrade in unpredictable ways, the process by which that unpredictability operates is itself predictable.

The crucial point is this: pure randomness or unpredictability cannot exist in the presence of limits; by virtue of its very existence, everything which exists is limited; therefore pure randomness and unpredictability cannot exist. Anything which resembles chaos must exist within some set of limits.

Matter cannon were developed by the application of chaos theory to the relationship between matter and energy.

Once the postulates of chaos theory are grasped, no conceptual obstacle prevents the hypothetical existence of forms of chaos which are transformed by their own limits into forms of order under certain conditions. And if such forms of chaos can exist, they can also be made to exist: they can be designed and generated in such a way that they will resolve themselves into forms of order when given parameters are satisfied.

In metaphorical terms, then, a matter cannon emits a beam of light-constant energy which "freezes" upon contact with matter. This energy takes on mass from any object in its path—mass which for mere picoseconds exists at the speed of light, and which is therefore at least theoretically infinite.

No object in the material universe can withstand light-constant collision with an infinite mass. For that reason the effectiveness of matter cannon is limited only by practical considerations: by the amount of power available to the cannon, for example; by the cannon's ability to emit a beam which resists dispersion over distance; by the presence of other energy fields which conduce to dispersion; or, where the technological capacity exists, by particle sinks which attempt to bleed off the infinite mass as it forms.

If chaos is a more subtle and perhaps more essential form of order, then destructiveness of matter cannon is a more insidious and perhaps more compelling form of material stability.

MIN

As soon as *Punisher* finished her initial burn and began tracking *Trumpet* across the gap, Min Donner slept again. Better now than later. *Trumpet* had a significant lead. And she wasn't easy to follow. After each crossing her homing signal had to be reacquired before *Punisher* could continue. And *Punisher*'s internal spin displacement was affecting navigation, throwing her thousands or tens of thousands of kilometers off course each time she went into tach. She might well need as much as a day or two to get close enough to *Trumpet* to keep pace with her.

If the displacement didn't get worse. And nothing else went wrong.

In the meantime *Punisher*'s drone required a certain number of hours to reach UMCPHQ. And Warden Dios wouldn't respond immediately. He couldn't: he would have to wait to reply until UMCPHQ attained a window on a listening post within effective reach of *Punisher*'s presumed course. After that, more hours would pass while the answering drone raced to its destination.

Better to rest now.

Once *Punisher* gained velocity comparable to *Trumpet*'s, the cruiser needed thrust only for course correction. *Trumpet*'s signal enabled *Punisher*'s helm to set gap parameters which would slowly draw the cruiser closer to the scout without overrunning her. As long as *Trumpet* didn't accelerate, *Punisher* could coast in pursuit using only her gap drive.

Because she was who she was, Min woke up for every course shift, every slight change in *Punisher*'s ambient vibrations. Nevertheless she was able to sleep for the better part of eight hours without being disturbed by hard g.

Once again her intercom awakened her.

"Director Donner, this is the bridge. Director?"

This time she roused easily. Everyone else aboard needed days or weeks of rest, not hours; but until recently she hadn't been under anywhere near as much strain as they had.

As she slid out of her bunk to answer the intercom, she discovered that most of her aches were gone, and her ears no longer registered everything against a background of pain. Nevertheless her anger remained.

At the last Warden had told her that Morn Hyland might survive. Before that—for *months* before that—he'd let, no, encouraged her to believe that Morn would be left to die.

What could she trust now?

How could she be sure that Morn's rescue was anything more than a prelude to another betrayal?

Well, she was glad that Morn was alive, *glad* from the back of her throat to the pit of her stomach. Still she was in no mood to be forgiving.

While her ears, the soles of her feet, and the nerves of her skin sensed *Punisher*'s condition, she toggled her intercom. "Bridge." By small increments the internal spin displacement was getting worse. "Captain Ubikwe?"

"Director Donner," the voice which had awakened her replied, "I'm Command Fourth Stoval, Hargin Stoval." Unlike most of the other officers, he sounded phlegmatic; immune to fatigue. "Captain Ubikwe wants to talk to you. He's in the galley."

"Fine," Min answered. "I'm on my way." But she didn't want to wait that long for news. "Where are we? What's going on?"

"With respect, sir," Stoval replied stolidly, "I think you should talk to Captain Ubikwe."

Min didn't bother to respond. She punched off the intercom, then stood glaring at it for a moment. Dolph, you goddamn prima donna, what're you doing? What're you afraid of?

Why don't you want your people to talk to me?

But she knew why. His ship and his people were damaged, raw with weariness, alone. He was chasing a UMCP gap scout, of all things, with at least one hostile vessel presumably in pursuit. And Min hadn't told him what was at stake.

Dolph Ubikwe was not a man to take such treatment calmly.

For his sake, as well as for her own, she made a particular effort to regain her own poise before she left her cabin to find the galley.

One of the innovations she'd imposed on the UMCP fleet when she became ED Director was the elimination of separate facilities for officers and crew. She desired hierarchies, chains of command, which were founded on respect and commitment, not on privilege—or isolation. Everyone aboard *Punisher,* including her captain, was served by the same foodvends and dispensers, ate in the same mess.

As a result, the galley was not a place Min would have chosen for a private conversation.

She suspected, however, that Captain Ubikwe wanted to talk to her there precisely so that their conversation would not be private. He intended to make her take responsibility for what she revealed, as well as for what she concealed. And he wanted his people to know that he withheld nothing from them which affected their chances of survival.

Min respected his attitude without sharing it. She hated the position Warden had put her in too much to like the prospect of discussing it openly.

She felt a small relief, quickly suppressed, when she found Dolph alone in the galley. The door to the mess stood open, of course, and half a dozen of the crew sat there at the tables, eating or talking; in easy earshot. But at least if they overheard her they might not see her squirm.

Captain Ubikwe sat at the galley table with a mug of coffee steaming between his hands. The table was intended to hold trays and plates while the dispensers and foodvends were being used, but a couple of chairs were kept available for people who needed to eat fast and leave. Dolph hunched in one of them, propping himself up with his elbows as if he needed the support. When he caught sight of Min, he nodded her toward the other chair.

"Get yourself something to eat, Director," he rumbled. "Sit down. We have to talk."

Min needed food, but she was in no mood for it. Instead of asking, Why now? What's changed? she countered, "You want to talk here?"

He shrugged. "Why not? I'm not the one who keeps this ship alive. I don't make her run. Her crew does that. So I don't keep secrets from them."

Standing, she towered over him. She hardly noticed the way her fingers alternately stroked and gripped the butt of her handgun. "You know," she muttered softly, "I could order you to discuss this with me in my cabin—and keep it to yourself afterward. I have the authority, Dolph."

"Sure," he responded with a show of confidence which belied his tension. "But you won't. You aren't that much of a hypocrite."

The man was insufferable; but Min stopped herself on the verge of telling him so. In truth what she found insufferable wasn't him as much as the pressure he exerted on her; the way he pushed her to acknowledge the ambiguity of what she was doing. He didn't deserve her anger. It belonged to Warden Dios.

Nevertheless it refused to go away. She helped herself to a mug of coffee from the dispenser, a bowl of stew from the foodvend, then thumped them down on the table and took the chair Dolph had indicated. Glaring at him like a hawk, she murmured harshly, "Damn it, Captain Ubikwe, I wish you would stop treating me like the enemy. I'm Min Donner, not Maxim Igensard. And I'm as sure as hell not Holt Fasner. For a change of pace, why don't you give your sense of outraged victimization a rest and just tell me why you wanted your command fourth to wake me up?"

Dolph didn't look away: he had anger of his own to match hers. When he spoke, however, he lowered his voice enough to keep his accusation between the two of them.

"You may not be the enemy," he rasped, "but you sure as hell are a problem. You ordered me to turn my back on one ship which may very well be committing an act of war, and another which looks like she might be engaged in some kind of high-level treason, just so we could go haring off after one of our own ships. She arrived out of forbidden space, and you know why she went there, you were expecting her to show up when she did, so I presume you also know where she's going. But you haven't told me why. Why we're here, why you're here, why she's here.

"*Do* you know where she's going?"

The vehemence of his demand took Min aback. She shook her head, sat as still as a gun while she waited for him to explain.

"In that case," he growled more loudly, "I'll tell you." Perhaps it was a mark of respect that he didn't call her a liar. "Massif-5. Valdor Industrial. Which by some amazing coincidence happens to be where we just came from."

Oh, shit, Min groaned to herself. No wonder Dolph was angry.

But he wasn't done. "You may have forgotten," he went on with more and more vitriol in his tone, "so I'll remind you that we were holed twice. We've got internal spin displacement playing hob with navigation, we've got micro-leaks in some of the hydraulic systems, one of our scan banks is useless, and *four of my people are dead,* Director." He visibly restrained an impulse to pound the table. "Eleven more are hurt too bad to work. And *that's* where this gap scout of yours is headed. Unless she changes her mind, she'll reach the system in twenty-four hours.

"Once she gets there, even a Class-1 UMCP homing signal may not be enough to help us follow her—which we'll have to do if you really want us to keep that Amnion ship from catching her.

"Do you think we haven't suffered enough? Are you planning to make us sail that damn Sargasso until navigational displacement if not ordinary bad luck contrives a head-on collision with an asteroid?

"Director Donner, I want to know what this is all about."

Min let out a sigh of recognition. "I can see why." Under the circumstances, she couldn't think of a reason to keep what she knew to herself. "I'll give you the best answer I can.

"But I have to warn you. What I tell you may not be complete." The euphemism tasted like bile in her mouth. "ED is peripheral to this operation. Hashi Lebwohl and Warden Dios planned it together"—I *assume* they planned it together—"without paying much attention to my opinion. So there could easily be things I don't know about it.

"I presume you read *Trumpet*'s flare?"

Dolph faced her squarely. "Sure."

"Then you don't need me to draw you a map. I told you we—that is to say, DA—launched a covert attack on Thanatos Minor. That was *Trumpet*. We put out the story she'd been stolen, but the truth is we gave her to a former illegal named Angus Thermopyle.

"I say 'former' because once Hashi got his hands on him, Captain Thermopyle stopped making his own decisions. He's been welded—he's a cyborg, complete with zone implants and a datacore. And he's been programmed to do whatever Hashi tells him. He could approach Thanatos Minor because he was an illegal in a stolen ship, but we sent him there to blow up the whole planetoid."

Dolph opened his mouth to ask a question, then bit his lip and remained still, letting Min tell the story in her own way.

"But we knew going in," she went on, "that the situation on Thanatos Minor wasn't simple. A man named Nick Succorso was there, along with his ship, *Captain's Fancy*. He's one of Hashi's less reliable operatives. Most of the time he pretends to be illegal, but actually he works for DA. That's why he has a 'mutagen immunity drug' in his possession."

Mordantly Dolph growled, "I didn't know mutagen immunity drugs existed. That's a hell of a discovery to keep secret."

Scowling, Min shrugged. "I'll get to that. Let me finish this first.

"Succorso went to Thanatos Minor from Enablement Station. Don't ask me why—I don't know what the hell he thought he was doing. But *that,* I assume, is why the Amnion now know about the drug—and why he knows about their near-C acceleration research. What must have happened next is that Thermopyle managed to rescue some of *Captain's Fancy*'s people before Thanatos Minor blew.

"If that were all, it might be enough to make the Amnion risk an encroachment. But you read the flare—you know it gets worse.

"Captain Thermopyle has a rather special group of people aboard. Just the fact that Succorso is with him is a surprise, considering that Hashi never would have gotten his hands on Thermopyle if Succorso hadn't framed him for a crime he didn't commit. But there's more.

"Morn Hyland is an ED ensign."

Dolph dropped his jaw in surprise; but Min didn't stop.

"Thermopyle captured her off *Starmaster* when that destroyer went down. Then Succorso took her from Thermopyle. One of them must have gotten her pregnant, which is why she now has a son—'force-grown,' whatever that means." The thought made Min want to spit. "Apparently something about the process has implications the Amnion didn't foresee. Now they want him back because they think he holds the key to replicating Amnion as human beings. Which could be the only weapon they need to destroy us."

Grimly Min held Dolph's stare. "Does that sound like enough? Do you think *Trumpet* needs protection? Do you think the Amnion would risk an act of war for stakes like that?"

He cleared his throat with a guttural rasp. "I would. If I were them. Which I'm beginning to think I might be."

Min forced her hand off her gun to pick up her mug. "What's that supposed to mean?"

"No, please," Dolph retorted sourly, "you first. Finish your story. Then I'll take a turn."

"All right." Deliberately she studied her coffee as if she thought it might quiet her apprehension. "Have it your way."

What happened while I was asleep? What else is going on?

"The reason I'm here is simple enough." On the surface, anyway. "The UMCP needs somebody on the spot who can make decisions and back them up. Somebody who has the authority to demand help and get it anywhere.

"You're here because you were the only ship available.

"I didn't know Thermopyle was going to head for Massif-5. But I can tell you how it happened, and I can guess why.

"He's a cyborg. He's also one of the worst illegals I know—which means no one actually wants to let him make his own decisions. He was sent out with a man who was supposed to control him, adjust his programming as circumstances changed. That was Milos Taverner—the one who turned traitor.

"Well, Hashi knew that might happen. Hell, *I* knew it might. So safeguards were built into Thermopyle's datacore. In effect, Taverner's priority-codes were erased. New codes were initiated. Unfortunately they're useless unless he has somebody with him who knows what they are. For the time being, at least, Thermopyle is out of control to some extent.

"But Hashi anticipated all this. Thermopyle's programming has instructions that require him to report. And activate that homing signal. Then the only thing he has to do is stay away from Earth and UMCPHQ—and stay alive. He can go wherever he wants until we have time to determine how dangerous he is and issue new orders.

"That's another part of our job. As soon as Director Dios says so, we'll maneuver close enough to *Trumpet* to invoke Thermopyle's new codes."

Captain Ubikwe frowned darkly, but didn't interrupt.

"Anyway," she continued, "he chose to head for Massif-5 on his own. Maybe he just thinks he'll be safe there—but I doubt it. He doesn't know that system. So it's my guess he picked Massif-5 because he has Succorso and Shaheed aboard."

And maybe because Morn is there.

"Go on," Dolph muttered.

"Do you recognize the name Vector Shaheed?" she asked, although she had no reason to think he would. "He's a genetic engineer—he used to work for Intertech, back in the days when Intertech was doing research into mutagen immunity drugs. As far as anyone knows—publicly—the research was shut down because it involved dangerous genetic tampering. But the truth is that the research was turned over to DA. Hashi completed it. He's been using people like Succorso to test it—and maybe to play a few mind games with the Amnion. After the Intertech project was stopped, Shaheed ended up with Nick Succorso. A case of 'disaffected loyalty,' according to the psy-profile in his id file.

"I think that's why Thermopyle is heading for Massif-5. Succorso has an immunity drug, and Shaheed knows how to analyze it. Where else could Thermopyle find a bootleg lab to study that drug, and keep himself alive in the process?"

A sneer of disbelief twisted Dolph's face. "You think he wants to duplicate this drug? And do what with it? Mass-produce it? Go into business selling it—to illegals, I presume? Hashi Lebwohl's pet cyborg?"

Min resisted an impulse to snarl back, What do you think I am, a mind reader? Instead she returned, "I think that's what Succorso has in mind. He's capable of it. Maybe Shaheed is, too. Thermopyle isn't. But he is capable of going along with it because he doesn't know what else to do until his computer gets new orders."

"I see." Captain Ubikwe chewed his lip for a moment, consulted his empty mug. "Unfortunately that just makes matters worse."

"How?" Min was tired of oblique gibes. "What do you care what Succorso has in mind? Thermopyle's in command—and we can control him as soon as we get close enough to send him a message."

Dolph snorted to himself. Still studying his mug, he asked, "Are you done? Is there anything else I should know?"

She shook her head brusquely.

"In that case"—he put his palms flat on the table like a man who meant to start shouting—"it's my turn."

Here it comes, Min thought. Because she needed the discipline, she forced herself to begin eating her stew as if nothing he could say would hurt her.

"I suggested," he began harshly, "that I feel like I might be working for the Amnion without knowing it. Turning my back on alien incursions has that effect on me." He appeared to swell with outrage as he spoke, taking on bulk as well as passion from his own words. He didn't raise his voice: nevertheless it seemed to resonate off the walls. "Turning my back on ships that might be engaged in treason has that effect. And hearing that I work for an organization that develops mutagen immunity drugs and then keeps them secret so men like this Captain Succorso can have them to play with produces the same goddamn sensation.

"But I'll tell you what really makes me feel like I enlisted on the wrong side." He shoved a fist into one of his pockets, pulled out a crumpled sheet of hardcopy. "While you were sleeping, we passed a UMC listening post."

For a second Min choked on her stew. But she didn't lift her head; didn't let him see her struggle to swallow.

"Not UMCP," he insisted, "United Mining Companies. What the

hell it's doing out here, I can't tell you. *You* could probably tell *me*, but I'm not sure I want to hear any more secrets right now.

"The post log was holding a message for us. Not you—us. It's coded for *Punisher*." Which was his only conceivable excuse for not waking her up right away and giving her the message directly. "But it's not from Command Operations. Hell, it's not even from Center. It's from Warden Dios himself.

"It makes me sick."

"Fine." Min slammed down her spoon so hard the stew slopped over the edges of the bowl. "*You* be sick." She stuck out her hand. "*I'll* read the message."

Abruptly she caught a glint of malicious humor from his eyes. "Here." He dropped the hardcopy on the table beside her hand. "After you read it, you can be sick on the floor. The bosun doesn't mind—he's used to messy galleys by now."

Stifling obscenities, Min picked up the sheet and smoothed it out so that she could see what it said.

He was right: the transmission was from Warden Dios. And coded for *Punisher*. As if he didn't trust her to obey him—

The first part of the message contained warnings. Sorting through the codes and the official locutions, she gleaned the information that *Free Lunch* was a mercenary working for Hashi Lebwohl. Contracted to DA as an observer, Captain Scroyle had returned from Thanatos Minor just ahead of the carnage. Now, however, he had a new assignment. For reasons which Warden didn't bother to explain, *Free Lunch* was now under contract to destroy *Trumpet*.

Hashi, you sonofabitch! You God *damn* son of a bitch.

Punisher was instructed to take any steps necessary to protect the gap scout.

In addition, Min learned that *Soar*, a ship reported in the vicinity of Thanatos Minor by Captain Scroyle, had been tentatively identified as *Gutbuster*. *Gutbuster* had been an illegal armed with super-light proton cannon, formerly presumed dead or lost; but now Hashi or his people thought she might be operating as *Soar*, with stolen id and a retrofit gap drive.

Warden guessed she might be the vessel heading out of forbidden space in pursuit of *Trumpet*. If that were true, she was an enemy to fear: *Gutbuster* had several kills to her charge, and only the lack of a gap drive had prevented her specialized cannon from doing even more damage.

All that was bad enough. What followed was worse.

With the highest possible priority, and on Warden Dios' personal authority, *Punisher* was commanded to flare a signal to *Trumpet* as soon as she could get within reach.

The text of the signal was brief.

It said:

Warden Dios to Isaac, Gabriel priority.

Show this message to Nick Succorso.

That was all. The words were embedded in coding that Min didn't recognize and couldn't read—some kind of machine language, apparently, intended to enforce compliance from Isaac's computer. But those twelve words were enough to make her vision go gray around the edges and fill her heart with gall.

Succorso wasn't stupid. He would figure out what the signal meant. He might not know why it was sent to him, but he would know how to use it.

Morn Hyland was aboard *Trumpet* with the two men who had abused her most. And her only protection was the fact that a programmed UMCP cyborg was in command. Because of who he was, Angus wouldn't let Nick hurt her. Because he was welded, Angus wouldn't hurt her himself.

But after he got this message—

Succorso would take command. In his own way, he was about as trustworthy as Milos Taverner. With a ship like *Trumpet*—and with a cyborg backing him up—he might be impossible to stop.

Morn certainly wouldn't be able to stop him.

Warden. *Warden*. You've betrayed us. Morn. Angus. Me. Humankind. You've betrayed us all.

"The truth is," Dolph said abruptly, "I trust you." He made no effort to keep his voice down: he might have been making an announcement to the whole mess. "I've always trusted you—I can't stop now. And at the moment Warden Dios' 'personal authority' doesn't mean shit to me. He let Hashi Lebwohl hire a mercenary to attack his own people. I don't know what that means—or what *this* means"—he slapped a gesture at the sheet of hardcopy—"but I can guess who's behind it. Holt Fasner. Or Cleatus Fane doing the Dragon's dirty work.

"So it's up to you. You decide. We'll do whatever you tell us. And fuck the consequences."

Min held his gaze with her eyes burning and her palms afire; she clutched her handgun as if it were the only thing left that made sense to her. In her name he was prepared to defy a direct order from the director of the UMCP—

"You know," she murmured, nearly whispering, "I could court-martial you right here for saying that."

A grin bared his teeth. "I know. But you won't." For the second time he told her, "You aren't that much of a hypocrite."

Oh, really? Full of sudden disgust, she had to clench her teeth and grip her gun hard to prevent herself from flinging her stew across the galley. Then what *was* she? What did all her years of dedication and loyalty come to now?

Warden was forcing her to commit an act of treason. Treason to humankind. Or treason to her oath of service.

What did he want from her? Did he assume that the faithful Min Donner, so faithful that some people called her his "executioner," would blindly go ahead and carry out his orders? Or did he believe, hope, pray that her commitment to the ideals which the UMCP supposedly served would compel her to disobey him?

How could she decide without knowing what he wanted?

Who *was* she?

While Dolph waited for her reply, she found an answer. It was there in his face, although he didn't know it—and might have disavowed it if he did. At a word from her, he was willing to commit a crime which would doom him and his whole command. And he was willing for the simple, sufficient reason that he knew her. She was the UMCP Enforcement Division director in the purest sense of the term: as disinclined to treason as to lies; and passionately loyal to her own people.

For that same reason, she had no choice now. She was *Enforcement* Division, not DA or Administration, Command Operations or PR. Put crudely, she was the fist of the UMCP, not the brain; not even the heart. And a fist that imposed its own decisions on other people was only a bully, nothing more.

If there was treason here, it was Warden's, not hers. She didn't make policy. It would be a crime of another kind—a violation of her essential commitments—if she arrogated to herself the responsibility for choosing humankind's future.

So she knew what to do. She hated it; but she did it.

"You're right," she told Dolph. "It's up to me."

She seemed to feel pieces of her heart breaking off as she announced, "I want you to flare that signal to *Trumpet* before she reaches Massif-5." Each raw chunk she lost had Morn's name on it, or Warden's. "Which means you're going to have to catch up with her first."

Which in turn would put even more pressure on his ship and his crew. With displacement affecting navigation, *Punisher* would have to work hard to gain on the agile, undamaged gap scout.

"The sooner you get started, the better."

Dolph Ubikwe's name may have been on one of the pieces which cracked away.

He didn't appear lost, however. Under his fat, his features hardened; his shoulders hunched up as if he were absorbing blows. But he didn't protest or complain: the glare in his eyes held no grievance. He appeared to be measuring her—or measuring himself against her, wondering if he could match her.

After a moment he let out his breath in a long sigh. "Shit, Min. And all this time I thought being one of the good guys was supposed to be fun."

Puffing out his cheeks lugubriously, he heaved his bulk out of the chair.

The acceptance behind his sarcasm touched her more than she could bear to show. In plain gratitude, however, because he'd given her one less bereavement to carry, she made an effort to respond in kind.

"One more thing, Dolph." She didn't look up at him: she didn't want him to see her face. "The next time something like this happens"—she flapped Warden's message—"don't keep it to yourself. It just upsets you, and when you're upset you're a pain in the ass."

"Aye, sir, Director Donner, sir." He sounded like he was grinning. "Whatever you say."

She longed for the ability to grin herself, but she was too full of grief. She'd made her decision. If humankind suffered for it, she would shoulder the responsibility.

Nevertheless as Captain Ubikwe left the galley to carry out her orders, she couldn't shake the conviction that she'd sent him to do Morn Hyland more harm than any mortal man or woman could sustain.

ANGUS

Once *Trumpet* had attained a steady course and velocity away from the Com-Mine belt, and he and Mikka Vasaczk had recovered from the immediate effects of g-stress unconsciousness, Angus began taking his ship by easy stages across the light-years toward the Massif-5 system and Valdor Industrial. He didn't rush her between crossings. And he made no effort to pick up more velocity so that she could cover greater distances. Instead he waited—sometimes half an hour, sometimes an hour or more—after *Trumpet* resumed tard before he reengaged her gap drive and sent her leapfrogging the void.

As a result, a trip which might have been accomplished in twelve hours was going to take the better part of two days.

He told Mikka and the rest of his passengers that he did this to minimize the strain on Morn. Every time *Trumpet* resumed tard, the ship had to be ready for emergency maneuvers. The chance always existed that navigational imprecision might drop her down a gravity well, or place her uncomfortably close to an obstacle. And of course no astrogation database could possibly include every rogue lump of rock prowling the vast dark. In consequence Davies had to put Morn to sleep before each crossing so that sudden g wouldn't send her into gap-sickness.

Angus told his companions that he wanted to spare Morn the ordeal of being paralyzed by her zone implant control all the way to Valdor Industrial.

And he used the same excuse to explain why he did nothing to evade pursuit from any of the three ships which *Trumpet*'s sensors had recorded when she'd come out of the gap on the edge of the Com-Mine belt. One of those ships was parked right over the listening post Angus had used; another drove toward human space from the direction of Thanatos Minor; the third showed every sign of being a UMCP warship primed for battle. Any or all of them might come after *Trumpet*—yet Angus did nothing to confuse his trace.

He didn't want to subject Morn to evasive maneuvers, he said. Not after what she'd been through. And *Trumpet* would be difficult to follow in any case. A pursuer would have to quarter the vacuum for hours after each crossing in order to pick up her particle trail. And even that effort would be wasted if the pursuer couldn't estimate accurately how far the gap scout went with each crossing. On top of that, even if the pursuer guessed *Trumpet*'s destination and simply headed for Massif-5, there was no guarantee—perhaps no likelihood—that the gap scout could be located in that huge, complex, virtually unchartable system.

Nick sneered at this explanation. Mikka faced it with a scowl of disapproval. Morn insisted that she was willing to spend as much time locked in artificial dreams as necessary to help *Trumpet* reach Massif-5 safely.

Angus ignored them.

It was all bullshit, of course. In fact, it was *stupid*. It outraged his instincts, appalled his fears. He could feel ships of every kind harrying him like Furies across the dark as if they were already within reach of scan; perhaps within reach of fire.

But the truth was that his programming wouldn't let him either hurry or dodge. As if *Trumpet*'s homing signal weren't enough of a betrayal, his datacore required him to behave with the mindless predictability of a moron; to ensure that any ship that followed him would find him impossible to lose.

With every passing hour, the taste of freedom turned more sour in his mouth. What good did it do him to make his own decisions if he had to carry them out like an idiot?

The men who'd programmed him scorned his desire for escape. Even when they loosened their control over him, they didn't let him go.

Warden Dios had said, *It's got to stop. We've committed a crime against your soul.* He must have been lying: every transmission from *Trumpet*'s homing signal proclaimed that this particular crime was far from over. Yet why had he lied? He'd called Angus a *machina infernalis*. What kind of man lied to a machine?

Angus wanted to believe that Dios hadn't lied. He needed to believe *some*thing. But each slow, imposed step of *Trumpet*'s voyage to Valdor insisted that he was deluding himself.

And cowards who deluded themselves paid for it with abuse, humiliation, and death.

Eventually he stopped talking to the people around him or answering questions—even when Morn asked them. If he couldn't say, *You've been betrayed, we've all been betrayed*, he couldn't bear to speak at all.

From time to time Ciro brought him sandwiches and coffee. Under pressure from his sister, Ciro had taken on the duties of a cabin boy. Apparently he considered this a demotion, and he didn't like it. Nevertheless he was plainly capable of discipline as well as loyalty. And he'd already shown that he had courage. He only allowed himself a hint of sullenness as he served Angus and Mikka at the command stations, or offered food to anyone else who happened to be on the bridge.

Mikka remained at the second's station for several hours after *Trumpet* left the Com-Mine belt behind. If Angus wanted a little help, she gave it. The rest of the time she spent familiarizing herself with the ship. When she reached the end of her stamina, he sent her off the bridge to sleep and ran the ship alone until she came back.

He could have asked almost anyone aboard to take her place, but he didn't. He had no intention of giving Nick access to *Trumpet*'s databases and programming again. Morn couldn't stay on the bridge while *Trumpet* went into tach; and she needed Davies with her. Between crossings, Vector virtually lived at the auxiliary engineering console, belted to the stool so that he wouldn't drift away, but he wasn't working for the ship. Instead he used the console to reconstruct as much as he could of his research at Intertech, and then to write programs which would help him analyze Nick's antimutagen. And Sib Mackern had assigned himself the job of guarding Nick. He was no good with a gun—Angus had already seen him in action—but he seemed to consider Nick the worst danger *Trumpet* was likely to face, and he was determined to prevent Nick from doing any more damage.

As for Nick, he appeared to have slipped into a state of cheerful lunacy. He understood what was said in his presence well enough to sneer at it, but he didn't talk himself. When he wasn't in his cabin, he floated the bridge, bobbing around and around the command stations like some frail old fool who'd lost contact with gravity or reality. At intervals he smiled to himself as if he'd slipped into senility while his medtech wasn't looking. His scars were pale under his eyes, the color of cold ash. Despite the fact that Sib was always with him, always watching, he ignored the nervous man as if Sib were invisible.

Angus trusted none of this. For one thing, he didn't believe that Sib was actually capable of handling Nick. And for another, he felt sure that Nick's amiable dissociation was nothing more than a pose. Nevertheless he didn't lock Nick away. His datacore didn't give him that option. Instead he was forced to rely on Sib—and anyone else who happened to be nearby.

Twelve hours passed; then twenty-four; thirty. Mikka's calculations and Angus' agreed that *Trumpet* was still roughly ten hours from the fringes of the Valdor system at her present pace. Five minutes after he informed his passengers that he intended to coast for an hour before the next crossing, Morn and Davies came to the bridge.

Perhaps by coincidence, everyone else was there as well. Mikka had resumed the second's station. Nick orbited her seat and Angus' under Sib's anxious stare. Ciro had just brought another light meal from the galley. And Vector concentrated on the auxiliary engineering console as if he'd forgotten that he was human and needed rest—as if his awareness had shrunk down to his hands and the small screen, precluding people and distraction; precluding sleep. While he worked, his mouth pursed and relaxed, pursed and relaxed, according to some rhythm of its own. Angus had the impression that the geneticist whistled soundlessly through his teeth as he entered data or wrote programs, then paused when he considered the results.

Morn surveyed the bridge; she and Davies accepted foodbars and g-flasks of coffee from Ciro. In the absence of internal spin, they couldn't stand anywhere. But her training had taught her the knack of floating in a stable position. Apparently Davies had the same ability.

After a bit of her foodbar and a sip of coffee, she turned to Angus.

"How is it going?" Her tone was carefully neutral. "Where are we?"

She didn't look much better than she had a day or two ago. She hadn't yet had enough food and rest to cure her core exhaustion. However, she wasn't suffering from withdrawal; and the release of that particular strain showed in the small muscles around her eyes, the shape of her mouth, the lessened fever of her movements. In addition, she'd used the san until her hair and skin gleamed with cleanliness. She might have been trying to scour away her hours as a prisoner of the Amnion. Or perhaps it was Nick's touch she wanted to scrub from her nerves.

Or the memory of what Angus had done to her.

Simply seeing her made his stomach hurt like knives twisting inside him.

Instead of speaking, he keyed an astrogation plot to one of the main screens and let her interpret it for herself.

She looked at it, glanced toward Davies. The two of them nodded like twins: they both drew on the same education and experience to understand the display.

"When will we get there?" she asked Angus.

He scowled without replying. I've been betrayed. You've been betrayed. Something has got to stop, that's obvious, but it sure as hell won't be the crimes of the fucking UMCP.

"Angus—" Morn began as if she meant to warn him; threaten him.

Davies swam closer to the command station.

"I don't know what his problem is," Mikka put in brusquely. "At a guess, I would say sleep deprivation is making him psychotic." Nick snorted at this, but didn't interrupt. Flashing a glare in his direction, Mikka continued to Morn, "He doesn't answer questions anymore.

"But he gave me projections." Now Mikka had Davies' attention as well as Morn's. "He had to—I couldn't plan a course through the system until he told me when we would reach it. I don't think there's a complete chart on Massif-5 anywhere in human space, but even the ones we have would be useless if we didn't know the time. We can just about estimate the positions of the twelve planets and Valdor itself, but without the time we couldn't predict where even the twenty-five or thirty largest planetoids, comets, and asteroid swarms are in their orbits.

"He told me we'll hit the edge of the system in"—she checked a readout—"9.3 hours. For the first fifteen or twenty hours of this trip, I thought he was crazy to take it so slow. But now I can see at least one advantage. If you don't count a few hundred uncharted asteroids and maybe even a singularity or two, arriving nine hours from now is going to give us a relatively clear insertion into the system. We won't have to start right out dodging major gravity wells and rock.

"After that—" She shrugged. "Then it gets messy."

Everyone except Vector and Nick watched her while she spoke, letting her tell them what they already knew as if hearing it from her might help them get ready; defuse their fears.

"Massif-5 is a binary system," Mikka said stolidly, "and all that stellar mass has attracted a staggering amount of rock and rubble. There are twelve main planets, all on different orbital planes. Some of them move at really astonishing velocities in loops around both stars, others circle just one or the other, and a couple circuit the whole well. They all have moons —some as many as thirty—and four of them have rings. In addition there are asteroid swarms flung in all directions like shrapnel. There are maybe a hundred planetoids, some of them with truly crazy orbits around the stars and several of the planets. We have nine comets on record, some of them pretty big. Then there's the debris—everything from fist-size rocks burning at .2 or .3 C to the drifting hulks of wrecked ships."

Angus growled to himself as he studied the problem. He wasn't especially worried about his ability to navigate the system—*he* could do that better than anyone—but he hated the prospect of taking *Trumpet* through that maze slowly enough to be safe.

"All that would be a hell of a challenge in any case," Mikka continued, "but unfortunately there's more. Apparently singularities breed in the gravitic stresses of binary systems. The good news is that only five have been found. So far. The bad news is that their orbits are unstable—and they have so much pull that they distort the orbits around them. Which means," she added grimly, "that any given piece of information in our databases could well become obsolete at any time.

"In other words, the system is a fucking nightmare."

She knew what she was talking about. She and Ciro had been born on Valdor Industrial.

"Of course"—she shrugged again—"it's also a treasure house. That's why Valdor was put here in the first place. Massif-5 has resources on a scale you can't imagine. But now there's another reason. VI has become the main research facility in human space for studying singularities, trying to find some way to harness all that power."

Her tone hardened. "Which is also why there are more pirates and bootleg operations in this system than in most of the rest of human space put together."

Running commands with blunt ease, she brought up a 3-D schematic of the Valdor system on one of the displays. "We're going there." A couple of keys made a small swirl of dots roughly a third of the way across the system blink amber. "As you can see, it's not exactly close to our point of insertion.

"It's an asteroid swarm that doesn't have enough inertia to escape the gravity well. Unless a singularity pulls it aside, it'll curve inward and finally plunge into Lesser Massif-5 maybe twenty years from now. But in the middle of it, protected by several thousand other pieces of rock, is an asteroid big enough to be a moon.

"That's where the lab we're headed for is located."

Davies was listening hard, but his manner no longer resembled Morn's. She was focused on Mikka; but he looked repeatedly away to see what Nick was doing or to watch for Angus' reaction. Angus suspected that he hadn't slept much since he'd come aboard: he seemed to burn at too high a temperature for rest.

He held Morn's zone implant control: he turned her on and off for every gap crossing. But what did he do while she was helpless?

Angus couldn't refrain from imagining what Davies might do with his power; what Angus himself would do in his son's place.

The idea left him sick with desire.

Desire and dismay. He'd already proven that he couldn't beat Morn: that his efforts to degrade and master her were nothing more than wasted attempts to get out of the crib. He'd spent his whole life in that struggle, but he'd never been able to break free.

He hardly heard Davies ask Mikka, "Have you been there?"

Mikka shook her head. "All I know is rumors and scuttlebutt—the kind of stories you would expect to hear in a system full of illegals. Nick says he went once. If he did, I haven't heard him talk about it."

Nick waved a hand dismissively, but everyone ignored him.

"The people who *do* talk," Mikka said, "don't give it a name. They just call it the Lab. But it's more like a complete research facility.

"I don't know if the cops know about it." She didn't wait for Morn or Davies to tell her. "I assume they do. It's been there for twenty-five years. But they've never tried to shut it down. With all that rock running interference, it's damn near impregnable. You have to go in slow—and some of those asteroids have matter cannon emplacements dug into them.

"In any case, it's not a good target. It doesn't have any dealings with the Amnion. It's more like one of those med labs on Earth that researches ways to make rich people look richer by experimenting on protected animals—like human beings.

"In fact, this place does plenty of med research. They study zone implants. They make cyborgs. A lot of BR surgery was invented here. So were the techniques that let people survive self-mutilation. But it's not primarily a med lab. That's just a sideline to finance what they really do."

Make cyborgs, Angus thought in a spasm of disgust. His anger was growing, accumulating hour by hour, but it had nowhere to go. No wonder the cops didn't shut "the Lab" down. They probably sent their own researchers to work there, to help them learn how to perform the kind of surgery they'd done on him.

Mikka took a deep breath. As she went on, her scowl deepened until it seemed to clench the bones of her skull.

"The man who built it and runs it is called Deaner Beckmann, and he's no ordinary illegal. According to his reputation, he's more of a lunatic libertarian—or an anarchist. He doesn't believe in the kind of laws that prevent him from doing whatever research interests him. And what interests him—so they say—is gravitic tissue mutation. He wants to evolve genetic adaptations that will allow organisms to survive the stress of working close to singularities. Eventually he wants to evolve human beings who can study singularities up close."

"Why?" Ciro asked in surprise.

"Because," Mikka answered tightly, "he thinks humankind's future lies inside. I guess he thinks all the stuff black holes suck in must *go* somewhere. But *people* can't go there if they can't take the pressure." She snorted sardonically. "So he wants to make a few changes."

"Unfortunately for him," Morn put in as if she were still trying to warn Angus, "that kind of research is illegal. As illegal as the unauthorized use of zone implants."

Davies nodded like an echo.

Drifting around the bridge, Nick snickered satirically.

Mikka gave him a glare as if she wanted to hit him, then finished what she was saying.

"The story about Beckmann is that he got started with a grant from Holt Fasner. But he lied about what he actually wanted to accomplish—or where he intended to work on it. He's been in the middle of that asteroid swarm ever since. Since he doesn't believe in anything that limits research, he lets other people come and work with him. Or so I've heard."

"Sounds perfect," Vector murmured without raising his head from his work. "He'll have everything I need."

Sib Mackern squirmed like a man who was trying not to throw up. "You actually want to go there?" he asked the engineer. "A place where they do BR surgery and make cyborgs?" Old fears twisted his face. "How is that different than being Amnion?"

"Because if they were Amnion," Morn said stiffly, "they wouldn't get to choose." Her hand moved toward the back of her head as if she were remembering the ways her zone implant could be used against her.

"Don't worry about it," Vector told Sib. "It'll be fun—I'll be in my element." A self-mocking smile crossed his face. "And I've always wanted to be the savior of humankind. I don't care where I do it."

" 'The savior of humankind.' " Nick aimed a false grin at Vector. "I like that. You couldn't save your way out of a sack of shit if they *gave* you the damn lab. The only time you ever do anything right"—just for an instant his grin cracked into a snarl—"is when you panic."

Furiously Mikka swung the second's station to face Angus. "Are you going to shut him up"—she jerked a vehement nod toward Nick—"or do I have to do it?"

Angus glowered back at her. Programmed inhibitions seemed to fill his throat, tightening until he felt that he was being strangled.

"Let him talk, Mikka," Vector put in quietly. "He's just trying to pretend he still exists. Sneering is all he has left."

"I don't *care*," Mikka spat. "I spent too many years believing in his fucking superiority. I don't want to *hear it* anymore."

Angus hated it. More than anyone else aboard, he needed to rage and strike; needed the kind of violence which would break him out of his prison. He would willingly, gleefully, have killed Nick with his bare hands, raped Morn right there, or beaten his own head to pulp, just to prove he could do it. But everything was impossible. He couldn't even explain why he'd let Morn and Vector persuade him to head for Massif-5.

"Then get off the bridge," he told Mikka harshly. You've been betrayed. *We all have*. Do you think I *like* listening to people who can say whatever they want? "You're relieved. Don't come back until we reach Massif-5."

Nick floated to a bulkhead, paused on one of the handgrips. His grin was so abhorrent that Angus howled to himself; but he made no sound.

"Angus?" Morn asked tensely. "What's wrong?"

She knew him too well.

"We've got to do *some*thing about him," Sib insisted, pointing at Nick. He sounded uncharacteristically determined. "If we don't at least lock him up, he's going to drive us all crazy."

"Angus, this is backward," Davies said earnestly. "Sib is right. Mikka's not the problem. Nick is."

Angus didn't answer his son. He didn't face Morn's question, or respond to Sib, even though his own voiceless protests and appeals tore at his heart. His datacore declined to let him lock up a UMCPDA operative.

Mikka confronted him squarely, searching him with her hard scowl. When he refused to reply, she bit her lip suddenly, then gave a tight shrug.

"I need rest anyway." She spoke to Morn without looking at her. "He'll want my help later. Unless he decides to let Nick replace me. In that case there's no reason for me to be here."

Keeping her eyes to herself, she undid her belt and pushed out of the g-seat, floating in a precise somersault for the companionway. When she reached the handrails, she pulled along them and rose out of sight.

"*Damn* it." Anchored with his other hand so that he wouldn't drift away, Davies thumped his fist on the edge of the command console. "I thought we could trust you," he rasped at Angus. "I thought you'd changed."

"He has," Morn said in a concerned tone. "He hates Nick. He wouldn't do this."

With a visible effort, she forced herself closer to Angus' station. When she was directly in front of him, she raised her eyes to his. They were deeply bruised, dark with damage—and yet somehow inviolable, as if she could remain whole under any kind of assault.

"Angus, something is wrong. We need to know what it is. *I* need to know."

She might have added, And *I* have the right to ask.

"Too bad," he retorted as if he were sneering at her; as if he were capable of that. "You can go to your cabin, too. We're going to hit tach in five minutes."

Consternation pulled at the corner of her mouth. "But you said—"

"I changed my mind."

He couldn't win a test of wills with her: he wasn't strong enough. If he tried to hold her gaze and face her down, he would end up whimpering like a baby in his g-seat. But his zone implants were more insidious than hers—and they were active. He scowled at her like the impact head of a mine-hammer until she dropped her eyes and turned away as if he'd beaten her.

"Come on," she murmured to Davies. "It's still his ship—he makes the rules."

Davies looked like his chest was congested with shouts. He was full of fever and extravagance, which he fought to suppress. All his movements seemed constricted, as if he were holding himself back from some extreme act by sheer willpower. When Morn spoke to him, however, he bit his mouth shut and coasted after her up the companionway.

Angus didn't watch her go. He didn't meet Sib's moist gaze, or Ciro's immature outrage; didn't answer Vector's quizzical expression. Above all he didn't look at Nick. He didn't want to give any of them a reason to approach him.

If they did—if they came closer to the command station—they might notice that a scan blip had appeared on his board.

CHAOS AND ORDER

A ship.

Not close: the lag to the vessel was nearly eight minutes. But she had resumed tard almost directly behind *Trumpet*, as if she were on the same course.

As if she were following the gap scout.

No one else moved; but Nick left his handgrip and sailed toward Angus, catching himself at the last moment on the edge of the station. Deliberately he braced his arms on the console so that he could leer into Angus' face.

"You know what your problem is?" he said in a casual, infuriating drawl. "You hate yourself. You don't want friends. No, it's more than that —you don't even want allies. You don't think you deserve them.

"You raped that bitch's brains out. *He* remembers every bit of it. And *still* both of them want to be on your side. As for Mikka—she's so jealous, she would form an alliance with a snake if it just despised me enough.

"They all *want* to help you."

Angus looked straight at Nick; but with his peripheral vision he studied his readouts. The following ship was definitely on *Trumpet*'s course. And moving faster: scan and data estimated her velocity climbing past .3C. That wasn't enough gain to give *Trumpet* any immediate problems. Still it made his heart squirm in his chest.

Who was she?

"But you won't have it," Nick went on. "You hate yourself too much. You can't *stand* anybody who doesn't treat you like you're the foulest motherfucking sonofabitch in the whole created cosmos."

Angus felt dangers crowding around him. A ship on his trail. At least one enemy who knew him too well.

Driven by electrodes deep in his brain, he tensed for action as Sib soared toward Nick, gripping his handgun in his fist.

Nick froze, deliberately made no effort to defend himself. Nevertheless his grin curdled, and his skin seemed to fade to the ashen color of his scars.

Sib stopped himself on the arm of Angus' g-seat.

"But Morn and Davies and Mikka aren't like that, Nick." He touched Nick's temple with the muzzle of his weapon; despite his fears, he held the gun steady. "And they aren't alone. The only one I hate is you."

He, too, was driven: his fears were as deep as electrodes. In an oblique way, he might have been declaring his loyalties—not for Nick's benefit, but for Angus'.

"Don't forget me," Ciro added, even though his voice quavered. "You hurt Mikka. I'm not going to forgive that."

Like Sib, he spoke to Angus as much as to Nick.

The data scrolling in front of Angus clarified as scan improved its fix on the pursuing vessel. She was too big, emitted power on too many bandwidths, to be anything except a warship.

Was she UMCP?

Or was she an Amnioni, risking war to hunt down *Trumpet*?

While everything inside him stormed and wailed, Angus simply glared back at Nick and waited for his tormentor to go away.

Nick didn't move until Sib lowered his gun and faded back. Then, however, he shoved himself off the console. As he arced to one of the bulkheads, then rebounded toward the companionway, he tightened his grin. He may have been trying to conceal relief.

"You'd better hit tach as soon as you can," he told Angus. "We don't want anybody to catch up with us.

"I'll be in my cabin."

Curling his lip at Sib, he left the bridge.

Angus swore to himself. Nick had seen the blip.

Too bad.

Determined and grim, he started running commands.

As he fed coordinates to the helm and power to the gap drive, as he charged matter cannon and focused scan, he announced, "Tach in thirty seconds."

Vector, Sib, and Ciro would need that long to reach the relative protection of their cabins.

He wanted to cut the time short; wanted to go *right now,* while he still could. If he let a UMCP ship catch him, he was finished. Some cop would invoke his priority-codes, and then his brief, ambiguous freedom would end.

But his datacore didn't let him cheat. He gave the people who relied on him their full thirty seconds before he sent *Trumpet* plunging into the gap.

MORN

Morn came out of deep dreams with the vaguely disturbing sensation that someone had flipped a switch. One moment she was far down in slumber so delicious and comforting that it seemed to soothe her from the surface of her skin to the center of her aggrieved heart. The next she was awake, with her eyes open and her limbs weak; aching because her hurts were still there after all, unassuageable by dreams or rest.

She recognized the phenomenon. It was the stress of transition from artificial sleep and peace to ordinary, vulnerable mortality. But the recognition did little to console her. She'd become so dependent on the emissions of her zone implant that even helpless unconsciousness seemed preferable to the limitations and pains of being human.

Across the small cabin from her, Davies sat on the edge of his bunk, securing himself against weightlessness with his knees. The gaze he fixed on her was dark and haunted—a stare as restless and concentrated in its own way as the yellow malice of his father when Angus had raped and degraded her.

In one hand he held her zone implant control.

Like Angus.

And like Nick. For a time Nick also had possessed her by means of the electrode in her skull.

Like both of them, Davies was male—

For an instant the sight filled her with revulsion and dismay. Once again she'd fallen under the control of a man who meant to abuse her.

Male or not, however, he wasn't like them. She insisted on that while he studied her. His hand hung limp: none of his fingers moved on the buttons. He was her son; his mind echoed hers. What haunted his gaze wasn't malice. It was concern. Distrust of Nick. Doubt of Angus. And the inevitable, unpredictable aftermath of being nurtured in her womb at a time when she was filled almost constantly by a storm of imposed energies. He'd been conditioned to metabolic extremes which no normal baby could have endured.

She wondered what he did for rest. He looked like he hadn't slept since they'd left Billingate.

Maybe he couldn't.

On the other hand, how long could he stay sane without sleep?

When he'd watched her wake up for a moment, he asked, "Are you all right?" His voice came out in a knotted croak, as if he'd spent hours with his throat clenched, waiting for her.

She nodded. Drained by transition, she fumbled at the g-seals which secured her in her bunk; opened the inner sheath, the outer webbing. With her fingers wrapped in the webbing so that she wouldn't float away, she swung her legs over the edge and sat up.

Giddiness and the lack of g swept through her. She had the uncomfortable impression that *Trumpet* was spinning; tumbling end over end like a derelict. But after a moment her zero-g training reasserted itself, and her disorientation passed.

Swallowing at the taste of lost dreams, she murmured, "Where are we?"

He replied with a frown like his father's. "Angus says we're one crossing away from Massif-5. Once we get there, we'll have to be ready for hard g almost constantly, so he wants to give us a chance to move around now. Tach in seventy minutes. He says." Davies' mouth twisted in disgust. "Unless he changes his mind again."

Morn sighed at the reminder of Angus' belligerence. It scared her more than she wanted to admit. "He won't if we don't give him an excuse. We can keep away from the bridge. Maybe he'll stay calm."

Davies snorted. Apparently the idea of simply trying to stay out of trouble didn't satisfy him. The muscles at the corners of his jaw bunched and released, chewing bitterness. His hand tightened on her black box. "What's wrong with him?" he protested abruptly. "What changed? He wasn't like this before we left forbidden space. Then I thought he was actually on our side. Now he acts like he's nursing some kind of grievance."

Morn bowed her head in the face of Davies' distress. How could she help him? She knew nothing about the aftereffects of force-growing and mind-transference; or of gestation and birth under the influence of a zone implant. And she could hardly function herself without artificial support. Angus was a subject she didn't want to examine. She was still in his power, even though he no longer held her zone implant control. Everything she did and said, everything she *was*, bore the taint of his brutality.

His and Nick's.

And yet Davies was her son.

Holding herself to the bunk, she shrugged. "You know as much about him as I do."

"I know more," he retorted harshly. "I spent time with him before he got you away from the Amnion. I know he doesn't care about me. Having a son doesn't mean shit to him." Morn shook her head slowly, but Davies didn't stop. "He only rescued me because Nick tricked him into thinking he could trade me for you.

"It's *you* he cares about." Davies' gaze burned as if he had a grievance of his own; as if he blamed her for the fact that his father didn't value him. "He wants you—but it's more than that. He wants to please you. That's why I believed he was on our side. He wants to do whatever you want him to do.

"Or he did. Now I can't tell what's going on."

His pain made her heart ache. Oh, Davies. My poor boy. You didn't ask for this. You don't deserve any of it.

Nevertheless she kept that kind of comfort to herself. He was too old for it. His body was at least sixteen. And his mind, his comprehension, was both older and younger than hers—aged by her sufferings as well as his own; yet immature in experience.

"That bothers you," she said carefully.

For a moment he forgot to hold himself down. The burst of vehemence which ran through him sent him tumbling for the ceiling. Fiercely he thrust himself back to his bunk, clung there.

"Morn, I'm alone here. I mean *here*." He hit his forehead with the heel of one palm. "Everything I remember tells me I'm you. I know that's not true, but my memories say it is. I need—

"I don't know how to put it." In anguish he broke out, "I need a *father*. Something to anchor myself on. An image to help me hold on to who I am.

"He could do that for me. He's a butcher and a rapist and worse—I know that, I can't get it out of my head—but at least I *look* like him. He's the only image strong enough to help me. But every time I try to concentrate on it, he does something that makes me want to hit him with a matter cannon.

"It's like he rapes me inside, violates—"

Davies stopped as if he were choking. Now his air of grievance was gone. He looked like a young kid, appallingly young, with nowhere to turn.

Morn wanted to weep. The thought that her son, *her son*, needed Angus—that he had hungers which only Angus could satisfy—seemed to be more than she could bear. Wasn't it bad enough that every part of her own being had been marred and stained by Angus' abuse? Did her son require his imprint as well?

Yet how could she protest? What right did she have? His dilemma was of her making. The responsibility was hers; absolutely; beyond appeal.

And Angus was her responsibility as well. Instead of abandoning him to the trap which Nick had set for him, she'd accepted her zone implant control from him and let him live. In the name of her own hungers, her naked and irreducible inadequacy, she'd spared him the death sentence which would have followed his conviction for unauthorized use of a zone implant.

She had no choice: she had to bear it. Davies needed some kind of answer from her.

"Try thinking about my father instead." Simply mentioning that Davies Hyland, whom she had loved and killed, lacerated her. Nevertheless she made the effort, even though it seemed to tear at her chest, filling her lungs with blood. "The man you're named for. You remember him as well as I do.

"If the cops are corrupt, that's Data Acquisition and Administration. Hashi Lebwohl and Warden Dios. Not Min Donner. ED is clean.

"But even if she's like them, my father wasn't. Angus told me—" Her throat closed on the words. She had to swallow a rush of grief before she could go on. "After I crashed *Starmaster*, there were still a few of us alive. My father was one of them. Angus says he was flash-blinded in the explosion. But even blind he didn't stop fighting for his ship. Didn't stop being a cop.

"When Angus boarded the wreck, my father tried to arrest him. Tried to commandeer his ship. Tried to bluff it through, even though he couldn't see—"

Her throat clenched shut again. Until the memory released her, she couldn't speak. Then she finished, "That's the best I can do. He's all I have." And Bryony Hyland, his wife, Morn's mother, who had loved and believed and fought with all her heart; who had died saving her ship and her shipmates from *Gutbuster*'s super-light proton cannon. "There isn't anything else."

But they were enough. For her, if not for her son: they were enough.

"Come on," she said quietly, fighting to recover her composure. "Let's get something to eat. We're going to need it."

At first Davies didn't react. He watched her with a tightness like Angus' anger around his mouth and a look of desolation in his eyes. And yet she guessed that he was helpless to contradict her. All the deepest parts of his mind insisted that he was her; that the captain of *Starmaster* had been his father.

Slowly he took a breath, let go of her with his gaze. Briefly he considered her zone implant control as if he'd learned to hate it. He would never have been born if she hadn't used it to win her contest with Nick. And she would never have gotten pregnant if Angus hadn't put a zone implant in her head.

Scowling like a wasteland, he opened his fingers with a small flick which floated the control toward her.

She caught it in her free hand and shoved it down into a pocket of her shipsuit without taking her eyes off him.

"You're right," he muttered distantly. "We need food."

He didn't look at her as he left his bunk, coasted to the door, and keyed it open. There, however, he stopped. Holding on to one of the handgrips by the door, he met her aching gaze.

"I don't blame you," he said quietly. "I remember too much. What happened to you. How you felt. Why you did what you did." He made an abortive attempt to laugh. "I would have done the same thing."

Pushing against the handgrip, he drifted backward out into the passage which ran through *Trumpet*'s core.

As she followed him, Morn had to fight down a different desire to weep. His understanding felt like forgiveness for crimes and failings which should have been unforgivable.

Like *Captain's Fancy*'s, *Trumpet*'s galley was hardly more than a niche in one wall of the central passage. However, its foodvends and dispensers as well as other furnishings were designed for use during weightlessness. The dispensers pumped coffee, soup, and other liquids into g-flasks; the foodvends primarily offered pressed foodbars and compact sandwiches which wouldn't break into crumbs and drift away. Stools bolted to the deck lined the one narrow table, and restraints could be attached to cleats on the sides of the stools and along the walls.

Several hours ago, during one of Angus' longer pauses between gap crossings, Davies had located a locker full of equipment like zero-g belts and clamps, and had appropriated a couple of belts for himself and Morn. When they'd prepared their meals, they were able to hook themselves to the stools and eat without bobbing away from the table whenever they moved their arms.

They ate in silence until Sib Mackern eased into the galley and asked if he could join them.

Morn gestured toward a stool. Davies mumbled, "Sure," around a mouthful of food.

Awkward with anxiety, Sib pushed himself around the niche until his meal was ready. Then he moved to a stool across the table from Davies and Morn. Like them, he'd found or been given a zero-g belt. When he'd clipped himself down, he frowned at his foodbars and g-flask as if he couldn't remember why he'd thought he was hungry.

With her head lowered, Morn studied him unobtrusively past the fringe of her hair. Aboard *Captain's Fancy* he'd let her out of her prison so that she could try to save Davies from the Amnion. Like Mikka and Vector in different ways, he'd risked betraying Nick for her sake; risked having his heart cut out— But the former data first didn't look like a man who took such chances. He seemed to give off an air of vague desperation. His pale features had an apologetic cast; his thin mustache might have been nothing more than grime on his upper lip. His determination to keep guard on Nick had left him drained and ragged.

She still wondered why he'd helped her. In one sense, all opposition to Nick struck her as reasonable, natural. But Sib had served aboard *Captain's Fancy* for some time; had presumably fallen under the spell of Nick's apparent infallibility. Why had he changed his allegiance? In her cabin, before he'd let her out, he'd said, *Since I joined him, we've done things that made me sick. They gave me nightmares and made me wake up screaming.* His revulsion came back to her as she remembered how he'd helped her. *But nothing like that. Nothing like selling a human being to the Amnion.*

I've **seen** *them, Morn. Those mutagens are evil.*

What had he seen?

Hoping that he would be willing to talk, she tried to start a conversation by asking, "Where is everybody?"

Sib didn't appear to feel any reluctance. His apprehension needed an outlet. "Nick's in his cabin. Sleeping, probably. Or maybe he just sits there grinning at the walls." Sib shuddered at the thought, but he made a palpable effort to keep himself calm. "There's nowhere he can go without passing the galley, so I decided I could afford to get something to eat."

For a moment he stopped as if Nick were the only question that mattered. When first Morn and then Davies looked up at him, however, he went on, "Vector's still working—he acts like he's forgotten that even engineers need food and sleep. Sometimes I forget how much his joints hurt when there's g. He seems to have a lot more energy when he's weightless.

"I guess Mikka and Ciro are in their cabin." The harmonics of strain sharpened in his tone. "I haven't seen them since Angus sent her off the bridge."

A frown pinched Davies' forehead. He swallowed a gulp from his g-flask, cleared his throat, and said abruptly, "We're looking for theories." He indicated Morn with a glance. "What do you think Angus' problem is?"

Sib shrugged with an air of helplessness. To all appearances he'd been out of his depth ever since Nick promoted him to be *Captain's Fancy*'s data first. Nevertheless he tried to answer.

"He and Nick are natural enemies. They hate each other. But the way they hate each other—" His voice trailed off into dismay. Then, however, he rallied. "They would rather be allies then take sides with anybody else."

Morn shook her head. Her impression of Angus was that his essential hatred was undifferentiated—at once so diffuse and so global that it made no real distinction between illegals and cops. It simply attached itself to anyone available. In any case, she couldn't imagine the circumstances under which Angus might forget—never mind forgive—the fact that Nick had framed him; beaten him.

Unfortunately there were other possibilities—

Why *was* Angus here, aboard a UMCP ship, surrounded by people he didn't like or need? And why had he accepted the idea of heading for a bootleg lab? Because he'd made some kind of deal with Hashi Lebwohl: so he said—or at least implied. To save his life, he'd agreed to carry out a covert attack on Billingate, and to rescue—Morn herself? Nick?—if he could.

Nick was an occasional DA operative: he'd worked for Lebwohl. Did Angus have further orders he hadn't mentioned, orders which required him to ally himself with Nick in order to carry out some additional part of his deal?

Without transition the galley seemed to become uncomfortably warm, as if the foodvends were overheating. Morn felt sweat trickling down her spine, running like lice across her ribs.

"We're in trouble." She was hardly aware that she spoke aloud. "We're in deep trouble."

Davies turned toward her, opened his mouth to ask her what she meant. Sib was caught up in his own fears, however; he thought Morn was sharing them with him.

"I know," he agreed. "But I don't think it matters what Angus is doing. *Nick* hasn't changed. He's still—" His throat worked convulsively. "He's still willing to sell any of us. As soon as he gets the chance."

Fighting nausea, she warned Davies to silence with a brusque gesture. Her memories were a black hole: they threatened to drag her down. She wanted to hear whatever Sib might say; wanted *anything* which might help her cling to the present.

"You told me once"—her voice throbbed with effort—"you've seen what the Amnion do. You called it 'evil.' "

Sib bobbed his head. "Yes." He tried to smile, but the attempt only made him look lost. "That's not a word you hear illegals use very often. But I know what I'm talking about."

He wanted to tell his story: that was plain. He couldn't face it without squirming, however, despite its importance to him. He spoke in awkward bursts and pauses, like a man who didn't know how to forget pain. Blinded by recollection, he stared through Morn as if he were alone with his past.

"I never really belonged on a ship like *Captain's Fancy*. You knew that—I'm sure you could see it as soon as you came aboard. Nick used to tell me I didn't have the guts for it, and he was right. But that's not the only reason I didn't belong.

"My family was merchanter. We had our own ship—this was about fifteen years ago"—Morn guessed that Sib may have been near Davies' age at the time—"and like practically everybody else who owned a ship, we were orehaulers. Actually we did most of our work where we're going now, in-system around Valdor Industrial, but we had a small gap drive, so we could pick our markets when we needed to. We weren't exactly getting rich, but we weren't doing badly, either."

Like Morn, he seemed to feel the galley getting warmer. Sweat formed slow beads on his temples and oozed down his cheeks.

"Our last run, we were hired to pick up a load of selenium and most of the miners from an operation on one of the moons of a planet that orbits Lesser Massif-5. The planet was about as far away from Valdor as it ever got, but its orbit was ready to carry it between the suns—which was like dropping it into a smelter. The mine had to be abandoned, at least for a year or two.

"We picked up the miners, no problem, and as much of the selenium as we could hold, and headed back around the suns for Valdor. But we had to swing wide to avoid a particularly violent asteroid swarm, so we ended up closer to the fringes of the system than we liked—we were too far away from the main shipping lanes and the UMCP patrols to be comfortable about it. But we'd done things like that before, when we had to. We didn't know any reason why this time should be different. Add a month or two to the trip, then we would be back in port."

Sweat gathered on his forehead. His eyebrows were dark with moisture. He wiped at it with the back of his hand, then clutched his fingers together in front of him.

"Of course, it *was* different. This time a blip that looked like just part of the swarm turned out to be illegal. Right when we stopped worrying about it, she came after us. They hit us with some kind of gun, I still don't know what it was, but it peeled us open like a storage container. We couldn't begin to defend ourselves, our own guns went out at the first hit. Then they grappled on and burned their way aboard.

"They took the selenium. You would expect that, under the circumstances. But they didn't kill any of us. I mean, not after the fighting was over. We thought we were going to be torched, or maybe just shoved out the airlock, but we weren't.

"I was hiding between the hulls, in an EVA suit. I've never been really brave, but for some reason when we were hit I had the crazy idea I might be able to reach one of the guns and get it working again, so I climbed into a suit and went outside. That's the only reason I'm still here. Still human—"

For a moment his voice trailed away. His hands seemed to writhe against each other as he forced himself to go on.

"We—my family—all those miners— We weren't killed. I'd never heard of illegals like that, I didn't know they existed. They weren't ordinary pirates, they were traitors, they worked directly for the Amnion." He seemed unconscious of the sweat trickling into his eyes. "Instead of killing us, they lined us up and started injecting us with mutagens."

Davies snarled deep in his throat—an involuntary growl of anger and protest. Morn put her hand on his arm to keep him still, but her eyes didn't leave Sib's face.

"I had a video link with the bridge," Sib said as if he were haunted by the memory; hunted by it. "I saw everything. If they were just being killed —my family—the others—I would have gone back inside and tried to fight for them. I might have. I was desperate enough. But I saw them injected. I saw them change. It paralyzed me. I started screaming—I couldn't help that—but I cut off my pickup first.

"My whole family and all those miners, the ones who weren't already dead— They were made into Amnion. Eventually they boarded the other ship and left me."

With an effort, he pulled his fingers apart, separated his hands. But then they seemed to have nowhere to go. Slowly they crept together, clung to each other again.

"I kept on screaming until I lost my voice. I thought as long as I could hear myself I wouldn't go insane." He swallowed like a spasm. "For some reason I was afraid I might be turned into an Amnioni just by watching it happen to my family. But of course that didn't happen.

"None of it had to happen." Blinking at a blur of sweat, he brought his gaze back into focus on Morn. There was no anger in his tone: he lacked her ability to hold a grudge; didn't have that defense against what had happened to him. "We'd been sending status reports to Valdor ever since we encountered the asteroid swarm. And as soon as we spotted that ship, we started yelling for help.

"We knew someone heard us because we got an answer. From the cops. UMCP cruiser *Vehemence*, Captain Nathan Alt commanding. She wasn't all that far away, maybe half a billion k.

"She told us she couldn't respond. She said she was on an impossible vector, g-stress would kill her if she tried to turn hard enough to reach us in time."

A clutch of loss lifted his shoulders like a shrug. "She never did reach us. I probably should have died—that would have been simpler—but just when I was starting to run out of air, I was found by an illegal that came to scavenge before the hulk was picked clean by an authorized salvage. That's how I became illegal myself. The cops didn't respond. And my whole family was gone. I didn't have any reason to do anything else.

"When I got the chance a few years later," he finished softly, "I joined Nick."

Morn nodded, a blaze in her eyes. For the moment she'd forgotten Angus and corruption; forgotten Nick. Instead she seemed to feel all the anger Sib needed for himself and couldn't find. The cops didn't respond. She might have become a pirate herself under those conditions.

How many illegals were like Sib?—like Vector? How many of them had been driven to violence by the inadequacy or malfeasance of the organization she'd tried to serve? How much of the piracy which threatened humankind's survival against the Amnion had the cops themselves caused?

When was it going to *stop*?

Then Davies interrupted her inward fuming. "Captain Nathan Alt," he muttered harshly. "I"—he glanced at her, caught himself—"you've heard of him."

He was right: the recollection came back to her as soon as he mentioned it. And it was important.

"I remember Captain Alt." Her voice shook until she controlled it. "By the time I went through the Academy, he'd become a legend. He was court-martialed because he didn't help a ship under attack in the Massif-5 system.

"The story we heard"—it was part of a seemingly endless series of lectures on the duties and responsibilities of being a cop—"is that Min Donner hit him with every charge she could think of. His datacore confirmed he couldn't have changed course hard enough to reach that ship in time—not without damaging *Vehemence* and maybe killing some of his own people. But Director Donner said he should have made the attempt anyway. Better yet, he should have anticipated the situation. He'd received that ship's status reports—he knew she was being pushed toward a part of the system where she might get into trouble."

Davies nodded once, hard, as if he shared the ED director's conviction.

"The court believed her," Morn finished. "He was stripped of his commission and drummed out of Enforcement Division."

Sib couldn't meet her gaze: his eyes slid off as if they'd lost their grip. Some necessary part of him had screamed itself away into the void while his relatives were injected with mutagens. And yet somewhere he'd found the courage to help her when she'd needed it most; the courage to risk his life against Nick—

"I'm sorry, Morn," he murmured toward his twisted hands. "That doesn't help. What good are cops, if they don't even try to do their jobs?"

"You've got it backward," Nick drawled from the passage outside the galley. "It's worse when they do try to do their jobs."

Sib flinched in surprise, jerked up his head. Together Morn and Davies turned on their stools, pulling against their zero-g belts to look at Nick.

He floated at the edge of the niche which contained the galley, holding himself stationary on a handgrip. Because he was weightless, he could move in complete silence. And Sib had been looking down. As a result, Nick had been able to come up behind Morn and Davies without being noticed.

She panicked as soon as she saw his face.

His eyes burned as if they were lit by madness; as if a magnesium flare of insanity had gone off inside his skull. A grin like a snarl stretched his mouth back from his teeth. His scars were sharp with blood, as distinct and dark as the work of claws.

"You've all got it backward." He sounded lethal and relaxed; master of himself as well as of them. "*This* is what happens when the cops try to do their jobs."

She knew him too well: she knew what his expression meant. Without thought, without taking so much as a second to wonder what in hell had gone wrong, she slapped at the cleats on her stool, unclipping her belt so that she could move; so that she could reach the zone implant control in her pocket.

Even then she wasn't fast enough. She'd suffered too much damage: her nerves and muscles were slow. Nick pivoted against his handgrip, bringing up his leg in an arc to kick at her head, and she could see that he wasn't going to miss. His boot came at her as if she were motionless; as if she were waiting for it.

But Davies was quicker. He had his father's reflexes; he'd been bred to adrenaline and urgency. And he also knew Nick too well; knew him with her memories, her pain. His fear was as swift as hers. Instinctively he flung his g-flask at Nick's face. With his other arm, he threw a block against Nick's leg.

Because he was anchored to his stool, he was able to stop the blow.

For the same reason, the impact slammed him onto the edge of the table. Morn thought she heard a snapping sound from his arm or his ribs. Even though Nick was weightless, his kick was charged with mass as well as inertia. And Davies' mass had nowhere to go.

The g-flask caught Nick's cheek and bounced away, leaving a round pale mark like a stain on his flushed skin. Momentarily out of control, he rebounded from Davies' block, tumbling for the far wall of the passage.

The instant her belt came free, Morn flipped forward, using the table to somersault her toward the foodvends; away from Nick.

Sib had frozen for a second. Panic had that effect on him; incomprehension had that effect. And for another second he made the mistake of scrabbling at the cleats to detach his belt.

Then he forgot about getting loose and wrenched his gun out of his pocket. His hand clenched on the firing stud before Nick could recover from Davies' block.

Before Davies could duck out of the way—

But Nick wasn't alone. Angus drifted in the passage beside him, his toes barely touching the deck, his face black with murder. Steadying himself on a handgrip, he caught Nick's recoil easily, steered Nick's momentum aside as if the movement were effortless.

In the same motion he raised his hand toward Sib.

Almost too quick to be seen, a thin streak of coherent light shot between his fingers. Before Sib could finish squeezing the firing stud, Angus' laser slagged a hole through the center of the handgun.

Yelping in pain and shock—hurt by the heat rather than the laser itself—Sib flung the useless gun away.

Oh, shit!

Laser fire? From his *hand*?

Morn couldn't understand what she'd just seen, and didn't try. Reacting in pure pain, she snagged a grip on the nearest dispenser, cocked her legs against the surface of a foodvend, and launched herself like a projectile at Angus.

For a splinter of time that seemed to sear her brain, even though it was too short to be measured, she stared straight into his eyes.

His whole face was black with blood, as if hundreds of blood vessels had ruptured at once, burst by the internal pressure of his heart. His eyes were as mad as Nick's; but they were insane with anguish, not glee; not triumph. Rictus stretched his mouth back from his teeth as if he were screaming; yet he made no sound. Nothing could get past the destructive pressure tearing through his chest.

The hand which had burned Sib's gun swung to meet her.

Again Davies was faster than she was. In that instant he came back off the edge of the table. Still secured to his stool, and hampered by damage, he nevertheless managed to hack his fist against Angus' arm.

Too fast for Davies to defend himself—too fast for Morn to see how he did it—Angus recoiled into a blow which struck the side of Davies' head with a crushing sound, like rock being pulverized. Davies slammed onto the edge of the table again.

This time he didn't get up.

The blow swung Angus out of the way of Morn's attack.

Out in the passage, Nick had recovered control. Now he seemed to pour at the galley like a breaking wave, ready to hammer down on Morn's head.

Instead of trying to hit Angus, she caught her fingers in the back of his shipsuit and used his bulk to pull her into another somersault. With every gram of strength and momentum she could focus, she drove her bootheels into Nick's face.

The impact knocked him nearly cartwheeling down the passage.

At the same time it shoved her hard against Angus' back.

Fighting for her life, she made a desperate effort to heave herself off him.

Easily, as if she'd used up her capacity to affect him, he caught her wrist in a grip as hard as a C-clamp.

Too late, much too late, Sib cried out, "*Morn!*" and grappled with the attachments of his belt.

A heartbeat later Mikka arrived.

She must have heard the sounds of trouble outside her cabin and come as fast as she could. Hurling herself along, she delivered a punch at Nick as he plunged past her; but she didn't pause to follow it. She was already committed to helping Morn.

Her brother floated behind her, directly in Nick's path. As Nick careened toward him, he raised his stun-prod.

Heavy with muscle, Mikka drove into Angus' arm.

Morn slipped free as if he'd thrown her away.

Spinning wildly, barely able to keep her head from colliding with the bulkheads, she dashed for the bridge like a feather in a torrent.

Somewhere behind her, she heard a cry that might have been pain; might have come from Ciro. She heard a harsh grunt of effort; heard blows as loud as shots. But she didn't stop. Driven by fury and terror, she shoved and heaved and rolled forward as fast as she could go. In panic she thought she could feel Angus' fingers clutching for her, grabbing at her. Thrashing her arms and legs so that she would be hard to catch, she flung herself along the passage until she reached the companionway.

There she could stop her mad tumble on the handrails; steady herself. Still she didn't pause or look back. From the support of the rails, she pitched into another flip which carried her over the empty bridge stations almost headlong into the bulkhead near the auxiliary engineering console.

Vector looked up in shock. "Morn—?" Surprise seemed to take him by the throat, choking him. He'd been concentrating too hard to hear anything. "What—?"

She locked her fingers into a handgrip, pulled herself off the bulkhead, swung down beside him.

His blue eyes were stunned with fatigue and incomprehension; unable to speak, he stared at her as if she were starting to mutate in front of him.

She had no idea what had gone wrong, but she knew what it meant. Angus and Nick had joined forces. And Angus could do things she'd never suspected—

"*Self-destruct!*" she cried urgently; blazed at Vector like a gun. "Blow us up! Do it *now,* while you still can!"

"Morn?" He gaped at her; hardly seemed to recognize her. "Morn?"

"God *damn* it!" He was too slow. "Let me at that board!"

Frantically she shoved him aside so that she could take his place in front of the console.

Self-destruct. Now or never. She would never get another chance. At any second Angus might shoot her in the back with his impossible laser. Davies was already lost, and she didn't believe that Mikka and Sib could beat him. There was no other way to stop him.

And yet the bare idea brought up agony from the core of her heart, filled her head with screams she didn't know how to utter.

Self-destruct.

How many times did she have to face the same horror before she finally succeeded at killing herself?

"You can't!" Angus barked from the head of the companionway. "You can't access those functions. I've locked everything except Vector's research."

As soon as he spoke, she knew he was telling the truth. Despite his exertions, he wasn't out of breath; didn't seem to be in a hurry. He wasn't afraid of anything she could do.

"Give it up," he told her. "Don't make me hurt you."

She wanted to howl and weep, beat her fists bloody on the edges of the console. He was telling the truth: she couldn't stop him this way. Nevertheless she had no time for frustration; couldn't afford to give vent to her agony and despair. She needed them herself.

Still clinging to her handgrip, she turned to face the man who had raped and brutalized and now betrayed her.

Angus hadn't left the head of the companionway. He seemed to think that he'd already won; that he didn't need to approach her in order to master her. Yet his face showed no triumph—and certainly no satisfaction. He was sweating so hard that his skin resembled molten wax, and his teeth ground against each other as if he were chewing pain. The congested anguish in his eyes made him look like a man who knew what being raped meant.

"Christ!" Vector breathed softly. "What went wrong? What happened?"

Angus didn't answer the engineer. His attention was focused exclusively on Morn. He might have been trying to think of a way to plead with her.

There was no pleading in his tone, however. Harshly he said, "Nick gave Ciro so much stun he's puking his guts out. Mikka and Davies are unconscious. And Sib looks like he's having some kind of seizure."

Looming out of the passage, Nick drifted to Angus' side. With one hand he caught the companionway railing to stop himself; in the other he held up the small stun-prod which Milos Taverner had left aboard *Trumpet*. The spot on his cheek where Davies'd struck him had turned a bright, mortal red, contrasting strangely with the darkness of his scars.

"Not anymore," he announced, nearly chortling. "He's puking, too. The air's full of it back there. When they recover, they're going to have fun cleaning it all up."

A sound that might have been a laugh or a snarl burst between his teeth.

"Nobody's left to help you," Angus told Morn. "Give up before I have to do something worse."

Vector shifted his position as if he wanted to protest, then thought better of it.

"No," Morn panted. Now that she was motionless, she found that she could scarcely breathe. Strain and fear cramped her lungs; she was only able to force out a few words at a time. "I won't. Put up. With any more of this.

"I would rather be dead."

Her free hand slid into her pocket and brought out her zone implant control. Wrapping her fingers over all the buttons, she put the black box behind her and held it there; shielded it with her body so that Angus couldn't fire his laser at it without killing her first.

"Morn," Vector whispered in horror. "Don't— I'll help you somehow. They need me—they want my research. I'll stop working if they hurt you."

She ignored him.

So did Nick and Angus. Instead Nick tensed, flashed a glare at Angus. "Why didn't you take that thing away from her? I told you to grab it."

Angus didn't bother to answer. Sweat dripped away from his eyes like tears. His face was livid with stress, as if he were strangling on his own tongue.

"Well, *stop* her," Nick rasped. Without transition his mad glee had become fury. "That's an order. I want her alive. After what she's done to me, I *want* her alive."

Angus might have moved to obey. The distress in his gaze seemed to imply that he took orders from Nick, even though he hated them. But Morn didn't wait to find out.

"You aren't listening," she retorted. "I haven't got anything left. So there's nothing you can do to stop me. If you come"—somewhere she found the strength to shout—"*one step* closer, I'm going to clench my fist. I'll burn out my brain before you get anywhere *near me*!"

"No!" Vector croaked desperately.

Morn glimpsed his movement out of the corner of her eye, but the warning came too late. Anchoring his weightlessness against the auxiliary engineering console, he hacked her across the side of her neck with the blade of his hand, then grappled frantically for her zone implant control.

Ripped it out of her grasp.

And turned.

Launching his mass from the platform of the console, he slammed her black box against the bulkhead; drove it onto the hard surface with the heel of his palm.

Blood splashed from the impact as the box shattered into half a dozen sharp fragments, shredding the skin of his hand. Squirming red globules stained the bulkhead, swam through the air in all directions. The jolt seemed to shoot pain through his arthritic joints.

He hadn't hit Morn hard enough to stun her. Even though she was already lost, already doomed, she recovered in time to see his blue eyes glaze over as if he were about to faint. Beads of his blood struck her face like little wounds.

The sight of his mangled hand and the shattered box made hysteria bubble and froth inside her: as extreme as lava; as corrosive as acid.

Vector must have thought he was saving her life—repaying his debt to her by freeing her from external coercion. Nick couldn't replace her black box. He didn't know its transmission frequencies, its hardwired codes.

But Angus did. He could make another zone implant control for her whenever he wanted.

DAVIES

Muzzy-headed with pain and cold fury, Davies hissed an obscenity when Mikka pulled him up from the edge of the table. It wouldn't have been so bad if he'd been able to float weightless, but he was still belted to the galley stool. Mikka's effort to raise him set the bones of his upper arm grinding against each other like the teeth of a saw; sent long knives of hurt probing between his ribs.

A spasm raked his face like claws. Locking his teeth together so that the pain wouldn't surge up from his chest and choke him, he snarled again, "Shit!"

Mikka released him slowly, letting him do what he could to hold himself. From what seemed like a great distance, she asked, "How bad is it?"

He closed his eyes to help him concentrate. Through the dark he tried to measure the severity of the damage. Then he muttered, "Sonofabitch broke my arm. And some ribs." As he spoke, he identified another hurt. "Feels like he split my skull."

"You're not alone," she retorted harshly. "Unfortunately I can't help you. We've been ordered to the bridge."

Ordered. To the bridge. Davies tried to make sense of the words and found he couldn't. He was distracted: pain and a hot, primal desire to strike at least one killing blow interrupted his attention. And the smell—

Vomit.

The reek seemed so close to his face that he thought he might have done it himself.

When he opened his eyes again, his vision labored in and out of focus as if it couldn't support the pressure of his heartbeat. After a moment, however, he succeeded at clearing his sight.

Across from him, Sib Mackern sprawled facedown on the table. His posture looked unnatural for zero-g: ordinary muscular contraction would have caused him to float against the attachment of his belt. Apparently he was stuck in a puddle of his own puke. Viscid bile and lumps of food smeared his face and the tabletop: fine, rank beads seemed to orbit above him like constellations.

He was breathing, but he wasn't conscious.

In the galley and the passage, the scrubbers strained to clean gouts and streamers of drifting vomit from the air, but they hadn't succeeded yet. The pads would have to be replaced soon, or *Trumpet*'s air would start to go bad.

"What happened—?" Davies' voice caught as the stink and his own pain made him gag. "What happened to him?"

"Stun," Mikka retorted shortly. "Nick took that prod away from Ciro. If it were any bigger—if it delivered more charge—he would be dead. Ciro, too.

"Can you move? If you get out of my way, I'll pick him up."

Davies wanted to snort, Move? Sure. I can probably get as far as sickbay. If you and God help me. But he didn't have the strength for it. And she didn't deserve his bitterness—

Where had she been when Nick and then Angus attacked Morn?

Where were they now?

What the hell was going on?

Gritting his teeth despite the pain in his head, Davies struggled to bring the rest of his mind into focus.

"You said—" He tried to remember what Mikka had said. "We've been ordered to the bridge." He swallowed a lump of anger. "Says who?"

"Says Nick." She had too much bitterness of her own: she wouldn't have noticed Davies'. "He's taken over. Apparently Angus has secrets he hasn't bothered to explain. Like why he suddenly lets Nick give him orders. Or how he did that." With his peripheral vision, Davies saw her point at the slagged handgun bobbing above the foodvends.

"Or," she finished, "how he got to be so strong."

Snagged by the timbre of despair in her tone, Davies turned against his pain until he could look at her.

The sight made him flinch and cough as if he'd driven a rib into one of his lungs.

She'd been hit, all right—hit *hard*. Glints of bone showed through the pulp above her right eye. That eye had already swollen shut, but the wound hadn't stopped bleeding yet. Seeping from the red-black mess of her forehead, a wet sheen covered the whole right side of her face. Her skull must have been a mass of fractures.

She needed sickbay more than he did. She had a concussion: in all likelihood she was already on her way into shock. And there must have been bleeding inside the bone. If she developed a cerebral hematoma, she could die.

"Fuck the bridge," he told her. Coughing hurt, but he could bear it. It wasn't as bad as the danger she was in. "You need treatment. Go to sickbay. I'll get myself there in a minute."

And Sib, too. He might have swallowed some of his vomit; might be dying—

She shook her head. "You don't understand." She sounded bleak and beaten, lost in a void of dismay. "Nick ordered us to the bridge. Right now. No matter what condition we're in." In a tight voice, as if she could hardly force up words, she explained, "He's got Morn."

Davies flung a look like a cry at her.

She replied with a small shrug. "We're finished. Even Vector is hurt. She's the only one of us who isn't either bleeding or unconscious"—Davies could see her brother in Mikka's eyes, somewhere beyond help—"and I think she's gone into hysterics."

"Then she needs me." A rush of serotonin and noradrenaline cleared his brain; he didn't hesitate. *He's got Morn.* His right arm was useless. Shifting so that he could reach the cleats with his left, he unclipped his belt from the stool. *I think she's gone into hysterics.*

Almost at once weightlessness seemed to ease the pain in his arm. With his ribs twisting against each other, he kicked his way out of the galley and headed for the bridge.

Despite the pressure inside him, he moved carefully, protecting his injuries. Zero-g grips along the walls helped him control his drift until he reached the companionway. There he caught one of the handrails and paused to scan the bridge.

Nick sat at the command station, grinning like a skull; he flashed his teeth and his dark scars at Davies as if they were pennons. Angus had taken the second's g-seat: he sat motionless, all his muscles locked down; he didn't turn his head to glance at his son. Belted to the stool in front of the auxiliary engineering console, Vector hunched forward as if he were in danger of fainting. He'd opened his shipsuit and pulled it off his shoulders so that he could wrap his right hand in one of the sleeves. Blood soaked the fabric. Pale in the flat white light of the bridge, his bare skin looked flaccid, almost lifeless.

None of them seemed to feel the slightest interest in helping Morn.

She floated near the ceiling, bobbing gently against the metal, with her face hidden between her knees, and her arms clamped around her shins. The strain with which she clung to herself was palpable. She'd made herself small because she had no other protection: all her defenses and hopes were gone.

For a moment Davies couldn't move. He could only stare up at her, dismay throbbing through him, while he thought, as distinct as a jolt of stun, That's not hysterics. That's insanity. She's snapped.

Nick must have taken her zone implant control. Feeling his power over her again must have been more than she could bear.

It was more than Davies could bear. Forgetting his broken arm and snapped ribs, his cracked head, he dove off from the companionway; aimed himself with all his strength at Nick.

Angus stopped him.

Davies didn't see how it happened. Angus must not have been belted down; must have turned his head in time to spot Davies' movement. Before Davies reached Nick, Angus collided with him, knocked him off course.

For an instant his brain went blank at the impact on his arm and ribs. Red flushed across his vision. By the time his sight cleared, Angus was behind him, holding him with one forearm like a steel bar across his throat.

"Stop it!" Angus grated in his ear. "You've lost—there's nothing you can do. Don't make me hurt you again."

"He's my bodyguard," Nick remarked to Davies. "Nobody comes at me until they get past him. Offhand I would say he's pretty damn good at his job."

Angus and Davies hit the bulkhead, rebounded toward the display screens. One more impact made no difference to Davies: he could hardly feel it. But it shifted Angus' position behind him.

A good squeeze would be enough to crush Davies' windpipe. Anybody could have done it: it didn't require Angus' strange strength. Davies was already choking. His broken bones cut inside him like knives. Nevertheless he focused his whole life in the blow as he slammed his left elbow into Angus' belly.

Angus absorbed it with a low grunt; his grip on Davies' throat held tight. Perfectly in control, he snagged the toe of one boot on the back of Nick's g-seat, slowing his momentum and turning himself in the air so that he struck the screen softly, cushioned Davies' body with his own.

"*Stop* it," he repeated. "At least find out what's going on before you give Nick an excuse to kill you." Then, as if he knew what Davies needed to hear, he hissed, "Vector broke her zone implant control. That's how he tore up his hand."

Davies discovered that he wasn't breathing. Broke—? As he and Angus recoiled slowly from the screen, he looked at Vector.

Vector met his gaze and nodded.

Broke her zone implant control.

Davies went limp as the worst of his fears drained away.

Until he remembered that Angus knew how to program a parallel control into his board.

"I wish you hadn't told him that," Nick drawled laconically. "I like seeing him upset. It would have been fun to let him go on thinking I could force her to tear his balls off for me."

"Then make your fucking orders more fucking explicit!" Angus shot back. He sounded enraged; almost frantic. Davies could feel his muscles shivering with hindered violence. "If you don't *tell* me to do it, it won't *get done*!"

Nick grinned at Angus' anger. "That's OK," he retorted. "I like seeing *you* upset, too."

Davies seemed to feel tremors run through Angus; neurons misfiring like a suppressed storm. He didn't care, however. He looked at Morn, waiting for Angus to let him go. He still couldn't see her face: she was clamped too tightly around herself. But he could take her in his good arm, hug her against him: she might be able to feel that. If he spoke to her, she might hear—

"Stay away from her," Nick told him sharply. "Looks like she's gone autistic on us, doesn't it. Well, let her. I don't want you to make the mistake of thinking you can comfort her. It won't save her."

Davies couldn't stifle his rage, even for Morn's sake. "You bastard! She needs help!"

"Help?" Nick snorted at once. "You're an optimist, you know that, you little shit? In case you haven't figured it out, we've got an addict on our hands. She didn't crack like that because *I* got her fucking control. She cracked because Vector broke it, and she can't live without it.

"Well, now she's in *real* trouble. When we reach Massif-5, we'll have to be ready for hard g all the way to the Lab. That means she has to be ready for gap-sickness. If she isn't catted out of her mind, she'll spend the whole trip trying to kill all of us. You couldn't help her if I wanted you to.

"Which I don't. I'm going to make her pay *blood* for every lie she ever told me. This is just the beginning.

"If you go anywhere near her, Angus will break your other arm for you. You got that?"

Davies swallowed curses; swallowed bile and blood and pain. Nick was right, of course. Morn's gap-sickness would make Valdor's system a personal hell. Without her zone implant she had no defense except drugs against a madness which her son could remember as if it were his.

Aboard *Bright Beauty* she'd told Angus about it.

I could see you on the screens. But I didn't care. The whole inside of my head was different.

I was floating, and everything was clear. Like a vision. It was like the universe spoke to me. I got the message, the truth. I knew exactly what to do. What I had to do. I didn't question it.

Then she'd keyed the self-destruct sequence into her board on *Starmaster*'s auxiliary bridge.

From that crisis—from the undetectable flaw which the gap had found in her brain, a weakness triggered by heavy g—all her sufferings had followed as if they were inevitable.

Nevertheless Davies felt a keen frisson of hope as soon as he heard Nick mention cat.

Nick thought she needed drugs. He didn't know it was possible to rig a parallel zone implant control to replace her black box. He hadn't discovered that fact for himself.

And Angus hadn't told him.

In surprise Davies wrenched his head to the side so that he could stare at his father.

Angus confronted Nick as if he were waiting for new orders. Still Davies could see his face—

Davies hadn't looked when Angus had attacked him in the galley; hadn't had a chance. Now for the first time he saw the black anguish which congested Angus' face, the yellow murder in his eyes. Despite the steadiness of his movements, the poise of his posture, he appeared frantic and homicidal, as if he were crazier than Morn; as if he'd already been driven completely and irremediably insane.

He took orders from Nick. But he hated them.

Davies understood none of it. Nevertheless his heart leaped. Nick didn't know it was possible to program a parallel zone implant control, so he couldn't order Angus to do it for him.

If you don't tell *me to do it, it won't* get done*!*

Morn, did you hear that? Do you know what it means?

Giddy with relief, Davies nodded to Nick. "All right," he croaked. "I don't want to make it worse for her."

Nick studied him for a moment, then shrugged at Angus.

With a twitch like a spasm of revulsion, Angus let his son go.

At once Davies kicked away toward Vector and the auxiliary engineering console. While Angus returned to the second's station, Davies anchored himself by bracing one knee under the console so that he could keep his good arm free. Glowering to conceal his relief, he massaged his aching throat.

When Vector glanced at him, he nodded once, thanking the engineer for several things simultaneously.

Morn floated above him in a clenched, fetal ball, as unreachable as if she were on the other side of the dimensional gap. He left her there for the same reason that she'd once let Nick give him back to the Amnion: because he had no choice. And because he didn't want to risk betraying his hope.

"You're obviously in command," he rasped to Nick. "If Angus takes your orders, the rest of us can't fight you."

Nick grinned or grimaced as if his scars were on fire. "That's fucking right."

"But you don't need me here," Davies went on stubbornly. "I should be in sickbay. It won't cost you anything to let me go."

"Tough shit," Nick snapped back. "I don't care how much any of you hurt. In fact, I *want* you to hurt. It's a small price to pay for what you've done to me. So you're going to stay here and"—he broke into a shout—"*pay it* until I'm done with you!"

Angus swallowed as if he were having trouble breathing.

Almost immediately, however, Nick relaxed again. "Who knows? You may find it interesting.

"Where the fuck is everybody else?"

"We're here," Mikka said from the head of the companionway.

Her voice sounded painfully thin, as if she were close to collapse. As she bled, the damage to her forehead looked worse. Yet she managed to support both Sib and Ciro, one on each side of her. They were conscious, pallid with strain; but they couldn't control their bodies well. Small jerks and twitches shook them as if their nerves were still under attack.

"We're following orders," she murmured defensively. "It's hard for people to move after they've had that much stun."

"Really?" Nick sneered. "I had no idea." Then he added, "Get down here before I ask Angus to do a little surgery on your internal organs."

Like a kid about to cry, Ciro buried his face in Mikka's shoulder. Sib may have wanted to do the same, but he fought the impulse. Instead he flopped an arm onto the railing and used it to help Mikka propel the three of them to a handgrip across the bridge from the auxiliary engineering console.

Slowly they settled to the deck. Still twitching, Sib separated himself from Mikka to find another grip, leaving her to hold her brother alone.

"Good." Nick relaxed in his g-seat, at home and unassailable at the command station. "Now we can get started."

Deliberately Mikka turned away from him. Across the length of the screens, she asked Vector, "What happened to you?"

"He broke Morn's zone implant control," Angus put in before Vector could reply; before Nick could stop him. "Smashed it—cut up his hand. He—"

"Angus, shut up," Nick snarled quickly. "Don't say anything. If I want you to talk, I'll ask you a question."

At once Angus' jaws locked together as if they'd been wired closed. Murderous and thwarted, his eyes ached like wounds.

"God, Vector," Mikka breathed. She made no effort to conceal her relief. "You're a genius. I should have thought of that myself."

Vector gave her a crooked gray smile like a line drawn in a sheet of ash.

Grinning again, Nick drawled, "No, Mikka. You've got it wrong as usual. You should stop talking and listen. I'm about to explain the facts of life to you mindless, mutinous shits, and this is your only chance to understand them."

"Fine," Mikka shot back at him. "You do that." She might have been taunting him, trying to provoke him into an attack. Despite her bleeding face and her weakness, she held his gaze. "Let's see if the 'facts' make you look as good as you think."

For a moment Nick tightened as if he meant to spring at her. But then he eased back against the cushions. His eyes glittered with ominous restraint.

"Angus, if she says another word—any word at all—I want you to use that little laser of yours on her. Cut off one of her fingers. If she screams or swears or even groans, cut off another finger. Cut them off one at a time until she learns how to keep her mouth shut."

Ciro wrenched his head away from Mikka's shoulder, turned his face toward Nick. His eyes were aghast; white with horror.

Involuntarily Sib hunched over his stomach, trying to vomit again; but he had nothing left to bring up.

Overhead Morn floated motionless, lost in fear and desolation.

"Don't push him, Mikka," Davies warned urgently. "He means it. And Angus will do it."

We need you. Morn and I need you.

And we need to hear what Nick's going to say.

Mikka bit down on a retort. She could see Angus' face as well as Davies could: she could see that he would do exactly what Nick ordered. With an effort she closed her eyes, let her shoulders sag; took a deep breath and released it softly.

When she opened her eyes again, she didn't speak.

"Shit," Nick said to her. "I don't know what's the matter with you morons. Don't you ever *learn* anything? Davies came in here with a broken arm. Your skull is in splinters. And you both still think you can mess with me.

"Well, I've got news for you. Your *messing* days are over." He snapped the words between his teeth. "I don't need you. Angus is *mine*—that's what counts. Vector I'm going to keep. He can be useful. But the rest of you— You can all go disembowel yourselves, and it won't make any difference to me. The only reason I haven't killed you already is because I might be able to think of something better."

Davies ignored the threat. He knew it was real, but it changed nothing. And he ignored Morn as well, although she pulled at his heart: she had to wait. With his good arm, he hugged his ribs and waited for Nick's explanation.

"In the meantime," Nick went on sardonically, "I'm going to tell you a little story. I want you to understand what's going on here, so you'll *know* I don't need you.

"Remember Com-Mine?" He settled himself in his g-seat. His familiar, dangerous poise made him seem comfortable, completely at ease. Nevertheless his tone betrayed a raw edge of bitterness and anger. "Remember framing Angus? Milos and I did that, but it wasn't our idea. We had orders from Hashi Lebwohl. From Data fucking Acquisition. They wanted to get their hands on the infamous Captain Thermo-pile."

Angus didn't react. Clotted with distress, his eyes showed nothing except malice.

"After we left Station, they reqqed him from Com-Mine Security, and Milos with him. Took them both to UMCPHQ. Then they did a little surgery on him—what the poor old Bill would have called 'bio-enhancement.' Made him into a cyborg. He has needle lasers installed in his hands, UV prostheses built into his eyes. He can emit jamming fields"—Nick glanced at Davies—"which explains how he managed to get you past all those bugeyes and guards. He has the strength of a fucking ape.

"But here's the important part. His skull is full of zone implants. You feel sorry for Morn because she has one. He must have at least six. And they're all run by a computer. Every neuron in his ugly skull is run by a computer. He has a datacore somewhere that tells him what to do, tells him everything. The fucking bastard can't take a piss without Hashi's permission.

"Look at him." Nick flicked a gesture at Angus. "You can see I'm telling the truth."

Davies looked; but he already knew. Nick's revelation fit. And he could see the truth in the congealed blackness of Angus' expression, the pressure of dark blood straining against the skin. Angus might have been a fanatic, a kaze; a madman who could set himself off at any moment, blasting the people around him to pulp. And yet the sheer lost extremity in his eyes showed that he had no choice.

"He wants to butcher me." Nick made a determined effort to sound casual, but his anger still scraped and sawed in his voice. "If hate could kill, there wouldn't be anything left of me but grease. But he can't do it. His computer controls him.

"Angus," he rasped abruptly, "say, 'Yes, master.'"

Past the helpless clench of his jaws, Angus pronounced, "Yes, master."

Sib gaped as if he couldn't imagine the kind of programming which would make Angus do that. Ciro turned a face full of questions at Mikka, then grabbed her arm to remind her not to speak.

God! Davies groaned past the pain in his head and arm and chest. Is it that bad? His father was ruled by Nick; absolutely under Nick's control. Nothing Angus had ever done to Morn was worse than that.

Nick nodded in brutal satisfaction. His scars were as dark as Angus' face.

"So why did DA do all this?" he demanded rhetorically. "You know why. To blow up Billingate. And rescue Morn. Who else could they send? Who could get in? They needed an illegal so slimy he wouldn't be questioned.

"But that's not all they needed. They also had to give him cover—a believable explanation for how he managed to get away from UMCPHQ in a UMCP ship. And they had to be sure they could keep their grip on him. No matter how good they are, they couldn't write an instruction-set for every contingency.

"So they needed Milos. To cover him. And keep him under control. They gave Milos priority-codes that would force Angus to do what they wanted."

Fighting dismay, Davies concentrated for his life on every word Nick said.

Nick's voice trailed away briefly. As if he were talking to himself, he murmured, "I thought Milos was going to help me. I thought that was why Hashi sent him."

Davies imagined he could see *Captain's Fancy* in Nick's eyes.

Almost at once, however, Nick came back to his explanation. "Lucky for us, they had a pretty accurate idea how far they could trust Milos." His bitterness sharpened as he spoke. Words seemed to grate against each other in his mouth. "Hashi expected problems. When Milos went over to the Amnion, his priority-codes were automatically replaced.

"Are you with me so far?" He didn't appear to be aware that he'd raised his voice. "Angus does his job on Thanatos Minor. He rescues Morn —and us with her only because he needed us to break her out. We get away. But now what? Everything he does, even everything he says, is being run by instruction-sets that are more obsolete by the hour. As far as Hashi and DA are concerned, he might be dangerous. He can't escape his programming—but it's conceivable his programming could fail. If something unforeseen creates a logic loop, he might go into a cyborg's version of meltdown. Or he might get loose.

"DA can't risk pulling him in until they're sure he's safe."

Nick paused, looked around the bridge. "In other words"—he made an unsuccessful attempt to sound triumphant—"they need a replacement for Milos."

Of course they did.

"Don't say it," Vector put in unexpectedly. His pain-dulled eyes met

Nick's glare. Although his voice was as pale as his face, it hinted at firmness; a refusal to be cowed. "We can see it coming.

"DA chose you."

Morn remained locked in herself, as small and hard and lost as she could be.

An involuntary snarl twisted Nick's mouth. "As it happens, there's a ship after us. UMCP cruiser *Punisher*. She's pretty far back—but about an hour ago, right before we went into tach, she managed to catch us with a transmission." He showed his teeth. "The cops have given me Angus' new priority-codes.

"If you saw that coming, you know what comes next. Now *I* run him. He's *mine*. And he can't disobey or ignore or even threaten me because his programming won't *let* him.

"Are you *listening*?" Nick flared around the bridge. "Do you get the message? I've already ordered him to protect me. You bastards may think you can team up against me, but you're dreaming. You can't touch me unless you get past a cyborg with machine reflexes and lasers first.

"And I'm not quite helpless myself." He waved Milos' small stun-prod, then used it to slap at the command console. "I have his codes for the ship. *She's* mine, too."

He couldn't sit still any longer; couldn't sustain his relaxed pose. He'd been too badly beaten: no amount of power could turn him back into the man who never lost. Driven by his bereavements, he made short, punching gestures with his fists as he spoke, as if he were fighting an invisible enemy. His voice sounded shrill and bloody, like the cut of a drill through bone.

"I'm sure Hashi Lebwohl in his infinite wisdom thinks he can reason with me. Or outmaneuver me. Or at least bargain with me. So that I'll do what he wants. And maybe he's right. I won't know until I hear what he has to offer.

"But if he thinks he can persuade or trick or pay me to give up what I've got now, he's out of his goddamn contorted mind. I've got a ship with enough firepower to take on a battlewagon. I've got a second who can do tricks nobody's ever heard of before—and who can't argue with me. Once Vector does his job at the Lab, I'll have something I can sell for enough credit to buy my own station." His whole face seemed to concentrate around his scars. "Then I'm going to start teaching you and a few other people what real revenge is all about."

Darkly Davies muttered, "If you don't go crazy and get yourself killed first."

Nick swung his station hard, brought his anger directly to bear on Davies. "*You* I'll probably keep alive. You'll make good bait." Then he raised his head so that he could rage more easily. "But the rest of you better start trying to think of ways to convince me I need you. You better figure out some way to make me forgive you.

"And that goes for *her*, too." He stabbed the stun-prod in Morn's direction. "I want her *compliant*, you got that? No more of her fucking self-righteousness, no more lies, no more resistance. Otherwise I'll blow the whole shit-faced lot of you out the airlock and never look back."

Sib released his handgrip, let himself float in the air beside the screens. Nick's demand for Morn seemed to be more than he could bear. He was as pale as Vector, but his twitching had stopped. The nausea in his eyes wasn't physical.

He'd assigned himself the job of guarding Nick. And he'd failed.

"Do it now," he said softly. "What are you waiting for?"

Nick turned again until he faced Sib, Ciro, and Mikka. Instead of shouting, however, he spoke almost casually; almost as if he'd recovered his self-possession.

"Right now I don't have time. We're too near our insertion window for Massif-5. And after that I'll be even busier. Until we get to the Lab.

"Besides," he added in a fatal drawl, "I want to watch you suffer. I want to see you sweat yourself dry trying to come up with some way to persuade me I shouldn't make you go EVA without a suit."

Davies couldn't keep quiet. He had to *do* something—had to get off the bridge, away from Nick, so that he could try to reach Morn. She needed him, and he'd given her nothing.

Everyone needed him. Sib's shame had pushed him as far as he could go. Mikka knew Nick too well to ignore his threats. Ciro was plainly out of his depth, appalled by what was left of a man he'd once idolized—and maybe also by how easily he'd been bested. And Vector looked too weak to move, much less make decisions.

"In that case," Davies put in stiffly, "how much time *is* there? Vector can't do lab work with that hand. Mikka can't survive heavy g without treatment. I might not be able to stand it myself. And if you want Morn 'compliant' "—that word hurt like a violation, but he used it in an effort to sway Nick—"you'd better let me take her to sickbay. Cat might bring her back, but I can't measure the right dose myself."

Nick started to say something that may have been, I don't care. But then he thought better of it. "All right." His eyes were full of schemes—

schemes which apparently left *Trumpet* and his immediate victims far behind. He glanced at his readouts. "You have twenty minutes. If you aren't strapped down by then, you can kiss yourselves good-bye.

"But"—he cocked a fist in warning—"don't think you can use anything in sickbay against me. I can monitor you from here. I'll know it if you try to arrange any surprises. And you aren't going to like what happens if Angus has to defend me again."

Davies didn't waste time on a retort. Twenty minutes. He was in a hurry. Releasing his anchor on the auxiliary engineering console, he pushed off from the deck; floated up over the bridge stations toward Morn.

Mikka nudged Ciro to follow. Sib and Vector were already moving.

As he passed overhead, Davies caught one more glimpse of the stark excruciation in Angus' eyes.

His father needed him, too.

DAVIES

Needed him—and would kill him if he did anything to help.

No. Davies couldn't afford to think about that. First things first. Twenty minutes until *Trumpet* went into tach. Twenty minutes to treat Mikka's injuries, and Vector's, and his own. Twenty minutes to try to reach Morn somewhere inside the protective ball of her body.

As carefully as he could, he wrapped his good arm around her and moved her in the direction of the companionway.

He couldn't control his movements, however—not with one arm broken and Morn hugged in the other. Awkwardly he tried to stop at the head of the companionway by hooking his leg on the nearest handrail, but his inertia pulled him over the rail toward an impact with the treads. He was useless like this, *useless*, couldn't even navigate zero g, when he hit it was going to hurt—

Sib Mackern crowded up the companionway behind him. At the last moment Sib managed to tuck a shoulder between Davies and the hard steps. Bright flares of pain burst across Davies' vision as his and Morn's combined mass landed on his broken bones. Nevertheless Sib's body absorbed most of the collision.

Apparently Sib wasn't hurt. As Morn and Davies rebounded, he lifted with them. Gripping the rail with one hand, he caught hold of Davies' shipsuit with the other.

"Thanks," Davies murmured through a clamor of flashes.

Sib didn't bother to respond. His face was etched with misery.

Steered by Sib's hold, Davies carried Morn toward sickbay.

Pressure swelled in his chest: he might have been bleeding internally. With his sight confused by neural eruptions, the passage resembled a tunnel, long and dim, ending in darkness. The small sickbay was toward *Trumpet*'s stern, out of the way of traffic between the galley and the bridge, the cabins and the lift. Surely it was possible to get there somehow. Pain was only pain: he ought to be able to ignore it for a minute or two.

Angus' zone implants and computer explained his quickness, but they didn't account for the superhuman force of his blows. *Strength of a fucking ape*. He must have other resources as well.

Abruptly Morn raised her head. Before Davies understood that she was moving, she extended her arm and snagged a handgrip.

In surprise Sib instinctively clung to Davies' shipsuit. Pivoting around her, they bumped to a stop against the bulkhead.

Davies croaked out a whisper. "Morn?" Then in panic he jerked his head around, scanned the passage. He didn't want to risk being overheard; exposing her. Where was the nearest intercom? Outside each of the cabins, of course: here; there; there. Others farther away. But they weren't active. All their indicators were blank.

"Morn?" he breathed again. For an instant his relief was so childlike that he feared he might break into tears.

She flicked a glance at him—a swift, urgent appeal for support. Then she turned away.

Vector and Ciro reached the passage, herded along by Mikka. As soon as they saw Morn, however, they all grappled for handgrips or each other, anything they could use to stop themselves. In a moment they were clustered around her, shoulder to shoulder with Davies and Sib.

"Morn—" Mikka bit her voice between her teeth to keep it low. Fresh blood seeped from her temple. "Are you OK? Did you hear all that? What're we going to do? We've got to fight."

"I can at least refuse to do their work for them," Vector offered thinly. "They can't force me to use my mind."

"*Don't*," Morn whispered back. "Don't fight. Don't refuse. Stay alive—don't give him an excuse to kill you."

"Why?" Sib protested in a choked moan. "We're better off dead. You more than any of us. You're the one they really want to hurt."

She shook her head vehemently, as if she were stifling curses. "We haven't got time for this. There's a lie here. Somebody's lying. We need to stay alive until we find out what it is."

Angus had said almost the same thing.

Mikka's eyes glared out of her stained face. "What lie? Angus is a cyborg. Nick controls him. What else is there?"

"Sickbay," Morn countered. "Go. We all need it. I'll try to explain."

She was right. Apparently she'd been able to postpone the things Nick meant to do to her by feigning collapse, but she still needed treatment to stave off her gap-sickness.

"Quickest first," Davies put in, riding a new rush of adrenaline. Pain made him light-headed: his fear began to seem like excitement. Morn needed him as well. She couldn't care for herself without him. "Sib and Ciro, that's you. *Go*—get what you need and get out of the way. Then Vector. Then you, Mikka. You can't survive hard g like that. I'm last. Morn can take as much cat as she needs while the rest of us are being treated."

As if they were accustomed to accepting his orders, Sib and Ciro pushed themselves into motion along the bulkhead. Vector started after them. But Mikka balked.

"No, *I'm* last. Morn needs you with her. If we run out of time, I'll be safe enough on the surgery table. It can probably take care of me even if we're under attack."

Davies didn't argue with her. "All right. Just go."

He would feel better talking in the confines of a closed room. Out here he couldn't predict what sounds might carry as far as Nick's ears, or Angus'.

Morn didn't need to be carried now. He could use his right hand and arm to control his movements. As soon as she pushed off along the passage, he followed.

As his vision cleared, the distance shrank to a more normal perspective. Coasting carefully, he reached the sickbay in a matter of seconds.

It was built into a chamber half the size of one of the cabins, with a heavy door to protect its equipment and occupants from the actions of the rest of the ship. Morn crowded through the doorway after Mikka. There was barely space for Davies to squeeze in behind her and shut the door.

Like the intercom indicators in the passage, the ones here were blank.

Fortunately *Trumpet*'s sickbay was as good as any he'd seen: compact and efficient; ready for emergencies. Sib had already finished entering a few quick commands on the console near the head of the surgery table. As Davies closed the door, the dispenser produced capsules to help Sib and Ciro recover from stun and vomiting: some mixture of stim and cat, metabolins and analgesics. Sib swallowed one convulsively, handed the other to Ciro, then gestured Vector to the table.

At once Vector took a handgrip, rolled himself onto the padded surface, and lay still while Mikka and Morn attached restraints to immobilize him so that the cybernetic systems could work on his hand.

Sib coded the console for urgent repair, more wounded coming; instructed the computer to concentrate on Vector's hand. After that he shifted out of the way as gleaming metal arms and needles flexed from the walls to anesthetize, clean, probe, mend, and suture Vector's slashed palm and fingers.

"Morn," Mikka insisted.

"Right." Morn gripped the edge of the table with one hand, pushed her hair back from her face with the other. A look of frenzy glinted from her eyes, a desperation strangely like Angus'. Nevertheless she kept her voice steady, tight; as hard and closed as a fist. "I'll try to make sense."

Painkillers and cat glazed Vector's eyes. Still he concentrated his gaze on Morn's face as if she alone could save him.

"DA is corrupt," she began. "We know that. I'll believe anything I hear about Hashi Lebwohl. But I'm Enforcement Division. I work for Min Donner. And she's honest."

Mikka scowled at this assertion.

"She has to be," Morn insisted. "Otherwise I wouldn't be a cop. If ED was corrupt, somebody in my family—my father, my mother, somebody—would have known. We would have resigned. The whole Hyland clan. And I wouldn't have followed them to the Academy."

This was true: Davies believed it as soon as she said it, even though he hadn't thought of it himself. It matched his memories too closely to be wrong.

"My family trusted Min Donner. And none of them were stupid. Or blind. So I trust her, too."

"So what?" Mikka retorted.

Morn didn't hesitate. "Think about it. That message didn't come from DA. It came from ED. From *Punisher*. The last I heard, a man named Dolph Ubikwe is in command, and he has the kind of reputation honest cops are willing to die for. He wouldn't do this. Min Donner wouldn't order him to do this.

"Unless there's something else going on."

Something to hope for.

The appeal in Mikka's eyes was as plain as beggary. "Like what?"

Vector's wounds were deep, but not structural. In moments the swabs and needles finished with his hand. Too weak to move well on his own, he let Sib and Ciro release the restraints; let Ciro support him against the wall.

Sib gestured at Davies.

Wary of his ribs and arm, Davies mounted the table gingerly until his back settled against the cushions; then he let his legs straighten. With his good hand, he unsealed his Amnion shipsuit; Mikka and Sib pulled down the strange black fabric until his torso was bare. As they attached the restraints, he reminded Sib, "Morn needs cat."

"Right." Sib typed in the commands to care for Davies, then added orders to dispense a supply of oral cat.

Morn watched her son as if she feared that the sickbay systems might hurt him.

Almost groaning, Mikka repeated, "Like *what*?"

A hypo from the wall tapped into Davies' forearm, piped out blood for the computer to analyze. He felt rather than saw a nearly subliminal flash of X ray. Limpet sensors on his skin tested for evidence of internal bleeding. Then cat, analgesics, and antibiotics washed into him from the hypo. Almost at once he began to drift away from his pain.

After that he heard voices as if they could barely reach him; as if the drugs had sent him into the medical version of tach, leaving everyone else on the far side of a perceptual gap.

"I don't know," Morn answered. She seemed to keep her tone hard so that she wouldn't wail. "Some way to stop Nick when DA is finished with him."

A clamp took hold of his broken arm, adjusted it until the bones were properly aligned. A gleaming extension set the fracture with tissue plasm, metabolins, and a nearly weightless acrylic cast.

"Maybe there's a restriction we don't know about built into Angus' programming. Maybe we've stumbled into a covert operation that has to be kept secret."

Then the clamp shifted to his shoulder; pushed in one direction while the table twisted in another to straighten his ribs.

Next the table retracted to make room for a nozzle which sprayed a more flexible acrylic around his chest. When it hardened—a few moments at most—this cast would shield his ribs, as well as restrict his movements so that he couldn't hurt himself.

"Or maybe," Morn finished, "Min Donner is just going along with Hashi Lebwohl until she figures out what he's up to and can stop him.

"There has to be *some*thing."

Whatever it is, it might help us.

Mikka groaned as if she were close to fainting. "And you want us to stake our lives on *that*?"

"Yes."

Yes, Davies echoed.

Sickbay diagnostics informed him that his skull had suffered a small crack, but that there was no internal damage. Other drugs would protect him against shock and concussion while metabolins speeded the healing of his fractures.

Above him, Sib handed Morn a vial of tablets. She glanced at the dosage label, then shook a couple of pills onto her palm. Glaring at them as if she thought they might kill her, she swallowed them.

Drugs muffled Davies' senses, confused his mind. Nevertheless he did what he could to back Morn up. From the other side of an imposed gulf, he struggled to say, "Angus is fighting it. He isn't giving Nick any more help than he has to."

"Bullshit." The more Mikka bled, the weaker she sounded. "He's a *cyborg*. He follows orders. How much help do you think Nick needs?"

Davies glanced at the intercom. Its indicator remained blank.

"Angus knows—" he mumbled across the void, "knows how to program a parallel control. For her zone implant. He's done it before. He can replace the one Vector broke—whenever he wants." Had he said everything yet? No, there was more. "But Nick doesn't know that." More. "Angus hasn't told him."

Morn nodded. Her eyes shed hints of gratitude and pride. Unfortunately he couldn't answer them. Medication seemed to occupy all the available space inside him, crowding out words.

This was wrong. He was supposed to be taking care of her, not lying here stupefied, as useless as an invalid. For some reason, his restraints had been released; but when he tried to rise, he found that he couldn't tell the difference between one direction and another. He had to watch while Morn and Sib pulled his shipsuit up onto his arms and shoulders, sealed the front.

Without warning tears blurred his vision. "I'm sorry," he told Morn. His voice sounded constricted and forlorn, as if he were crying. "Too many drugs. I can't help you."

She lifted him off the cushions. He was weightless; she supported him as easily as a baby. "You already have." With both arms she held him out of the way while Mikka settled toward the table. "And you will again. I took enough cat to put me out for four hours." Already it had begun to drain the urgency from her voice. In moments it would drain her of consciousness as well. "By then you'll be able to give me whatever I need."

He felt that he could sink down into her embrace and never rise again. Only his strange endocrine heritage kept him awake.

"Four minutes," Sib announced tightly. "You'd better get to your cabins."

"You, too," Mikka told him while he and Ciro fixed her in place. "Tell the systems to take hard-g precautions. Then go. Take Ciro with you. I'll be all right."

Vector put his undamaged hand like a gesture of reassurance on Ciro's shoulder. "Come on," he murmured. "I'm too weak to get there alone. And I need someone to seal my g-sheath."

"Mikka—" Ciro began as if he wanted to protest, stay with her. Almost at once, however, he pushed away from the table to open the door for Vector.

Morn followed, drawing Davies with her.

Already half-unconscious, they swam leadenly toward their cabin. The air had grown viscid with mortality; it opposed their movements. And the passage had become longer while they were closeted in sickbay. It stretched immeasurably ahead of them, like a corridor in a nightmare. Davies could hardly keep his eyes open. Still he resisted the cloying pull of the drugs. Morn was in worse shape than he was: more deeply exhausted; not bred to crises. They would both die if they fell asleep now.

She lasted long enough to reach their cabin, open the door, swing him inside. After that, however, she went limp, tugged out of herself by cat and weariness.

Through a dim, thick haze of somnolence, he steered her into her bunk, sealed her sheath and webbing. Then, while his mind frayed out into the hungry dark, he made an effort to do the same for himself.

He barely succeeded at closing his seals before drugs and loss carried him away.

ANGUS

There were no words. No words for it at all. He existed in a world from which all language had been removed, all meaning stripped away; all release denied. The message had come in from *Punisher*, and he had read it, and his last sanity had cracked open like a crushed shell, spilling out passion and escape and doomed outrage wherever he turned.

Warden Dios to Isaac, Gabriel priority.

Dios had given him back to his mother. The inside of his head had become the crib, where he lay helpless in his anguish. Like a child with nowhere else to turn, he fled for the recesses of himself, seeking darkness and death; seeking the vast void where his unanswerable pain could be extinguished.

Show this message to Nick Succorso.

Yet he wasn't a child: he was a man and a cyborg, and his zone implants permitted nothing. Death he couldn't have, and insanity couldn't save him. Alone on the bridge, with only Nick and ruin for company, he ran *Trumpet*'s helm from the second's station, and lay in the crib, and made small mewling noises no one could hear through his locked teeth.

While he piloted the ship—not *his* ship, never again his—he watched Nick study her; suck up data from Angus' board, Angus' codes, and become her master.

"Shit!" Nick remarked from time to time, usually in amazement. "I didn't know they could make ships like this. I didn't know it was fucking *possible*. She's a goddamn *treasure*."

Angus had lost *Bright Beauty*. He'd lost Morn and his life. Now he lost *Trumpet*. But his mother didn't care. Dios had restored him to her; and she cared for nothing in all the world except his weak cries and his capacity to be hurt.

Still none of his agony showed on the outside, none of his excruciation; or only a little—only the appalled, conflicted labor of his heart, the unsteadiness of his hands, the anguish in his eyes. His datacore ruled everything else.

When he'd first received *Punisher*'s transmission, his datacore had taken him to Nick's cabin, where he'd handed Nick a flimsy hardcopy of the message. His programming had required him to wait while Nick groped through the implications of the words; it had compelled him to supply Warden Dios' answers to Nick's questions. Then it had enforced every instruction Nick gave him: every blow; every protection; every piece of brutality.

Now it drove him to pilot *Trumpet* through the elaborate chaos of Massif-5's system on Nick's orders; guide what had once been his ship at high speed and under heavy g past obstacles by the hundred; on and on for hours at a time, with only an occasional pause to refine the focus of his instruments, or to meet the needs of his flesh.

As he lay in his crib, babbling pain and blood, too profoundly harmed to summon an infant's thin wail of protest, he also served Nick Succorso and the complex treacheries of the UMCP with the wordless precision of a machine.

Massif-5 was a nightmare, but he didn't fear it. He had no external fears. And his madness was no threat to his instruction-sets, or his databases: they didn't need his sanity to aim the ship past the loud infernos of the opposing stars, or among the charted and uncharted hazards which clotted the system.

"What the fuck do *you* want?" Nick had demanded from his bunk when Angus had entered his cabin. "Can't you see I'm sleeping?"

Angus hadn't replied: his datacore gave him no answer, and his own were gone. Instead he'd simply poked the flimsy sheet from the command board's printout into Nick's face.

"Shit."

Nick had hauled himself upright against his g-sheath and snatched the hardcopy. Then his face had turned blank with dumb, stupid surprise. Slowly his mouth had formed words as if he were reading the message aloud to himself; as if he couldn't understand it without moving his lips.

After a moment he'd stared up at Angus with his eyes glazed. His scars pulled at his face like a mask.

"Where did this come from?" he asked dully.

Angus recited his response as if it were written somewhere in his datacore, waiting for Nick to need it.

There's a UMCP cruiser after us. *Punisher*. We passed her when we first came out of forbidden space near the belt. Just before we went into tach this last time, she got close enough to reach us with that transmission. You saw the blip.

"Isaac," Nick murmured to himself. He seemed unable to think. "Gabriel priority. What's that supposed to mean?"

It means you're in command now. You give me orders. I carry them out.

Nick swallowed heavily; swallowed again. His gaze sharpened. He couldn't stop staring at Angus. "Why would you do that?"

I can't help it. I'm a cyborg. The cops welded me. I'm run by a computer that makes me obey anybody who uses my codes.

"A cyborg." Nick bared his teeth. "A fucking machine." By degrees the effort to grasp what he was hearing seemed to bring him back to life. "What makes you think I'm going to believe a load of crap like that?"

Angus wailed at the walls of his crib, but he was too small to break free. He'd always been too small. His long flight from the abyss was no more than an illusion; a coward's desperate, necessary way of lying to himself.

Nothing. But I'm sure you can figure out a way to test it.

"Fine. I can test it." Nick crumpled the sheet of hardcopy. "Here, Gabriel." He tossed it to Angus. "Eat this."

Angus caught it. He chewed it to a compact wad and choked it down as if it were one of Milos' nics.

Nick's eyes began to burn. A hard, red pulse tugged at the edges of his scars.

"Why?" he demanded. "Why did they do that to you?"

Angus told him.

Dangerous hope seemed to flare in Nick's stare. An end to his losses. A new start. He flung out of his g-sheath, bobbed to a zero-g grip so that he could bring his growing excitement and passion closer to Angus' face.

"Fine. Let's pretend that makes sense. Why are they giving you to me now?"

Angus told him. He told him about Milos.

Nick swore viciously, eagerly: fatal as thermite, he blazed on the verge of an explosion. "And you expect me to *trust* that? You expect me to stake my life on it? You expect me to believe you aren't setting me up?"

Angus' programming didn't reply. It didn't need to.

"I'm going to test you, all right," Nick promised; he spoke as if the words were fire. "What kind of equipment did they give you to blow up Billingate?"

Angus' programming didn't reply.

"Isaac, you fucking sonofabitch," Nick snarled, "this is Gabriel fucking priority. *What kind of equipment did they give you to blow up Billingate?*"

Pain. Despair.

UV prostheses so I can read electronic fields and circuits. Jamming fields so I can disrupt bugeyes. Lasers so I can cut open doors and people.

Madness. Ruin.

His datacore didn't mention the plates that protected him, the reinforcements that made him strong.

Nick thought for a moment, then protested, "Shit, Isaac. If you can do all that, why did Milos let you go? He could have used you for anything he wanted. Are you asking me to believe he just walked away from a chance like that?"

There were limits to what he could make me do. I have restrictions to prevent me from killing UMCP personnel. That includes you. And he thought he was betrayed. Hashi Lebwohl told him I wasn't going to rescue Morn.

"But Hashi *lied*." Nick jumped at the idea. A craziness of his own flamed on his face; a thermonuclear sense of possibility. "And poor miserable Milos panicked when you started doing things he couldn't control.

"All right." He sounded like he was shouting, even though he kept his voice low. Blood filled his scars; it seemed to fill his gaze. Heat poured off his skin. "You're going to prove it to me. You're going to help me take over the ship. You're going to protect me. And—"

Abruptly he caught himself as another idea occurred to him. "No, wait a minute. Wait a minute. How can I—?"

Then he had it.

"Isaac," he articulated distinctly, "this is Gabriel priority. From now on, you are going to follow my orders exactly, even if I never say 'Isaac' or 'Gabriel' again. Do you hear me? I'm talking to your computer. This is Gabriel priority. Every order I give you has the force of Gabriel priority. You don't need to hear the codes in order to obey me. If you never hear the codes again, you will still obey me.

"Tell me you understand."

I understand.

Nick eyed Angus harshly. "Tell me what you're going to do about it."

There were no words. No words for it. All language had been burned out of him, all meaning extirpated; he would never be released. His last sanity was gone.

I'm going to obey.

"*Right!*" Nick rasped through his teeth in triumph. Frenetic with eagerness, he launched his passion toward the door. "Let's get going! I've got something I want to *teach* those bastards!"

Angus had obeyed because Warden Dios had given him back to the crib, and his cries were too thin for anyone except his mother to hear. On Nick's orders, he'd hurt Mikka and Davies, slagged Sib's gun; cornered Morn on the bridge and driven her into hysteria.

Now he ran the ship so that Nick would have a chance to prepare himself for what lay ahead.

Trumpet had already come far from her point of insertion: she challenged the system in a kind of navigational combat, soundless and lethal. Trajectories arced across the display, bent off true by doppler effects and changing perspectives. His readouts shouted their warnings at him, blips signaling in confusion as dangers surged close and then receded. Asteroid swarms heaved like igneous hurricanes across scan and fell astern when he avoided them. The small scrap of planets and ships punched *Trumpet*'s impact deflectors. G plucked and sawed at her from all directions, distorting her vectors, falsifying her helm. She was lured toward collisions too massive to be deflected, gravity wells too potent to be escaped.

Yet he mastered the hazards almost easily, showing no strain: his computer and the gap scout were made for this. Faster than any sane ship, *Trumpet* dodged toward her destination.

When Nick had learned all he could absorb at one time, he sometimes napped, sometimes ate; sometimes he talked. Once he said cheerfully, "You're probably wondering why I need bait. Everything would be so much tidier if I just had you slaughter them in their bunks. Or if your restrictions got in the way, I could do it. Jettison them from the airlock and be done with it.

"But I'm ahead of you. Way ahead." He spoke as if Angus had nothing to think about except him. "You haven't figured out what happens after Vector learns how to synthesize that drug."

He glanced over at Angus. His scars grinned like the fond hunger of a barracuda. "Ask me what we're going to do."

What are we going to do?

"Go after Sorus," Nick announced as if the decision made him proud. "Sorus fucking Chatelaine. And *Soar*. And for that I need bait.

"She works for the Amnion—and the Amnion want your dear, sweet son. She'll jump at it if I give her a chance at him. She'll know it's a trap, but she won't be able to help herself. *They* won't listen to excuses if she fails them."

He mused for a moment, then added, "Of course, the cops aren't going to leave us alone while we do that. I need something I can offer them to keep them off my back. Morn would do"—he clashed his teeth together viciously—"but they can't have her. I've got other plans for her. And I have options. Between them Mikka and that pitiful asshole Sib know everything I do about those Amnion acceleration experiments. If *Punisher* starts to cause trouble, I can dangle that in front of her nose."

Angus said nothing. Phosphors danced across his screens and readouts, echoing the system's silent, random pavanne of destruction. Coercion was the only answer he had left.

"How much longer?" Davies demanded from the intercom.

"Shut the fuck up," Nick retorted happily. "We're busy."

Davies persisted. "I need to know how much cat to give Morn."

If he feared Nick, he didn't show it. That was good. Angus was afraid enough for everyone.

"I don't give a shit," Nick answered. "Just don't think you can protect her by letting her go crazy. You won't like what I do to her if that happens. Or what I do to you."

Grinning at Angus, he silenced the intercom.

Angus' mother had smiled that same way when she leaned over the crib.

Sometime later Nick pointed at a readout and swore. "A homing signal, you sonofabitch? You didn't mention that. No wonder *Punisher* was able to catch us."

He chewed his lip for a moment, thinking hard; then he relaxed. "Under the circumstances I probably shouldn't complain. But I can't imagine what the hell you thought you were doing. Tell me why—no, I can guess why you did it. Tell me why you didn't mention it."

Angus answered like a corpse.

You didn't ask. I don't make choices—I just follow orders. If you don't ask, I can't tell you.

That was his only defense, his one secret. It had protected him once during DA's interrogation. Now it warded him again; let him keep this last, useless piece of himself intact.

Nothing required him to tell Nick that he knew how to replace Morn's shattered zone implant control.

"Well, let's not make it easy for them," Nick drawled. "They've already given me all the help I need. I don't think I want to hear what they're going to tell me to do when they're sure I've got you under control."

His fingers punched at the command board. On a readout, Angus saw that the homing signal had been deactivated.

Useless, yes. Empty and insignificant. Yet Angus clung to it.

And to one other thing as well; one other useless, empty, insignificant act. While he worked in Nick's service—and Warden Dios'—he kept *Punisher*'s transmission visible on another readout. Let Nick notice what he was doing and be suspicious: let Nick think he needed to be reminded of his compliance. He didn't care. He couldn't. Whenever his programming and Nick's orders gave him a chance, he scrutinized that readout with the fixed incomprehension of a madman.

Warden Dios to Isaac, Gabriel priority.

Show this message to Nick Succorso.

The words were embedded in coding that he didn't recognize and couldn't read—some kind of machine language, apparently, intended to enforce obedience from Isaac's computer. Nevertheless he studied them whenever he could; stared and stared until his vision swam and his choked wailing filled his ears.

Warden Dios had told him, *We've committed a crime against your soul.* He'd said, *It's got to stop.*

Angus hunted for the end of his despair, the bottom of the abyss, but he couldn't find it.

Six hours. Twelve. Eighteen. The strain should have been too much for any man, even a welded cyborg. It would have been too much if he hadn't used all his knowledge, skill, and cunning to thread a course which minimized *Trumpet*'s reliance on thrust. Ordinary mortality needed sleep: even tortured babies in their cribs slept when they couldn't bear any more. And Nick rested when he felt like it. Yet Angus' zone implants kept him awake, alert; compliant to the pitch of desperation, despite the fact that his small limbs were bound to the slats so that his mother could *fill him with pain*.

Warden Dios to Isaac—

Deep in the lost background of his mind, after each new penetration, she still *comforted him as if it were him she loved*.

Show this message—

At last their destination loomed on the fringes of scan—the asteroid swarm, according to Mikka, where a lunatic researcher named Deaner Beckmann had hidden his installation. By some bitter coincidence, his lab just happened to have received its original financing from Holt Fasner. The same man who owned the cops.

Angus' databases and *Trumpet*'s instruments confirmed that this particular swarm was doomed to eventual immolation in Lesser Massif-5. But he hadn't been given any indication that the UMCP knew of the Lab's existence. And *Trumpet*'s scan had no hope of piercing deep enough into the swarm to detect its emissions. Distance was only part of the problem: that many thousand gigatons of shattered rock simply shed too much interference of all kinds. And a hot singularity less than a parsec off the swarm's course through the system distorted everything the gap scout could see.

Mikka had said that the Lab was located on an asteroid *big enough to be a moon* in the middle of the swarm.

With all that rock running interference, she'd explained, *it's damn near impregnable. You have to go in slow—and some of those asteroids have matter cannon emplacements dug into them.*

Nick tapped in commands. Angus watched without interest as his board lost helm.

"I'll take her from here," Nick explained. "I know where the Lab is. And I know how to talk us in. You'll just get us blown apart."

Show this message—

Angus had shown it all; every word; every scrap of code. But Nick had ignored the machine language to concentrate on the words.

"You have targ," Nick went on. "Screens, dispersion sinks, all our defenses. Data and damage control." Those functions came to life on Angus' console. "Your reflexes are probably faster than mine. If we get in trouble, you'll have to do our fighting for us. I'll handle the rest."

Mikka had said that the Lab did *a lot of med research. Most of the BR surgery you've ever heard of was invented here. But that's just a sideline to finance what they're really doing.* Which was Deaner Beckmann's real research. *Gravitic tissue mutation.*

He wants to evolve genetic adaptations that will allow organisms to survive the stress of working close to singularities. Because he thinks humankind's future lies inside. But people *can't go there if they can't take the pressure. So he wants to make a few changes.*

Like the cops.

Warden Dios to Isaac—

It's got to stop.

The Lab might be the only illegal installation in existence where Angus could be unwelded. But he didn't have that choice.

The swarm's image on scan grew sharper quickly—too quickly, considering the dangers. A sane ship would have decelerated in order to approach the vast stone torrent more carefully. But no sane ship would have crossed this system as fast as *Trumpet* did: she had no sanity aboard. Nick was crazy with freedom and power, and his excitement burned like fission as he brought the gap scout around to begin matching the vector and velocity of the asteroid swarm. Movement through that careening chaos of rock would be impossible unless the ship first assumed the same course at the same speed.

A flat hand of g pushed Angus into his seat as *Trumpet* turned, but he could bear it. Nick had to work within his own limitations. If he pushed himself too hard, he might lose consciousness; might lose everything. And Angus was much stronger. In addition, *Trumpet*'s bridge gimballed smoothly on frictionless bearings, adjusting its orientation to compensate for g. Any strain Nick could stand, Angus could stand easily.

Davies and Morn could endure it, too, if they were sealed in their bunks. Vector, Sib, Mikka, and Ciro ought to be able to survive the same way.

By degrees lateral thrust eased. The ship had come into line with the swarm's trajectory through the cluttered void. Almost immediately, however, that force was replaced by deceleration. *Trumpet* had too much velocity; at this speed she would crush herself on the first asteroid she encountered.

Angus couldn't feel the difference. G was g, always pulling in the same direction as the bridge revolved to meet it. The ship knew the change, however. She made it obvious. Braking roared through the hull, a raw, almost subliminal howl of energy, at once louder and more profound than the oblique stress of lateral thrust.

The screens flickered and broke up for a second or two while scan algorithms recalculated for deceleration; Angus' readouts offered him a heartbeat of gibberish. Then the displays sprang clear. Data began to pour in: distance, size, composition, relative velocity from half a hundred obstacles at once. A particle storm of input raged past *Trumpet*'s hull, was interpreted by her computers, and appeared in front of him as if it were coherent; as if so many instances of mass thrashed by so many conflicting forces could be seen as anything other than chaos.

Proximity alarms began to signal in the background. Nick was bringing *Trumpet* too close too fast. Angus, who wouldn't have hesitated to attempt the same maneuver himself, didn't trust Nick to handle it. Yet Nick ran helm precisely, despite his relative unfamiliarity with the ship. Filled by a rising chorus of klaxons, she finished her deceleration as she breached the fringes of the tumbling river of rock. Then she started dodging among the stones toward the distant heart of the swarm.

The screens became an impossible jumble of positions and vectors. For any ship to navigate past so much mad rock—and to do so at this speed—would have been an enormous challenge if the asteroids had been stable in relation to each other; if time and distance and entropy had deprived them of individual motion, so that they traveled as one. But of course they didn't. Conflicting gravitic fields from Massif-5's stars and planets, from the nearby singularity, and from the swarm itself affected each of the asteroids differently, according to its mass and composition. As a result, each rock shifted constantly within the general plunge. Stones the size of ships or stations rolled against each other and either cracked apart or rebounded on altered vectors: the whole swarm seethed as if it were seeking to coalesce. Only the sheer confusion of collisions and g prevented the asteroids from collapsing around their center like a black hole.

Navigation was still possible. If it weren't, the Lab could never have come into existence. But movement had to be done slowly, as close as feasible to the exact velocity of the immediate stones. *Trumpet* was in danger as much from Nick's pace as from the surrounding torrent.

He ran the ship as if he were trying to prove something to Angus; as if he meant to show Angus that he was as good as any cyborg. Swearing gleefully, brandishing his teeth and scars, he drove the gap scout among the mute thunder and rebound of the rocks as if he were superhuman; elevated once again by instinct and skill to the stature of the man who never lost.

Proximity alarms squalled at him like pierced souls. An asteroid as big as a warship knocked against its neighbor and was instantly, silently, transformed into a small fleet of gunboats reeling off into the jumble. Energies from the ripped solar winds, fed by magnetic resonance, fired lightning in long, blinding sheets against *Trumpet*'s shields. The displays broke apart as scan scrambled to redefine itself in new patterns. Nevertheless Nick found his way unerringly toward the swarm's defended center.

He ran helm like a magician. In that sense, at least, he knew what he was doing. Warden Dios had known what he was doing.

Show this message to Nick Succorso.

With no duties except to study his readouts and stay ready, Angus rode out his personal nightmare and the ship's like the damned familiar of some demented wizard, dangled by curses from the wand of his master.

Punisher's transmission had been embedded in codes which Nick hadn't been able to read any better than Angus could. If that part of the message had been meant for him, he'd missed it or ignored it. Unless he ordered Angus to show it to him again, it was lost.

Yet it was etched in the neurons of Angus' brain. He could have recited it from memory at any moment. He stared at it on his readout, not because he'd forgotten it, or had any hope of understanding it, but because he had nothing else.

"It gets easier," Nick explained as if he had a lump in his throat. Despite his exaltation, he was feeling the strain. "The Lab has been clearing space for itself for years. Cutting up asteroids for fuel and minerals, rare earths, that sort of thing. Clearing the approach. Improving the field of fire for those emplacements Mikka told you about. We should be able to pick up a signal from one of their transmission remotes soon. After that we'll be under their guns most of the way in."

Angus had no idea why Nick spoke at all, except to show off his expertise. Before long, however, the screens began to indicate that he was right. The stone confusion diminished slightly. One k at a time, scan range improved. The middle should have been the densest part of the swarm; but it wasn't.

As the swarm thinned, Nick slowed his pace. *Trumpet* ducked and dodged toward her destination less recklessly. He spent more time studying his communications readouts, searching the bandwidths for a transmission source close enough to reach him past the moil of rock, through the disruptive barrage of static.

Warden Dios had called Angus a *machina infernalis*. An *infernal device*. He'd said, *We've committed a crime against your soul*.

Whatever was left of Angus' soul writhed in protest.

Abruptly Nick stabbed a key. "There!" He snatched up a PCR from its socket in his board and jacked it into his left ear. His hands continued to run helm commands while he focused one of *Trumpet*'s dishes on the transmission source he'd just identified.

"Got it."

One screen showed the source: a remote on an inert ball of rock with a relatively stable trajectory. Presumably the remote was shielded against collisions and lightning, and programmed to reorient its antennae as needed. But no signal from that rock could reach deep enough into the swarm to find the Lab. It was part of a whole network of remotes, all bouncing signals back and forth to each other until they gained a clear window on the Lab.

As Nick listened, a different tension came over him. The sharp concentration with which he navigated became false insouciance. In a tone of feigned relaxation he announced, "Lab Center, this is Captain Nick Succorso, UMCP gap scout *Trumpet*. Ship id follows." He hit a series of keys. "Don't panic—we aren't spies. We stole this ship from a covert UMCP operation against Thanatos Minor in forbidden space. Otherwise we would all be dead.

"Voiceprint comparison will confirm my id. I've been here before. But none of the rest of us have." More keys. "Crew manifest follows."

A glance at his own readouts told Angus that Nick's "manifest" made no mention of Morn or Davies. Or of Angus himself.

He could have listened in to Center's side of the conversation by using the second's personal communications receiver. Nick hadn't told him to do that, however.

With one part of his broken mind, he hunted for matter cannon emplacements so that he could fix targ. With another he studied indecipherable strings of machine code as if they held the secret of his life.

"I know that, asshole," Nick told his board pickup casually, dangerously. "I'm not fucking stupid. Give me a chance, and I'll tell you why it's worth the risk."

But his tone was misleading. Now he became cautious, despite his earlier hurry. With a few soft gusts of braking thrust, he slowed *Trumpet* to hold her within range of the remote; out of reach of the Lab's defenses. Then he waited.

The transmission distance was negligible to microwave remotes. The Lab delayed responding so that its authorities could talk to each other. Or so that guns could be made ready.

When Center spoke again, Nick stiffened.

"No, I will not give you a datacore dump," he drawled as if he were immune to threats or apprehension. "I'm not here to sell my soul. I just want to use your facilities for a while. Maybe just a couple of hours. Maybe a couple of days."

Without shifting his concentration, he adjusted *Trumpet*'s orientation to avoid a slow scattershot volley of errant scree from a broken asteroid.

Jamming hard things—

This time Center answered more promptly.

Nick's gaze sharpened at what he heard. After a moment he retorted, "Is your whole operation completely out of touch with reality? Doesn't the name 'Vector Shaheed' mean anything to you? It's right there on my crew manifest. Vector Shaheed. He's fucking famous, for God's sake." Nick's mouth sneered, but he kept his scorn for Vector out of his voice. "He's a geneticist—he wants to use your genetics lab."

Down his throat—

Angus had stopped listening.

Perhaps Nick had ignored the machine language of *Punisher*'s message because he simply couldn't read it. In that case, it probably hadn't been meant for him. Even Hashi Lebwohl wouldn't have sent out instructions or promises in a code his operative couldn't decipher. So who was the message for?

What was it for?

Presumably it was written in machine language because it was intended for a machine.

And laughing.

What machine? *Trumpet?*

Angus' brain had gone blank when he'd read the words. He hadn't noticed—couldn't have noticed—whether the ship's computers had reacted to the transmission.

As if it were him she loved—

On impulse, without caring if Nick noticed, he typed *Punisher*'s entire message into his board.

The command entry readout replied before he was finished.

<Input error. Verify coding and retry.>

"Yes, *that* Vector Shaheed," Nick said with elaborate patience, as if he were speaking to idiots. "From Intertech."

Angus tried again. This time he left out the words, entered only the code-strings.

The response was the same:

<Input error. Verify coding and retry.>

Hopelessness boiled up from the bottom of his mind. He seemed to remember hearing his mother say, *You can't get away*, even though he'd been far too young to understand any language except pain and comfort, *No, no, you can't get away. I can't get away from them, and you can't get away from me. That's why you're my son. Why you'll always be my son.*

Nick silenced his pickup, turned a conspiratorial grin on Angus. "I think I'm talking to Deaner Beckmann himself," he whispered as if he didn't want to be overheard. "Someone there has actually heard of Vector. These obsessive researchers all like to talk too much. They keep secrets from everybody else, but they'll tell each other anything. Beckmann probably knows what Vector was working on before he left Intertech."

Why do I care? Angus wondered. Why should I care?

Him she loved—

What was left? How many other machines did *Trumpet* have aboard?

He only knew of one.

It's got to stop.

Isaac, he said in silence. Are you listening to me, Isaac? Can you hear me, Isaac?

That was his name. But it was also his access-code. When his brain formed the exact pattern of neural activity which represented that word, a window opened in his head so that he could access some of his databases, query some of his programming. All the knowledge and guidance held in his datacore would have been wasted if he hadn't been allowed to tap a certain amount of it voluntarily, under the right conditions.

"How do I propose to pay for it?" Nick snorted into his pickup. "I propose to pay for it with *results*. If Vector succeeds, you can have a piece of whatever he learns. I can't tell you what that'll be because I don't know. But I can tell you *this*. The Amnion know things about mutation"—he might as well have said *gravitic tissue mutation*—"that could be right in line with what you need."

If that gambit didn't gain what Nick wanted, nothing would.

That's why you're my son.

Angus' zone implants couldn't literally read his thoughts. They could recognize a finite number of specific synaptic patterns; but they interpreted his mental state primarily by identifying the presence of individual neurotransmitters, the changes in his blood chemistry. Their control operated directly on his motor centers. They weren't capable of managing—or even understanding—the ambiguous activity of his volition.

Why you'll always be my son.

Can you hear me, Isaac?

"Got you!" Nick crowed abruptly. "*Got* you."

At once he swung his station to face his second as if he expected Angus to be impressed.

"They're going to let us in. There!" He pointed triumphantly at a schematic as it etched itself across one of the screens. "That's our course past the guns. It's all coming in"—he glanced at his readouts—"approach protocols, traffic and navigation data, ship id, everything we need.

"If Vector doesn't fuck up, we're going to be *rich*. Beckmann is going to shove credit-jacks at us with both hands."

Angus didn't respond. He couldn't. All his attention was turned inward: he was too full of desperation and pain to notice Nick. His wrists and ankles were *tied to the slats*, and he'd never had the strength to free himself.

When his datalink opened, he began to recite *Punisher*'s message to himself, hoping that it would reach through the window to his datacore; hoping that the same resource which enabled his datacore to hear and comprehend Nick's orders would also enable it to receive his own mental voice.

Nick studied his readouts again; this time he stared as if he couldn't focus his eyes. The next instant something like a blow slammed him back in his g-seat. All the blood drained from his face, his scars; his eyes glared white, as pale as bone.

Then he flailed the air with his fists and gave a cry like the one with which he'd greeted *Captain's Fancy*'s destruction—the howl of a man whose heart was being torn open.

A moment later he looked back at Angus.

His face had changed like a mask. Stark pallor left his cheeks the color of his eyes; but his scars were livid with blood, so dark they seemed black. They underlined his white glare like streaks of violence.

"*Soar* is here," he breathed; whispered. "She beat us—she's already in."

His fists clenched convulsively. A spasm twisted him against his belts.

"That bitch," he pronounced distinctly, as if he were still in control of himself; as if he still knew what he was doing. "That fucking bitch. This is her last mistake. Now she's *mine*!"

Angus finished his recitation.

He waited.

Nothing happened. He wasn't strong enough. His datalink remained active until he closed it; but nothing changed.

ANCILLARY DOCUMENTATION

SYMBIOTIC CRYSTALLINE RESONANCE TRANSMISSION

Theorists had argued for decades over the possibility of instantaneous communication across interstellar distances.

In practical terms, of course, the possibility didn't exist. All known means for the transmission of data were at once too inflexible and too vulnerable to be efficient across the vastness of space. Waveforms such as radio, photon emissions such as lasers, line-pulses of the kind employed by electronic telecommunications: all were light-constant (therefore too slow when the distances involved were measured in light-years), and all were to varying degrees susceptible to distortion by gravity wells, electromagnetic furnaces, and plasma flares—not to mention obstruction by planetary or solar bodies, or even by the seas of dust which swept uncharted through the great void.

Furthermore, humankind had developed an alternative: the gap courier drone. By storing the data to be communicated and transporting it across the dimensional gap as a physical object, humans could obtain results which far exceeded anything mere microwaves or lasers might accomplish.

In practical terms, then, the whole question of instantaneous communication across interstellar distances was foolish: impossible on the one hand; unnecessary on the other.

Theorists who relished the foolish, ignored the impossible, and doted on the unnecessary were not daunted.

Many of them rationalized their efforts in these terms: In normal space, waveforms traveled significantly faster than objects. Objects simply could not be accelerated up to the speed of light. As they approached *c*, their mass experienced time dilation until at the last, unattainable moment it became infinite. Therefore, as objects approached *c*, more and more force was required to accelerate them. The final, nearly infinite increments demanded nearly infinite energies.

And yet, *in effect*, objects were able to travel much faster than light by the dimensional legerdemain of crossing the gap. The physical properties of objects enabled them to go into the gap—where no waveform could reach them—and emerge intact.

Well then, if such sleight of hand could be practiced upon objects—legerdemain that depended on the very physical properties which restricted matter to velocities lower than the speed of light—why could not an analogous sleight be devised for waveforms, a sleight specific to the unique material properties of microwaves and light?

So some theorists argued. Their imaginings remained purely speculative, however, even fanciful, until the results of some rather specialized inquiries into the characteristics of certain crystalline structures became known.

Working in zero-g environments, crystallographers were able to design and produce crystals of a purity unknown on Earth: a purity which never occurred in nature. The original purpose of the inquiry was to study the relationship between the crystallographic planes and the "seed" atoms from which those planes were projected, on the plausible assumption that the planes represented a form of code which when deciphered might reveal new insights into the atoms themselves. And, of course, the purer the crystal, the more accurate the code. However, the research soon produced the secondary discovery that certain pure anisotropic crystals grown in pairs from nearly identical "twin" atoms had a property which became known as "symbiotic resonance." When one such twin was subjected to mechanical strain in order to induce a piezoelectric effect, the other exhibited an equal—and simultaneous—response.

It was as if both twins had been subjected to exactly the same strain at exactly the same moment, even though the crystals were not in physical contact with each other. In fact, the twins had been grown in separate containers and were insulated from each other by a variety of fluids and barriers.

Subsequent research determined that the range across which symbiotic resonance took place was a function, first, of the purity of the crystals and, second, of the similarity between their seed atoms. In particular, the more nearly identical the seed atoms were, the greater the obstacles—both of space and of matter—which the twins could ignore in their response to each other.

Theorists interested in the possibility of instantaneous communication across interstellar distances were ecstatic.

Clearly, symbiotic resonance had the potential to be a means of data transmission. Piezoelectric responses could be produced as code in one twin and decoded from the reaction of the other. And if such communication could take place—without any measurable time lag—between one side of a lab and the other, why not between one side of a station and the other?

Why not between the station and Earth? Between Earth and her planets? Between Earth and the stars?

Crystallographers were unable to advance any theoretical objections. Certainly their research repeatedly confirmed that this resonance occurred independent of time. Yet practical objections abounded—and these were effectively insurmountable.

In order to achieve symbiotic resonance across distances greater than a few dozen meters, the seed atoms of the twins would need to be identical to standards so strict—identical down to the precise orbital placement of the component electrons—that they were virtually inconceivable to human minds; quite unattainable by human methods. The purity of the crystals themselves could be improved; but how could the seed atoms be made identical? Just as Einstein had defined the limits of physical velocity, Heisenberg had established the limits of atomic predetermination.

Crystallographers found it easier to believe that objects would one day be accelerated past the speed of light than to credit that individual seed atoms could ever be made identical.

Naturally the theorists were no more daunted now than they had been earlier. If communication by symbiotic resonance was effectively impossible for human minds using human methods, that didn't necessarily imply that it was impossible for other minds using other methods. Was it not conceivable, they argued, that the techniques of the Amnion might be equal to the challenge of symbiotic crystalline resonance transmission?

That was just a theory: no more inevitable than any other act of speculation. Nevertheless, the bare idea was enough to make the men and women charged with the defense of human space—men like Warden Dios, women like Min Donner—break into a cold sweat.

DARRIN

Captain Darrin Scroyle, master of the mercenary vessel *Free Lunch,* sat naked in his cabin, absentmindedly scratching the grizzled hair on his chest while he studied the readouts from his personal data console.

Displayed on one of the small screens was a schematic of the Massif-5 system. His last reading of *Trumpet*'s homing signal showed him the gap scout's point of insertion into the system. At the moment she was one easy gap crossing ahead of *Free Lunch.*

For that matter, so was *Punisher. Free Lunch* had been following the UMCP cruiser across the dark at a considerable distance; far enough back to be beyond the plausible reach of *Punisher*'s scan; close enough to keep track of her. With the information from *Trumpet*'s signal waiting in the vacuum like a series of signposts—and with *Punisher*'s particle trace leading the way—*Free Lunch* could have followed her target indefinitely.

Unfortunately she wasn't being paid to simply follow the gap scout. And *Punisher* stood between her and the fulfillment of her contract.

No doubt *Punisher* and *Free Lunch* had diametrically opposed reasons for pursuing *Trumpet.* If *Free Lunch* attacked the gap scout, *Punisher* would fight to protect her.

Such things had happened before in Darrin Scroyle's experience. More than once he'd seen righteous Min Donner and conniving Hashi Lebwohl work at cross-purposes. At UMCPHQ the right hand had no idea what the left hand was doing.

He didn't find this amusing.

On the other hand, he wasn't disconcerted. He didn't care what

Donner's loyalties were in this situation, or Lebwohl's. The only question which interested him was: Did *Punisher* know what he was doing now? Had she received warning of Hashi Lebwohl's intentions? Did she know that *Free Lunch* had been given the codes to interpret *Trumpet*'s homing signal?

If *Punisher* had been warned, *Free Lunch* might have an unusually difficult time fulfilling her contract.

The cruiser was likely to be a formidable obstacle. According to his reputation, Captain Dolph Ubikwe had a casual attitude toward UMCP protocol; but there was nothing casual about the way he carried out his orders.

If Darrin Scroyle couldn't outmaneuver *Punisher* somehow, he wouldn't be able to avoid a fight with the warship.

He wasn't afraid of that. Still he intended to avoid it if he could. His contract with Hashi Lebwohl didn't require him to be stupid.

Among mercenaries he was an old man. He had gray hair on his chest and head. He'd learned to forgive his paunch for being flabby. He let himself limp when his sciatica flared up; instinctively he distrusted the nerve implants which might have cured the ailment for him. By now he was old enough to know that nothing was ever simple.

That no longer bothered him. He and his ship had survived their uncompromising life for so long because he was relatively simple himself: he could concentrate on the complexities which affected him, and let the ones which didn't go.

"How does it look?"

Alesha asked her question from the master's bunk, where she lay waiting for him to finish what he was doing. Like him, she was naked. And like him, she was no longer young. Time made her once-proud breasts sag at the pull of *Free Lunch*'s internal spin. Her habitual seriousness had been twisted awry, so that her frown of concentration now resembled a crooked grin. She had less stamina than he remembered, and perhaps a bit less appetite.

Nevertheless she was precious to him. He loved the comfort of her soft skin, even though it was no longer as taut as she wished; loved the taste of her nipples, even though they no longer hardened so readily against his tongue. And he treasured her refusal to dismiss complexities which meant nothing to him.

She was Alesha Hardaway, his targ first; but she was also his first cousin. Mercenary ships were like that: often interbred. They took on outsiders rarely. Outsiders who shared the same code, the same commitment—outsiders who could be trusted—were hard to find. Most of Darrin's crew had come from other mercenary vessels after time or violence, bad luck or bad judgment, had cost them the ability to fulfill their contracts. Alesha had been with him aboard *Free Lunch* from the beginning.

"About as we expected," he answered. Like her question, his reply was easy, companionable. "According to *Trumpet*'s last signal, she's crossed into Valdor's system. *Punisher* has already gone after her. We'll do the same as soon as I tell the bridge how I want it done.

"As for that other ship—the one coming in from Thanatos Minor—we haven't seen her for twenty-four hours. I don't know where she is. So I'm going to assume she's there, too"—he tapped his schematic, although Alesha couldn't see it from where she lay—"trying to get to *Trumpet* ahead of all of us."

Alesha considered for a moment, then asked, "How *do* you want it done?"

He turned his back on the board so that he could look at her. She faced him on her belly, with her chin propped on her folded arms. Dimpled by time, her flanks curved toward the cleft between her legs.

"I guess I've known you too long," he responded. "For some reason I'm sure that's not the question you want to ask first."

She gave him her twisted frown. "Am I that obvious?"

He pursed his mouth. "I wouldn't have called it 'obvious.' I've just known you for a long time. As a general rule I do try to learn from experience."

"All right, then." Her gaze held his thoughtfully. "I wish you would tell me again why we're doing this. It's going to be dangerous."

She may well have been the only person aboard who would have asked such a question. He hoped so. Nevertheless he had no trouble thinking of an answer.

"Because we're being paid what the danger is worth."

That was his code: *the* code. Get paid what the job was worth. Then do it. Or turn it down and forget about it. No second-guessing; no after-the-fact scruples; no self-pity; no cold feet. Get paid for the job and then do it. Otherwise life didn't make much sense.

The alternative was vampirism: living off other people's blood and sweat. If life didn't make sense, he might as well have been an illegal. Or a cop.

Alesha didn't think that way, however. She shared his commitments, but she was bedeviled by gray areas and complications.

"How can you be sure?" Her sober gaze held him. "The whole thing stinks of plots and counterplots. How can you know how much the danger is worth?"

He shrugged. "I can't. But I'll stand by my own decisions. I didn't take the job blindly. And I like what we're getting paid for it."

She shook her head. "There are different kinds of blindness. Did Lebwohl tell you why he wants *Trumpet* killed?"

"You know he didn't. He's a client. I don't expect him to tell me what his reasons are."

"Then how—?"

"All right." Darrin didn't need to feign patience. If she hadn't asked him such questions, he would have valued her less. And he wasn't afraid to admit that the circumstances were complex. Only his commitment to his own actions needed to be kept simple. "Here's how I see it.

"*Trumpet* is a UMCP ship." While he explained, he resumed scratching through the hair on his chest. "She went to Thanatos Minor with a famous illegal in command and Com-Mine's former deputy chief of Security for crew—presumably some kind of covert operation. Maybe she was sent to blow up Billingate? I don't know. But I do know this. While she was there, the Bill managed to lose the contents of an ejection pod which was originally supposed to be delivered to the Amnion by Nick Succorso.

"Succorso met Thermopyle in a bar. During the fight before the planetoid blew, Succorso and the Amnion each lost a ship. But by that time *Trumpet* had considerably more than a crew of two. We know because we saw them go EVA—and come back. It sure looked like *Captain's Fancy* got herself killed to keep them alive.

"After that *Trumpet* left just in time to escape being caught in the shock wave. But she didn't head for human space, which was what any sane ship would have done. Instead eight or ten hours went by before she came back over—and when she did, it wasn't from the direction of Thanatos Minor.

"In the meantime Min Donner had already sent out a reception committee to welcome her back. But she didn't stop for it. In fact, none of us would have seen her at all if she hadn't paused to flare that listening post. And then she turned straight for Massif-5, acting like a ship who wanted to have nothing to do with the UMCP—except for the fact that she left a nice, convenient homing signal behind her, and came here by careful stages, so she would be easy to follow."

With mild vexation, Darrin noticed that he was making the skin of his chest raw. Scratching too hard. Alesha would have reminded him to stop if she hadn't been concentrating on what he said. Frowning at his hand, he set it down on his thigh.

"At the same time another ship appeared out of forbidden space, burning as hard as she could straight from Thanatos Minor after *Trumpet*."

He spread his palms. "How smart do I have to be before I can guess what all that means?"

Alesha listened as if she were memorizing every word. "Tell me."

He couldn't suppress a smile. Sometimes he liked her so much that he wanted to laugh out loud. However, he didn't hesitate to answer her seriously.

"Succorso had a cargo the Amnion want back. He promised it to them so they would let him live, but then he diverted it to Billingate. He and Thermopyle stole it from the Bill—they've got it with them now.

"Naturally they don't want to hand it over to the cops. They want it for themselves. They're illegals—they won't do what the cops tell them unless someone holds a gun to their heads. At the same time they have no intention of facing an Amnion incursion on their own. For all they know, the ship after them is *Calm Horizons*. They wouldn't stand a chance against her, despite *Trumpet*'s fancy equipment. So they leave a trail for *Punisher* to follow. They're trying to keep the cruiser between them and that other ship.

"*Punisher* wants their cargo. And of course she doesn't want the Amnion to get it. But Hashi Lebwohl doesn't trust a mere UMCP cruiser for a job like that. He doesn't want the Amnion to get that cargo. He doesn't want Succorso and Thermopyle to keep it. And maybe—just maybe—he wants to keep it away from Min Donner. Maybe he doesn't like to think about what someone that pure will do with it. Whatever it is.

"So he hires us."

"For insurance," Alesha put in softly.

"Insurance." Darrin nodded. "Exactly. He's paying us to cover his ass."

He paused for a moment to let her examine the implications, then went on, "In other words, I don't think anyone is plotting against *us*. If Hashi Lebwohl is afraid of us because we 'know too much' about what happened on Thanatos Minor, he could have given *Punisher* orders to take us out. Captain Ubikwe would have done it—he was itching for the chance. As far as ED is concerned, anybody who uses Cleatus Fane for cover must be illegal.

"But Lebwohl didn't do that. Instead he offered us a contract. He told us about that homing signal. And he gave us what looks like a pretty complete rundown on *Trumpet*'s capabilities. He isn't worried about what we know or don't know. He can trust us to keep it to ourselves. And there's no other reason why he might want to get rid of us.

"What do you think?" he finished with a small smile. "Are we getting paid what the danger is worth?"

Alesha didn't answer immediately. Instead she countered, "That brings me back to my original question. What are you going to tell the bridge? As long as we're this far behind *Trumpet* and *Punisher*, we'll never fulfill our contract. We need to get ahead of them somehow—or between them, if we can't get ahead. But how can we do that? We don't know where they're going."

However, Darrin had a counter of his own ready. "As long as we're guessing, what do you suppose that cargo is?"

She lifted her shoulders. "I have no idea. I can't think of anything the Amnion would value low enough to let Succorso steal it, and yet high enough to risk an act of war to get it back."

He tightened his mouth so that he wouldn't grin. "You're worrying about reasons again. They're just smoke—they confuse the issue.

"What do we know about the cargo itself?" Because he liked explaining himself to Alesha, he didn't sound pedantic. "Succorso sent it toward *Tranquil Hegemony* in an ejection pod. What kind of cargo—what kind of treasure—fits in an ejection pod?

"Something physical, that's obvious. It isn't just data or secrets. And nothing raw or unprocessed. That wouldn't be worth an incursion into human space." As if it had a mind of its own, his hand rose to his chest. He pulled it down firmly. "Some kind of equipment? A device? I don't think so. The Amnion can reproduce their own devices whenever they want—and they know we can't. Human methods can't replicate their technologies."

Alesha seemed able to study his face, watch him think, for hours at a time. "What's left?"

"Something organic," he replied promptly. "Something living. Maybe even something that needs an ejection pod's life support to survive."

He could be sure of this because he was sure of himself.

"Like what?" she asked.

"That doesn't matter." He waved both hands to dismiss the question. "We don't need to know. The point is that we can guess where *Trumpet* is headed."

For a moment she frowned in confusion. Then her eyes widened, and she gave a sigh of recognition.

"Deaner Beckmann. The Lab. Because the cargo is organic."

Proud of her—and secretly pleased with himself—Darrin nodded firmly.

"So we're going to stop following this nice trail they've left us. Instead we're going to choose our own point of insertion into Massif-5." He turned back to his board and indicated a spot in the schematic, even though she couldn't see it. "There. Which is about as risky a gap crossing as we can make and still plan on living through it."

His crew and his ship had done such things before, when circumstances required it. He trusted them. Nevertheless he spent a moment reconsidering his decision while he explained it.

"That will put us—oh, roughly a million k on the other side of Beckmann's swarm." If she could find a flaw in what he meant to do, he wanted her to say so now. "By the time we set it up—change course and velocity, go into tach, resume tard, pull back around to the swarm—we can be pretty sure we won't beat *Trumpet*. But we'll be hours ahead of *Punisher*.

"And we'll be in position. We can use the swarm for cover while we hunt *Trumpet*. If we're lucky, *Punisher* won't even spot us there."

Once again he put his back to the board, waiting for Alesha's reaction.

"What about that other ship?" she asked.

He frowned thoughtfully. "That's a problem. We can't know where she is at this point. But here's how I see it.

"If she knows about the Lab—if she can guess *Trumpet* is headed there—she isn't Amnion. She's a human ship working for them, maybe because she likes what they pay her."

His mouth twisted ruefully. More than once he'd asked himself if he would accept a contract from the Amnion. Was his commitment to the code really as simple as he liked to believe? He didn't know. All his life he'd avoided the question by making sure the situation never arose.

"That means several things," he continued. "It means she doesn't carry as much firepower as a warship. *Trumpet* might be able to survive an engagement. And it means she probably won't attack while *Trumpet* is anywhere near the Lab. She won't want to have Beckmann's guns turned on her. Also she might not want him to know whose side she's on.

"If she's anywhere close enough to give us trouble, I think we'll have time to figure out what we want to do about her."

Alesha nodded as he finished, agreeing with him. Apparently she couldn't find any flaws. Slowly one of her rare smiles grew across her face.

"Have I ever told you that I think you're good at this?"

Grinning, he drawled, "You've mentioned it from time to time. Not that I mind hearing it." Then he let the way he felt about her make him grave. "I just hope you're right. I'm not in the mood to do anything stupid. I like living too much."

Without warning, her eyes turned moist. Blinking, she dropped her gaze. "I know how you feel." At last she answered his earlier question. Are we getting paid what the danger is worth? "I'm growing old. That seems to make everything harder. I don't want to lose you."

Because he was the master of his vessel, responsible for her and all her people, he was tempted to say, Don't worry, you won't lose me. Whatever happens will happen to both of us. But he knew Alesha better than to offer her false comfort.

Instead he used his console intercom to talk to the bridge, give his orders. Then he went to bed.

He might not get another chance.

MIN

Bobbing and weaving down the corridor, Min Donner fought to remember her zero-g reflexes and cursed Dolph Ubikwe for summoning her from her cabin. It was craziness to be out here, working her way along the passages, when the klaxons might sound at any moment, warning her that she was about to be slammed to pulp on the ship's steel.

She'd been station-bound too long. And when she traveled, she was usually aboard ships with internal spin. She'd grown accustomed to comfortable g; to weight as well as mass; to environments where her nerves and even her veins knew which way was up. *Punisher*'s version of freefall—punctuated by abrupt jolts, hull roar, and pressure whenever the cruiser shifted course—was making her sick.

Either that, or she'd become old without realizing it.

Punisher hadn't been designed to run this way. She fought without g, of course: centrifugal inertia restricted her maneuverability. But for other duties she'd been built to use spin. There were too many people aboard, engaged in too many different activities. They could all move and work, sleep and recreate more effectively when they were anchored by their own weight.

But Captain Ubikwe had ordered the ship to secure for zero g so that she could catch up with *Trumpet*. Core displacement was distorting navigation across the gap. Each time *Punisher* resumed tard, she lost too much time reacquiring the gap scout's homing signal. And the displacement was getting worse. With every passing hour, it became more and more likely that *Free Lunch* or—was it *Soar?*—would reach *Trumpet* first. If they knew or could guess where she was headed.

Punisher's crew had been sailing under what were, in effect, battle conditions for the better part of twenty-four hours before the cruiser achieved insertion into the Massif-5 system.

And now she had no choice except to go on without g. For ships moving at *Punisher*'s speed, and *Trumpet*'s, Valdor Industrial's system was a lethal maze of obstacles and hazards. The added burden of centrifugal inertia was too dangerous.

Without *Trumpet*'s homing signal to guide her, the encroaching ship from forbidden space may well have lost the trail a long way back. But *Free Lunch* might conceivably be ahead of *Punisher*. Min couldn't begin to guess where the lies she'd been told ended. As far as she knew, it was perfectly possible that Hashi Lebwohl still controlled where Angus was headed, and had already passed that information to *Free Lunch*.

For that reason *Punisher*'s best communications people were doing their best to break the code in which Warden Dios' message for Nick Succorso had been embedded.

Maybe those code-strings don't mean anything, Dolph had said. But if they do, I want to know it.

The cruiser urgently needed to understand what was going on.

In the meantime *Punisher* forged ahead. Despite her far greater mass, the difficulties of reacquiring *Trumpet*'s signal, and the effects of a truly unfortunate insertion into the system, Captain Ubikwe's command strove to keep up with the swift, agile gap scout.

It was *craziness* for Min to be out of her cabin under these conditions. She should have stayed webbed into her bunk. But this wasn't the first crazy thing she'd done, when it needed doing. If she lived long enough, it wouldn't be the last. Dolph had chimed her intercom and summoned her. Without hesitation she'd unsealed herself to respond.

He wanted her to meet him in sickbay.

He hadn't offered her an escort, and she hadn't asked for one. She knew the way. And the fewer people who were exposed to this kind of danger, the better. It was bad enough that he took the same risk he asked of her.

Something had happened.

Again.

She didn't waste energy wondering what it was. Instead she concentrated on trying to regain her reflexes; on piloting herself down the corridor with as little wasted motion as possible.

The instant she heard the klaxons, she dove for the nearest hand-grips; cleated her zero-g belt. The bridge crew would give the ship as much warning as they could, but sometimes that wasn't much. One grip in each fist, her back against the bulkhead, she waited for thrust to hammer her in some direction she couldn't predict and might not be able to survive.

Straight deceleration: she recognized it as soon as it hit. It wrenched her forward so hard that her aft hand pulled loose. If she hadn't attached her belt first, the sudden weight would have flipped her face-first into the wall. But the belt caught her; snatched at her like the recoiling crack of a whip. Fortunately she remembered to go limp when her grip failed. Otherwise she might have ripped the muscles in her back.

Five seconds of hard burn. White lighting yawed across her field of vision, then cracked into bits of darkness. Her pulse moaned in her ears: her body twitched and jerked under the strain. Then it ended. She spent a moment bouncing back and forth across her belt's attachment while her mass dissipated its stored inertia.

At this rate she might need sickbay herself. She could already tell that some of these bruises were going to *hurt*.

Resting, she waited for the bridge to tell the rest of the ship what would happen next.

Another bleat of the klaxons: less intense than the first; shorter. Almost immediately forward thrust eased to life, firing the dark to regain lost velocity. Because this push was more gentle, it took longer; but after a couple of minutes the ship-wide intercom piped an all clear.

"Secure from collision stations," a woman's voice told the ship. "We have twenty-eight minutes until we start jockeying for position on the next obstacle. Use the time."

The intercom clicked silent like the sound of the carabiner on Min's zero-g belt as she unclipped it from the bulkhead cleat. At once she kicked herself into motion again.

Damn it, Dolph, she muttered silently. What's the damn hurry? Why couldn't you wait?

She knew, however, that Dolph had called her from his quarters rather than the bridge. Probably he'd been resting. When he'd asked her to meet him, he might not have been aware that *Punisher* was near a patch of open space.

Grimly she wondered what the hell was urgent enough to make him risk himself as well as her like this.

• • •

She saw a hint of the answer when she floated out of one of the main personnel lifts into the passage which led to sickbay, twenty meters off to her right.

The corridor was festooned with g-hammocks: at least twenty-five of them arced at intervals up and down the walls on both sides of the entrance to sickbay. And they were all occupied. Sickbay itself had space for ten, counting surgical tables as well as berths. This was the overflow.

Some kind of accident? Explosive decompression? Matter cannon attack? That wasn't possible. Min would have felt it. Any damage powerful enough to hurt this many people would have sent shock waves of concussion and clamor throughout the ship.

Concentrating too hard to curse, she coasted past the hammocks; slapped the palm-plate which opened the sickbay doors. They slid shut automatically behind her as she entered.

Dolph was waiting for her inside, along with another man identified by his uniform and insignia as *Punisher*'s medtech. They sat with their belts cleated to mobile stools which were slotted into tracks in the deck and run by servos so that sickbay's personnel could work under zero g or combat. The two tables were empty, but all eight of the bunks were in use.

The medtech saluted Min. "Director Donner." His id patch said "Foster." He sounded wan; stretched too thin.

"Hope you weren't hurt," Dolph grunted in greeting. "I didn't think this could wait until we hit clear space."

Min returned Foster's salute from the anchor of a handgrip, but her attention was fixed on Dolph. "What's happened?"

He met her gaze for a moment, pursed his black lips. "A couple of things." Then his eyes slid down to the deck as if he was too tired to go on looking at her. "But let's take them one at a time." He gestured toward the medtech. "Foster."

"They aren't hurt, Director," Foster said on command. "I mean the ones outside. I couldn't monitor that many of them if they were, but they aren't. They're sick. I've"—he faltered briefly—"never seen anything like it."

From Min's perspective, he didn't seem old enough to have seen much of anything.

More than twenty-*five* of them? she protested to herself. What was this, some kind of epidemic? Resisting a surge of impatience, she asked, "Sick how?"

Foster shrugged like a wince. "Nausea. Vomiting. High blood pressure. Disorientation. Hallucinations." He glanced at Dolph as if he were hoping for confirmation, then added, "Five of them told me separately that the walls are leaning on them. Trying to squash them.

"None of them are in danger. They aren't sick enough to die. But the way they feel, they might prefer dying."

Nearly half the crew—

Min growled through her teeth. "Sounds like they've been overdosing on stim and hype."

Tension clenched Dolph's shoulders; instinctive rejection. But he didn't interject a retort.

"Actually"—Foster gave another uncomfortable shrug—"it sounds like SAD. Space adjustment disorder," he explained unnecessarily. "The symptoms are classic."

Because she feared that he might be right, she had to stifle an impulse to shout at him. "SAD?" *Punisher* was damaged, shorthanded, and worn-out. "A goddamn *epidemic* of SAD?" The whole vessel had already suffered too much in this system. "On an experienced ship like this?"

Now Dolph spoke. "That," he breathed heavily, "is the problem. You don't believe it. I don't either.

"Director Donner"—he pronounced her name and title with special precision as his weary gaze rose to her face—"I think we have a sick-out on our hands."

Abruptly Foster slotted his stool away to one of the walls and began working at the main sickbay control panel, ostensibly checking the condition of his immediate patients. Apparently he agreed with his captain. Perhaps his sense of medical ethics barred him from saying so.

Sick-out. Stung by alarm and indignation, Min stilled herself; became as poised and motionless as her handgun. Not an epidemic: a protest. Mute, passive resistance to her orders. Disobedience which stopped short of mutiny. But the UMCP Code of Conduct made no provision for such an action. It was called "malingering": it was a court-martial offense.

"Captain Ubikwe," she asked softly, "what kind of ship are you running?"

Dolph's mouth twisted bitterly. "As far as I can tell, it's the kind I've been told to run." Anger ached in his stained eyes. A moment later, however, he said, "She's my ship, Min. My problem. I'll deal with it. But there's something I need from you first."

Min waited like a weapon aimed at his head. *Punisher* had been turned aside from a much-needed leave so that she could chase a UMCP gap scout all the way to Massif-5—and then put Nick Succorso in command. This was the result.

That wasn't Dolph's responsibility. It was Min's. And Warden Dios'.

"I said a couple of things have happened," Dolph went on, holding her glare. "The other may be worse." He paused to search her face, then announced, "*Trumpet* has switched off her homing signal."

She didn't move; didn't react. Nevertheless her hands burned as if magnesium flares had been lit in her palms. If Nick Succorso had been there in front of her, she might have started breaking his bones, one at a time.

"We didn't lose it," Dolph asserted flatly. "Class-1 homing signals are just too damn helpful to be lost. They tell you everything you need to reacquire them. And when they're switched off, they tell you that, too.

"*Trumpet*," he concluded, "is trying to get away from us."

Min looked back at him as if she were impervious to surprise or shock. Past a fire which only felt like pain because she couldn't act on it, she asked, "What is it you need from me?"

"I need an *explanation*," he broke out in sudden passion. "I need to know *who's* doing what to *whom* in this goddamn farrago." But an instant later he stopped himself. "No, forget it. That was uncalled for. If you knew, you would have told me already."

Controlling his emotions with formality, he said, "Director Donner, I need to know what we're going to do now. How can we follow *Trumpet* if we don't know where she's headed?"

In silence, Min chewed flame and obscenities.

Warden Dios, you misguided, secretive sonofabitch, what the hell do you *want* from me?

Of course she saw Dolph's point. To confront his crew's fear and resistance would be costly for the whole ship. If his people refused him, hardened their position, they might all end up facing courts-martial. But if they backed down under pressure, they would lose respect for themselves—and cops more than anyone else survived on the strength of their respect for themselves. Why should Dolph try to persuade or intimidate his people back to work, if *Punisher* no longer had anything to do?

So what were Min's choices?

Give up? Head home? Forget that she, too, needed self-respect? That questions which affected all human space rode with Angus, Nick, and Morn aboard the gap scout?

Or search for *Trumpet*'s particle trace? Quarter the complex sargasso of the system until the cruiser's entire crew came down sick in earnest from simple strain and exhaustion?

Or call in VI Security, req help? Help which might take days to get organized?

Or give up in another way? Find a listening post, flare UMCPHQ, ask for instructions?

Or guess. Stake everything on her own judgment or intuition.

Slowly, choosing her words with care, she answered, "I said they might go looking for a lab. Let's assume I'm right. How many bootleg research facilities are there in this system?"

Punisher had left her tour of duty around Massif-5 only a few days ago. Dolph Ubikwe had everything he'd ever known about the system at his fingertips.

"Six. That we're aware of."

Six? Shit. Min wrapped a hand around the butt of her gun to cool the fire in her palm. Massif-5 was heaven for illegals. "How many of those could *Trumpet* reach on the general heading of her last signal?"

Dolph gazed at her without blinking. "Two."

"Just two? That helps." She chewed her options for a moment, then asked, "Which of them is equipped to study drugs and mutagens? Which is likely to recognize Vector Shaheed's reputation and let him work there?"

Nothing moved in Dolph's face. He might have given up breathing as well as blinking. "Deaner Beckmann's."

Then he added, warning her, "But it's murder to get to. A gap scout—any small ship—can maneuver in there a hell of a lot better than we can."

As if she were saying, I don't give a damn, Min announced, "That's where we're going." She glanced at Foster's back, cocked an eyebrow toward the corridor full of hammocks. "Unless you have a better idea."

Snorting softly, Dolph lowered his head. "Shit, Min, *all* my ideas are better than that. But if I were in your place, I might make the same decision. At least I hope I would." Memories of Massif-5 and damage seemed to weigh on his shoulders. Slowly at first, then faster and harder, he scrubbed his hands on his thighs. He might have been trying to generate courage by sheer friction.

Then he slapped his knees and looked up at her again. He'd reached a decision of his own. "In the meantime," he drawled, "it would help if you happened to consider this an appropriate occasion to yell at me."

He surprised her. Angrily she snapped, "Say what?"

"Chew me out," he explained. "Give me a dressing-down." Hard humor pulled at the corners of his mouth. "Blame me for this sudden outbreak of SAD. Say whatever you want, just so long as you mean most of it. And you're loud about it." When she went on staring at him as if he'd lost his mind, he grimaced. "I want them to hear you outside.

"You can do that, can't you?" Sarcasm gave his voice a taunting edge. "You've been wanting to tear into me ever since you came aboard. As far as I can tell, the only real secret of command is being able to pick your occasions to get mad. So get mad at me now. Be in command."

He met her glare of consternation with a sardonic smile, as if he'd tricked her somehow.

She wanted to retort, Chew yourself out, you bastard. You're a big boy now—you can supply your own abuse. But the humor behind his provocative smile told her that she'd missed the point. He thought he had something to gain if his sick-out crew heard her—a phrase popular in the Academy—"stripping the paint off his hull."

Maybe he knew what he was doing.

So she took a deep breath, held it for a moment while she tapped the depths of her old outrage. Then she spent the next three minutes doing her best to burn blisters into Dolph Ubikwe's fat cheeks.

When she finished, Foster was staring at her with his mouth open. Mute laughter shook Dolph's shoulders.

"Now you tell me," she rasped, keeping her voice low. "Why is that funny?"

He shook his head. "Wait. You'll see."

Lugubriously, pretending that even in zero g his bulk was difficult to move, he unclipped his belt and drifted off his stool. Wearing a look of exaggerated pathos, he palmed open the doors. As he floated out of sickbay, however, his expression resumed its earlier fatigue and concern.

Min followed him far enough to hold the palm-plate so that the doors stayed open.

Out among the g-hammocks, he paused briefly as if he were surveying a battlefield. Then, apparently at random, he selected one and bobbed toward it. Curling his fingers in the mesh, he frowned sadly at its occupant. "How're you doing, Baldridge?" He could have read the man's id patch, but Min was sure that he knew all his people by name. "You must feel like hell."

"Aye, sir," Baldridge answered thinly.

"What's going on? What's happening to you?"

The hammock shifted as if Baldridge were squirming. "Don't know, sir. I was working my board like always, just sitting there, and my eyes went spotty. Couldn't see the readouts. Then I started puking. Spots were so damn big, I couldn't help trying to heave them up. My duty officer had to bring me here."

"Sounds miserable," Dolph rumbled sympathetically. "They're going to have to make the sickbays on these tubs bigger. You shouldn't have to hang out here in a damn hammock."

"Aye, sir." The uncertainty in Baldridge's tone was plain.

Again without any obvious reason for his selection, Dolph approached another invalid. This time a woman answered him. He asked her the same questions in different words: she gave him her version of the answers. He patted her head through the mesh as if he wanted to comfort her, then moved to a third hammock.

Glancing aside, Min saw that Foster had come to watch from the doorway with her. He seemed full of his responsibility for his patients: perhaps he wanted to be sure that Captain Ubikwe didn't mistreat them.

When Dolph had expressed his solicitude a third time, he stopped moving around. Instead he told the man he'd just questioned, "You know, almost the same thing happened to me once."

He spoke as if he were talking to the man personally; but now his deep voice was pitched to carry, so that everyone in the corridor could hear him.

"It wasn't on my first ship, it was the second. I mean, I wasn't still wet behind the ears. At least I didn't think so. But it happened to me anyway. Our medtech—he was a crusty old SOB who'd been through the gap a few times too many—told me I didn't just have SAD, I was fucking *depressed*."

A grin flashed across his face. Then he became serious again.

"Before it happened, I thought I was doing pretty good. Only my second ship, and already I'd worked myself up to targ third. On my way to the upper ranks, where they get to make their own decisions practically every day. The fact is, I thought I was hot shit. Unfortunately that turned out to be true."

His mouth hinted at another smile, but he didn't stop.

"We hit heavy action, four illegals, one really huge hauler and three gunboat escorts, and they were trying to duck us in an asteroid belt. It wasn't my first action, or even my first heavy action, that first tour wasn't what you could politely call a cakewalk, but for some reason it scared me different than I'd ever been scared before. The hauler wasn't agile, but those gunboats could spin rings around us, especially when we were moving slow enough to survive in a belt. They were coming at me from every direction at once, I couldn't keep all those trajectories on my readouts at the same time, not to mention in my mind. And for reasons which weren't exactly clear to me, the old man—our captain wanted us to call him that, God knows why—didn't let me put targ on automatic and just blaze away. No, he wanted to pick his own targets in his own sweet time.

"For a couple of minutes there, I thought I was about to die. My hands were sweating so hard my fingers skidded off the keys. By the time I got around to firing after the old man gave me an order, there was nothing to fire *at* except rocks and vacuum. He swore continuously whenever he didn't have something else to say, and I knew he was swearing at me."

Dolph paused as if he were lost in memory, then sighed. "That's when it happened."

He fell silent; might have been finished.

In spite of herself, Min wanted him to go on. His voice or his story had a mesmerizing quality: it carried her with it. And she wasn't alone. She could see at a glance that every head in the corridor was turned toward him. Foster bit his lip while he waited as if he didn't like the suspense.

Compelled by the unexpected silence, someone offered tentatively, "Hallucinations?"

Dolph shook his head. "Worse than that." Suddenly his dark face broke into a grin like a sunrise. "I fouled my suit.

"I mean the *whole* suit." Laughter welled up in him from some core of personal amusement. "Talk about hot shit!" He started chortling, then began to laugh as if he were telling the best joke he knew, the best joke of his life. "You would think I hadn't been to the head for a week. By the time I was done, the bridge, I mean the *entire* bridge, stank like a backed-up waste treatment plant. Our communications third actually *puked* because she couldn't stand the smell."

His mirth was infectious. Several of his people laughed with him as if they couldn't help themselves. A dozen others chuckled.

While his laughter subsided, he concluded, "Our medtech was right. I was fucking depressed for *weeks*."

Shaking his head, he pulled himself past the hammocks and coasted away in the direction of his quarters. As he left, his shoulders continued to quake as if he were still laughing.

Together Min and Foster drifted back into sickbay and let the doors close.

The medtech didn't look at her. Frowning like a man who wasn't sure of the propriety of what he'd just witnessed, he asked, "Is that story true, Director?"

She nodded. "Yes. His captain told me years ago. I'd forgotten all about it." A moment later she added, "But the way his captain told it, it wasn't funny."

Sounding wiser than his years, Foster murmured, "It wouldn't work if it weren't true." Then he returned to his console and monitors.

An hour later, during another brief patch of clear space, Dolph chimed Min in her cabin to let her know that twenty-one of his SAD-afflicted people had released themselves from sickbay and gone back to their duties.

She still wasn't sure what it was he'd done, but obviously it'd succeeded.

"You couldn't have faked that," she informed him sternly. "You really think that old story is funny."

She wanted to ask him, How? How do you do that? But the words stuck in her throat.

"Of course," he replied through a yawn. "I wanted to give them some other way to think about how they felt. I don't mean physically. How they felt emotionally. Mentally." Almost echoing Foster, he explained, "It wouldn't work if I had to fake it."

Another yawn came across the intercom. "Forgive me, Min. I'd better take a nap while I have the chance."

Her speaker emitted a small snik as he severed the connection.

For a while as *Punisher* wrenched and dove through the system in the direction of Deaner Beckmann's lab, Min lay sealed in her g-sheath and tried to imagine herself laughing at Warden Dios. Or laughing with him at the way she felt about some of his recent actions.

She couldn't do it.

DAVIES

With Morn's training as well as his own experience, Davies listened to the ship. He felt the complex pressure of the drives, gauged the various vectors of braking and maneuvering g. When *Trumpet* entered the asteroid swarm which surrounded and protected the Lab, he knew the difference.

The change was obvious. Quick variations on a comparatively low velocity had a different effect than changes to avoid obstacles at high speed. And each course shift as *Trumpet* had crossed the Massif-5 system had been followed by a matching return to the original heading: pressure on one side; then pressure on the other. But in the swarm every g-kick of thrust belonged to an ongoing series of new trajectories as *Trumpet* dodged back and forth among the rocks.

Lying paralyzed in his g-sheath and webbing tormented Davies. All his energies—mental, emotional, metabolic—burned at too high a temperature: most of the time he needed movement more than he needed rest. In addition the discomfort of his ribs and arm and head galled him. Despite his elevated recuperative resources and all the drugs sickbay had given him, his body couldn't heal fast enough to suit him.

A restlessness as severe as panic impelled him. As soon as *Trumpet* broached the swarm, he risked getting off his bunk.

He could use his arm: his cast gave the still-fragile bones enough protection. And the more flexible acrylic around his ribs supported his chest adequately. As long as Nick didn't hit him with too much g, he could move without damaging himself.

Simply because his need was so great, he spent ten minutes pumping himself like a piston between the deck and ceiling of the cabin—the zero-g equivalent of push-ups. Then he used the san cubicle; scrubbed himself in the needle spray for a long time, trying to clean away the sensation of Angus' betrayal.

But when the vacuum drain had sucked the water away and dried his skin, he decided not to put on a clean shipsuit. He'd worn the same strange black Amnion fabric since the hour of his birth. It wasn't especially comfortable, but he needed its alienness—needed external reminders of where he'd come from, who he was. Whenever he let his defenses down, he forgot that he wasn't Morn. Sleeping, he dreamed her dreams.

Maybe that was the real reason he couldn't endure much rest.

Thrust punched his shoulder against one wall. Not hard: just enough to remind him that he should be careful. And that he had to check on Morn.

Wrapped in her webbing and sheath, she slept the flat, helpless sleep of too much cat. Repeated doses which he'd pushed between her slack lips had kept her unconscious so long that he began to wonder if she would be able to wake up. The medtechs in the Academy had enjoyed telling cautionary tales about men and women overdosed with cat who sank so far down into themselves that they never returned.

He looked at the cabin chronometer: she was due to receive another capsule—or begin waking up—in forty minutes.

After a moment he decided he couldn't wait that long. In spite of the danger, he unsealed her from her bunk and lifted her out.

At once he noticed that she'd fouled her shipsuit. Nobody could sleep as long as she had and stay clean.

Without transition the rank, sweet smell triggered memories—

This had happened to her before; happened to him. When Angus had first brought him aboard *Bright Beauty*, Angus had strapped him down on the sickbay table to immobilize him. Fresh with horror from the destruction of *Starmaster*, the slaughter of the Hyland clan, Davies or Morn had cried and wailed, screamed against the deaf walls until he'd lost his voice; lost his mind. Then Angus had shot him full of cat—

—and when he'd awakened, still in the EVA suit which had brought him to *Bright Beauty* from *Starmaster*'s wreck, this smell was everywhere, filling the sickbay, filling his head. Angus' power over him began with murder and gap-sickness; blood and the clarity of self-destruct.

Asleep in her son's arms, Morn whimpered softly and turned her head aside, as if he'd disturbed her with bad dreams.

Her small sound and movement brought him back to himself.

Sudden sweat streaked his cheeks. His heart labored as if he were fighting for his life. That was *Morn's* smell; *her* ordeal, not his: it was *her* memory. Her nightmare—

When he lost the distinction, let himself forget who he was, he became as mad as she'd been then.

Oh, Morn.

No doubt he ought to be crazy. Nevertheless while he could still tell what sanity was, he clung to it. Morn needed him; that came first. Later he would try to get rid of the stink in other ways.

Grim with determination, he drew her weightless body into the san. His stomach twisted as he pulled off her shipsuit and propped her in the cubicle. At least she would be spared this one memory: she was still asleep. He set the jets to produce a fine mist which wouldn't drown her. While the water ran, he disposed of her soiled shipsuit, then hunted for a clean one that might fit her.

More jolts knocked him from side to side as *Trumpet* dodged. Each one hit like a stun-prod of alarm: he feared its effect on Morn. But they weren't hard enough to hurt him. They probably weren't hard enough to trigger her gap-sickness.

When he went back to check on her, he heard her coughing in the mist. She sounded conscious.

He raised his voice so that she could hear him. "I'm right here. Nick hasn't said anything yet, and I guess the others are still in their cabins, but I know we're in the swarm. I assume we're going to reach the Lab soon. I couldn't stand to give you any more cat, so I decided to take the risk of waking you up."

After a thin spasm of coughing, she murmured, "Thanks."

She was awake. And sane. A sudden rush of relief left him light-headed and vulnerable; close to tears. No gap-sickness: not this time. Until that moment he hadn't realized the extent of his fear. As far as he could remember, Morn had never tried controlling her mad certainty with cat. He hadn't known it would work.

Shaking, he left the san and closed the door.

While he waited for her to finish, he did more zero-g push-ups, working his body until the alien fabric of his shipsuit chafed his skin and he began to sweat so hard that he needed another shower; working the dread out of his muscles.

She emerged clean and dry; but too many hours of enforced sleep had done nothing to improve her appearance. She looked pale and thin, almost emaciated, as if she hadn't eaten for days. Lingering cat dulled her gaze. Despite the absence of g, her movements seemed frail, confused. It was hard to believe she was the same woman who'd insisted, *Don't fight. Don't refuse. Stay alive—don't give him an excuse to kill you.*

There's a lie here. Somebody's lying. We need to stay alive until we find out what it is.

But Angus hadn't told Nick how to make another control for her zone implant. That memory belonged to Davies; he trusted it. He remembered it while he looked at her so that her weakness wouldn't fill him with fresh panic.

She didn't meet his gaze. Maybe she couldn't focus her eyes. "Now what?" she asked wanly.

He shrugged. Droplets of sweat detached themselves from his face and became perfect globes. They caught the light like glass beads as they floated toward the scrubbers. "I guess we wait." Wait for *Trumpet* to reach the Lab. Wait for Vector to attempt his analysis of the mutagen immunity drug. Wait for Nick to make a mistake. Or for Min Donner to perform some inconceivable intervention. "I don't have any better ideas."

She shook her head. She didn't either.

Trumpet remained relatively motionless for what seemed like a long time, then started moving again. Now every shift of course and nudge of thrust was gentle, cautious: the ship slid forward as if she were picking her way through a mine field. Davies fought an impulse to watch the chronometer. Instead he tried to guess by sheer intuition what *Trumpet* was doing.

She'd stopped so that Nick could talk to the Lab, get permission to approach. Now she was moving in. Slowly, so the Lab wouldn't see her as a threat. So the Lab's guns wouldn't open fire on her. She must be close to her destination. If the matter cannon emplacements were too far out, rock and static would make accurate targ impossible. Scan installations might be anywhere in the swarm, reporting their data along long chains of remote transmitters, but the guns would be nearer the Lab.

OK: assume that made sense. How much longer? An hour? More? Less? Deliberately he avoided the chronometer. Because he needed movement, any kind of movement, he began doing push-ups again. Gradually, without noticing it, he increased his pace. Up. Down. The directions were meaningless, of course—simply a frame of reference. Up down. Nevertheless the action of his body generated its own g; its own significance. Updown.

"Waiting is hard enough," Morn murmured distantly. "You're wearing me out. Why do you do that?"

He stopped himself on the edge of his bunk. Breathing hard—but steadily, as if he could have gone on for hours—he said, "I don't like sitting still. I don't even like rest. It scares me."

As her last dose of cat wore off, some measure of elasticity had returned to her muscles, especially in her face. Her expression had slowly become more alert, less exposed. She tried to smile, with limited success. "How did I get a son like you? I feel just the opposite. I think I could rest"—she shrugged, grimaced—"practically forever. It's movement that scares me. I'm afraid of what happens next."

Then she added wryly, "I guess I'm turning into a coward in my old age. Considering the fact that I'm almost as young as you are, that isn't easy to do. I'm probably going to set some kind of record."

But Davies was in no mood for jokes. "Considering the fact," he retorted harshly, "that you've already been through a lifetime of hell, you've earned the right to be afraid. It's about time some of the rest of us started helping you. But you're too far ahead of us. We can't catch up." Sib's attempt to guard Nick had been a debacle. Neither Mikka nor Davies himself had been able to handle Angus. "For some reason, you're always the one who helps us."

Morn frowned. "I'm sure you're right," she countered. "I distinctly remember rescuing myself from the Amnion."

"That was Angus and Nick," Davies protested. Mikka and Sib. And *Captain's Fancy*. "All I did was stand guard."

Suddenly Morn was angry. "*All you did*," she snapped back, "was stay sane when you should have gone completely crazy. *All you did* was scare the Bill so much that he couldn't just hand you over to Nick or the Amnion. *All you did* was keep Nick from tricking Angus. How many of us would still be alive if you hadn't done that? And since then you haven't done anything except take care of me.

"*Don't* tell me you aren't helping. I can't stand it—I need you too much."

Davies felt a rush of chagrin he couldn't stifle. "I'm sorry. I didn't mean it that way. I'm just"—shame and ineffectuality affected him like rage—"just lost. I don't know who I am, or what I'm doing. You saved me twice when Nick tried to give me to the Amnion." Once on Enablement. Once in the ejection pod. "When you call yourself a coward, it sounds like you're telling me there's nothing left I can count on."

Morn took a deep breath, let it out in a long sigh. "I know. I don't mean to be so touchy. All this waiting—" She pushed her hands through her hair, pulling herself back under control. "It wears on me. It goes on and on, and I don't know what I'm still trying to hope for. Sometimes I can feel myself crumbling."

He knew that feeling—or one just like it. Gritting his teeth, he clung to the edge of the bunk so that the restless pressure inside him wouldn't take over.

He and Morn went on waiting.

They knew it when *Trumpet* came into her berth. The hull sounds of approach and dock were unmistakable. First came the steadily more gentle pressure of braking thrust, the slim fire of attitudinal jets: then the clangor of metal, amplified by constricted space, as the ship met the berth guides and slid along them: then the slap and groan of grapples, the final settling. And after that came the insertion of air hoses and communications lines, power cables and waste pumps—each with its characteristic hiss or thud or click, its telltale echo.

Gradually the distant, visceral whine of *Trumpet*'s drives subsided. She was at rest.

The apprehension coiling around Davies' spine pulled itself another notch tighter. Morn's fingers clenched and unclenched as she combed them through her hair: she might have been resisting an impulse to yank strands out by the fistful.

Abruptly the intercom crackled.

"All right, assholes," Nick announced cheerfully. "On the bridge. Right away would be good. Right now would be better. It's time for orders."

Immediately Morn bobbed up from her bunk as if she couldn't afford to hesitate; as if she knew that once she hesitated she would lose her capacity for movement altogether. But the sight of her stricken gaze and her pallor wrung Davies' heart. He caught her by the shoulder, turned her in the air to face him.

"I can tell him you're still asleep. He'll have to believe me—he doesn't know how much cat I gave you. You can probably stay in here as long as you want."

I can protect you that much.

She shook her head. "That would mean more waiting. I want to do something. Anything." A rueful smile shaped her mouth for a moment. "I guess I'm more like you than I thought."

He couldn't think of a response. His own need for activity left no room for argument. In any case he wasn't sure which one of them was protecting the other.

With his courage clenched in both hands, he pushed off toward the door.

He felt a downward drag as he moved—the light g of the asteroid, perhaps marginally augmented by gravitic fields from some of Deaner Beckmann's experimental equipment. By the time he'd reached the door and keyed it open, his boots touched the deck.

Perfect. Just enough weight to confuse his zero-g training; not enough to let him move normally.

Fear spiked along his pulse as he floated in a flat arc toward the head of the companionway.

He was the first to arrive: only Nick and Angus were on the bridge. When he started down the treads, Nick flashed him a feral grin, full of black scars and threats; but Angus sat motionless—shoulders hunched, head bowed—as if he'd fallen asleep at his board.

Then Morn reached the companionway behind Davies.

Nick's grin stretched wider. "You're sane again," he observed harshly. "I don't know whether to regret that or enjoy it."

"Enjoy it." Morn's tone was quiet and steady: she spoke from some distant place where Nick's malice didn't reach her. "You can't hurt me when I'm out of my mind."

Despite her plain weakness, her obvious vulnerability, she followed her son downward.

She may have been trying to defy Nick; but he didn't react to it. He was on fire with a strange, personal ecstasy. The passion that heated his gaze and darkened his scars gave the impression that he'd achieved a state of exaltation in which he, too, couldn't be reached.

Something had happened—something as acute and fatal as *Punisher*'s transmission.

"You underestimate me," he retorted. "But at the moment I don't give a shit. While you've been sleeping your damn brains out, the game has suddenly gotten a whole lot bigger."

"Why?" Davies and Morn asked simultaneously. "What do you mean?" she pursued. "What's going on?" he added.

"Good." Nick nodded in satisfaction. "I like that. You two are so fucking identical, you might as well be twins. Maybe if you make a special effort to keep me happy, I'll let you entertain Beckmann and his collection of tech bozos by reading each other's minds."

"Fine," Mikka said from the head of companionway. "Morn and Davies are in charge of entertainment. Where does that leave the rest of us?"

She stood with Sib and Ciro on either side of her as if she needed their support. Sickbay had patched and bandaged her forehead: no doubt it had given her transfusions as well, pumped her full of drugs. Nevertheless the damage to her skull required more time to heal. She looked wan and uncharacteristically fragile, as if she'd broken more bones than sickbay could treat.

Behind her Vector moved stiffly, awkwardly: apparently his joints hurt even in this low g. Bandages made his cut hand thick and imprecise, like the head of a mallet, but he still had the use of his fingers. If he needed them. He was probably capable of operating the Lab's equipment with one hand.

Sib and Ciro were in better shape physically. Short of neural breakdown, the aftereffects of stun didn't linger. But Sib's cheeks were hollow, and his eyes had sunk in his head; he looked like he was being eaten alive by his fears and failures. And Ciro appeared to suffer from a kind of emotional nausea. Perhaps he felt sickened by the fact that he'd let Nick take his stun-prod away from him.

"It leaves you with me," Nick answered. His tone was like a ghoul's mimicry of his former ominous casualness. "I'm going to take Vector to meet Beckmann and use his facilities. You're coming along.

"Let me tell you something about that, just in case you're still groggy enough be stupid. You're going to take orders. You will fucking *do* what I fucking *tell* you."

He hit keys to clear his board, then unbelted himself from his g-seat and stood up, at least in part so that everyone else could see the impact pistol clipped at his waist. At some point during the past several hours, he must have paid a visit to the weapons locker.

"Never mind the fact that I'll shoot you if you don't. Fucking heroes like you probably don't care. No, you're going to take orders because you can imagine what I'll make Angus do to Morn if you don't.

"Is that clear enough so far?"

Mikka and her companions hadn't moved from the top of the companionway. Her bandages seemed to twist her frown into an act of brutality. "I take it that means Angus and Morn aren't going with us. What about Davies?"

Nick shook his head. "He's staying behind, too. To tell you the truth" —his expression might have looked impish if his scars hadn't been so dark —"Center doesn't know they're aboard. I left them off the manifest. As far as Beckmann and his guards are concerned, there's only the five of us. Which means Angus here can give us all the cover we need while we're off the ship."

He turned toward his second. "You listening, asshole?"

Angus' voice was confined in his chest, caught by conflicting pressures. "I'm listening."

He didn't lift his head or look around.

"Good," Nick rasped. He spoke to Angus as if none of the other people on the bridge existed. "Listen hard, because I'm not going to put up with any bullshit.

"The five of us are leaving. We probably won't be back until Vector gets somewhere with that drug. Depends on how good he is. Right now he probably thinks he'll gain something by being slow. But after he's considered the situation, he'll realize that the longer he takes, the more people are going to get hurt.

"Until then"—Nick drifted a step or two closer to the second's station—"you'll cover us." Leaning forward, he demanded, "*Are you listening?*"

Davies held his breath. Angus must be Nick's weak point, the place where his plans could go wrong. If his control over Angus failed while he wasn't here to enforce it, he wouldn't have a ship to return to.

Angus still didn't look up. "I'm listening."

"You damn well better," Nick shot back. Saliva gathered at the corners of his mouth like froth, but he appeared unaware of it. "I'll tear your heart out—and you know I can do it."

Angus didn't retort or protest; he hardly seemed to be alive. His nod was like the shudder of a broken machine.

But that was enough for Nick.

"Monitor every communications and scan channel you can tap," he ordered, "watch for trouble. If you see or hear anything that sounds like we've got problems, charge the matter cannon and start making threats. This ship has enough power to gut the whole installation from here. That's something Beckmann will listen to. His research is too precious—he won't risk it."

To himself, Davies admitted that Nick was right. Deaner Beckmann had made a serious mistake when he'd let Nick get this close to him.

Now Nick turned his baleful grin on Davies and Morn, although he continued speaking to Angus.

"In the meantime"—fires laughed in his hot gaze—"the Hyland twins are yours."

Davies thought he could feel his heart stop. He heard Sib choke in shock and chagrin, heard Mikka breathe a low curse; but those sounds meant nothing to him. For an instant the bridge constricted around him, shrank to darkness. In the void helpless memories beat about his head like black wings: Angus with the zone implant control; Angus cocking his fists; Angus erect past the seams of his shipsuit, charged with violence—

He jerked a glance at Morn, saw the thin blood drain from her face. She held herself still, poised, as if she could bear anything; but the sudden pallor of her cheeks and the white rim of panic around her irises betrayed her fear.

Nick clapped sarcastic applause. Then he told Angus, "If that computer in your malicious little head will let you play with them, go ahead. I don't care."

Don't care, Davies heard. Don't care.

"Just don't let them out of your sight. Don't let them touch anything."

Anything.

"Don't let them do or say or even *think* anything that gives them the impression they can get out of this.

"And don't kill them," he added abruptly. "I'm not done with them.

"Is *that* clear?"

"It's clear," Angus answered in a dead tone.

Angus—

"Good." Nick flashed his teeth. "When I get back, you can tell me all about it."

Morn, help me. Tell me how to help you. We've got to get out of this.

Mikka still hadn't moved; her companions hadn't moved. "It's not clear to me," she put in roughly. "You expect us to take your orders because we're afraid of what Angus will do to Morn if we don't. But you just told him to do whatever he wants. What have you got left to threaten us with?"

Despite her weakness, she was trying to put pressure on Nick; force him to give Morn and Davies some protection.

Nick swung toward her, flung his voice at her like a fist. "I didn't threaten you with what *he'll* think up. I threatened you with what *I'll* think up *for* him."

Mikka shrugged stiffly. "Is that worse?"

"Try me," he countered, nearly shouting. Flecks of saliva sprayed from his lips. "*Try* me."

Mikka faced him without flinching; but she didn't answer. Maybe she couldn't.

Angus hadn't told Nick how to replace Morn's zone implant control. He may have been saving that for himself.

"You try him if you want to, Mikka," Vector said unexpectedly. The blue calm in his eyes disturbed Davies, like a glimpse of something unfathomable. "I'm going to take orders like a good boy."

Ciro's eyes widened as if he were dismayed; as if he expected Vector to resist. Mikka shifted her weight so that she could confront Vector without putting pressure on her neck.

"The truth is," Vector continued, "I don't really care what he does with this antimutagen. Assuming I can actually figure out the formula. I just want to know if I was on the right track—if the research I did for Intertech could have worked."

"Do you *mean* that?" Sib protested. "You really don't care what he's going to *do*?"

The former engineer shrugged gently. "It's not as callous as it sounds. By itself the formula is useless to him. I could give him every chemical miracle in the galaxy, and he couldn't synthesize one of them. He doesn't have the equipment. The formula means nothing until he sells it.

"And every sale is a form of dissemination. Maybe it's not as good as actually making the drug public, but it goes in that direction. The more people who know about it, the closer it comes to being common knowledge. A discovery like this does good simply by existing. I'll spread it any way I can."

He was out of his mind. Apparently he believed Morn's insistence that there was *something else going on*. Something to hope for. But Nick had given Morn and Davies to Angus to *play with*. There was nothing left.

Through her teeth, Mikka told Vector softly, "That's not good enough."

"Shut up, Mikka," Nick snapped. "I don't have time for this. You're going to take orders, and you're going to start *now*." He closed his fingers threateningly around the butt of his handgun. "Center knows we have injuries aboard. That's why they aren't harassing us already—they think we need time to pull ourselves together. But if we don't go soon, they'll start asking questions. The wrong questions. I don't want that.

"Are you going to *do what I tell you*, or do I have to shoot a few chunks out of your brother to convince you?"

For a moment Mikka stiffened. She leaned toward Ciro as if she meant to step in front of him. From under her bandage her good eye flashed a glare of belligerence. But she must have been able to see that there was nothing she could do. Gradually her instinct for combat faded.

"I'm sorry, Morn," she sighed. "I don't know what else to do. It's too much for me."

"Don't worry about it." Morn's tone held firm, even though her gaze ached with doom. "I would make the same decision."

Davies wanted to protest, I wouldn't. *I* wouldn't. But he knew better. He had no idea what else any of them could do.

Without warning the bridge speakers came to life.

"*Trumpet*, this is Center," a tense voice announced. "We thought you were going to disembark. Is there a problem? Do you need help?"

Nick swore impatiently. Bounding back to the command station, he keyed his pickup.

"Center, this is Captain Succorso. I don't mean to keep you waiting. I just wanted to give sickbay time to finish with Vector and Mikka. They're ready now. We'll be opening our airlock in five minutes."

Palpably insincere, Center replied, "Take your time. *We're* in no hurry."

With the pop of a toggle, the communication channel closed.

Nick silenced his pickup.

"Now. Let's do it."

Unexpectedly slow, almost languid in his movements, he turned for the companionway. He seemed completely at ease; altogether sure of himself. Nevertheless his scars looked like streaks of acid under his eyes, burning deeper and deeper into his cheeks. Heat poured off him as if he were overflowing.

"The lift," he told Mikka and Vector, Sib and Ciro. "Go."

Mikka and her companions hesitated for a second. But after a quick glance at each other they shoved off from the handrails and began drifting backward along the passage.

Davies couldn't let Nick go. His fear was Morn's: he had to do something about it. "Wait a minute," he objected; insisted. "You still haven't told us what happened. What are you so excited about? What's going on?"

He thought Nick wouldn't answer. Nick had gone too far into his strange personal exaltation: he might not be able to hear ordinary questions—or deal with them if he heard them.

His reaction surprised Davies. He squinted up the companionway to be sure that Mikka and the others were out of earshot. Then he gave a burst of febrile laughter, a quick, spasmodic clench of his fists. "Sorus," he announced. He began with a chuckle; but almost at once the name seemed to stick in his throat. "Sorus fucking Chatelaine." For a moment he gaped as if he couldn't breathe. Then he croaked, "She's here."

He might have been strangling on joy.

Davies wanted to demand, *Soar?* Here? Doesn't she work for the Amnion? But memories of the woman who'd helped the Bill interrogate him stopped him. She was the same woman who'd cut Nick because she despised him—and hadn't considered him worth killing. The Bill had told her to question Davies. Torture him, if that was what it took. She hadn't done that: apparently she didn't go to those extremes unless she was sure they were necessary. But he'd believed that she would do it.

She would have done it, if Angus hadn't rescued him—

—the same Angus who was now under Nick's control. Who had been given permission to *play with* Davies and Morn.

The same Angus who sagged over his board as if his spine or his spirit had snapped.

Still moving slowly, Nick coasted toward the companionway. Then, suddenly, he grabbed for the back of Angus' g-seat, pulled himself around beside his second. His whole body seemed to emit malice as he leaned forward to pat Angus' cheek as if Angus were a kid of whom he'd become inordinately fond.

"Have fun," he said cheerfully. "Opportunities like this don't come along every day, you know."

Grinning at Morn and Davies, he somersaulted to the treads as if he were showing off, handed his way up the railing, and disappeared toward the lift.

A moment later Davies heard servos hum as the lift opened; closed. Hydraulic systems gave off a nearly inaudible whine while the lift moved. Nick and his involuntary crew were about to unseal the airlock. About to go meet Deaner Beckmann.

Davies and Morn were alone with his father—the man who'd first ripped her life apart.

Deliberately he shifted his position so that he stood between Morn and Angus.

She put one hand on his shoulder. She may have intended her touch to comfort or restrain him in some way; remind him of his importance to her. But slowly her fingers dug into his flesh, gripping him as if she couldn't find any other strength to support her.

Angus hadn't moved. He leaned like a broken thing over his board, a puppet with his strings cut—severed from will and passion and hope by the inexorable demands of his datacore.

"Come on, Angus," Morn said abruptly. Her voice was harsh with dread and raw, helpless defiance; full of memory. "Get it over with. Show us your worst."

Davies' heart struggled against his ribs like a prisoner. Instinctively he braced himself to fight.

Released by Morn's words, a tremor ran through Angus. Shuddering, he raised his head. For a time he fumbled at the catch of his belt: his hands appeared to be stiff with cramps. Then, one painful muscle after another, he pulled himself upright.

Unsteady as a derelict, he turned to face his victims.

The sight of them seemed to shock him. They were only two meters away, but he squinted at them as if they were almost out of sight; beyond comprehension. He began breathing harder: his chest heaved as if he were trapped in an EVA suit with no air. Damage glazed his yellow eyes. By degrees pressure blackened his face. His hands crooked into claws, straining for bloodshed.

Abruptly Angus jerked up his arms and hammered both sides of his head with the heels of his palms.

Davies flinched involuntarily. Morn's fingers gouged his shoulder.

As if his life depended on it, Angus struggled to say something. But he couldn't articulate the words through his hoarse gasping; couldn't force them out clearly enough.

Davies watched in dismay while Angus hit himself again; and again.

Then the pressure inside him appeared to burst and fall away. Grinding his teeth, he rasped like an obscenity, "I'm not your son."

His voice rose into a rending shout, as if his throat were torn by clarion triumph or wild despair.

"I am not your *fucking* SON!"

At once he broke into a fit of coughing that sounded like sobs.

MORN

Angus' cry shocked her like stun. Charged with fear, her muscles turned to jelly; the marrow seemed to bleed from her bones. She wanted to protest, What?

What?

What are you *talking* about?

But she couldn't find the words. Words were strength—anything she might have said, any response was a kind of strength—and all the strength had burned out of her. The torn triumph or pain in Angus' voice had left her helpless.

I'm not your son.

Frantically she glanced at Davies.

He, too, had been hit hard. He remembered Angus as well as she did. And his ability to distinguish himself from her was fragile: he'd only had a few days in which to try to re-create himself as a separate human being. Something labored in him, strove to rise against the blow—some defense or rejection, some instinct for intransigence or violence. She could see the struggle on his face. Nevertheless for the moment he was caught the same way she was; trapped and held by the sheer extremity of Angus' shout.

I am not your **fucking** *SON!*

Now he, Angus, broke into coughing as if he'd ripped open his lungs—

—and stopped. Just like that: between one heartbeat and the next. Tears of pain smeared his cheeks, but he ignored them. Maybe he didn't know they were there. He looked as stunned as Davies, as stunned as Morn herself.

Slowly, as if he, too, had only jelly to support him, he turned back to the second's station.

Morn recognized that instant transformation. His datacore had taken control: emissions from his zone implants had stifled his coughing, forced down his despair, smothered his triumph. He was a welded cyborg, ruled by decisions made for him days or weeks ago by men who didn't care what he felt or how he suffered; who cared only how he could be used. Briefly his raw human distress had burst its bounds. But now the inexorable pressure on the neural centers of his brain had recaptured him.

Whatever he did here, it would be because Warden Dios or Hashi Lebwohl—or their proxy, Nick Succorso—required it of him, not because he chose it.

She understood from experience. Oh, she'd never been welded. But Angus had imposed the same kind of submission on her. Later, voluntarily, she'd imposed it on herself. Time and again she'd felt an appalled outbreak of need and pain collapse in the face of electromagnetic coercion.

I'm not your son.

Davies opened his mouth. He was going to say something hostile; try to defend her by attracting Angus' malice to himself; she saw it on his face. With an effort that caused her to shudder as if she were shaken by fever, she brought up her hand in a warning gesture, cautioned him to silence.

He looked at her with his father's fear and fury clenched in his features. Nevertheless he clamped his jaws shut. The only sound from him was a low, visceral snarl.

Artificially steady, Angus began tapping keys on the second's board.

Morn couldn't do anything except gape as a flimsy sheet scrolled from the console's printout.

Angus tore off the hardcopy slowly, as if it were precious. His datacore demanded precision. Ineffably meticulous, he pivoted in the asteroid's slight g and left the second's station. Despite the pressure of his zone implants, he appeared almost at ease, almost graceful, as he moved.

His boots touched the deck in front of Davies. He stopped himself with a palm on Davies' shoulder.

Davies didn't move. Stiff with incomprehension, he bore the contact without flinching; without striking out. His attention was fixed on the sheet Angus carried.

Still slowly, as if the situation had become too urgent for haste, Angus handed the sheet to Davies.

For no reason she could name, Morn found herself holding her breath like a woman who wasn't sure whose son Davies truly was, hers or Angus'.

Davies peered at the hardcopy. He seemed unable to read it. Perhaps he was having trouble focusing his eyes. Or perhaps he simply couldn't believe what he saw.

"Jesus," he sighed—a long, soft exhalation, as if he were draining out of himself. By degrees he turned toward Morn.

Angus turned with him: they faced her together. The resemblance between them was uncanny. Davies was less bloated: he had less muscle, less fat. His black shipsuit contrasted strangely with Angus' grimy outfit. But those differences were trivial. Only Davies' eyes—eyes like Morn's—distinguished him from his father.

Suddenly Davies flailed his arms at the ceiling and yelled as if he were crowing, "*We've got him!* We've *got* him!"

She jerked backward involuntarily. She couldn't help herself: his unexpected savagery hit her like an attack. His shout echoed in her ears. For a moment she couldn't hear anything else. Between them, he and his father had deafened her.

Angus' cheeks were still wet: his eyes bled tears he couldn't control. He didn't glance at Davies. Instead his yellow gaze clung to her as if he were begging her for something.

Understanding? Forgiveness?

Help?

Her heart labored for several beats before she was able to find her voice.

"What is it? What does it say?"

With an effort Davies forced himself to speak more quietly. "It's from *Punisher*." Yet his eyes burned, and his whole body appeared to emit a furious joy. "We've got his codes. Angus' codes. Now we can beat Nick!"

Dumb with supplication, Angus stared at Morn like a beaten animal.

The words were plain enough. *We've got his codes*. Yet she couldn't grasp what they meant. *Angus' codes*. Panic and hope and old pain filled her chest until she could hardly breathe, crowded her heart while it struggled to beat.

Now we can beat Nick!

What do you mean?

Her question was inaudible. She'd asked it of herself, not of her son. Or of Angus.

And she didn't know the answer.

She tried again.

"What do you mean?"

"I mean"—Davies' hand shook with eagerness as he shoved the flimsy sheet at her, urging her to take it—"we can *countermand* him. We can cancel his orders. We can give Angus new ones.

"We can *beat* Nick."

Fighting a constriction in his throat, Angus said thickly, "It's not that simple." His gaze was flagrant with need, but he couldn't articulate his appeal.

Dumbly Morn accepted the hardcopy so that she could read it herself.

Warden Dios to Isaac, it said, **Gabriel priority.**

Familiar codes identified *Punisher* as the source of the transmission. But ciphers she didn't recognize surrounded the words themselves; encysted them. They might have been some specialized machine language. Certainly they didn't resemble any normal UMCP routing or command sequence.

Show this message to Nick Succorso.

Punisher had given control over Angus to Nick. Now Angus had given it to Davies.

And to Morn.

All at once everything mattered too much. She couldn't afford to make a mistake. Without forewarning or preparation, with nothing to go on except instinct and desperation, she'd arrived at a crisis in which any error would be fatal.

God help her, she wasn't *ready*.

Davies was so full of excitement that he bounced toward the ceiling. He couldn't contain himself: he didn't see the danger. The intensity of his desire to protect her blinded him.

The burden fell on her.

Ready or not.

Her heart beat in her ears, as loud as drums, and heavy as thunder: the venous funeral march of her inadequacy. It didn't matter whether she was ready or not. No one cared. She couldn't afford to care herself.

Nevertheless she was as careful as the pounding in her ears and the frenzy in her soul allowed.

"Isaac," she pronounced unsteadily, "this is a Gabriel priority instruction. Answer my questions.

"Is this the message that came in earlier—the one Nick told us about?"

He swallowed once, convulsively. Beggary bled from his eyes.

"Yes."

"Did you obey it?"

"I didn't have any choice."

"You showed it to Nick?" she insisted, wanting to be clear; wanting him to tell her precisely where she stood.

Angus nodded as if his neck were in pain. "Yes."

"Of course he did," Davies put in impatiently. He was too excited: he didn't seem to have noticed that the situation had become lethal; that his life as well as hers was at stake in every sense. Moment by moment Angus' betrayal grew more terrible. "Those are his *priority-codes*. He *can't* refuse them."

Morn ignored him.

"And since then"—she needed to be sure, *needed* to hear Angus say these things—"he's been telling you what to do? You've been taking his orders? That's why you turned against the rest of us?"

"Yes." If his zone implants had allowed it, he might have sighed.

She took a deep breath, let it out slowly in an effort to calm herself. Fear yammered in her ears—a whole mob of panics clamoring to be heard. The hardcopy shook in her hand.

"Then why are you showing it to us now? Did Nick tell you to do this? Is it some kind of trick?"

That struck a spark in Angus. Hints of anger showed past his mute supplication. "He doesn't know."

Davies settled to the deck. "Is that what you're worried about?" he asked tensely, as if he were running to catch up with her. "You think this is part of some game Nick is playing?"

Morn didn't answer. She had no attention to spare. Everything in her was concentrated on Angus.

"Then who ordered you to do this? And how did they do it?" The sheet trembled. "This doesn't say anything about giving us your codes."

"I don't know who." A small tremor ran through Angus as if he were trying to shrug. "I can only tell you how.

"It's that coding," he explained harshly, "that machine language. I can't read it, but my datacore can. When I entered those strings, it ordered me to show the message to Davies.

"But not right away," he added. "I couldn't do it if Nick would see or hear me. I didn't know I was supposed to do it until he left the ship. My datacore didn't tell me—" Another tremor. "They don't want him to know."

"In any case," Davies objected, "it doesn't matter. We *have* the codes. We can use them, no matter what Nick knows."

For a moment Morn turned away from Angus' appeal to face her son. She held his gaze, let him see the demand in her eyes, until his enthusiasm receded into a scowl. Then she shifted back to Angus.

"What did you mean, 'It's not that simple'?"

The tension in his shoulders and arms told her that she was moving closer to his need; to the thing he wanted to ask of her.

"You can countermand him," he replied in a hoarse rasp. "Fine. He can countermand you. You'll cancel each other out. What happens then? Maybe you can beat him, maybe you can't. But I'll be paralyzed—I'll be useless."

Morn could almost hear him wailing, Please, *please*! as if his pain was beyond language. The sheer scale of the harm which Warden Dios and Hashi Lebwohl had done to him shocked her.

But Davies couldn't contain himself. "We still have the advantage," he interrupted. "Nick doesn't know he's in trouble. We can attack him first. Angus can open the weapons locker. We'll meet Nick in the airlock with guns. Nail him before he reaches Angus. Lock him away where Angus can't hear him. Kill him if we have to. Let's see him countermand *that*."

Angus never looked aside from Morn. His datacore had required him to give his codes to Davies; but she was the one he focused on.

"It's not that simple," he repeated. Pressures which should have driven him into madness—or at least into motion—gripped and released in his muscles, yet his zone implants held him stationary. "What if he calls me from the Lab? What if he uses the exterior intercom to talk to me while you're waiting in the airlock?" His moment of anger was over. "I have to obey him. If he asks me what's going on, I'll tell him."

Davies opened his mouth; closed it again: Morn's expression stopped him. Like Angus, he stared at her as if he wanted to ask her for something, beg—

Now she knew the question Angus wished her to put to him. It came to her as clearly as if it were written on the hardcopy in her hand. Yet as soon as she identified it she quailed.

Everyone might live or die according to what she did—Mikka and Ciro, Sib and Vector, as well as Nick and Angus, Davies and herself. That was terrible enough. And yet mere death seemed simple in its own way: its implications could be understood. Angus' betrayal and need thronged with larger issues.

She'd promised herself that she would cling to the legacy of her parents, her family: that she would commit herself to the convictions and dreams she'd learned from them: that she would be a cop in the pure sense, even though the cops were corrupt, even though men like Warden Dios and Hashi Lebwohl were capable of inflicting such extreme hurts on humankind—and on individual humans. Precisely because she was weak and flawed, she would make the effort to be strong.

Now that seemed impossible.

Unable to take the next step, she turned aside.

"But why are we going through all this?" To herself she sounded plaintive, almost self-pitying; overtaken by vulnerability. Nevertheless she continued, "If Warden Dios wanted us to have those codes—or Hashi Lebwohl—why not just give them to us?" This was important, perhaps crucial, despite the fact that it didn't touch Angus. "Why hand them to Nick first? He might have killed us before Angus ever got a chance to enter those code-strings."

Davies was nearly frantic with urgency or vexation. "That doesn't matter, either."

She jerked her head toward him. A flare of anger burned across her fear. "It matters," she snapped. "Who are we working for now? Who's trying to use us? Whose side are we supposed to be on?"

Davies didn't flinch or hesitate. "Our own," he answered as if he were sure. "The side we choose."

She fought an impulse to yell at him. Wake up! she wanted to shout. *Grow* up! There's a rift in UMCPHQ. Maybe in all of human space. Warden Dios gave Hashi Lebwohl orders, and Lebwohl subverted them because he didn't want to obey. Or Dios didn't want Lebwohl to know what his real orders were, so he hid them. Or Min Donner didn't like what either of them did, but she didn't want to risk overt insubordination, so she sneaked her own orders into the transmission. It *matters*! Where we go from here, everything we do or try to do from now on, *depends* on who wants Nick to control Angus. Who wants us to take that away from him.

And *why*!

After no more than a heartbeat or two, however, she found that she no longer needed to yell. Her anger had served its purpose: it had denatured some of her fear. Unwittingly Davies had goaded her into becoming ready for the next step.

Without transition her hearing cleared. The drumming thunder and the echo of shouts were gone. She could hear Davies' urgency and Angus' clenched, constricted respiration. The small electronic insistence of the command systems reached her; the phosphors humming in the display screens; the background susurrus of the air-scrubbers. And behind them, almost masked by tangible reality and emotional distress, she identified the subliminal crackle of treachery.

Once again she faced Angus.

He remained still, dumbly aching. His datacore denied him the means to articulate his appeal. If she didn't ask him the right question, he would never be able to tell her the answer.

"All right," she said as if she, too, were sure. "We countermand Nick. He countermands us. We get a stalemate. You get paralyzed.

"What alternatives do we have?"

Just for an instant Angus dropped his gaze as if he couldn't bear what he had to say. But then he brought his yellow, pleading eyes back to her face.

"Kill me."

Suddenly bitter, Morn snapped, "Not counting that one."

A spasm like an outbreak of pain pulled at the corner of his mouth. "Help me."

" 'Help' you?" She didn't let go of her bitterness; she needed it. "What does *that* mean?"

"Help me," he said, picking up the words like litter off a ruined street, "get away. From my datacore."

His eyes spilled tears which meant nothing to him.

A flush of instantaneous panic set fire to Davies' skin. He opened his mouth to start shouting.

Morn forestalled him. *It's not that simple*. The same memories which stung her son cried through her, demanding terror. To combat them, she clutched at Angus' extremity; at the helpless appeal on his face. She remembered the rending anguish with which he'd wailed, *I am not your* **fucking** *SON!*

"Somehow," she answered like acid, "I knew that was coming." Her deepest dread had told her. "Help you get away from your datacore. Set you free. So you can make your own decisions.

"How?"

Electronic emissions stifled the spasm in Angus' cheek. They held him still as if he'd been sculpted in bone.

"You can cut it out. I'll tell you how.

"But if you do that," he went on, not hurrying, not emphasizing what he said in any way, "you'll lose me. Everything in my databases, all the extra things I can do. I'll just be—" His programming allowed him a stiff shrug like a wince. "The whole system will freeze if you pull the chip. Some of the stasis commands are hardwired. My zone implants act on them automatically. I'll lock up, and you wouldn't be able to reach me. Eventually I'll die."

He stopped.

Davies watched her in dismay.

"Or?" she prompted grimly.

"Or," Angus replied through a throat congested with wildness, "you can help me change it."

"*Change* it?" Davies had moved to the nearby rail of the companionway: he couldn't hold down his protest without some anchor. He had Morn's anger, her primal, necessary outrage: he'd suffered her hurts everywhere except in his own body. "That's impossible." He needed it to be impossible. "You can't rewrite those SOD-CMOS chips. They can't be altered. If they could, what's the point of having them?"

But his anger wasn't hers: not really. Her share of his mind stopped in an Amnion crèche on Enablement Station. From that moment until Angus had freed him, he'd spent all his time as a prisoner; isolated from her.

While she—

"Why are we even listening to this?" he went on hotly. "You won't help him. You *can't*. Not after *Bright Beauty*. You're just getting his hopes up for nothing. He probably already knows what he's going to do to you—to both of us—as soon as he's free.

"*Stop* this," Davies insisted; demanded; begged. "Give him orders. Or let me do it. Nick is the real problem. Let's start getting ready for *him*."

She shook her head.

While her son had been a prisoner, she'd taken over *Captain's Fancy*, held the whole ship and most of Enablement hostage, to get him back. Later, locked in her cabin and nearly autistic with dread, she'd sat pulling her hair out for hours until Sib Mackern had found the courage to release her. More than once, she'd been through withdrawal. And then Nick had delivered her to the Amnion. With their mutagens in her veins, she'd sat waiting for the ribonucleic convulsion which would deprive her of her humanity as well as her mind.

Her anger was of another kind.

"Davies," she said distinctly, "shut up. We need to hear this. We need to know what our choices are.

" 'Change it'?" she asked Angus.

He hadn't reacted to her exchange with Davies. His attention had contracted until it included only his need, his supplication, and her: there was no room for anything else. As soon as she spoke to him, he answered, "I can edit it. If you'll help me get at it."

"How?"

She meant, How can you do that? But she also meant, How can you conceivably know how to do that? How is it possible that you can do a trick which no one else in human space can even imagine?

He seemed to understand her. "The Amnion taught me." Each word cost him an effort, as if he had to bring it to the surface from a terrible depth. Or as if he dreaded her reaction to it.

In a dead voice, the voice of a machine, he explained, "It was years ago. I hijacked an orehauler. *Viable Dreams*. Crew of twenty-eight. But I didn't kill them. I wasn't after their cargo."

Abruptly Morn wanted him to stop. She felt herself growing colder, as if the void through which the swarm plunged were leaking into the ship. She didn't think she could bear to hear more.

"I took them to Billingate," he went on mechanically, "and sold them to the Amnion. All twenty-eight of them.

"As far the Amnion were concerned, that was the richest prize any illegal ever offered them. They paid me by teaching me how to edit *Bright Beauty*'s datacore."

Strange chills started in the core of her belly and spread outward, making her bones tremble, her heart shiver. Nick had given her to the Amnion. He'd tried to give Davies. But Angus had sold *twenty-eight*—

He produced another stiff shrug. "That's the only reason Com-Mine Security didn't execute me while they had the chance. The only reason I'm here. Like this." His tears didn't mean that he was weeping. They were the essential sweat of his anguish. "*Bright Beauty*'s datacore didn't have any evidence they could use."

Chills reached her shoulders, shuddered along her arms. Somehow she'd been touched by a piece of absolute cold—the utter and irredeemable ice of the abyss.

A man who'd sold twenty-eight human beings to the Amnion wanted her to give him back his freedom.

"You bastard," Davies panted through his teeth, "you vile bastard. How do you live with yourself? How can you stand it?"

Angus didn't reply; but Morn knew the answer. Her comprehension was as intimate as rape. He didn't stand it. He'd spent his whole life fleeing from himself, running from violence to violence in an obsessed effort to escape his own darkness.

"How?" she repeated. Her voice quivered as if she were hypothermic. "How do you do it?"

Her question was entirely unlike her son's.

Angus understood her. "SOD-CMOS chips don't change state," he recited. "They add state. Physically, they can't be edited. Everybody knows the only way to affect them is, write in a filter that masks some of the data during playback. The data is still there. It just doesn't show.

"But that's useless. The filter shows. It plays back along with the rest of the data. Everybody knows that, too."

Morn shivered as if Angus were sneering at her.

"The trick," he continued inflexibly, "is to write a *transparent* filter. It shows, but nobody sees it because everything else looks normal. But even that's impossible. The chip only *adds* state. Everything in it is linear. Sequential. Even a transparent filter becomes obvious because it was written after the data it masks. Otherwise the filter wouldn't work."

He seemed to pause involuntarily, caught at the cusp of a logic-tree; trapped between UMCP programming and his own desperation. The colder Morn felt, the more his face streamed with sweat. His eyes rolled, giving off glints of yellow.

"Go on," Davies muttered. He sounded out of breath, almost exhausted; strained taut. "Don't stop now."

Abruptly Angus said, "Unless you know how to write a filter that looks exactly like the lattice of the chip itself." His voice scraped like a rusty blade in his throat. "Now it isn't transparent, it's invisible. You can't see it during playback because it's just like the physical chip—and you never see the physical chip. You only see the data."

Morn clasped her arms around herself to contain her shivers, but they were too strong. Long tremors shook her. Her teeth clicked against each other until she clenched them tight.

"I can't do that," Angus told her, "but the Amnion can. Their instruments and coding are that good. All they did was teach me how to use the information."

His eyes oozed need like running sores.

"If my datacore and *Bright Beauty*'s were made the same way," he finished, "if the lattice is the same, I can write in a filter to block my priority-codes. Mask them. Nobody else will be able to give me orders."

Full of gelid, shivering detachment, she thought that probably they *were* made the same way. The UMCP was humankind's only authorized supplier of SOD-CMOS chips. She couldn't think of any reason why their manufacturing methods might have changed.

"Shit." Davies stared at Angus in horrified fascination: despite his instinctive rejection, he'd been snagged by what Angus proposed. "Can you go deeper? Can you filter the original programming? Substitute your own?"

Angus shook his head. "No." He treated the question as if it came from Morn. "I don't know what code it's written in. I can only work with data I recognize."

"Like your priority-codes," Davies said for him.

"Like my priority-codes," Angus acknowledged stiffly.

No, Morn groaned to herself. She couldn't do it. It was too much. Absolutely too much. How often had he abused and humiliated her—raped her—hit her? Davies was right: she couldn't set Angus free.

Yet there was one more question she had to ask, in spite of her dismay and the tearing cold. One more crucial detail—

"Angus, who knows you can do this?"

Which one of the plotters and counterplotters back at UMCPHQ could have planned for this?

Now he didn't respond. An ice of his own held him frozen. Thronging with supplication and agony, his gaze clung to hers, but no sound came from his mouth. He'd run into one of his prewritten restrictions, and his zone implants closed his throat. He might have been strangling on words he couldn't say.

Harsh with self-coercion, she rasped, "Isaac, this is Gabriel priority. Answer my question.

"Who knows you can do this?"

A shrug like a spasm shook him. "Warden Dios." He might have been shouting, crying, *I'm not your son.* "As far as I know, he's the only one." *I am not your* **fucking** *SON!* "But he didn't make me explain it. And he said he couldn't tell anyone else. Too dangerous. He used the word 'suicide.' "

Suicide? Morn paused as if she'd fallen into the still point between one wave of chills and the next. This gambit—giving Angus' priority-codes to Davies, cursing her and her son with the burden of decision—had been set in motion by Warden Dios. But it wasn't aimed at Hashi Lebwohl. Or Min Donner. They were his subordinates: they simply weren't strong enough to threaten him. There was only one power in human space great enough for that.

Only Holt Fasner could destroy the director of the UMCP.

She was in the early stages of zone implant withdrawal. Prolonged doses of cat had postponed the crisis; but now it'd caught up with her, sinking its claws into her nerves, drawing her chills into a high-pitched wail of cold.

Warden Dios had given Davies control over Angus.

Why? What did he want from her son? What did he think Davies could do to save him from the Dragon?

How much more suffering did he think she could survive?

Davies pushed toward her from the rail of the companionway. The small impact as he gripped her shoulders moved her backward, away from Angus. Shivers rose against his hands; she trembled as if she were about to shake apart in his grasp.

He brought his face close to hers, forcing his resemblance to his father on her.

"Morn, I keep saying the same thing." His voice was soft and fatal—a whisper like the sound of atmosphere venting to the void. "*None* of this matters. Not *here*. Not to *us*. We can't guess whose side we're supposed to be on. We don't know whose game this is, or what they want from us. *That* isn't our problem.

"Our problem is *Nick*. We need to get ready for him.

"We don't know when he's coming back. Once he puts Vector to work, he might decide to wait here for the results. Playing with us to pass the time.

"We can't let him catch us before we're ready."

His fingers dug into her shoulders as if he thought the pressure might stifle her chills.

"Start giving Angus orders," he insisted softly. "Or I'll do it, if you hurt too much. We need to *move*."

Angus didn't argue. Apparently he'd come to the end of his appeal. Sweat beaded on his skin, squeezed out by the pressure of his need, but he stood still, saying nothing, asking nothing.

He wanted Morn to set him free.

All her life she'd been a woman who knew how to hold a grudge. She'd never forgiven her parents for leaving her in the name of their service to the UMCP. Because she was a child then, she'd never forgiven herself. When her mother had died saving *Intransigent* from *Gutbuster*, she'd made the decision to be a cop herself, hoping to turn her old, unanswered grievance outward; appease her guilt. That commitment had failed, however, when her gap-sickness had destroyed *Starmaster*. On some primal level—beyond reason or logic—her guilt had been confirmed. *Starmaster* died because she hadn't forgiven her parents. That was the source of her gap-sickness; the flaw in her brain. Welded to her grudge, she'd brought about her parents' deaths.

And then Angus had taken her: the incarnation and apotheosis of the punishment she deserved. She'd turned her grudge against herself with a vengeance. After all the harm she'd done—and all she'd received—she hadn't been able to conceive any way out of her plight except by accepting her zone implant control from Angus and casting in with Nick; by dedicating herself to the profound falsehood of confirming Nick's illusions. She'd disdained rescue so that she would continue to be punished.

But Davies had changed her. Having a child had forced her to step outside her grudges and self-brutalization in order to consider other questions; larger issues. Vector had told her that the cops were corrupt. At the time that information had horrified her. But how was their suppression of Intertech's antimutagen research different from her use of her black box against Nick? Or against herself? If she wanted her life and her son's to be any better than Nick's—or Angus'—she had to begin making decisions of another kind.

As far as I'm concerned, she'd once told Davies, *you're the second most important thing in the galaxy. You're my* **son.** *But the* **first,** *the* **most** *important thing is to not betray my humanity.* And later, when he'd wanted to lock Nick out of *Trumpet*, she'd said like a promise, *You're a cop. From now on, I'm going to be a cop myself. We don't do things like that.*

Fine sentiments. But they meant nothing if she didn't act on them.

Yet if acting on them meant setting Angus free—

Shivering in revulsion, she turned the question back on him. Past her son's shoulder, she asked, "Why should we help you? Davies is right—we can find some way to deal with Nick that doesn't get you paralyzed. You'll work for us, you'll have to, you'll take our orders instead of Nick's, and we won't need to be afraid of you all the time." Use him as a tool, the same way Warden Dios and Nick did. Less brutally, perhaps. Or with more subtlety. But still as a tool. A thing. "Why should I think for a second that either of us will be safe with you?"

"Morn!" Davies protested, grinding his fingers into her shoulders and shaking her.

She ignored her son. The necessary focus of her attention was as constricted as Angus'. For the moment nothing mattered except his answer.

"Because I could have stopped you," he said on the heels of Davies' outcry. All trace of belligerence had left his face: only his need remained, naked and pure.

"Bullshit!" Davies flung away from Morn, wheeled to face Angus. "You couldn't stop anything. You were *beaten*, Nick *beat* you, you didn't have any choices *left*. You would have sold him your soul to keep yourself alive, but he didn't give you the chance. You handed her the control and let her go"—his fists lashed the air—"because there was *nothing else you could do*!"

Angus shook his head as if his neck were breaking. Still he spoke only to Morn.

"I could have proved I was framed. I knew about Nick's link with Com-Mine Security. I could have traced the link to Milos. All I had to do was say something, and Security would have stopped you. You and Nick. Even if they didn't believe me, they would have stopped you. Until they learned the truth. Then you were finished.

"That link was real. It would nail Milos. And he would sell anything to save himself. Maybe they would have executed me—if I couldn't bargain with them—but I would have taken you and Nick down with me.

"But I didn't. And I didn't do it later, after you were gone. I didn't defend myself at all. Not even to save *Bright Beauty*." Dumb pain ached in his eyes. "I let them do whatever they wanted to me. So they wouldn't go after Nick. So you could get away."

He surprised her; almost shocked her. For a heartbeat or two the cold let go of her, allowing her to concentrate.

"Why?"

Why did you care?

His voice dropped until she could barely hear him. "Because I made a deal with you." He sounded incongruously vulnerable, like a wounded child. "I gave you the zone implant control. You let me live. And I kept my end. Whether you kept yours or not."

In a small, sore whisper, he admitted as if he were laying bare his heart, "When I hurt you, I hurt myself."

"Angus," Davies began harshly, "God damn it—" But then his protest trailed away. He seemed to have no words for what he felt. With his back to Morn, he stood as if he were huddling into himself, crouching against a pain he couldn't understand.

She put her hand on his shoulder. When she felt his muscles knotting under the strange fabric of his shipsuit, she knew what she had to do.

She had to make this decision; make it now and act on it. Warden Dios had sent it to her son, but it didn't belong to him.

He'd been force-grown with her mind, but he wasn't *her*. His father was part of him as well. And he was caught between them—between his memory of her pain and his recognition of Angus'. Anger was his only defense. When it failed, he was lost.

This decision was beyond him.

She, on the other hand—

You're the second most important thing in the galaxy. You're my **son.**

She was the woman Angus had raped and degraded. Whether he knew it or not, he'd given her the right to choose his doom.

But the **first,** *the* **most** *important thing is to not betray my humanity.*

Everything she'd learned came to this: revenge was too expensive. Humankind couldn't afford it.

Deliberately she set a lifetime of grudges and self-punishment aside.

"We'll do it," she told Angus, although her voice nearly stuck in her throat, and the hammering of her heart brought her chills up again with redoubled force. "We'll trust you."

More for Davies' benefit than for Angus', she added, "It's not just you. We'll trust whoever wrote your core programming." Shivering like the damned. "I think it was Warden Dios. I think he's trying to find some way to fight Holt Fasner. And if he is, I think we should help him."

Shivering as if the cold had become metaphysical—a tremor of the soul which only incidentally affected her body.

Nevertheless she finished, "We're cops. We don't *use* people."

Angus began to clench and unclench his fists while his mouth slowly pulled back into a feral grin.

She started to weep as soon as Davies turned and put his arms around her.

NICK

Nick Succorso walked in the light g of the Lab's asteroid like he was riding a cloud. He was elevated by triumph, nearly giddy with aspiration. Hungers which had hag-ridden his life were about to be fed; *were* being fed. *Trumpet* had become *his*. For reasons which meant nothing to him and didn't interest him, Warden Dios had given him his own pet cyborg. Mikka and Vector were stuck taking his orders. Soon he would possess an effectively limitless supply of UMCPDA's mutagen immunity drug—all the wealth he would ever need. Morn herself was *his* as surely as *Trumpet* and Angus, ripe to be hurt.

And *Soar* was here, Sorus Chatelaine was *here*.

His heart and head were so full that they seemed to lift him from step to step, almost carrying him off his feet. He could hardly keep track of the deck.

With Mikka and Vector at his shoulders, Sib and Pup behind him, he left *Trumpet*'s airlock to enter the access passage which led into Deaner Beckmann's installation.

Mikka glared murderously past her bandage, but Vector had perfected his look of mild calm, and his face showed nothing. As for Sib and Pup, Nick didn't give a shit what they thought or felt. He intended to sacrifice them in any case. Get even with them for daring to turn against him. Only Vector truly mattered. Mikka was just cover. And he'd made sure that she didn't know *Soar* was in. She wouldn't interfere because she wouldn't be able to guess his intentions.

The passage was featureless: a straight concrete corridor toward another airlock, lit by long, flat fluorescents which flickered as if their power source were unstable. Nick didn't see any scan fields and detection sensors. The Lab relied on other defenses, and he'd already passed most of them.

Bouncing to the interior lock, he thumbed the intercom and announced, "Captain Succorso. We're here. Sorry to keep you waiting." He glanced backward to confirm that *Trumpet* had resealed herself, then added, "My ship's lock is tight." The installation didn't need to hear this from him. Routine dock communications covered such points as a matter of safety. Nevertheless he always checked. "You can let us in."

"Thanks, Captain." The response suggested stifled impatience. "Stand by. We're opening now."

Servos hummed. A small gasp of air equalized the slight pressure differential. Then the airlock irised, letting Nick and his people into the warmer light of Beckmann's domain.

The lock admitted them to a room like a holding area—the Lab's version of Reception. It seemed full, almost crowded. Nick counted six guards in addition to three women and two men in labsuits—an entire reception committee.

The guards carried impact pistols. And they all sported prostheses of various kinds—scanners, communications gear, augmented limbs, and, presumably, concealed weapons. To that extent, they might have been transplanted here from Billingate. But the fact that they lived in a world substantially unlike the Bill's showed in their eyes, which were clear of the complex haze of chemical dependencies: stim or cat, nerve-juice or pseudoendorphins. Most of the surgery which they'd undergone was probably voluntary. In certain ways they were more dangerous than the men and women who'd served the Bill.

Nick didn't recognize any of the women in labsuits. He'd ignored the women the last time he was here: in his experience, women who dedicated themselves to research and labs were usually too ugly to live; certainly too ugly to notice. But he knew one of the men by sight.

Deaner Beckmann: the founder, driving force, and embodiment of the Lab in person.

Either Vector's name or Nick's hints had struck sparks in high places.

The director of the Lab was a short, squat man who looked even shorter and thicker because of the way he seemed to hunch into himself as if he was trying to increase his mass by an act of will. He alone might have been on drugs. His researchers projected alertness or subservience to varying degrees, but he had an air of being distracted and driven, almost frightened, as if he were crazed by dreams which were in danger of failing.

Gravitic tissue mutation, Nick snorted to himself. No wonder the man looked like he was losing his mind. If Beckmann wanted to live in a black hole, all he had to do was find one and let go. That would fucking cure him.

Nevertheless Nick kept his contempt private. As far as he was concerned, the more spaceshit crazy Beckmann was, the better. It would make the scientist easier to outmaneuver.

In any case Beckmann may have simply been concerned about the nearly subliminal unsteadiness which afflicted his lighting like an electron palsy.

"I'm Captain Succorso," Nick announced with a cheerful smile to the whole group. "Thanks for letting us in." Disingenuously he added, "I don't think you'll regret it."

"Captain Succorso, I'm Dr. Beckmann." In contrast to his anxious expression, his voice was clipped and decisive; impervious to doubt. "Forgive the guards. They aren't here to make you feel like a prisoner."

"We're here," one of them put in abruptly, "because your ship is a Needle-class UMCP gap scout." Chevrons above the black sun sigil on his uniform distinguished him from the other guards. "The last time you were here, your vessel was a frigate of"—he pursed his mouth sternly—"questionable legality, *Captain's Fancy*. Now you look like you're working for the cops."

"This is Chief Retledge," Dr. Beckmann commented by way of introduction. "He runs Security for us."

Apparently Chief Retledge's duties didn't require a deferential attitude. As if Dr. Beckmann hadn't spoken, he went on, "I want to hear a better explanation than the one you gave us, Captain Succorso."

Nick didn't hesitate; he was beyond hesitation. Ignoring the guards, he faced Beckmann.

"Dr. Beckmann, let me introduce my crew. Mikka Vasaczk, command second." He indicated each of his companions with a nod as he said their names. "Sib Mackern, data first. Our cabin boy, Pup. And I think you know Vector Shaheed, at least by reputation. He used to be my engineer." With a shrug, he added, "Of course, we all have different duties now."

Dr. Beckmann paid no attention to the others; his troubled gaze concentrated on Vector. He didn't interrupt his chief of Security, however.

"Saying you aren't a spy is easy, Captain Succorso," Retledge continued coldly. "We're at risk here. We're always at risk. Between them, VI and the UMC would make you rich for betraying us. We cut into their profits too much. Sure, we let you in. That was easy, too. But you won't leave until I stop worrying about you.

"Make me stop worrying, Captain Succorso."

Nick thought that he could hear *Soar*'s presence in Retledge's tone. The guards and researchers seemed more nervous than they needed to be. On that assumption, he asked innocently, "Have you heard what happened to Billingate?"

A couple of the guards glanced at each other, but no one answered.

No question about it: *Soar* was responsible for the chief of Security's distrust. He would certainly have demanded information from her. And Sorus Chatelaine wouldn't have scrupled to reveal some of the facts, if for no other reason than to account for her presence here. But Retledge didn't want to admit that; didn't want to give Nick any hint of where he stood.

The situation was tricky. How much Nick should say depended on what Sorus had already told Retledge. He would have to guess what that was. But he wasn't afraid: he feared nothing now. He was Nick Succorso, and he could play this game better than Retledge, Sorus, and Hashi Lebwohl combined.

"It's complicated," he explained blandly to Beckmann's concentration and the group's silence. "I need to be careful—I don't want to give you the impression I'm promising something I can't deliver. Here's how it happened.

"I took *Captain's Fancy* to Enablement Station. That worked out well in one way, not so well in another. I got what I went for—the same thing that brought me here." One lie was as good as another. "But the Amnion didn't like it. They came after me.

"My gap drive failed while they were chasing me. Billingate was as far as I could get, and the Amnion were on my heels. Frankly, I thought I was finished." Nick smiled as if the idea amused him. "But by coincidence"—he spread his hands—"at least I assume it was coincidence—*Trumpet* arrived about the same time. The story I heard was that she'd been stolen by an illegal named Angus Thermo-pile"—Nick couldn't resist the old insult—"and the deputy chief of Com-Mine Security, Milos Taverner, who happened to be working with Thermo-pile. Apparently Taverner sprung Thermo-pile from UMCPHQ when he was on the verge of getting caught himself, and the two of them took *Trumpet* for a ride.

"I don't know if any of it's true." Nick retailed this kind of bullshit with perfect equanimity. "At the time I didn't care. All I cared about was a ship. One with a gap drive. I knew Thermo-pile—we did business occasionally. So I let him think we could team up. While he and Taverner were out in Billingate, I got some of my people aboard his ship. Then I sent *Captain's Fancy* to create a diversion while we borrowed *Trumpet*."

At his side, Mikka ducked her head as if she were swallowing curses. Vector gazed back at Beckmann like a man whose questions had all been answered; but Mikka had trouble keeping her composure. Nick knew her well; he knew the signs—the dangerous angle of her hips; the way her shoulders hunched against the fabric of her shipsuit. She wanted to call him a liar.

He wasn't afraid of her, any more than he feared Sorus. For Morn's sake—and her brother's—she would keep her mouth shut.

"Unfortunately," he continued with no hint of regret, "Thermo-pile and Taverner were left behind." He showed his teeth. Deaner Beckmann may have been an illegal for the research rather than the money, but he was still illegal. He wouldn't be able to pretend that he was shocked by what Nick claimed to have done. "They probably would have been all right, but someone sabotaged Billingate's fusion generator. For all I know, they did it themselves. I didn't ask—I just took their ship. Barely in time, as it turned out. We only got out seconds ahead of the shockwave.

"Once we were clear, we headed here."

Retledge's expression didn't shift. For a moment after Nick finished, none of Beckmann's people reacted. Then the chief of security rasped, "Interesting."

"I've always said—" Dr. Beckmann began.

Retledge cut him off. "It's a pretty story, Captain Succorso, but it doesn't give us much reason to trust you."

"I know that," Nick retorted. "But it gives you a reason to take the risk. As I've already said."

He turned to the director of the Lab. "Dr. Beckmann, all I want from you is a little time for Vector in one of your genetics labs. That and some supplies, which I'll be able to pay for—if the risks *I've* taken pay off. Did you hear me say," he asked as if the point were unclear, "that I stole something from Enablement? Or that it's valuable? Otherwise the Amnion wouldn't have tried so hard to get it back.

"If you'll let Vector analyze it—whatever it is," he concluded, "I'll give you a share of the results."

Dr. Beckmann hadn't objected to Retledge's interruption. On the other hand, he didn't let himself be deflected.

"I've always said," he repeated, "that money is a petty reason to do anything. It begs for pettiness in response." Somewhere in the background of his voice ran an undertone of passion as acute as savagery. "If human beings never dreamed higher than money, they wouldn't be worth saving."

Apparently "saving human beings" was what he thought he and his Lab were doing. Maybe he was no longer sane.

Nick started to respond, "But money buys—"

"Excuse me," one of the women said unexpectedly. "Dr. Shaheed?"

Vector turned his head toward her, gave her the benefit of his mild smile. "Yes?"

"Dr. Shaheed"—she spoke like a woman with a dry throat; a woman who hated calling attention to herself—"I used to know the man who ran your computers. At Intertech."

Nick looked at her closely for the first time. She was a small creature with unfortunate hair and a flat, inherently expressionless face—the kind of face, he thought in a flash of confident inspiration, that medtechs sometimes produced when they were trying to repair extensive damage on the cheap.

"Orn Vorbuld," Vector answered as if he weren't surprised by her remark. "He and I joined Captain Succorso together. After UMCPDA shut down my research." Unlike Mikka, he seemed more than willing to go along with Nick. "But we lost him weeks ago."

Nick didn't doubt for an instant that the woman had known Vorbuld.

"He committed what you might call suicide," Mikka put in darkly, confirming Vector's reply. Her tone told Nick, however, that she was making a subtle effort to cause trouble.

But the woman didn't react to Mikka's hint: she was looking for something else. Without quite meeting Vector's gaze, she asked, "Dr. Shaheed, how would you expect me to feel about that?"

It was one thing to know Vorbuld's name: it was another to know what he was like. This was Dr. Beckmann's oblique way of verifying Vector's identity.

Now everything depended on the former engineer.

Fearing nothing, Nick smiled at Beckmann's people and let Vector take his time.

Vector frowned ruefully. With just the right combination of understanding and detachment, he answered, "At a guess, I would say that you're glad—or perhaps simply relieved—to hear that he's dead. He hurt women whenever he had the chance. But"—Vector lifted his shoulders delicately—"you may also regret that you didn't have a hand in killing him."

The woman nodded slowly. Her eyes had slipped out of focus, as if they were turned on memories which she would never voluntarily describe to anyone. Nevertheless a sense of tension eased out of the room. Vector had just passed his id check.

Mikka clenched her fists; but she didn't mention Vorbuld's "suicide" again.

"Dr. Shaheed," Beckmann said as if he hadn't been staring at Vector for minutes, "welcome. It's good to meet a colleague of your reputation. I hope you understand that we need to take precautions. None of us has ever had the honor of meeting you. From our perspective it would be painfully easy for someone to steal your id tag and pretend to be you. We wouldn't know the difference unless we subjected you to a full gene scan."

No illegal Nick knew had ever willingly submitted to a gene scan—not if the results could be compared with the data stored in his id tag. As a rule only spies made that kind of mistake. And of course they passed: their id tags were forged. But the fact that they submitted told against them in places like the Lab.

"Dr. Beckmann"—Vector showed his palms in a gesture of deference—"the honor is mine. Certainly I understand. I don't object to your methods. I admire your resourcefulness."

Nick nodded bland approval.

"Unfortunately," Dr. Beckmann went on without pausing, "this research that Captain Succorso has in mind troubles me. Naturally I'm interested in any artifact or compound which comes to us from forbidden space. As a scientist it's my duty to be interested, regardless of any conceivable relevance to my personal research. And of course the possibility of relevance always exists. You know of our work here, Dr. Shaheed?"

"Only in the vaguest terms," Vector conceded. "I've read your seminal papers on"—he mentioned a couple of topics which meant nothing to Nick—"but that was a long time ago. Since then I've only heard rumors."

"And?" Deaner Beckmann pursued.

Vector considered his options momentarily. He may have wanted to ask Nick for guidance, but he resisted the impulse. Instead he said, "Frankly, I can't speculate. I know what I'm hoping to learn here, but I really have no idea what you need."

"What I need most, Dr. Shaheed," Beckmann returned incisively, leaving no room for Retledge to interrupt him, "is time.

"We live in a difficult era. The Amnion that Captain Succorso so blithely visits have given the UMCP the excuse which police-minded men have sought throughout history—the excuse to impose a tyranny of choice and knowledge on the citizenry they purport to protect. The fact that the threat which the Amnion represent is real only confirms the moral imperialism of Warden Dios and his henchmen. And the result, the true cost, of such tyranny is here."

One or two of the people in labsuits shifted their feet, lowered their eyes uncomfortably. No doubt they'd heard Deaner Beckmann deliver this speech on any number of occasions. But he didn't notice their reaction; he didn't pause. A fanatic's passion had risen in his voice. He might not have been able to stop if he'd wanted to.

Nevertheless the director of the Lab hadn't survived so long under such precarious conditions by being stupid. He must have a reason for what he was saying.

Despite his eagerness to move against Sorus, Nick forced himself to remain quiet and appear patient.

"Have you noticed our lighting, Dr. Shaheed?" Dr. Beckmann demanded.

Vector kept any disconcertion he may have felt to himself. "Not particularly, I'm afraid."

"It is *unstable*," Beckmann pronounced. "It *flickers*, Dr. Shaheed, for the simple reason that our source of power is inadequate to sustain all the demands we must place upon it.

"We need to generate energies comparable to the forces which compose singularities, but we can't. We cannot. We scavenge this asteroid swarm constantly for raw materials, we barter for new technologies and equipment by every means available to us, we commit crimes ourselves and reward the commission of crimes in our name, and still we can barely supply power for small real-time simulations of our true experiments, our essential work.

"Why is this?" he asked rhetorically. "Because the UMCP force us to operate as illegals. Instead of sanctioning our work, instead of investing civilization's resources in the quest which offers humankind its only true hope—the quest for salvation through knowledge—the 'cops' compel us to exist on the fringes of the very society we seek to serve.

"My research, Dr. Shaheed," Beckmann insisted, "*my research* has the potential to secure humankind's future against any conceivable threat the Amnion can or may present. Yet I am effectively outcast, and I can only obtain what I need for my experiments by stealing it."

Nick struggled against a desire to sneer. You fucking researchers are all alike. Of course you feel sorry for yourself. Self-pity is all you're really good at. Nagged by a mounting need for action, he had more and more difficulty concealing his impatience.

Sorus had *cut* him. She'd fucked him and betrayed his hopes and *cut* his cheeks and abandoned him. And now she was *here*.

Still Dr. Beckmann wasn't done.

"Yet even the UMCP would not present an insurmountable obstacle," he went on, "if we were not confronted with another problem. We face an unalterable deadline. This asteroid swarm faces an immolation which nothing can alter. Measured by the standards of organic matter, we are powerful enough. On the scale of star systems, however, we are paltry beyond imagining. In a few short years, Massif-5 will furnace us from existence, and everything we do here will have been wasted, meaningless."

He paused for a moment, then added harshly, "Unless we succeed. Unless we find and develop the knowledge we seek in time.

"Have I made myself clear, Dr. Shaheed?"

Vector considered the question. "I think so, Dr. Beckmann."

"Nevertheless let me be explicit," Beckmann insisted, "so that there will be no misunderstanding. You wish to use our equipment. In other words, you wish to use our power. Which of our functions, which of our experiments, should I pause or postpone so that you will have power?"

His point was obvious. My resources are stretched thin. I won't share them with you unless you have something I need.

Nick didn't wait for Vector to answer. Letting his tension show as irritation, he put in, "Under the circumstances I don't see how you can take the risk of *not* helping us."

Slowly Beckmann turned away from Vector as if he had difficulty taking anyone else seriously.

"Your chronometer is running, Dr. Beckmann," Nick said trenchantly. "You can count the number of seconds you have left. If we might produce something that helps you, even accidentally, you can't afford to miss the chance." Then he shrugged. "If what Vector learns is worthless to you, of course, we'll have to repay you in some other way."

For several heartbeats Beckmann faced Nick. With his distracted, fanatic's expression, he looked like a man who wondered whether he should trouble himself to step on an insect. When he spoke, however, he addressed Vector without dropping Nick's gaze.

"What do you need, Dr. Shaheed?"

To himself Nick crowed abruptly, *Got* you! But he wasn't talking to Beckmann.

Vector immediately named several items, but Nick ignored the tally of equipment and supplies. As soon the geneticist finished, Nick said, "That's not all." *Now*, Sorus. Are you ready for this? "Sib has a list of what we need from your engineering section." The fact that this was the first Sib had heard of it didn't worry Nick. "He can take care of that while Vector works. And I want Pup to req some of your food stores." He felt Mikka flinch beside him, but he ignored her. "Naturally," he told Beckmann, "you won't give us anything until we pay for it. But I want to have everything ready so we can leave as soon as possible when Vector's done."

"Nick—" Mikka fixed her good eye balefully on him.

At the same moment Pup said, "Mikka?" in a frightened voice, and Sib began, "Nick, I—"

This time, however, Chief Retledge didn't let anyone get in his way. Overriding Nick's people, he asked sharply, "What's your hurry, Captain Succorso?"

Deliberately Nick turned away from Retledge. Facing Mikka, he said through his teeth while his mouth smiled, "You knew it would be like this. Just trust Security. They'll take care of your brother. You can guard the lab while Vector works."

Before she could retort, he swung around to Sib. More harshly than he'd spoken to Mikka, he told Sib, "You know how much depends on this. Don't fuck up."

Tightening the screws on Sib's alarm. Ensuring that Security would keep close watch on him, as well as on Mikka.

Making Pup look harmless by comparison.

Nick wanted to laugh out loud. But he couldn't take the time to enjoy Sib's sweaty dismay—not now. Instead he returned his attention to the chief of Security.

"I think what we have is pretty valuable," he replied before Retledge could repeat his question. "If I'm right, then it's also true that there are ships after us. Ships that want what we have. The way I see it, the sooner I get out of here, the less chance they'll have to turn this place into a battlefield."

To the director of the Lab, he remarked, "I would like to get started, if you don't mind, Dr. Beckmann. One way or another, the chronometer's running for all of us."

Deaner Beckmann had made his decision: he didn't hesitate to act on it. "Dr. Shaheed can use thirty-one, Sven," he told one of the men in labsuits. "I'll ask you to escort him there and help him settle in. As long as you consider it reasonable, let him have whatever he needs."

Did the director mean, Keep an eye on him? Watch what he does? Nick didn't know—and didn't care. He had no intention of concealing the results of Vector's analysis. Telling the truth here was the most dangerous thing he could do to Beckmann. With luck *Soar* might destroy the Lab for him after he was gone; Sorus might go that far to protect her Amnion masters from the threat of an antimutagen.

"Linne," Dr. Beckmann went on, speaking to the woman who'd confirmed Vector's identity, "tell Dr. Hysterveck to put his TCE simulation on hold until further notice. That should release enough power for the equipment Dr. Shaheed wants.

"Chief Retledge," he concluded as he led the way out of the room, "I'll leave Mr. Mackern and Mr.—ah—Pup to you."

Nick began to think that this might be a good time to take up singing. His spirit needed music for its feral joy.

He wasn't going to be content with cutting Sorus' cheeks. He was going to leave the marks of his knife on her fucking heart.

SORUS

From the bridge *Soar*'s captain watched her target ease through the asteroid swarm and settle into the berth Lab Center assigned. She listened to the Lab's operational communications until she heard that Nick Succorso and four other people had disembarked to explain their reasons for coming here to Deaner Beckmann. Then she thumbed her intercom and told the team she'd prepared to stand by.

She was morally certain that those four people with Succorso were all former members of *Captain's Fancy*'s crew. Earlier she'd noticed that the manifest which *Trumpet* had transmitted to Lab Center made no mention of Angus Thermopyle, Morn Hyland, or Davies Hyland. Succorso was keeping their presence secret.

Unless he'd already gotten rid of them somehow? Sorus dismissed that idea. She didn't believe that Succorso was capable of killing a UMCP cyborg. And he must have known that the Hylands were too valuable to kill. So he'd left them aboard the gap scout to keep them secret; keep them safe.

She didn't care. Someone from *Captain's Fancy* would suit her better in any case. Taverner would no doubt have approved if she could have put her hands on Thermopyle or the Hylands. However, some lesser member of the crew would be a better candidate for what she had in mind.

How long would Succorso talk to Beckmann? How much time would he need to convince the director of the Lab to give him what he wanted? That would depend on how much he was willing to reveal. If he told Beckmann he wanted to analyze a mutagen immunity drug, he would receive cooperation immediately. Beckmann might sacrifice half his installation for a share of information like that. But Succorso might not be willing to expose himself to that extent—in which case he would have to work harder to convince Beckmann to help him. And Sorus herself had told Retledge enough about what had happened to Thanatos Minor to make the Security chief nervous.

Succorso and Beckmann might spend quite a while arguing with each other before *Trumpet*'s people began moving around the installation; before they became vulnerable.

Sorus had been coming here for years. She and Retledge had known each other a long time: on one occasion they'd been lovers. And she'd told him Succorso would do anything he could to hurt her. She'd told him why.

At the moment there was nothing more she could do except wait and see whether Retledge took the hint; whether he believed it would be in the best interests of the Lab to let her know what Beckmann decided to do about Succorso. If or when he did that, it would be time to send out her team.

Milos Taverner studied her without blinking: his lidless eyes, yellow and slitted, had no human need for moisture, despite the humanness of his appearance. Not for the first time, he asked her, "What is your intention, Captain Chatelaine?"

His alien tone seemed insufferably steady. He sounded impervious to pain, disconcertion, alarm, or any of the other emotions she carried on her tired back like succubi.

He'd been standing beside her command station for so long now she'd begun to feel that he would be there for the rest of her life; that every decision she made would be scrutinized and challenged by alien exigencies; that every breath she took until she died would be tainted with alien pheromones. Tainted as she was herself: false in the same way. Taverner kept her company whenever she was on the bridge as if his real purpose here was to remind her of facts and compulsions which she could never forget.

She hated that. She'd been showing the Amnion for years that she was smart enough to understand the facts and act on them without their superintendence.

Nevertheless he wanted to know what her "intentions" were.

She faced him bleakly. Even though she doubted that he would understand the connection, she countered, "Did you believe me when I told you *Trumpet* would come here?"

That had been an intuitive triumph. She might have felt vindicated, if she'd had the energy—and if she hadn't had so much cold despair locked away at the bottom of her heart. By rights *Trumpet* should have gotten away clean. The gap scout had escaped Amnion space in a way which should have made it impossible for anyone to follow her.

After *Soar* had rendezvoused with *Calm Horizons*—to take on new equipment and a supply of specialized mutagens and drugs, as well as to transfer Marc Vestabule and the shuttle crew to the big defensive—the Amnion vessel had moved off to track *Trumpet*'s emissions across the debris- and static-cluttered void while *Soar* had headed toward the frontier of human space. In the absence of any better ideas, Sorus had aimed her ship at the part of the frontier where the Com-Mine belt bordered Amnion space. That, she'd believed, was the most logical, as well as the safest, place for *Trumpet* to go. The belt offered almost any amount of cover to a ship on the run. And Com-Mine Station was nearby. The Station could provide assistance even if the cops weren't ready and waiting.

Before she'd reached her chosen position, however, Sorus had heard from *Calm Horizons*. The warship had lost *Trumpet*'s trail. The astonishing accuracy of Amnion instruments had enabled *Calm Horizons* to follow *Trumpet* as far as a red giant well inside Amnion space; but there the screaming emissions of the star had proved loud enough to conceal the gap scout's trace.

Once again Amnion thinking had been inadequate to deal with human cunning and treachery. Without Sorus to help them, the Amnion would have lost *Trumpet*. In all likelihood they would also have lost the present, unstable peace. Their undeclared war against humankind would have been doomed.

But Sorus had guessed well when she'd selected her position near the frontier. And after that her guesswork had risen to the level of pure inspiration.

She'd seen a UMCP cruiser arrive near the belt—presumably intending to meet and protect *Trumpet*'s return to human space. She'd seen the cruiser pause unexpectedly to exchange transmissions with some other vessel, one *Soar*'s scan couldn't reach through the intervening rock of the belt.

And then Sorus had seen *Trumpet* arrive out of the gap, flare her own transmission in the direction of the hidden ship, and head away, plainly making no effort to contact—much less join—the UMCP cruiser. Almost immediately the cruiser had turned in pursuit of the gap scout. If Sorus had remained where she was, she might have caught sight of the hidden ship if or when that vessel emerged from the belt. But *Trumpet* would have been lost.

Soar hadn't remained there, however. *Trumpet*'s strange behavior had given her the information she'd needed—the kind of information which made exalted guesswork possible.

"Give chase," Taverner had ordered her. "*Trumpet* must be caught. The ship must be stopped. If you do not act now, they will attain reinforcements. Your weaponry will enable you to defeat the warship."

The weaponry he'd referred to was *Soar*'s super-light proton cannon. Apparently he assumed—as Sorus herself did not—the cops didn't know that *Soar* had formerly been *Gutbuster:* that the space-normal illegal which had once done so much damage with her proton gun now ran under another name—and was gap-capable. Sorus hadn't bothered to argue with him. Or to obey him. Instead she'd issued orders of her own, building up velocity as hard as she could for an entry into human space and the gap.

"Captain Chatelaine," Taverner had asked then as he asked now, "what are your intentions?"

She'd answered him then—but only after *Soar* was well under way.

If *Trumpet* was acting directly—and willingly—for the UMCP, why hadn't the gap scout simply tucked herself into the cruiser's shadow and let the warship protect her all the way back to Earth? Sorus hadn't been able to think of a reason. Therefore she'd jumped to the conclusion that either Succorso or Thermopyle had his own ideas.

Ideas which might not please the cops.

Instinctively she'd dismissed Thermopyle, not because he was insignificant, but because he was a welded UMCP cyborg, incapable of initiative or disobedience.

So what in hell was Succorso doing?

Taverner had told her that Succorso had a mutagen immunity drug which Hashi Lebwohl had given him.

What would she have done in his place?

Knowing that the Amnion couldn't follow her—and that the cops couldn't follow fast enough to stop her—she'd have headed for the best and most secure bootleg lab she knew, so that she could try to analyze and profit from her precious cargo before the cops or anyone else interfered.

Only one place fit that description. And it just happened to lie on *Trumpet*'s heading away from the Com-Mine belt.

Driving her crew to their limits, Sorus Chatelaine had brought *Soar* by great leaps to the Lab. To Deaner Beckmann's brilliant—and brilliantly defended—exercise in futility.

Yet now, here, where any fool could see the benefits of leaving matters in her hands, Milos Taverner challenged her to justify herself again.

She didn't expect him to understand her retort, but she stood by it anyway, grimly claiming responsibility for her own damnation.

At first he didn't appear to comprehend her question. " 'Believe' is not an Amnion concept," he answered in his inflectionless voice. His mutation had taken place scant days ago, yet already he seemed to be losing his ability to think like a human—the very ability for which he'd been assigned "decisiveness" aboard her ship. But a moment later he added, "In your terms, however, it might be correct to say that we did 'believe' you. You are human. Among humans false dealings are endemic. Perhaps they are congenital—an organic flaw. Yet we have the means to ensure that you are not false to us." He placed no stress on the threat. He didn't need to: it had been a fact of her life ever since she'd stumbled into the hands of his kind. "And I acceded to your judgment in this matter. Does that not indicate 'believe'?"

Sorus snorted to herself. She wasn't interested in Amnion hairsplitting.

"Was I right?" she demanded.

Taverner considered the question as if it weren't rhetorical. "Your prediction of Captain Thermopyle's actions has proved to be accurate. Your perception of his motives may also be accurate."

"Then leave me alone," she rasped. "Let me work. I'm still human. I know how to go about this. Having to explain myself all the time just wears me out."

Taverner studied her for a long moment. His unblinking eyes and pudgy face gave no hint of what might be in his mind. Then, however, he surprised her by stepping closer to the command station, bending forward, and crooking one index finger as if he wanted her to put her head near his.

Taken aback, she leaned to comply.

In an oddly conspiratorial, almost human whisper, he breathed so that no one else could hear him, "Captain Chatelaine, you must be made aware that the Amnion have developed airborne mutagens. These are slow acting and somewhat crude, but they suffice to meet the present need."

She stared at him. Airborne— Panic clutched her stomach. Only years of dark resolve and bitter discipline enabled her to keep herself from grabbing her gun and blasting him in the face so that he wouldn't say what came next.

"Sacs of them," he went on quietly, almost inaudibly, "have been set upon the scrubber pads of this vessel." That must have been done while equipment and supplies were being loaded from *Calm Horizons*. "I am able to trigger their release. If you deal falsely with us, I will provide that your crew does not."

Constricted rage and hopelessness boiled inside her, blocked from any outlet. "You bastard," she murmured through her teeth, "that wasn't part of the deal."

What did I do it for, all these years of betrayal and harm, if you're going to take even my crew away from me?

But her protest was a lie, and she knew it. She hadn't done it for them: she'd done it for herself.

His response was as low as the murmur of *Soar*'s support systems. "Your statement is not correct. We did not enter into a 'deal' with you. You are ours. Until now your crew has been left human so that they might function in human space effectively. However, the present need transcends former policies.

"You do not wish to explain your intentions. Very well. Do not. Your humanness remains necessary. But understand the consequences if you deal falsely with us."

Sorus understood. Oh, she understood. The Amnion had owned her for years. Taverner had only raised the stakes, not changed the nature of the game.

A sense of fatigue as crushing as stone settled into the curve of muscle where her neck met her shoulders. She couldn't make him go away, so she sighed instead, "I told you. I know what I'm doing." For a moment gray weariness seemed to fray the edges of her vision. Then she added, "And if I'm wrong, we'll still have time to do it your way."

Taverner appeared to accept her assertion. Nevertheless he stayed at her side while she waited to hear from Chief Retledge.

"Captain Chatelaine?"

The Security chief's voice on her intercom sounded clipped and sure of itself. Retledge was like Beckmann in that respect; he didn't try to second-guess his decisions when he made them.

Sorus shook herself alert. "Chief Retledge. Thanks for calling. Am I allowed to ask what's going on?"

Milos Taverner gazed at her incuriously, as if he didn't care what she did.

"Dr. Beckmann has given Captain Succorso and Dr. Shaheed permission to use one of the labs," Retledge reported crisply. "The rest of *Trumpet*'s people are here, too. My men are keeping an eye on them."

There: confirmation. Sorus had been right all along. Vector Shaheed was going to analyze Lebwohl's mutagen immunity drug so that Succorso could start selling the formula. She resisted an impulse to shake her fist in Taverner's face.

But Retledge couldn't know what his information meant to her. His thoughts were elsewhere. He paused for an instant, then went on, "Captain Succorso didn't mention you." A note of grim humor came across the intercom speaker. "A curious omission, I think. If you believe him, the enemies he worries about are all somewhere else."

Sorus cocked an eyebrow in surprise, but didn't respond.

"Of the two of you," Retledge went on, "I know which one I would rather trust. But I'm not going to let anything happen. *Trumpet* came in. She does what she's here for. Then she goes. Clean and simple. Is that clear, Captain?"

Sorus controlled a retort. Life is trouble. Nobody gets out alive. If you don't cover your own ass, don't expect me to do it for you. Instead she drawled, "Sure, Chief. Leaving that sonofabitch alive was the worst mistake of my life." Her mouth twisted on the lie, but she kept her tone casual. "I don't want to make any more."

Succorso hadn't mentioned her? What the hell did *that* mean?

Retledge said, "Good." Her intercom clicked as he silenced his pickup.

She felt too tired to move. Lowering her head, she closed her eyes and fell into fatigue as if she were plunging down the gravity well of her buried despair. But Taverner didn't take his gaze off her: she knew that without looking to confirm it. His attention leaned on her, making demands she couldn't refuse.

What game was Succorso playing *now*?

She didn't know. After half a minute she pulled the ragged pieces of herself together and sent out her team.

Forty-five minutes later she met their return in the airlock which connected *Soar* to the Lab.

Milos Taverner stood beside her. She would have preferred to leave him behind, but she hadn't wanted to argue with him. However, she'd insisted that he wear eyeshades to conceal his alienness.

The four members of the team weren't necessarily her best people, but they were well suited for this assignment. One of them, her targ second, was so large and loud that his friends said of him that he couldn't sneeze without setting off proximity alarms on nearby ships. Another, *Soar*'s cabin boy, was simply the most beautiful youth she'd ever seen—a flagrant invitation to pederasty enhanced by his own rapacious appetites. The third, one of the engineers, was a woman with a weird talent for appearing demure while nearly falling out of her shipsuit.

Sorus had chosen them because they were good distractions. Without much effort they could hold every eye around them almost indefinitely.

The fourth member of the team was her command third. She'd put him in charge because he was quick, decisive, and knew how to make total strangers do what he told them.

As ordered, her people had brought a boy with them. He might have been fourteen or sixteen years old, but the white fear on his face made him look younger.

Grinning harshly, the command third saluted Sorus. "Captain." Then he pointed at the boy. "According to *Trumpet*'s manifest, his name is Ciro Vasaczk, but Succorso calls him Pup."

He was exactly what Sorus needed.

Pup was stocky, a bit too wide in the hips. A plain shipsuit a size too large for him rumpled at his wrists and ankles, but at least it was clean. The pallor of his skin seemed to emphasize the whites of his eyes; his mouth hung slightly open. Nevertheless he didn't struggle or shake. His gaze attached itself to Sorus as if he knew immediately that his life was in her hands; hers and no one else's. If she didn't take pity on him, no one would.

Just a kid, she thought, gripped by a self-disgust she couldn't afford. Perfect.

"Pup?" she said quietly. "I prefer Ciro."

One of his eyebrows twitched. He looked too frightened to speak. But then he surprised her by saying through his fear, "Captain Succorso won't like this."

She studied him gravely. "Of course he won't. That's the point.

"Any problems?" she asked her command third.

The man shook his head. "We found him in what Beckmann calls the refectory. He was sitting at one of the tables, trying to fill out a req. You think he's scared now, but he wasn't any calmer when we located him. I guess Succorso told him to order supplies, but didn't bother to let him know what they needed." He glanced to the other members of the team.

"Security never saw us with him. They had other things on their minds. As far as they know, he wandered off while they weren't looking."

Sorus nodded. "Good." Retledge's men would begin hunting as soon as they noticed the boy's absence, but the nature of the search would be conditioned by the idea that Ciro had gone somewhere on his own—perhaps simply exploring, perhaps acting on Succorso's orders.

She intended to put him back where he could be found before Security had time to become urgent.

Saluting, she dismissed her team. They filed out of the airlock behind her, leaving her alone with Ciro and Taverner.

Taverner hadn't spoken. He might have been blind behind his eyeshades—blind and deaf, unaware of anyone else's presence.

She considered suggesting that he do her dirty work for her. But she didn't want that, in spite of her self-disgust. Her responsibility for her own actions was all that kept her sane—and human.

"Ciro," she asked distantly, as if she were lost in thought, "do you know who I am?"

The boy didn't react. He stared white panic at her, betrayed nothing else.

"Do you know who this is?" She indicated Taverner with her head.

Ciro didn't so much as flick his eyes in Taverner's direction.

She let a little weariness creep into her tone. "Why do you think I had you brought here?"

A moment passed before he decided to answer. "I thought you wanted crew. Ships like this do that. I've seen Nick do it, when he was desperate. Steal crew—" Slowly the muscles at the corner of his jaw tightened, thrusting out his chin. "I'm not really a cabin boy. I've been trained for engineering.

"But that's not it." Just for an instant his voice rose as if it were about to break. Then he controlled it. "You aren't interested in me. You said so. You want to use me against Nick." He swallowed hard. "Or *Trumpet*."

Sorus sighed to herself. So Ciro could still think, despite his alarm. And he had engineering experience. That was good, from her point of view. But it would make what was about to happen that much worse for him.

"That's right," she answered. "In fact, you're essentially irrelevant—I mean you personally. I could have used anyone. You just happened to be available.

"Pay attention to me now," she told him as if she thought he might be capable of attending to anything else. "Your life depends on it. I want you to understand this situation. I want you to understand that I'm serious."

He gave a quick nod like a jerk. His eyes never left her face.

Taverner stood without moving. Just once she would have liked to see him appear restless or uncomfortable. The fact that the Amnioni didn't fidget made her feel jittery by comparison.

Harsh with vexation, she began, "I'm Captain Chatelaine. This ship is *Soar*—we were at Thanatos Minor when *Captain's Fancy* went down. I'm the woman who cut your Captain Succorso.

"I serve the Amnion."

Involuntarily Ciro's jaw sagged.

"I don't mean I work for them." Sorus didn't mind letting her anger and revulsion show. She wanted to scare the boy—scare him right to the edge of paralysis. "I *serve* them, Ciro. I'm going to tell you why.

"Years ago," in a different life, when Sorus had turned illegal because that was the path she chose, "this ship had another name. But she wasn't gap-capable then, and eventually the cops caught up with us. They couldn't take us—she's too powerful—but they did us real damage. Enough to finish us. It was just a matter of time, we were crippled. Limping to our grave." She remembered it all too well. "The next time the cops found us, they were going to tear us apart.

"But the Amnion found us first. We were doing business with them anyway, and we missed a contact. They came looking for us."

Ciro stared back at her dumbly; close to terror.

"They weren't nice about it," she rasped. "When they saw how bad we were hurt, they didn't offer to help us. Not them. Instead they handed me an ultimatum. Meet their terms or die. They were going to let us sputter away until we starved or crumpled, unless I gave them what they wanted."

Can you guess what's coming, boy? Do you know how much trouble you're in?

"What they wanted was to use me in an experiment. They'd developed a new—I guess you could call it a drug—and they wanted to know if it worked on humans. *If* it worked, they told me, I would still be human when it was done. I could have my ship back, they would save us, give us a gap drive, anything we needed."

Sorus paused to let some of the pain of the memory pass, then said, "If the experiment *didn't* work, I would turn into one of them."

She shrugged to loosen the tension in her shoulders.

"I figured I knew what would happen if I said no. They wouldn't risk a fight—they didn't want damage. So they would leave us alone until we were too far gone to defend ourselves. Then they would board us and do their damn experiments anyway. One way or another, we were all lost. The Amnion would get what they wanted, and I would get nothing.

"So I let them have me to experiment on."

If Ciro had showed any reaction, she might have started to yell at him. She needed an outlet for the gnawing pain of her despair. But for some reason his focused, unresponsive fear daunted her, like Taverner's immunity to restlessness.

"It worked," she told the boy bitterly. "I'm still human."

Again she shrugged. "But they hadn't bothered to tell me what kind of drug it was. I didn't find out until afterward.

"It's not an antimutagen, it's more subtle than that. It doesn't stop their mutagens. It postpones them. Like a temporary antidote. The mutagen stays in you, it stays alive, it works its way into every cell and wraps itself around your DNA strings, but it doesn't change you as long as you have this other drug in your system. How long the delay lasts depends on how much of this other drug you have in you—or how often you get it. You can stay human until you're cut off from your supply. After that"—she snapped her fingers—"you're an Amnioni."

She shifted her feet, adjusted her balance against the asteroid's light g.

"That's why I serve them, Ciro. If I don't, they'll stop giving me the antidote.

"And that's why *you're* going to serve *me*."

Sliding her left hand into a pocket of her shipsuit, she brought out a loaded hypo.

For a kid, the boy was quick. His face stretched and then crumpled as if he were panicking; he flinched backward a step. But his retreat was a feint. Too fast for real panic, he launched a flying kick at the hypo.

Fortunately Sorus was ready for him. She shifted to the side, pulled her left hand out of the way, blocked him past her with her right forearm.

The force of his kick glanced toward Milos Taverner.

Without effort, Taverner caught the boy's boot, spun him in midair, and wrapped both arms around him from behind.

Ciro struggled fiercely, wildly; making no sound. But he might as well have been trying to break free of an armcuff. The Amnioni had more than enough strength to hold him.

Now Sorus didn't hesitate. If she did, the darkness of her own actions might well up and drown her. Swift and relentless, she slapped a grip onto Ciro's wrist, stretched his forearm out from its sleeve to expose a patch of bare skin, and jabbed her hypo into him.

In two seconds the hypo was empty.

Nick Succorso's so-called cabin boy had approximately ten minutes of humanity left.

She stepped back quickly, in case he tried another kick. But she saw at once that he was done fighting. He hung rigid in Taverner's grasp; gaped at the tiny red stigmata which the hypo had left on his skin. Then he drew back his head and opened his mouth for a scream of absolute horror.

With a long sweep of her arm, Sorus struck him across the cheek. The blow did nothing to ease her revulsion, but it stopped Ciro's cry.

"I told you to pay attention!" she barked. "*Look* at me."

As his head recoiled, he'd dropped his eyes to his forearm again; the mark of the hypo seemed to pull his gaze down. When she demanded it, however, he slowly brought up his face.

His expression made her feel like shooting him.

Trembling somewhere deep inside, she put the hypo away and took out a small vial.

"Think for a minute, Ciro. If I turned you into an Amnioni, you wouldn't be able to help me. Succorso would never let you back aboard.

"You're right. You have a mutagen in you. But it's slow. Are you listening? It's *slow*. It won't start to work for ten more minutes.

"*This*"—she held the vial up in front of his face—"is the antidote. The drug that keeps the mutagen passive."

His eyes seemed to claw at the vial as if he wanted to swallow it, plastic and all.

"There are six capsules here," she went on. "Each one lasts for an hour. I can give you six hours of your life back right now. And there's more where this came from. *Plenty* more. Enough to keep us both human as long as we live.

"But I want you to *think*."

Abruptly Ciro thrashed against Taverner, threw himself into a fury of resistance. But the effort was useless: no doubt Taverner could have held Sorus as easily as he gripped the boy. After twenty seconds Ciro slumped, dangling in Taverner's arms.

"You want to know why we're here." Now he didn't look at Sorus or the vial; his head hung as if his neck were broken. "You want me to tell you." His voice struggled like a groan out of his constricted chest.

"Wrong." His dread touched fury in her. "I already fucking *know* why you're here. I know all about Shaheed's research. So try again."

He flinched. "Then you want me to do something for you. Something to Nick. Or the ship."

"*Think*," Sorus insisted.

"You can't want me to try to kill any of them," he breathed. She couldn't see his face; she could barely hear him. "I'm just a kid. I wouldn't stand a chance.

"You want me to do something to the ship."

"Go on."

"I don't know how to work the command boards," he protested. "I don't have the priority-codes. And anyway I'm never alone on the bridge."

She nodded slowly. "That's probably true. You'll have to think of something else."

He held his breath for a moment, then let it out in a burst like a muffled sob. "You want me to sabotage the drives."

"*Both* of them," she pronounced so that he couldn't misunderstand her. "You've been trained in engineering. You know how to do it.

"That's all. You make sure *Trumpet* can't outrun me. I'll handle the rest. She's finished if she can't run. I'll beat her, grapple on, cut my way in if I have to, take what I want. Then you can come with me. I'll keep you supplied for the rest of your life."

"Give me the pills," Ciro begged in a whisper.

"Not yet," she countered, tightening her fist on the vial. "There's one more thing I want you to understand.

"When I let you go, you could tell Succorso what I've done. As you say, you're just a kid. You might decide to be a hero. Or maybe you'll think I've been lying to you.

"But you can't hurt me. Try to understand that. I'm going to leave dock as soon as you're off the ship. Without more of this drug, you'll turn Amnion. Your friends will have to kill you. And I won't be any worse off than I am now. I can still tackle your ship in the swarm, before she can run.

"Is that clear, Ciro?"

She thought that he would nod: he appeared beaten enough to agree to anything. But she was wrong.

Still without raising his head—still hanging as if his neck had snapped—he objected, "What if it takes longer than six hours? I've never seen those drives. I've never even seen how they're accessed. What if I need more time?"

Now his head came up, lifted by the pressure of his racing heart. "Or what if Nick isn't done? What if I'm stuck here and you're out there when I run out of time?"

This time his voice cracked like a cry.

She met his flaring gaze and held it. Despite her years of service to the Amnion and her many visits to Billingate, she'd never before done what she was doing to him. Nevertheless she'd witnessed enough brutality, experienced enough, to foresee his argument—and prepare for it.

"All right," she sighed as if she were relenting. From another pocket she withdrew a second vial. "Six more hours." She wanted him scared, even terrified—not overwhelmed. "But that's as far as I go. If I don't have what I want in twelve hours, you're on your own."

He was a kid: twelve hours might seem like a long time.

His features twisted on the verge of tears; but she waited until she heard him breathe like a whimper, "All right." Then she told Taverner to let him go.

The instant Ciro was released, he snatched the vials from her and fought one of them open, fumbling to get a capsule into his mouth before his ten minutes ran out.

Sorus Chatelaine knew exactly how he felt.

A few minutes later her command third took Ciro off the ship. His orders were to deliver the boy to Chief Retledge; explain that Ciro had been found lost or snooping near *Soar*, and was being delivered to Security in order to avoid trouble with Captain Succorso; then return for an immediate departure.

When the outer lock had closed behind them, Sorus faced Taverner and demanded, "Good enough?"

Taverner's eyeshades made him seem more human, but they had no more expression than his alien gaze. Instead of answering her question, he asked one of his own.

"Do you believe that this ploy will succeed?" He didn't stress the word "believe": their earlier conversation stressed it for him.

She snorted angrily. "Maybe you've forgotten what human fear looks like. I haven't. That boy is *afraid*. He'll do what I told him."

She was sure. Men like Succorso didn't inspire the kind of loyalty that would lead Ciro to sacrifice himself.

"But that doesn't mean I think it'll work," she went on. "It might—or it might not. If he's scared enough, he might give himself away. What I 'believe,' " she sneered, "is that it's worth trying."

Taverner's pause might have been the Amnion equivalent of a shrug. Then, while they were alone in the airlock, and no one else could hear him, he announced flatly, "This installation must be destroyed."

She'd seen too many installations destroyed recently; too many lives lost. Despair filled her throat as she retorted, "Somehow I knew you were going to say that."

Taverner was insistent. "The knowledge which Captain Succorso seeks must die here. This installation must be destroyed."

Pain and darkness made her savage. Turning, she thumbed the control panel to open the inner doors. "That's one of the things a super-light proton cannon is good for."

As soon as the lock hummed aside, she pushed herself into motion, nearly bounding along the corridor in an attempt to put as much distance as possible between herself and the Amnioni who'd been assigned to haunt her.

MIKKA

She couldn't remain where she was; not now; not like this. Nick had told her to stay on watch outside the lab where he and Vector were presumably working—or where Vector worked while he watched—but she couldn't do it.

He was scheming: the signs were unmistakable. His efforts to keep the people aboard *Trumpet* secret, like his unexpected decision to separate Sib, Ciro, and her made no obvious sense. They must be part of some plot.

Whatever he was plotting, it was going to hurt—her, or someone she cared about. She knew Nick well enough to recognize the malign exhilaration in his eyes.

The thought left her sick with dread and anger. She absolutely could not remain standing here indefinitely, useless, while harm moved against her brother and the few people she wanted to call her friends.

Regardless of the price Morn and Davies might pay later for her disobedience, she nodded to the guard Retledge had assigned to watch with her, told him that she'd thought of a few things Sib and Ciro needed to include on their req lists, and walked away from the locked door.

The man didn't object or follow. She was secondary: what happened in that lab was his primary responsibility. And Beckmann's installation had plenty of other guards to make sure she didn't cause trouble.

In fact, she relied on encountering any number of guards. She'd never been here before, didn't know her way around. She would have to ask directions. And she didn't want anything she did to appear even remotely furtive. If or when Nick challenged her, she wanted to be able to name witnesses who could confirm what she told him.

Movement helped: acting on her own decisions helped. Her heart seemed to settle in her chest as she walked. At first she simply retraced her approach to the room where Vector worked. But as soon as she reached one of the Lab's main hallways, she began scanning for Security.

Techs and researchers in labsuits moved up and down the hall—so many of them that she suspected the installation's complex labs and experiments had reached a shift change. How many people lived here? She didn't know. This place was big; but still relatively small compared with shipyards like Billingate. Ordinary piracy attracted more illegals, if only because stealing was so much easier than the kind of work Beckmann carried on.

In five minutes she spotted a guard ahead of her, moving away. She strode after him.

He walked as if he were looking for someone. When she touched his arm to get his attention, he turned sharply and glared at her as if she'd interrupted something important.

She disliked him immediately. For some reason his tension sent anxiety crawling along her nerves like skinworms.

Nevertheless she made a point of noting the name on his Security id badge: "Klimpt." Witnesses with names were more useful than those without.

"Excuse me," she answered his glare. "I'm Mikka Vasaczk. Off *Trumpet*. I'm trying to find my brother. Ciro."

Like Nick, she'd called her brother "Pup" ever since he'd joined *Captain's Fancy*. But in the past few days that nickname had begun to pain her. Ciro deserved better.

The guard looked away, ran his eyes along the hallway, then faced her again, making no particular effort to be polite.

"Who?"

Under her bandage, Mikka's face clenched into its familiar scowl, but she kept her tone neutral. "Captain Succorso referred to him as 'Pup.' He has orders to req supplies from wherever you keep your food stores. I need to talk to him."

Klimpt's glare sharpened. Bending toward her aggressively, he demanded, "Why?"

She shrugged to show how little she feared his hostility. "We need some things Ciro might not know about. I want to be sure he puts them on his list."

The guard's belligerence receded, and a harried expression took its place. Wary of being overheard, he muttered quietly, "Then you can help me. The little shit wandered off somewhere. We're supposed to find him."

Mikka felt her heart stumble. She wanted to hit Klimpt for calling her brother a "little shit." At the same time she wanted to tear her hair, yell, go running in all directions. *Wandered off?* Ciro? When he was scared for his life—and knew even less than she did about what was going on?

But panic was useless; as useless as hitting the guard. With an effort, she kept herself under control.

"Nice work," she snarled. Now she knew where Klimpt's hostility came from. "How did you let that happen?"

"I didn't *let* it," he retorted defensively. "It just did."

She started to say, Where have you looked? but caught herself. That wouldn't help. She didn't know the Lab: she would only slow Klimpt by expecting him to account for himself. Instead she asked, "Have you checked with Sib? Sib Mackern?"

Klimpt shook his head.

"Tell me how to find him. I'll talk to him while you go on looking. If he knows where Ciro is, I'll contact Security."

The guard accepted her offer with a hint of gratitude. The more people who hunted for Ciro, the sooner he would be found. And the sooner he was found, the better Klimpt's chances of staying out of serious trouble. He pointed Mikka back the way she'd come, rattled off a quick series of directions, then turned to continue along the hall.

Where are you, Ciro? What has Nick done to you?

She was headed for General Stores. Concentrating hard to hold Klimpt's instructions in the front of her mind so that she wouldn't make a mistake—and wouldn't panic—she moved as fast as she could without running into the researchers and techs, or causing some other kind of commotion.

What had Nick done to her brother?

She was concentrating hard: too hard. For a moment she didn't notice that one of the rooms she passed resembled a station transit lounge. Twenty or thirty chairs measured the floor; data terminals stood around the walls at intervals; a series of information screens depended from the ceiling.

Mikka stopped. What use did the Lab have for a transit lounge?

None that she could think of.

The room was empty, so she entered to look at the screens.

As soon as she saw what they displayed, she understood. Not a transit lounge: more like an observation deck. Two of the screens gave what appeared to be progress reports on various experiments. One showed several researchers hunched over a piece of equipment she didn't recognize. Another offered a lecture of some kind: the man at the podium droned on as if he knew no one was listening. From this room spectators could watch experiments, check the results of someone else's work, or hear abstruse topics explained.

Where was Ciro? What had Nick done?

Mikka was about to leave when one more screen caught her eye. It displayed the installation's dock status—showed which berths were in use, by which ships.

Three of them she didn't know: they may have belonged to the Lab itself. One was *Trumpet*, numbers and blips winking to indicate that the ship was active.

One was *Soar*.

God *damn* it!

God damn *you*, you son of a bitch!

So that was what Nick was up to. By pure intuition and hard experience, she knew the answer. *Soar* was in: nothing else mattered. Somehow Nick had just sacrificed Ciro as a pawn in his deranged quest for revenge on Sorus Chatelaine.

Bounding forward as fast as the asteroid's g allowed, Mikka left the room and hurled herself recklessly along the route Klimpt had described.

Fortunately the halls were becoming less busy. Her pace was dangerous—more so because only one of her eyes focused well, and her depth perception was poor. If she made a mistake, she could easily break an arm or a leg; crack her ribs. The adrenaline pounding in her veins hurt her head as if she'd been hit again. But she didn't slow down. Nick had set Ciro up: he'd separated Ciro and Sib and her so that Ciro would be vulnerable.

Vulnerable to *Soar*. Nick had known she was here, that was obvious; the Lab's operational data would have told him even if *Trumpet*'s instruments didn't. For some reason he'd decided to dangle Ciro in front of Sorus Chatelaine like bait.

Mikka couldn't imagine what he hoped to gain. At the moment she couldn't imagine how *Soar* had known he was coming here. Nevertheless she was sure, as sure as fear, that Ciro was in danger; that Nick meant to use him against his old enemy.

She didn't pass any more guards. Maybe they were all busy looking for her brother.

The thought made her want to puke.

Hitting a wall hard enough to shock her lungs, she rebounded into the room where Klimpt had told her she would find Sib Mackern.

The room was little more than a cubicle, with a data terminal set into one wall opposite a reinforced door like an airlock. A sign over the door said GENERAL STORES. Deaner Beckmann kept his supplies and equipment sealed away as if they were in a vault—which made sense, considering the kind of people who came here to do business with him.

Sib stood in front of the terminal, frowning at the readout—or at the sweat dripping onto his hands whenever he used the keypad.

He was alone.

His head jerked up when he heard her thud against the wall and rebound. Relief broke across his strained features. "Mikka! Are we done? Can we—"

Her expression cut him off. His face froze; he stared at her, motionless, while she fought to catch her breath.

"Did Ciro come here?" she choked out.

Sib shook his head.

"Damn it!" She beat her fists on her hips in frustration and alarm. Damn damn damn. Now what could she do? How could she find him?

"What's happened?" Sib whispered thinly as if he feared that Security might be eavesdropping.

Panting, she told him. Her voice caught as she finished, "And *Soar* is here. In dock. I don't know how she found us, but she's here."

Sorus Chatelaine had cut Nick—

"Wait a minute," Sib murmured. "I don't understand. You think this has to do with her? How?"

Her fists swung harder. "He separated us so we'd be vulnerable. Especially Ciro."

"But why?" Sib protested. "What's he trying to do?"

Mikka was accustomed to her own competence; to knowing what to do—and being able to do it. But now she felt stunned by the danger Ciro was in.

"I don't *know*. I'm just sure. He separated us so Chatelaine could get at one of us. Maybe he just wants to get rid of us. I don't think so. It's not that simple. He's trying to set *her* up somehow."

Sib chewed his lower lip. His eyes seemed to stare past her. She feared that he didn't believe her; that he was thinking of ways to argue with her. After a moment, however, he surprised her by saying, "Then we'd better go over there." His fear was plain on his face. "Maybe we can find him. Or maybe—if we warn her"—he grimaced like a wince—"she'll give him back."

A gratitude Mikka couldn't name turned her heart to water. Trying to manage her sudden weakness, she objected, "We don't know the way."

Sib didn't look at her. Instead he turned back to the terminal. With a few keys, he bypassed the General Stores req protocols to access the Lab's public informations programs. They included schematic maps for most of the installation. Presumably Deaner Beckmann didn't want new residents getting lost.

Mikka told Sib which dock *Soar* occupied, then watched over his shoulder while he scrolled through the maps to discover where that berth lay in relation to General Stores. But she let him search by himself. Another fear had occurred to her. The weak water of her heart was becoming acid.

"If we do this," she murmured softly, "Nick will tear Morn's heart out."

Sib ducked his head, rubbed sweat or apprehension out of his eyes. Still whispering, he replied, "She'll understand. She would do the same thing."

Then he pointed at the screen. "There." He'd called up a series of red blips to indicate the most direct route between General Stores and *Soar*'s berth.

Mikka had the strange impression that he'd somehow become stronger than she was. Nevertheless she didn't hesitate. "Let's go." She couldn't afford to falter now.

He keyed off the terminal, turned to accompany her—and stopped as Chief Retledge came into the room.

Retledge had another guard with him. Both men made a point of the way they gripped their impact pistols.

The Security chief faced Mikka with a humorless smile. "There you are," he drawled. "When it comes to wandering off, you're as bad as Pup. I don't know why Captain Succorso bothers to give you orders. You obviously don't pay any attention to them." Then he nodded brusquely to Sib. "No offense, Mr. Mackern. At least you have enough sense to stay where you're put."

Mikka swallowed a howl; locked her arms across her chest so that she wouldn't raise her fists. Through her teeth she told Retledge, "In effect I'm Captain Succorso's second. While he's busy with Dr. Shaheed, I thought of a few things we need. I considered it my duty to make sure Pup put them on his req.

"Your man Klimpt told me he'd 'wandered off,' " she continued. "I came here to see if he was with Mr. Mackern."

"Of course," Retledge rasped. "Naturally I believe you. You don't look like a woman who wants trouble.

"But just to be on the safe side," he added, "I'm leaving Vestele here with you." Scowling, the other guard tightened his hand on his gun. "He'll make sure you keep the rest of your 'duties' to yourself until Captain Succorso wants you.

"As for Klimpt," Retledge finished, "I'll have his ears for this. Dr. Beckmann doesn't tolerate incompetence."

Familiar with the thin g, he turned hard and strode out of the room.

Vestele aimed his scowl like a warning at Mikka and then Sib. Slowly he withdrew to the entryway, putting a little extra distance between himself and the possibility of attack. After that, however, some of his tension or distrust eased. He let go of his pistol and raised his hand to tap his right ear.

"I'm wearing a PCR." His tone was unexpectedly mild. "I'll know when they find Pup. I won't keep it to myself. And if Captain Succorso asks for you, I'll hear the message."

Mikka should have thanked him for his consideration. She meant to. But she didn't have the strength. Her legs folded under her, and she sank to the floor. Clamping her arms around her knees to keep what was left of her heart from leaking away, she put her head down and closed her eyes.

Nick had found her weak point—the place where her defenses failed. Nothing he'd ever done to her had hurt like this. Even his most casual seduction and callous rejection had left her whole by comparison; essentially intact despite her grief and anger; still able to function. Now, however, she was in so much pain that she literally couldn't stand. Everything in her quailed. The harm which Nick and Sorus Chatelaine might do her brother was too great to be borne.

He deserved better.

Sib murmured her name a few times, but she didn't react. Eventually he fell silent and left her alone.

In one sense the wait was painfully long; in another, surprisingly short. She didn't measure it. Instead she hugged her knees and rode the long solar wind of her distress until Vestele surprised her out of herself by clearing his throat.

She looked up in time to see him lift his hand halfway to his right ear, cock his head as if he were listening. For a moment his attention seemed to slide elsewhere.

Without realizing it she surged to her feet.

The cramped vehemence of her muscles sent her toward the ceiling. At once the guard's eyes jerked into focus on her: he raised his gun as if he thought she might attack him. But Sib caught her arm, held her back. As she touched the floor again, she opened her hands and showed them to Vestele so he could see that she was harmless.

Vestele kept his pistol aimed at her; but the pressure of his grip loosened.

"What is it?" Sib asked tensely. "What did you hear?"

Vestele's reply was cautious. "They found Pup. For some reason he was in one of the service corridors outside the cargo dock. Said he was lost—said he was trying to find Captain Succorso and just got lost." The guard refrained from commenting on the plausibility of this. "He's being held in the entry room. Where Dr. Beckmann greeted you."

"Is he—" Mikka's throat choked shut before she could finish the question. Relief and alarm filled her chest until she could hardly breathe.

"Is he all right?" Vestele asked for her. "Center says so. He looks scared out of his mind—maybe scared enough to be telling the truth—but he isn't hurt."

Mikka gulped for air. "Take me to him."

The guard shook his head. His gun didn't waver. "Sorry. Chief Retledge wants you to stay here. Until we hear from Captain Succorso." Then he added more considerately, "Don't worry. Pup will be safe. We don't want trouble any more than you do."

She was tempted to yell at him; threaten him; try to bluff her way past him. A deep sense of uselessness stopped her. She'd never been equal to Nick's schemes: he was always ahead of her. Ever since she'd fallen under his spell and joined his ship, her competence had been a mask for this futility—a way of concealing from herself the fact that she meant nothing and accomplished less. What she thought or wanted or did only mattered to people who were as substantially ineffectual as she was.

People like Ciro and Sib. Vector.

Morn and Davies.

She didn't say anything. There was nothing left to say.

"What is it you want to hear from Captain Succorso?" Sib put in. Maybe he hadn't noticed his own futility yet. Or maybe he'd grown accustomed to the idea.

Vestele shrugged. "I'm just a guard. I don't make policy." After a pause, however, he added, "Mostly I think Dr. Beckmann wants to hear how Captain Succorso is going to pay him."

Which might mean that Mikka and Sib were stuck here until Vector completed his analysis of UMCPDA's antimutagen.

That could take hours. It could take days.

She wondered whether Morn and Davies would still be alive—and sane—when she and the rest of Nick's people finally returned to *Trumpet*. Or whether Sorus Chatelaine would ever let them get that far.

In fact, two more hours passed before Vestele listened to his PCR again. He nodded to superiors who couldn't see or hear him. Then he announced, "Dr. Shaheed is done. He and Captain Succorso are leaving thirty-one. Captain Succorso wants you two to meet him where Pup is—in the entry room. And he wants to talk to Dr. Beckmann."

Sib scrubbed his hands up and down his face. "I'm not ready," he murmured. "Two hours ago I was. Now I'm not."

Mikka ignored him. Her heart thudded in her chest—as hard as a mine-hammer, but too erratic for anything mechanical. "Let's go," she told Vestele.

The guard examined her narrowly; looked at Sib. After a moment he slid his handgun into its holster.

"This way." He gestured toward the outer passage.

Driven by panic, Mikka left the room as fast as she could without losing her purchase on the floor.

Sib and then Vestele followed her quickly. At the first intersection she let the guard take the lead. In an effort to control her pulse—if not her dread—she concentrated on matching her pace to his as he guided her and Sib through the complex.

He was listening to his PCR again, receiving new orders. When they reached what appeared to be another of the Lab's main corridors, he stopped; gestured for Mikka and Sib to halt. "We'll wait here."

She couldn't help herself. "What for?"

"Mikka," Sib breathed, warning her.

Vestele didn't bother to retort. Instead he pointed down the corridor.

Nick and Vector had just come into sight. The man Dr. Beckmann had addressed as "Sven" was with them, in addition to two more guards. But Mikka ignored the Lab's personnel. While the men approached, she scrutinized Nick and Vector as if the answers she needed might be legible on their faces.

They both looked vindicated, triumphant.

There the similarity between them ended, however. Vector's smile and his mild, blue eyes had an ineffable glow, like those of a man who had been washed clean in the waters of a sacrament. He walked buoyantly, as if his joints no longer caused him any pain, and his lips moved as if he were singing to himself.

Nick, on the other hand—

His triumph was bloodthirsty and malign; full of threats. His scars were as stark as shouts under his eyes—so crowded with passion that they seemed to swell and throb—and his grin resembled a sadist's perfect love for his victims.

The answers were plain enough: Mikka couldn't mistake them. He'd staked Ciro out like a Judas goat. And Sorus Chatelaine had taken the bait.

He looks scared out of his mind—

For a moment red fury nearly blinded Mikka's good eye.

Nick, too, walked quickly, in a hurry to follow up his advantage. As he passed her, he snatched at her arm, pulled her into motion beside him. His fingers dug like fire into her muscles; his whole body seemed to radiate heat like a furnace.

Bending to her ear, he whispered, "You like to live fucking dangerously, don't you. I told you to guard the door until we were done."

Slowly her vision cleared. She couldn't fight him; argue with him. Not here, like this. Maybe never. In a dead voice she gave him the same story she'd told Klimpt and Retledge. She didn't expect him to believe her: she was only trying to buy time until she saw Ciro.

Stupidly helpful, as if he thought Nick might listen to him, Sib put in when she was done, "That's true."

Nick didn't listen to Sib: his contempt for his former data first was palpable. "I don't care," he answered Mikka softly. "You were too late to interfere. That's what counts." His joy glittered like a scalpel. "And you're going to pay for it as long as you live. Which may not be much longer at this rate.

"Think about *that,*" he advised her in a fierce murmur. "You'll be dead—and I'll still have Pup."

The pain of his grip on her arm meant nothing. But the pain of being so close to him was more than she could bear. Planting her feet, she wrenched her arm out of his grasp. Before anyone could react, she pulled back to the wall of the corridor; separated herself at least that much from his triumph.

At the same time Sib hurried forward so that he came between them. Regardless of his fears, he intended to shield Mikka. Perhaps because he'd failed in the self-appointed duty of guarding Nick earlier, he seemed determined to sacrifice himself for someone as soon as he could.

Nick sneered at him harshly, then strode on.

As Mikka moved to follow, she found herself beside Vector.

He also put his hand on her arm—a gentle touch which nevertheless slowed her pace until she was five or six strides behind Nick. Like Nick, he bent toward her so that he could whisper into her ear.

"He's wrong." Vector spoke so softly that she could barely make out the words. "He's missed the point.

"God, we were *close*." He must have meant his research team at Intertech. "If the cops had left us alone for another month—or another week—we would have gotten it. I cracked the formula so fast because I already knew most of it."

Bitterly, Mikka breathed back, "And you think *that's* the point?"

"Don't you see?" Vector tightened his grip for a moment, then remembered to ease it. "It won't be a *secret* any longer. As soon as he makes his deal with Beckmann, it'll be out of his control. People will *know*, more people every day. The cops are going to lose their stranglehold on human space. Right now they have so much power because they're vital. They're humankind's only defense. But that won't be true once *this* gets out."

Vector smiled like a rebirth. Still whispering, he concluded, "Nick is obsessed with revenge. He can't see that he's already started to cut the ground out from under his own feet."

Mikka understood him. He may even have been right. But she didn't care. "That doesn't help," she answered. "He's still got *us*."

Us and Morn. Angus and Davies.

Vector sighed; straightened his back. "There's nothing we can do about that." He seemed to think that she, too, had missed the point. "We've been doomed ever since we joined *Captain's Fancy*. No one recovers from that kind of mistake."

Thanks a bunch, Mikka rasped to herself. You're a real comfort. But she kept her bitterness silent. She couldn't blame Vector for the fact that he didn't have a younger brother.

One of the guards listened to his PCR, then turned and spoke privately to Sven. Sven nodded and left the group; apparently he'd been sent to other duties.

Accompanied only by guards, Nick, Sib, Vector, and Mikka reached the entry room where they'd first met Deaner Beckmann.

The director of the Lab was already there, along with Chief Retledge and half a dozen more guards. Their numbers in the small room almost concealed Ciro, who stood by the entrance to the airlock: they might have forgotten he existed.

Beckmann paced back and forth between the other men as if he were fuming or feverish; ruled by hungers he didn't know how to feed. As soon as he saw Nick, however, he stopped with a jerk.

"Captain Succorso." His voice sounded like the action of a metal cutter. "It's time for some answers."

Almost in unison the guards dropped their hands to the butts of their impact pistols. They knew their orders.

Nick halted as promptly as he could in the light g. Behind him Sib, Vector, and Mikka did the same.

The director of the lab didn't wait for his Security chief to speak. "You come here asking for help," he snapped, "and all you offer in return is a vague share of Dr. Shaheed's unspecified research. That's fine—I'm willing to take a risk on a man of Dr. Shaheed's reputation. But another ship, a ship we've known for years, tells us that you're here to cause trouble. And what happens? You haven't been here an hour before two of your people *apparently* disobey your orders. In fact, one of them"—he slapped a gesture toward Ciro—"disappears completely. And as soon as we find this *Pup* of yours again, the other ship leaves. If he didn't look so frightened himself, I would almost think he scared her away.

"I want answers, Captain Succorso, and I want them now. What kind of harm are you doing at my expense?"

He spoke severely, but Mikka hardly heard him. Her attention was focused on Ciro. He was barely visible past the shoulders of the guards, but she seemed to see him as clearly as if they were alone.

He was too young to hide what he felt. By an act of will he kept his face still; stood without squirming. Nevertheless his entire body shouted that he was in mortal terror—that he'd been violated as profoundly as any rape and didn't know how to bear it. Mikka knew him too well to be mistaken. His dismay and need were flagrant to her. Sweat oozed like wax from his skin; his bones might have been melting.

She thought she'd imagined the worst, but she saw now that she had no idea just how bad the worst could be.

She didn't listen to Beckmann's question; didn't give Nick time to answer. Carried by a flood of anguish, she began thrusting her way among the guards to reach her brother.

"*Mikka!*" Nick barked after her.

Some of the men shifted out of her way. Others drew their guns. By the time she reached Ciro, there were at least three pistols leveled at her head.

She took no notice of them.

What has he done to you?

Her arrival only seemed to increase his distress. Chagrin pulled at his features as if she'd caught him doing something shameful. Unable to contain the frenzy rising in her—a wildness like a scream, shrill and tearing—she flung her arms around him, hugged him against her. But he didn't respond; all his muscles were rigid with rejection. His fear had consumed him completely, swallowed him down to a place where she couldn't reach him.

What have they **done** *to you?*

"Mikka!" Nick shouted again. And Sib croaked like an echo, "Mikka!"

She let go of her brother; whirled to confront three guns so close that their muzzles brushed her face.

Chief Retledge was saying something that might have been, "—pushing your luck, Vasaczk."

She ignored him; ignored the guns and the guards. Instead she aimed her frenzy like a shaft of rage at Nick.

"I'm going to take him aboard." Her voice was almost steady. "I need to talk to him. And you don't want us here."

Can you *hear* me, you bastard? Are you *listening*? You don't want us here because if you try to stop me I'm going to take one of these guns and blast your *face* off. And if I can't do that, I'm going to tell Retledge what the *fuck* I think you're doing.

Nick appeared to understand her unspoken threat. She might say something which the Lab would pass along to *Soar;* which would warn Sorus Chatelaine. At once he said to Retledge, "It's all right, Chief." In one cheek small spasms tugged at the edges of his scars, but he didn't seem to be aware of it. "We might as well let them go. The kid needs cat, or he won't be able to talk to anybody. And she's too worried about him to be good for anything else.

"Sib and Vector will stay here with me," he reassured the Security chief. "We all have plenty to discuss." An involuntary twist of his mouth showed a flash of teeth. "I won't even mention leaving until you and Dr. Beckmann are satisfied."

Past the guns Mikka saw Chief Retledge glance at the director of the Lab.

Deaner Beckmann nodded once, decisively.

A slight easing of tension ran like a sigh through the room. Slowly three guards withdrew their weapons from Mikka's face. A fourth stepped past Ciro and began tapping codes into the keypad of the lock.

Mikka turned her back on Nick so that he couldn't see how close she came to screaming.

"Take him aboard, Mikka." He didn't shout, but his voice slid along her spine like the tip of a blade. If he shoved on it, it would cut between her vertebrae and sever the cord. "I'll deal with his insubordination later. And yours."

Fine, she rasped. You do that. I'll take my chances.

But she knew that she'd already lost all her chances.

Ciro still hadn't moved. Maybe he couldn't. He stood facing Nick and Sib, Retledge and Beckmann; his back to the airlock; rigid as the rigor of death. A different kind of knife had cut the link between his limbs and his mind.

Why did seeing her make him feel worse?

She put her hands on his shoulders, turned him forcibly, and pressed him forward as the door opened. Awkwardly she impelled him into the airlock.

Behind her the guard keyed the inner door shut again. After a quick series of automatic safety checks, the outer door irised aside. At once she hauled Ciro into the blank access passage which led to *Trumpet*.

What had they done to him? How could they have scared him so badly? He was her brother, but she'd never seen him afraid like this. Never.

The light was flat, vaguely inhuman. She didn't spot any bugeyes or sensors. Maybe there weren't any hidden pickups. She didn't know the codes to open *Trumpet*'s airlock herself: she would have to ask Angus to her let her aboard. But anyone who overheard her would realize that the gap scout hadn't been left empty. That might unravel Nick's schemes; but it would also doom everyone she cared about.

Assuming that Ciro wasn't already doomed—

They reached the ship. Irrationally concerned that he might turn and run, she trapped him between her and the wall, leaned against him while she snapped open the cover which protected the exterior control panel, then thumbed the intercom.

"It's Mikka." She hissed the words softly so that she wouldn't yell or scream. "Let me in."

No one answered. The indicators on the panel showed that the intercom was active, but no reply came.

She hammered the ship's hull with her fist. "I've got Ciro with me. We're in trouble. Let me in."

Of course Angus wasn't going to answer. Nick had told him, *The Hyland twins are yours. If that computer in your malicious little head will let you play with them, go ahead.* He probably couldn't hear her at all. He was too busy raping Morn. Or slowly flaying Davies alive—

Helpless to contain her anguish, she punched the hull again. Her knuckles left a smear of blood on the metal, but she didn't feel any pain. She was past recognizing minor hurts.

"Goddamn you, let me *in*."

"Mikka," Ciro croaked brokenly, "please—"

"Please?" She jerked around as if she were turning to hit him. "*Please?*"

His eyes ached at her, raw for lack of moisture. He couldn't have wept if he'd wanted to: he had no tears to weep with.

"Kill me." His voice strained against a constriction in his throat. "Now. While you have the chance."

Lights winked on the control panel as the airlock began to cycle open.

Mikka ducked her head. Dismay and rage mounted inside her. Howling through her teeth, she snatched Ciro off the wall and heaved him inward as *Trumpet*'s outer seal eased out of the way.

Sailing in the light g, he crossed the lock, smacked against the inner door, and rebounded toward the access passage as if he were trying to escape.

She leaped after him, caught him in the air, drove him back again.

If she hadn't been moving so fast, Davies' blow might have cracked her skull. As it was, she caused him to mistime his swing. The gun in his fist missed her head. Instead the butt pounded deep into the muscles of her left shoulder. Instantly her arm went numb as if she'd received a blast of stun.

"Shit, Mikka!" he protested softly, urgently. "What the hell are you doing?" Then he demanded, "Where's Nick? We thought he was with you. What's going on?"

Out of the corner of her eye, Mikka saw Morn at the airlock control panel, entering commands as fast as she could to close the door.

Davies. And Morn. But not Angus.

She didn't try to understand it. Her left arm was useless; so completely numb that it might as well have been cut off. She had to release Ciro in order to key open the inner door and the lift. At once, however, she gripped him again, even though he hadn't tried to get away.

"Mikka!" Davies barked. With the airlock sealed, he no longer needed to keep his voice down.

"Mikka, we're sorry," Morn said more quietly. "We didn't mean to attack you." Like Davies, she had a gun—a laser pistol, charged and ready. "We thought Nick was with you—we thought he might be trying to take us by surprise."

Servos swept the lift doors out of Mikka's way. She pushed Ciro inside, entered the lift after him, then turned.

"Vector's done," she told Morn and Davies as clearly as she could. "He and Nick are dickering with Beckmann now. Nick kept Sib with them. They should be coming soon." Desperation leaked past the edges of her self-control. "Ciro and I need to talk, so *leave us alone*."

Davies seemed deaf to the complex stresses in her tone. "What's going on?" he demanded again. "What happened out there?"

Strange stains marked the front of his alien shipsuit. They looked like blood.

"Where's Angus?" Mikka countered harshly. "What's going on in here?"

Morn put her hand on Davies' arm like a warning.

His mouth closed sharply.

Snarling under her breath, Mikka shut the lift and sent it upward. She barely heard Davies shout after her, "Stay off the bridge! Angus doesn't want to be bothered!"

Doesn't want to be bothered? What was going on? Morn and Davies had guns. They were trying to ambush Nick in the airlock. And Angus didn't want to be *bothered?*

Later: she would worry about all that later. If she could still bear it. When the lift opened, she pulled Ciro out.

The central passage was empty: the whole ship sounded empty. For the first time since she'd joined *Trumpet*, the door at the head of the companionway was shut. But she didn't pause to analyze the situation. If anything happened now to delay her, she might begin to tear her hair; might beat her skull on the bulkheads. In four strides she reached the cabin she and Ciro shared. The door responded at the touch of a command.

She thrust her brother inside so hard that he staggered; nearly fell.

While he caught his balance and slowly, fearfully, came around to face her, she closed the door; locked it. If she could have dropped an iron bar across it to keep it shut, she would have done so. A glance at the intercom confirmed that the pickup wasn't active.

Lungs heaving for air, she confronted Ciro across the small cabin. "Now." Her breath scraped in her throat. "You're going to tell me what happened.

"Whatever it is, we'll face it together."

He stared back at her, dry-eyed, as if she'd offered to reach into his chest and rip out his heart.

MORN

Morn could feel withdrawal beginning to burn in her nerves like a slow fuse lit by Mikka's frantic passage through the airlock. Until now she'd been too busy—and too scared—to take notice of her own condition; too full of adrenaline to want or need the artificial stimulation of her zone implant.

Angus wasn't ready. In fact, at the moment he was virtually helpless. Even Ciro, despite his obvious fright, could have killed the cyborg now.

Angus' struggle to free himself dismayed Morn. He was the victim of his zone implants: she knew what that was like. His helplessness touched sore places in her heart which she didn't want to examine.

At the same time, she didn't want him to succeed. She'd made the decision to let him try. Now it horrified her.

Yet without him she was lost. Her life—and her son's—depended on him. And her ability to endure the things which had happened to her, as well as the things she'd done, depended on her determination to make decisions the way a cop should.

Because Angus was vulnerable, she and Davies were here in the airlock, waiting for Nick. Until he completed his self-transformation, he couldn't defend himself; certainly couldn't protect anyone else. Morn and Davies had to beat Nick themselves.

Just shoot him, Davies had suggested. They had guns. Angus had opened the weapons locker before they began his operation.

But Morn had refused.

Why not? Davies had pursued. If he's dead, he can't hurt us. And he can't mess with Angus. We won't have to stake *everything* on this weird idea that Angus can edit his datacore.

Because we're cops, Morn had answered. We don't do things like that.

And we might need him. We might need him to talk us out of here, in case Lab Center refuses to deal with anyone else.

And—the mere idea appalled her—we might need his help if Angus goes out of control. If his changes backfire. Or if he taps his core programming to somehow cancel his restriction against harming UMCP personnel.

Besides, we can't be sure we won't hit Vector or one of the others.

Nick would be here soon: Mikka had said as much. *Vector's done*. The geneticist had succeeded at analyzing UMCPDA's mutagen immunity drug: he knew the formula. *He and Nick are dickering with Beckmann now*. And Beckmann would want a share of that secret, if only for the wealth it represented. Under the circumstances, "dickering" wouldn't take long. Nick would get everything he asked for and be ready to leave in a matter of minutes.

What had happened to Mikka? What had happened to *Ciro*?

Their distress brought back another nagging question: why had *Soar* left? Morn had assumed that Sorus Chatelaine was taking her ship out into the asteroid swarm to prepare an ambush. But Mikka's actions, and Ciro's face, suggested other possibilities.

Nick had committed some new atrocity.

Or he himself had been betrayed. Beckmann had turned against him —perhaps because *Soar* had set him up.

Morn had no intention of telling anyone, not even Mikka, how exposed Angus was until she knew what had happened in Deaner Beckmann's domain.

I need time, Angus had insisted. You've got to keep Nick away from me until I'm done and one of you plugs the datacore back into my computer. After that I can defend myself, even if I'm still wired to the ship.

But I can't rush it. It's complicated anyway, but the really hard part is getting around the stasis commands. They're hardwired. That's how Hashi fucking Lebwohl's techs used to handle me. They could pop my datacore in and out whenever they wanted because the stasis commands aren't on that chip. They kick in automatically if my programming doesn't countermand them.

So you can't just cut me open, pull my datacore, and hand it to me. I won't be able to work on it.

The solution he'd devised was elaborate as well as uncertain. It had involved opening his back to expose his computer and then running a complex series of leads between it and *Trumpet*'s command circuits—in effect using the ship's datacore to override his hardwired instruction-set so that his own datacore could be removed without sending him into paralysis.

Will that work? Morn had asked.

Who the hell knows? Angus had answered. But what's it going to hurt? Even if you end up frying what's left of my brains, you won't be any worse off than you are right now. At least you'll have a better chance against Captain Sheepfucker. And maybe I'll get to stop screaming inside where nobody hears me.

So Morn and Davies had agreed. As far as she was concerned, they'd had no choice. And once he'd been persuaded to take the risk of freeing Angus, he'd become eager to act on it.

She'd left the cutting and wiring to him—but not because he was eager. She hadn't wanted to get that close to Angus. Hadn't wanted his blood on her hands. While Davies stained himself red in the task of reaching Angus' computer, peeling skin and muscle aside to lay bare his equipment, and then attaching leads exactly as Angus instructed, she'd helped by wiring those same leads into the command board.

At the same time she'd watched scan and communications, studying the Lab as well as the surrounding swarm for data or warnings. When she'd seen *Soar* undock, she'd spent a while on targ, tracking the other ship with *Trumpet*'s guns until she was sure that Sorus Chatelaine didn't mean to attack the gap scout while *Soar* was still within reach of the Lab's matter cannon.

In that way Morn had kept herself busy; distracted. Otherwise her apprehension and the smell of Angus' blood might have made her weep.

The job had been long and arduous. But at last Angus had said, All right, we're ready. As far as I can tell, everything tests out. Go ahead—pull the chip.

Now or never. Kill me or save me.

When Davies unplugged the datacore from its socket between Angus' shoulder blades, Angus had rolled his eyes, grimaced like a convulsion, muttered a curse. Then both he and his son had begun to laugh like demented schoolboys; crazy with relief.

Maybe the three of them had a chance after all. Maybe by the time Vector finished his research Angus would be whole again, able to use his lasers and databases and other resources; and freed from the compulsion of his priority-codes.

But Mikka had keyed the ship's exterior intercom too soon. And there'd been no advance notice from Lab Center. Angus wasn't ready—he was still sweating over his datacore. While it was unplugged none of his equipment functioned. In fact, he couldn't even move around: he was effectively trapped by the wiring which connected him to the command circuits.

A sitting target.

Snatching up their guns, Morn and Davies had run for the airlock.

On their way off the bridge, they'd closed the bulkhead door at the head of the companionway. That wouldn't protect him unless he remembered to lock it, however. Morn feared that he was concentrating too hard to think about things like that.

But it was out of her hands. In a rush she and Davies had taken their places in the airlock on either side of the doors; braced themselves for Nick.

Club him, she'd hissed to her son. If you can knock him out, our problems are solved. Even if he's just dazed, we can handle him. And if you miss— Stiff with dread, she'd shrugged. I'll have to try.

Davies had nodded bitterly. He still ached to kill Nick.

But when Morn unsealed the doors, Mikka came through the airlock like a flare of panic, thrusting Ciro ahead of her as if he were too frightened to make himself move.

Vector's done. He and Nick are dickering with Beckmann now. They should be coming soon.

"What's going on?" Davies demanded. "What happened out there?"

"Where's Angus?" Mikka countered. "What's going on in here?"

Then she and Ciro were gone, riding the lift upward.

"Jesus," Davies breathed in shock. "What's wrong with them? I thought this place was just a lab, not some House of Horrors like Billingate."

Morn felt the raw touch of withdrawal crawling along her nerves. She didn't know the answer. Somehow Mikka's fear, and Ciro's, pushed her to the verge of another attack. She'd been deprived of her zone implant's emissions too long— Only hours of cat had postponed the onset of her mad hunger for clarity. Now it was overdue.

The same questions ran her in circles.

What had happened to Mikka and Ciro? What had they *done*?

Davies tightened his grip on his impact pistol. His body gave off tension like static. "You ought to go back to the bridge," he told Morn. "One of us should be there to plug in that datacore as soon as Angus is ready. And if I can't deal with Nick, you'll still have a chance."

To explain his concern, he added, "We don't know what's wrong with Mikka and Ciro. They could turn Angus off just by tugging on one of those leads."

"I know," Morn sighed. A familiar acid licked small streaks of pain along her limbs, through her joints. The back of her head throbbed. "But if I'm going to trust Angus, I'm certainly going to trust Mikka. No matter what's happened, she doesn't want Nick to run this ship." Again she shrugged. "And I can't leave you," she admitted thinly. "I'll lose my mind if I have to wait up there with him alone."

Davies growled, but didn't try to dissuade her. "Then we'll have to do better than we did with Mikka. You go first this time. Step in front of him, point your gun at his face—whatever it takes to distract him. All I need is two seconds to key the door and then hit him."

She nodded dumbly. Fear or withdrawal dried her mouth, desiccating what was left of her courage.

But she didn't have time to be afraid. Before starting his operation, Angus had opened ship-wide channels for *Trumpet*'s internal communications. Now the airlock intercom chimed, and almost at once Nick's voice crackled across the silence.

"Open up." He sounded ebullient, nearly manic with eagerness. "I'm back. Whatever you're doing"—he must have been talking to Angus, although the Lab's personnel would have thought he addressed Mikka—"stop it. Get the ship ready. It's time to leave." He coughed a laugh. "Time to go have some fun."

Fun. Sure.

Morn clutched her handgun.

They couldn't afford to hesitate now. Nick would expect immediate obedience from Isaac. Any delay might warn him that he was in trouble.

Davies thumbed the airlock controls. He and Morn tucked themselves into the corners on either side of the outer door.

Her heart beat hard enough to make her woozy. Step in front of him. Point her gun at his face. *Arrest* him. She was a cop, wasn't she? She was supposed to know how to do this.

But between them Angus and Nick had nearly dismantled her. She was a zone implant addict. Weeks of overexertion and fear had exacted their toll. And the cops she'd trained to serve were corrupt. The laser pistol felt like an alien artifact in her hand: a construct she didn't understand and couldn't use.

And Nick sent Sib and then Vector into the lock ahead of him as if he wanted to make sure the way was safe.

Her hand, no, her whole arm had already begun to tremble by the time Nick crossed between her and Davies.

Sib turned at the lift, caught sight of her. His involuntary surprise betrayed her.

She jumped forward with her gun straining for Nick's head. As if she were still a cop, still believed in herself, she barked, "*Freeze!*"

But she'd already failed. Her motion was too intense for the slight g. The pressure in her legs drove her past Nick toward the ceiling; out of control.

Sib's surprise warned Nick; the sound of the airlock closing warned him. He ignored Morn. Sudden and savage, he whirled on Davies. Morn's frantic shot scored the deck beyond his feet, but didn't touch him.

Davies wasn't braced for it. He was expecting to attack, not be attacked. As Nick spun, he jerked up his hands too late to stop Nick's elbow from catching him squarely on the cheekbone. His head hit the wall with a sodden double smack like the sound of fruit being pulped.

The doors whined shut; sealed the fight inside.

Morn clashed against the ceiling and rebounded, flailing to aim her laser. But now Vector blocked her. Trying to get out of the way, he blundered in the wrong direction.

Nick swung at Davies' head. Davies was stunned, barely able to move. Still Morn's old training saved him. Reflexively he tossed up his forearm hard enough to deflect Nick's fist.

An instant later Nick crashed into him. They both stumbled against the bulkhead as Sib drove into Nick's back with all his weight and force.

Sib had failed too often, shamed himself with his own fears too much. Now his desperation transformed him. His eyes blazed as he planted himself and began hammering Nick's back with his elbows, throwing the torque of his shoulders and the strength of his arms like projectiles at Nick's ribs and kidneys.

Roaring with pain, Nick flung himself off Davies; twisted to fall away from Sib's elbows.

"Angus!" he howled. "*Angus!*"

In a frenzy of alarm, Morn heaved Vector aside; thrust herself headlong after Nick.

She would have failed at that, too, if Vector hadn't helped her. Awkward with old pain, he braced his arms and legs, anchored his body so that she could launch off him accurately.

She landed across Nick's back as he sprawled on his face.

She couldn't hold him down with her own weight; couldn't fight him physically. She didn't try. As he bunched under her to pitch her off, she knotted her free hand onto the collar of his shipsuit and jammed the muzzle of her pistol into his ear.

"I said *freeze*! I can't miss from here! You can't flip fast enough to make me miss! If you don't *freeze*, I'm going to burn a red hole right through the middle of your *brain*!"

She didn't know whether or not he believed her. She wasn't sure that she believed herself. Nevertheless he faltered—

An instant later the butt of Davies' impact pistol came down on his skull like a cudgel.

His body flopped raggedly, then slumped still. A small sigh like a groan escaped him. "Angus, you bastard—"

After that he was gone.

Blood trickled through the hair on the back of his head. More blood marked the deck under his face. Nevertheless he went on breathing thinly, like a man who didn't know how to die.

"Shit," Davies panted somewhere above Morn. "I'm sorry. I can't seem to beat him. Every time I fight him he does something I don't expect."

Slowly Morn lowered her head, rested it for a moment between Nick's shoulder blades while she let herself go faint with relief. She may have looked like she was grieving for him, but in truth she was suddenly so full of gratitude that she could scarcely contain it.

"Don't be too hard on yourself," Vector breathed to Davies. His own relief was palpable. "As far as *I'm* concerned, you're absolutely amazing. Whenever I make the mistake of thinking you Hylands have limits, you do something like this. How did you—" He cleared his lungs with a loud gust. "You take my breath away. How did you get past Angus? I thought he was unreachable. Not to mention invulnerable."

"Can you move?" Sib murmured close to Morn's head. "I'll help you. If you can get off him, I'll try to make sure we don't have to go through all this again."

Make sure we don't—? With an effort she raised her head and saw that he had a roll of strapping tape in his hands.

"This stuff is as strong as flexsteel," he told her quietly. "If I tie him up with it, maybe we can stop worrying about him."

Vector began to laugh, a clean, happy sound like a blue sky. "Sib, you maniac, do you *always* carry a roll of strapping tape?"

Sib blushed. "I put it in my pocket after Nick took over. I couldn't find anything that looked like a weapon. This seemed like the next best thing." He met Morn's gaze for a moment, then looked down. "I've been praying for a chance to use it."

Morn managed a smile. "Do it." Carefully, as if her relief were fragile, she rolled off Nick.

At once Sib set to work. He strapped Nick's wrists together snugly behind him, ran loops of tape around his upper arms to secure them, then hobbled his ankles, leaving only enough slack to let him take small steps. Finally Sib stretched more tape between the hobble and Nick's wrists so that he wouldn't be able to jump or kick.

Davies watched with grim approval. When the job was done, he said, "Keep that roll handy. If his mouth starts to bother us, you can tape it shut."

Sib nodded. If he felt any relief, it didn't show.

Morn let some of her fear out in a long sigh. She met Davies' questioning glance; nodded assent.

Thumbing the intercom toggle, he chimed the bridge.

"Angus? We got him." He paused, perhaps considering how much to say, then simply repeated, "We got him. So far, so good.

"Vector and Sib are here," he went on. "Mikka and Ciro already came aboard." He looked at Vector for confirmation before he finished, "Vector got what we came for."

Vector tapped the side of his head with one forefinger. Loud enough for Angus to hear, he said, "It's all here. If I had the facilities, I could start mass-producing it." His smile was positively beatific.

After a moment Angus answered, "I'm almost done." Harsh strain twisted through his voice. "Come on up."

Davies turned to Morn. A grin of his own spread across his face. All at once he looked inexpressibly young—much younger than his father; *decades* younger than Morn felt. A jig seemed to gleam in his eyes, as if he were dancing inside. "What're we waiting for? Let's go."

Morn shook her head. Her relief had begun to curdle, soured by withdrawal and comprehension. Her nerves felt the touch of acid again. And the pain was growing: organic adrenaline couldn't feed her hunger for artificial stimulation. Nick was only one of her personal demons. Others still harried her, defying exorcism. "First we need to talk."

Everything she and her companions did mattered too much.

"We've got Nick. That's a step in the right direction. But let's not forget to be cautious."

Let's not forget what's at stake. Or how precarious it is.

Trusting Angus came hard.

"I agree," Vector said promptly. "Don't misunderstand me. I'm so glad I can hardly think. But I still want to know how you got past Angus. I thought Nick had him"—the geneticist hunted for an adequate expression and couldn't find one—"under control. What did you do to him?"

Morn put that question aside. "It'll be easier to explain when you see him. But there are things Davies and I need to know right now." Things we might not want Angus to hear, if he isn't being honest with us. "For a start—

"Mikka said Nick and Beckmann were 'dickering.' What did Nick want?"

Sib referred the question to Vector, but Vector passed it back with a gesture.

"When we first went in," Sib began, "Nick said we needed supplies. Which didn't make sense—but I guess that's not the point. As soon as Vector was done, Nick told Dr. Beckmann he'd changed his mind. He wanted something else.

"He gave Dr. Beckmann the formula. For confirmation he let him have some of the capsules."

Vector nodded. Mutely he held up Nick's original vial. Only five or six capsules were left.

"We got permission to leave," Sib went on. "And this." He bent over Nick, rummaged in his pockets, and produced a small metallic rectangle like an id tag. "It's a data-jack. According to Dr. Beckmann, it holds everything the Lab knows about the swarm. The best chart they can put together. Composition. Internal vectors. External stresses." He offered the data-jack to Morn, but she waved it to Davies. "If it's accurate," Sib finished, "we ought to be able to navigate out of here blind."

"Sounds good." Davies closed the data-jack in his fist. His eyes asked Morn as clearly as words, Can we go now?

No, she answered soundlessly. Small tremors of withdrawal rose in her. She hadn't accepted the data-jack because she hadn't wanted anyone to see her hand shake.

Facing both Sib and Vector, she said, "It seems pretty straightforward. What went wrong? What happened to Mikka and Ciro?"

Vector glanced at Sib, then returned his gaze to Morn. "I was hoping you could tell us."

She shook her head. "She and Ciro came aboard like she thought he was dying. But she didn't explain anything."

Ciro and I need to talk, so **leave us alone.**

Sib grimaced. After a moment he offered, "Maybe she thinks he *is*."

"What's that supposed to mean?" Davies put in. Being reminded of Mikka and her brother renewed his tension.

"It was strange," Sib answered in a perplexed tone. "As soon as Vector got permission to work, Nick separated us. He sent Ciro off to req food stores we don't need. He told me to put in a list for other supplies—which we also don't need. And he didn't let Mikka go with either of us. Instead he ordered her to stand guard outside the lab where Vector was working.

"She didn't obey." Sib shrugged. "I guess she couldn't. She went looking for Ciro.

"But he was gone. Security said he 'wandered off' somewhere. So she came to find me. We were getting ready to start a search of our own, but then Security found him. They said he wasn't hurt, just 'scared out of his mind.' But they wouldn't let us go to him. We had to wait until Vector was done. We never got a chance to talk to him."

"Go on," Morn murmured.

Sib paused like a man who needed to clear his head. Then he admitted, "I don't know why any of this happened. But Mikka—

"She thinks it's because of *Soar*. She thinks Nick used Ciro as bait. Otherwise why did he make up that lie about needing supplies? He's trying to trick Sorus Chatelaine, trap her somehow."

Sib spread his hands to show his bafflement.

"Because she's the woman who cut him," Morn breathed softly.

"That's right. *Soar* had a different name then, and maybe Sorus Chatelaine did, too. He didn't know it was her until he saw her on Billingate. But I guess now all he can think about is getting revenge."

"Wait a minute," Davies demanded. His eyes darkened expectantly. "What name?"

Sib shrugged anxiously. "I don't know what she called herself. Nick didn't say.

"But in those days *Soar* was called *Gutbuster*."

Without warning a new pain struck through Morn. It was as visceral as withdrawal, but it was a different kind of hurt altogether—an intuitive and primal anguish so acute that she nearly gasped and might have fallen to her knees. Even though she hadn't known it was there, it had crouched like a predator in the core of her heart for years, waiting its chance to spring—

Waiting for this moment to tear her completely apart.

Gutbuster.

She hardly heard Davies' strangled shout; didn't know that she herself had cried out. *Gutbuster!* Vector reached for her. Sib groaned, "Morn, what's wrong, what did I say?" But she couldn't understand either of them. Old bereavement ripped her open, and nothing else could reach her.

"*Gutbuster,*" she and Davies breathed in unison—the nearly voiceless wail of lost children, umbilically linked by her past.

The memory returned like the acid of withdrawal; it filled her head with vitriol.

She was a little girl held in her father's arms while he told her of her mother's death.

His voice was steady and clear—the voice of a man who valued what his wife had done too much to protest against it. Yet tears ran from his eyes, collected along the certainty of his jaw, and dropped like stains onto Morn's small breast.

We picked up a distress call from the ore transfer dump off Orion's Reach. An illegal came in on them hard—

She called herself Gutbuster. *She wasn't fast, and she didn't show gap capability. But she was heavily armed—as heavily armed as a battlewagon.*

Her first blast ripped one whole side of Intransigent *open.*

A pure super-light proton beam.

We immediately lost targ. Another beam like that would have finished us.

Your mother was on station in targeting control. And targeting control was in the part of Intransigent Gutbuster *hit. That whole side of* Intransigent *had been ripped open to vacuum. Targeting control began to lose atmosphere.*

She could have saved herself. But she didn't. While her station depressurized and her air ran out, she worked to reroute targ function so that we could use our guns.

That's why Intransigent *survived. She restored targ in time. We hit* Gutbuster *with everything we had.*

But your mother was lost.

She gave her life—

Then her father had made his promise. *No one in the UMCP will ever rest until your mother has been avenged. We will stop* Gutbuster *and every ship like her.*

By the time his story ended, Morn had decided in his arms that she, too, would be a cop. She'd been too ashamed of herself to make any other choice.

That was the defining moment of her childhood, the center of her losses: the moment which had made her into what she was when *Starmaster* died—a cop who couldn't defend herself against Angus. Her shame was too old; ran too deep.

She hadn't seen Davies move, but he stood in front of her now. His hands gripped her shoulders as if he were lifting her out of herself. Except for his eyes, his face was a younger version of his father's—squat and bitter, congested with venom. Nevertheless his eyes transformed him.

They flamed with her memories. Fed on the same fuel which burned her.

Through his teeth he told her, "We're going after her."

And she answered, "Yes."

But her heart cried, No! *No.*

Revenge was too expensive. She'd learned that the hard way. Hadn't she? She'd seen what it cost Nick: his ship and his reputation; the only things that kept him sane. And ever since *Starmaster* died she'd been paying the price of her old grudge against herself. It didn't *matter* who Sorus Chatelaine was; what *Soar* had once been. Only Vector's research was important: only making his antimutagen known meant anything. Revenge was for lost souls. No one else could afford it.

Why else had she decided to risk freeing Angus?

And yet she couldn't give Davies any answer except, "Yes." Her mouth refused to form any other response. She was ruled by her losses. Without them she had no idea who she was.

No one in the UMCP will ever rest until your mother has been avenged. We will stop Gutbuster *and every ship like her.*

Maybe that wasn't wrong. Davies obviously didn't feel the way she did—and his mind was almost hers. The fire which ate at her seemed to have the opposite effect on him: he burned with certainty, purpose; life. Maybe she'd been prey too long; had spent too many days and weeks thinking like a victim. Maybe it was time for other predators to hunt.

She could have saved herself. But she didn't.

Remembering her mother, Morn found that she could stand on her own: her legs were strong enough. The neural sobbing of withdrawal didn't control her. Abruptly she laughed—a mirthless sound, raw with the harmonics of strain and regret. "We don't need to. She thinks she's coming after us."

Slowly Davies nodded. His hands let go of her. He was ready.

"Morn?" Sib asked apprehensively. "I don't understand. What are you talking about?"

Nick was still unconscious, breathing thinly against the deck. That helped. With an effort, she forced herself to look at Sib and Vector.

Vector shared Sib's uncertainty. Nevertheless he didn't appear alarmed. He had sources of calm his companion lacked.

"Davies and I have a score to settle with that ship," she murmured weakly. "*Gutbuster*. We're going after her."

Sib's mouth shaped questions he didn't voice. Instead he observed tensely, "That's what Nick wants." His gaze brimmed with fears.

"Too bad," she sighed. "This isn't for him. It's for us."

But she didn't believe that, in spite of her efforts to convince herself.

"Let's go," Davies insisted. "The longer we delay, the more time she'll have to trap us."

Morn nodded.

At once Davies took Sib's arm and pulled him toward Nick.

Sib's anxiety remained in his eyes, but he didn't hold back. Together he and Davies heaved Nick up so that they could drag him between them into the lift.

Morn gestured Vector ahead of her. She entered the lift last, keyed shut the airlock, then sent the lift sliding upward to the core of the ship.

By the time they all reached the bridge, her scant strength had begun fraying. The memory of her mother wasn't enough to fend off her fear of Angus.

Davies had been born with her mind, but they didn't think alike. His months in her womb had conditioned him to levels of stimulation which would have killed an ordinary kid. In that sense his physiological state resembled her zone implant addiction. Nevertheless the difference between them was profound. His needs could be met by his own organic endocrine resources; hers required external intervention.

Doubts nagged at her.

She couldn't forget Mikka and Ciro.

She couldn't forget that the conflicting messages which had betrayed Nick as well as everyone else aboard were intended to serve unexplained purposes in a larger conflict; purposes she didn't understand and couldn't evaluate.

Above all she couldn't forget that she didn't know how to trust Angus Thermopyle.

As Davies opened the door at the head of the companionway, she saw Angus sitting exactly where they'd left him: directly in front of—almost under—the command board.

"Shit," Sib croaked. "What did you do to him?"

Angus' bare back was a mess. Cut and torn tissues oozed blood the same way his face oozed sweat; trails of blood ran down his spine into his shipsuit. From the wide wound Davies had made between his shoulder blades, fine silver leads webbed him to the underside of the command board—a delicate and apparently random tracery protecting him from stasis.

Small tools, keypad modules, a first-aid kit, and wiring were scattered around him within easy reach, but he wasn't using any of those things now. Instead his fingers held a computer chip in front of his face. He studied it as if he might penetrate its secrets by sheer divination.

His datacore.

Davies ignored Sib. "Are you done?" he asked Angus harshly.

"One way or the other." Angus' voice was a frail sigh, scarcely audible. The desperation which had driven him to this gamble was gone; burned out. He sounded like a small boy who was too frightened to hope. "I can't—" His throat closed. A moment passed before he was able to say, "I can't do any more."

Pulling Nick with him so that Sib had to follow, Davies started down the treads. "Then let's try it."

Angus continued holding his datacore up to the light; but his head slowly sank until his neck bent as if he were waiting for the ax.

Davies and Sib dropped Nick behind the second's station. Davies gave his impact pistol to Sib, then immediately moved to stand in front of his father. If he wanted to hunt *Gutbuster*, he needed Angus.

Vector glanced at Morn. When she didn't move, he shrugged and descended the companionway behind Sib.

She thought that she would go after him. Yet she remained where she was, immobilized by uncertainty. She told herself that she hesitated because she wanted to go check on Mikka and Ciro. The truth was that she suddenly wanted to flee; ached to *get out of here* before Angus recovered the power to harm her.

"Morn?" Davies asked; urged. He stood poised beside Angus, waiting for her permission.

No! her fears answered. No! He's a murderer—a rapist. He *broke* me. I'm a zone implant addict because of him. I would rather see him dead. I would rather be dead myself.

But she knew better.

Revenge was for lost souls.

You're a cop, she'd once told her son. *From now on, I'm going to be a cop myself*. Cops were predators, but they didn't hunt for vengeance. If she went after *Soar*, it would be because Sorus Chatelaine was humankind's enemy, not because *Gutbuster* had killed her mother.

Even though Angus terrified her, and every moment of anguish he'd ever caused her stuck in her throat, she'd said to him, *We'll trust you*.

Now or never.

Gripping the handrail for support, she started downward.

"Go ahead," she said through her terror. "We've come this far. There's no point in stopping now."

"Yes!"

Davies plucked the datacore from Angus' fingers, moved around behind his father, and dropped to his knees.

"Go ahead with what?" Sib objected. He sounded nauseous with ignorance and anxiety. "I don't understand any of this. What are you *doing*?"

Morn finished descending the steps. As she left the railing, she put her hand on Sib's shoulder, partly to reassure him, partly to help her keep her balance.

"Angus says he knows how to edit datacores." This was the best answer she could give: she didn't have the bravery for a complete explanation. Sib would have to fill in the gaps as best he could. "We're going to find out if that's true."

"Ah," Vector sighed in comprehension. "You don't believe in half measures, do you. This is the old kill-or-cure treatment with a vengeance." He paused, then asked, "Could I persuade you to tell us how? Editing datacores is supposed to be impossible."

Later. Morn raised a palm to put him off. If we survive. And if we have time.

Davies studied Angus' back; swore under his breath; withdrew. From the first-aid kit he snatched up swabs and began vigorously blotting the welter of blood so that he could see the chip's socket.

Angus' head hung hopelessly. He endured Davies' pushing and prodding as if the removal of his datacore had deprived him of all normal sensation.

Abruptly the bridge speakers snapped to life.

"*Trumpet*, this is Lab Center. We're waiting."

Waiting? Oh, shit! In an instant Morn's brain seemed to go numb. Waiting for what?

Davies froze.

Panic flared in Sib's eyes; but before he could say anything, Vector intervened.

"You'd better talk to them, Sib." His calm suggested that he had complete confidence in the former data first. "They'll be surprised to hear from you, but there's nothing we can do about that. Morn, Davies, and Angus can't do it—they aren't supposed to be here. And Center won't believe me. I'm just a geneticist. As for Nick"—Vector smiled phlegmatically—"he looks like he's going to be tied up for a while. That leaves you."

Sib couldn't stifle his alarm. His face seemed to sweat failure. Nevertheless Vector's confidence steadied him in some way. Or perhaps he remembered that without his help Morn and Davies wouldn't have beaten Nick. Despite his fear, he moved to the second's station.

While Morn still groped to imagine what Center was waiting for, he punched open a communications channel.

Vector didn't pause. "If you'll give me that data-jack," he said to Davies, "I'll start feeding it in. I can do that from the auxiliary engineering board. Then we'll be able to get out of here"—he glanced at Angus—"no matter what happens."

Scowling, Davies passed the data-jack to Vector. At once he resumed working on Angus' back, trying to swab away enough blood so that he could see what to do.

"Lab Center," Sib said almost firmly, "this is *Trumpet*. Sorry for the delay. We're just about ready."

Vector smiled impartially around the bridge. Then he headed for the auxiliary engineering board.

"All right," Davies muttered into Angus' open back. He picked up a small circuit clamp, clipped the datacore onto it. "Now maybe I can do this without plugging it in backward."

Holding his breath so that his hands wouldn't shake, he probed the datacore toward Angus' computer.

"*Trumpet*," Lab Center demanded sharply, "who is this? Where's Captain Succorso?"

Morn didn't know the voice.

"Sorry, again," Sib responded. "Chief Retledge, this is Sib Mackern. I guess I should explain. The truth is"—with an effort he managed to make his anxiety sound like embarrassment—"I'm afraid Captain Succorso and Dr. Shaheed couldn't wait to start celebrating. They're in the galley, already half null— I could probably get the captain to talk to you, but at the moment I don't think he cares whether we ever undock."

Once he began, Sib didn't falter. His approximation of assurance improved steadily. "Mikka Vasaczk is tending her brother in sickbay. It looks like he has some kind of health problem we didn't know about. Suddenly it was too much for him.

"That just leaves me.

"As soon as our computers finish reading your data-jack, we'll be ready to receive departure protocols."

"Alone, Mr. Mackern?" Chief Retledge didn't try to conceal his incredulity. "You propose to take *Trumpet* out alone?"

"There," Davies breathed through clenched jaws. "It's in." He leaned back: unaware of what he did, he wrapped his arms around himself as if he needed comfort. "Can you still hear me, Angus? Did I do it right? Can you tell if I did it right?"

Angus didn't move; didn't answer. He squatted on the deck as if he'd surrendered to execution.

Withdrawal twisted through Morn's stomach. She felt herself hyperventilating. She wanted to tell Sib, Get us out of here. Make them give us permission. But she didn't dare; she couldn't risk being overheard.

"Chief Retledge," Sib countered, "this is a gap scout, not an orehauler—or a warship." He spoke loudly to cover Davies. "Her manifest only requires a crew of two. If your data is accurate, I can run this swarm in my sleep." He paused, feigning doubt, then added, "Captain Succorso doesn't care at the moment. But when he sobers up, he's going to be more than just furious if I don't carry out his orders."

Nick seemed to react to the sound of his name. He groaned softly: his shoulders hunched: he tried to rise. But the effort was too much for him, and he slumped back to the deck.

Retledge was silent for a long moment. Then, grudgingly, he snorted, "*Trumpet*, we're standing by to initiate undock on your word. We'll assign departure protocols when you're clear. Lab Center out."

The bridge speakers emitted a faint hiss and fell silent.

"Almost done," Vector murmured to no one in particular.

Without warning Angus moved his arms.

Morn flinched; she couldn't help herself. Skinworms of fear chewed along her nerves.

His muscles tensed. His back straightened. Slowly he stood, pulling himself taller. He might have been a piece of equipment coming back online.

"Angus?" Davies asked uncertainly. "Angus—?"

A low moan began to leak up out of Angus' chest like a prayer. Quiet at first, it built louder as his heart beat and his arms flexed; as tension moved up and down his spine like a systems check. Morn wanted to implore him, Stop it, stop! but she couldn't. He transfixed her. She could only stand and listen as his moan rose to a roar, as guttural and extreme as the howl of a tortured beast.

Suddenly he whirled away from the command station, ripping himself free of the board, slinging a spray of blood and wires around him.

"It works!" he cried like a shout of rage. "*It works!*"

Morn took a step toward him. There was no one else to do it. Davies knelt where Angus had left him, too shocked to move. Sib and Vector might have been paralyzed. Somehow Nick had squirmed his knees under him, but he couldn't lift himself any higher. Morn had to face Angus alone.

Her laser was in her hand; of its own volition, her hand pointed itself at Angus' head. Panting as if she'd lost the power to breathe, she asked, "How do I know that? How am I supposed to believe you?"

His passion wasn't rage: it was a feral joy, as savage and necessary as murder; as pure as fury. Bloody from working on his datacore, his hands closed and unclosed like a torn heart.

"Try me," he rasped. "*Try* me."

Try him? She wanted to turn and run. No, she wanted to burn him through the head before he thought to defend himself. Involuntarily her fist tightened. Shame and fear from the core of her being begged her to press the firing stud.

We'll do it. We'll trust you.

We're cops.

Gasping to force up words, she ordered, "Isaac, this is Gabriel priority. Put your head down."

Nick let out a groan of pain and betrayal. "You bastard."

Fierce with exaltation, Angus jutted his chin toward the ceiling.

"I'm free." Wild relief congested his voice as if he were sobbing. "I'm *free*."

"You bastard." Heaving on the tape which bound his wrists to his ankles, Nick pulled himself up onto his feet. Pain glazed his eyes, thickened his tongue. "Motherfucker." He hardly had the strength to stand; his bonds didn't let him move. Nevertheless he fought to articulate his despair. "Treacherous bloody piece of shit."

Morn ignored him. "That's not what you told us," she protested to Angus. Her arm began to shake: she couldn't control it. The muzzle of her laser pistol wavered across the display screens behind his head. "You told us you could mask your priority-codes. But you can't circumvent your core programming. That's what you said. How free *are* you?"

Angus' eyes rolled as if he needed to howl again. Her distrust seemed to torment or transport him.

Abruptly his attention caught on Nick. With a snarl, he sprang forward. His left hand grabbed Nick by the collar of his shipsuit: his momentum and strength carried Nick backward, slammed him against the bulkhead.

Deliberately Angus bunched his right fist in front of Nick's face, aimed his prosthetic laser into Nick's eyes.

No! Morn thought. *Yes.* No!

She'd killed Nick with a question. How free *are* you? His death was on her head.

But Angus didn't fire. Strain whitened his knuckles, stretched the cords of his hands taut. His fingers clenched until his hand shook as badly as Morn's. His desire to kill Nick filled his face like a scream.

Yet his laser didn't fire.

"See?" Convulsively he flung Nick away from him, whirled to face Morn again. His voice rose into a shout of grief and protest. "*See?* I can't *do* it! I can't even *hit* him! My *programming won't let me hurt UMCP personnel!*"

Nick fell to his knees, toppled onto the deck. His eyes stared past his pale scars. From somewhere deep inside him, a sound like laughter trickled out of his mouth.

"Come on," Angus pleaded with Morn, "*try* me! Don't stand there thinking I didn't keep my deal with you!"

By degrees his shout sank to a bitter growl. "I'm free of *him*." He slapped the back of his hand in Nick's direction. "And I'm free of *you*." He stabbed one strong finger like a blow at the center of her chest. "You can't *use* me the way he did.

"But I'm not free of the goddamn UMCP. I'm not free of Warden Dios." His eyes spilled memories as dark as hers. "I won't be free of him and Hashi fucking Lebwohl until they're dead.

"Give me a way to prove I keep my deals. The ones I care about. Tell me what you want me to do."

Without apparent transition Davies stood at Angus' shoulder, holding the open first-aid kit under one arm. Morn hadn't seen him move. Her concentration had contracted until only Angus seemed to exist.

"For a start," Davies said acidly, "you might try standing still. If I don't do something about your back, you're going to bleed to death."

Angus didn't agree or object. He waited for Morn to reply.

Davies glanced at her, then took a tube of tissue plasm out of the kit and began squeezing the contents into Angus' wound.

"I think—" Sib put in hesitantly.

"Don't." Unexpectedly sharp, Vector cut him off. "This is between them. You and I haven't earned the right to an opinion."

Morn turned away. The tremors which weakened her aim had become more than she could bear. She needed her black box: without it, she was too frail, too mortal. Angus had cost her too much. She'd made the decision to let him free; but now she wasn't brave enough to face the outcome.

When she turned, however, her eyes met Nick's.

In spite of his cracked head and his bonds, he grinned like a skull. "You stupid bitch," he murmured softly. "You thought I was bad." His tone was raw malice. "This is going to be worse."

At the sight of his twisted features and the sound of his voice, something in her stiffened—an echo of the resolve which had carried her when she'd decided to help Angus.

We'll trust whoever wrote your core programming. I think it was Warden Dios. I think he's trying to find some way to fight Holt Fasner. And if he is, I think we should help him.

Angus hadn't hurt anyone here until Nick took control of him.

She could have saved herself. But she didn't.

Holding Nick's gaze, she retorted, "Just for the record, Angus didn't betray you. He couldn't. He couldn't fight his priority-codes. The people who sent you that message did it."

Nick made another small inarticulate sound; but now it seemed less like laughter.

She put her laser down: she didn't need a weapon anymore. Without it, her hand stopped shaking, and she was able to face Angus again.

"I want you at the command station," she told him. "Sib has to talk to Lab Center, but we need you to get us out of here." So that Davies, Sib, and Vector would hear her as well, she went on, "We're going after *Soar*. But we probably can't beat her unless you help us. You're still the captain of this ship."

Gratitude and fierce joy bared Angus' teeth, but he didn't answer her. Instead he pulled away from Davies and vaulted into his command g-seat. With his shipsuit still rucked down around his waist and blood smearing his half-sealed wound, he began entering the commands which brought *Trumpet* to life.

Nick was laughing again, but Morn ignored him. Trying to shore up her courage, she recited a litany of hope.

One man who'd hurt her was bound; helpless.

The restrictions in Angus' datacore still held—and yet he was free to do what Morn asked of him. Warden Dios had given her that.

Her son and her friends had survived.

Vector knew the formula for an antimutagen.

And *Soar* used to be called *Gutbuster*.

Maybe Davies was right. Maybe it was time for other predators.

ANCILLARY DOCUMENTATION

THE AMNION LANGUAGE AND INTELLIGENCE

In dealing with the Amnion perhaps more than at any other time in humankind's history, language was the only available tool for understanding.

Communication was necessary for the negotiation of trade agreements, the determination of frontiers, and the resolution of disputes—what humankind called "diplomacy." For that reason, the Amnion had taught themselves to translate as much as they could of human speech, and had made their own speech accessible for humans to study. However, humankind knew virtually nothing about what lay behind that speech: it had no context.

This ignorance stretched across the whole spectrum of sentience. At one extreme, humankind had no idea how an Amnioni experienced sensory input. What gave an Amnioni physical pleasure? What constituted pain? How did the visual field appear? Were members of the species attracted to each other? And at the other, humankind had no information about Amnion culture. What relationship, if any, did individual Amnion have with their offspring? Did they in fact have offspring at all, or was every member of the species impersonally manufactured in some way? And did they produce art? Did their social structures provide for imaginative creation? If so, of what did it consist?

No one knew.

Language was the only tool humankind had to work with.

This was like using a pair of field glasses to study the wonders of the galaxy. The tool had neither the range nor the precision for the task.

Obstacles abounded, not least among them the fact that Amnion intraspecies communication did not rely exclusively on sound. The projection and manipulation of pheromones also played a significant part, as did —according to some theorists—light and color.

But precisely what part did pheromonic signals play? Were they analogous to "body language" in humans—a more or less conscious form of posturing—or were they denotatively encoded? If the former, they were of secondary importance: translation could function without taking them into account. If the latter, however, they were essential to comprehension.

In addition, finding accurate approximations or analogies for alien concepts was inherently difficult. Each species was hindered in its attempts at comprehension by the very limitations which enabled or enriched its own language. A case in point was the Amnion use of the word "defensives" to refer to "warships." Was "defensive" truly the best human word the Amnion could find to indicate the intended function of a warship? Did the Amnion perceive their own genetic imperialism as a form of "defense"? Or was the word merely an instance of the rhetorical legerdemain diplomats and politicians loved—an effort to make a threat appear benign through the manipulation of language?

Precision would have been useful in such matters. Instead it was impossible.

One of the most critical examples involved understanding the apparent lack of personal pronouns in the Amnion language. When diplomats or other "decisive" figures spoke, they made no reference to themselves as individuals. They claimed no individual agendas, acknowledged no individual desires. Regardless of the scale of the issues under discussion, they either spoke for the Amnion or did not speak at all. Only human beings incompletely altered by mutagens used such words as "I," "me," and "my."

A corollary problem involved the apparent absence in Amnion speech of a number of abstract concepts much relied on by humankind, among them "good," "evil," "justice," "mercy," and "loyalty." It was theoretically possible, however, that such concepts did exist between Amnioni, but could only be communicated by means of pheromones. The ideas themselves may have been considered too intimate or revealing for speech.

By contrast the use of personal pronouns—at least in human terms—was at once so ordinary, so ubiquitous, and so practical that any language which didn't employ them seemed almost imponderably unwieldy and restrictive.

What did the lack of personal pronouns imply about the nature of Amnion intelligence and thought patterns, or the character of Amnion ambitions?

These questions were urgent because Amnion genetic imperialism was taken as given. Knowledge of the enemy was a necessary weapon. If the Amnion couldn't be understood, how could they be defeated?

Efforts to account for the known characteristics of Amnion language revolved around one or the other of two distinct hypotheses, each with its own adherents and detractors, each with its own implications for humankind's dealings with forbidden space.

One postulated what was sometimes called a "hive mind." Drawing analogies from certain species of insects, this theory suggested that all Amnion partook of a communal intelligence which had its physical center or nexus, its "queen," somewhere deep in alien space. Individual members or units of this mind had a separate corporeal being, but no separate thoughts or volition. Instead each was effectively a neuron or ganglion of the hive mind, transmitting data inward—and action outward.

Proponents of this theory used it to explain why the first human experiment with a mutagen had driven its host mad. As the woman who had volunteered for the experiment was transformed, she had lost her reason because distance—if nothing else—had cut the now-Amnioni off from her/its source of identity and purpose. Under this hypothesis, great store was placed on reports that some humans had heard Amnioni make reference to an entity, construct, or concept called the "Mind/Union." What could this be, if it were not the "queen" of the "hive"—the center of intelligence and intention for the whole species?

If the hive mind theory was accurate, then the single most effective tactic humankind could use against the Amnion would be to locate and extirpate the "Mind/Union." Without its "queen," the entire species would collapse into its own kind of madness.

The opposing hypothesis was more insidious—and, in a sense, more frightful. Its proponents dismissed the "Mind/Union" as a corporeal entity or nexus; rather they considered the term to be an abstract concept—the equivalent of words like "good" and "evil," which humans used to rationalize their actions. And they dismissed also the argument that the woman who had first accepted a mutagen had gone mad because of her separation from the "Mind/Union": they insisted instead that her madness had been a consequence of having her genetic identity ripped away.

The opposing hypothesis held that the Amnion were driven, not by a collective intelligence or hive mind, but by the essential coding of the nucleotides which comprised their RNA. They had no humanlike abstract concepts for the same reason that they had no humanlike personal pronouns: they needed none. Their imperialism was genetic in content as well as in form; in inspiration as well as in effect. Commandments analogous to the human lust for reproduction impelled their actions. They were unified and moved by impulses at once more profound, more global, and more imaginable than the directives of some impossibly distant—as well as impossibly homogeneous—"queen."

Adherents of the genetic imperative theory argued that no surgical strike anywhere in forbidden space could have a meaningful impact on the threat which the Amnion presented. The motley and multifarious pageant of life in the galaxy would never be safe until every single Amnioni was stricken from existence.

HASHI

Hashi Lebwohl considered the quantum mechanics of reality as he shuffled through the corridors of UMCPHQ toward the docks. Werner Heisenberg, that strange man, had named the truth decades ahead of his time when he'd postulated that the position and velocity of an electron couldn't be determined simultaneously. When one knew where a given particle was, one couldn't identify its movements. When one quantified its movements, one could no longer establish its location. Knowledge precluded knowledge: in some sense the effort to understand reality prevented comprehension. And yet without that effort humankind would never have known that electrons existed; that the macroverse depended for its predictable solidity on the indefinable activities of the microverse.

Hashi himself was a kind of atomic particle, transforming realities as he moved; bringing new facts to life and losing old as he slopped along in his untied shoes toward the berth where the Suka Bator shuttle waited.

The conceit pleased him. The UMCPDA director assigned no moral valence to truth. Nevertheless he admired it enormously. To his eyes, the quirky yet seamless flux of facts and interpretations which defined reality was a process of surpassing beauty.

He was on his way to define certain truths, thereby causing others to become unknowable.

No one had asked him to ride Koina Hannish's PR shuttle down the gravity well to Earth in order to attend the next session of the Governing Council for Earth and Space. Protocol wasn't among his duties. Whatever happened when the GCES met in extraordinary session to consider Captain Vertigus' still-secret Bill of Severance, it was none of Hashi Lebwohl's business.

Similarly, Security on Suka Bator wasn't his concern. His mandate, levied onto his chagrined head by an openly angry Warden Dios, was to pursue the UMCP's investigation into the terrorist attacks which had killed Godsen Frik and very nearly done the same to Captain Sixten Vertigus.

Such considerations didn't stop him. Regardless of the fact that his responsibilities were presumably elsewhere, he dug his id tag and other credentials out of his pockets, flapped them like a scarecrow's hands in the surprised faces of the dock guards, and talked himself aboard the poised craft as if he had a sovereign right to be there.

He was the UMCP's director of Data Acquisition; difficult to contradict. Certainly none of UMCPHQ Security's personnel were likely to refuse him. Instead they would consult with Director Dios. If Warden Dios disapproved of Hashi's actions, the guards could always decline to let him leave the shuttle.

He didn't think Warden would disapprove. Despite the unfortunate contract Hashi had given Darrin Scroyle and *Free Lunch*, he guessed—or perhaps simply hoped—that Warden would continue to trust him a little longer.

Subatomic particles combined and recombined constantly to form new facts, new realities; new truths. Hashi intended to repay Warden's trust. If that required the DA director to put himself at risk, he accepted it.

Authorized or not, his attendance at the GCES session would be dangerous. Koina Hannish had relayed to him a warning from Captain Vertigus. *Tell Director Lebwohl I'm afraid there's going to be another attack.* The Captain's exact words, apparently. *During the next session. Tell him if he's ever been a real cop—if he cares at all about the integrity of the UMCP, or the rule of law in human space—or even if he just wants to clear his reputation —he's got to keep kazes away from the hall.*

Hashi in turn had informed ED's Chief of Security, the man charged with the safety of the Council. Other people might have dismissed the warning as the frightened delusion of a senile old man: Hashi didn't. In his view, an opponent who deemed Godsen Frik worth murdering was capable of anything.

But of course fulsome, futile Godsen wouldn't have died if he'd obeyed the summons of the great worm; if Warden Dios hadn't restricted him to UMCPHQ in an apparent effort to protect him. A fascinating coincidence, full of implications and uncertainty. If one knew what events were, one couldn't tell where they were going. If one knew where they tended, one could no longer identify them.

Sixten Vertigus' warning was one reason Hashi had decided to attend the extraordinary session.

Another was that he wished to talk to Warden's new UMCPPR director, Koina Hannish.

As he stepped through the passenger hatch of the shuttle, he caught her attention. She'd been studying a sheaf of hardcopy—briefing documents, no doubt, intended to prepare her for her first GCES session. Surprised, she looked up at him with her eyes wide and her lips slightly parted. Her instinctive grace didn't desert her, however: she may have been taken aback, but she wasn't—as dear, departed Godsen might have said—"flummoxed." Her face showed nothing as Hashi offered himself the g-seat at her side, sprawled into it, and cocked his head against his shoulder in order to regard her over his smeared glasses. Instead she smiled, using only the corners of her mouth.

"Director Lebwohl," she murmured, "you astonish me. Is this a social visit, or do you think"—she fluttered her sheaf of hardcopy wryly—"I haven't been adequately briefed? You'll have to be quick, I'm afraid." She glanced at the cabin chronometer. "We're scheduled to launch in two minutes."

In reply Hashi gave her his most amiable grin—the one which made him resemble a doting uncle, cheerful and slightly mad. "My dear *Director* Hannish"—he stressed her title humorously—"I would not presume to *brief* you." This was a joke: it was often said of him that he did nothing briefly. "You understand your own duties far better than I. And I would not impose myself on you socially at such a time."

As if that were a sufficient explanation, he subsided.

An ED Security guard stood at the front of the cabin, looking across Hashi, Koina, and the other passengers: two of Koina's aides, a Security communications tech, and Deputy Chief of Security Forrest Ing. Clearing his throat uncomfortably, he said, "Director Lebwohl, you'd better belt yourself in. We've been cleared for launch as soon as the hatches are sealed."

Hashi blinked as if he found the admonition incomprehensible. But then he sighed in understanding and fumbled for the g-seat straps. When he was done, he smiled at Koina again.

"I have been haunting my lair in the bowels of UMCPHQ far too long. I forget the more mundane details of travel."

Koina's mouth had taken a more serious line. For a moment she considered Hashi gravely. Her tone was neutral, neither encouraging nor impatient, as she said, "I'm waiting, Hashi."

"Do not be concerned," he replied like a jocund gnome. "Your shuttle will surely depart at its appointed time."

As if on cue, the guard answered a signal by tapping on the hatch keypad; and at once the heavy door slid into its frame. With an audible thunk, the seals locked. The guard ran a quick safety check, then belted himself into his own g-seat.

A rumble of engine noise began to carry through the hull. It was too soon for the shuttle's drive. Some of the muffled roar came from the dock's passive launch projector—colloquially called "the palt"—which would slingshot the craft out into the dark. The rest was the throaty growl of the huge motors that opened the space doors of the dock.

Against that background, the intercom crackled. "Launch in thirty seconds. Brace for two g acceleration."

Two? Hashi thought. My, my. There was no theoretical reason why the palt couldn't waft the craft outward so gently that the pressure would be impalpable. Koina Hannish was in a hurry.

Just for a moment he wondered whether he was healthy enough to withstand being slammed backward by a force equal to twice his own weight. Then he grinned. Too late to worry about that: far too late. As if he were dependent on them, he removed his glasses and cradled them in his fingers so that they wouldn't be ripped from his face.

Koina tightened her grip on her hardcopies when the throw of the palt hit. Other than that she showed no sign of discomfort.

Then it was over: the shuttle coasted free of UMCPHQ. Weightlessness took hold of Hashi's stomach, floating it against the back of his throat—a queasy sensation which would pass when the shuttle began to feel the tug of Earth's gravity well. He discovered that he'd been holding his breath. He let it out slowly. A mental damage inspection informed him that his systems appeared to be functioning as well as could be expected.

Settling his glasses back on the end of his nose, he returned his attention to the PR director.

She regarded him as if their conversation hadn't been interrupted. "I'm waiting," she explained evenly, "for you to tell me why you're here."

Hashi nodded his approval. The impenetrability of her mask pleased him. She was growing into her duties. In only a few days, her self-possession had become stronger. She was clearer, better focused. At this rate she would soon be worth a dozen Godsen Friks.

"Well, then," he announced, "I will tell you. It is true"—ubiquitous word—"that I do bear with me a small fact or two which I wish to submit for your consideration. However, I am primarily 'here' "—he indicated his g-seat—"rather than ensconced elsewhere in the hope that you will *brief* me."

Koina cocked a noncommittal eyebrow, but didn't reply.

"You see," he went on, "it is my intention to attend this unique as well as extraordinary session of our much-to-be-respected Governing Council for Earth and Space. It is conceivable that the esteemed Members will wish to question me." This was the smallest of Hashi's reasons for making the journey; but he didn't feel constrained to mention the others. It was common knowledge that Special Counsel Maxim Igensard had issued a standing and unconditional demand for the right to question Hashi Lebwohl further. "Naturally my responses will be more accurate—or perhaps I should say, more accurately tailored to UMCP policy—if they are intelligibly prepared. And I am certain, my dear Koina, that you will be able to prepare me intelligibly." After a barely perceptible pause, he added, "If you so choose."

Did Koina's forehead suggest a frown? He wasn't sure. He didn't have Warden Dios' special sight; couldn't read the play of tension in the muscles under her skin. Nevertheless there was no mistaking the tension in her next question.

"Does the director know you're doing this?"

The underlying issues were plain. Does he approve? she wanted to know. Did he send you?

"Alas, no," Hashi answered. His equanimity was untroubled. "For some time now he has been too busy to speak with me.

"That is to say," he amended, "I assume he has been too busy. It is unquestionable that his offices continue to perform their functions in their ordinary fashion. But does this necessarily imply that Warden Dios is busy? Perhaps not. I can only say with certainty that he has declined to speak with me."

All factual, as far as it went. Hashi had no intention of giving the PR director any cause to complain on that score.

"But you're going anyway?" she pursued.

"My dear Koina"—if his smile had been wired to a rheostat, he would have dialed it higher—"I did not rise to my present elevated position through reluctance to display initiative or accept responsibility."

She nodded slowly. No doubt she was aware of how inaccessible Warden had become recently. Since his most recent visit to Holt Fasner's home office, he'd been virtually incommunicado, dealing with DA, PR, and even ED almost entirely through subordinates. Hashi had the odd impression that Warden was hiding, keeping his anxieties private while he waited for some revelation or development which would clarify his dark game with—or against—the Dragon.

That impression reinforced Hashi's chagrin at the knowledge that his contract with *Free Lunch* had damaged Warden: chagrin both that he'd inadvertently done his director a disservice which he couldn't undo, and that he'd failed to grasp the complexity of Warden's game. By his own lights he'd always supported his director honorably. But Warden wanted Morn Hyland alive—even though Hashi had raised the possibility that she might be a kaze of more than one kind.

Hashi wasn't accustomed to thinking that any man's mind could see deeper or reach farther than his own. The idea disturbed him profoundly. He felt a gnawing need to prove in some way that he was equal to Warden's intentions.

That was the real reason he was here.

Koina knew nothing of his personal concerns, however. "Still," she mused, "I'm not sure it would be appropriate for me to brief you further." That "further" was unnecessary—a subtle reference to the way she'd shared facts and secrets with him in the past. "If the director wanted you to attend this session, he would have briefed you himself."

Hashi fluttered his hands airly, as if her scruples cost him nothing. "My dear Koina, I trust your judgment explicitly. As evidence of my good faith, I will tell you my new little facts without what our so-lamented Godsen would have called 'strings attached,' and you will decide freely whether to answer my questions in return."

She didn't insult him by saying, And you don't mind being overheard? By now she must have known him well enough to understand that he hadn't chosen this venue carelessly—although she might not have been able to guess why he now wanted to keep his dealings with her in some sense "public." Instead she murmured, "Fair enough," and waited for him to go on.

"Are you acquainted with Lane Harbinger?" he asked.

Koina shook her head. "I know the name. She's Malcolm Harbinger's granddaughter. But we haven't met."

"A shame," he remarked speciously. "You have much in common." But then he cautioned himself to restrain his sense of humor. Nervous, driven Lane was the PR director's near opposite—and he'd decided on a policy of factual accuracy. "However, that is of no moment. More to the point are her recent labors. In the name of Data Acquisition, she had been conducting a study of the physical evidence which we have obtained from the site of Godsen's murder."

He sensed movement behind him. At the edge of his vision, he glimpsed Forrest Ing shifting to a closer g-seat in order to hear better. ED Security—bless Min Donner and all her blunt, diligent minions—hadn't found any physical evidence for themselves.

"A careful scrutiny," he continued without pausing, "of your former superior's former office uncovered a minute fragment of the kaze's id tag. More specifically, a minute fragment of the tag's SOD-CMOS chip." Are you able to eavesdrop adequately, Deputy Chief Ing? These details are contained in reports which DA Processing has already delivered to Enforcement Division. "Since then, it has been Lane's task to extract the data which surely remains intact in that portion of the chip.

"Are you interested in technical considerations?" he asked Koina solicitously. When she shook her head again, he promised, "Then I will be concise.

"Putting the matter simply, a CMOS chip changes state—or, in the case of a SOD-CMOS chip, adds state—when an appropriate signal is applied to its source and drain. In essence, the data is read back from the chip by reversing the process. Sadly a fragment as *little*"—he pinched the ends of his fingers together to suggest tinyness—"as this lacks such conveniences as its own source and drain. Deprived of all ordinary methods for reading the chip, Lane has been compelled to improvise.

"In the past few hours, my dear Koina, she has transcended herself. So that you will not be inundated by technical considerations, I will merely explain that she has devised means to bond our fragment to another, more accessible chip. By that contrivance she has been able to obtain the chip's contents."

Koina cocked a delicate eyebrow to show her interest, but didn't interrupt. At his back, Hashi felt Forrest Ing's presence lean closer.

Smiling, he settled into his lecturer's mode.

"As you might surmise, those contents are as fragmentary as the chip itself. They are, however, provocative—one might almost say, extremely so.

"You are doubtless aware that we—the United Mining Companies Police—are humankind's only authorized supplier of SOD-CMOS chips. In addition, the UMCP and the Governing Council are humankind's only authorized consumers of such chips. All other use flows from one fount or the other. However, the actual manufacturer is a corporate entity curiously named Anodyne Systems. You may also be aware that Anodyne Systems is a wholly owned subsidiary of the United Mining Companies."

Therefore Anodyne Systems was in some sense open to Holt Fasner, even though the UMCP provided all working personnel and security.

"As I have suggested," he went on, "our honorable Council has no direct dealings with Anodyne Systems. The Council's SOD-CMOS chips come from us. For that reason our investigation has until now excluded the busy denizens of the GCES complex. Each chip delivered to them can be accounted for. Instead our operational assumption has been that a stolen chip could only have been obtained directly from Anodyne Systems —and that only our personnel or the Dragon's could have effected the theft.

"Lane's research has thrown that assumption into confusion. From her fragment she has extracted two—one might call them legible—code-strings. Neither is even remotely complete, yet both are complete enough to be traced.

"SAC programs have determined incontrovertibly that both are small portions of source-code."

He paused to study the PR director's mask of calm interest. Captain Vertigus had given her reason to think she might be in danger. Doubtless that explained Forrest Ing's presence aboard the shuttle: the deputy chief had been assigned personal responsibility for Director Hannish' safety. Nevertheless the particular beauty of her features kept her emotions private.

"Are you familiar with the term?" Hashi asked her; but he didn't wait for a reply. "Security such as ours and the Council's relies on continuously shifting patterns of passcodes and verifications to establish authorization. But because they shift continuously, these patterns must be generated continuously within each id tag and credential according to parameters and restrictions determined by their designers. This function is performed by a code 'engine.' In essence, the engine 'drives' the modulation of passcodes and verifications.

"The term 'source-code' refers to the specific language—the grammar and vocabulary, if you will—in which the engine is written.

"Clearly"—he spread his hands to indicate that he was being entirely candid—"the engine represents a more profound secret than the coding it generates. In addition—being itself constant—it is also more identifiable."

While Koina waited, he settled his shoulder blades deeper into his g-seat. Then he came to the point.

"Of the two portions of source-code which Lane has identified, one belongs to the code engine currently in use by Anodyne Systems." He grimaced like a shrug. "So much was to be expected. The chip would not have passed testing without being coded for clearance.

"But the other—" Hashi rolled his eyes in mock dismay. "Ah, my dear Koina, it is the other which sows consternation among our investigative assumptions.

"The other," he pronounced distinctly so that Forrest Ing couldn't fail to hear him, "is a portion of source-code from the code engine employed by GCES Security."

At last he was rewarded by a small flaring of alarm in Koina's eyes; a glimpse of hidden dread. She was in more danger than she'd realized.

As if he were pleased, Hashi remarked, "The implications are dazzling, are they not? QED, the source of our kaze's id tag finds both Anodyne Systems and GCES Security accessible. The logic is immaculate. The difficulty—as I've already suggested—is that GCES Security has no dealings with Anodyne Systems."

When he was satisfied that he'd made himself clear, he concluded, "I wish to attend this extraordinary session of the Council because I believe that my investigation leads there."

Attend me well, Deputy Chief, he added in silence. I, also, may require your protection.

Koina regarded him with darkness stirring in the depths of her gaze. The restrained tension of her cheeks and forehead hinted at the bleak bones beneath the skin. Not for the first time, Hashi wondered what her mission to the Council was; what mandate Warden had given her. He wanted an answer, but he no longer believed that she would offer him one.

At last she spoke. Her voice was a soft whisper.

"Did you tell Warden?"

Hashi bridled despite his self-command. "Do not insult me, Koina." His chagrin left him strangely vulnerable. "As Godsen would have said, I know my job."

Eventually she nodded. By degrees her gaze slipped down to the sheaf of hardcopy in her hands as if she were asking herself what purpose all those sheets of information served.

He was in no hurry. The ride down the gravity well to Earth and Suka Bator gave him all the time he needed; more than enough. He could afford to be patient. So he waited without speaking—an exercise in self-effacement of which some of his subordinates wouldn't have believed him capable—until at last she raised her head and looked at him again.

"I assume you don't really want me to give you a formal briefing." Her tone was low, but steady. "I'm sure you already know everything I've told them." She nodded toward her aides. "Why don't you just ask a specific question? That way I can make a specific decision about answering."

Hashi renewed his avuncular smile. He needed it now; his own anxieties were too near the surface. Could he ask, What are your instructions from Warden? What position will he take toward Captain Vertigus' Bill of Severance? No: that would be too crude. And not particularly suitable for Forrest Ing's ears.

Instead he said, "If recollection serves, you recently had a matter of some importance to discuss with our esteemed director."

Her nod acknowledged that she remembered the conversation; but she didn't rise to the bait. Her self-possession would have exhilarated Hashi if he hadn't been feeling uniquely exposed at the moment.

He cleared his throat. "May I ask how he responded?"

The PR director appeared to weigh a variety of considerations before she answered. When she spoke, her tone was careful, stressing nothing.

"He told me I'm not in any danger. I think his exact words were, 'That's not what this is about.' "

Indeed. Indeed and forsooth. Hashi stifled an impulse to attempt several different rejoinders simultaneously. At such times he envied his computers—and his own mind—their capacity for multitasking. Conversation was sadly linear. To fill the time while he chose which line to take, he flapped a gesture in Forrest Ing's direction and commented, "I see that you do not entirely credit his reassurance. Or Enforcement Division Security does not." But he didn't mean the observation as criticism. "I approve, naturally. It is always wise to take precautions."

He took them himself. He'd gained one of his ends by "publicly" informing the PR director of the results of DA's investigation. Willingly or not, Forrest Ing would report that Hashi had done what he could to provide for Koina's safety.

In the meantime, other issues were more important.

As casually as a man who didn't care, Hashi murmured, "Forgive my curiosity. What was the director's reaction to your tidings themselves?"

Koina studied him without blinking. An impression of hardness gathered in the background of her gaze. Only the corners of her mouth smiled as she replied, "I'm sorry. To use one of Director Frik's words, that's 'privileged.' "

The days when she could talk to him freely about things which were none of his business were gone. Since her elevation to Godsen's post, she'd been overtaken by new loyalties. Like so many men and women before her, she was no longer able to distinguish between her attachment to Warden Dios and her service to the UMCP.

Hashi Lebwohl would get no help from her.

To his cost, he understood. He suffered from a like confusion, despite his best efforts to remain unclouded by the emotional murk—the value judgments and moral posturings, the irrational commitments and blind faiths—which soiled all human truths. With a sigh, he eased his thin limbs farther down into his g-seat.

"In that case, I believe I will avail myself of this opportunity for a *brief* nap." He chuckled aimlessly. "While we still may count ourselves wrapped in the peace of space."

After he closed his eyes, he heard Koina shuffling through her sheaf of hardcopy; resuming her studies for what lay ahead. Behind him Forrest Ing murmured to the communications tech, who in turn relayed transmissions elsewhere, no doubt using the shuttle's dishes to reach both UMCPHQ and ED Chief of Security Mandich on Suka Bator. But Hashi ignored them all.

That's not what this is about.

Though the question pained him, he wondered whether he was capable of playing a game as deep as Warden's.

G and the shielded hull roar of reentry brought him back to attention. Polymerized ceramics protected the craft from heat, but no defense could entirely seal out the howl of violated atmosphere, or the fire of the drive. In this stage of the shuttle's trajectory, braking thrust exerted more pressure than gravity. However, the cabin g-seats had pivoted automatically to meet the force backward. Hashi's lean frame seemed to bury itself in the padding as his weight pulled against him. G now was greater than it had been at launch—greater than any physical stress Hashi had felt for a number of years—but because it accumulated incrementally it was less traumatic.

He turned a glance at Koina, saw her features stretched in the characteristic rictus of added g, and at once looked away to allow her at least the illusion of privacy. Under these conditions even the faces of the finest human specimens bore a naked—and nakedly undignified—resemblance to skulls.

Reentry was mercifully quick. For a few minutes he felt himself dragged backward down the gravity well; then the shuttle planed to a more level course, and braking thrust eased. The skin of his face seemed to slump on its bones as if it had lost elasticity, but he began to breathe more easily, and the constriction of too much weight receded from his heart.

In twenty minutes the craft would heat its skids almost to slag on the glazed tarmac of Suka Bator's spaceport, and shortly after that the DA director would set foot on his planetary home for the first time in more years than he cared to count.

Now was as good a time as any for him to take his next step, his next precaution.

"Deputy Chief." In effect, Hashi now sat behind Forrest Ing. Nevertheless a lifetime of intercoms and transmitters had accustomed him to addressing people he couldn't see. "I require a word with you before touchdown."

Koina looked at him curiously, but didn't interrupt.

The deputy chief craned his neck awkwardly to meet Hashi's gaze around his g-seat. He had a blunt, square face which didn't wear perplexity well. In addition, the strain of his posture showed in his expression. After a short stare, he retreated out of sight. "Yes, Director?"

"Deputy Chief," Hashi began amiably enough, "Director Hannish's attendance at this extraordinary session of the Governing Council for Earth and Space is expected. Mine is not. Indeed, I hope that my presence will occasion considerable surprise. This may prove fruitful.

"In order to meet events effectively, I must be assured that you will comply with any requests or instructions I may mention."

He thought he could hear Ing squirming. "Forgive me, Director," the deputy chief said. "My orders from Chief Mandich don't give me much leeway. I'm personally responsible for Director Hannish's safety. Frankly, I'm not even supposed to let her go to the san without calling in an inspection team first. And I'm instructed to take her orders, no one else's. If there's something you want me to do, I'll have to clear it first."

In plain words, Hashi muttered to himself, you decline to trust me. Min Donner's righteous scorn blinkered every mind in Enforcement Division.

"Then clear it now," he retorted more sharply. "My point is precisely the one you raise. If I ask you to 'do something,' I will need it done without the delay of applying to your chief for permission."

The man's discomfort became more palpable. "What kind of trouble are you expecting, Director?"

Hashi let a waspish wheeze into his voice. "I expect nothing. But I mean to be prepared."

In its own way, that also was factually accurate. His sense of possibilities was at once precise and indistinct, defined by Heisenberg's profound uncertainty. He felt intuitively that he knew where events were going. *That's not what this is about*. Therefore he couldn't know what those events were—or would be.

However, Forrest wasn't satisfied. "Director," he began hesitantly, "with respect—" Then he forged ahead. "Chief Mandich is going to want something more concrete to go on."

Hashi had expected this. He also disliked it. His disdain for the ED director and all her blind oversimplifications seemed to rise into his throat. His tone turned to a rasp.

"Then kindly inform Chief Mandich that I require him to assign personnel to me who have been given his authorization"—he nearly snarled the words—"to do what I tell them."

Trapped by indecision, the deputy chief turned to Koina. "Director Hannish?"

Koina—bless her self-possessed heart—didn't hesitate. "Do it, Forrest," she said calmly. "I don't know what Director Lebwohl is worried about, but whatever it is, I'm sure it's important. If nothing comes of it, we haven't lost anything."

The deputy chief hesitated a moment longer. Then Hashi heard him murmur instructions to his communications tech.

With an effort, Hashi stilled his anger. Instead of muttering imprecations on Min Donner and all her ilk, he turned to Koina and smiled. Softly, so that he wouldn't be overheard, he breathed, "Thank you, Director Hannish."

His gratitude was real, although nothing he felt or meant was simple.

She regarded him with a somber frown. "Hashi," she replied, also softly, "why do I get the impression that everything I've been preparing myself for"—she flexed her sheaf of hardcopy—"has suddenly become irrelevant?"

His smile deepened. "My dear young woman, that impression overtakes us all, early or late. The knowledge of existence precludes the awareness of motion, just as awareness of motion precludes knowledge of existence. And yet neither is of any significance without the other."

The frown tightened its grip on her brow. For a moment he thought that her reserve might crack; that she might snap at him. However, she didn't allow herself to speak until she could ask coolly, "Meaning?"

Hashi shrugged against his belts. His own control seemed to slip while hers held. "I expect nothing." The wheeze in his voice was growing worse. "But I mean to be prepared.

"As I have already said," he added hoarsely.

She continued studying him until he looked away. Then she remarked distantly, "I suppose that's fair. I didn't answer your question either." Holding her stack of hardcopy sheets in both hands, she began tidying them for touchdown.

He felt an impulse to retort, Indeed you did not. I am gratified that you remember. His irritation was misplaced, however. It belonged on his own head. The fact—perhaps the truth—was that he had no answer to give her. Uncertainty stood in his way.

Warden Dios had outplayed him once. At least once, he amended. If he didn't raise the level of his game—and soon—other people would begin to do the same.

SORUS

Soar was already moving back into the asteroid swarm, returning toward the heart of Deaner Beckmann's domain, when her communications first opened a channel to Lab Center and persuaded Center that Captain Chatelaine needed to talk to Chief Retledge.

Soar's course kept her hidden from her own outbound particle trace. If Retledge declined to help her, Sorus would have to rely on the assumption that *Trumpet* meant to track her outward. Succorso would want to come after her. And even if sanity prevailed—even if Succorso decided not to risk his ship against *Soar*—he would still try to follow her: he couldn't count on avoiding her unless he knew where she was. So Sorus had left him the clearest emission trail she could. Now she doubled back, intending to get on his tail when he began to trace her.

Unless Retledge gave her something more concrete to go on.

For once, Milos Taverner didn't question her. He stood beside her command station, mutely superintending everything that was said or done on the bridge, but he kept his thoughts to himself. Whether Retledge helped her or not, the Amnioni had already given her his orders. If she didn't return to the vicinity of the Lab, she couldn't carry them out.

She recognized the chief of Security's voice over the bridge speaker before he identified himself.

"Captain Chatelaine? Chief Retledge. This is a surprise. I thought you were heading out. Didn't you tell me you don't want trouble with Captain Succorso?"

Sorus took just a moment to summon her waning resources. Her bridge crew was frightened: she could see that. All her people were scared. To varying degrees they seemed to wear the same fear she'd inflicted on Ciro Vasaczk.

Now more than ever she had to sound confident; needed to be sure of what she did.

Retledge knew her voice as well as she knew his. "That's what I said," she told him without preamble. "I didn't want trouble—not on your turf. Other factors aside, I would rather not make myself unwelcome the next time I decide to visit."

Involuntarily she glanced at Milos; but his face revealed nothing. He still wore the eyeshades she'd given him earlier. Had he forgotten to take them off? Was that possible for an Amnioni? Even if he removed them, however, his pudgy face and alien eyes would have masked his thoughts. The cost of human slaughter no longer had any significance to him.

"But I also told you," she went on, speaking into her command pickup, "that leaving him alive was the worst mistake of my life." She paused long enough to inhale. "I want you to help me correct it."

Her signal bounced along half a dozen or more relays until it reached him. Distance and static flattened out his reply.

"How can I do that?"

"Give me clearance to come back in," she answered promptly. "And answer a couple of questions."

Then she waited.

Out of the dark, Retledge inquired, "Such as?"

"Such as, has he left yet? How long ago? And what course did you assign him?"

Exactly where in this seething tumult of doomed rock was *Trumpet*? How much time did Sorus have to do all the things the Amnion wanted from her?

"Captain Chatelaine"—a burst of static distorted Retledge's tone—"you know we don't give out that kind of information. We're a stationary target here. Our guns give us some protection, but we need more than that. As a matter of policy, we do what we can to stay on good terms with the ships that visit us. Even if those ships aren't exactly friendly with each other."

Did he sound angry? She couldn't tell. Just in case, however, she gave her voice a placating tone.

"I understand that, of course, Chief Retledge. Unfortunately I still have a problem. Succorso is sure to come after me. He's going to be a threat as long as he lives." Gently she concluded, "What can I offer you that might make you feel like helping me?"

Milos watched her, listened to her, as if he were blind and deaf.

"Captain Chatelaine," the speaker replied, "you're cleared to return, if that's really what you want. Approach course and protocols follow."

The helm first studied his board, then murmured, "Got it, Captain," as codes and routing came in. Apparently Retledge wasn't angry.

Nevertheless he added a warning. "But if you intend to pick a fight with Captain Succorso, don't waste your time coming back here. We don't want any part of your petty feuds. Go away and leave us alone. Retledge out."

Center's transmission fizzled to silence.

You self-righteous sonofabitch, Sorus thought harshly. Damn you, don't you know I'm desperate? Do you think I would do *any* of this if I had a choice?

You're already dead. It wouldn't cost you anything to help me.

After a moment an ache in her fingers made her aware that she was clenching her fists.

Damn you all to hell.

Sighing, she instructed helm, "Take us in. And don't forget to be careful. But make it as quick as those protocols will tolerate." More for her own benefit than for his, she remarked, "I assume Retledge would have said so if *Trumpet* was still in dock. Time is precious."

She turned to Milos. "Looks like we're on our own." A rasp of weariness crept into her voice: he had that effect on her. "I don't like the odds. You've given me conflicting priorities. If I concentrate on one, I risk losing the other.

"You told me you can call for help." The Amnioni had said that when *Soar* had left her rendezvous with *Calm Horizons*. "Maybe you'd better do it."

As if he were performing an act of courtesy, Milos shifted his stance slightly toward her.

"Why do you need help, Captain Chatelaine?"

"Because," you Amnion bastard, "if *Trumpet* left the Lab too soon after we did, she might get out of this swarm before we can catch up with her." God, she hated explaining herself to this former human being. She was *tired* of it. "Once she has a clear line of acceleration, she can go into tach. Then we're going to have hell's own time trying to find her again.

"We need another ship out on the fringe to turn her back if she tries to run."

Milos shook his head—an atavistic gesture which meant nothing. "I do not understand. Do you now believe that Ciro Vasaczk will not sabotage *Trumpet*'s drives, as you instructed?"

With an effort, Sorus kept her obscenities to herself. "I've already answered that question. I believe it's stupid to assume nothing will go wrong. That's why I want *help*." A moment later she added sourly, "Although you haven't bothered to mention what kind of *help* you think you can whistle up in the middle of a system like Massif-5."

The Amnioni appeared to consider the implications of her sarcasm. Then he announced impassively, "I am in contact with *Calm Horizons*."

"What?" Sorus couldn't contain her incredulity—or her indignation. "All the way from here to forbidden space? Don't bullshit me, Milos. Even with drones you would need at least a day just to get a message there—and you haven't been using any drones. But that's not all. A tub like *Calm Horizons* might take as much as two more to reach us. Two more *days*, Milos.

"You told me you can get us help when we need it. You didn't say anything about having to wait for three *days*."

Milos studied her. Like his eyes, his emotions—if he had any—were hidden.

"I am in contact with *Calm Horizons*," he repeated evenly. "The contact is instantaneous. I am able to transmit and receive communication without measurable delay. The device which makes this possible was brought aboard from the defensive after the destruction of Thanatos Minor.

"At present its range has not been perfected beyond 2.71 light-years. For that reason *Calm Horizons* began an encroachment into human space when we set course for this system."

Sorus fought an impulse to gape at him. Her bridge crew were already staring.

"A covert encroachment," he said without emphasis. "Marc Vestabule is confident that *Calm Horizons* has not been detected.

"The defensive's position is presently 1.38 light-years from ours. Only course and velocity require adjustment. *Calm Horizons* can attain any position you desire outside this asteroid swarm in approximately three hours."

He stunned her. Amnion technology was capable of achievements she could barely conceive. Deep in her belly, despair and frustration seethed and spat, as hot as outrage.

" 'Instantaneous contact'?" she snarled. "And you didn't tell me you could do that? You didn't think I might need to know?"

The Amnioni remained still. Somehow his immobility suggested a shrug.

Sorus growled her disgust, but there was nothing she could say that would make a difference. All her dealings with the Amnion were like this. They could listen to reason—or to her human, unreliable version of reason—but they offered nothing, exposed nothing; ignored every appeal.

"Just tell her to get here," she sighed roughly. "I'll give you an exact position when I know what course *Trumpet* took away from the Lab."

Milos bent forward from the waist: he may have been trying to remember how humans bowed. Then he turned to leave the bridge.

Apparently his instrument for "instantaneous contact" wasn't an implant. He must have kept the device in the quarters she'd assigned to him when he came aboard.

Before Milos completed his exit, however, the communications first spoke.

"Captain, it's the Lab. Chief Retledge wants to talk to you again."

Sorus held up her hand, advising Milos to wait. "Let's hear it," she told the woman on communications.

The snap of a toggle brought the bridge speaker to life.

"Captain Chatelaine?" the chief asked. "This is Retledge."

Sorus faced her pickup, took hold of her waning courage, and said firmly, "Now it's my turn to be surprised, Chief Retledge. I thought you'd already explained your position."

Retledge cleared his throat. "Sorry about that, Sorus. Too many people listening in Center. Now I'm alone. This is a secure transmission."

"I see." She softened her tone. "In that case, it's nice to hear from you. Can I assume you've reconsidered?"

The chief didn't answer directly. Instead he said, "As it happens, there *is* something you can offer me."

"Name it," Sorus returned promptly.

Retledge took a moment to choose his words. "You think Captain Succorso is a threat. You want to put a stop to it. That gives us something in common."

She glanced over her shoulder to be sure Milos was still there, then replied, "I'm listening."

Carefully Retledge said, "Dr. Beckmann made a deal with Captain Succorso. More particularly, he made a deal with Vector Shaheed. He doesn't break those kinds of agreements. He figures no one will come here if we start taking sides in feuds like yours. And he has quaint ideas about 'professional courtesy.' He wouldn't consider mistreating a 'colleague' like Shaheed."

The chief paused. When he continued, his grimness was plain, despite the distance and static.

"But Security is *my* problem, not his. I have to worry about keeping us alive. And I don't think we can survive the secrets *Trumpet* is carrying.

"They're—explosive, Sorus. Take my word for it. When they go off, we're going to get caught in the wave front."

You're already caught, she thought. You're already dead. But she didn't say that aloud.

"I'll answer your questions," he finished, "if you promise me you'll destroy that ship. Completely. No survivors. Nothing left but dust."

Sardonically he added, "I'll tell Beckmann Succorso suffered a 'navigational mishap.' "

Sorus didn't believe him. He didn't care whether Shaheed's "secrets" were explosive: he cared whether they were exclusive. What Beckmann had learned from Shaheed would be far more valuable if no one shared it.

But his reasons didn't matter. His information did.

"My friend," she said before he could think that she was hesitating, "you have a deal. Complete destruction. No survivors." Including you. "Nothing left but dust."

Like her heart.

"Then you'd better get started," Retledge responded quickly. "Shaheed finished his research faster than I was expecting. Succorso is already on his way."

"I'm still coming in," Sorus warned. Images of slaughter twisted like nausea in her stomach. She and the chief of Security had been lovers once. At the time the experience had been a pleasure; nothing more. But now the memory scraped like a dull knife across the strings of her despair. "I want to get behind him. Once I reach you, I'll turn and trail him until we're out of your range. That way you won't know anything embarrassing."

Retledge hesitated momentarily, then said, "All right." Through a random scatter of electrons, he advised her, "Stand by to copy *Trumpet*'s departure course and protocols."

A few seconds later helm reported again, "Got it, Captain."

"We have it, Chief," Sorus informed Retledge. "We'll turn as soon as we reach your immediate control space." Hurrying to end the transmission before her voice betrayed her, she said, "Captain Chatelaine out," and silenced her pickup with her fist.

Good-bye. I'm sorry. For whatever that's worth.

"Captain Chatelaine," Milos observed behind her, "the falseness of your kind is without end." Then he asked, "Can you now identify the position you wish *Calm Horizons* to attain?"

Full of flaming curses, Sorus swung her station toward him. But his stolid stance and covered eyes stopped her. Just a few hours of his company had been enough to make her forget that he'd once been human. And she knew the Amnion well enough by now to understand that no individual member of that species would ever have given in to the pressure they'd exerted on her.

Maybe she deserved what they were doing to her. Maybe she'd always deserved it.

Through a black gloom she called *Soar*'s charts of the swarm up onto one of her display screens; overlaid the data Retledge had just supplied; ran some quick calculations. Then she gave Milos the coordinates he was waiting for.

At once the Amnioni left to apply himself to his "instantaneous contact" device.

As *Soar* moved back into the asteroid swarm, deeper toward the heart of Deaner Beckmann's domain, targ began using spare thrust capacity to charge her super-light proton cannon.

MIKKA

Through the hull, she heard the hiss of hoses pulling free, the snap as cables jerked from their sockets; she felt the visceral jolt of grapples unclamping. Metal rang as if it were in distress. *Trumpet* was leaving dock. For better or worse, the gap scout was free of that place.

Still she didn't move. Crouched at one end of her bunk with her back pressed into the corner of the wall, she remained where she'd been ever since she and Ciro had come into their cabin. As *Trumpet* drifted loose and lost the asteroid's weak g, she tucked one of her legs under the bunk's webbing so that she wouldn't start to float. Other than that, nothing changed. Leaving the Lab didn't really make any difference.

Ciro lay in front of her with his upper body propped on her knees and his head turned away; her arms were wrapped around him. He refused to speak. He hadn't said a word since he'd begged her to kill him. *Now. While you have the chance.*

Please.

Now, she'd panted back at him, almost gasped, when they'd reached the privacy of their cabin. *You're going to tell me what happened.* What Sorus Chatelaine had done to him. What Nick had sacrificed him for. *Whatever it is, we'll face it together.*

He'd stared at her as if she were threatening to tear out his heart; as if she'd already started— Tearless, and as pale as death, he'd stared at her until she couldn't bear it; until she was the one who looked away. But he hadn't answered.

Tell me! she'd howled at him: a cry so fierce that it seemed to rend her throat; and yet only a small thing, barely a whimper, compared with the extremity of her dismay. *Tell me, God damn you! I can't help you if you don't* tell *me!*

He hadn't answered. Instead he'd rolled himself onto the nearest bunk and turned his face to the wall.

Needing to breathe, desperate for air and hope, she'd pushed onto the bunk with him; squeezed into the corner; pulled him toward her until he lay across her knees and she could hold him. Still he didn't say anything. He refused to let her see his face. Eventually she found that she didn't care whether or not she could breathe.

Her brother. And her responsibility: she'd brought him to this. He'd joined *Captain's Fancy* because of her; Nick had accepted him because of her. Now he was the only person left that she still knew how to love.

She'd survived losing Nick. But if she lost her brother—

For a while after she'd realized that he wasn't going to talk to her, she'd wept. That was over now. As dry-eyed as he was, she crouched in the corner and simply held him while *Trumpet* eased out of dock and slowly, almost unnoticeably, began to adjust attitude for departure.

Across the Lab's immediate control space. Back into the long, jockeying moil of the asteroid swarm.

How long would it take? A gentle nudge of thrust moved the ship. First the relative void around the Lab. Then the swarm itself. Then the Massif-5 system. How long before Nick took her and her brother and the whole ship beyond the reach of any imaginable help?

How long could she suffer Ciro's silence?

Presumably Morn and Davies had ambushed Nick in the airlock. Had they succeeded? Mikka didn't think so—not when he could get Angus' help just by commanding it. No, it was more likely that Morn and her son were dead. Unless Nick kept her alive because he was addicted to hurting her—

Why had Angus given them guns?

Ciro shifted against Mikka's arms. In a small, strained voice, he murmured, "I want to be alone."

Involuntarily her muscles clenched as if she'd been hit by a stun-prod.

"They need you on the bridge." He kept his face stubbornly away from her. His voice was muffled by her arm; he sounded like a little boy. A boy who knew that nothing good could happen unless he was left to die. "I'll be all right. I just want to be alone."

She would have said, No. Would have said, I won't do it. I can't leave you like this. But she couldn't unlock her throat.

"If you don't go, they're going to come here. Vector or Sib. Or Nick, if he still wants to punish you. I can't stand it. If you go, you can make them leave me alone."

He was lost. Nick had sacrificed him to Sorus Chatelaine, and now he was completely gone.

Mikka swallowed, trying to moisten her throat and mouth. She couldn't help him. He didn't want her help: he was out of reach. The only gift she had left to give was the dignity of letting him face whatever had happened to him on his own terms.

She tried to say, All right. If that's what you want. But when she opened her mouth, nothing came out. She'd already exhausted her capacity for tears.

"Please, Mikka."

She was going to do it. As soon as she could undo the knots in her muscles, she would get up from the bunk, go to the door—

The chime of the intercom stopped her.

"Mikka?" Morn's voice. "Ciro?" *Morn's*. "Are you all right? May I come in? I need to talk to you."

At once Ciro began to babble. "No, Mikka, don't let her, I don't want to see her, I can't see her, don't let her in—"

A sudden thunder of blood and need nearly deafened Mikka. Her damaged forehead throbbed. She shot a look at the intercom. No, Morn couldn't hear him. The pickup hadn't been activated.

"I'm sorry it took me so long to come," Morn went on. "I know you're in trouble. I want to help. But there's been so much— Please let me in. We need to talk."

There's been so much—

Through the thunder Mikka suddenly understood what she was hearing. *Morn's* voice. Morn was alive. And making her own choices regardless of Nick.

Why hadn't he killed her?

That question was urgent enough to reach Mikka in spite of her distress; urgent enough to outweigh Ciro's pleading. She wasn't able to dismiss all the lives that hinged on it.

Moving roughly because she couldn't yet unclench her arms and legs, she shifted Ciro aside and pushed off from the bunk. He was still babbling —"Mikka, no, please, don't, no"—but she ignored him. As soon as she reached the control panel, she keyed in the code to unlock the door.

Ciro stopped as if she'd cut his vocal cords.

Morn waited in the passage, holding a handgrip outside the door. She was alone. Her eyes seemed unnaturally dark; almost fatal; haunted by doubt and worry.

As the door swept aside, she showed Mikka an uncertain smile, then came determinedly into the cabin. There she let *Trumpet*'s gentle acceleration tug her to a halt. After a glance at Mikka, her gaze turned to the bunk where Ciro lay with his back toward her and his face hidden against the wall.

"My God," she whispered. "What happened to him?"

Mikka drew a shuddering breath. Without transition the thunder became fury. Rage rolled and crashed like a storm in her head. "Nick set him up. Left him as bait. *Sacrificed* him. He wanted *Soar* to take him—I don't know why. Some kind of scheme."

Her throat closed. No words could convey what she felt. She made a helpless gesture. "He's been like this ever since she let him go. First"—it was impossible to say this, it hurt too much, but somehow she forced it out—"he told me to kill him. Now he wants me to leave him alone."

Morn's eyes widened: the darkness haunting them grew deeper. Her mouth formed the words, "Kill him?" Then she bit her lip.

Mikka started to speak again. Or she thought she did. She meant to. Meant to ask, Where's Nick? What's going on? Why are you alive? What did Angus do to you? But she didn't make a sound. Her head hurt as if she'd just been hit. The bandage on her forehead obscured her vision in one eye. And Morn was looking at Ciro as if she saw his doom in the taut lines of his back.

Mikka knew this about Morn: she'd been Nick's victim as well as Angus'; only her zone implant had kept her sane. But she hadn't had that support when the Amnion had pumped their mutagens into her veins. She understood doom.

"Ciro."

She said his name softly. Nevertheless her voice was enough to make him flinch.

"Turn around, Ciro. Look at me. I need to talk to you, and I want you to look at me."

Ciro pressed himself harder against the wall.

With her eyes, Morn asked Mikka's permission to go on. Mikka nodded roughly, and Morn nudged herself toward Ciro's bunk. When she reached it, she closed one hand in the webbing, pulled herself down to sit on the edge of the bunk, then rested her other hand on Ciro's shoulder.

She made no effort to draw him toward her: she simply let him feel her presence through his tension.

"Ciro," she repeated. "We beat Nick. Sib tied him up. And Angus doesn't take his orders anymore. He's helpless."

Surprised out of herself, Mikka broke in, "How—?" How in hell did you manage *that*? At once, however, she set her teeth on her tongue. She didn't want to interrupt.

A subtle change showed in Ciro's body. He didn't move, but Mikka could tell that he was listening.

"The message that gave Nick Angus' priority-codes came from *Punisher*," Morn answered quietly. "From Dolph Ubikwe. I told you I thought there was something else going on. Something to hope for. This time I was right.

"Somehow that message programmed Angus' computer with new instructions. As soon as Nick and the rest of you left the ship, Angus told us the same codes. He handed himself to us. Then he told us how to set him free. How to help him free himself. Now he doesn't have any priority-codes. They're blocked—they don't effect him. He can make his own choices again."

"Wait a minute," Mikka protested. She couldn't help herself: what she heard horrified her. "You had his codes—you had that bastard in your control—and you set him *free*?"

Morn didn't look up at Mikka. She didn't need to.

"He used my zone implant to hurt me. So did Nick. I can't treat other people that way."

Mikka pressed a hand over her bandage to contain the pain. She was doomed; they were all finished. Morn couldn't *treat other people that way*. Great. Wonderful. So instead she put herself at his mercy. Again. He was still a cyborg, wasn't he? Now he had the power to treat everyone else the way he'd once treated her.

No wonder she looked haunted. She'd gone over the edge. Like Nick.

Yet she didn't sound crazy. *I can't treat other people that way*. She sounded like a woman who'd made up her mind to take risks which terrified her.

Mikka tried to swallow the futility rising in her gorge. "So what choices is he making?"

Morn lifted her head. For a moment she closed her eyes, as if that might help her bear the pain of her memories.

"Somehow," she murmured distantly, "a long time ago, he and I made a deal. A commitment to keep each other alive. He gave me the control to my zone implant. I took it and went with Nick. Instead of turning myself in to Com-Mine Security. That way Security didn't have enough evidence to execute him. And I got what I thought I needed to go on living.

"Apparently that—I don't really know what to call it—that accommodation still holds for him. He honors it. And maybe he thinks I honored it by letting him free himself."

Slowly Morn opened her eyes and turned to face Mikka. Now the darkness in her gaze looked like a wail of loss.

"Right now he's leaving the choices to me."

Mikka tried, but she couldn't hold Morn's eyes. Not for the first time, she felt weak and limited in Morn's presence; essentially ashamed. Morn should have been the weakest person aboard. Certainly she was the most damaged. And yet she was stronger than anyone else. She just didn't know it.

Despite the tremor of need which made her voice shake, Mikka asked, "So what choices are *you* making?"

Morn considered the question for a moment. She seemed to flinch inwardly as she answered, "We're going after *Soar*."

That struck a nerve. Without warning Ciro thrashed around to face Morn. His expression ached with an intensity Mikka couldn't interpret—hope or despair so extreme that they were indistinguishable from each other.

Now, however, Morn didn't look at him. Instead she concentrated on Mikka as if she'd forgotten about him.

Intuitively Mikka understood. She, too, refused to look at him—she didn't want to drive him back into his clenched rejection. Instead she asked Morn sourly, "Now why would you go and do something like that?"

A small frown pained Morn's forehead. "That ship used to have another name. She was called *Gutbuster*, and she killed my mother. She killed the only mother Davies remembers. In a strange way, she's the reason he and I both became cops. So we could try to get the ship that killed our mother."

Ciro raised himself on one elbow as if he wanted to see Morn's face better. His free hand started to reach toward her, then fell back.

"He wants that more than I do," she went on. "Or I want it, but I don't trust it. Revenge is too expensive. And maybe we have more important things to do.

"But our minds started diverging as soon as he was born. We've been changing in different ways. There's enough of Angus in him to affect the way he thinks. And everything that's ever happened to him has been twisted— He needs simple decisions. They help him hang on to who he is."

Morn shrugged. "And I'm supposed to be a cop. I need that. So maybe if I'm going to turn myself into the kind of cop I can believe in, I have to start from the beginning."

Soft as a whimper, Ciro protested, "No. Don't—"

Still without turning away from Mikka, Morn spoke to him.

"Do you understand what I'm saying, Ciro? We're going after *Soar*. And *Soar* did something to you." An undercurrent of anger began to surge in her voice, whetting her words like knives. "Sorus Chatelaine wants to use you against us somehow.

"Not just against Nick," she insisted. "Do you understand that, Ciro? I don't know what she told you, but this isn't aimed at him. He's irrelevant. She works for the Amnion. And they want *us* dead. We have an immunity drug. We have Davies. We know about their near-C acceleration experiments. If they can't take us, they need to kill us.

"She's hunting us right now. No matter where we go, she'll come after us. We'll never be safe. That's as good a reason as any to hunt her ourselves."

"Please," Ciro moaned as if she were cutting at him; as if what she said flensed the skin from his bones. His eyes clung to her like pleading. "Don't do this to me."

"I'm not," Morn retorted. "*She* is. Sorus Chatelaine did this to you. I'm just trying to help you understand it."

Slowly she shifted on the edge of the bunk until she could face him. Mikka held her breath as Morn moved her hand—so slowly that it seemed inexorable—to Ciro's chest and gripped the front of his shipsuit. With her fist, she lifted him upright to sit in front of her.

He stared naked dread at her. His eyes were so full of white fear that they appeared to have no irises. His mouth hung open. But he didn't resist. Somehow she'd taken control of him.

"Maybe you can change it," she told him. Anger and pain made her strong. "If we leave you alone, and you do whatever it is she wants from you, we'll all die. One way or another. If we don't die fighting her, they'll make us Amnion. All of us, Ciro. Not just Nick. Not just Angus. Mikka and me. Sib and Vector and Davies. A handful of antimutagen pills—which is all we have left—won't save us.

"If we lock you up so you can't do anything, we can probably keep her from taking us. But she still might kill us. That ship has a super-light proton cannon. One hit is all she needs."

Mikka winced. Super-light—? Oh, shit!

"Leave him alone," she breathed at Morn. "Don't you think he's scared enough already?"

Ciro's lower lip quivered. His fear seemed to leave him mute.

Morn went on as if she'd forgotten remorse and knew nothing about terror. Each word was as distinct as an incision.

"But if you tell us what she wants you to do, we might be able to use that against her. We might have a chance. And if you tell us what she did to you, we might be able to help you.

"It's up to you, Ciro," she finished. "But you'd better make up your mind soon. We don't have much time."

Still she didn't let him go.

"I mean it, Morn," Mikka warned thinly. Pain and thunder muffled everything. She could hardly hear herself. "That's enough. It would be kinder if you just tortured him."

Morn ignored her. Her gaze and her grip on Ciro's shipsuit didn't waver.

He squirmed against her grasp. His voice shook. "You're going to kill me."

"Maybe." Morn didn't shirk the possibility. "Maybe we will. But before it comes to that we'll do everything in our power to save you. And right now, with Angus and this ship on our side, we have a *lot* of power.

"Ciro," she added more gently, "tell us. Please. Give us a chance to show you you're not alone."

"*Alone?*" His voice cracked, but he didn't stop. Morn had tapped a core of frenzy in him—a passion as knotted and extreme as his sister's. "You're going to show me I'm *not alone*?

"What about Mikka? How *alone* is she?"

Mikka gaped at him in surprise.

"You're a cop," he cried, "a cop, you keep telling us you're a *cop*. Well, *she's* an illegal. So is Sib. Even *Vector's* an illegal. What're you going to show *them*? What are they going to have left when you're done being a cop? Why is it worse for them to die now? At least they can fight. They don't have to sit around waiting to be *executed*!"

Morn flinched as if he'd flung acid in her face.

When she heard him—and saw Morn's reaction—Mikka snapped; she couldn't endure any more. Flailing her nearly weightless limbs, she swam to the edge of the bunk, grabbed it, hauled herself down, and drove her desperate fury at her brother.

"Don't give me that *bullshit*! I don't *care* about being executed! I don't care about anything that might happen days or weeks or *months* from now, if we're lucky enough to live that long. I care about *you*!"

Struggling to control herself, she lowered her voice. "And after that I care about fighting the bastards who got all of us into this mess. I can take responsibility for my own crimes."

But the effort of restraint seemed to hurt her as much as his fear. She needed to howl; needed to raise her head to the ceiling and wail while her heart tore.

"If you want to betray us," she rasped bitterly, "then *do it*. But don't use *me* as an excuse. And don't use Sorus Chatelaine, either. All she did is lean on you. She isn't here holding a gun to your head."

Ciro couldn't match her when she was like this. She could see what was left of his resistance crumbling under her scorn. He was already broken: Sorus had shattered something that he depended on to keep him whole. Morn had brought him out of his defenses in order to put pressure on him. And now his sister snarled at him as if he were contemptible—

"No," he admitted like a whipped child. "She isn't. It's worse than that."

Like Morn, Mikka stared as if she were paralyzed. Angus had cracked her skull. Why hadn't he deafened her as well? She didn't want to hear this. It was more than she could bear.

But Ciro had made his decision. Crouched and beaten on the bunk, with his heart in his eyes and his throat full of pain, he told her and Morn what they'd asked to hear.

"She serves the Amnion because they gave her a mutagen. A special one. It's slow. Then they gave her an antidote. One that just postpones the mutagen. She stays human as long the antidote lasts. As long as they keep her supplied. But if she doesn't take it—or if they don't give it to her—the mutagen starts up again."

His voice sank as he spoke. And yet no matter how low it was, Mikka could still hear it. The clamoring reverberation in her head gave her no protection. She was powerless to forgive herself. Nick had sacrificed him, and it was her fault. She'd given her brother to Nick as surely as if she, too, had considered him only bait.

"She did the same thing to me. She and some man. I think he might have been Milos Taverner."

Tears began to spill from his eyes, but he didn't notice them. Mikka herself hardly noticed them.

"If I sabotage the drives so we can't run or fight, she'll take me with her. She'll keep me supplied." His throat closed on a sob. "So I can stay human."

Take me with her. Mikka groaned. "And you believe that?"

"I have to," he answered simply.

Have to? Of course he did. Sorus Chatelaine had injected a mutagen into his veins. There was nothing else left for him to believe.

Mikka's need to howl mounted until she couldn't contain it. Pushing back from the bunk, she brandished her helpless fists and brought up a scream from the bottom of her heart.

At once, Morn caught her by the front of her shipsuit, held her the same way she'd held Ciro. Her eyes were cold and dark, as bleak as ice. Lines of authority marked her face like emaciation. "Mikka! We don't have *time* for this!"

Her shout hit Mikka like a slap. Mikka swung a wild blow at Morn's head. But there wasn't enough g to anchor her. Her own force tossed her away from the impact, out of control.

By the time she'd reached the wall and recovered, Morn was at the intercom.

Ignoring Mikka now, Morn thumbed the pickup toggle.

"Vector. Are you there? I need you."

"I'm here, Morn," Vector answered promptly. Metallic circuits or concentration made him sound abstract; too far away to be reached. "Give me twenty minutes. I don't want to stop in the middle of this."

"Vector—" Morn began.

"It's going to be great," he went on as if he hadn't heard her. "I'm coding a transmission. It's in my name—maybe that will give it some credibility. In essence, it says that since I left Intertech I've finished the research I was doing there. I've developed an antimutagen. I'll include the formula. Maybe suggest test procedures for verification. We can set it to broadcast constantly, wherever we go. Anybody who hears it can produce the immunity drug for themselves.

"God, Morn, I've *dreamed* of doing something like this. I still can't believe it's happening. It's going to make everything else worthwhile."

"But *not now,*" Morn cut in fiercely. Outrage bristled in her voice. "Vector, I *need* you! That can wait. This can't."

The intercom was silent long enough to make Mikka think that Vector would refuse. Then the tiny speaker crackled.

"All right. I'm on my way. Where are you?"

"Mikka's cabin."

At once Morn silenced the pickup.

Mikka clung to a handgrip. After a moment she realized that she was gasping. She couldn't think; didn't understand— Somehow Morn's growing anger seemed to consume all the air in the cabin.

A faint glitter that might have been hope showed in Ciro's gaze. "What can Vector do?" he asked hesitantly.

Morn faced him as if she were resisting an impulse to shout. "Damn it, Ciro, what do you think antimutagens are *for*? I don't know if this can work. An immunity drug isn't the same as an antidote. It's supposed to be in your system *before* you get the mutagen. I don't know what happens if the mutagen is already there. But," she promised, "we are going to find out. It is by God worth a try."

Ciro stared at her, then put his hands over his eyes as if he were afraid to think that she might be right.

To her chagrin, Mikka found that she couldn't keep up; couldn't bounce from despair to hope like this. Her torn emotions refused. She needed to do something to contain her turmoil. So that she wouldn't start to scream again, she thrust herself toward the door and keyed it open in case Vector didn't know which was her cabin.

She caught him outside with his hand raised to knock.

Vehemently—she didn't care how vehemently—she grabbed his shipsuit and swung him through the doorway, then closed the door after him.

Taken by surprise, he flapped his arms in a wasted effort to manage his trajectory. At once, however, Morn moved to help him stop; put both hands on his shoulders to steady him—and herself.

His blue eyes shone: he was as close to excitement as Mikka had ever seen him. But he'd always been a man who knew how to concentrate. As soon as he saw Morn's face, and Ciro's, and Mikka's, he put his personal eagerness aside.

Calmly he asked, "What's wrong? How can I help?"

Morn took a deep breath, held it for a moment as if she needed time to marshal her courage. Then she gave Vector a quick summary of Ciro's story.

When she was done, she added, "You know more about mutagens than the rest of us—and antimutagens. Tell us what to do."

As an engineer, Vector Shaheed may have been only competent. In other areas, however, he was considerably more than that. A slight frown creased his round face—a mild acknowledgment of Ciro's plight—but he knew how to respond.

"First things first," he told Ciro in a blunt, avuncular tone: the tone of a man who saw no reason to panic. "Don't stop taking that antidote. It may be temporary, but it gives us time.

"By the way, how much time *do* we have?"

Mikka hardly understood him; she was full of chaos and doom. But Ciro faced Vector's question as squarely as he could. Although his larynx bobbed convulsively, he was able to say, "She gave me enough pills for twelve hours. I'm due for another one in"—he flicked a glance at the cabin chronometer—"nine minutes." From a pocket of his shipsuit, he brought out a small vial. "This is all I have left."

Vector nodded. "That should be enough." Without hesitation he turned toward the door. "I need a hypo. I'll be right back."

Mikka foundered; she might have been drowning. She didn't know how to deal with her fear that Morn was wrong; that Vector had come too late to save Ciro. Panting for air, she rasped, "What good is that going to do?"

Vector cocked an eyebrow at her. "I need a blood sample," he explained. "The sickbay systems can analyze it. They might not be able to answer all my questions, but they can tell me how closely this mutagen resembles the ones Nick's antimutagen can handle." As if the point were incidental, he remarked, "I know a lot more about that drug's limits than I did a few hours ago."

Ciro seemed to cling to every word as if Vector might keep him human simply by talking to him. Nevertheless Mikka couldn't stop. If she let herself believe that Vector could help Ciro, and he failed, she might kill him.

Nearly choking, she demanded, "And what good is knowing *that* going to do?"

Vector shrugged. "If there's enough of a resemblance—and if the antidote really keeps this mutagen passive—our antimutagen should work. Remember, it's not an organic immunity. It doesn't make human DNA resistant. The drug is essentially a genetically engineered microbe that acts as a binder. It attaches itself to the nucleotides of the mutagen, renders them inert. Then they're both flushed out of the body as waste.

"Of course, it wouldn't normally accomplish anything to take this drug after a mutagen was injected. That's because most Amnion mutagens act immediately. But if this mutagen is just sitting there, our drug should have time to catch up with it."

Morn nudged him toward the door. "Do it now," she urged him. "We can talk about it later."

Vector nodded. Still he paused long enough to let Mikka raise more objections.

She set her teeth on her lip and knotted her fingers in the thighs of her shipsuit to make herself shut up.

Vector inclined his head like a bow. The movement seemed curiously formal—an indication of respect. A moment later he bobbed to the door and let himself out of the cabin.

At once Mikka left the wall to reach the bunk and Ciro.

This time when she wrapped her arms around him he returned her embrace.

"I'm sorry," she murmured. "I didn't mean to be so hard on you. I'm just scared out of my mind."

He nodded mutely and tightened his grip.

From someplace far away, Morn said, "I'm going back to the bridge. They need to know what's happening." She meant Sib, Davies, and Angus. "And maybe Angus can help us. One of those UMCP databases might tell him something useful."

The bandage blurred Mikka's vision. She didn't reply. She was too busy holding on to her brother.

DARRIN

Deep in the asteroid swarm protecting Deaner Beckmann's installation, Darrin Scroyle sat at his command station and watched three of his people work. They'd gone EVA, but they were easily close enough for *Free Lunch*'s lights and cameras to reach them. He watched them on the largest of the display screens.

Through the fabric of his shipsuit, he scratched his chest absentmindedly. He didn't take his eyes off the screen. His bridge crew would tell him quickly enough if their instruments picked up hints of trouble from the seething space around the ship; but if his people outside encountered any difficulties, he wanted to see what happened himself. That might enable him to react in time to save them.

They clung with grapples and compression pitons to the rough surface of an asteroid not much larger than *Free Lunch*'s bridge. At the moment they were anchored beside a concrete emplacement which held one of the relays that bounced scan data and operational communication to and from the Lab.

If the information Darrin had gleaned the last time *Free Lunch* visited the Lab was still accurate, his ship had reached this position without being detected by Beckmann's scan net. Lab Center didn't know he was here.

Unless he'd made a mistake—

He shrugged mentally. Mistake or not, he was here. And if his people did their jobs right, he would soon know if he'd miscalculated, one way or the other.

The sight of fragile human beings bobbing like bubbles amid the imponderable rush of so much rock made his stomach queasy. That was normal for him—he always found EVA easier to do than to observe—but he didn't shirk it. If his people risked their lives outside the ship, the least he could do was to endure a little nausea in order to keep an eye on them.

After a few minutes, the bridge speaker emitted a spatter of static. "I think we're done here, Captain." A woman's voice: his command second, Pane Suesa. "It looks like it should work. How's it coming through?"

"Data?" Darrin asked without glancing away from the screen.

"Clear enough, Captain," the data first answered. "At this range, we can handle the static, no problem. But we'll have to crack their coding."

"Is that going to be a problem?" Darrin inquired even though he knew the answer.

Data chuckled sardonically. "For me? No." If he hadn't routinely justified his high opinion of himself, he would have been insufferable. "We'll know everything the Lab knows by the time our people reach the airlock."

"Good." Darrin leaned toward his pickup. "Pane," he transmitted, "it's coming through fine. You're done. Get back in here before I get spacesick watching you."

"Aye, Captain," the speaker replied.

After another moment his command second and her two companions aimed their maneuvering jets and began riding gusts of compressed gas in the direction of *Free Lunch*.

From her place at the targ station, Alesha turned a grave look toward Darrin. Like him, she was belted into her g-seat. The ship floated without internal spin: centrifugal g would have made *Free Lunch* too hard to handle in the swarm. Alesha had to twist against her restraints in order to face Darrin.

"Are you sure they won't detect what we're doing?"

" 'They'? Succorso and Thermopyle?" His attention was consumed by Pane and her crew: for an instant he didn't understand Alesha's question. Then he said, "Oh, you mean Lab Center."

She nodded.

He shook his head. "Yes and no. If I've made a mistake—or they've moved their emplacements—they might know we're here. But even if they do, they can't detect our transmitter. It's completely passive. It doesn't add or subtract anything, interrupt anything, distort anything—or leave any ghosts. All it does is read the signals passing through the relay and echo them to us. So we're safe, at least for a while."

The cameras tracked *Free Lunch*'s people as they coasted for the ship.

Changing focus slowly blurred the image of the asteroid in the background. More to calm his stomach than because Alesha needed the explanation, Darrin went on, "When data gets it decoded, that echo will show us everything in this quadrant of Beckmann's scan net. We'll hear every message Lab Center gets from this vicinity—or sends out here.

"We'll know where *Trumpet* is. If she's left the Lab, we'll know where she's going. We'll know if there are any other ships around her—or after her."

Darrin considered what he'd said briefly, then finished, "Also—if the occasion arises—we can blow our transmitter and knock out this whole sector of the net. That'll blind anybody who happens to be relying on it."

"Sounds good," Alesha remarked with a hint of challenge in her tone. "In fact, it sounds too good. Too easy. If we can do this, why can't *Trumpet*? Why can't *Punisher*, or the ship that followed *Trumpet* out of forbidden space?"

"They could." The closer Pane and her companions came, the less queasy Darrin's stomach felt. "But *Trumpet* won't take the time. She'll be in a hurry to get out of the swarm. And *Punisher* isn't here yet." His shipsuit protected his chest: he could scratch as much as he liked. "I don't know where the hell that other ship is. She might not be in this system at all. Or she might be lurking right on top of *Trumpet*. That's one reason we're tapping into the scan net. We need to know who else we have to deal with."

Alesha nodded again. "I know. I just wanted to hear you say it."

On several occasions over the years, she'd told him—sometimes with more than a little exasperation—that he had the gift of making even the most impossible situations sound manageable. But there was no exasperation in her voice now. She'd put her larger anxieties aside in order to concentrate on the present; on doing her part to keep *Free Lunch* alive.

The cameras tracked the three EVA suits all the way to the waiting airlock in the ship's scarred flank.

With obvious satisfaction, the data first stabbed a key. "Got it, Captain." He made no effort to conceal his smugness. "I'm relaying to scan and communications now."

"Looks good, Captain," scan commented as he studied his readouts. "If you're done watching Pane, I'll put it on the big screen."

Pane had taken hold of a cleat outside the airlock; she was ushering her companions inside. Darrin decided to believe they were safe. With a small sigh of relief, he said to data, "Nice work." Then he told his scan first, "Do it."

At once the video image flickered off the display, and a 3-D scan schematic took its place.

A maze of blue dots indicated rocks. Green showed scan emplacements and relays; yellow pointed to guns. A voice filled one corner of the schematic: the clear space around the Lab. The image wavered slightly as Beckmann's net adjusted itself to account for the shifting positions of the asteroids.

Two red blips amid the maze marked ships.

They were identified in the schematic by code rather than name. Nevertheless Darrin could see at a glance that neither of them was *Free Lunch*. Neither was this close to a relay. And both were moving.

The Lab didn't know his ship was here. Therefore he could be morally certain no one else did, either.

One of the blips picked its way through the center of the quadrant, heading away from the Lab. The other was nearing the installation's control space at the fringes of the schematic.

After a moment helm added a yellow blip to the image: *Free Lunch*'s position. She was no more than a couple of thousand k away from the vessel in the middle of the screen.

"Have you got id on those ships?" Darrin asked.

"I'm coordinating now, Captain," the communications first answered. Transmissions between the ships and Lab Center were separate data-streams, distinct from the flow of scan. However, a quick time-slice comparison would enable him to determine which data-stream belonged to which blip.

Within five seconds, a name replaced the code over the red blip in the center of the screen.

Trumpet.

Unmistakably moving away from the Lab, out of the swarm. And only two thousand k beyond *Free Lunch*.

"Target acquired," Alesha announced to no one in particular. At this distance through this much confused rock, she couldn't have hit *Trumpet* if she'd fired all day. The gap scout was totally blocked from *Free Lunch*'s scan. Nevertheless Alesha's words lit a small incendiary excitement in Darrin's chest.

Tension or eagerness tightened his bridge crew in their g-seats, sharpened their movements. Automatically, without orders, the helm first projected *Trumpet*'s course, plotted an interception, and posted both in the schematic.

Free Lunch would be able to cut off the gap scout and attack in three hours.

Darrin was about to say, Let's go, when communications named the second red blip. The information surprised him to silence.

Soar.

"Damn," Alesha breathed as if she were speaking for the whole ship. "She was at Billingate. What's she doing here?"

Darrin knew. He didn't need intuition; the logic of the coincidence was too obvious. "*Soar*," he pronounced quietly. "Captain Sorus Chatelaine. According to her reputation, she worked for the Bill. And sometimes the Amnion.

"That's who followed *Trumpet* out of forbidden space."

He was sure.

"Problems, people," Alesha warned the bridge. Experience and her relationship with Darrin gave her the right to say such things. "We've got complications. Be ready."

He cleared his throat.

"If she knows where *Trumpet* is," he said, organizing his thoughts, "we have competition." He ran some rough estimates on his board, looked at the results. "She could turn right now and get to *Trumpet* before we do." The gap scout's pace through the maze was efficient and steady, but unhurried. Anybody willing to take enough risks could chase *Trumpet* down. "Even if she waits until she reaches the Lab's control space so she can follow *Trumpet*'s particle trace, she'll still be close.

"If she doesn't know, of course, she's out of it. She's heading the wrong way. By the time Beckmann tells her what she needs, she'll be too late to catch up with us."

"What do you think, Captain?" communications asked casually. Not Alesha: Darrin assumed that his targ first had already made up her own mind.

He paused for three beats of his heart, simply looking at the schematic and letting the logic of the coincidence complete itself. Then he shrugged and took his chances.

"She knows. If she's good enough to track *Trumpet* here, she's good enough to finish the job."

It was possible for him to take such things simply and act on them, as if they were facts instead of speculations.

A moment later he added, "But the Amnion don't want *Trumpet* destroyed. They want her captured—they want her cargo back. Which means"—he looked around the bridge, faced each of his people in turn to confirm that they were prepared—"we'd better make sure we get to her first."

No one hesitated. "I'm on it, Captain," helm murmured as data and scan fed information to his board. At the same time Alesha began tapping power to charge the ship's matter cannon.

Darrin glanced at his indicators, saw that the airlock was secure. Pane and her people were out of danger.

He gave the order, and *Free Lunch*'s thrust kicked to life.

He didn't recognize what he was feeling until he looked at Alesha. From this small distance, he could see delicate beads of sweat gathering at her temples. In all the years he'd loved her, he'd only seen her perspire when she was scared.

Then he knew that he, too, was afraid.

DAVIES

"We're not closing."

Davies was on fire. Hunger, rage, and a strange species of madness were burning him up.

"We're going to lose her, Angus."

Angus didn't bother to answer.

In one sense, Davies had been living this way too long. But in another, he was dependent on it. He needed the pressures of his circumstances and his metabolism to deflect him, defend him, from the central confusion at the core of his being. He'd been born with the knowledge that he was a woman, despite what his eyes and his nerves and other people told him. He was a woman, he was *Morn,* in ways which had nothing to do with the shape of his flesh or the nature of his hormones. His bond with his mother was fundamentally false.

But if he allowed himself to dwell on the discrepancy, he would crack. The stress would burst his brain like a rotten fruit.

Unfortunately his defenses left him vulnerable to other forms of craziness.

When he'd learned that *Soar* had once been known as *Gutbuster,* the oddly fragile balance between his enhanced resources and his acute confusion had failed. He'd begun to burn inside like magnesium under water, devouring bound oxygen until he could reach atmosphere and take true fire.

Gutbuster had hit *Intransigent* with a super-light proton beam. His mother's no Morn's no *his* goddamn it *Bryony Hyland's* station in targeting control had lost structural integrity. She'd died because she'd stayed at her board to save *Intransigent*.

Davies remembered that. He'd become a cop because of it.

As a young girl, Morn Hyland had sworn in the silence of her heart that someday she would *get* that ship; avenge her mother. And she'd known how to hold a grudge. Somewhere in the depths of her aggrieved soul, beneath all the harm which Angus and Nick and the UMCP had done to her, she'd kept that purpose fresh until it was imprinted on Davies.

Now he'd lost his ability to care about anything except retribution. It seemed to eat at his sanity like vitriol. Morn was able to think about other things, take them into account: he couldn't. Instead he fulminated inwardly because Angus refused to go faster.

Trumpet was moving too slowly, following *Soar*'s particle trail and Lab Center's departure protocols too cautiously; Angus was worrying too much. Davies wanted to make the ship burn like his heart, but Angus paid no attention. Instead he concentrated on data Davies couldn't interpret, on questions Davies didn't consider worth asking.

Despite the blood on his back and the shipsuit still rucked down around his waist, Angus had never seemed more like a machine than he did right now: blind, literal, and impervious.

Davies hardly noticed when Vector left the bridge. He ignored Sib's moist anxiety as the former data first drifted around the command stations, explicitly keeping watch on Nick even though Nick could barely move. While Angus worked and Sib sweated—while Nick alternately gasped and chuckled to himself like a man fighting an internal battle which sometimes struck him as funny—Davies ran insistent course projections, feverishly comparing Angus' decisions with Lab Center's operational input and the swarm charts Deaner Beckmann had supplied; calculating and recalculating the lag between *Trumpet* and *Soar*.

"We're going to lose her," he rasped for the ten or even the twentieth time.

Angus keyed commands as if he were oblivious. "What's Morn doing?" he asked without raising his head. "What does she need Vector for?"

Davies' casts and the itch of healing fretted him: another distraction. He ground his teeth. "We're going to *lose* her. You're letting her get away."

Artificially calm, Angus looked up from his readouts.

"You're wasting my time," he told Davies flatly. "If you can't shut up, say something useful. Explain to me why Lab Center gave us exactly the same course as *Soar*."

Apparently that was true. Despite the hot static of the swarm, *Soar*'s readings matched *Trumpet*'s assigned departure too closely for the similarity to be coincidental. Every step and turn that Angus had been instructed to take between the rocks aligned itself neatly with *Soar*'s residual trail.

"Who cares?" Davies retorted bitterly. "Maybe they're too lazy to plot us a new way out. What difference does it make?"

If we already know *Soar*'s heading, we can go faster.

Sib didn't wait for Angus to answer. "It isn't normal," he put in uncomfortably. He seemed unable to relax: old anxieties kept him tense, even though Nick was effectively helpless. "Places like the Lab spread out traffic as much as they can. They don't want one ship covering another to disguise an attack. And they don't want trouble between ships. If there's trouble, they lose business, no matter who wins.

"But that's not all." Sib kept his gun in his hand. "The kind of ships that come here don't want to be too close together. They don't know who might turn out to be hostile. And they don't want anyone else to see where they're headed."

Nick let out a clenched laugh, as if he were strangling.

Angus aimed a scowl at Davies. "Sure looks like that fucker Beckmann wants us to go after *Soar*, doesn't it?" When Davies didn't reply, he went on, "The problem is, I can't figure out why. What's he got to gain? What could Chatelaine've told him that would make him want to help us sneak up behind her?

"I'm not going faster," he finished, "until I know whose game we're playing here."

Davies bit his lip so that he wouldn't shout, What *difference* does it make? Who *cares*?

God damn it, Angus, we're going to lose her!

"It's a setup," Nick croaked unexpectedly. The mention of Sorus Chatelaine's name translated him out of his self-absorption. "Beckmann's on her side. Maybe she's getting old, but I bet she can still fuck. Give her a few hours, and she'd have him eating her shit. He's setting us up."

Davies didn't listen. He couldn't. According to *Soar*'s emissions, her thrust was heavier than *Trumpet*'s. And it was working harder. *Gutbuster* was pulling away. Angus could have caught her—*Trumpet* was swift and nimble enough to catch almost anything in this swarm—but he was letting her escape.

Seething, Davies toggled his intercom, opened a ship-wide channel. He didn't know where Morn was, but he could reach her this way. She'd told Angus that they were going after *Soar*. And Angus obeyed her—Davies didn't understand or care why. He meant to call her back to the bridge so that she would make Angus carry out her orders.

Before he could speak, however, he seemed to feel her behind him as if her presence had a palpable aura which altered and defined the atmosphere around the command stations.

He turned, saw her drifting down the companionway, guiding herself with her hands on the rails.

"Morn—" he began.

The focused outrage on her face stopped him. She looked as angry as he felt: furious enough to kill.

Something had changed since she'd left to check on Mikka and Ciro.

When Angus glanced toward her, she told him, "It's worse than I thought." Her control showed in the iron lines of her face, the precise delineation of her movements. Nevertheless a tremor she couldn't suppress serrated her voice so that it cut.

Sib Mackern caught a handgrip on the bulkhead beyond the command station and froze, his face pale. Nick rolled his eyes and croaked out another chuckle.

"Meaning what?" Angus asked brusquely.

Morn floated to the back of Davies' g-seat so that she could face Angus more easily. "I don't know if he knew what he was getting Ciro into." She didn't need to say Nick's name: the focus of her anger was obvious. "Whether he did or not doesn't matter now. But it's worse than I thought."

Sib groaned softly. Angus opened his mouth, then shut it again and waited.

"Ciro—" For an instant Morn's restraint faltered. While she fought to regain it, she swung toward Nick and whispered like a lick of flame, "You did this." Then she faced Angus again.

"Sorus Chatelaine gave him a mutagen."

Sib raised a shocked hand to his mouth to keep himself from crying out. Recognition filled his eyes like nausea. Angus sat still; suddenly motionless as if all his internal functions had been suspended.

Forget it, Davies tried to say. That just gives us another reason. We already have plenty. At this rate we're never going to catch *Soar*.

But his throat refused to work. He was as crazy as Nick; strangling like Nick. Confusion he didn't want to acknowledge or confront built up against his defenses, stoking the fires. Sorus Chatelaine had killed Bryony

Hyland. She'd given Ciro a mutagen. For some reason Davies couldn't make a sound.

"Apparently it's the same one they used on her." Morn sliced out words as if her voice were a blade. "Then she handed him an antidote. That's how they control her. It doesn't stop the mutagen, it postpones it. Puts it on hold. According to her, he can stay human as long as he takes the antidote.

"She promised to keep him supplied. But first he has to sabotage *Trumpet*."

Manic triumph flashed in Nick's gaze. "It worked," he announced as if everyone on the bridge were waiting to hear what he would say. "I left the bait under her nose, and she took it. Now we can get her."

A small quiver ran through Angus. The threat to his ship seemed to bring his systems back on-line.

Ignoring Nick, he asked Morn, "He told you that?"

With his peripheral vision Davies saw Morn nod as if she were too angry to speak.

"It's perfect," Nick rasped. "She thinks we're going to be sabotaged. So we fake sabotage. Suck her in. Then we burn out her fucking heart.

"Burn out her fucking heart *at last*."

Davies wished that Nick would shut up. Nevertheless he understood how Nick felt.

If *Soar* intended to come back in for the kill, it was safe to let her pull away at first. *At last* he would have a chance to get the revenge he needed; the revenge which had set him ablaze.

"And you believe him?" Angus pursued. "Why should he tell the truth? The only way he can stay human is by doing what she wants. Now that we know, we can stop him. He's doomed."

This time Morn shook her head. "I believe him," she pronounced like a woman who was beyond question.

Angus continued facing Morn; held her gaze steadily. They looked like they were testing something between them. He didn't challenge or contradict her, however. Maybe he couldn't.

"At *last*," Nick repeated. His voice sank to a murmur as he retreated into himself.

Davies understood that, too. If Nick attended to what went on around him, he would eventually realize that he himself would play no part in the attack on *Soar*. And then his heart would surely burst.

A twitch lifted Morn's shoulders in a tight shrug. "Vector might be able to help him," she went on. "Nick's antimutagen may work. But he's so scared—" She took a deep breath to ease her distress. "Even if he survives, this could break him.

"And Mikka is doing everything she can just staying with him. I hope you won't need her for a while. If you do, we're out of luck. She isn't available."

Angus turned back to his board. "We'll manage."

That was fine with Davies. Earlier Angus had picked Mikka to be his second, but Davies yearned to have the second's station himself, ached to run targ. He didn't want to be emasculated like Nick—prevented by tape and distrust from carrying his essential passion through to its conclusion.

And yet he couldn't have named that passion, even to himself. It flamed in him as if he, too, were driven by zone implants; but somehow its significance eluded him. He called it "revenge" only because he was too confused and frantic to look at it more accurately.

No one could emasculate him: he was already a woman. Everything he knew about himself was founded on that. Therefore everything was false. His entire existence rested on a lie.

Fiercely he scratched at the edges of the cast on his arm. When he didn't ask them to do anything else, his hands hovered instinctively on the targ keys, smearing them with moisture and oil. He called his passion "revenge" so that it wouldn't destroy him.

"What does Vector think?" Sib asked tentatively. "Does he know what to do?"

Morn sighed. For a moment an old weariness seemed to well up in her. The cat she took to muffle her withdrawal may have been wearing off.

"He knows more about that antimutagen than anybody else. Maybe even Hashi Lebwohl." Slowly she relaxed against the back of Davies' g-seat. Her hand slid down the padding until it rested on her son's shoulder. "He sounded pretty confident.

"Oh, one more thing," she said as an afterthought. "There was a man with her. He helped her inject Ciro. Ciro thinks he was Milos Taverner."

As he worked, Angus' eyes betrayed a smolder of mute fury.

Davies didn't respond to her touch. Unable to contain himself, he ran another course projection, measuring *Soar*'s emissions against *Trumpet*'s route and speed. There was no question about it: *Soar* was still increasing the gap. Soon she would be so far ahead that even *Trumpet* wouldn't be able to catch her.

He would have to wait until *Gutbuster* came back to get him.

In an odd way, Ciro's plight eased his frustration. If *Trumpet* was supposed to be sabotaged, he could more easily believe that his mother's killer would return.

Twenty minutes had passed when the intercom chimed.

Angus keyed his speaker so fast that Davies didn't have time to react.

"Vector," announced the geneticist's calm voice. "I'm in sickbay. Morn? Angus?"

His tone was neutral; hinted at nothing.

"Here," Angus answered at once.

"Angus," Vector acknowledged. "This sickbay of yours is amazing. I didn't know the UMCP built them like this. You've got analytical data available here that makes some of the hospitals I've been in look stupid. And if the equipment were any better, Deaner Beckmann could use it."

With a jerk, Morn pulled herself around Davies' g-seat. As soon as she reached his board, she toggled his intercom with a stab of her thumb.

"Is it going to work?" she asked urgently.

"Oh, sorry, Morn," Vector replied. "I didn't mean to keep you in suspense. Yes, it's going to work. I've already tested a blood sample. I saw it work."

Weakly Sib breathed, "Thank God." Angus nodded to himself, but didn't betray any other reaction.

Inside his Amnion shipsuit, Davies' skin oozed sweat like heated tallow.

Sudden relief seemed to catch in Morn's throat like a sob. She made a small, choked sound and released the board so that she could cover her face with her hands. The movement sent her drifting away from the second's station, receding from Davies as if she didn't want to be near him.

As if she couldn't bear standing too close to his fury for revenge.

Come and get me, he begged the crackling seethe of the swarm and the deep cold of space. Come on—do what the Amnion keep you human for. It's me you need. The Amnion want me alive.

Believe we've been sabotaged. Come get me.

Please.

Vector wasn't done. After a moment's silence he spoke again.

"Can I ask what's going on?"

"Don't," Angus returned roughly. His eyes followed Morn's drift as if he wanted to unbelt himself and go to her, touch her—as if he thought she might be able to bear his touch. "Take care of Ciro. Make sure he's all right. Then come see for yourself. Finish coding your message. We'll transmit as soon as we get a window on Valdor. If we survive this damn swarm."

He punched off his intercom. To no one in particular, he growled, "I still want to know whose game we're playing."

When her back touched the bulkhead, Morn wiped her eyes, rubbed her palms up and down her cheeks. Then she reached for one of the zero-g grips in case Angus used navigational thrust. But she didn't answer him.

"Well, if Nick's right—" Sib began. He couldn't complete the idea, however. "I guess I don't understand. What does *Soar* gain by trying to sabotage us? She's pulling away—she'll never know if Ciro succeeded."

He looked at Nick as if he wanted Nick to explain himself. But Nick gave no sign of hearing. Motionless and unreactive, he slumped in his bonds as if he'd been overtaken by autism.

Under his breath, Angus muttered, "That won't last."

Davies didn't know whether he was talking about *Gutbuster*'s escape or Nick's withdrawal.

Nevertheless Angus was right.

After fifteen minutes or so, Vector returned to the bridge, reported that Ciro's blood was clean, and resumed working at the auxiliary engineering console. And less than half an hour later *Trumpet*'s particle sifters jumped like Davies' heart. Across the spectrum, narrow bandwidths spiked as if they were screaming. Bombarded by subatomic intensities which had nothing to do with the natural rock and static of the swarm, the sensors chimed alerts.

"Shit!" Davies gasped. His hands leaped convulsively at the data keys, capturing the readings, coding them for analysis.

Again Angus was faster. By the time Davies finished entering his commands, Angus had already begun feeding results to one of the displays.

"Jesus!" Sib panted as numbers and implications scrolled to life in front of him. "Are we hit?"

Violent jags in the readings suggested weapons fire.

"No," Angus muttered as he worked. "But there's a shock wave coming."

The sensors showed a tremendous blast building behind the first violence.

Morn tightened her grip. She didn't look at the screens—or even at Davies. Pale and intense, she kept her eyes fixed on Angus.

After a second he added, "It won't reach us. It'll have to move too much rock to get out this far."

"Then what—?" Sib tried to ask.

Wishing Morn to look at him, Davies pointed urgently at the screen. "You know what that is?"

He had the answer himself: he didn't need to hear her say it. All he wanted was her attention. He no she had made an almost obsessive study of such things in the Academy.

She was him. He hungered for her confirmation.

She shook her head as if she couldn't turn away from Angus.

"What?" Sib repeated.

Twisting against his zero-g belt, Vector studied the display. "Some kind of beam gun," he murmured curiously. "But I don't recognize the signature. Too much distortion. Some other power source is playing havoc with our reception."

"Damn right," Davies snapped. "That's the Lab's generating plant. It just blew."

Distinctly Angus growled, "It was hit by a super-light proton beam. *Soar*'s behind us."

Morn flinched as if she'd been stung.

"You mean," Sib croaked in protest, "Sorus Chatelaine just destroyed the *Lab*? She doubled back and *destroyed* it?"

Grimacing a sneer, Davies twitched his head in Nick's direction. "She took the bait. He didn't just set her up. He set up the whole installation. She works for the Amnion. One reason she's here is to make sure nobody finds out about our antimutagen." Morn, *look* at me. "The Lab was doomed as soon as Nick started talking to Beckmann."

Nick, of course, hadn't given Deaner Beckmann any warning.

"They must have trusted her enough to let her inside their guns. They didn't have anything that could protect them from a super-light proton cannon."

Intransigent herself had barely survived.

"All those people," Morn breathed. "*All those people.*" She seemed to shrink in dismay, as if the shock belittled her. "Nick, what have you *done?*"

Nick's eyes flipped open. Slowly he raised his head and started grinning like a skull.

"There isn't likely to be another ship with that kind of cannon around here," Angus continued. "It's got to be *Soar*. So now she's behind us." With a shrug, he finished, "If Ciro sabotaged the drives, she wouldn't have any trouble catching us."

Sib chewed his mustache. "What're we going to do?"

A shiver of intensification ran through Nick. "Let me loose," he offered.

Apparently only Davies heard him. Vector, Sib, Morn, and Angus acted like he hadn't spoken.

"You know," Vector put in, "the thing that's always amazed me about illegals—including myself, of course—is the amount of ingenuity we're willing to expend so that we can get ourselves into trouble. It's staggering." As he talked, he keyed off the console, unclipped his belt, and drifted free. A push of his foot moved him toward the command station. His tone sharpened. "Deaner Beckmann was a brilliant man. A little wrongheaded, in my opinion, but brilliant. Half the people there were brilliant. And now every one of them—"

He swallowed hard and hunched over his chest as if emotions he'd forgotten long ago were crowding out of his heart. Distress occluded his blue gaze.

"Let me loose," Nick repeated. His tone hinted at fever or hysteria. "I'll stop her."

Vector caught himself on the arm of Angus' g-seat. Like Davies, he seemed to want Morn to look at him. Yet she focused on Angus as if he were the only one who mattered, the only one who existed; the only one who could help her.

"I think we should get out of here," Vector told her and Angus. His voice shook. "Run for open space and start broadcasting. Beckmann and his people were killed because they knew about the mutagen immunity drug. Our only real defense is to tell more people. Tell everybody. If we fight, we might lose. Then the Amnion win, and every one of us will have died for nothing."

"No!" Davies protested instantly. His inner fire spiked like the readings on *Soar*'s cannon. "You can't do that!" She killed my mother! "We have to hit her. Now, in the swarm, where we have the advantage"—where *Trumpet*'s agility could be most effective—"and she thinks we've been sabotaged. We'll never get another chance like this."

Words weren't enough. He couldn't articulate the fire. Only his hands on the targ keys would be able to do that.

At last Morn turned toward him. Stricken and reduced, she gazed at him with an ache in her eyes. Pain compressed her mouth. Softly she sighed, "Oh, Davies," as if she were grieving.

"I did this," Nick insisted more vehemently. "It's mine. Let me loose."

Angus cocked an eyebrow at his son. "You don't think Vector makes sense?" He might have been jeering.

A cry mounted in Davies' nerves, strained against the muscles of his throat. Don't you understand? I don't *care* if he makes sense! I don't *care* what it costs. *Soar* killed my mother. If we don't go after her, I'm *nothing*. That's all I have.

He restrained himself somehow. "Morn's already made her decision," he retorted weakly. "We're going after *Soar*." To his own ears he sounded small and useless, like a beaten kid, but he didn't know how else to defend what he needed. Morn was watching him with misery on her face, as if he'd failed her. "We're going after *Soar*," he repeated. "She's killed too many people. We're cops, we can't run away from this."

Abruptly he stopped in a flash of inspiration. His fire burned so hotly that it exalted him. Instead of protesting further, he said the only thing he could think of which might sway Angus.

"She has Milos Taverner with her."

When Davies said that name, old rage smoldered again in Angus' yellow eyes. His hate was almost autonomic: so visceral that even his zone implants couldn't control it. His mouth twisted as if he were remembering hurts which sickened him.

"It might be a good thing," he muttered, "to put Sorus Chatelaine out of her misery."

"Let me loose," Nick insisted. His fever was plain in his voice. "I'll stop her. I know what to do."

"That does it," Sib announced; unnaturally harsh and sure. "I don't want to listen to this anymore. I'm going to gag him."

Grimly Sib shoved his gun into one pocket and retrieved his roll of strapping tape from another.

"No!" Davies protested again. "Don't." Intuition ruled him now, as commanding as flame. Because he was desperate, he could see possibilities— "We need him."

Slapping at the clasp of his belts, he freed himself and swung out of the second's station to intercept Sib.

Sib stopped, stared at him in consternation. Morn opened her mouth as if she wanted to object. Vector must have swayed her; she wasn't on Davies' side any longer; she withdrew her support just when he needed it most. But instead of speaking she only watched him with dumb sorrow in her eyes.

"Him?" Angus snorted in scorn. "You mean Captain Sheepfucker? We must be in worse trouble than I thought. What in hell do we need *him* for?"

Davies didn't try to answer. When he saw Sib stop, he redirected his momentum toward Nick.

Nick rested against the rear bulkhead in a crumpled stance, as if his bonds prevented him from straightening his back. So that he wouldn't turn into a projectile when *Trumpet* maneuvered, Sib had strapped one of his arms to a handgrip: he dangled there like a dressed beast.

In a strange way, he looked like he'd been blinded by his scars. Their craziness consumed his gaze completely. Passion throbbed in them as if they were all he had left.

Davies caught himself on the front of Nick's shipsuit.

Nick leered back at him from under his eyebrows.

Ignoring the pressure of Morn's dismay and Angus' disdain, Davies met Nick's eyes.

"How?" he demanded. "How would you stop her?"

Nick replied with an immured grin. "Let me loose."

"Sure," Davies returned sharply; desperately. "Let you loose. Give you another chance to kill us all. Try to imagine Angus doing that. Try to imagine Morn doing it. Use your head, Nick. We're going to keep you trussed up here until you rot.

"You said you know what to do. I don't believe you. How could you stop her?"

A look of manic calculation came into Nick's gaze. He glanced past Davies' shoulders at Angus, at Morn, then focused on Davies again. Slowly his chin came up.

"Let me loose," he repeated in a conspiratorial whisper, as if he didn't want Angus or Morn to hear him. "Give me a gun. A laser rifle—a big one. And an EVA suit."

"Oh, perfect," Davies snapped. "What a great idea. That way you can fry us all without having to worry about it if you damage *Trumpet*'s integrity."

Nick shook his head impatiently. "Send me outside. Leave me. I'll stop her.

"She's following us," he breathed to Davies' hunger. Husky and strained, his voice throbbed with his own desperation. "She knows where we are. Lab Center assigned us the same protocols. She'll come after us on the same course.

"Leave me outside. I'll wait for her. She won't see me because she won't look." His chest heaved. "I'll peel her open like a bloated carcass. By the time she knows I'm there, she'll be venting so much atmosphere she won't be able to keep up with it. Then I'll cut my way inside. I'll cut her heart out—I'll give her scars she can't live with.

"Let me loose." He showed Davies his teeth. "I want to kill her."

Angus laughed like cracking wood. "You're out of your mind, Captain Sheepfucker. *Soar* is too big. She can absorb all the damage one laser rifle would do. You won't even slow her down."

Vector nodded. "You must think we've all lost our minds. How do you expect us to believe you won't start shooting at us as soon as you get your hands on any kind of gun?"

Davies didn't care what they said. He waited to hear Morn.

Vector fell silent. Angus didn't go on. Sib said nothing. Everyone on the bridge waited.

After a moment she cleared her throat.

"Davies," she murmured thinly, "this is impossible." The crime which Nick and Sorus had committed against the Lab distressed her too much: she couldn't see what was at stake. "What's happening to you? You want to get *Soar*. I understand. But if that means you're ready to start trusting Nick—"

Her voice trailed away as if she were sinking down to some inconsolable place where he would never be able to reach her.

Davies didn't turn. If he looked at her and saw that she was beyond reach, his veins would burst.

"*No!*" he shouted into Nick's madness. "I *understand* him—I understand him better than *you* do! I remember what *you* remember." The harm Nick had done to her was acid-etched in the channels of his brain. "And I'm *male*. Whatever that means. I know what he'll do!

"He needs this too much."

Nick's blind craziness urged him on. At the same time, however, it helped him control himself. He stopped shouting. Instead he spoke in a guttural rasp from the center of his chest.

"He won't bother to turn on us. We don't matter. We never did. Sorus Chatelaine is everything. She's all there ever was."

Nick nodded as if Davies' recognition pleased him.

"If we don't try to get *Soar*," Davies continued roughly, "if we can stand being that ashamed of ourselves, we might as well go into hiding for the rest of our lives." At last he let go of Nick so that he could confront the rest of the bridge. "She'll hunt us forever.

"But if we do try to get her, he can help us. He can hit her while she still thinks Ciro might have sabotaged us."

Let him pay for his own crimes. And give us a better chance.

Morn clenched her free hand in her hair and pulled as if she wanted to tug her mind out by the roots. "Do you think so?" she countered. "Look at him." Her eyes were full of darkness as she studied her son. "Do you like what you see? He isn't here anymore. There's nothing left of him. He died when he lost his ship. That's what's wrong with revenge. It kills you. It's just another kind of suicide."

God damn you, Davies groaned to himself. I backed you when you decided to free Angus. When you finally made up your mind, I stood with you. Why can't you stand with me?

He ignored her protest. Instead he retorted softly, "Do you really think it's *preferable* to keep him tied up here like a piece of meat?"

More than anything he'd said, that appeared to affect the people around him. Angus growled deep in his throat, but didn't argue. Vector blinked as if he were abashed; as if everything that happened surprised him with new emotions.

Pale and tense, Sib stared at his hands. He held the gun in one, his roll of tape in the other. He might have been weighing one against the other; choosing his fate.

The gun was heavier. Abruptly he shoved the tape back into his pocket, lifted his head. A cornered look gleamed like sweat on his pale features.

"I'll go with him," he announced. "Make sure he doesn't turn against you."

Vector and Morn gaped at him in shock.

"You're right, he can't destroy her." Shivers of apprehension ran through his voice. "But he could do some damage. He might hurt her enough so that you can beat her." His throat closed involuntarily. He needed a moment before he could force himself to say, "When you're done, you can come back for me."

"Motherfucker," Angus muttered to no one in particular. "Motherfucking sonofabitch. It might help."

"*Sib,*" Morn cried quietly. She was weeping again. Small constellations of tears drifted in front of her face; pieces of loss. "You don't have to do that. It's too much. What if something goes wrong? What if we don't find you in time?

"*What if she takes you?*"

What if she captures you and gives you one of her mutagens?

Sib shrugged as if he were breaking inside. "I've been afraid all my life. I've let the Amnion have too many people. I need to make up for it.

"When I let you out of your cabin, that was a start. Now I can't quit.

"And I think Davies is right. We have to stop *Soar* somehow. We can't just run away from her. She's too dangerous.

"If I go with Nick, I can protect you. And maybe I can help him damage her."

"Sure," Nick pronounced with approval. "Sure."

Morn turned away as if she couldn't bear to look at the men around her anymore.

Vector studied her for a moment, his concern plain on his face. Then he turned to Angus. "We ought to make a decision—while we still have time." Unfamiliar dismay and anger plucked at the corners of his mouth. "I've told you what I think. You've heard Davies, Nick, and Sib. Now I guess it's up to you.

"What're we going to do?"

Angus bared his teeth, unconsciously mimicking Nick's grin. He didn't hesitate. A feral light shone on his features as he swung toward Davies and Nick; put his back to Morn.

"I want to get rid of Succorso," he answered. "I would have done it myself already, but my programming won't let me. I want to pay back that fat bastard Taverner somehow. And I want help against *Soar*. That proton cannon is a hell of a gun. I don't like tackling her without—something extra.

"We'll take a chance. See if Captain Sheepfucker's as crazy as Davies says he is."

He considered Sib momentarily. Then he told Vector, "I don't need him. If he wants to cover us, I say let him."

Sib sighed as if he'd hoped Angus would refuse him.

Davies ducked his head to conceal a relief so intense that it brought tears to his eyes.

Without pausing Angus ran a command on his board, wheeled his station so that he could see the results on the screen. "We're coming up on a rock you can use. It's big enough to hide behind—not so big it'll get in your way. Time to move."

He aimed a glare at Sib. "Get it right," he growled. "If you screw up, we're all going to feel like shit.

"Take him to the EVA locker. Strap his arms behind him after he puts on a suit. You carry the guns. I'll take you close—you can drift to the rock. If you need them, the suits have jets. Don't cut him loose until we're out of range. After that he probably won't turn on you. If he isn't completely crazy, he'll realize he might need you.

"We won't be able to talk to you for long. Too much rock and static in the way. And we don't have Beckmann's relay net. But those suits have distress beepers we can use to find you later. If we don't come back, it'll be because we can't."

Angus made a rough gesture of dismissal. "Go."

Deliberately he began concentrating on his board as if Sib and Nick were already gone.

Davies scrubbed his eyes clear. For a short time, at least, his relief had changed everything. The fire in him had been temporarily appeased. In its place he felt abashed at the scale of the risk Sib had agreed to take.

Because he needed to express his gratitude somehow, he moved to help Sib with Nick.

Sib nodded as Davies untaped Nick from the handgrip, but he didn't say anything. His determination took the form of a dumb misery with no other outlet. His skin was damp with anxiety: the moisture in his eyes was liquid fear.

Nick paid no attention to them. He was murmuring to himself, happily repeating the same phrases and sentences over and over again. "Poor bitch. She's dead, and she doesn't even know it yet. She's laughed at me for the last time. Poor bitch."

Together Sib and Davies steered him to the companionway.

"Davies."

Morn's low voice stopped him like a hand on his shoulder. Bracing himself against the rail, he turned to look at her.

"What's happening to you?" she asked for the second time. Her eyes were as dark as gaps opening on the abyss between the stars. "Who are you?"

At once his relief died: flames leaped up to devour it. A blaze that might have been rage filled him like his father's hate. When he needed her, she turned her back on him. Instead of backing him, helping him, she was afraid of him.

"As far as I can tell," he answered her, grinding the words between his teeth, "I'm Bryony Hyland's daughter. The one she used to have—before you sold your soul for a zone implant."

Leaving a sting of bitterness in the air behind him, he tugged Nick and Sib up the companionway off the bridge.

SIB

Sib Mackern wanted to be spared.

In retrospect, he thought that must have been what he'd wanted his entire life. Perhaps it was because he'd been spared so little. Unheeded supplication was his whole story.

Spare me.

No.

Right from the beginning—

His name was short for "Sibal": his mother had wished for a girl. Ever since he'd become conscious of it, he'd wanted to be spared his own name.

No.

He'd never liked data work, never liked space or ships. In particular he hadn't liked his family's orehauler. Spare me, he'd said—not in so many words, but in every other way he could think of. Nevertheless his father had compelled him, because he was needed. And that had led him to the one crucial occasion on which he'd tried to spare himself.

When an illegal had peeled upon the orehauler, he'd hidden between the hulls in an EVA suit. At the time he'd had the crazy idea that he might reach one of the guns and use it. An idea as crazy as Nick's. *That's the only reason I'm still here*, he'd told Morn and Davies. *Still human—*

We weren't killed. Instead of killing us, they lined us up and started injecting us with mutagens.

I saw everything. If they were just being killed, I would have gone back inside and tried to fight for them. I might have. I was desperate enough. But I saw them injected. I saw them change. It paralyzed me.

Then he'd started screaming. He hadn't been able to stop. But first he'd deactivated his suit pickup.

Sparing himself—

He'd gone on screaming until he'd lost his voice. He was irrationally sure that as long as he could hear his own voice he wouldn't be turned Amnion just by watching his family mutate.

Of course, events had shown that there was a price to pay for being spared. Always. Inevitably. He'd been rescued by a pirate looking for illegal salvage. That had been bad enough. But a few years later, still hoping to evade his endless fear, he'd tried to change his fate by joining Nick Succorso.

Crime after crime, Nick had taught him to hear that implacable *no* whenever he found himself begging the blank stars for mercy he couldn't have and probably didn't deserve.

In a sense, when he'd first turned against Nick by helping Morn out of her cabin, he might have been trying to deserve what was going to happen to him anyway.

Now he was doing it again. Only this time it was much worse. This time he was helping Davies guide Nick along *Trumpet*'s central passage toward the suit locker. He was going to go EVA *again* in the wild hope that he would be able to protect the people he cared about *again*. And he was doing it in the company of the man he feared and distrusted most. He could feel everything inside him sweating with horror.

Spare me.

No.

He must have been out of his mind.

"She's dead," Nick muttered cheerfully, "and she doesn't even know it. Poor bitch."

Davies ignored Nick. As they passed sickbay, he said suddenly, "Just a minute." Releasing Nick, he opened the door and went inside. When he came back out, he had a scalpel in his hand. "For cutting tape," he explained.

"She's laughed at me for the last time," Nick promised nonchalantly.

Steering him between them, Sib and Davies moved on to the suit locker.

Indicators above the compartment showed that it was unlocked: Angus had entered the necessary codes from the bridge. Sib and Davies positioned Nick in front of the locker. Then Sib drifted a meter or two away and drew his handgun while Davies began slashing Nick's bonds.

As soon as his arms came free, Nick stopped muttering.

In a spasm of activity, he stripped the rest of the tape off his limbs, wadded it up, flung it away. At once Davies floated out of reach. Instinctively Sib tightened his grip on the gun. He couldn't hold it steady—he'd never been any good with firearms—but he hoped Nick would believe that he couldn't miss at this range, no matter how much he wavered.

Nick stretched his arms, twisted his back until his spine cracked. "That's better," he announced. "Now we're getting somewhere."

Without transition he looked like his old self—confident, cunning, and unbeatable. All sign of the tic which had once distorted his insouciance was gone. He cocked an eyebrow at Sib's gun, bent his mouth in mock chagrin, then chuckled to himself and turned to open the suit locker.

"Which one did I wear last time?" he asked rhetorically. "Oh, here it is."

Whistling tunelessly through his teeth, he pulled an EVA suit from its hangers and began climbing into it.

He checked the suit's indicators and seals casually, as if he already knew that nothing could go wrong. The helmet went over his head and locked into place. He snapped the faceplate shut; his features slowly vanished as he tuned the plate's reflective surface. With a hiss, air processing inflated the suit.

"Are you ready?" Sib asked, although he wasn't sure that Nick could hear him.

But Nick had activated his suit's transceivers. His external speaker crackled. "Do it," he instructed. "I want to get this part over with."

He put his arms behind him, making it easy for Sib and Davies to bind him.

His confidence scared Sib almost as badly as what they were planning to do. But Sib had made this decision himself: he needed to go through with it. If he didn't, the pain of being refused mercy *again* would be more than he could bear.

He tossed his roll of tape to Davies and kept his gun aimed at Nick while Davies strapped Nick's arms.

Then it was his turn. He didn't hesitate: he'd been hesitant all his life, and it only made matters worse. There was a price to pay for being spared. Always. Inevitably. He gave his handgun to Davies, picked out an EVA suit, and settled into it.

The sensation of the waldo harness around his hips reminded him that he hadn't been able to control his maneuvering jets on Thanatos

Minor. Maybe they would be easier to use in zero g. Or maybe he would misfire them; send himself tumbling away from the ship and Nick, out of reach, beyond hope—

If that happened, he would have to beg *Trumpet* to save him.

He trusted Morn and Davies. He trusted Mikka and Vector. Nevertheless he already knew the answer.

Spare me.

No.

"Give me a line of tape," he told Davies, "so I can hold on to him. I'm no good with these jets. If we're separated, I might not be able to get back to him."

Davies nodded: he'd seen Sib's difficulties on Thanatos Minor. While Sib finished checking his suit and sealing himself into his helmet, Davies attached ten meters of tape to Nick's wrists and folded it over its adhesive to form a rope.

His suit's air processor built pressure in Sib's lungs. The indicators inside his helmet told him that the suit's atmosphere was identical to *Trumpet*'s. Still he felt that he couldn't breathe. With the controls on his chestplate, he reduced the volume of air, increased the proportion of oxygen. Gradually some of his claustrophobia eased.

He'd forgotten to toggle his transceivers. Davies moved his mouth soundlessly for a moment, then reached out to key a frequency on Sib's chestplate. At once the internal speaker came to life.

"Pay attention, Sib," Nick said. "If you can't hear me, we might as well stay here. We'll be useless."

At the same time Sib heard Davies say, "I'll give Angus your frequency. We'll hear you as long as you're in range. Which won't be more than a few minutes under these conditions. But if you need help during that time, we can probably do something."

Sib nodded dumbly, then realized that Davies couldn't see his face. Swallowing against the dryness in his throat, he replied, "All right."

Davies moved to the nearest intercom to talk to Angus. He kept the gun pointed at Nick's head.

Because he'd left himself no choice, Sib drifted past them toward the weapons locker.

Angus coded the locker open as Sib reached it. Determined not to hesitate, not to freeze—not to let the vast cold outside the ship consume him—Sib selected a laser rifle the size of a portable missile launcher for Nick, picked a smaller rifle for himself. Without waiting for Nick's approval, he closed the locker.

"Fine," Nick pronounced as soon as he saw Sib's choices. "If I can't cut into Sorus with that, I'm wasting my time. That matter cannon Angus lugs around doesn't hold enough charge."

"They're ready, Angus," Davies told the intercom. "We're going to the lift now."

Ready? Sib thought. Ready? He wasn't sure the word made sense. Had he ever been ready for anything?

But Nick was ready. Even though his arms were taped behind him, he seemed primed for action. He kicked himself in the direction of the lift before Davies finished talking to Angus.

Sib followed as if he were being tugged along by Nick's eagerness.

The lift was waiting. By the time Sib and then Davies reached it, Nick had already entered the car.

The bulk of the rifles made Sib awkward. He missed his hold and carried past the lift. Floundering, he tried to recover, but his momentum took him down the passage. The suit's humidity indicators climbed as he sweated and gasped.

Davies caught him. He gave Sib a look like one of Angus' glares, angry or contemptuous, and steered him back to the lift.

"Thanks," Sib murmured, nearly panting.

Covering Nick with his handgun, Davies guided Sib into the car and keyed the door shut.

Nick's snort seemed to fill the inside of Sib's helmet with scorn. "I told you to pay attention. This is getting ridiculous. If you navigate out there as well as you do in here, you'd better cut my arms free and give me that rifle right now. You might not get another chance."

"Stop it, Nick," Davies snapped. "If he weren't going with you, we wouldn't let you do this at all. You would still be tied up, and whatever happens to *Soar* would happen without you."

Nick gave a short laugh like a burst of static, but he didn't retort.

As the lift slid upward, Davies activated the intercom. "We're at the airlock," he reported. No doubt Angus already knew this: he could see it on his maintenance status readouts. Apparently Davies kept talking to control his own tension. "I'll wait in the lift until they're off the ship. And I'm keeping the gun. If Nick tries anything in the lock, I might be able to stop him."

Again Nick laughed roughly.

"Sib?" Morn put in unexpectedly. "Can you hear me?" Her voice sounded anxious through the speakers; too personal to be meant for him.

"Yes, Morn."

He might have been choking. The pressure in his suit still felt high. He resisted an impulse to lower it further.

"Sib," Morn replied as if she were in a hurry; as if she, too, feared freezing. "I just wanted to say thank you. I don't know why you think you're not brave. You help me when I need it. It's never easy—it wouldn't be easy if you were crazy with courage. But you do it anyway."

Spare me, Sib thought. Misery kept him mute.

"As far as I'm concerned," Morn finished, "that's better than being brave."

"Please," Nick put in cheerfully. "Let's not get all mushy here. This is supposed to be fun."

Davies snarled a low curse, but Nick ignored him.

"Two minutes," Angus announced. "Get in the airlock. We're coming up on that asteroid. If you miss it, I'll have to double back."

"Right." Davies thumbed the intercom and began entering codes to open the doors between the lift and the airlock. While the doors slid aside, he turned to Sib.

He showed Sib his scalpel, then tucked it into a utility pouch on the belt of Sib's suit. "In case you don't feel like lasering that tape off his arms," he explained.

Once again Sib nodded invisibly inside his helmet.

"Come on," Nick commanded. Bumping a shoulder against the wall of the car for thrust, he pushed himself through the doors.

In spite of himself, Sib hesitated. He knew too well what he was getting into. This was his last chance to change his mind: right here, before the airlock sealed and started decompression. He could free Nick's arms, hand Nick the rifle; he could stay with Davies while Nick carried his lifelong hatred of Sorus Chatelaine to its logical conclusion.

He could avoid the cold dark and the memory of his own raw screams. Leave someone else to strike out at the Amnion for the harm they'd done to Ciro and Morn and his whole family.

You do it anyway. That's better than being brave.

Certainly it was better than begging for mercy and being refused over and over again while the people he loved died or worse because he couldn't defend them.

"Say good-bye to Mikka and Ciro for me," he told Davies. "I'm glad I knew them."

Davies didn't say, You'll see them again. We'll get you back. Maybe he didn't believe it.

Swallowing terror, Sib coasted into the airlock.

Angus' voice spattered in his ears. "Do it now."

At once Davies turned to the control panel. Servos pulled the doors shut with a solid, interlocking thunk; sealed Sib alone with Nick. A moment later the EVA suits distended as pumps sucked air out of the lock.

"Don't look so pitiful," Nick gibed. He couldn't see Sib's face, any more than Sib could see his: he was talking to be heard on the bridge. "This is going to be the goddamn highlight of your life. From here on all you have to do is cover my back. They'll think you're a fucking hero, even if the only thing you really do is fill your suit with shit."

"God damn it, Nick—" Morn began. And Davies barked, "Back off, you bastard! If he doesn't cut your arms loose, you're still helpless."

But Sib didn't care what Nick said. All that mattered now was the outer seal of the airlock—the last thin doors between him and black space. They eased aside when all the air was gone, opening *Trumpet* to the deadly, imponderable rush of the swarm.

He saw midnight outside. Unseen shapes and ineffable seething crowded the dark. A momentary glare of static limned the rock Angus had chosen with strange fire. Then the light vanished, making the darkness deeper.

"Let's *go*," Nick breathed urgently.

Awkward because of the guns he carried, Sib turned on his suit's headlamps. Around one gloved fist he wrapped the end of the line which Davies had attached to Nick's bonds.

"OK," he croaked out.

At once Nick cocked his hips, fired his jets.

Gusts of gas and the line of tape pulled Sib like cargo from the airlock into the absolute cold of the asteroid swarm.

He could scarcely remember what happened next. The racket of his pulse and the labor of his breathing must have deafened his brain; fear must have blinded it. Momentary fragments came back to him—drifting in the bottomless dark, pressure on the line he gripped for his life, Nick's harsh voice—and then faded again; he couldn't retain them. Nothing stayed in his head except the echo of old screams until after he'd spent half an hour clinging to the rock at Nick's side, anchored by compression pitons while he watched the elaborate aftermath of the Lab's destruction flare and blaze like a distant light show.

Nick must have pulled him to the asteroid: he couldn't have managed that on his own. *I kept on screaming until I lost my voice*. Apparently he'd cut Nick's bonds, surrendered one of the guns: Nick's arms cradled the laser rifle in front of him, and the tape was gone. *I thought as long as I could hear myself I wouldn't go insane.* Probably someone—Nick or a voice from *Trumpet*—had told him there were pitons in his utility pouch. *Afraid I might be turned into an Amnioni just by watching it happen to my family.* Otherwise how would he have known?

None of it had to happen.

On the other hand, he didn't need anyone to explain the light. He seemed to understand it by direct intuition, as if the raw glare and glow of coruscation from deep within the swarm found echoes among his recollections of dismay. He'd been *Captain's Fancy*'s data first: he had at least a theoretical understanding of super-light proton cannon. And he could easily imagine what kind of nuclear furnace had powered Deaner Beckmann's domain. The forces devouring the Lab wouldn't burn themselves out until every attainable particle of matter had been cracked open and consumed. Fed with static generated by the complex boil of the swarm, those forces crackled in the pit of the dark like lightning and St. Elmo's fire gone mad. Blast after blast, light etched the asteroids in the distance until they seemed to writhe, hurt like living tissue by the fury they absorbed. And after each blast, lingering pressure in his optic nerves left him utterly blind.

I saw everything. If they were just being killed, I would have gone back inside and tried to fight for them. But I saw them injected.

Recollection froze him like the total cold of the void.

Trumpet was long gone. Her voices in his helmet had broken up and then faded some time ago; he wasn't sure when.

But *Soar* was coming. If she survived the havoc she'd made of Deaner Beckmann's installation—

"Jesus," Nick breathed as if he were proud of himself. "Isn't that something? I've never seen anything like it.

"I've been waiting for this all my life. I'm going to light a fire like that in her heart. When she dies, she'll consider hell an improvement."

Nick was crazy: Sib knew that. No matter how totally they took Sorus Chatelaine by surprise, one or even two laser rifles simply could not do a ship *Soar*'s size all the damage Nick hungered for. Nevertheless Sib didn't argue. He no longer cared what Nick said. Deep inside himself, he concentrated on holding his thoughts and memories and actions together so that finally—for perhaps the first time—he could choose what happened to him.

His life had come to this. There was nothing else left.

After watching the Lab's lambent, unsteady ruin for a few more minutes, Sib asked, "When will we feel the shock wave?"

"We won't." Nick was sure. Over the years he'd claimed any number of times that he could do algorithms in his head. "Captain Thermo-pile was right about that. There's too much rock in the way—too much inertia. It'll absorb the actual concussion. We can relax, enjoy the show." He might have been talking about some naive bit of theater.

"What about *Soar*?" Sib pursued. "She must have been sitting right on top of that blast. What did it do to her?"

Nick turned toward Sib. His headlamps shed smears of refraction down Sib's polarized faceplate.

"Sib Mackern," he snorted, "you never fail to amaze me. You are so fucking *slow*. Don't you get it? Has this whole sequence of events"—he sneered the words—"gone over your head?

"She didn't need to use a super-light proton beam. She could have hit Beckmann with matter cannon and not made it so absolutely fucking obvious who was doing it. But then his power plant wouldn't have blown.

"She used her damn proton gun because she wanted that explosion. She wanted the shock wave.

"Sure, it's going to scrub out our particle trace. It'll erase every decipherable emission in the whole sector." His voice was heavy with contempt for his companion. "But she doesn't need to track us. She knows our course. All she has to do is clean the garbage out of the way and come after us.

"That's what this blast is for. If she burns just right, she can ride the wave front—let it clear the way and carry her along at maybe five or six times *Trumpet*'s velocity. Of course, she'll have to brake as the front dissipates, do her own work after that. But in the meantime she'll cover a lot of distance."

As if Sorus Chatelaine's ingenuity pleased him, he finished, "She probably gained two hours in the first ten seconds after she fired that damn cannon."

Oh, God, Sib panted to himself. New fears crawled around his abdomen. "You mean—"

"That's right," Nick jeered. "She's going to get here long before you figure out how to be as brave as that shit-crazy bitch"—he didn't need to say Morn's name—"thinks you are."

Light throbbed and glowered in the heart of the swarm. Secondary discharges traced jagged lines from rim to rim of Sib's vision, defining impossible horizons. The aftermath of the Lab's destruction appeared to be generating its own coriolus forces, mounting in savagery instead of diminishing—

Soar might come into range at any time.

"In that case," Sib said thinly, "you'd better tell me what we're going to do."

The sudden vehemence of Nick's reaction nearly pulled him free of his anchor. "*You* aren't going to do *anything*," he rasped inside Sib's helmet. "You're a self-righteous, mutineering asshole, and I'm sick to death of you. I'm sick of you and Vector and Mikka and all you bastards who think you have a right to do anything except take orders. I will *fry* you before I let you interfere with me.

"Are you listening to me? You can hang on to that little squirt gun. If you want, you can stick it in your mouth and suck on it. But Sorus Chatelaine is *mine*. You are going to stay right where you fucking are and keep out of my fucking way."

Sib's rifle pointed at Nick's chest. He didn't want to be killed here, now, while unresolved fears filled his head, and he could still hear himself screaming. The idea that Nick intended to spare him closed around his heart like the cold of space.

Nick didn't want him to do anything. He could wait where he was while *Soar* passed by. Stay alive: stay out of Sorus Chatelaine's hands. If *Trumpet* came back for him, he would know mercy at last.

It might happen. If he let it.

Half an hour passed. More? Less? He didn't know. Gradually he concluded that the Lab's death storm was lessening. Light still streaked like cries through the chaos of rock, but by degrees it lost its garish intensity. The Lab was gone, burned down to its atoms and discharged into the void. The illumination would die when it exhausted its final fuel.

Nick had begun murmuring over and over again, "Anytime now," repeating himself as if he were unaware that Sib could hear him. "Anytime now. Count the minutes, bitch. You don't have many left."

Sib didn't listen. In this place—small as an atom himself within the jostling confusion of the swarm—he could believe that the moral order of his life might be overturned.

He caught his first glimpse of the ship because she seemed to emerge straight from the heart of the Lab's diminished deflagration; created by violence and ravage. Backlit with fire, she loomed out of the dark like a black behemoth, dwarfing Sib and Nick and the asteroid to which they clung; dwarfing every chunk of rock in the vicinity.

"There!" Nick announced in a husky whisper, as if his voice was stuck in his throat, trapped by passions he couldn't swallow.

Her lights were on, searching the vacuum around her: no sane captain navigated an asteroid swarm without using video to complement scan, in case some freak emission echo or sensor glitch masked an obstacle. In a few moments Sib saw her outlines clearly. Roughly ovoid, studded with antennae, receptors, dishes, and gun ports, and sliding forward without a sound, as if she floated on oil, she soon seemed to fill the visual window of his faceplate, even though she was still two or three k away.

Her lights showed the scars of old battles, the marks of fresh damage. One dent licked along her prow; another left an impression like a crater amidships. And farther back her hull had been holed: torn metal opened on darkness inside her. A cargo bay, Sib guessed.

That was the way in. If the interior bulkheads could be cut, one or two laser rifles might actually do the ship some harm. Not enough to stop her; but maybe enough to slow her down—weaken her.

He'd stopped sweating. His suit indicators warned that he was in danger of dehydration.

Keep out of my fucking way.

He still didn't have an answer. He'd spent years obeying—and fearing—Nick.

Nick crouched against his pitons. His helmet cocked back and forth as he studied *Soar*, measured her progress, then checked his rifle to confirm that it was fully charged.

"Cut me, will you?" he muttered. "Come on, bitch. Just a little closer. Come find out what that costs."

He didn't speak to Sib again. As far as Sib could tell, Nick had forgotten that he existed.

"It's time to pay."

The ship was less than a kilometer away when Nick released his pitons, launched himself with a kick toward her looming bulk. He didn't use his jets; didn't need them. Instead he coasted like a stone for the huge ship.

Sib watched with his heart full of old cries. Despite the warmth of his suit, he could feel black cold soaking into him.

Stay right where you fucking are. Let *Soar* go on past. Stay alive alone in the dark. Hope that the resources of his suit held out until *Trumpet* could come back for him; that *Trumpet* survived long enough, or cared enough, to come back for him.

Or go. Defy Nick one last time; stop begging to be spared. Try to strike some kind of blow for all the people he loved.

You do it anyway. Maybe that was true. Maybe Morn had made it true by saying it aloud.

If he let Nick spare him, he would have to pay for it.

Nick sailed away. Every few seconds *Soar*'s lights touched him, gleaming along his suit like a hint of stars. He'd aimed himself well ahead of the ship: his trajectory looked like it would intersect hers in another moment or two.

Sib didn't wait for mercy. He said *no* himself.

Jamming his feet under him, he thrust off from the asteroid.

He didn't breathe. He wasn't sure there was still air in his suit. He couldn't tell whether he'd jumped straight or hard enough to reach the ship. He concentrated on Nick as if he thought that Nick could somehow draw him where he needed to go.

Adrift like a mote in the rush of the swarm, he sailed toward the huge ship.

Now he saw that Nick wasn't heading for the breached cargo bay in *Soar*'s flank. Instead he aimed at her prow. As fatal as spikes, her forward guns jutted from their ports—sleek laser tubes, massive matter cannon shafts, complex proton emitters.

Somehow Sib had contrived to jump in the right direction. Several heartbeats ahead of him, Nick reached the hull, caught a handgrip. Sib would touch the ship himself no more than five meters away from Nick.

But there weren't any handgrips on the surface ahead of him.

Hit; bounce off; drift away— Back out into the swarm. The ship would glide past him, leaving him in the void.

No. His boots could generate a magnetic field. Any decent suit had that capability: it was essential to EVA survival.

He slapped the switch and flipped into a somersault.

When his boots touched metal, they held.

At some point he started breathing again. For what seemed like ages, relief and anoxia left him blind; he couldn't focus his eyes.

But it was time. Here and now. No more hesitation. No more paralysis. Time to strike his blow.

He blinked his vision clear.

His laser rifle was too small. It would take long minutes to burn into *Soar*'s outer hull; or damage even one of her guns. But there were other targets—

By the illumination of his headlamps and *Soar*'s running lights, he scanned the surface of the ship for particle sifters, cameras, receptor dishes; anything vulnerable.

There: a video camera; one of several searching the dark.

He pointed his rifle, clasped the firing stud. First he missed. Then a red slash slagged the camera from its mounts.

A blow. Sib bared his teeth. It wasn't much, but it was *some*thing. Something he'd never done before. If he'd had the chance, he might have yelled aloud until his mute, screaming fear became a howl of defiance.

Nick cut him off.

"I warned you."

He wheeled; saw Nick in front of him.

"Sorus is mine." The voice of murder.

Frozen with surprise, he watched as Nick raised his arms and brought his rifle to bear.

In a flash of coherent light, Sib Mackern was spared.

SORUS

Sorus Chatelaine rode the shockwave out from the Lab's destruction with Deaner Beckmann's blood on her hands and more killing on her mind.

The blast of her proton gun and the detonation of the Lab's generator echoed inside her as if she'd lit an inner chain reaction as hot and consuming as the one she'd left behind. There was no turning back from that slaughter: it could only carry her forward. Her actions were like atoms splitting themselves from violence to more violence.

As the wave front defeated itself against the charged rock of the swarm, *Soar* slowed her headlong ride and began hunting *Trumpet*'s emission trail. For that job Sorus trusted her scan first. In any case, there was nothing she could do personally to help the search. Despite her appearance of attention to the ship and the bridge—and to the mutated man beside her—she concentrated on other things.

From violence to violence—

The man she really wanted to kill wasn't Nick Succorso. He was Milos Taverner. As far as she was concerned, Succorso was trivial. When she'd manipulated and discarded him all those years ago, she truly hadn't cared whether he lived or died: she didn't care now. On the other hand, no other action would have given her as much harsh joy as murdering the Amnioni. And not only because he was here, watching her, prepared to criticize: not only because whether or not she survived the dissatisfaction of her masters depended on his evaluation of her.

She also wanted to kill him because he'd forced her to destroy the

Lab. Even in her nightmares—the only dreams she had—she hadn't foreseen that kind of slaughter. He'd driven her to kill people she'd known and sometimes respected; illegals like herself.

So much killing. Each new link in the chain reaction twisted her heart. Her life nauseated her. Only the violence itself kept her going—

She didn't have anything else to hope for.

She was supposed to capture *Trumpet* somehow: she understood that clearly enough. The Amnion would be dissatisfied by any other result. Unfortunately she didn't believe it would be possible. Despite her gamble with Ciro Vasaczk, she couldn't imagine anything except death.

If the Amnion were merely dissatisfied, however, they might not withdraw her humanity. She had too many other uses.

Then other outcomes became conceivable.

If she could put off her doom for a while—

"Got it, Captain," the scan first announced suddenly. "*Trumpet*'s emission signature. No mistake."

"Good," Sorus said crisply, although she hardly noticed what she was doing. "Compare it with the course Retledge gave us—put any discrepancies up on the screen so we can look at them. And route it to helm.

"Helm, it's time to get serious about catching her." Orders were unnecessary now. Her people already knew what to do. She spoke primarily to show Taverner that she was carrying out his instructions diligently. "Scan should be able to give you a velocity estimate. We need to go faster. We've already closed a lot of the distance. Now we'll cover the rest.

"If Ciro Vasaczk did what I told him," she added grimly, "we should get hints from her particle trace before long."

Unless something went wrong—

She faced Taverner grimly, defying him to challenge her.

Maybe this time, she prayed privately, something will go wrong for you, you inhuman bastard.

An hour or two ago he'd brought a strange box as big as her command board to the bridge. It was covered with controls and readouts which meant nothing to her. Despite its size, he wore it in a harness around his neck so that he could enter commands and see the results easily. Its weight meant nothing in zero g.

He'd told her what it was, although she hadn't asked: his SCRT; the device—he claimed—which gave him instantaneous contact with *Calm Horizons*. The time was near when the two vessels would need to work together without delays in communication—and preferably without being overheard.

Maybe he was telling her the truth. Maybe his box worked.

Maybe *Calm Horizons* was near enough to join the hunt.

In that case, Sorus might be able to carry the logic of violence a step farther.

Where was the UMCP warship she'd last seen stationed near the Com-Mine belt, obviously waiting for *Trumpet*? Even though she'd found no hint of the cruiser, she felt sure it was somewhere close.

If Taverner was telling the truth, *Calm Horizons* had already been seduced into committing an act of war. With any luck at all, the big defensive would eventually find herself in a pitched battle with the UMCP warship.

That gave Sorus hope; the only hope she had left. She pictured the defensive and the warship pounding each other to derelicts. She pictured herself shooting Milos Taverner right between the eyes—before he could trigger the mutagen sacs he'd set on the scrubber pads. If necessary, she pictured firing on *Calm Horizons* herself to make sure the defensive died. Then she pictured her people salvaging what she needed most from *Calm Horizons'* drifting carcass: the antidote which kept her human. A supply so large that it would last her as long as she lived.

If all those things happened, she would be free. She and her people—

The chain reaction carried her forward. It was irresistible anyway: she didn't try to alter or deflect it. Her proton gun had brought down ruin on the Lab like an instant of sunfire. Now she preferred to take her chances; risk her own destruction.

But first she had to stop *Trumpet*.

That probably wasn't going to be easy. By reputation, at least, both Nick Succorso and Angus Thermopyle were formidable opponents. In addition Thermopyle was a UMCPDA cyborg, with resources even Taverner didn't understand. *Trumpet* had secrets of her own. And Sorus' gamble with the Vasaczk kid might too easily be caught.

Nevertheless she intended to gain this one more piece of death for her masters. So that she could go beyond it.

A palpable tension afflicted the bridge. Taverner had that effect. Potential disasters charged the air. Her people sweated over their boards; clung to their duties fretfully.

She knew how they felt. Still their tightness worried her. Men and women with their nerves pulled this taut made mistakes—

"Captain!" The communications first's voice cracked. "I'm getting audio transmission."

Atoms split along Sorus' nerves, carrying fear like a nuclear pile. "Out here?" she demanded. "Who's trying to talk to us out here?"

What the hell is going on?

"Milos—" she began. Is *Calm Horizons* already here? What's she doing? But his unreactive face stopped her. He still wore the eyeshades she'd given him to conceal his Amnion features. When she stared at him, a black strip gazed back, as fathomless and unreadable as the gap.

"It's not aimed at us," the woman on communications answered quickly. "General broadcast—we just happened to overhear it. I've been scanning every frequency we can get, just in case something leaks through that might help us. For a while the reaction behind us fried all the bandwidths. But now we're past it."

General broadcast? That made no sense. Who in their right mind would transmit a general broadcast in this asteroid swarm under these conditions, with the Lab's destruction still flickering and spitting in the background?

"Locate the source," Sorus ordered.

"Sorry, Captain. I've already tried. It was just one short burst. We didn't have a chance to triangulate. And it wasn't coded for position, time, anything like that. Just plain voice transmission. I can give you the quadrant, that's all."

Sorus chewed her lower lip for a moment. "All right," she replied. "Let's hear it."

"Aye, Captain." Communications tapped keys, reversed her log to the data she wanted, then activated the speakers.

At once the bridge fell silent. No one breathed or moved.

"Cut me, will you?" a man's voice said out of the dark. "Come on, bitch."

His tone had a curious hollow resonance which made it sound constricted in some way. Yet it was almost unnaturally clear—distance and static should have affected it more.

"Just a little closer. Come find out what that costs."

The voice nagged at her memory. She nearly recognized it—

"It's time to pay."

"Captain Chatelaine," Milos Taverner put in as if even he finally felt something which might have been surprise, "that is Captain Succorso."

She knew he was right as soon as he spoke. Nick Succorso. Somewhere nearby—too near. *Come on, bitch.* Setting a trap, calling her into it.

Why did he sound so hollow, constricted?

Just a little closer.

She should have known the answer; should have recognized it, too; but she didn't have time.

"Scan, damn it!" she barked urgently. "What's out there? What're we getting into?"

"Nothing, Captain," the woman on scan protested. "Nothing except rock. I've got *Trumpet*'s trail, but she's still ahead of us, we haven't caught up with her without knowing it. And I can't see anything else. We're the only ship here."

Sorus didn't hesitate. "Targ, stand by. Helm, evasive action on my order. Taverner, you'd better anchor yourself somewhere. We're going to start kicking around pretty hard."

Taverner stepped in front of her console and clamped himself there with one hand. The other remained on the controls of his SCRT.

"There's nothing *out* there," scan insisted, staring wide-eyed at her displays.

It's time to pay.

"Tighten your video sweep," Sorus commanded harshly. "Get me visual all around the ship."

With her thumb she set off alert klaxons throughout *Soar*.

"Ready, helm?"

Before helm could respond, scan gasped, "Shit! Captain, we just lost one of the cameras!"

Sorus let herself shout. "*Get me visual!* Damn it, I want to see what's out there!"

At the same instant the woman on communications hissed, "Captain!" and keyed the speakers again.

Hollow and deadly, like a voice from the grave, Succorso said, "I warned you. Sorus is mine."

Christ!

This time communications had no difficulty fixing the source. "God!" she cried, involuntarily frantic. "He's right on top of us!"

Scan was focused too far away, that was the problem—looking for objects that were too big. Right on top of us. That odd, constricted resonance in his voice: Sorus had almost recognized it. Of course. She should have understood immediately.

But how could she or anyone have guessed that Succorso was crazy enough to do something like this?

"Captain," scan shouted at her, "we're hit! Laser fire!"

"Confirm that," the man on data barked from his readouts. "We're under attack. We've got damage."

What damage? Where were they hit?

One thing at a time.

Sorus drove her voice through the fear and consternation of her people. "Where's *visual*?"

"Coming, Captain!" scan croaked.

An instant later the main screen split into images as three of *Soar*'s external cameras swiveled toward the point of attack. From conflicting perspectives—shock, nausea, rage—Sorus saw figures in EVA suits.

Just two of them: two lone human shapes in the vast swarm, assaulting her ship as if they thought they could beat her on their own. And one was already out of action; unquestionably dead: drifting away from the hull with a weightless fountain of blood where his faceplate should have been.

Soar was being attacked by one man. One lunatic who'd just lost or killed his only companion.

But he knew what he was doing.

Clamped magnetically to the metal, he stood facing the super-light proton port. In his arms he held a laser rifle; a big one. Etched garish and fatal out of the dark by searchlights, he fired and fired into the base of the cannon.

"What the fuck's he doing?" helm asked as if he couldn't trust his eyes; couldn't understand what he saw.

Targ knew the answer. "Captain," he announced in shock, "I've lost the proton cannon. It's dead. Completely."

"Confirm that," data said again. "He's burned the power conduits. Now he's slagging the mounts. It's already more damage than we can repair ourselves. We'll need a shipyard."

Suddenly the data first wheeled his station to face Sorus. "Captain," he told her hoarsely, "that's a hell of a laser rifle. In another thirty seconds, he'll cut deep enough to breach the inner hull."

As if in response, the figure in the EVA suit—Succorso—stopped firing. He raised his head. Searchlights glared off his faceplate as he looked around.

With a quick thin shaft of ruby light, he killed one of the cameras. The images on the display broke up, then resolved from three to two.

That must be what had happened to the first camera.

Almost casually, Succorso swung to face the next one. "Keep watching, bitch," he said as if he was sure she could see him. "You're next."

It's time to pay.

One of his images disappeared in red flame. Only one remained.

More damage than we can repair ourselves.

Sorus didn't hesitate. She'd survived for so many years because she could make decisions when she needed to, and her instincts were good.

Pounding commands into her board, she jettisoned the entire proton cannon assembly.

At the same instant the last camera died in laser fire.

Massive iron thunder rang throughout *Soar* as an array of shaped charges went off simultaneously. As precise in their own way as Succorso's laser, they sheared bolts and welds, detached plates, sealed conduits, cauterized wiring. The whole ship staggered like a wounded beast when the big gun ripped free.

But the screen was blank. Sorus didn't get to see the explosions tear Succorso in half; the spray of blood from his ruptured torso. She could imagine it, but she hadn't seen it.

Repercussions seemed to echo through the hull, spreading the violence. The data first shouted into his pickup, sealing bulkheads against the possibility of lost atmosphere; marshaling damage control teams. Everyone else stared at Sorus as if she were as crazy as Nick Succorso.

Communications told her he'd stopped transmitting.

That wasn't enough to comfort her.

Her nerves burned like laser fire with shock, nausea, and rage as she confronted Milos Taverner. Somehow, somewhere, if she ever got the chance, she was going to shoot him square in the center of his smug, pudgy face.

"Have you got the picture now, Taverner?" she rasped. "Have you figured it out?

"He set us up. Succorso *set us up*! I don't know why he thought damaging us like this was worth dying for," no, that was the wrong question, the damage was obviously worth doing, what she didn't know was why he'd taken it on himself, "but he tricked us into this. We've been playing his game all along.

"He let us have the Vasaczk kid to suck us in. We thought we were ahead of him, but he was just laying bait. There won't be any sabotage. If *Trumpet* acts hurt, it'll be another sham, that's all.

"Without that cannon, we're only about half as dangerous as we were a couple of minutes ago."

The Amnioni considered his alien priorities. "Yet Captain Succorso is now dead," he observed.

"Only because he didn't know I would jettison the cannon!" Her action had been almost as crazy as his; almost as desperate. And she hadn't seen the explosions hit him— "Otherwise he would still be blazing away at us. In thirty seconds he would have breached the hull! Then we would be in *real* trouble."

But yelling at Taverner gained nothing. With an effort, she restrained her fury, swallowed her nausea. "If you're really in contact with *Calm Horizons*," she finished, "you'd better make damn sure she gets here in time to help us. We're going to need it."

She couldn't see Milos' eyes, but the angle of his head told her that he was consulting his strange box.

"Help will come, Captain Chatelaine," he pronounced quietly. "*Calm Horizons* has already entered the Massif-5 system."

Data and scan kept working as best they could. The rest of the bridge crew gaped at him in surprise. They hadn't believed that something like this was possible.

Slowly Taverner raised his head. "I argued against this," he explained for reasons Sorus didn't understand. "Something here"—in an oddly naive gesture, he touched his hand to his chest—"warns of danger. Such men as Nick Succorso and Angus Thermopyle are fatal. But the exigency of our requirements makes the risk necessary.

"The defensive will be in position to prevent *Trumpet*'s escape from this asteroid swarm in less than an hour. If she attempts to flee by attaining adequate gap velocity, she will be destroyed. And if she seeks to evade or resist capture in the swarm, *Calm Horizons* and *Soar* will trap her between them.

"I will coordinate communications," he concluded, "so that no mistakes will be made."

No mistakes. Right.

Sorus looked away from him to study her readouts. This whole situation was a mistake—disastrous from first to last. Succorso had outplayed her. Worse, Thermopyle was still doing it. She'd lost her best weapon, and all her gambles were being turned against her.

She wasn't ordinarily a woman who prayed; but now she begged her nameless stars to give her one good UMCP warship.

ANCILLARY DOCUMENTATION

WARDEN DIOS: BACKGROUND INFORMATION

[These notes—among others—were found in Warden Dios' files when Data Acquisition Director Hashi Lebwohl succeeded at breaking the former UMCP director's private codes.]

I often think about how I got into this mess.

In a sense, of course, "how" doesn't matter. I'm here. I did it to myself. Dealing with it isn't optional. As long as I call myself a cop—and I've been doing that all my adult life—I don't have any choice. What it costs me is irrelevant. Especially when I consider the price humankind has already paid for my mistakes. And that price can only increase. Unless I find some way to really do my job.

I'm painfully familiar with the argument that despite its terrible flaw the present arrangement should be preserved because it's better than the alternatives. The lesser evil. After all, if I succeed in bringing about my own destruction, the UMCP will inevitably be what Hashi would probably call "unmanned." No one else knows the danger as well as I do, or can use our resources as effectively. No one else has my fatal gift for inspiring loyalty, or my rather ambiguous skill at pulling strings. Until whoever takes my place—Min Donner, God willing—has time to grow into the job, human space will be vulnerable as never before.

But that argument doesn't move me. I reject the idea that the cops can serve humankind better by being stronger-but-corrupt than by being weaker-but-honest. Nothing corrupt can ever be truly strong. Look at Holt Fasner. He has every imaginable kind of power. On top of that, he's my boss. My master. And yet there's nothing he can do to stop me from bringing him down. If I fail, it won't be because he was strong enough to beat me. It will be because my proxies, Angus and Morn, have paid too high a price for my complicities—the corruption I've condoned in order to prevent Holt from seeing the truth.

That's why I don't resign. I simply can't leave the harm I've done for someone else to clean up.

Still I find myself thinking about the past, looking for hints which might help my successors avoid my mistakes.

All my life I've been obsessed by strength.

The foster family that raised me after my parents were killed lived in one of Earth's urban borderlands. On one side, the guttergangs ruled. On the other, saner civilization prevailed. And on the border between them, safety and violence struggled back and forth like tides as the balances of power shifted.

I thought then, as I think now, that the question was one of strength. Within their territories the guttergangs were strong. They imposed their own order. Elsewhere more benign structures were potent enough to resist encroachment. But in the borderlands everyone suffered because no one was strong enough to defy chaos.

Here, I thought, there should be cops. The borderlands needed men and women with the force to extract safety and order from the conflict—and the goodness to do their jobs without becoming just another kind of guttergang. There was no other cure.

In a sense, I've been fighting on behalf of the borderlands ever since. First the borderlands of Earth's orbital space, where stations and corporations battled for scraps of wealth and survival, and no planetary authority had the strength to control them. And later the vaster borderlands created by contact with the Amnion, borderlands which now exist in virtually every place that can be reached by warships with gap drives.

In the specific borderland where I grew up, I did what I could to organize the homes and families around me for their own protection. I suppose I must have been trying to defend my foster parents from the deaths that took my mother and father. But we had no resources. We were good—at least I think so—but we weren't strong.

At the first opportunity, I allowed myself to be recruited by SMI

Internal Security. I had no loyalty to Space Mines Inc. itself—or even to the idea of trying to procure humankind's survival by doing research and exploiting resources in space. On the other hand, I was enormously attracted by the work SMI IS was supposed to do, which was "to secure" the safety of SMI personnel, operations, and contracts in that one small section of the orbital borderland. I had goodness to spare—or so I imagined at the time. Recruitment by IS gave me access to the support and money, the equipment and people I needed to make my "virtue" useful.

Valuable work as far as it went. But it wouldn't have contented me for long if I hadn't learned that Holt Fasner was ambitious. For a man with my obsessions, SMI Internal Security's "turf" was simply too small. I knew I could do a better job—far better—if I had more to work with.

Holt had bigger dreams. He was in the process of expanding his domain, and therefore my "turf," at an exhilarating rate. In addition, he was already old. Perhaps that was why he seemed—this sounds impossibly naive, even when I admit it to no one but myself—he appeared wise to me. Certainly his profound understanding of the uses of power gave an impression of wisdom.

And during my early years with SMI IS I was still junior personnel, in spite of some fairly rapid promotions. Holt didn't trust me enough to let me see inside his decisions. As far as I could tell, IS was clean. Everything we did looked legitimate.

Finally my new prosthetic eye afflicted me with a kind of hubris. Or maybe it allowed an older hubris to come to the fore. IR vision enabled me to "read" people so well that I began to think I was infallible. An immaculate judge of truth.

I was young and driven. Though it shames me now to say it, I had an easy time convincing myself that there was no inherent conflict between Holt Fasner's dreams and my own—that, in fact, the benevolence of his dreams was demonstrated by the way they carried mine with them.

But I began to catch glimpses of the truth in the heady days after I became chief of Internal Security. That was the time of SMI's acquisition of Intertech after the Humanity Riots. The time of first contact and first trade with the Amnion. A borderland situation if ever there was one. I was in my element as never before when I was forced to recognize that IS didn't spend so much time and effort on corporate espionage simply in order to secure SMI from predators. Holt used stolen secrets to make himself a more effective predator.

For example, with information IS supplied, he exposed some of Sagittarius Exploration's political dealings, which left SagEx ripe for acquisition. And Internal Security's files on the "votes" who chartered corporations enabled him to engage in what he calls "surgical interventions" to protect SMI's interests.

Well, blackmail by any other name is still extortion. I was horrified. And confused. And damn near drunk on the exhilaration of IS's growing "turf" and resources. The conflict threatened to tear me apart.

But Holt has a genius for these situations. He knows when to push and when to hold back. When to seduce and when to use force. He sat me down and confided a tailored version of his dream.

He dreamed, he said, of making SMI such a dominant player in human space that IS would be the only viable candidate to serve as humankind's cops. If I gave him my support, IS would become *the* police for all the borderlands between the stars.

I was won over, in spite of my reservations. I believed him. Or rather, I chose to believe him. I needed some way out of the conflict between exhilaration and horror. My desire to think he was telling the truth was so intense it made me frantic.

But frantic men make mistakes. Mine was complicity. I let, even helped, Holt commit his secret crimes so that I could go on serving the public good.

That's no excuse, of course. It's simply a description. A hint. It shames me—but it's worth knowing.

Years passed before I understood how badly I'd gone wrong, and by then there were no clean solutions left. I couldn't think of any way to undo the harm of my mistakes except by going ahead.

By pushing my complicity as far as it would go. And by doing everything in my power to turn that complicity against the man who taught me how to play this game.

HASHI

By some alchemy which he hadn't expected and barely understood, his equanimity was restored by the warmth of Earth's sun on his head and shoulders as he stepped off the shuttle. How many years had it been since he'd last exposed himself to his native solar radiance? A dozen? More? Now it shone down on him out of a sky as clear as innocence. An azure expanse untainted by centuries of humankind's despoliation arched over him. Imponderable and vast, it reminded him of something which men and women who lived on stations too easily forgot: his own littleness. Nothing that he encountered within UMCPHQ had the scale to dwarf him as this sky did. And of course the station's steel skin closed out the vaster dark so that little human minds like his wouldn't go mad with insignificance.

This warmth, this light, that sky: they were positively therapeutic. If Hashi Lebwohl proved himself stupid and met humiliation before several billions of his own kind, this light and that sky would take no notice. Reality in both its subatomic and its galactic manifestations would remain untroubled. He could only do what quarks and mesons did: ride the electron flux. Combine and recombine as occasion suggested.

Learn and—perhaps—serve.

His nagging sense of inadequacy seemed to melt off his shoulders in the heat of distant solar fire. By the time he and Koina reached the main entrances to the GCES complex and moved in out of the light, he'd recovered his poise; his openness of mind. He was prepared to observe what transpired, respond as he was able, glean what he could, and be content.

In the interim, Koina's two aides, Forrest Ing, and the communications tech had been absorbed into an entire retinue of guards and functionaries, newsdogs and ushers. She and Hashi were escorted like visiting potentates—which, in a sense, they were—into the main building and along the high, diplomatic halls until they gained the formal meeting chamber of the Governing Council for Earth and Space.

The room was easily large enough to hold a hundred or more people without undue crowding. This was a practical necessity. The Council comprised only twenty-one Members—twenty-two including President Abrim Len—each sitting at his or her place at the large, half-oval table which defined the lowest level of the hall, each with his or her own data terminal and stacks of hardcopy. But behind each Member sat tier after tier of aides and advisers, secretaries and advocates. And around the wall above the last seats stood the guards assigned by UMCPED Chief of Security Mandich to protect this session—at least two dozen of them. The result was an aggregation of individuals and intentions which felt unwieldy, almost unmanageable, even though twenty-one was not an unreasonable number for such a body.

Koina had good timing. The session wasn't scheduled to start for another ten minutes: enough time for her to pay her courtesies and take her place; not enough for the Members or their aides to accost her with their private agendas.

As the doors admitted her and Hashi to the hall, leaving most of their new entourage behind, a wave of sound washed over them—the undifferentiated gabble of aides briefing their Members, Members issuing instructions to their secretaries, advisers arguing among themselves. The noise was abruptly cut off, however, when the two directors entered. The Members and most of their personnel would have noticed Koina Hannish's arrival; some would have stopped talking to acknowledge her. But Hashi Lebwohl's presence took them all by surprise. Recent events had made him an electric figure here. And he hadn't attended a GCES session in person for at least a dozen years.

He paused inside the entryway and scanned the startled hall as if the sudden silence were a mark of respect. All the Members were already in their places: two from each of Earth's six political subdivisions, one from each of the nine major stations. Hashi knew them as well as it was possible to know men and women he'd never met. Their dossiers had familiarized him with their names and predilections, their voting records and personal histories. And his prodigious memory supplied the same information for most of the aides and advisers. His own people in DA sometimes referred to him as "Data Storage with legs"—for good reason. If the need arose, the only people in the hall he couldn't have addressed by name were the guards.

Most of the Members were seated; but Abrim Len stood at the center of the table, bowing like a marionette to everyone who required his attention. With the exception of the President, Members were randomly assigned new places for each session, to avoid any impression of favoritism. It was, therefore, a matter of chance that two vehement critics of the UMCP had seats beside the President: Sen Abdullah, the Eastern Union Senior Member, on his right, and United Western Bloc Junior Member Sigurd Carsin on his left. Nevertheless the coincidence didn't auger well.

Other faces were especially familiar for divergent reasons. Blaine Manse, the Member from Betelgeuse Primary, was renowned for her persistent and embarrassing peccadilloes. Punjat Silat of the Combined Asian Islands and Peninsulas had produced fascinating—if admittedly speculative—writings on the philology of intelligence. Com-Mine Station Member Vest Martingale had played what she must have considered an excruciating role in the passage of the Preempt Act.

Halfway down the table opposite Martingale rested Captain Sixten Vertigus, the old hero of humankind's first contact with the Amnion, and the reason for this extraordinary session. His frail head leaned against the back of his chair, and his eyes were closed: he was apparently asleep.

Maxim Igensard sat behind his sponsor, Martingale. More than ever the Special Counsel resembled a predator disguised as prey. Under other circumstances, his gray attire and undistinguished features might have caused him to blend into the crowd of aides and secretaries. Now, however, he radiated tension like a nuclear pile. Hashi suspected, or perhaps merely hoped, that when Igensard learned the nature of Captain Vertigus' legislation, he would—in the argot of UMCPHQ—"go critical."

Many other faces were known; but in the silence which his arrival had occasioned, Hashi found his gaze riding a frisson of excitement and apprehension along the table to its end. There he received a nervous shock of his own.

At the same moment Koina murmured, "Hashi," as if she were warning him.

In the last chair—a position notable for its lack of a data terminal or hardcopies—sat Cleatus Fane.

Holt Fasner's First Executive Assistant: a man who was said to speak with the voice and hear with the ears of the great worm himself.

He was a rotund figure in any case, but by sheer force of personality he took up so much space that he appeared even fatter. His eyes were the unreadable green of deep seas, and his plump lips smiled mercilessly. Beneath them an expanse of white beard concealed his neck and sternum. His whiskers were wiry rather than soft, however: his beard moved like a blade whenever he spoke or turned his head. Nevertheless he bore more than a passing resemblance—as any number of people had remarked—to Santa Claus.

He met Hashi's surprised look and smiled benignly, as if he'd come to speak the Dragon's blessing on this chamber and all who did the work of governing humankind.

Father Christmas, dispenser of the UMC CEO's gifts.

But Hashi wasn't misled. Not coincidentally, Cleatus Fane also exacted his lord's punishments.

What was he doing here? Hashi had no difficulty imagining an answer. Abrim Len, bless his timid, conciliatory heart, may have informed Holt Fasner's Home Office that this extraordinary session had been called to consider legislation proposed by Captain Sixten Vertigus. Knowing the good captain's reputation, the Dragon would certainly have guessed that Sixten Vertigus' bill wasn't intended for his benefit. Hence he'd dispatched his most practiced and reliable subordinate to witness—and perhaps respond to—whatever the UWB Senior Member did.

The restrained clamor in the hall resumed as abruptly as it'd stopped: all at once everyone present found something compelling to say to his or her neighbors. Some of them were surely wondering what Hashi Lebwohl's appearance and Cleatus Fane's had to do with each other.

To cover his momentary lapse of composure, Hashi bowed in Cleatus' direction. His mouth shaped the words, "My dear First Executive Assistant, how piquant to see you." Then he leaned toward Koina and whispered, "It appears that the stakes of the game have been raised." Hidden by the hubbub of the Members and their retinues, he asked, "Do you believe that Captain Vertigus will proceed under these circumstances?"

Koina looked at him, let him see that the corners of her mouth were smiling again—only the corners. Then she moved to descend the tiers toward her honorary place at the end of the half-oval table across from the great worm's representative.

Hashi followed behind her aides and Forrest Ing, noting as he passed that Abrim Len had begun to put on dignity like a man who meant to assume his duties. However, he had no real interest in the President's posture, dignified or otherwise. Other questions held him; questions which gathered a new urgency from Fane's presence. What answer had Chief of Security Mandich given Forrest Ing? And when would Deputy Chief Ing deign to mention it to the DA director? Hashi couldn't risk expressing either his offended vanity or his legitimate concerns to the deputy chief in front of this assemblage, but his instinct for caution had suddenly become stringent.

He could no longer say accurately that he expected nothing. Therefore his need to be prepared had grown stronger.

As Koina reached her chair, sat down, and commenced the ritual of logging onto the data terminal so that she could open a transmission channel to UMCPHQ in case she needed it, Hashi put his hand on the deputy chief's arm to detain him.

"I am still waiting for a reply," he announced just loudly enough to be heard; just sharply enough to threaten Ing. "Sadly I do not wait well."

The man cocked an uncertain eyebrow as if he couldn't remember what Hashi was talking about. Then he said quickly, "Forgive me, Director. I've been distracted."

Turning away, he snapped his fingers; and at once a young UMCPED Security ensign came forward from the rear of Koina's diminished entourage. Hashi hadn't noticed him earlier: he must have joined the PR director's retinue outside the hall. Although he must surely have been at least twenty years of age, his fine blond hair and pale skin made him appear almost prepubescent.

"Ensign Crender," Ing said by way of introduction, "you have your orders. You're here to do what Director Lebwohl tells you. *Whatever* he tells you." The deputy chief smiled coldly. "Within reason, of course."

"Yes, sir." The ensign's voice nearly cracked. He looked frightened, as if he feared that Hashi might instruct him to draw his impact pistol and open fire on the Council.

Within reason? Within *reason*?

With some difficulty, Hashi restrained a rush of anger. Mandich, he swore in silence. Donner. Ing. Be warned. If this whelp fails me, the price will be laid on your heads. *I* will lay it there.

Brusquely he took the nearest seat at Koina's back. Then he closed his eyes and spent a moment experiencing the surge and pull of blood in his temples as if his pulse embodied the electron flux; calming himself with metaphors of uncertainty.

He looked up again as the Members and their people grew quiet. The session was about to start.

A last guard entered the hall, and the doors were closed. Seeing this, President Len turned to the table and took up the ceremonial miter—privately Hashi considered it a "cudgel"—which symbolized his office. Now all the Members, advisers, and secretaries sat down, leaving only the President and the guards on their feet. Summoning up his dignity, Len brought his miter down on the tabletop with a thump which somehow conveyed hesitation despite its weight.

"Your attention, Members of the Governing Council for Earth and Space," he announced sententiously. Again he thumped the surface in front of him. "Today we meet in extraordinary session, and we are ready to begin."

After a third thump, he set his miter down.

In a less formal tone, he went on, "As you know, this session has been convened to consider a matter which the Senior Member for the United Western Bloc, Captain Sixten Vertigus, wishes to bring before us." He nodded toward Captain Vertigus, who continued to doze. "This Council has a number of pressing issues to consider"—he may have been asking the old Member to pay attention—"including, but by no means limited to, the recent, appalling terrorist attack on Captain Vertigus himself, the even more recent murder of the UMCP's then-director of Protocol, Godsen Frik, and the public confirmation of his successor, Koina Hannish." The President bowed politely in Koina's direction. "However, Captain Vertigus has claimed Member's privilege. By virtue of his long service to the Council, as well as to humankind, our charter grants him precedence. Other matters will be raised as time and circumstance permit.

"Are there any objections," he concluded, "before I ask Captain Vertigus to speak?"

This call for objections was a mere formality, one of the codified courtesies which gave government its illusion of collegiality. Hashi was surprised when Sen Abdullah immediately took his feet.

"President Len"—the EU Senior Member's voice was unfortunate: it whined like a maladjusted servomechanism—"fellow Members, I must object. Without disrespect to Captain Vertigus, the present situation is too extreme for any of us to claim privilege. A kaze has attacked him, a kaze has killed Godsen Frik. And this occurred only a short time after we conducted a video conference which might mildly be called 'provocative' with UMCP Director Warden Dios and Data Acquisition Director Hashi Lebwohl."

He didn't glance at Hashi.

Cleatus Fane studied the speaker with a hooded gaze, revealing nothing.

Abdullah cleared his throat as if Fane's scrutiny made him uncomfortable. "President Len, fellow Members, the Special Counsel appointed by this Council to investigate allegations of malfeasance against Director Dios and the UMCP has uncovered several issues which are cause for grave concern. The UMCP have risked covert operations within forbidden space, employing persons of doubtful character. The Data Acquisition director has admitted delivering one of Enforcement Division's ensigns into what might be called prostitution—if it is not called enslavement. A notorious illegal, Captain Angus Thermopyle, has escaped from Data Acquisition in the company of a traitor.

"And now"—Abdullah gestured toward Hashi with a chop of his hand—"here sits the same director of Data Acquisition who so horrified us when he spoke for Director Dios. We will be derelict in our duty if we miss this opportunity to question him.

"Captain Vertigus," the EU Senior Member whined, "I must ask you to yield your privilege. I will use it to provide a forum for Special Counsel Maxim Igensard's investigation."

Igensard leaned forward in his seat, eager to stand.

Like everyone around him, Hashi turned toward Captain Vertigus. Sen Abdullah's demand would have been difficult to refuse at the best of times. With Cleatus Fane watching him, the old man might find refusal impossible.

Captain Vertigus still sat with his head back and his eyes closed. His open mouth emitted a small rasp like a snore.

"Captain Vertigus." President Len disliked rudeness—not to mention assertiveness—and his discomfort made him unnecessarily peremptory. "You must answer. Will you yield your privilege to Senior Member Abdullah?"

The old man twitched. His head came down: he opened his eyes, then gazed blearily around him as if he'd forgotten where he was. "What?" he asked. At once, however, he went on, "Oh, very well." His voice held a pronounced quaver.

From where he sat, Hashi saw Koina's shoulders tighten. Several of the Members seemed to have stopped breathing.

"I'll be glad, delighted, to yield to my esteemed colleague," Captain Vertigus said thinly.

Igensard started to rise. Fane hid his reaction behind his beard.

"As soon as I'm done," the UWB Senior Member finished.

Shock jolted the chamber like a static discharge. Hashi allowed himself to smile as Igensard's face twisted and Abdullah bit back a retort. "Nicely played, Captain," he murmured, only half aloud. Sixten Vertigus had looked the dotard for so long that most people had forgotten his old courage.

Koina didn't react; hardly moved. She couldn't afford to betray the fact that she knew what Sixten intended.

Hurrying to avoid conflict, President Len put in, "You won't reconsider, Captain? I'm sure we'll have time for you when Special Counsel Igensard is done."

Captain Vertigus sighed. "No"—strain showed in his voice as he stood up—"I won't reconsider. This is too important." Supporting himself on the tabletop with his arms, he added, "And it's not irrelevant to all those 'provocative' subjects my esteemed colleague mentioned.

"Don't worry, Abrim," he muttered with a touch of asperity. "This probably won't take as long as it should."

"Very well, Captain Vertigus," Len sighed. His hand on Sen Abdullah's shoulder urged the EU Senior Member to sit down. "The session is yours."

Bowing, the President seated himself.

"This better be good," Sigurd Carsin murmured to no one in particular. She was Sixten's Junior Member, but she'd never concealed her impatience at giving precedence to a man she considered "senile."

" 'Good'?" Captain Vertigus cocked his head at her. "I don't think so. These days I'm not sure 'good' exists anymore. But if you'll pay attention, I'll offer you something better than what we have now."

Carsin glared at him, but didn't speak again.

Slowly the captain raised his head between his hunched shoulders so that he could address the whole chamber.

"You're right, of course," he began. "I was attacked. Poor, pompous Godsen Frik was killed. Warden Dios and Hashi Lebwohl nauseated us—some of us, anyway—with what they said during that conference. Captain Thermopyle has escaped, and what we know about DA's covert operation in forbidden space stinks. Events are moving too fast for us to control. The Special Counsel probably has good reason to think he's on the trail of the worst kind of malfeasance."

His old voice seemed to lack any of the force which would have made it effective. Nevertheless Hashi found himself listening as if he were entranced. Sixten had a quality which counted more than force: he had frailty; the kind of earned human frailty that only grew from long years of valor and probity. He was persuasive because he'd earned the right to be.

"I support the United Mining Companies Police," he announced as if his quavering were a form of strength. "I always have. I believe in the job they're supposed to be doing. What's happened makes me even more nauseous than the rest of you.

"I want to do something about it. All of it—everything you've mentioned. And everything Hashi Lebwohl hasn't bothered to tell us yet. I want to clear the obstacles out of the Special Counsel's way so he can do his job *right*."

Hashi feared that the captain's voice would crack when he pushed it; but it held firm.

"As it happens, I know how. I've already done the work. All you have to do is vote on it. Then our situation can start to get 'better.' "

A hundred people watched the old man as if they were as rapt as Hashi; eager for what came next. They all heard Fane remark amiably, "You fascinate me, Captain Vertigus." A none-too-subtle reminder of his presence—and of the man he represented. "What can you possibly propose that isn't already being done?"

Sixten ignored the distraction. Still leaning on his arms, still speaking in a high, thin voice which threatened to waver out of control whenever he raised it, he said distinctly, "President Len, fellow Members, I wish to propose legislation which I call a Bill of Severance. This bill will decharter the United Mining Companies Police as a subsidiary unit of the United Mining Companies and reconstitute that organization as an arm of the Governing Council for Earth and Space."

Decharter—?

Reconstitute—?

The ensuing consternation gave Hashi a keen sense of pleasure. Members gasped. Some of them actually turned pale; others turned to hiss urgently at their aides. Secretaries clutched each other's arms; advisers floundered. Igensard slumped backward like a man who'd been poleaxed. In contrast, Fane rocked his bulk forward as if he meant to launch it into the air. After a stunned moment fifty or a hundred voices began gabbling at once.

Through the confusion, Hashi heard Koina say softly, "Thank you, Captain," although her voice wasn't loud enough to reach Sixten. "Thank you."

"Please!" President Len was on his feet, shouting to lift his appeal above the noise. "Members, *please*!" With his miter, he pounded the table as if he were belaboring an assailant. "We must have *order*!"

After a moment his shout—or perhaps the possibility that he might break his miter—had an effect. Slowly the tumult eased. Flustered Members adjusted their garb, straightened themselves in their seats; aides and advisers stopped talking and started attacking their data terminals; some of the secretaries made shushing sounds which others eventually heeded.

The guard who had entered the chamber last left his post at the doors and took a few steps along the wall across from and above Hashi's position, then stopped and stood still. Apparently he'd moved in order to improve his view of the chamber.

Hashi thought that Cleatus Fane would demand a chance to speak; but he didn't. Instead he subsided in his seat, brandishing his beard like a shield.

"That's better." The President sounded like a peevish aunt. No doubt he was hard-pressed to manage his own surprise—as well as his congenital fear of consequences. When the noise had sunk to a persistent rustle of hardcopies and whispers, he said, "I think you'd better explain yourself, Captain Vertigus."

Sixten had stood without moving while confusion poured down the tiers at him; now he gave no indication that he'd heard any of it. As if he hadn't been interrupted, he resumed.

"The entire bill has already been written. It can be enacted as it stands. If you want to look at it, it's available on your terminals." In a flurry Members and aides hurried to confront their screens. "Log onto the public files and bulletins of the United Western Bloc, query my name, and enter the code word 'survival.' " A sharp rattle of keypads followed, but he ignored it. "My proposed legislation is there, complete."

The strain of holding his head up showed in a slight wobble, but he didn't let himself relax.

"While you read, let me answer some of your more obvious questions.

"Because of the crises we're facing right now, my bill provides that the present resources, personnel, and functions of the Police will be preserved intact. The GCES Police won't miss a moment in their defense of human space. And funding will be supplied by a proportionate tax on all chartered corporations which operate in space. Procedures for levying the tax are included in the bill. On that score, also, the new Police will have no reason to falter.

"But if so little is going to change, what do we gain by enacting this legislation?"

"My question exactly," someone put in—Hashi didn't see who.

"In the short term, obviously," Captain Vertigus answered, "the primary benefit is that the Police will now be accountable to *us*, not to the UMC. Special Counsel Igensard will be able to pursue his investigation whether Holt Fasner *or* Warden Dios approve of it or not. But in the long term that one benefit will produce hundreds of significant improvements."

He paused, summoning strength or determination, then went on more firmly.

"If we pass this bill, we will finally be able to do the work we were elected for—the work of defining and preserving humankind's future in space." Despite its quaver, his voice took on a trenchant edge. "As matters stand, all we really do is argue about decisions someone else has already made. Right now, today, it is Holt Fasner who sets human policy. And his subordinates carry out that policy. Occasionally he allows us to ratify some small part of his designs. The rest of the time we might as well as be *asleep*.

"I want to change that. We can. *We* can. We have the power. As humankind's elected representatives to the Governing Council for Earth and Space, we *have* the power. All we need to do," he finished, "is make up our minds to pass this bill."

Finally his head dropped. He supported himself on his arms with his head bowed as if he were waiting for someone to pray over him.

In front of Hashi, Koina sat with her hands at her sides like a woman restraining an impulse to applaud.

If she'd started clapping, he would have been tempted to join her himself.

How many Members, he wondered, felt the same way? Sigurd Carsin appeared nonplussed, dismayed by involuntary admiration for her Senior Member, whom she'd always despised. Abrim Len fussed with his miter: he seemed to think his dignity depended on the proper placement of his ceremonial rod. Vest Martingale looked back and forth between Cleatus Fane and Captain Vertigus as if she wanted to flee, but didn't know where safety lay. Punjat Silat beamed like a benevolent idol. Despite her reputation for serving on the Council only because it supplied her with opportunities for sexual conquest, Blaine Manse studied Sixten with a new glow of purpose on her face.

Hashi would have looked farther, but his attention was attracted by movement among the guards opposite him. The man who had stood at the door earlier changed positions again, moving another three or four meters away from his original post. Then he stopped once more. His face was partially in shadow: Hashi couldn't see his features clearly.

Now what, Hashi asked himself, do you suppose that man has in his mind?

"Captain Vertigus," the Dragon's First Executive Assistant asked solicitously, "do you feel well?"

Sixten didn't turn his head. "Read my bill, Mr. Fane. It will tell you how I feel."

Cleatus Fane shifted his weight in a way which caused him to appear larger. "Then I'm forced to say—with all deference to your years and reputation—that this is preposterous."

His tone had a cloying, medicinal quality, as if he kept it sweet to make its underlying bitterness palatable.

"In the name of the United Mining Companies, as well as for the benefit of this Council, I must mention several points which you have apparently chosen to overlook."

He didn't ask permission to speak. He didn't need it; he spoke for Holt Fasner, and President Len made no attempt to stop him.

"First, your assertion that the charter of the UMCP can be transferred to this body without disruption—without 'missing a moment'—is pragmatically absurd. Such things may be imagined in the abstract. In practice they do not occur. Structural change has structural consequences. At a time when humankind's survival depends on the Police as never before, you ask this body to ignore the inevitable upheavals—and their inevitable cost."

Leaning his elbows on the table in order to face Sixten more directly, Fane seemed to expand again. His voice grew sharper; mordant behind its sweetness.

"In addition, Captain Vertigus, you ignore the irrefutable fact that as a branch of the United Mining Companies the Police are more effective than they can ever be as an arm of the GCES. Under the present arrangement, the UMCP and the UMC share resources and information, personnel and research, listening posts and other tools. They must because those are Holt Fasner's instructions. However diverse their actions may be, their authority comes from a single source.

"At present the UMCP are better informed, more mobile, and more powerful than they could hope to be under any other arrangement. *Not*, I hasten to say, because the UMC would ever withhold cooperation, information, or support from a separate Police, but because the GCES and the UMC are inherently discrete entities—unlike the UMC and the UMCP."

Cleatus Fane looked around the chamber, inviting the Members to agree with him—or to disagree, if they had the nerve.

However, Hashi no longer watched the First Executive Assistant's performance. In a sense he'd stopped listening. The guard who'd left the doors was moving again. When he stopped, he was almost directly behind the section of the table where Vest Martingale sat. Another shift of the same distance would put him behind Sixten Vertigus: two more after that, behind Cleatus Fane.

Hashi studied the guard, trying to get a clear look at his face.

When none of the Members offered an opinion, Fane continued.

"Finally, Captain Vertigus, I feel compelled to observe that your insistence on *accountability* is misleading. With all respect to this body, it is plain that accountability to any group of men and women can not be as clear and absolute as accountability to a single authority. At present the UMCP must answer to Holt Fasner for everything they do. His personal commitment to the integrity and effectiveness of the UMCP protects against any corruption."

He paused to give this assertion force. He might have been asking, "Is there anyone here who dares to say publicly that Holt Fasner is not honorable?"

No one did.

Fane smiled. He could afford to be magnanimous.

"Matters may appear dubious at the moment," he conceded, "but I can assure you from long and direct experience that the UMC CEO's investigation will root out malfeasance and punish treason better than any Council. The diligence and dedication of the Council's Members can't compete with Holt Fasner's more intimate knowledge of the UMCP's people and operations.

"If you insist on disrupting the Police when so many crises are upon us, you will lay all human space open to kazes—and worse. Yes, worse," he insisted. "In fact, I fear that any sign of confusion in the UMCP now would give all our enemies the occasion they need to attack."

Now at last the features of the guard Hashi scrutinized caught the light squarely.

Quoting shamelessly in surprise, the DA director whispered, "Now there's a face that flits upon my memory."

Nathan Alt. At one time Captain Nathan Alt, commander, UMCP

cruiser *Vehemence*. Until Min Donner had court-martialed him for what she chose to call "dereliction of duty."

Hashi didn't doubt for an instant that he was right. He trusted his vast memory. But what in Heisenberg's name was *Nathan Alt* doing here? In the uniform of a GCES Security guard?

At once the DA director turned in his seat and gripped the arm of the boy Forrest Ing had assigned to him, Ensign Crender.

"Come with me."

Without waiting for a response, Hashi rose and began working his way up the crowded tiers to the back of the hall.

Sixten Vertigus was a frail old man who might as well have been beaten. He made no effort to look up or turn his head. Nevertheless he was the only one in the chamber who answered the First Executive Assistant.

Wearily he retorted, "That's all beside the point, Mr. Fane." Despite his fatigue, however, his words were distinct. "It changes nothing. You would say exactly the same things with exactly the same conviction if your Holt Fasner had sold his soul to the Amnion."

A gasp of shock hissed around the hall. Abrim Len turned toward Sixten with a jerk, gaped aghast at the UWB Senior Member. No one had ever said anything like that aloud in front of the GCES.

Hashi admired Sixten's reply, but he didn't pause. When he reached the last tier and the wall, he turned to Ensign Crender again, pulled the boy toward him.

"Stay close," he demanded softly, so that the nearby guards wouldn't hear him. "Be ready."

Shuffling in his untied shoes as if he felt no need for haste, Hashi began to walk around the back of the hall, hoping to intercept the object of his interest in time to learn whether he was making a fool of himself.

Ensign Crender followed doggedly.

Below and across from them, Cleatus Fane dug his beard into the air. "I will ignore your insult for the moment," he snapped. "What *is* the point, Captain Vertigus?"

Sixten sighed. He may have been exhausted, but once again he mustered enough force for a retort.

"You keep talking about the practical application of power. 'Diligence and dedication can't compete.' Of course they can't. But that's not the subject of this bill. It has to do with *ethics*, Mr. Fane—ethics and responsibility.

"*We* are humankind's elected representatives. Holt Fasner is not. The responsibility for guiding and controlling the actions of humankind's Police belongs to *us*, not to him."

Bravo, Captain, Hashi thought. Still he kept moving. As he walked, he concentrated on projecting the impression that he was engaged in some trivial activity—perhaps that he'd lost his way to the san. Above all he didn't want the guards to begin watching him rather than the Members and their aides.

Cleatus Fane snorted through his stiff whiskers. If Sixten's answers—or determination—took him aback, he didn't show it. And he certainly didn't lack for answers himself.

"I think you'll find," he drawled sardonically, "that the Police themselves aren't so sanguine. And they may also have something to say about your absurd claim that Holt Fasner can't be trusted to keep them honest. In fact, I don't hesitate to predict that Warden Dios himself will denounce this bill, for the same reasons I've already given you. I've heard him discuss 'ethics and responsibility' many times, and I'm sure of what he'll say."

Abruptly he turned toward Koina.

"Director Hannish?" Like his beard, his bulk aimed itself at her like a demand. "I know you haven't had an opportunity to consult Director Dios on this, but perhaps you can comment on the UMCP's position."

Hashi had reached a point on the curve of the hall which allowed him to see Koina's face. Her mask was immaculate, untroubled: she wore her beauty like a shield. But to his eyes the pressure of her hands as she gripped the edge of the table betrayed her tension. Cleatus Fane had just demanded that she proclaim the UMCP's allegiance to the UMC—her own as well as Warden Dios'. In the circles where Holt Fasner wielded his might, no subordinate could refuse such a demand.

A tension of his own clutched at Hashi's heart. He'd urged Koina to let Warden know about Captain Vertigus' bill; but she'd declined to tell him how Warden had reacted to the information. Just for a moment he halted to hear her response.

She didn't stand. She didn't need to: every eye in the chamber was on her; she had the Council's complete attention.

"On the contrary, Mr. Fane," she replied, "we've discussed this bill many times." A low throb of emotion in her voice showed that she grasped what was at stake. "Not this specific bill, of course. How could we? I mean that my fellow directors and I have often considered the idea of a Bill of Severance. We have debated its merits and formed our opinions. I don't need to consult my director now in order to inform you of our position."

"Please, Director Hannish," President Len put in, making at least that one small attempt to regain control of the proceedings. "Go ahead."

The First Executive Assistant nodded as if to say, I'm waiting. An intake of breath caused his body to swell ominously.

Sixten didn't raise his eyes to Koina. His posture suggested that he was resigned to abandonment.

"Thank you, President Len." Her apparent calm seemed to emphasize the background intensity of her tone. "Mr. Fane, Captain Vertigus, Members of this Council"—she regarded the chamber with a firm gaze—"our position is one of absolute neutrality."

Startled, Fane opened his mouth to protest; but Koina didn't let him interrupt her.

"In the most necessary sense," she explained, "we disavow responsibility for it. That responsibility is yours and yours alone. Our function, *our* responsibility, is to serve humankind according to the terms and conditions of our charter. If we seek to determine the nature of those terms and conditions, we will inevitably become a force of tyranny, no matter how benign our motives may be. *That* responsibility must rest with you. When our organization began, you chartered it as a branch of the UMC because you saw fit to do so. If you now see fit to alter our charter, we will abide by it without question.

"As individuals we all have personal opinions and beliefs. But as the United Mining Companies Police Director of Protocol, I am forced to contradict Mr. Fane. I say—and Director Dios will say with me—that this decision rests on you. What you decide, we will accept. If we do otherwise, we have betrayed your trust, and humankind would be better off without us."

Bowing her head, Koina concluded, "Thank you for allowing me to speak."

The Council had suffered too many surprises in one session. The Members and their people peered at her as if they were stunned. Cleatus Fane's resemblance to Santa Claus had become an illusion: the glare in his eyes was murderous and dark. Wonder shone on Sigurd Carsin's face. Len strove to close his mouth, but his lower jaw had become too heavy for him. Maxim Igensard seemed to bounce in his seat as if he were frantic to address the gathering. Slowly Captain Vertigus raised his head to look at Koina: he may have had tears in his eyes.

Hashi was more than pleased: he was profoundly relieved. To this extent, at least, he hadn't been wrong in his assessment of his director.

What you decide, we will accept. Warden's strange game—whatever it might be—was being played against Holt Fasner.

As a result the complex question of Hashi's own loyalties was simplified.

To confirm that Ensign Crender was still with him, he glanced aside at his companion.

The guard looked impossibly pale, drained of blood, as if he were about to faint. In a blink of intuition, Hashi realized that the youth understood the struggle taking place in the hall. He was merely young, not stupid.

The DA director had no time for delay, however. A movement caught the edge of his vision: Nathan Alt was coming closer. Now the man Hashi hunted had reached a position against the wall above and behind Captain Vertigus.

"My point remains the same," Fane growled harshly; but he may have been blustering. "If this Council does anything to disrupt the Police—if they're weakened in any way at a time like this—I think we're all going to regret it."

Praying God or Heisenberg that the ensign was intelligent enough to react quickly, but not so intelligent that he paralyzed himself, Hashi started forward again, quickening his pace to narrow the gap before Alt noticed him.

President Len had begun to speak, hesitantly calling the GCES back to order, but Hashi paid no heed. Alt was too near Captain Vertigus. Worse, he was closing the distance between himself and Cleatus Fane. Concentrating exclusively on the former UMCPED captain, Hashi hastened around the wall.

Three meters from Nathan Alt, he stopped. At last he was close enough to read the id patch on the man's uniform, the clearance badge clipped to his breast pocket.

Both identified Alt categorically as "GCES Security Sergeant Clay Imposs."

Hashi was taken aback. Caught in the uncertain swirl of subatomic possibilities, he studied the man.

Alt didn't so much as glance at the DA director. His disfocused stare was fixed, opaque; aimed at nothing. Unequal dilation distorted his pupils. Pallid and waxy, the skin of his face hung slack on his cheekbones.

Hashi knew the signs. He'd worked with such things often enough to be sure of them.

Nathan Alt was in a state of drug-induced hypnosis.

Woodenly he continued his incremental progress in Cleatus Fane's direction.

Too late, it was already too late, Hashi had delayed too long, letting uncertainty carry him when he should have been sure. Only Alt's chemical stupor saved him.

Wheeling on Crender, he barked, "Arrest that man! Get him out of here!"

The boy froze. Youth and inexperience betrayed him. Instead of springing forward, he blinked openmouthed at Hashi's demand as if he found it incomprehensible.

"He is a *kaze*!" Hashi shouted; almost screamed. "*Get him out of here!*"

Then he leaped at Alt himself.

Ignoring the instant pandemonium around him, the cries of the aides and secretaries, the surging of the guards, he clawed the clearance badge from Alt's uniform, ripped open the front of Alt's uniform in order to snatch at the id tag around his neck.

An instant later Crender burst past him, slammed Nathan Alt away. Yelling in fright, the ensign half drove, half threw Alt back toward the doors.

Almost immediately Forrest Ing roared orders. Two more guards rushed to help the boy. Together they manhandled Alt along the wall as fast as they could. On the far side of the hall, Ing shouted at his communications tech, warning Chief Mandich and the guards outside.

Drugged and oblivious, Alt put up no resistance. Perhaps he wasn't aware that anything was happening to him.

Nevertheless he might explode at any moment. The fact that he was hypnotized, volitionless, only meant that the bomb inside him was controlled by other means: an internal timer; an external radio signal.

Taking the only precaution he could think of, Hashi flung himself headlong down the tiers into the terrified frenzy of bodies and seats.

In his fists he clutched Imposs/Alt's clearance badge and id tag as if they were precious enough to ransom his entire species.

More guards rushed into the confusion. At last their training took hold: half a dozen of them forced an aisle through the wailing tumult; others threw open the doors; still others helped move Imposs along. Abrim Len shrieked at the Members to clear the hall. If they'd been able to obey, the crush would have made it impossible to remove Imposs. But reinforcements arrived in time to block the Members and their staffs out of the way.

At a run, Ensign Crender and the other guards impelled Imposs or Alt from the hall. Immediately Chief Mandich ordered the doors closed again. Men and women who didn't know what they were doing kicked Hashi from side to side. In self-defense, he picked himself off the floor just as the high portal slammed shut.

Across the moil and din Ing shouted fiercely, "Sit down! Sit *down*! Get below the blast!"

His yell produced an instant of frozen silence. But before anyone could move, obey, a detonation as heavy as thunder shook the chamber.

The blast was too close to the doors: they cracked from top to bottom. The floor bucked in the concussion. People staggered; some lost their feet. Powdered plaster, paint, and cement filled the air as the shock wave hit the walls and ceiling.

Then it was over.

The Members stared at each other with shock on their faces and dust in their hair. For a moment they seemed stunned to find that they were still alive.

Unaware that a smile stretched his thin face like a rictus, Hashi stooped to the floor and started looking for his glasses.

Apart from Nathan Alt/Clay Imposs, only one man died. A GCES Security guard too close to the explosion was blown to pulp. And only one was seriously injured: Ensign Crender lost his left hand and forearm. For the most part, however, Chief Mandich had taken effective measures to muffle the blast and protect lives. A number of Security personnel—both GCES and UMCPED—suffered damaged eardrums and other symptoms of concussion, but they were spared any lasting harm.

When the ensuing pandemonium had eased, and order had been restored, President Len offered to adjourn the session so that the Members would have time to recover. To his surprise, virtually all of them declined. Under the circumstances, the consensus of the Council was that the UWB Senior Member's Bill of Severance should be brought to an immediate vote.

The Bill was rejected by a significant margin. The Members were too shaken to approve it. They heeded Cleatus Fane's assertion that severance would disrupt the efforts of the UMCP to protect them. Any kind of centralized authority seemed preferable to terrorist attack.

In their fear, the Members felt too vulnerable to accept responsibility for their own survival.

The fact that Cleatus Fane himself had been the kaze's apparent target gave his arguments added weight. The threat came, not from humankind's enemies, but from the UMC's. Therefore the UMC should deal with it.

When the extraordinary session was adjourned, Captain Vertigus limped out of the hall. However, his carriage was erect, uncowed. He might have been on his way to make humankind's first contact with the Amnion.

Koina Hannish couldn't contain her indignation. To that extent, her professional mask failed her. "How did he get *in*?" she demanded repeatedly of Forrest Ing. "Is this the best ED Security can do? Why did I work so hard to put Chief Mandich in charge of Security here, if he isn't capable of stopping a kaze? A kaze *I* warned him about?"

The deputy chief, poor man, had no answer.

But her ire had another, truer question behind it. Implicit in her outrage was the assumption that if a kaze hadn't gained entrance to the chamber, the Bill of Severance might have passed.

Hashi deemed that plausible. He'd heard Captain Vertigus' arguments, and they were better than Cleatus Fane's. Even Members bought and paid for by the UMC might have been swayed.

Nevertheless the DA director considered the session a success.

Warden Dios had assured Koina she was in no danger. Apparently he'd meant that the danger wasn't aimed at her personally. The earlier attacks on Captain Vertigus and Godsen Frik didn't imply that she was next. They had another significance entirely.

In the aftermath of Nathan Alt's death and Sixten Vertigus' defeat, Hashi Lebwohl could see that significance clearly. Events in flux had resolved themselves: he was sure of their position.

On the other hand, he had no idea what might happen next.

MIN

She was already on her way to the bridge when *Punisher*'s fire alarms began yowling like banshees.

The cruiser was nearing the huge asteroid swarm where Deaner Beckmann had hived his bootleg lab, and Min wanted to be at the center of information and command. Nevertheless the unexpected squall of the klaxons seemed to change everything. Her instincts hadn't warned her: she hadn't felt the ship's ambient vibrations mounting toward an emergency.

Surprised by disaster, she launched herself forward in the zero g equivalent of a run.

Dolph Ubikwe hadn't arrived yet when she coasted onto the bridge, stopped herself on a handgrip. Command Fourth Hargin Stoval sat at the command station, barking orders at the intercom. Data and engineering shouted back and forth: the other bridge stations clung fiercely to their tasks while her people fought to assess and answer the damage.

"Status!" Min demanded as soon as Stoval paused for breath.

He hadn't seen her enter the bridge. When he heard her voice, however, he flung his g-seat around to face her and snapped a salute. "Director Donner. We're on fire." He named a section of the ship's infrastructure near the core. "So far we don't have a clue what started it, but it's pretty bad. Hot enough to feed off every bit of plastic, debris, and oil it can find. We already have two dead, others hurt."

He hesitated momentarily, then said, "I should get down there. If you'll take the bridge, Director—"

Min jerked a nod. "Go." From what Dolph had said about him, she guessed that Stoval was the best man aboard to take charge of the damage-control parties. Captain Ubikwe wouldn't feel slighted if she watched over his command for him briefly.

As Stoval unbelted himself and headed off the bridge, she left her handgrip for a new hold on an arm of the command station. From that position she could see the console and readouts without assuming Dolph's authority.

After a quick glance at the indicators and screens, she turned to the other officers. "Anything else I should know right this minute?"

The bridge crew came from a mix of watches: individual duty rotations had shifted to compensate for lost personnel. Glessen on targ and Cray on communications shook their heads. "We've reached the trailing edges of the swarm, sir," Patrice reported from helm. "In another hour we'll approach the main body."

Porson, the scan officer, punched vehemently at his board until Min gave him her attention. Then he muttered, "Looks like we've lost that entire sensor bank for good, Director. The one we've been working on ever since you came aboard. Fire must have got the wiring."

"Compensate," Min instructed him. "Tell helm what you need to cover us. We can't afford blind spots.

"Data," she went on, "this is your department. What happened?"

The data officer was a young woman named Bydell. When Min spoke to her, she flinched. "Engineering—" she began. "The computer—" She was too young for her duties; too vulnerable to the prolonged strain *Punisher* had endured. "I don't know—"

She conveyed the impression that she was coming apart.

"Reconstruct it," Min answered firmly. Bydell's distress was Dolph's problem. Min didn't know his people well enough to take their individual personalities into account. But she had no intention of letting them slip into paralysis while their ship burned. "That's what computer simulations are for. Let's not make Captain Ubikwe wait for answers when he gets here."

"Aye, sir." The data officer did her best to confront her board like a woman who knew what she was doing.

Min turned back to the command board, tapped a few keys to call up new information, then paused to think.

Any fire was bad enough aboard a ship; but this one was more than that. If it spread, it might do severe damage to *Punisher*'s control systems.

Worse, it could conceivably breach the core— If Stoval didn't put it out quickly, it could cripple the ship.

Already one of the sensor banks was gone. She confirmed that on the command console, even though she didn't doubt Porson for an instant. One whole scan array had failed, leaving *Punisher* blind forward across an arc of nearly thirty degrees.

A bit of weight nudged her toward her boots as helm began adjusting the ship's attitude in relation to her course.

Min clenched her fists against the familiar fire in her palms and waited for Captain Ubikwe.

He arrived no more than five minutes after she did. Surging onto the bridge as if he were shouldering off fears and weakness, he coasted straight to the command station, pulled himself into his g-seat, and clasped his belts. "Thanks, Director," he said to Min. His voice projected the power and certainty of a pneumatic hammer. "Sorry I kept you waiting. I took the time to talk to Hargin. We've got the moral equivalent of an inferno in there. What's the situation here?"

Min glanced at Bydell and decided to take a chance. "Data was just about to tell us," she drawled calmly.

"Right, sir," the woman said as if she were gulping for air.

"I didn't see what happened," she began at once. "We didn't get any warning—at least not any warning we understood. But I've been running simulations, trying to construct a scenario that fits. This is what I've been able to come up with."

We've got micro-leaks in some of the hydraulic systems, the bosun had told Min when she'd first come aboard. *We haven't had time to trace them.* But she'd already known that: she'd read *Punisher*'s reports. And there hadn't been anything she could do about it.

Now she was learning what her decision to take this ship despite the cruiser's condition cost.

The sequence of events, as Bydell reconstructed it, was this. Acid from one hydraulic line and oil from another had drifted together. That should have been impossible, of course: such lines lay in sealed conduits. But if lines could crack, so could conduits. While *Punisher* ran in zero g, without internal spin or navigational thrust, the leaks had accumulated until they formed considerable quantities of fluid. Then the cruiser began veering and hauling her way through Massif-5, ducking obstacles by the hundreds to follow *Trumpet*. Pools of acid and oil were sloshed and pulled in every direction until they found cracks. And those cracks led to other conduits, more cracks.

In the meantime *Punisher*'s people were still at work on the wiring to one of the main sensor banks. External repairs had been jury-rigged earlier: now the internal lines were being restrung. To do the job, repair techs needed repeated access to a portion of the ship's infrastructure. Unfortunately the bulkhead door they used was sticking. At times its servos cycled for three or four seconds before they built up enough pressure to shift the door.

While they labored they generated heat as well as pressure, more and more heat as the action of the door deteriorated.

Somehow considerable quantities of oil and acid had come together in the lines around the straining servos. When the fluids caught fire, they exploded with such force that they crumpled the bulkhead, killed two techs, flash-burned two more, and started a blaze which *Punisher*'s people, hampered by zero g and navigational thrust, didn't know how to control.

In the process, of course, the sensor bank was lost.

Captain Ubikwe felt the strain: it showed in one of his familiar outbreaks of irascibility. "Damn it," he muttered as if he didn't think anyone was listening, "this is too much. I'm starting to believe in curses. How long has it been since any of us were on a ship that actually caught fire?"

No one responded. Min flexed her fingers and counted the beats of her pulse to keep herself from issuing orders.

"*Damn* it," he repeated. "We've got decisions to make."

Abruptly he changed his tone. "Confirmation on that sensor bank, Porson? It's really dead?"

"Worse than useless, Captain," scan replied. "I can't even get static out of it. The computer has already routed around it like it isn't there."

Dolph nodded. "How are we compensating?"

"I'm stretching the arc on the other banks, Captain," Porson continued, "but I can only pick up a few degrees. The rest is up to helm."

"Sergei?" Dolph asked the helm officer.

"Usual procedure, Captain," Sergei Patrice answered, "if anything about this situation is 'usual.' I'm rotating the entire ship around her core. You can feel the tug—we've picked up a couple of pounds of g. So what we have in essence is a one-second blind spot sweeping our scan field. We can make it shorter or longer, whatever you want.

"But, Captain—" Helm hesitated.

"Spit it out," Captain Ubikwe rumbled. "I'm already in a bad mood. You aren't likely to make it worse."

"Sorry, Captain." Patrice grinned humorlessly. "I just thought I ought to say—we can't go into combat like this. We can't afford the inertia. At some point we'll have to choose between defending ourselves and being able to see."

Dolph smiled back at him. "I was wrong. You can so make it worse."

At once he thumbed his intercom.

"Hargin," he called. "Can you hear me? Hargin Stoval. I want a report."

The intercom speaker brought distant shouts over a roaring background to the bridge. Then the connection popped as the pickup on the other end was activated.

Stoval's voice shed frustration and alarm like sparks. "We aren't getting anywhere, Captain. The automatic systems can't handle it. And it's so damn hot, we can't get close enough to use portable extinguishers.

"This g hurts us," he added. "Seems to concentrate the fire. It's hotter all the time."

Captain Ubikwe grimaced. "I hear you, Hargin. Stand by. We need to change something. I'll let you know as soon as I decide what."

He clicked off his pickup and turned to Min.

"Director Donner." His tone was steady, incisive, but the dull, combative smolder in his eyes made him look desperate. "This is your mission. I have to ask you. Is there any reason why we shouldn't cut all thrust and let ourselves coast while we fight this fire?"

Min allowed herself a sardonic snort. "If I tried, I could probably think of six. But none of them will matter if we let a fire cripple us. Do what you have to do, Captain. We'll deal with the consequences later."

A flicker of gratitude showed in his gaze. He didn't take the time to articulate it, however. Wheeling his station, he began, "All right, Patrice—"

"Shit!" Porson croaked in sudden dismay. At once he murmured tensely, "Sorry, Captain," running commands as fast as he could hit the keys. Scan readouts on the screens jumped and blurred as he changed them. As if he couldn't help himself, he groaned again, "Shit."

Dolph growled a warning. But he didn't need to demand an explanation. Min didn't need one. Porson had already put the data which shocked him up onto one of the main displays.

Out of nowhere ahead of *Punisher* another ship had appeared.

Literally out of nowhere. Scan identified the characteristic burst of distortion—the impression that physical laws were being fried—which followed vessels emerging from the gap.

Counters along the bottom of the display measured lag. That ship had come out of the gap practically on top of *Punisher:* less than sixty thousand k away. She could have opened fire already if she'd known *Punisher* would be there. And if she hadn't resumed tard at nearly .2C; three times the cruiser's velocity.

She angled toward the main body of the asteroid swarm at a speed which any human captain would have considered insane.

"Lord have mercy," Glessen breathed from targ as he studied the display. "They're out of their minds."

"Id!" Dolph demanded sharply. "I want id."

Was the vessel friendly or hostile?

She was *big:* scan already made that clear.

"She's not broadcasting, Captain," Cray answered. "I don't hear anything except gap distortion and emission noise."

"You've got her signature?" Captain Ubikwe asked scan.

"Aye, Captain." Porson pointed: the numbers were already on the display.

Min recognized them long intuitive seconds before Dolph said, "Bydell, what do you have on that emission signature?"

Flustered, Bydell was slow coding an analysis. "Sorry, Captain," she muttered, repeating herself like a stuck recording as she entered commands, accessed databases. "Sorry, Captain."

Min couldn't wait. "Targ, lock onto that ship," she snapped. "Matter cannon, torpedoes, whatever you have ready. Prepare to attack."

If the stranger fired, *Punisher* would get no advance notice at all. Light-constant blasts would reach her as fast as scan. Her only hope of warning depended on scan's ability to detect whether the other ship's guns were charged.

Dolph flashed a look at her; apparently decided not to question what he saw. "Do it, Glessen," he confirmed. "Full alert. Screens and shields on maximum."

A heavy finger on his console set *Punisher*'s battle klaxons screaming.

Then he keyed his intercom. "Hargin?" Without waiting for a response, he called, "We're going to battle stations. Don't stop what you're doing. That fire takes precedence. I'll give you fair warning if we have to hit thrust."

"I hear you, Captain," Stoval answered. "We're doing our best."

"Locked on, Captain," Glessen announced. "We're out of effective torpedo range. Lasers probably aren't powerful enough for a target that big. Matter cannon might take a piece out of her—if we don't hit a particle sink. But at the rate she's pulling away, we're losing her. In another twenty seconds, she'll be out of reach."

Out of reach. Min swore to herself. Right in front of her, an Amnion warship had arrived out of the gap to commit an act of war. But the UMCP cruiser charged with defending human space was on fire. In another twenty seconds, the Amnioni would be safe.

Fiercely she bit down an impulse to order an assault. *Punisher* was in no condition to engage an enemy. The cruiser wouldn't be able to defend herself against return fire unless she solved other problems first.

"Captain"—Bydell's voice shook—"I've got tentative id."

"Let's have it," Dolph rasped.

"According to the computer," Bydell replied as if she were feverish, "that ship is a Behemoth-class Amnion defensive. The biggest warship they make. UMCPDA reports say she has enough firepower to nova a small sun. And"—the data officer swallowed convulsively—"she carries super-light proton cannon."

Glessen croaked an involuntary curse. Cray turned away to hide her face.

An act of war. Combative fury scalded Min's palms. An Amnion warship had come all the way here from forbidden space to stop *Trumpet*. The Amnion considered the stakes high enough to justify risks on that scale.

Was this what Warden wanted? An incursion to shore up his political position by demonstrating how necessary he and the UMCP were? Was this why he'd chosen Milos Taverner to go with Angus?—to set this up?

How would Succorso react when he learned how much trouble he was in?

"Captain Ubikwe," she said harshly, "we've got to go after that ship."

He didn't look at her. His eyes studied the displays while his hands worked his board. "Is that an order, Director Donner?" His shoulders clenched as if he were suppressing a shout. "Are you instructing me to ignore the fact that we're on fire?"

"Yes," Min snapped, "that's an order." Then she added, "No, I'm not instructing you to ignore the fact that we're on fire."

For a moment Dolph didn't react. He bowed his head: his bulk seemed to shrink down into itself as if his courage were leaking away. He looked like a man who'd been instructed to kill himself.

But he didn't comply. Instead he slammed his fist onto the edge of his console, launched his station around to face her. *"Then what do you expect me to do about it?"* he roared. "I can't take on a goddamn *Behemoth-class* Amnion warship if I can't maneuver—and I can't maneuver without killing my people fighting that fire!"

Min held his angry glare. Her gaze was as strict as a commandment; absolute and fatal.

"Captain Ubikwe," she articulated through her teeth, "you have enough plexulose plasma sealant aboard to reinforce the entire inner hull. Pump some of it between the bulkheads onto the fire. Use it to smother the flames."

Dolph's mouth dropped open: he closed it again. Shadows of outrage darkened his gaze.

"Bydell"—his voice rasped like a scourge—"how hot is that fire?"

Data consulted her readouts. "According to the computer, it must be" —she named a temperature. Then, inspired by her fears, she jumped to the point of Dolph's question. "Captain, that's hot enough to set the sealant on fire."

"No." Min was sure. She had an encyclopedic knowledge of everything that went into UMCPED's ships. "Plexulose plasma doesn't become flammable at that temperature until it hardens. The foam won't burn. If Stoval works fast enough, he can smother the fire before the sealant hardens."

"He can't get that *close* to it!" Captain Ubikwe protested like a man who wanted to tear his hair.

Min faced him without wavering. "Tell him to put his people in EVA suits," she retorted. "They'll be able to work right on top of the blaze—at least for a couple of minutes."

Until the suits' cooling systems overloaded and shut down.

Dolph's mouth twisted as if he were tasting another yell. Gradually, however, the darkness in his eyes cleared. An emotion that might have been amazement or respect pulled at the lines of his face.

"You know," he breathed, "that might work. It's crazy, but it might work."

His surprise lasted only a moment. Then he slapped open his intercom and started issuing new orders to Hargin Stoval.

As soon as the command fourth confirmed that he'd heard, Dolph returned his attention to the bridge.

"Sergei," he instructed sharply, "stop this damn rotation. Hargin has enough to deal with. Position us so we can track that ship with one of our good sensor banks. Then give me steady one-g acceleration along her heading."

"Aye, Captain." Patrice was already keying in commands.

"That won't catch her," Dolph explained as if he thought Min might question him, "but it'll keep us in scan range until she starts braking.

"She *is* going to start braking," he asserted, addressing his people now rather than Min. "A Behemoth-class Amnion warship didn't come all this way just to give us a thrill. She's here to hunt for *Trumpet*. That means she'll have to slow down.

"Cray," he went on without pausing, "tight-beam a flare for VI Security. Full emergency priority. Tell them they have an Amnion warship on their hands. Give them her position. Tell them to scramble every ship they have out here."

"And tell them to flare UMCPHQ," Min put in quickly. "Tell them to use the fastest gap courier drone they have. On my personal authority."

"Do it," Captain Ubikwe confirmed.

"Aye, Captain." At once Cray went to work.

Dolph considered his readouts, then turned back to his intercom.

"Hargin," he called, "we're about to lose rotation. Instead we'll have one-g thrust straight ahead. That might make what you're trying to do a little easier." Stoval's firefighters would be able to stand—and to trust the surface they stood on. "Brace yourself."

"I hear you, Captain," Stoval answered. His voice had the hollow resonance of an EVA suit pickup. "We're rigging the hoses now. We'll be ready in a minute. Tell Bydell to start the pumps on my signal. We'll be frying our suits that close to the fire. We can't afford any delays."

"Got that, Bydell?" Captain Ubikwe demanded.

Determination clenched the data officer's features. Her hands fluttered and flinched on her board. "Aye, Captain."

"We're standing by, Hargin," Dolph told his pickup. "Pumps at full pressure. We'll give you sealant as fast as the hoses can spray it."

He continued issuing orders; but Min had stopped listening. She was watching the warship's blip recede in the center of the main display screen. The Amnioni was pulling away as if she would never stop.

Min knew better.

A Behemoth-class defensive, armed with super-light proton cannon. Hunting *Trumpet*.

An act of war.

Damaged by six months of running battles in this system, blind in one sensor bank, her core off true, and now threatened by a fire hot enough to gut her, *Punisher* was heading for the worst fight of her life.

MORN

Morn was losing control: she could feel it. The urgency and outrage which had sustained her were crumbling; falling apart. She was at the mercy of a withdrawal as poignant as the sick loss which afflicted her when she was deprived of her zone implant's support. Her relief that Vector had been able to help Ciro had left her drained and vulnerable. Now horror seemed to gnaw in her bones.

Horror at what Nick had done to the Lab. At the destructive madness which had driven him to leave the ship so that he could pit himself against *Soar* in an EVA suit. At Sib's willingness to accompany him.

At the fact that what Nick was doing made sense to Davies—

As far as I can tell, I'm Bryony Hyland's daughter. The one she used to have—before you sold your soul for a zone implant.

Oh, Davies, my son. What's happening to you?

Did I teach you this? Did you learn it from me?

Is it part of me?

Maybe it was. But if so, it'd died in her when she first came down with gap-sickness—the culmination and apotheosis of her old grudge against herself.

She more than anyone else couldn't afford revenge.

A few minutes ago Davies had returned from the airlock. Without glancing at her or anyone else, he'd seated himself at the second's station, secured his belts. His face was closed—as dark with bile as his father's, but somehow less readable. He'd put up walls she couldn't penetrate; swallowed or buried the near hysteria of his insistence on hunting *Soar*. His hands on his board were vehement, but steady: he keyed commands with brutal precision.

"You feel better now?" Angus had asked indifferently.

Davies hadn't bothered to reply.

Status indicators on one of the screens showed that he was running targ diagnostics, making sure that *Trumpet*'s guns were fully charged, fully functional.

He couldn't handle targ as well as Angus. Human desperation or passion were no match for Angus' microprocessor reflexes. Nevertheless his attitude toward his board gave Morn the impression that he was prepared to be as relentless and bloody as his father.

Just a little while ago—an hour or two at most—she'd made decisions and stood by them. But now she could hardly hold up her head. She'd learned to desire revenge on *Gutbuster* at the same time and in the same way that she'd learned to be ashamed of herself. As a child, her secret disloyalty to her parents' calling had undermined her self-esteem; left her feeling culpable for her mother's death. And since then that flaw at the core of her convictions had eroded everything she did.

Now her shame came back to her in a new way.

As far as I can tell, I'm Bryony Hyland's daughter.

She couldn't see any way out of it. After everything she'd done and endured, the logic of her illness still held her.

And she was useless. She couldn't help Vector work. Nor could she take either of the command stations. There was combat ahead—urgent maneuvers and hard g. As soon as *Trumpet* faced action, Morn would have to return to her cabin, dope herself senseless with cat, and lie passive in her g-sheath while other people determined whether the ship would live or die.

As useless as Nick in his bonds—

The thought made her feel like weeping again. If she couldn't comprehend Nick, she understood all too well the pressure which had impelled Sib to go with him.

As for the rest—

I understand *him*, Davies had protested. *I understand him better than* you *do! I remember what* you *remember. And I'm* male. *Whatever that means. I know what he'll do!*

He needs this too much.

Morn was familiar with absolute commitments. She had her own, which had carried her to extremes she would have found unimaginable scant weeks ago. Nevertheless her heart refused to accommodate the sheer scale of Nick's hunger to repay Sorus Chatelaine.

How much time did she have left?—how long before she was forced to return to her cabin and hide herself in drugs?

Do you really think it's preferable *to keep him tied up here like a piece of meat?*

At the moment she felt it would be preferable to put the muzzle of an impact pistol in her mouth and squeeze the firing stud.

"That's it," Angus muttered abruptly. "We've lost their transmission. Sib and Captain Sheepfucker are out of range. If Succorso wants to kill him, he can do it anytime now."

Morn looked at him. He seemed to squat like a toad over his console; his face and movements burned with concentration. He still hadn't troubled to pull up his shipsuit. She could see his bloated chest too well: remembered it too well—the black triangle of hair covering his heart like a target; his pale skin stained with sweat. Yet he was changed in some way, subtly different from the butcher and rapist she knew. And different as well from the clenched, bitter machine who'd rescued her on Thanatos Minor. Something essential had been set loose in him when she'd allowed him to edit his datacore. His concentration was as hard as his old malice and brutality; but it had new implications.

She searched for ways to test him; to discover what the changes in him meant. Facing him with the screens behind her, she asked unsteadily, "Are we really going to go back for Sib?"

Have we sent him out to die just so you can get rid of Nick?

Angus paused with his fingers on the helm keys. Slowly he lifted his yellow eyes to meet her gaze. She saw shadows of hunger in them; hints of grief behind his certainty and focus. Before *Trumpet* left forbidden space, she'd asked him, *What do you want?* And he'd answered, *I want you.* But when she'd told him, *I would rather make myself into a lump of dead meat,* his reaction had surprised her.

He'd seemed almost relieved. As if her revulsion spared him a vulnerability he couldn't afford.

She understood now that he'd always wanted his freedom more than he'd ever wanted her. To the extent that she could trust him here, it was because she'd released him from the coercion of his priority-codes.

At the auxiliary engineering console, Vector cocked his head, obviously listening for Angus' reply. Davies gave no sign that he'd heard her question.

Angus studied her for a moment. Then he shrugged. "If we get the chance. Why not? He got rid of Succorso for me. That counts for something. And if he's that crazy, he might be useful again."

His gaze held hers as if he never blinked.

"You don't care about anything else?" she pursued. "Sib himself doesn't matter to you?"

"I'll tell you what I care about." Angus clenched one fist and started tapping it softly on the edge of his console. However, the rest of him showed no emotion. He had zone implants to keep him steady. "I care about why you didn't want to let Captain Sheepfucker go."

Morn frowned. What was he getting at?

"You broke my heart," he said gruffly. "You know that? You always wanted him. You wanted him the first minute you saw him, that time in Mallorys." As he spoke, his voice became more guttural: it sounded like the exhaust of a combustion engine. "I would have killed to have you look at me that way. Hell, I would have killed everybody on the whole damn station." His mouth twisted. "I would have stopped hurting you if you'd ever looked at me that way."

As sudden as a cry, he demanded, "Is that what's going on now? Are you fucking falling apart right in front of me because you think you're never going to see him again?"

He shocked her. Too quickly to stop herself, she caught fire; the needy tinder of her spirit burst into flames of protest. He'd hurt her too much for too long, far too long, she'd believed he was destroying her. Pain as hot as a smelter seemed to roar and devour through her.

"*Wanted* him?" she yelled into his bloated face and yellow eyes. "You think I *wanted* him? Do you think I'm *crazy*? I never *wanted* him. Wanting to *die* would have been easier!"

Her shout jerked Vector around in his seat, made even Davies look up at her. But she ignored them.

"All I *wanted*," she flung at Angus, hurling words like knives to tear at him, "all I *ever* wanted was somebody to help me *get away from you*!"

Abruptly she stumbled silent. Again he shocked her. Instead of drawing back or looking away—or answering with his own anger—he watched her with a grin dawning on his face as if she'd filled him with sunrise.

"Is that true?" he asked in amazement. "Do you mean it?"

Bitter as acid, she finished, "I was sick of men. Anything male revolted me. But Nick was the only one I saw who looked like he might have a chance."

Angus went on grinning. Slowly he began to chuckle like a maladjusted turbine.

"Shit, Morn. If I'd known that, I wouldn't have spent so much time wishing he was dead."

He was too much for her. Revulsion crackled and swirled inside her, as fresh as when he'd first degraded her; as fresh as fire. She wanted to flay his skin from his bones—draw blood for all the damage he'd done her.

"Of course." She strove to make her voice as harmful as his. "Of *course*, you sonofabitch. *You* don't care what happens to Sib. *You* don't care what Nick was like. *You* don't care who he hurt, or how he did it, or what it cost. All *you* care about is that I didn't *want* him more than I wanted you."

Angus shook his head. By degrees his strange mirth subsided; the sunrise faded from his expression. Her attack must have reached him. "Maybe that's true," he admitted. The admission seemed to pain him, however. Her attack restored his familiar anger. "And maybe it doesn't matter.

"I'm a machine," he rasped with his accustomed harshness. "A goddamn machine. That's all. Warden Dios tells me what to do, and I do it. Sometimes he pulls the strings. Sometimes I get to make my own choices. Sometimes I can't even tell the difference. What the fuck do you *expect* me to care about?"

"You aren't being fair," Davies put in unexpectedly. Despite his youth, he sounded as stern as her father delivering a reprimand. "He got you away from the Amnion. Since then he's been on your side. As much as Nick let him. We would all be dead without him. What more do you want?"

Carried by conflagration, she wheeled on her son. He was too much like Angus, too male and belligerent: he hadn't earned the right to reproach her.

" 'Bryony Hyland's daughter,' " she quoted trenchantly. " 'The one she used to have' before I sold my soul—the pure one." The one who hated Nick and *Soar* so much he was willing to let Sib die for it. "I want you to care about what you're doing. I want you to care about what it costs."

Davies met her squarely. He didn't shout or argue; didn't so much as raise his voice. "You don't know anything about what it costs me."

She couldn't stop: she was too angry. "I'll tell you what I don't know. I don't know why you feel so sorry for yourself. And I don't want to know.

It doesn't interest me. I gave you life, whether you want it or not. I've kept you alive ever since." Angus had only rescued Davies in order to trade him for her. "If you aren't willing to talk about what's eating you, at least stop sneering at me."

That stung him. Abruptly furious, he faced her with a look like black hate. Straining against his belts, he cried, "I killed my father! I killed my whole family! The universe spoke to me, and I did what it said! I did it with my own hands. And *it wasn't even me*! I don't *exist*. I'm just a shadow of you!"

Then his voice dropped to a low snarl. "I need to be the kind of cop you should have been. And you don't," he repeated, "know anything about what it costs me."

As effectively as a splash of foam, he doused the flames in her, quenched her desire to draw blood. He was right: she couldn't begin to guess what his life cost him. And she had no idea what Hashi Lebwohl and UMCPDA had done to Angus; no idea how much he suffered for it. They didn't deserve her indignation.

But without it she had nothing left except shame.

"You're right." She couldn't meet his eyes, or Angus'. "I'm sorry. It's withdrawal— I don't know how to handle it."

"You know," Vector offered quietly, "we might be able to find a dosage of cat that protects you without leaving you unconscious. If we titrate it right."

Morn didn't respond. She meant withdrawal from the artificial stimulation of her zone implant. But she also meant withdrawal from the ability to transcend her limitations, rise above her flaws. And for that loss there was no drug to help her.

Angus ran the swarm as smoothly as he could. With the chart Beckmann had supplied, Lab Center's earlier operational input, and *Trumpet*'s penetrating sensors, he found ways through the throng of rock that didn't require sudden course changes, emergency evasions. The gap scout slid from side to side on relatively gentle thrust, dodging out of the depths of the swarm.

G pulled Morn in every conceivable direction. Her feet drifted off the deck; her body arced slowly this way and that. But the pressure didn't threaten her. With one hand on a zero-g grip she was able to control her movement enough to avoid bruising herself against the bulkhead.

Angus should have sent her off the bridge to protect her; or to protect *Trumpet* from what she might do if her gap-sickness took her. Instead he took care of her in other ways. Under the circumstances, she could afford to wait awhile.

She clung to the bridge the same way she clung to her handgrip, using her presence at the center of decisions and action to help her manage the stresses pulling at her heart.

At the second's station, Davies worked obsessively, verifying and refining his mastery of the gap scout's targ.

Clinging, Morn studied the data he routed to one of the displays, and was dumbfounded by the power and complexity of *Trumpet*'s weaponry. The ship was a gap scout: according to her public specifications, she was totally unarmed. In any case, she should have been too small to carry heavy guns. But the UMCP's researchers must have achieved miracles of miniaturization. The weapons *Trumpet* shouldn't have had could deliver more destruction at greater distances than Morn would ever have guessed.

Trumpet wasn't equipped with lasers. They were problematic in any case; vulnerable to EM distortion as well as to the jolts and line fluctuations of the ships powering them. In battle it was difficult for human technologies to maintain coherence. But the gap scout had enough other armaments to make the absence of lasers seem trivial.

She had impact guns for close combat; matter cannon for strikes at greater range; plasma torpedoes; static mines. And—amazingly—she also carried singularity grenades; devices at once so dangerous and so difficult to use that Morn's instructors in the Academy had dismissed their value in actual combat. Theoretically, under the right conditions, they detonated to form black holes—tiny instances of mass so dense that their gravitic fields could suck down anything within their event horizons. Practically, however, the right conditions were nearly impossible to obtain. The grenade only produced a black hole if it detonated in the presence of enough other power—for instance, if the grenade went off inside an active thruster tube. Without external energies to feed it, the singularity was so tiny that it consumed itself and winked away before it could do any damage.

The fact that Hashi Lebwohl—or Warden Dios—had seen fit to supply *Trumpet* with singularity grenades made Morn shiver so hard the muscles in her abdomen cramped.

They had expected the gap scout to fight for her life. Probably alone —and probably against massive odds.

What other expectations did they have for her?

"Done," Vector announced suddenly. Satisfaction and eagerness sharpened his voice. "I'm copying it to your board," he told Angus. "You can start transmitting whenever you want.

"Assuming we get the chance," he added while he relayed his results. "Which I certainly hope we will. All this talk about fighting *Soar* and not being ashamed of ourselves"—he glanced pointedly at Davies, who ignored him—"is fine as far as it goes, but this message is a more effective weapon than any gun."

Morn nodded dully. He was right: his information about UMCPDA's mutagen immunity drug was the most important thing *Trumpet* carried. In the end transmitting his message mattered more than whether or not the ship survived; whether Angus could be trusted, or Sib died; whether Morn or Davies lost their souls.

The minute that data reached anyone who could understand it and disseminate it, the entire complex of plots and imperialism which humankind and the Amnion played out against each other would be transformed.

Warden Dios might come down. The entire UMCP might topple. Holt Fasner himself could be threatened. And the Amnion would suffer a blow which might force them to end this war now, by attack or retreat, while they still had the chance.

Whatever else happened, whatever it cost, *Trumpet* needed to transmit Vector's message.

"Got it," Angus answered when the data transfer was complete. "We're set to broadcast as soon as we get out of this swarm. We'll spray it in all directions like a distress call. Eventually every receiver in the system will pick it up." He bared his teeth. "That way whoever wants to stop us will know they've already lost.

"Now get off the bridge."

Vector frowned as if Angus had insulted him.

"Where you're sitting isn't exactly a combat station," Angus explained. "You'll be dead meat as soon as we hit hard g. Probably wreck the console, too. Go web yourself into your bunk."

"Ah," Vector sighed in comprehension. "Of course." He nodded. Projecting an air of pain, as if a flare-up of arthritis had settled in his joints while he worked, he unclipped his zero-g belt, drifted off his seat.

Instead of moving for the companionway, however, he floated toward Angus' station. When he reached it, he caught the arm of the g-seat. Facing the displays instead of Angus, he remarked wearily, "I didn't think I would ever say this, but I miss the days when I could stay on the bridge. If I'm going to die out here, I want to see it coming—God knows why.

Maybe I hope I'll have time to seek absolution at the last minute." He smiled crookedly. "I wouldn't want to risk repenting prematurely.

"Will you tell us what's happening?" He was looking at Morn, but his question must have been meant for Angus. "Mikka probably wants to know. I certainly do."

"If I have time," Angus retorted impatiently. "Just go."

Vector sighed again; shrugged. "Right."

From Angus' g-seat he launched himself stiffly toward the companionway. In a moment he'd climbed the rails and moved into the midship passage out of sight.

Seeing him go like that, alone and unapplauded, touched Morn with sadness. He'd accomplished so much, and received so little for it. No matter what crimes he might have helped Nick commit, he didn't need absolution; not as far as she was concerned. He'd already done something better than repent.

"He could have stayed," she murmured. "It wouldn't have hurt us to give him a little companionship."

"No, he couldn't," Angus growled, concentrating on his board and the screens. "You should go, too. This isn't safe."

His tone scraped a sore place in her, a raw nerve of panic. Urgency flushed her skin. He'd seen something, felt something—

"What is it?"

"I'm getting a scan echo." Angus' hands spidered over his board, scuttling to sharpen images and data. "If it isn't a ghost, there's another ship out here."

Davies gripped the edges of his console. "Is it *Soar*? Has she caught up with us this fast?"

"It's an echo," Angus returned sourly. "It doesn't have a fucking emission signature.

"I mean it," he shot at Morn. "Get off the bridge. I've already seen what you're like under heavy g. I don't want to repeat the experience."

As if she were obedient, abraded with panic, she pushed off from the bulkhead in the direction of the companionway. But when she reached the rails, she reversed her trajectory, rebounded to the back of Angus' g-seat.

Whether or not the ship survived—

She had no intention of leaving unless he physically forced her away.

Despite her fear, she believed she could prevent him from doing that.

"You're spending too much time on the guns," Angus snapped at Davies. "Concentrate on our defenses." *Trumpet* had glazed surfaces to deflect lasers, energy shields to absorb impact fire, particle sinks to weaken matter cannon blasts. "The cops're experimenting with dispersion fields. Might be more effective against matter cannon. There."

He hit keys, jerked data onto the screen Davies used.

"But they aren't automatic. If they were, we couldn't fire through them. You have to be ready."

Davies looked up, studied the information. "All right," he muttered. "I'm on it."

A small part of Morn's mind was filled with wonder. A dispersion field was an elegant idea: project an energy wave to disrupt the matter beam before it took on mass from its target; disperse the forces. As Angus had said, however, none of *Trumpet*'s guns could be fired while the field was being projected. And the resulting boson bleed-off would be staggering.

The rest of her simply held to the back of Angus' station as if she were praying.

Past his shoulder she could see his readouts; his efforts to identify the scan echo. He was fast—God, he was *fast*. She'd never seen anyone run a board so swiftly. In some sense, he *was* a machine: a nearly integral extension of his ship.

Elusive and undifferentiated, the echo seemed to flee under his fingers, becoming something else whenever he snatched at it. Yet it was too persistent to be a ghost. The conditions which could produce a ghost through the swarm's static were evanescent: a false image would have vanished as suddenly as it appeared.

"I'm getting a profile." Angus might have spoken to himself. "Doesn't look like *Soar*. Not as big. Damn this static.

"It's almost familiar. Shit, almost—"

Familiar? Was it *Punisher*? Not likely: not if the ship was smaller than *Soar*.

Morn couldn't stay silent. She had to say, "If she isn't *Soar*, she might not be hostile."

"That's naive," Davies snorted without glancing at her. "Whoever she is, she's illegal. Around here she couldn't be anything else. And by now she must know the Lab's gone. She'll have to assume we had something to do with it. She'll shoot first, worry about the consequences later.

"Besides, we can't be sure *Soar*'s alone." He sounded more like his father all the time. Leaving Morn behind— "She had plenty of friends back on Billingate."

"I told you," Angus snapped at Morn, "to *get off the bridge*."

But he didn't move to make her go. Maybe he assumed she would obey. Instead he thumbed his intercom, opened a ship-wide channel. "Secure for combat. Somebody's after us."

How long before *Trumpet* reached the fringes of the swarm? Angus had left a navigation schematic running on one of the displays. Projections indicated that she had at least an hour to go. But she could do it in less—maybe much less—if Angus accelerated; ran helm with the same inhuman speed and precision he used to analyze scan.

Angus, Morn meant to say, go faster. Get us out of here. We'll be harder to hit. And we need to reach a place where we can start broadcasting.

The words stuck in her throat.

Without warning, the ship's alarms shrilled. One of the screens broke up, scrambling to display new input: then it started scrolling data too fast for Morn to read.

"There!" Angus barked. "God damn it, I've seen that signature before!"

Scan had located another vessel, nudging her way between the rocks ahead.

She emerged from behind an asteroid large enough to occlude a battlewagon, navigational thrust roaring to orient her on the gap scout. She was big, not the size of *Soar,* but several orders of magnitude bigger than *Trumpet,* possibly a merchanter, more likely an illegal hauler. Her emissions shouted signs of power: drive ready to burn; charged guns.

Davies' hands came down on his keys so hard that his shoulders hunched and his torso wrenched against his belts. Instantly *Trumpet* unleashed a barrage of impact and matter cannon fire.

He hadn't taken enough time to focus targ: his need to strike had betrayed him. Impact blasts licked along the other ship's hull or skidded past her: the matter cannon shot wide.

At once the ship nearly vanished from scan as asteroids burst like fragmentation bombs, filling the void with tons of debris which yowled and ricocheted up and down the spectrum.

Bombardments of rock clanged off *Trumpet*'s skin and shields. The whole ship cried like a carillon.

A heartbeat later the gap scout staggered and went blind as the other ship's matter cannon covered her like the fall of an avalanche.

The scan displays crackled and spat with distortion. Metal stress rang through the hulls: klaxons squalled like demented spirits. Hammering keys, Angus hauled *Trumpet* out of the line of fire, practically cartwheeling her in a blaze of thrust to put stone between her and the other ship's guns.

Morn knew what he was doing, even though she couldn't see or hear him. She knew because her feet lifted from the deck; her own weight snatched her hands off the back of his g-seat as if her strength were trivial.

Helpless as a cork, she swirled in the air and dove headlong toward the starboard bulkhead.

She tucked her head, arched her shoulder; turned in time to avoid shattering the bones of her head. Still her mass hit with its own hard g.

The impact slapped her flat, pounded the air from her lungs, drove the blood from her brain. She seemed to slip out of herself as if she were being sucked into the wall.

Somewhere nearby she heard Davies shouting.

"It works! That dispersion field works!"

No wonder *Trumpet* had gone blind. Her sensors and sifters couldn't see anything except the raving chaos at the heart of the matter beam.

I've seen that signature—

Then Morn lost consciousness. She never knew whether the other ship fired again.

DARRIN

Darrin Scroyle stared at the chaos which had taken the place of his scan displays; for a moment he froze. Around him his people gaped in astonishment and alarm.

Trumpet was gone. Disappeared in a fury of boson madness. Until the sensors cleared, *Free Lunch* was blind and deaf; she might as well be weaponless. Scan and data fought with their instruments and programs, struggling to see through the particle storm; but it was too intense for them. And too unfamiliar—*Free Lunch* had never encountered anything like this before.

Despite the emission carnage, however, Darrin was sure he hadn't hurt the gap scout. No normal matter cannon blast caused results like *that.* If *Trumpet*'s drives had blown—if the ship had broken down to her component atoms—*Free Lunch*'s computers would have understood; would have filtered out the distortion in order to see the results.

The gap scout was gone. Darrin couldn't be sure that he'd so much as touched her.

What in the name of sanity was going on?

"How did she *do* that?" Alesha demanded. A note of panic sharpened her voice. "We hit her dead on, I swear it. Even if she's nothing but a particle sink, we hit her hard enough to smash her."

Darrin held up his hand to stop her. He needed silence; needed to think.

Alesha frowned at him, bit her lip; but she obeyed.

No one else spoke.

Darrin scratched his chest, trying to pull his confusion into some form of order.

Trumpet had fired at almost the same instant she came onto *Free Lunch*'s scan—too quickly for her targ to focus accurately. So she must have known *Free Lunch* was near; her targ officer must have been riding with his fingers on the keys, poised to attack.

How had she known?

When the Lab ceased operational transmission in a blaze of static which suggested total disaster, Darrin had realized that the stakes in this contest were higher than he'd suspected; perhaps higher than Hashi Lebwohl had suspected. The only ship close enough to do the installation any damage had been *Soar*. Presumably *Soar* had come here from lost Billingate hunting *Trumpet*. Had *Trumpet* shared her cargo with Deaner Beckmann? Was that the reason his facility had experienced a disaster?

Had *Soar* attacked the Lab?

Deaner Beckmann had been betrayed: that was plain.

Who was next?

Darrin's instinct for survival screamed at him. It was time to cut and run. The stakes had become too high. Too high for what he was being paid; too high for what he knew about the other players. If *Trumpet* could do *that*, what else could she do? If an illegal ship like *Soar* was willing to attack an illegal installation like the Lab, what else would she do?

Darrin Scroyle had survived for so many years because his instincts were good.

"Any luck?" he asked scan.

"We can't handle it, Captain," the man on scan answered. "The computers don't know what to do with it. But it *is* dispersing. We should start getting data we can interpret in"—he consulted a readout—"make it two and a half minutes."

Two and half minutes before *Free Lunch* could see. Was *Trumpet* blind, too? Or did she know how to penetrate this charged storm? Was she moving now, taking a position to tear her opponent apart?

"Too long," Darrin decided. Because his people were afraid, he made a particular effort to sound calm. "We can't wait.

"Helm, back us out of here. You'll have to assume nothing's changed since we went blind. I don't care—just do it. I'm not interested in being a sitting target. Try to put that asteroid between us and the center of the storm. Maybe the rock will shield us enough to clear scan."

"Right, Captain." The helm first's tone spiked like a nervous tic, but he started working immediately.

G nudged Darrin against his belts as *Free Lunch* reversed course. If the bigger rocks in the vicinity hadn't shifted too much, helm ought to be able to move the ship safely—at least for a couple of k—by following her most recent thrust vectors backward. That might be enough—

Was he going to run? A little occlusion might reduce the particle barrage to manageable levels. Then *Free Lunch* would be able to see, navigate: she would be free to burn—

Get out of this damn maze while she still could.

But as soon as he asked the question he knew he wouldn't do it.

He'd accepted a contract.

He'd survived so long because his instincts were good—and because the rules he lived by were simple. He trusted his code. *Get paid what the job was worth. Then do it.* The truth was, he couldn't really know what this job might be worth. He may have evaluated it wrongly. But then, he never knew what any job might be worth; not really. Surprises, miscalculations, even disasters happened all the time: too often to be faced on any terms except simple ones. He trusted his code because the alternatives were worse. *Otherwise life didn't make much sense.*

As always, he preferred to make his own commitments and stand by them than to live by anyone else's rules.

"It's working, Captain," scan reported abruptly. "That asteroid is starting to cast a shadow we can see. I should be able to get real information in a few seconds now."

Darrin returned his hands to his board, put questions aside.

"Hold us where we are, helm," he ordered. "But stay alert. If *Trumpet* wants to come back at us, we need to be ready to burn.

"Concentrate, Alesha. They brushed off a direct hit once. We have to hope they can't do that too often."

Almost at once, scan announced, "Clearing now, Captain. Range is still only one k—no, two. But *Trumpet* isn't there. We have at least that much empty space around us."

He meant empty of ships. The images he rebuilt on the displays showed plenty of rock. The blast which had blinded *Free Lunch* hadn't been of a kind to push asteroids around.

Darrin had asked himself his questions, reminded himself that he already knew the answers that mattered. Now he didn't hesitate. "All right, people," he pronounced firmly. "Time to get serious.

"We knew *Trumpet* is formidable. Hashi told us that. He just didn't trouble to explain how formidable she is. From now on, we'll treat her like we would a warship.

"I'm guessing she was blinded as much as we were. That means she isn't moving in on us. She's running for clear space so she can see. And the safest way she can do that is retrace the way she came. Retrace it exactly.

"We're going to dive back into that distortion storm. As much acceleration as you dare, helm. If the storm hasn't dispersed enough for us to handle it, targ, we'll start firing matter beams in all directions. We'll keep firing until scan clears. Then we'll see if she's there. We'll see if maybe we hit her by accident—or if she can make more of those storms."

"What if she can?" Alesha asked tensely.

Darrin snorted. "Then we won't see her. But I'll take the risk. I think she won't be able to see us, either.

"If scan clears," he went on, "or stays clear, and we don't spot her, we'll sniff out her particle trace and go after her. When we catch up with her, we'll try lasers or torpedoes on her. She must be vulnerable to *something*."

Most of his people didn't look at him, but he knew they were listening. After years of experience together, he trusted their determination as much as their competence. They didn't always agree with him, but they always did their jobs as well as they could. That was their code as much as his.

Without pausing he continued.

"One more thing. We're heading back down into the swarm. That's where *Soar* is. As I read our contract, there's only one breach worse than not killing *Trumpet* ourselves, and that's letting some other ship capture her. Especially *Soar*. So we might have to take *Soar* on.

"*She* doesn't have any amazing new defenses against matter cannon. *That* I'm sure of. But rumor has it she carries a super-light proton cannon." Everyone on the bridge had heard the same rumor, but Darrin repeated it anyway. "If we start shooting at her, we'd better make damn sure we give it everything we've got.

"All right?" he finished. "Questions? Are you ready?"

No one questioned him. Of course not. He was their captain. He'd kept them alive for a long time; taught them his code; trusted them; made them moderately wealthy. Most of them loved him as much as he loved them.

After a moment Alesha drawled, "Let's get it over with. I'm so sick of this swarm I could almost puke."

Helm laughed nervously as he poised his hands on his keys.

Quickly data extrapolated a course from scan recordings of the vicinity made before *Trumpet* had appeared; he copied it to one of the screens while he routed it to helm.

When Darrin gave the order, his ship went to fulfill her contract.

MORN

Acceleration held her to the deck—pressure full of clarity and dreams. Through the pain of impact moved grand visions, majestic as galaxies, pure as loss; phosphenes spoke to her of truth and death. She was in the presence of ultimate things.

And while she dreamed and labored, Angus fought to save the ship, even though she couldn't see or hear him.

He snatched *Trumpet* out of her wild cartwheel when instincts or databases screamed at him that he was about to hit rock. Somehow retaining his sense of orientation despite *Trumpet*'s vertiginous career, he hammered thrust against the spin, pulling the gap scout away from her attacker's guns, away from the scan madness which her dispersion field had created out of matter cannon fire; back the way she'd come; down into the depths of the swarm.

If he took the time to check on Morn, she didn't know it. She was unconscious on the deck, small beads of blood oozing from half a dozen abrasions on her back and scalp.

Davies shouted things like, "Who *was* that?" and, "Where're we going?" and, "Damn it, Angus, *talk* to me!" but Angus ignored him. He was deep in the uncluttered concentration of a machine, focused like a microprocessor on keeping his ship alive while she hurtled among the asteroids at three times her former velocity. If he made plans, or his programming made plans, they were buried where no one could argue with them.

I've seen that signature before!

In moments *Trumpet* cleared the worst of the distortion. One at a time her instruments recovered their sight. The swarm became real again around them as if it had been re-created from the raw materials of the boson storm.

"*Gutbuster*'s back this way!" Davies yelled when scan and Deaner Beckmann's charts enabled him to identify where the gap scout was, where she was headed. "If you keep going like this, we might run right into her before I have a chance to fire!"

Angus may have known better. It was possible that some mechanical part of his mind had already calculated *Soar*'s likely position and taken it into account.

In an entirely different way, Morn also seemed to know better. Instances of clarity opened in her unconsciousness like flowers which spread their blooms at the first touch of sunrise. So much certainty: so little fear. Life questioned nothing; death dreaded nothing. If she remained here, all things would become plain.

But of course she couldn't stay here. The time had come to move on. Fear was essential to the blood in her veins, the delicate web of electrical impulses in her brain. It was her mortality: she wasn't human without it. Her tangible flesh hurt too much to go on without fear.

Angus struggled to save the ship. In the same way, she fought to pull herself past the wall of darkness in her head.

She'd been under heavy g. She'd hit the bulkhead hard enough to go mad; Angus had used enough thrust to make her crazy. For a moment she seemed to pass the wall into gap-sickness.

I was floating, and everything was clear. It was like the universe spoke to me. I got the message, the truth. I knew exactly what to do.

I keyed the self-destruct sequence—

She heard herself speaking as if she were Davies. She knew how he felt. Her whole existence revolved around self-destruct sequences.

As far as she could tell, only the pressure of g saved her; only the fact that her head and back *hurt*, and she weighed at least thirty kg more than she should have. She couldn't float. The certainty was still with her: she remembered the sound of commandments, immanent and inevitable. But as she strove to climb the wall and open her eyes, the universe seemed to lose its hold on her. Flashes of clarity burst in her bloodstream like embolisms; died away like failed hopes.

She opened her eyes as the force of thrust eased and her body began to shed its artificial mass.

From her perspective, Angus towered over her at the command station. Beyond him across the bridge, Davies worked the second's console: on his screens he labored to project a position for some other vessel.

Soar? Or the other ship, the stranger?

Morn wanted to know the answer, although she didn't care which it was.

With an effort she lifted her head. "Angus." Coruscations spangled the back of her head, rippled down her spine. "What happened? Where are we? Are we intact?"

Davies jerked his head toward her. "Morn?" he croaked in dismay. "Christ!" Apparently he hadn't realized she was still there. He'd been concentrating too hard to notice her. "Are you all right?"

Angus had no time to spare for Davies, but he did for Morn. When he heard her voice, he wheeled his g-seat as if he were trying to fling it free of its mounts. Rage mottled his skin; feral stains seemed to flush from his face down his neck into his torso. His eyes burned with coercion or hysteria.

"I told you to get off the bridge!" he roared. "God *damn* it, Morn, what the *fuck* do you think you're doing? You think we *need* you here? You think we can't make decisions or push keys unless you tell us what to do? Or are you just tired of living? It's been too long since you got to play self-destruct?" Clutching the edges of his board, he strained toward her against his belts. "Do you think I came all this way just so I could watch you lose your fucking *mind*?

"*This is my ship!* When I give you an order, you are going to *carry it out*!"

His fury was fierce enough to draw blood. Perhaps because fading embolisms of clarity still ran in her veins, however, he didn't frighten her. She was already bleeding: the bulkhead had drawn blood. Facing him as squarely as the pain in her skull allowed, she murmured, "I guess that means we're still intact."

He rocked back in his g-seat as if her reaction punctured him; deflated him somehow. "*Yes*, we're still intact." Surprise and speculation changed the mottling on his skin to dull grime. "This kid of yours doesn't have the sense to focus targ before he fires, but he has good timing with a dispersion field. That ship hit us hard without actually hitting us at all."

His eyes searched her as if he wanted to see inside her head.

"What're you trying to do to yourself?" Davies demanded thickly. "Why didn't you go? Don't you know how dangerous—?"

His protest trailed off.

"You didn't get gap-sickness." Angus' voice was harsh with doubt.

"Or you were out long enough for it to pass. Or I didn't give you enough g to trigger it. Or you used that damn zone implant so much you cauterized your brain. Shit, Morn, you—"

Whatever he might have said, he didn't finish it.

Groaning at the abrasions, Morn shifted her shoulders; climbed slowly into a sitting position. He was right: something had prevented her gap-sickness from taking hold. The g had been hard enough to make her crazy; she knew that. Had she been unconscious long enough to mute her illness? Had she driven herself so hard with her black box that she'd damaged neurons? Maybe. There was no way to tell.

Now that the crisis was past, she felt a touch of relief.

And a hint of sadness, as if she'd lost something she valued when the clear commandments of the universe receded.

She knew how Davies felt.

"So where are we going?" she asked while she tested the extent of her scrapes and bruises.

"That's right," Davies muttered. "*You* ask him." He sounded suddenly bitter. "He won't tell *me*."

Like a man throwing up his hands, Angus growled, "Back. Into the swarm." Grimacing in disgust or bafflement, he referred to the screens. "You can see that."

Davies snarled a curse, but Angus ignored him.

"You haven't studied Beckmann's charts like I have," Angus went on. "From where we are, there isn't any reasonable course out of this mess except the one where we met that other ship. Unless you like clearing rock out of your way by running into it. We're stuck between *Soar* and that other bastard. We could duck and dodge, maybe hide for a while, but eventually they're going to find us.

"I want to deal with them one at a time. If they hit us together, even dispersion fields aren't going to keep us intact. So I'll try *Soar* first, see what we can do. I know more about her." With his own bitterness, he added, "And there's always a chance Captain Sheepfucker damaged her. That might help us.

"Besides," he went on harshly, "I know that other ship. We've seen her before."

He didn't pause. Anger and desperation drove him. "Her name's *Free Lunch*. She was at Billingate the same time we were. She got out a couple of hours ahead of us. We heard her name from operational transmissions in Billingate's control space. Scan picked up her emission signature.

"Do I have to tell you what that means?" he snarled. Morn shook her head, but he didn't stop. "She knows us from Billingate. And she knows *Soar*. So it's no fucking coincidence that she turned up here just in time to start shooting at us."

"She's working with *Soar*," Morn said for him. Oh, God, more enemies. How many allies did Sorus Chatelaine have?

"If we try to face both of them at once," he finished, "we're dead."

He shrugged violently, as if he were restraining an impulse to hit something. Then he said more quietly, "And Sib's back there. For whatever that's worth. If *Soar* or Captain Sheepfucker didn't kill him—and he's out of the way when the shooting starts—and we can beat *Soar*—and *Free Lunch* doesn't catch us too soon—and we're able to find him—"

Angus let the rest of the sentence die into the background whine of *Trumpet*'s drives, the whisper of air-scrubbers, the nearly subliminal hum of charged matter cannon.

The thought of Sib Mackern alone in the vast crackling turmoil of the swarm, slowly dying inside his EVA suit while he waited for his air to run out or *Trumpet* to come for him, gave Morn a sharper sadness: the pang of it seemed to settle against her heart like a blade. He might be better off if Nick killed him, or *Soar* did. The distress of his old fears and losses deserved some clean end.

How long could he scream without dying inside?

How many allies did Sorus Chatelaine have?

By an act of will she set her questions aside. Speaking more to Davies than to Angus, she said softly, "So this isn't for revenge anymore. We're going after *Soar* because that's better than the alternatives."

Davies appeared to swallow a retort. He needed his hunger for revenge on *Gutbuster* and Sorus Chatelaine: she understood that now. It protected him from deeper terrors, keener madnesses. His own peculiar gap-sickness—the strange, demented gulf separating who he was from what he remembered—lurked in him avidly, waiting its time to strike. If he couldn't fight for his image of who he should have been, he might disappear between the dimensions of himself and never return.

Trying to help her son, she asked Angus, "Do you know how you want to tackle her?"

He shook his head; for a moment he didn't reply. He may have been consulting his databases or programming. Then he said, "Depends on how far away we spot her. How much cover we can use. Whether we get a clear field of fire. I can't be sure.

"But this time," he told Davies, "don't be so goddamn eager to shoot." His tone was gruff. Yet Morn thought she heard something more than disdain in it. Amusement, maybe? Recognition? "There's only one real defense against a super-light proton cannon. You have to take out the gun before they can use it.

"Sometimes your shields hold. If you're far enough away. And sometimes, if you're too fucking lucky to die, you can shove a matter blast right down the throat of the proton beam. That seems to fray it somehow, take the edge off. Then maybe your shields can hold. But nobody gets that lucky very often.

"So don't waste your time pulverizing a few rocks. Focus. If we get a good look at her, scan can identify her emitters."

Awkwardly, as if Morn's presence disturbed his concentration, Davies sent schematics to one of the displays, reminding himself of the configuration and emission signature which characterized super-light proton cannon.

Holding her breath against the throb in her head, Morn rose from the deck and reached for a handgrip. Maneuvering thrust held her against the bulkhead, but *Trumpet* wasn't turning hard enough to threaten her. Nevertheless she cleated her zero-g belt to an anchor. That was the only precaution she could take—short of leaving the bridge.

For a moment she studied Angus' scan plot. Then she asked, "How long do you think we have?"

Do I have time to go to sickbay for some cat?

Do I have to decide whether I'm willing to take more drugs?

"Minutes," Angus growled distantly. "More, less, I don't fucking know." He was sinking back into the mechanical focus of his microprocessor. "*Soar* isn't coasting, that's for damn sure. She wants to catch us before we can leave the swarm."

Not enough time to go to sickbay. Morn cleared her lungs with a sigh. She'd made her decision when she hadn't left the bridge earlier.

Had she simply been unconscious long enough to outlast her gap-sickness? Was that what had saved her? Or had something inside her changed? Had she crossed a personal gap into other possibilities?

Like identity—or like the relationship between identity and fear—gap-sickness was a mystery. No one understood it.

No one had enough time—

"*There!*" Angus stabbed keys, and a scan image sprang to life on one of the displays.

Thirty k away, past an oscillating jumble of rocks the size of EVA suits and other loose debris, a ship swung past the bulk of an asteroid big enough to block her from *Trumpet*'s sensors. While the image sharpened, the ship lined her prow in *Trumpet*'s direction.

Emission numbers along the bottom of the screen spiked rapidly. Targ tracking: the ship was about to fire.

Scan identified her profile instantly; configuration; thrust characteristics. She was *Soar*.

Under the circumstances, she was moving fast. Her velocity was nearly as high as *Trumpet*'s. They would be within ramming range of each other in twenty seconds.

"Shit!" Instantly frantic, Davies hammered his board, searching for his target. "I can't—!" His voice cracked. "Angus, I can't find her emitters!"

Morn clenched both fists on her handgrip and hung there, watching. If Davies couldn't see the emitters, *Soar* must not be oriented to use her proton cannon.

"Forget it!" Angus snapped back. "Pay attention! Fire torpedoes, then static mines, then matter cannon! Then get on that dispersi—"

He was cut off. Numbers shrilled red along the display: klaxons yowled.

Shoulders hunching like a strangler's, he jammed his fingers onto the helm keys, hauling *Trumpet* sideways with every gram of lateral thrust she could generate.

A small fraction of a heartbeat later, scan scrambled and shut down, foundering in *Soar*'s matter cannon barrage.

The gap scout staggered as if she'd run into a wall. Alarms and metal stress shrieked at each other like the fury of the damned. Morn slammed to the side; bounced back in time to see *Trumpet*'s particle sinks red-lining on one of the displays as they strained to bleed off the impact—absorb the impossible picoseconds during which the cannon's energy attained near-infinite mass.

In increments of time only a CPU could measure, the sinks failed: one by one they overloaded and seemed to burst like exploded glass. Yet they must have saved the ship. Or else the coincident static seethe of the swarm's electromagnetic friction had eroded some of *Soar*'s force. Or Angus' evasion had spared *Trumpet* a direct hit. Despite the clangor of stress and the howl of alarms, Morn would have heard the deep-throated, whooping shout of the klaxon which warned that the ship had broken open.

Would have, but didn't. Therefore *Trumpet*'s hulls held.

Through the racket, Angus raged, *"Do what I told you!"*

Bracing himself with one arm on the end of his board, Davies launched plasma torpedoes, sprayed out static mines. Using residual scan data to direct targ, he fired a blind volley of matter cannon.

He must have missed. He wasn't Angus; simply wasn't fast enough to extrapolate both *Trumpet*'s and *Soar*'s new positions and take them into account.

Thrust still clawed the gap scout to the side. Morn's arms strained in their sockets as if they were being torn out. Without the support of her belt, she would have lost her grip. On his board Angus ran commands like lightning; instructions so swift that they seemed to have no effect.

Scan took forever to clear: two seconds; three. Then the screens went wild as *Trumpet*'s systems raced to catch up with new input.

An instant later the displays resolved into fatal precision.

Their images froze Morn's heart. Involuntarily, uselessly, she cried out, "Angus!"

One of the static mines had already gone off, leaving an area of distortion like a migraine aura at the edge of scan. Past it, however, the sensors read *Soar* plainly, still driving toward her prey. Violent energies scorched along one flank, and her hull wore a corona of dissipating forces: a near miss from *Trumpet*'s cannon. Plasma blossoms studded the void around her. But she was whole: her shield and sinks had shrugged the assault aside. And she had a clear field of fire ahead of her.

That wasn't the worst of it, however. As scan cleared, the surrounding swarm became visible again.

The screens showed that Angus' efforts to evade *Soar*'s attack had sent *Trumpet* with lethal momentum straight at an asteroid so massive it threatened to crush her.

Angus didn't answer Morn's cry. He may not have heard it: he was too busy. As *Soar*'s targ readings spiked for another barrage, he cracked like a whip at Davies, *"Dispersion!"*

Wordless rage rose like a scream through Davies' clenched throat. Desperately he keyed his defenses.

For the second time scan collapsed in the heart of a boson storm as the dispersion field transformed matter cannon fire to chaos.

"Yes!" Angus brandished his teeth at the screens; pounded the side of his board with his fist. At once, however, he attacked his console again, entering commands Morn couldn't follow or interpret.

A jolt of thrust slapped her around her handgrip; her other shoulder thudded the bulkhead. She clung for her life: her hands and her belt were all that kept her from being thrown at the screens. Maybe the jolt was enough; maybe Angus could wrench the gap scout off the asteroid looming at her; maybe—

With a palpable lurch, *Trumpet*'s thrust died.

G suddenly vanished. At once the pressure of Morn's arms lifted her into the air. Then her belt snatched her back.

Without thrust—!

Blinded by the storm, proximity alarms went off only a heartbeat before *Trumpet* stumbled against the side of the rock.

An appalling screech seemed to pull Morn loose from her handgrip. She dangled from her belt as the pressure tried to fling her across the bridge. The ship's hulls and skeleton cried out in metal agony. Davies was tossed like a doll back and forth between his g-seat and console. In contrast, Angus' inhuman strength protected him: braced against his station, he locked himself rigid to endure the collision.

G doubled Morn over. Her forehead smacked on her knees. Her belt seemed to be tearing her in half. She couldn't breathe—

Caterwauling with damage and protest, *Trumpet* settled to rest as if she were embedded in the asteroid. Several different alarms continued to squall: damage-control alerts; power failure warnings; systems fluctuations. Metal groaned and rang as the hulls and infrastructure adjusted themselves.

Morn's hips and knees wailed as if they'd been dislocated; pain and threats of rupture burned in her abdomen; shards of pressure threw themselves like spears at the walls of her head.

Nevertheless she was alive. After a moment she was able to draw breath.

And the ship was alive. Morn still didn't hear the terrible, whooping klaxon of breached integrity.

But *Trumpet*'s thrust drive had failed. Without thrust she had no power to run her systems; no power to charge her guns. Energy cells might keep life-support and maintenance running for a time, but they couldn't help the gap scout defend herself.

Couldn't lift her away from the rock.

Without transition the asteroid had become her tombstone.

"Angus—" Davies panted; groaned. His voice limped like a crippled thing out of the center of his chest. "Oh, my God. Angus—"

Angus, what're we going to do?

As soon as *Soar* recovered scan, she would hammer the helpless gap scout to scrap.

"*Stop* it!" Angus flamed back. Terror or rage crackled in his voice: he blazed with fear or fury. "Pull yourself together. God damn you, *pull yourself together*! I *need* you!"

One brutal slap unclipped his belts. With acrobatic ease, he flipped backward up and out of his g-seat, heading for the companionway.

Leaving—

No. A shout of absolute protest echoed among the shards piercing Morn's skull. *No!* Not now: not like this. Not while she and her son were too nearly broken to save themselves.

Through a whirl of lacerations and keening, she straightened her torso and legs. G didn't hinder her now: the asteroid had very little; *Trumpet,* even less. Bobbing against her belt, she reached for Angus. Her fingers strained like prayers.

He was already out of reach. On the far side of his immeasurable desperation.

Yet he stopped on the rails of the companionway as if she'd caught his arm; dragged him around to face her. His yellow eyes seemed to strike at her like fangs, carious and poisoned.

"Angus," she insisted, pleaded. His name seemed to rise up from an abyss of abasement and horror. "Angus. What are you going to do?"

"Don't ask!" he shouted as if demons raved inside him. "I haven't got *time*! Succorso is crazy. He's also a fucking genius!"

Violent as bloodshed, he hauled his bloated distress up the handrails and left the bridge.

"Morn?" Davies croaked. "Morn? My God, I don't know what to do. We can't try to fix the drive—there's no time. Pull myself together? What's he talking about? What does he want?"

His dismay accumulated into a yell. *"I don't know what to do!"*

The boson storm would dissipate soon. *Soar* would be able to see. She would hammer the helpless gap scout—

No, that was wrong. She wouldn't try to kill *Trumpet. Trumpet*'s thrust was dead: she couldn't defend herself. Sorus Chatelaine had no reason to kill her.

Soar would come alongside, fix grapples. Her people would force their way aboard. Capture Davies. And everyone else. Recover the immunity drug. Silence Vector's transmission. Put an end to every threat the gap scout represented.

Waste every pain and passion which Morn and Davies and Mikka and Vector and Sib and Ciro and even Angus had spent on their humanity.

Because the thrust drive was dead.

Ciro might as well have sabotaged it—

Morn felt her heart stumble against her ribs as if *Trumpet* had run into the asteroid again.

Ciro hadn't sabotaged anything. Vector had cured him. In any case, Mikka would have stopped him.

Succorso is crazy.

He's also a fucking genius!

Hurts filled Morn's head like glimpses of clarity. As if she understood, she uncleated her belt. When she was free, she coasted to the back of Angus' g-seat. Gripping one of the arms, she swung around and into the g-seat; secured herself with the belts; put her hands on the console.

While Davies watched with anguish gathering in his stricken eyes, she assumed command of the ship.

ANGUS

He only had a small window of time to work with; an unpredictably small window. He needed to be in position and ready before *Soar*'s scan cleared. After that, if he kept his profile low enough, Chatelaine's people might not spot him. But if they had a chance to catch sight of him while he was still moving—

One little laser pop would fry him.

In that case, *Trumpet* was finished. He'd left her effectively defenseless.

From the companionway he headed straight for the suit locker.

He'd done everything he could think of to make this work. He'd used static mines and plasma torpedoes to confuse the effects of *Trumpet*'s dispersion field so that *Soar* would be less likely to grasp what had really happened. Then she might not realize that the blindness which the field produced was itself a gambit. And in the meantime he'd used the field to cover his next actions.

Without scan *Soar* had no way of knowing that *Trumpet* had lost thrust, not because the drive had failed, but because he'd shut it down—or that before he powered down the drive, he'd fired thrust to soften *Trumpet*'s impact. Chatelaine would see only the outcome of *Trumpet*'s collision: scored and dented hulls; torn receptors and dishes; dead systems.

Exactly what she would expect to see if Ciro had sabotaged the drives.

Then she might succumb to the temptation to capture *Trumpet*'s people instead of killing them.

Might come close enough for Angus to destroy her.

His shipsuit still hung around his waist. He didn't bother to pull it up. When he reached the locker, he stripped his shipsuit off, tossed it aside. He might sweat less unclothed; might be in less danger of dehydration. Naked as a baby, he opened the locker and took out his EVA suit.

His datacore commanded none of this. His computer was at his service. His zone implants gave him what he asked for—speed, accuracy, strength; self-control. But his programming held no provision for what he was doing now. He'd stumbled into a place where he was free to make his own choices.

Neither Warden Dios nor Hashi Lebwohl had foreseen just how desperate Angus could be—or how extreme he became when he was desperate.

Because he'd chosen to take this risk, it appalled him to the marrow of his bones. He would never *never* do it of his own free will. Nevertheless he didn't hesitate. When had he ever done anything of his own free will? Fear was more compulsory than will. The abyss cared for nothing but pain, horror, and the most abject loneliness.

Pulse pounding with terror, as if he were voluntarily submitting himself to the crib, he hauled on his EVA suit, settled the harness around his hips, shoved his arms into the sleeves and gloves, closed the chestplate, set and sealed the helmet. At machine speeds he ran through the checklists to test the suit's equipment, confirm its integrity. Then he slapped the door of the compartment shut and moved to the weapons locker.

The miniaturized matter cannon was the only gun he took; the only one he would get a chance to use. Lasers and impact rifles, handguns of every kind, blades, mortars—all were useless to him. The matter cannon should have been useless, too: wildly effective inside closed spaces, but essentially trivial against a ship with *Soar*'s sinks and shields. Nevertheless he jerked the gun from its mounts, inspected its indicators, made sure it was charged.

It was ready. Readier than he was. He was never going to be ready for this.

He did it anyway. Cursing the inadequacy of his zone implants because they couldn't or wouldn't spare him from horror, he closed the weapons locker and headed for the lift.

Neither Warden Dios nor Hashi Lebwohl could have imagined how extreme Angus became when he was desperate.

In the lift, he sent the car upward.

His respiration rasped and echoed in his ears, raw with fear. He was breathing too hard, and his helmet constricted the sound. He could feel the slats of the crib rising on all sides, confining and vast; his whole, narrow world. In another minute he would start to hyperventilate.

while his mother filled him with pain

He should talk to the bridge. It was time. He needed Davies. Without help nothing would save him. Or *Trumpet.* If *Soar* didn't get them, that other ship would.

Yet he didn't want to open his mouth. As soon as he did, his dismay would pour out—a flood of darkness deep enough to drown him. He dreaded the lost, pitiful sound of his own voice in this enclosed place.

He had to do it. All his risks would be wasted if he didn't talk to the bridge. Savagely he keyed his transmitter.

"You listening?" he snarled. "Pay attention, bastard." He needed brutality to control his fear. "I've got orders for you. If you fuck up, we're all dead."

Preparing for his gamble, he'd done several things before he'd left the bridge. One was that he'd preset *Trumpet*'s command intercom to receive suit communications on this frequency. Davies would be able to hear him.

He nearly cried out when Morn's voice answered him.

"We hear you, Angus. We'll do whatever you tell us. I think that dispersion storm is starting to dissipate. *Soar* might be able to see us again in three or four minutes."

Her tone—husky, full of need, driven by her own desperation—reminded him of the way she'd once spoken to him aboard *Bright Beauty*. No matter how much it hurt him, he couldn't stifle the memory.

I can save you, she said. I can't save your ship, but I can save you. Just give me the control. The zone implant control.

You're crazy, he retorted.

Give me the control, she pleaded nakedly. I'm not going to use it against you. I need it to heal.

That's the deal, isn't it, he groaned when he understood her. You'll save me. If I let you have the control. But I have to give up my ship.

After he hit her, he promised, I'll never give up my ship.

He'd said that; meant it. Nevertheless it was a delusion, like so many others. Empty talk. He *had* given *Bright Beauty* up. Surrendered her to scrap and spare parts. Because he hadn't wanted to die. And because that was the only deal he'd been able to make with Morn.

We hear you, Angus. We'll do whatever you tell us.

The lift opened while he stood paralyzed: the doors to the airlock faced him. Multitasking automatically, as if his computer ruled him, he entered the codes to unseal the lock. At the same time, however, his heart hung on the edge of screams.

"You can't do this, Morn!" he gasped frantically. "God damn it, what's happened to your brains? Are you fucking psychotic? *We need hard* g. I can't get back there in time to run the ship. And as soon as we start to burn, you'll go gap-sick." With the command board right under her hands! "Get out of there. Don't you understand? You have to leave the bridge! Let Davies do it.

"Davies, don't let her stay!"

"He can't handle it alone." Morn was sure despite her desperation. "You know that. There's too much of it—and neither of us has your resources. If he takes helm, maybe he can manage scan at the same time, but he won't be able to run targ. We'll be defenseless, even if we're moving."

"Which we won't be," Davies put in fiercely, "because we haven't got thrust."

Anger shivered in his voice. He may have thought Angus had betrayed him.

"So I'm taking helm," Morn continued reasonably, as if what she said made sense; as if anything she did made sense. "He'll have scan and targ. He knows targ well enough to handle scan at the same time."

Enclosed by the helmet, echoes seemed to beat about Angus' head, blinding him to the distinction between what he remembered and what he did. Unable to stop himself, he cried into his pickup, "You're crazy! *I'll lose my ship!*"

"Angus," Morn retorted tightly, "we're dead where we sit. Craziness is the only thing that might get us out of this. Why else are you going EVA? Stop complaining about it. Take your own chances. I'll take mine."

"And I'll lose my ship!" he shouted back. "Is this the same deal over again? You get helm, but I have to give up my ship?"

Morn didn't answer. Instead Davies' voice crackled trenchantly in his helmet speakers.

"Take it or leave it, Angus. She's right. And she isn't completely crazy. She's already come through hard g once.

"Are you sure you aren't the one who's lost his mind? I checked the weapons inventory—all you've got is that portable matter cannon. It's a goddamn *popgun*, Angus. *Soar*'s sinks will shrug it off like water. You'll hardly scratch her."

He had no time for this. Without noticing what he did, he'd already moved into the airlock and closed it behind him; already started the pumps cycling to suck out the air. Scan must be clearing by now. *Soar* would be able to see—

Oh God.

His resistance crumpled. He already had too many fears hunting like Furies in his head. Raw with distress, he accessed his computer; instructed it to steady his pulse, calm his breathing. His hands entered commands to open the airlock as soon as the air was gone. Then he spoke into his pickup again.

"All right. We've all lost our minds. We might as well be crazy together.

"Pay attention. I can't afford explanations right now.

"Thrust didn't fail. I powered down the drive. It's set for cold ignition. All you have to do is hit the keys and point her in the right direction."

I'm not your son. By degrees the stress of hearing his voice cramped around his head made him vicious. *I am not your* fucking *son!* His tone sharpened as he went on.

"I want you to play dead. Don't make a flicker, don't experiment with anything, don't focus targ. *Sit* there. Until I tell you." Until I blow that fucker's heart out. "Then hit those keys. Hit them fast. Get us out of here. Burn us back the way we came, full acceleration, all the g you can take."

"I'll do it," Morn replied promptly. She sounded distant with concentration. "I've got the keys. I'm laying in a course now. We'll be ready."

"And give me scan data," Angus demanded. "Talk to me—tell me everything you pick up. I need to know what's going on."

"Right," Davies muttered as if he was speaking to himself. "It's still a mess out there. You'll probably see better than we can. But the storm's definitely receding. The scan computer projects we'll start getting data we can use in eighty seconds."

Eighty seconds. Shit! That wasn't enough. He was never going to make it.

He didn't have any choice. He had to make it.

The airlock cycled open, leaving him face-to-face with a nearly invisible curve of rough stone.

He could only discern the shape and relative angles of the asteroid because the rock seemed somehow darker than the void around it; more absolute. And because erratic flickers of static limned its outlines at unpredictable intervals, leaving faint afterimages like ghosts on his retinas.

At once his terror mounted to an entirely new level.

He hated EVA, *loathed* it. From the core of his heart to the ends of his fingers, he'd always feared it. Whatever made him small made him vulnerable. Only babies could be tied down in cribs and searched with pain to the limits of their being.

Nevertheless he kicked out of the airlock and floated up the side of the ship along the rock as if he were driven by his datacore's commands instead of his own desperation.

DAVIES

Stricken with dismay, Davies watched as Morn belted herself into the command g-seat.

He didn't know which horrified him more: being abandoned by Angus, or seeing Morn's hands on the command board. Memories of gap-sickness flocked in his head, fatal as ravens: clarity and ruin seemed to thrash like wings against the inside of his skull.

When she felt hard g, the universe would speak to her, commanding self-destruct; and she would obey. That was the nature of the flaw which the strange physics of the gap had searched out in the tissue of her brain. She wouldn't be able to help herself. The voice of the universe overwhelmed every other need and desire.

But of course *Trumpet* wasn't about to experience hard g. Not now: maybe never again. Somehow Angus had lost or damaged the thrust drive. He'd crashed the gap scout so hard that she'd nearly broken open.

After that he'd fled as if his datacore or his own terrors had ordered him to cower and rave elsewhere.

Succorso is crazy.

He's also a fucking genius!

What in hell was *that* supposed to mean?

"Jesus, Morn," Davies breathed so far back in his throat that he hardly heard himself. "Don't do this. Please don't."

Apparently she couldn't hear him. Or she didn't care what he said. She was concentrating hard on the console, running her fingertips lightly over the keys and indicators; reminding herself of what she'd learned in the Academy about Needle-class gap scouts. Untended and unloved, her hair straggled across the sides of her face, half hiding her from her son.

"Morn—" He had to plead with her somehow. There must be some way to reach her; some need or fear or appeal he could name that she would acknowledge. His heart and all his synapses burned as if she'd punched the settings of her black box to full strength, filling him with a frantic, artificial, helpless rush of extremity; as if he were still in her womb, writhing and struggling through the imposed dance of her zone implant's emissions.

"Morn," he began again, louder now, impelled by noradrenaline. "Morn, listen. We need to do better than this.

"Nick and Sib must have failed. They're probably both dead. And Angus has run out on us. We're the only ones left. Mikka and Vector and Ciro—they're sheathed in their bunks, they can't defend themselves." Or help us. "We're all they have.

"Whatever we do, it's got to be better than this. They don't deserve to die just because you've got gap-sickness."

Morn's concentration didn't shift. Past the scrim of her hair, she murmured, "You think I can't handle it."

Too tense and dismayed to restrain himself, Davies cried back, "I think you're too dangerous to try!"

She nodded. "So do I." Her hands tested a sequence of commands. "Have you got a better idea?"

She was too far away: her focus made her distant. The scale of the gulf she'd set around her daunted him completely. A minute ago he might have been able to come up with several alternatives. Now, however, his brain seemed to hang open like his mouth. He was so full of anguish that he couldn't answer.

"Angus hasn't run out on us," she pronounced quietly, as if she addressed him from another star system. "He's planning something—something so wild he can't bear to explain it. He's going to need us here—he's going to need our help.

"Can you run this whole ship by yourself?"

Her question held nothing except distance and concentration. If she meant to criticize him, she didn't show it. Nevertheless he felt stung, as if she'd tossed acid at him. *Of course* he could run the ship himself—

But of course he couldn't. Only Angus had that much ability; that many resources.

Involuntarily Davies bared his teeth and wrapped his arms across his chest to contain his inadequacy.

"You've been studying targ," Morn went on. "You've paid attention to scan. Can you handle helm at the same time?" You're as weak as I am. "You probably don't know any more about it than I do." You have the same limits. "That means if you take helm you won't have the attention to spare for scan and targ.

"And that means we're going to die even if Angus succeeds. Maybe you don't call that self-destruct, but the results will be the same."

It's *different,* he retorted voicelessly, as if he'd fallen dumb. It's at least a way of *trying* to stay alive. It's not the same as doing something you know is suicidal.

But he couldn't shout his protest aloud because he knew she was right. He simply wasn't good enough to manage helm, scan, and targ simultaneously. Trusting the ship to him was as suicidal as gap-sickness because he was flawed with mortality.

She wasn't done, however. From somewhere out past Fomalhaut or deep in forbidden space, she offered softly, "Maybe we won't burn hard enough to set me off. And maybe all the time I've spent with my zone implant active has changed something inside my head. Nobody understands gap-sickness."

Slowly she turned to look at him. As if she were speaking directly to the core of his heart—as if she knew him so well that she could slip past all his fear to touch him at the center—she said gently, "You want me to be the kind of cop Bryony Hyland's daughter ought to be. What do you think she would have done?"

She had the power to daunt him. He couldn't beat it back. The more she controlled herself, the more he quailed. He knew what the mother he remembered would have done.

"If *Soar* captures us," Morn asked, "do you think Mikka and Vector and Ciro will be glad I didn't kill them? Do you think you're going to *like* what the Amnion have in mind for you?"

She was too much for him: harsh and kind; brutal and inarguable. Goaded by frustration, a frenzy rose in him like hysteria. He didn't try to hold it back.

"No, I won't *like* it! Don't you think I *know* that? *None* of us are going to like it! If they take us, one of us will have to be brave enough to kill everybody else.

"*But I know what gap-sickness feels like!* If you understand everything else, why don't you understand that? I know what it *means* when the universe speaks to you! And I know how much it hurts afterward. If you do that to yourself again, it's going to tear me apart."

Somehow he'd found a place where she could still feel pain. Like a ship from the gap, she seemed to spring fury at him out of nowhere. Her rage resumed tard so nearby that he felt its heat in the bones of his face.

"*This is the best I can do!*" she cried like the hull-roar of thrust, the quantum howl of matter cannon. "If you aren't able to run *Trumpet* by yourself, *shut up and let me work*!"

Without transition she swung away from him, leaving him scorched. Savagely she pounded her board with the blade of her hand to toggle her intercom pickup.

"Mikka and Ciro, Vector, pay attention." She didn't try to moderate her anger; or muffle the tremor of fear and grief running through it. "I don't have much time. You asked for reports. This is all I can tell you right now."

As she talked, however, her distress seemed to ease; or it faded into the urgent concentration she turned on the command board. Sentence by sentence her voice grew calmer, restoring the gulf which separated her from Davies.

"We came up on another ship, *Free Lunch*. From Billingate. We assume she's working with *Soar*. We fired on her—she fired back. That was the first attack, the first hard g. We ran.

"Angus wasn't sure how to tackle her, so he took us back the way we came. Toward *Soar*. He thought we had a better chance against her.

"When we met her, we tried evasive maneuvers. But then we lost thrust. We couldn't stop—we hit an asteroid. You felt that collision.

"Now Angus is trying some other kind of tactic. We don't know what it is. But *Soar* is blind—at least for a few more minutes. *Trumpet* has a dispersion field that turns matter cannon fire into distortion. *Soar* can't see us, and we can't see her. We're safe until her scan clears. Then she'll come after us."

Roughly Morn dredged her hands through her hair as if she needed to pull her thoughts away from her console in order to finish what she was saying.

"If Angus tells us what he has in mind—and if I have time—I'll pass it on. In the meantime, Davies and I aren't going to let *Soar* take us. If we run out of other choices, we'll try to set up a feedback loop in the gap drive, see if maybe we can drag *Soar* into tach with us when she gets close. We'll never come out again—but she won't either.

"Hang on. We aren't finished yet."

Roughly she silenced her pickup and returned her full attention to the command board.

Again Davies stared at her. He felt that he'd been staring at her in horror or amazement for hours. When she said the words "set up a feedback loop in the gap drive," his distress was transformed.

The helpless discrepancy of identity beneath his protest and rejection underwent a strange tectonic shift. Sure, set up a feedback loop. Why hadn't he thought of that? If she could find enough residual energy in the ship's systems, enough juice in the energy cells—

The idea should have scared him. If Morn's gap-sickness commanded self-destruct, she could turn the gap drive in on itself and be sure of death.

But he wasn't scared: his visceral dread had become wonder. The fact that Morn knew how to kill *Trumpet* was only part of the shift; only the catalyst. If she could contrive a feedback loop, so could he. He could destroy the ship himself.

Which meant that if she died or went mad, he could still save the ship and his friends from *Soar*. He could spare them all from ending as Amnion.

Could spare himself.

In the grip of an epiphany, he glimpsed the true passion behind his bloody hunger for revenge on *Soar*/*Gutbuster*/Sorus Chatelaine. His wildness and determination had more to do with what *Soar* wanted him for than with what *Gutbuster* had done to *Intransigent* and Bryony Hyland.

He wished absolutely to destroy Sorus Chatelaine in all her guises so that she wouldn't capture him and turn him into a weapon against humankind.

The understanding seemed to ease his anger at Morn; his fear of her. If he wasn't helpless to meet his deeper dreads, he could deal with his more immediate alarm as well. He could work with her—

She studied her keys and readouts as if her son had ceased to exist. The screens told him that the boson storm—matter cannon energies transmuted to secondary and tertiary quantum discontinuities—was starting to fray, pulled apart by particle dissipation and the sharp gauss of the swarm. Before long *Soar* would recover her sight.

If Angus was able to restore thrust—

Was that why he'd fled from the bridge? Was he trying to effect some last, desperate repair which would give *Trumpet* back her power?

Davies needed an answer.

Clearing his throat, he asked with as much calm as he could muster, "Why do you think Angus hasn't run out on us?"

Morn didn't glance up. "Because he doesn't want to die." She'd recovered her distance, walled herself around with emptiness. "An hour after his brain fries and his corpse falls apart, he'll still be fighting to live. I don't know where he's gone, but he is going to *do* something.

"If we're lucky, it might give us a chance."

That explanation made sense to him: it fit with what he remembered of Angus. On the other hand, it didn't help him comprehend why she seemed to know Angus better than he did, even though he was crowded to bursting with her memories.

The scan displays reminded him that he had no time for such questions. In minutes *Soar*'s sensors and sifters would recover their ability to identify their surroundings.

Without warning the command intercom crackled. Harsh as a blow, Angus' voice struck the bridge.

"You listening? Pay attention, bastard." He must have been talking to Davies; must have thought Davies had the command station. "I've got orders for you."

Quickly Morn searched her readouts. "He's in an EVA suit," she whispered. "Using suit communications. But he hasn't left the ship yet." Then she keyed her pickup.

As if she'd been expecting this, she answered, "We hear you, Angus. We'll do whatever you tell us. I think that dispersion storm is starting to dissipate. *Soar* might be able to see us again in three or four minutes."

When she spoke to Angus, she didn't sound distant. She sounded the way Davies remembered feeling when she'd asked Angus to give her the zone implant control, back aboard *Bright Beauty*.

Angus' shock at hearing Morn's voice was palpable despite the metallic inadequacy of the intercom speaker.

"You can't do this, Morn! God damn it, what's happened to your brains? *We need hard g.*

"Get out of there. Let Davies do it.

"Davies, don't let her stay!"

With a snarl of his own, Davies bared his teeth and started running commands which might force scan through the distortion. At the same time he called up a checklist of the weapons locker's contents. Surely Angus didn't intend to go EVA without guns.

Morn glanced at him, saw what he was doing. He had the impression that under other circumstances she might have smiled. Relief or gratitude? Hope? He didn't know.

"He can't handle it alone," she told Angus. "You know that. We'll be defenseless, even if we're moving."

"Which we won't be," Davies put in so that Angus could hear him, "because we haven't got thrust." He wanted Angus to know where he stood.

"So I'm going to take helm," Morn went on. "He'll have scan and targ."

"You're crazy!" Angus' voice seemed to echo with anguish. *"I'll lose my ship!"*

Morn thumped the sides of her board with her palms; pulled her hair back from her face. "Angus," she returned sharply, "we're dead where we sit. Craziness is the only thing that might get us out of this. Stop complaining about it. Take your own chances. I'll take mine."

"And I'll lose my ship!" he raged. "Is this the same deal over again? You get helm, but I have to give up my ship?"

Roughly Davies keyed his own pickup, tapped into the frequency Angus was using.

"Take it or leave it, Angus," he rasped. "She's right." He was on Morn's side again. His dismay at the risk had become something new. "And she isn't completely crazy. She's already come through hard g once.

"Are you sure you aren't the one who's lost his mind? I checked the weapons inventory—all you've got is that portable matter cannon. *Soar*'s sinks will shrug it off like water."

Answer that if you can. Then maybe you'll have a right to complain.

Angus was silent for several seconds. When he spoke again, he seemed beaten.

"All right. We've all lost our minds. We might as well be crazy together."

The tone of his defeat was strangely familiar. He'd sounded exactly like that when he gave her the zone implant control in Mallorys. *I accept. The deal you offered. I'll cover you.*

"Pay attention. I can't afford explanations right now."

Remember, I could have killed you. I could have killed you anytime.

"Thrust didn't fail. I powered down the drive. It's set for cold ignition."

Morn's eyes widened in surprise; she sucked a quick breath. At once she began hunting her board.

"I want you to play dead," Angus went on. "*Sit* there. Until I tell you." His tone had recovered its edge. "Then hit those keys. Get us out of here."

"I'll do it," Morn promised from the center of her concentration. "I've got the keys. I'm laying in a course now. We'll be ready."

"And give me scan data." Davies could hear Angus' attention shift to him. "I need to know what's going on."

"Right," Davies answered promptly. As if he were Morn, he felt focus taking over him; giving him distance. "It's still a mess out there. You'll probably see better than we can." One of his readouts supplied him with an estimate. "The scan computer projects we'll start getting data we can use in eighty seconds."

A gasp came across the speaker. Then Angus stopped talking.

Over the intercom Davies heard his father breathing hard, too hard; panting for air or courage.

He left his pickup active. Indicators showed that Morn had done the same. Grimly he resumed his efforts to pierce the dwindling storm with *Trumpet*'s sensors.

The storm's center was nearby between the gap scout and *Soar*. But the edges of the distortion would clear first: the center of the boson distortion would be the last to drift apart. When he finally, truly, applied his mind to *Trumpet*'s situation instead of to Morn, a new thought sent alarm hiving like insects along his nerves.

What if *Soar* didn't hold her position, waiting for sight? What if she altered her course and continued to advance, hoping to come around the storm and catch *Trumpet* blind?

Sweat smeared his palms. In contrast his mouth felt as dry as a wasteland. Angus, he tried to say, Angus, I just thought of something. But he couldn't find his voice: his throat refused to work. His hands shook as he pounded keys; redirected his instruments toward the fraying fringes of the distortion.

Angus continued to strain for air as if he were wrestling demons.

Almost at once blips signaled at Davies from several different locations. Ships on all sides of him; half a dozen or more.

But that was patently impossible. Ghosts, he was picking up ghosts: spooks and echoes. If scan claimed to see a ship when its view was blocked by solid stone, there was no other explanation. Nevertheless it was a good sign, no matter how much it scared him. If the sensors could see ghosts, they would soon be able to identify real ships.

Like moons or satellites trapped by orbital decay, the ghosts appeared to swirl and converge, coming together as scan labored to filter out the mad from the actual.

There.

No mistake.

Shit!

And no time—

"Angus," he barked urgently, trying not to shout, not to panic, "we've got company. Off to the side." He named the blip's relative position. Scan was still too hampered to supply an image. "She's coming in fast.

"It's *Free Lunch*." His voice cracked. Scan was sure. "The emission match is too close to be wrong.

"*God*, Angus! *Now* what're we going to do?"

Angus didn't answer. Only panting came over the intercom, guttural as a death rattle.

Davies looked at Morn, but she didn't answer either. Instead she stared at the screens, her face blank and helpless.

She'd routed a course projection overlay to the scan display: her course; the one she'd plotted for *Trumpet*'s escape. It told him that when she hit her keys, ignited cold thrust, the gap scout would burn almost directly into the path of *Soar*'s ally.

ANGUS

The airlock closed and sealed behind him, but he didn't notice it. He needed to reach the far side of *Trumpet*'s hull quickly—the exposed side. Get there and get back behind the relative shelter of the gap scout's mass in the few seconds left. He slipped the muzzle of his matter cannon into the nearest handgrip, left it there. Slamming his boots against the rock, he sailed up and over the ship.

The instant he rounded the occlusion of *Trumpet*'s bulk, a keen lance of pain drove through his EM prosthesis into his brain. Too swift for his zone implants to stop or manage it, it seemed to nail his optic nerves to the back of skull.

Oh Christ shit God! Involuntarily he slapped a hand over his faceplate, but that didn't help him. Even sheathed in mylar and plexulose, his flesh was too permeable to ward off the pain.

He'd forgotten to adjust the polarization of his faceplate against the boson storm; to filter out the savagery radiating on the bandwidths his prosthesis received.

Damn it! Where were those fucking databases when he *needed* them? Why hadn't his programming foreseen this?

He knew the answer. Neither Warden Dios nor Hashi Lebwohl had understood how far he would go when he was desperate.

Through a red, squalling, visual knife of pain, he found the controls on his chestplate, began frantically dialing changes to the polarization.

By the time the neural screaming eased enough to let him see again, he'd already drifted more than fifty meters from *Trumpet*. Out toward the center of the storm, where *Soar* waited—

How much time did he have left?

Fifty-five seconds and counting, his computer reported.

Viciously he toggled his jets; turned his trajectory with compressed gas so that he swung back in *Trumpet*'s direction.

As fast as his jets could take him, he gusted toward the place he wanted on his ship's flank.

He hit hard; nearly missed his grip and bounced away. But machine reflexes saved him. He closed his fingers on the cleat beside the access hatch.

Forty-seven seconds.

Trying to concentrate, forget pain and time limits, let his microprocessor carry him, he keyed open the hatch.

Unlocking it was another of the details he'd prepared before leaving the bridge. Otherwise he would have had to shout to Davies or Morn, tell them what he wanted, give them the codes. Now only his planning saved him. His breathing rattled so thickly in his throat that he didn't think he could speak, much less shout.

The hatch accessed the storage compartment which fed *Trumpet*'s singularity grenades to their launcher.

Earlier he'd wondered why his tormentors had bothered to equip the gap scout with singularity grenades. They were almost impossible to use. Launching them was easy enough: detonating them effectively was altogether more difficult.

At the moment, however, he didn't care what Dios' or Lebwohl's reasons might have been.

Thirty-nine seconds.

Quickly he unclipped the nearest grenade from its rack, levered it out of the compartment. That part was simple in zero g. And the grenade was no bigger than his chest: he could manage its size. But its mass was another matter. It weighed—a database told him this—over five hundred kg. It had inertia with a vengeance. He could pull the device into motion, but he would have to red-line his jets to make it stop.

He couldn't afford to fail. What was the good of all his reinforced strength, if it wasn't enough when he needed it?

Gasping for courage as much as air, he heaved the grenade up, toggled his jets to full power, and began to lift like a feather up the exposed curve of *Trumpet*'s side.

Twenty-four seconds.

Unless Davies' estimate was wrong. Maybe *Soar* could see him already.

He didn't risk a look in that direction.

Move, asshole! Motherfucking sonofabitch, *move it*!

Above the line which served him as *Trumpet*'s horizon, he shifted the vector of his jets. Straining until he feared his sinews might snap, he fought the grenade to a new heading.

Across *Trumpet*'s spine. Directly at the black asteroid. Down at the last moment toward the narrowing space where *Trumpet* met the rock.

Seventeen seconds.

He couldn't turn the grenade in time. It crashed into the asteroid. Shedding chips and splinters like hail, it rebounded away.

He was ready for it. He jammed the toe of one boot into a handgrip for an anchor: his hips cocked urgently to aim his jets. With a final lurch that nearly dislocated his arms, the grenade settled beside the ship and stopped moving.

Eleven seconds.

Shit, that was close! And he still wasn't done. He needed to nudge the grenade back upward until it was poised at the horizon. Then retrieve his small matter cannon; take up his own position.

Somewhere inside the lost crib of his EVA suit he had to find the strength to throw the grenade at *Soar*.

He wasn't strong enough. No one was. UMCPDA had equipped him for any number of things, but not for this. For the last time in his life his wrists and ankles were *tied to the slats*; utterly bound. Nothing he'd ever been able to do would prevent Sorus Chatelaine and the malign forces of the swarm from tearing him apart.

"Angus." Davies' sudden call seemed to crack open his head. Stress made his hearing wail like feedback. "We've got company. Off to the side." Davies gave coordinates which only Angus' computer understood. "She's coming in fast.

"It's *Free Lunch*. The emission match is too close to be wrong.

"*God*, Angus! *Now* what're we going to do?"

Soar's ally. Here. Already.

It was worse than being tied in his crib, worse than needles and pain. Angus wanted to scream, but he was gasping too hard.

Clutching like a wildman at cleats and handgrips, he wrenched his way up the hull to his chosen horizon and looked out at the seething midnight of the swarm.

It should have been too black for him to see anything. The erratic crackle and flare of static couldn't mitigate the dark. But in the deep distance the aurora borealis of the Lab's destruction still burned faintly, giving a nacreous, fatal glow to some of the asteroids, limning others with evanescence. And *Soar*'s running lights were on, etching her against the void.

She was there; *there*, directly in front of him; no more than fifteen k away.

And closing.

He could see *Free Lunch* up past the point of his right shoulder, at the edge of his faceplate's field of view. She, too, had her running lights on. But she was closer— God, she was *closer*! Five k at most. Point-blank range.

Angus hadn't planned for this. Nothing would help *Trumpet* against *two* attackers.

Helpless, he was always helpless, always, there was nothing he could do. The abyss hovered over him, loving and cruel. His own weakness tied him down: his own failures and fears stuck him full of pain.

"Give me orders!" Morn's voice cried. "Angus, tell me what to do!"

"I can see *Soar*!" Davies yelled. "They're both ready to fire! They're going to kill us!"

Tell me what to do!

Morn had set him free. Otherwise he might have given up and died. He would already have died inside himself, driven mad by helplessness and coercion. But Morn had set him free—

And his equipment didn't understand surrender. His programming made no provision for it.

Desperately he flipped back down *Trumpet*'s side, propped himself under the grenade, and shouldered it into motion.

Then he dove for his matter cannon.

That was enough. He had weapons. And terror was strength. Morn had set him free. His zone implants steadied him, refined his control, but took nothing away from his stark urgency.

As the grenade crested his horizon, he rose with it.

Stopped it with a sharp blast of his jets.

Took his position behind it.

He was too late. In that instant *Free Lunch* opened fire.

A second later *Soar* fired as well. Without transition the dark became a caterwauling blaze of light and discontinuities as matter cannon unleashed pure chaos.

But they were firing at each other. God, *they were firing at each other*! One of them had betrayed the other. *Trumpet* was too rich a prize to share.

And they could afford to ignore the gap scout. She already looked dead.

If *Soar* had used her proton gun, *Free Lunch* would have been finished; torn apart before she could deliver a second barrage. But Angus knew the energies of matter cannon; recognized them when he saw them. *Soar* fought back in kind—

That gave *Free Lunch* the advantage. She'd fired first; would be able to recharge her guns first. And she'd taken *Soar* by surprise. If either ship could win this battle, it was likely to be *Free Lunch*.

He made his choice by instinct—too quick for thought. Bracing himself, he heaved at the grenade with every gram and fiber of his enhanced force; fired his jets with all their power in the same direction.

What he did should have been impossible. The grenade weighed five hundred kg. And he was alone. But he'd been made for this in ways he didn't understand; trained for it in ways he couldn't imagine. Terror was strength. It was *life*. Trapped in the crib of his suit, he strained for freedom so hard that watching him should have broken his mother's heart.

Somehow he succeeded at launching the grenade straight at *Free Lunch*'s looming mass.

It would take forever to get there. Or it would have taken forever, but *Free Lunch* continued to advance, improving her position and angle of fire between barrages. She came to meet the grenade faster than the grenade itself moved.

Angus gave his computer a fraction of an instant to calculate relative trajectories, estimate the point and moment of impact. Then he dropped to *Trumpet*'s hull.

Frantic for speed, he clipped the belt of his suit to one of the handgrips; cinched it tight so that he wouldn't waver or fall away. He set his boots on the base of the nearest particle sifter, dialed up their magnetic field to help him stay in place. Swinging the muzzle of his gun around, he brought it to bear.

Another barrage. *Free Lunch*'s lambent fire enclosed *Soar* like a penumbra of ruin. Her sinks pulsed and burned like suns, throbbing to bleed off the damage. Frenetically she blazed back at her attacker.

If her fire hit the grenade before it reached *Free Lunch*— Before Angus could fire himself—

"*Now!*" he howled into his pickup. He could scream at last—scream from the pit of his torn heart, even though his voice seemed to fall dead in the dark around him; unheard; unheeded. "*Do it* now! *Hit those keys!*"

Indicators inside his helmet yammered at him, warning of dehydration, temperature overloads, exhausted jets, oxygen depletion. Clutching his matter cannon, he waited in the crib at Morn's mercy to find out whether he was going to live or die.

MORN

"It's *Free Lunch,*" Davies had croaked into his intercom. "*God,* Angus! *Now* what're we going to do?"

Morn could see the other ship's blip on the screens. She stared at its place in her course projection overlay as if her heart had failed. The terror of *Starmaster*'s murder filled her, and she couldn't move.

She understood cold ignition. Some ships were able to do that. The acceleration would be severe, but not cruel. From a cold start, *Trumpet*'s thrust drive wouldn't generate enough force to push her and Davies beyond their physiological limits. They had trained under hard g: they could bear it. If she didn't fall into clarity and craziness—

But her course projection was a problem of another kind; insuperable. The scale of thrust *Trumpet* could produce, the nearness of *Soar*, and the nature of the available route through the swarm had determined the course Morn had programmed. There were no alternatives.

As *Trumpet* pulled off the asteroid and came around, she would pass—would have to pass—straight in front of *Free Lunch*.

Davies' fingers hit and flashed on his board. Targ displays jumped up and down the screens: scan scrambled to find its way through the residue of the storm. *Free Lunch* took on definition, looming and fatal. It was obvious which of the two ships would survive a collision. And *Free Lunch* would be able to fire at point-blank range—

Morn had no choice. The helm computer showed her none. If *Trumpet* didn't go *there,* she would go nowhere at all.

Angus' stertorous respiration scraped and ached over the intercom as if he were dying.

Morn wanted to call out, *Help me*, God damn you! Tell me what to do! But she didn't believe he was in any condition to hear her.

Then another fear took hold of her.

What if *Trumpet did* go *there*? What if she survived? What happened then?

Morn couldn't reach past the immediate crisis. Beyond her course projection lay only darkness: asteroids and collisions; blank scan and blind navigation; hard g, unconsciousness, gap-sickness. She hadn't studied Deaner Beckmann's charts or the lost Lab's operational data. She didn't know how to think beyond the doom on the overlay in front of her.

But the gap scout and everyone aboard would die if she failed: if *Trumpet* survived *Soar* and *Free Lunch*, and Morn hadn't planned for what came next.

She'd already killed her father's ship and most of her family.

Trembling with fear, she copied *Trumpet*'s assigned departure protocols from the log, then dummied them back to her helm program so that they would run automatically. After that, she set the command overrides to slow or stop the ship if her preset course threatened to damage her.

Morn had no idea what else to do.

"Jesus, Morn." Abruptly Davies silenced his intercom pickup so that Angus wouldn't hear him. He turned his station partway toward her. "Do you know what he's *doing*?"

She shook her head. The course projection overlay held her, and her heart may have failed. She couldn't guess what Angus had in mind.

"He's taken one of the singularity grenades," Davies murmured in awe or dismay. "Manual launch. He thinks he can suck those ships into a black hole. My God, he must be planning to *throw* it at one of them."

Which might have worked, if *Trumpet* had faced only one enemy. And if by some miracle he could have contrived to place the grenade where it would absorb enough power from its target.

But now—

Morn fought a desperate desire to hit the keys he'd prepared *now*; initiate cold ignition and *move* while *Trumpet* still had a little room. Angus wasn't ready: he hadn't given the order. He was dying outside the ship, he might never give the order, perhaps his dread of EVA had already broken him. Nevertheless he was *Trumpet*'s only real hope; her last chance. Premature thrust might ruin what he was trying to do. Morn clenched her fists until her fingers burned, and waited.

Without warning Davies' readouts snatched at his attention. Hints of *Soar* began to appear. "There she is!" Emission data sharpened on the screens. When he saw it, he yelped, "They've seen each other! They're going to fire!"

He pounded his pickup. But Morn was faster. She had too much death on her hands.

"Give me orders!" she cried into her intercom. "Angus, tell me what to do!"

Davies shouted at Angus, but she hardly heard him.

Scan didn't detect targ from either ship. They weren't tracking *Trumpet*.

An instant later the screen displayed matter cannon blasts like inaudible screams. *Trumpet*'s picture of the surrounding swarm dopplered in and out of distortion as the computer labored to filter the chaos.

"They're not firing at us!" Davies gaped at the data. "They think we're finished. They're fighting each other.

"We were wrong! They aren't working together."

The gap scout seemed to have more enemies than Morn could count.

But *Soar* still hadn't used her super-light proton cannon. Maybe she couldn't—

Time seemed to freeze between one barrage and the next. There was room to live or die between the ticks of the command chronometer. Morn planted her fingers on the cold ignition keys, braced herself despite the plain doom written in her course projection. To some extent, *Soar* and *Free Lunch* would be taken by surprise. Davies was right: they thought *Trumpet* was dead or crippled. Otherwise they would have opened fire on her already. And surprise would give the gap scout a few seconds. Distortion would give her a few seconds. Neither assailant would be able to refocus targ instantly.

Whatever else happened, Morn had to stay out of gap-sickness; needed absolutely to keep herself sane. As soon as she hit those keys, she herself would become the most immediate threat to the ship. If the universe spoke to her again, she was ideally placed to obey. With helm under her hands, she could send *Trumpet* into collision with either of the other ships; with a rock; she could dive into the heart of the black hole Angus hoped to create.

How had she survived the last time? Her gap-sickness had come to life when she'd hit the bulkhead; she'd felt it overwhelming her mind with crystalline compliance. And then it had faded away, dying in her bloodstream like the waste of expended neurotransmitters.

Why?

What could she do to make that happen again?

All she remembered was pain: the crack of her head against metal; the heavy abrasions on her back.

Her injuries still hurt. But she was sure that they didn't hurt enough.

"I can see the grenade," Davies choked out, gasping like his father. "He's launched it somehow. Not at *Soar*—at *Free Lunch*. That makes sense. She's closer.

"I don't know how he does it." Despite the way he breathed, his tone hinted at wonder, admiration. "He may be crazy, but he's got good aim. The grenade's right on target."

If *Trumpet*'s sensors could identify the grenade, so could *Free Lunch*'s. But that ship might not think to look.

An idea caught at the back of Morn's mind.

"My God," she breathed like her son. "That's why he took the portable matter cannon. To detonate the grenade."

Detonate it with enough added energy to make it effective.

"Is that possible?" Davies whispered.

Morn didn't know. "Can we hit it ourselves?" she asked. "Set if off when it's close enough?"

"No chance," Davies panted. "Everything's moving. There's too much distortion. And cold ignition won't give us stable thrust. We'll be lurching like mad. We would be lucky to get within fifty meters of a target that small."

Then how could Angus hope to hit it?

He was a cyborg: human and machine. Maybe his eyes and his computer and his zone implants together were better than targ—

Free Lunch fired again, emptying her guns at *Soar*. *Soar* returned the barrage. The force they flung against each other would have torn any undefended vessel apart. If a blast hit the grenade too soon—

It hadn't reached the field of fire yet. While *Soar* and *Free Lunch* blazed back and forth, the grenade continued sailing toward its target.

Again scan broke apart. At this distance, quantum discontinuities combined with particle bleed-off from the sinks to create emission fury all along the spectrum. More distortion: a few more seconds of cover.

"*Now!*" Angus' voice shrieked across the bridge. "*Do it* now! *Hit those keys!*"

With all her strength, Morn obeyed.

At the same instant Davies activated his guns, set them to pull charge from the drive.

A shudder ran through *Trumpet* as if she'd taken an impact blast. Morn jerked against her belts, flopped back into her g-seat. Energies powerful enough to crack cold thruster tubes came to life in the drive. From *Soar*'s perspective, or *Free Lunch*'s, *Trumpet* may have appeared to be embedded in the rock; but she was only resting there. Stone scraped a nerve-rending cry along her hull as she flung herself dangerously into motion.

Pressure built up on Morn's bones: acceleration and maneuvering g. As soon as *Trumpet* cleared the asteroid, the gap scout began curving along her programmed course, turning to head away from the depths of the swarm.

Into the path of Angus' target: a ship that wanted her dead.

More shudders shook her like explosions in the tubes—metal and polymerized ceramics straining to absorb too much heat too fast and adjust to each other. Morn's head dug into the cushions of her g-seat; her back drove its abrasions against the padding.

She couldn't remember any defense except pain. *As far as she could tell, only the pressure of g saved her; only the fact that her head and back* hurt—*She couldn't float.*

Lurching like a derelict, *Trumpet* moved into the distortion toward the field of fire.

She was accelerating as hard as she could. She should have been able to generate more g than this; far more. But cold thrust was unstable. It couldn't come near its full power until the tubes were hot. And Davies charged his guns, drawing energy off the drive. She acquired velocity too slowly to open the universe in Morn's head.

At this rate of acceleration *Trumpet* might as well have been stationary. Either *Soar* or *Free Lunch* could nail her the moment they got a clear look at her.

Her energy cells lacked the capacity to satisfy her matter cannon. But they held enough power to project her dispersion field. If Davies' timing was perfect, he might be able to keep her alive until thrust stabilized; until she began to burn in earnest, and Morn went mad—

Even if the ship lasted that long, Angus might not survive the boson storm. Quantum discontinuities might reduce his equipment's signals to gibberish. His human eyes might not be able to pierce the emission chaos.

Blips on *Trumpet*'s screens seemed to spell out her death. She neared the field of fire between *Soar* and *Free Lunch*. In another few seconds she would run directly under *Free Lunch*'s guns. Scan and alarms shouted that both opposing vessels were charged for another barrage.

Both were hurt: their sinks overloaded, wailing of particle torture; their hulls scored and dented, ports and antennae smashed; their energy profiles rippling with stress. But *Soar* bore more damage than her attacker.

Earlier wounds left her vulnerable.

"*Soar*'s got us," Davies announced through his teeth. Sweat dripped in his voice; concentration strained his eyes. Scan detected targ from *Soar*'s direction, saw cannon swiveling in their mounts. Nevertheless he was done shouting. "*Free Lunch* is still aiming at her."

For Sorus Chatelaine, killing *Trumpet* must have been more important than defending herself.

Emission numbers jagged off the scale. At once Davies slammed keys fiercely with the heel of his palm, raising the gap scout's dispersion field.

Morn felt the timeless, fatal concussion of impact. *Trumpet* was hit—

For the third time scan failed completely as the entire discernible spectrum tore apart.

—no, not hit, that jolt came from the thruster tubes. Half a dozen warnings squalled simultaneously, but none of them cried of matter cannon impact or vacuum.

The next instant the thrust parameters scrolling down Morn's readouts stabilized; took on a smooth energy curve; began to mount. Suddenly *Trumpet* started to burn.

G squeezed Morn deeper into her seat. Blood roared in her ears as the pressure built. The skin of her face stretched over its bones. Her heart labored to sustain its beat.

Now or never. If her gap-sickness took her now, she would never get another chance to answer it.

She had no answer.

At least both *Soar* and *Free Lunch* were as blind as *Trumpet*. If the gap scout died now, it wouldn't be because she'd been hit. It would be because her course ran her straight into *Free Lunch*. Or because she struck an asteroid at full burn. Or because the universe began to speak—

With an odd, dislocated sorrow, Morn realized that she might never know whether Angus had succeeded or failed; whether his desperation had proved greater than hers.

But she knew. She *did* know.

She knew because g suddenly doubled; tripled.

At the same instant *Trumpet* staggered and began losing momentum as if she'd driven headlong into an obstacle as thick and fluid as water.

Gravitic stress klaxons filled the ship with demented wailing, but Morn didn't need them to tell her what happened.

Angus had detonated his singularity grenade. And his matter cannon had given it the power to make it live.

Trumpet was being sucked into a black hole.

Now time existed only in tiny increments of seconds. Morn's heart didn't have a chance to beat: g and gap-sickness filled her personal cosmos too swiftly to be measured by heartbeats.

Alarms screeched, warning of event horizons and implosion. Vibration rattled Morn's teeth, her bones, her brain. *Trumpet*'s drive should have been strong enough to pull her away. If she wasn't already past the point of no return, she should have been able to veer off, break free. But of course *Free Lunch* had already been caught: her energies fed the black hole as it swallowed her. Its hunger reached outward, ravening for fuel, too swiftly for *Trumpet* to outrun it.

Morn had no answer. Now she didn't need one. Full of clarity and death, she would dive into Deaner Beckmann's dream, and then she would never be confused again.

But Davies wasn't done. He had a response she hadn't thought of; could hardly imagine. Even though he needed every gram of his strength and will, every iota of his own desperation, to move his arms, he forced his hands to his board.

Stopped draining thrust for the guns.

Then he reversed the flow: sent the matter cannon charge—and everything in the energy cells—back into the drive.

It was enough. With that one extra kick of force, *Trumpet* began to win free.

More g: more than enough to crush out consciousness. Blackness filled Morn's head.

It would pass. Automatic overrides would slow and then stop the gap scout as soon as they could. But that changed nothing. When the dark passed, Morn would be gap-sick and deadly. Neither Davies nor Angus would live to understand what they'd accomplished.

She needed some way to confront the universe and remain herself.

She couldn't move her hands to her board: that was out of the question. She didn't have her son's bulk of muscle. And g was worse. The roaring in her ears had become absolute night, carrying her ineluctably into its depths.

Instead she fought her right arm slowly up the back of her g-seat. A centimeter at a time, a degree at a time; there *was* no time, her heart hadn't beat again yet, if as much as a second had gone by she didn't know it. Through midnight and roaring and urgency she raised her arm, shoving it along the pads which cushioned her from being crushed.

When her hand crossed the top of the g-seat, she stopped. She'd done enough. G finished the job.

Without support her hand—her whole arm—had no defense. The singularity and *Trumpet*'s thrust sank their teeth into her flesh.

They ripped her hand and arm past the seat back with ten times her limb's weight, dislocating her shoulder, shattering her elbow, cracking bones in her wrist.

She didn't know it. She was already gone.

MIN

Belted into one of the support personnel g-seats against the bulkhead behind Dolph Ubikwe's command station, Min Donner watched *Punisher* engage the encroaching Amnion defensive.

Tension and urgency were palpable in the air; so thick that they seemed to clog the scrubbers, tainting the atmosphere with CO_2 and fear. Scan and data conferred in bursts, reported their findings in voices like muted cries. Communications barked at Valdor Industrial, demanding help and information. Intercoms crackled incessantly as the bridge stations asked and answered questions for the whole ship. The hull carried a visceral roar of thrust. At times *Punisher*'s spine seemed to groan under the strain. Matter cannon fire filled the ship with a characteristic sizzling sound, as if the laws of physics were being panfried.

The men and women around Min seemed to wince and cower as they worked. She moved that way herself. The bridge crew were veterans to one degree or another, hardened by six months spent fighting for their lives in the Massif-5 system. And Min was so familiar with combat that she hardly noticed its more mundane difficulties. Nevertheless they all flopped like sacks in their g-seats, jerked from side to side by the complex dance of conflicting navigational vectors. *Punisher* seemed to jitter in space as if she were constantly trying to twitch out of harm's way.

Over the babble of voices and needs, the incessant demands and the thronging decisions, Captain Ubikwe presided like a man impervious to chaos. His bulk appeared to have settled in his g-seat as if he couldn't be moved; as if he were the stable point around which *Punisher*'s alarms and struggles revolved. Min had to catch herself repeatedly on the arms of her g-seat because she couldn't know which direction the cruiser would jump in next; but she never saw Dolph lean or recover.

She liked watching him. He was *good* at this. Of course, she would have preferred to take command herself; use the ship as a personal weapon. Her hands burned for action. But since her rank required her to respect Dolph's relationship with his ship, she was glad that he was who he was. She was lucky to be with him, instead of some more cautious or unimaginative commander.

The fire was out; that was the good news. Plasma sealant pumped between the bulkheads had succeeded at smothering the hot blaze. Hargin Stoval and two of his team were in sickbay, suffering from heat prostration and burns—they'd red-lined the tolerances of their suits, and some of the systems had failed. And damage control still hadn't finished measuring the ravages of the blaze. But *Punisher* herself—and most of her people—were safe.

If going into battle exhausted and damaged, with one sensor bank blind and the core off true, against an Amnion warship carrying super-light proton cannon, could be called "safe."

The bad news was that *Punisher*'s stores of plasma sealant were nearly exhausted. If she needed to seal a breach in this fight, she was as good as dead.

Punisher had gone after the alien vessel too slowly to catch her. That had worried Min, even though she'd maintained an air of grim confidence; it had worried her badly. However, Dolph's judgment of the situation proved accurate when the Behemoth-class defensive had commenced hard deceleration along the center of the asteroid swarm where Deaner Beckmann had built his bootleg lab. Soon *Punisher* narrowed the gap.

The alien began stabbing barrage after barrage in *Punisher*'s direction as soon as she came within range. At intervals the defensive's super-light proton cannon spoke, uttering destruction in coherent shafts ten thousand k long. If she could have fired continuously, instead of needing nearly two minutes between blasts to recharge that cannon, she would have killed her opponent already. One solid hit was all she required.

Punisher answered as best she could, using guile and agility to compensate for the fact that her guns simply were not as powerful as the Amnioni's. For the most part, she relied on evasive action to keep her alive.

That was Sergei Patrice's job. If the helm officer ever gave the Amnion warship a clear look at *Punisher*, and then held his position long enough for the defensive to focus her targ, he might not live long enough to know that he'd made a mistake.

Already the defensive had fired three deadly blasts. Two had shot wide by an adequate margin, but the third had skimmed a microwave dish off *Punisher*'s tail and nearly cracked one of her thruster tubes. A broken tube now, under these conditions, would have made the cruiser virtually impossible to manage.

Unfortunately helm had other problems as well. Patrice's assignment was the most complex on the bridge. To cover *Punisher*'s lost scan bank, her window of blindness, he'd resumed rotational thrust, sweeping the heavens with the cruiser's other sifters and sensors. That made the task of sustaining *Punisher*'s battle orientation—and of executing her evasive actions—brutally difficult.

The one advantage of helm's efforts was that they allowed Glessen on targ to keep the Amnioni under constant fire. As *Punisher* revolved, all her guns came to bear in turn. They could be recharged when they revolved away.

If this kind of attack didn't break through the alien's defenses, no weapon *Punisher* possessed would.

"How're we doing, Porson?" Captain Ubikwe's voice was a comfortable rumble, relaxed and focused, but it pierced the muted din of battle easily. The whole bridge heard everything he said. "Are we making a dent in her yet?"

"Negative, Captain." Anxious Porson labored over the scan console, struggling to sort out and interpret all the information *Punisher* needed. As far as Min could tell, his chief worry seemed to be that he would make some critical mistake. "That whole ship must be one big particle sink. We're hitting her—we're hitting her regularly—but we might as well be pouring fire down a sump. She isn't even taking evasive action. She just sits there, shrugging off what we give her and sending it back. If I didn't know better, I would think she's using our fire to charge her guns."

"That isn't possible," Bydell murmured. The data officer was scared in a more personal way than Porson, but she concentrated like death on helping scan make sense of everything the instruments registered. "It's the wrong kind of power. Too random."

It was more likely, Min thought, that the Amnioni had cross-linked her sinks, trusting that she wouldn't be attacked from any other direction while she fought off *Punisher*.

"Keep after her," Dolph ordered calmly. "If nothing else, we'll distract her until we figure out what we're going to do."

Glessen nodded. He fired constantly, maintaining a steady assault with all his guns instead of concentrating their force in barrages—no easy job, considering the way *Punisher* hauled and wrenched from place to place. Nevertheless he managed targ phlegmatically, as if he saw no essential difference between his duties now and his training in combat simulators.

"By the way, Director Donner," Dolph asked over his shoulder, "what *are* we going to do? If we can't overload her sinks and start hurting her, what can we hope to accomplish?"

Min considered several answers, discarded them. "I don't know yet," she replied, pitching her voice to carry through the noise. "Until we locate *Trumpet*, our only objective is to keep that ship occupied while we wait for help."

The Amnioni must have stationed herself over this part of the swarm for a reason. Min couldn't imagine how the defensive might know any more than *Punisher* did about where *Trumpet* was. Nevertheless the alien acted like she knew *some*thing. Min was prepared to trust that oblique information, at least for a while.

VI would send out ships. Then the Amnioni would be trapped. If she didn't run, she would die.

Assuming she didn't kill *Punisher* first—

Another proton beam scorched the vacuum past *Punisher*'s flank. A clear miss. Patrice did his job well. Fine sweat showed on his temples, his upper lip. His eyes had a glazed cast, almost disfocused, as if he were concentrating too hard to actually see anything. Still his hands ran his board steadily. Thrust vectors sawing and heaving through the ship kept *Punisher* alive.

And by routing his maneuvers to Glessen as he made them, he enabled targ to hold its fix on the Amnioni. Despite the constant lurch and stagger of *Punisher*'s movements, she sustained her unremitting assault on her opponent's particle sinks.

Obliquely Min wondered about the state of UMCPDA's research into the use of dispersion fields against matter cannon. The physics had looked good in simulation: prototypes had shown promise. But the equipment hadn't yet been tested in combat. Only a month had passed since Min had authorized installing experimental field projectors on one of ED's destroyers. And *Punisher*'s name had never been on the list of candidates. She needed too much time in the shipyards for other work.

Too bad. A dispersion field might have given her exactly what she needed now. Her sinks and evasive maneuvers were adequate against the alien's matter cannon at this distance; but the emission chaos caused by an effective dispersion field would have covered her while she attacked the defensive in other ways.

Hashi had requisitioned an experimental field projector for *Trumpet*. Maybe the gap scout would give Min a chance to see whether it was effective.

"Cray," Captain Ubikwe rumbled as if he were safe where he sat, "I'm still waiting for help from Valdor. What do they have to say for themselves? I refuse to think they're procrastinating when there's an alien warship in-system."

Cray on communications had been shouting most of the time as she relayed messages back and forth between Dolph and VI Security; Dolph and the rest of the ship. However, her loudness sounded like a control reflex rather than alarm or hysteria: she raised her voice because shouting helped keep her fears at bay.

"Captain," she answered, "VI has eight ships burning in this direction. Gunboats, most of them. One pocket cruiser. But we're too far off the main shipping lanes. VI Security doesn't usually patrol out here. The nearest of those gunboats won't be in range to support us for another eleven hours."

Eleven hours! Min snorted to herself. She wasn't surprised. In the ordinary course of events, sane traffic never went near asteroid swarms. Still the delay vexed her.

"So of course," Cray went on, "there aren't any merchanters nearby that VI can divert to back us up. We're on our own."

"What about our replacement?" Dolph asked. "UMCPHQ must have sent somebody to take over for us when we left."

The sarcasm in his voice may have been aimed at Min, but she didn't take it personally.

"Aye, Captain," Cray answered too loudly; always too loudly. "VI reports that *Vehemence* arrived an hour before we left."

Vehemence. Min sneered the name silently. That ship didn't have what anyone could call "a glorious record" around Massif-5. Nathan Alt had been court-martialed for his actions as her commander. And his predecessor had been patently incompetent. But later officers and crews hadn't fared much better. Some ships were jinxed—doomed to futility by fates which human will and skill couldn't alter.

"They say," the communications officer went on, "she's been charging around like a juggernaut, trying to be everywhere at once. But at the moment she's on the far side of Greater Massif-5." Occluded by the star.

"They can only talk to her if they use mining platforms and other ships as relays.

"Even if she knew we need her," Cray finished, "she would take forty or fifty hours to get here."

"Fine," Dolph growled. "Perfect. So we're on our own.

"Sometimes I think space is just too damn *big*. We're wasting our time pretending we can handle it."

He sounded almost cheerful.

"So what we need," he added in a musing tone, "is to know why that ship"—he nodded at the defensive's blip—"thinks this part of the swarm is special. Ideas, anyone? Porson, are you getting any hints we can use to help us jump to conclusions?"

What *Punisher* really needed, Min thought, was to break the embedded code of Warden Dios' message to Angus Thermopyle for Nick Succorso. Obviously the cruiser couldn't formulate a useful strategy without knowing where *Trumpet* was. But, more importantly, *Punisher* couldn't decide whether the gap scout was worth dying for without knowing what Warden wanted from Thermopyle, Succorso, and their ship.

Unfortunately *Punisher*'s off-duty communications people hadn't yet succeeded in deciphering the UMCP director's message.

That left Min with only one essential question. Did she trust him? Even now, after he'd given control over Isaac/Angus to Nick Succorso?

Of course. What choice did she have?

He'd told her that Morn Hyland was alive.

"I can't see much, Captain," Porson answered tensely, "if you call what I can pick up through this barrage 'seeing.' But there *is* something—"

Min wheeled her seat, fixing her attention like a hawk's on the scan officer.

"At this range," he explained unnecessarily, "the swarm looks like blank rock. Magnetic and gravitic pressures produce a lot of electrostatic energy, but that's inside the swarm. All we read is an occasional flicker, like heat lightning.

"But I'm picking up some odd stress indications. If the instruments aren't confused—and the computer isn't"—his uncertainty made him sound apologetic—"there's an anomalous kinetic reflection coming off the swarm.

"I don't know how to describe it. It's like an echo of something too big pushing through the rocks. Something that violates the normal forces of the swarm."

"It's like," Bydell put in unexpectedly, "a singularity. Like some accident of physics—or maybe a rogue experiment—has created a black hole in there." Abruptly she caught herself. "Captain." Weakly she added, "I'm sorry, sir."

Dolph dismissed her breach of bridge protocol with a flick of his hand. "A kinetic reflection anomaly," he breathed. "A singularity. Now what do you suppose that means?"

Min couldn't hold back. Her palms were on fire, and her pulse had begun to pound out distress in her temples. "Never mind what it means," she snapped. "Where *is* it? Can you locate it?"

Porson glanced at Captain Ubikwe. "Not exactly, sir," he replied as if Dolph had asked the question. "But that Amnioni has positioned herself right over it."

Min gripped the arms of her g-seat, anchored herself against the ship's evasive thrust. "In that case, Captain," she rasped harshly, "I can tell you what we're going to do."

Without any discernible effort, Dolph swiveled his station through conflicting vectors and g to face her. "I was afraid you might say something like that, Director," he drawled. His tone was laconic; the glare in his eyes hinted at insolence. "When I suggested I was interested in jumping to conclusions, I was hoping to start from someplace just a bit more plausible."

Plausible? Min wanted to bark at him. You want *plausible?* I haven't got it. Nothing about this goddamn situation is *plausible.*

Nevertheless she restrained herself. She couldn't take her frustration and anguish out on him. He didn't deserve them; Warden Dios did.

Instead she told him the truth. She'd already swallowed enough lies and misinformation to sicken her.

"It's plausible enough, Captain," she retorted. "*Trumpet* is a gap scout—and gap scouts aren't supposed to be armed. But this is a special case. She has matter cannon. Impact guns. Plasma torpedoes." A dispersion field projector. "And she's carrying singularity grenades."

Dolph's eyes widened; his jaw dropped involuntarily. Then a look that might have been fury filled his gaze. "Do you mean to tell me"—he gritted his teeth on the words—"you gave a rogue illegal and a cyborg a ship armed with *singularity grenades?* My God, Min, I thought they were *experimental.* I thought they were too *God damn* dangerous to use!"

"*Everything's* too dangerous," she shot back. "In case you hadn't noticed, we're already in a black hole ourselves." An impossible mass in an imponderably small space. "Just because it isn't physical doesn't mean it's not deadly. We passed the event horizon when we didn't blast *Trumpet* while we had the chance, off the Com-Mine belt. Now the only way out is through."

If she remembered what she'd read of Deaner Beckmann's theories—and if he was right—

"That echo tells us where *Trumpet* is. Or was." A black hole big enough to cast kinetic inconsistencies out this far could easily have consumed the gap scout and everything around her. In order to survive, she must have already fled the effects of her grenade. "If she tries to leave the swarm on this side, she'll come from there."

And if we get there in time, we might be able to cover her.

"Shit," Glessen muttered abruptly. "What—?" Without lifting his head from the targ board, he called, "Captain, I'm losing charge on one of the guns!"

Dolph didn't glance away from Min. "Bydell?" The anger in his eyes had been replaced by chagrin, as if he feared the ED director had lost her mind.

"I'm on it, Captain," the data officer croaked, hunting her readouts frantically. "Damage-control computer indicates a drain on the power line. The insulation is failing. There." She pointed at a schematic no one else could see. "Must be heat breakdown. That line conduits through one of the bulkheads where we were on fire. The leak's there." She gulped. "Captain, it's getting worse. That section of the bulkhead is already carrying a measurable charge."

Facing Min, his expression hidden from his people, Dolph winced like a snarl.

"Can you reroute?"

"Aye, Captain." A tremor frayed Bydell's voice. "But if I do, we won't be able to maintain a steady current for the other guns. The lines won't carry that much load."

Min saw a strange struggle on Captain Ubikwe's heavy face. His own conflicting vectors—fear for his ship, respect for his director, determination to protect his command, desire for battle—pulled him in too many directions at once. Opening his mouth wide, he drew breath as if he were about to howl. His gaze never left hers.

But he didn't howl. Instead he exhaled, chuckling softly to himself. Slowly he lifted his hands as if he were surrendering. His eyes glittered like cut gemstones.

"Well, this is fun," he rumbled. "When I signed on, they promised me adventure and excitement. I guess this is it.

"You'd better disable that line before we electrocute somebody,

Bydell. Glessen, you can live without one gun for a while. It'll make your job easier."

"Aye, Captain," they answered together.

Under other circumstances, a tech could have repaired the insulation in half an hour. But now any crewmember who left the protection of g-restraints would be dead in seconds, pounded to pulp by *Punisher*'s staggering maneuvers.

"All right, Director," Dolph announced. His voiced filled the bridge. "You've convinced me. You say we're in a black hole. I say we're up to our ass in alligators. Either way, we haven't got anything left to try except prayer. Maybe that'll work.

"What do you want us to do?"

Maybe prayer *was* the answer. Breathing silent gratitude for Captain Dolph Ubikwe, Min gave him her orders.

Take an evasive course toward the site of the kinetic reflection anomaly. Angle to put *Punisher* between the Amnioni's guns and that part of the swarm. Position the cruiser to cover *Trumpet*'s escape.

Position her to die for the strange game Warden Dios played with Angus Thermopyle and Nick Succorso. And Morn Hyland.

"Got that, Sergei?" Dolph asked the helm officer.

"Aye, Captain," Patrice responded.

"Then set course and go.

"I hope you're in the mood for a challenge," Dolph added cheerfully. "With this on top of everything else, you'll have your hands full."

Under his breath Patrice murmured something which might have been, "Piece of cake, Captain."

Rotational thrust. Evasive maneuvers. Now this. Piece of cake: sure. Min wasn't entirely confident that she could have handled the assignment herself.

"Captain," Porson whispered suddenly as if he were amazed—or horrified. "It's been too long."

"Too long?" Dolph made the inquiry sound impersonal; almost abstract.

The scan officer strove to be clear. "Too long since the defensive fired her proton cannon. She's been shooting at us every one hundred eighteen seconds. Exactly. I assume that's as often as she can. But it's been three minutes now. Three and a half. She hasn't fired."

Hasn't fired? Anxiety twisted like nausea in Min's guts. After three and a half minutes?

Dolph straightened himself at his station, clasped his hands on the arms of his g-seat. "In that case, Sergei," he pronounced as if he were enjoying himself; as if all his troubles had been lifted from his shoulders, "I think we'd better carry out Director Donner's orders at full burn. If a Behemoth-class Amnion defensive isn't using her proton cannon to defend herself, it must be because she's about to acquire another target."

Trumpet had been built full of surprises. But nothing the gap scout carried—or could carry—would be able to protect her from a super-light proton beam.

Only *Punisher* could do that.

And die.

SORUS

Taverner had told her to do it; *ordered* her. Even though she'd warned him it was a trick. She'd shouted at him that *Trumpet* was shamming; there was no sabotage; Succorso had been too far ahead of her; if the gap scout struck an asteroid and looked dead, she was doing it deliberately to lure *Soar* in. But Taverner had insisted that the risk was worth taking. That any chance of capturing *Trumpet*'s people alive was worth taking. When *Soar* had finally penetrated the strange storm of distortion—when scan had at last reacquired the gap scout, seen her playing dead—he'd forbidden Sorus to kill the small ship while she could.

This was the result.

Without warning, another ship had appeared. Scan had recognized her at once: she was known from Billingate's operational transmissions.

Free Lunch. Sorus knew nothing about her except her name. But she'd escaped Billingate scant hours ahead of Thanatos Minor's destruction.

Instantly *Free Lunch* opened fire, hitting *Soar* hard; straining her sinks and shields to their limits. *Trumpet* had allies in the most incomprehensible places. *Soar* was forced to throw all her energies into the battle. Otherwise she wouldn't survive.

Barrage after barrage, the stranger hammered her. She fired back frantically. But she'd already suffered too much damage. Succorso had hurt her; the ruin of Thanatos Minor had hurt her. Despite her best efforts to defend herself, she was foundering.

And then, just as Sorus had predicted, *Trumpet* came back to life.

The gap scout must have risked cold ignition. That was the only way she could have brought her thrust back to power and started moving so quickly. Staggering while her tubes heated, she pulled off from the asteroid—

—pulled off in a tight arc which carried her straight into the field of fire between the two combatants; straight under *Soar*'s and *Free Lunch*'s guns.

Thermopyle must have lost his mind. Or *Trumpet* was running on automatic, following a course which had been preset before *Free Lunch* appeared.

Which meant he was busy elsewhere; too busy to manage helm himself.

Busy setting another trap—

"Destroy *Trumpet*," Taverner demanded. Supported by the command console directly in front of Sorus, his alien strength held him as stable as a post. His hand on his SCRT didn't waver. Shades covered his inhuman eyes: they revealed nothing. His tone had become as inflexible as his mind. Nevertheless she couldn't mistake the note of urgency in his instructions. "Destroy her now. The other vessel will not grant you a second opportunity. And she must not be taken by our enemies."

Sorus obeyed, even though turning her guns off her attacker was as good as suicide. "You heard him, targ," she snapped. "Get the gap scout. Hit her *now*."

In a rush of keys, a flurry of desperation, targ did what she told him.

She obeyed Taverner—but not because she feared him. She'd left that old apprehension behind; or it'd been burned out of her by hope and extremity. *Soar* was too badly hurt; couldn't absorb much more punishment. Nothing remained in Sorus Chatelaine's heart except her prayers.

She obeyed because she thought she knew what was going to happen next.

And again she was right. The instant *Soar*'s matter cannon spoke, another wild tsunami of distortion struck: so much random boson fury that every spectrum which *Soar*'s sensors and sifters could receive dissolved in chaos, as if the entire material existence of *Free Lunch* and *Trumpet* and the surrounding swarm were a quantum joke.

The gap scout must have done that. She had a defense against matter cannon. The cops were developing weapons Sorus had never heard of. Weapons she could hardly imagine.

Nevertheless she was ready. *Trumpet* had already produced too many surprises. Sorus didn't intend to be caught by another.

A fraction of a second after scan failed, she shouted at helm, "Veer off! Get us out of here—hard and fast!"

She'd watched the man work for years: she knew he was good. He didn't need to be told that he could trust scan data which was only a few seconds old to help him pick his way through the hurtling torrent of rocks.

Instantly thrust slammed her to the side; strained her ribs to the cracking point on the arm of her g-seat. At the edges her vision seemed to drain away into darkness as thick as blood. Around her, her people fought g to run their boards. Taverner was forced to flex his knees in order to hold his position. The pressure snatched his eyeshades off his face, shattered them to splinters on one of the bulkheads.

While *Free Lunch* and *Trumpet* were as blind as *Soar*, Sorus' ship swung away from the battle. If *Free Lunch* fired again, scan couldn't see it —and the ship didn't feel it.

As *Soar* finished her swerve and came to a new heading, Sorus settled more comfortably into the support of her g-seat. Another few seconds, that was all she needed: if the ship burned for a few more seconds without a fatal miscalculation, a killing collision, scan would begin to clear. Then she could look around her; estimate her chances of turning in time to intercept *Trumpet*'s escape beyond the covering fire of the gap scout's ally. If helm kept the ship safe that long; if Sorus could go on breathing, resist unconsciousness, for those seconds—

Without warning *Soar* faltered as if she'd stumbled into a wall. Her thrust seemed to sag, leak away. Sorus feared for an instant that the ship had holed a tube. But at the same time g increased. Between one heartbeat and the next Sorus felt her weight double.

"Gravity!" data croaked. "Jesus, that's *gravity*! There must be a black hole back there!"

A black hole? Here? All of a sudden? Sorus couldn't understand it—and didn't try. Black hole or not, its pull was tremendous. And any force strong enough to suck at *Soar* this hard would affect everything around her. Already metal thunder pounded through the ship as asteroids of all sizes hammered the hull, trying to drive straight through *Soar* in their hurry to obey the hunger which summoned them.

If she couldn't break free, break free *fast*, she might be dead before the black hole took her. The rush of rock might smash her to pieces.

For no reason Sorus could imagine, Taverner said in a constricted tone, "An induced singularity. A weapon.

"We—I"—he had difficulty referring to himself—"I have heard of such things. Singularity grenades. When I was human. They were spoken of in rumors. It was said that they were impractical. Our research concurs."

Impractical? Sorus raged. If a black hole ate her ship, no one aboard would give a shit whether it was *impractical*.

Humankind endured by being impractical.

Uselessly she noticed that the screens were clearing. The force behind her drank down bosons even faster than it swallowed asteroids. *Soar* would be able to watch herself die.

"Full power, helm," Sorus ordered urgently, pitching her voice to carry through the thunder. A vise of g held her chest: she sounded like she was trying to scream. "Don't fight it directly—angle around it. If it's a black hole, maybe we can pick up enough lateral velocity to sling ourselves loose."

That would expose *Soar*'s flank to the stone torrent; make her a bigger target. But it gave her her best chance to escape.

"Stop charging," Sorus gasped at targ. "Feed your power back to the drive. Matter cannon won't save us now."

If anything saved the ship, it would be the fact that she'd turned away before the black hole came into existence.

The thunder swelled to a din—an endless battery, stone on metal; slower than cannon, but no less fatal. She couldn't hear. In another moment she wouldn't be able to think. G sang in her bones like a subsonic drill: she felt them turning to powder. Her skin seemed to flow and gather like hot paraffin. How long before a rock massive enough to open the hull landed? How long before the event horizon caught her; before hunger and time carried her backward to her death?

She didn't want to die like this. She couldn't move her hands, had no chance whatsoever to reach the impact pistol at her belt. And she'd sworn, *sworn*, that she would kill Milos Taverner before she died. Blast him straight in his fat face—one small payment for the long debt of harm she owed the Amnion.

She didn't want to die like this!

Prayer—

—was sometimes answered.

Slowly at first, almost too slowly to be felt, *Soar* began to win free.

Curving around the depths of the gravity well, she took on centrifugal inertia to combat the pull. At last the black hole's own force helped swing her hard enough to carry outward. Scant moments snatched away from the dark by will and yearning gradually drew Sorus Chatelaine's command out of the well.

The hammering eased as gravity receded. Fewer asteroids answered the singularity's hunger. They answered less avidly. Sorus was sure that one whole side of her ship had been flattened; that every gun, antennae, port, receptor, and vane on that flank had been beaten to metal ruin. Virtually every damage system and warning *Soar* possessed cried alarm. Yet the decompression klaxon was silent. The ship may have been battered almost to scrap, but she hadn't been breached.

As g let her go, Sorus started breathing again. For a moment the return of blood to her eyes and brain overloaded her optic nerves. Then her vision struggled like scan out of a phosphene storm, and she could see again.

Blips on all the screens shouted amber panic. Her command indicators and readouts burned fearfully, as if her board were full of St. Elmo's fire. But *Soar* was alive.

Helm was already at work, firing unmodulated bursts of thrust to control the ship's headlong trajectory. *Soar* staggered as she plunged, yawing and pitching while helm fought to impose a course. And a moment later scan resumed feeding useful data to the helm board. After that his efforts improved. One last clang ended the assault of rocks.

Taverner remained in front of the command station, braced there with one hand under Sorus' console. With his eyeshades gone, she could see his alien eyes.

He wasn't looking at her. Instead he studied the incomprehensible readouts on his SCRT while his fingers sped across the keys. Talking to *Calm Horizons*. Instantaneous communications. If he suffered from the effects of so much g, he didn't show it.

Sorus decided to ignore him. Whatever he was doing—whatever he wanted—could wait.

Sipping air past the pain in her chest, she breathed, "Data, give me damage." Then, because she hurt too much to concentrate on everything at once, she added, "Keep it simple. Just the highlights for now."

Blips on the command board signaled for her attention as well. They, too, could wait.

"Not good, Captain," data croaked. Roughly he scrubbed his eyes; squinted at his readouts. "Shit, I can hardly see.

"No decompression," he reported, "but we took a hell of a beating."

He recited a list of vanes, guns, receptors. "All gone. We're deaf, dumb, and blind on that side. Structural damage to both hulls. Metal stress way past our tolerances." After a momentary hitch, he went on, "We've lost a 30° arc of maneuvering thrust. And one of our main tubes was crushed flat.

"In clear space," he concluded, "we could probably limp along for a while. We might even be able to pick up enough velocity to use the gap drive. But it wouldn't do us any good. We don't have the control to choose a heading we can count on.

"Navigating this swarm will be like playing pinball."

Sorus listened to him as if he weren't pronouncing a sentence of death. *The control to choose a heading we can count on*. Gap capability meant nothing without precise heading and velocity. In other words, *Soar* couldn't escape the Massif-5 system. She couldn't save herself.

To keep the ship out of human hands, Taverner would order self-destruct. The Amnion were like that. If Sorus refused, he would release the airborne mutagens which he'd prepared in the scrubbers. Then everyone aboard would be changed—and his orders would be carried out.

Yet Sorus heard nothing but hope in data's report. Obliquely and unpredictably, her prayers were still being answered.

"Where are we?" she asked scan quietly.

The woman looked up from her board. "Hard to say, Captain. Suddenly our charts are"—she tried to chuckle—"out-of-date."

Perhaps she, too, understood something about hope.

"But at a guess, we're here." She routed a schematic to one of the displays. *Soar* appeared to be roughly thirty k past the limits of the singularity's gravity well—a considerable distance off the departure which dead Lab Center had assigned to *Trumpet*. "I can't speak for helm, but we ought to be able to find our way from here. It just won't be as clear as the course Lab Center gave us."

Sorus nodded. "Any sign of *Trumpet*? Any ships at all?"

"Not that I can see," scan replied. "As far as I can gauge it, *Free Lunch* was sitting right at the center of the singularity. She must have been the first thing it ate. And *Trumpet* wasn't as far away as we were. If she survived, she's got God on her side. It would take a goddamn miracle."

Sorus smiled at the woman. No question about it: the scan first understood something. Her rueful answering grin told her captain that Sorus wasn't alone.

One more answer, that's all I need, she thought. Just one. Is it too much to ask?

She took a moment to consider the blips flashing on her board. Most of them warned her about dangers she already knew; threats she expected. But one came as a surprise.

Someone had used an airlock. Specifically the airlock to the cargo bay which had been breached by debris from the destruction of Thanatos Minor.

Shit! That was insane. All her people knew better than to leave their g-restraints in combat. And any sentient being knew better than to enter a breached cargo bay under these conditions.

Nevertheless it was unmistakable. Someone had opened the airlock; used it; closed it again. Without sealing it. According to her status readout, the sealing mechanism was inoperative.

No. She didn't believe it. It was probably just stress damage—too much g, too much pounding. She'd seen stranger readings that turned out to be false.

And she didn't have the time or energy to worry about it. Her scant remaining resources were needed for prayer—

Shaking her head, she shifted her attention to Milos Taverner and inquired, "What do you want us to do?"

He didn't glance up at her. He was fixed to his SCRT, feeding and receiving data. Nevertheless he replied promptly, as if he'd heard everything she'd said. As if like God he had the power to grant miracles—

"Captain Chatelaine, analysis of *Trumpet*'s thrust-to-mass ratio during her escape from Thanatos Minor suggests that her drive is adequate to retrieve her from the singularity's event horizon. It is conceivable that she has survived. Indeed, it seems plausible that she ensured her capacity to survive before she activated her weapon. That is—"

He faltered as if he'd come to a translation barrier. His grasp on human language, like his ability to comprehend human patterns of thought, drained out of him with increasing rapidity. After a moment, however, he seemed to find a way to reach back to his former self; his former mind.

"That is," he repeated awkwardly, "consistent with what I know of Captain Thermopyle. He would sacrifice his companions and even his ship to survive." The idea may have pained him. "We must act on the assumption that *Trumpet* is alive."

More strongly he continued, "*Calm Horizons* has taken her position to guard against *Trumpet*'s egress from the swarm. It is probable that she will be able to destroy the gap scout. However, she is heavily engaged by a UMCP warship." Again he paused to grope for translation. "You would call the vessel a 'Scalpel-class cruiser.' At present the warship's cannon cannot penetrate *Calm Horizons*' defenses. Yet the warship's presence diminishes the likelihood that *Calm Horizons* will be able to ensure *Trumpet*'s destruction.

"We are instructed to advance to the edge of the swarm so that we may watch for the gap scout—and also so that we may assist *Calm Horizons*. I have the coordinates we must attain.

"The cost of *Trumpet*'s survival is too high to be met. She must be destroyed."

Yes. Sorus could hardly contain herself. *Yes!*

Thank God Taverner wasn't looking at her. If he'd glanced up then, he would almost certainly have seen the quick flare of glee and fury in her eyes, the sudden, killing hope on her face.

Everything she asked had been given to her.

Simply to preserve appearances, mask her joy, she rasped back, "This is your fault. I hope you remember that. If you hadn't stopped me from killing her when we had the chance, you would be on your way home by now."

Now at last Taverner raised his gaze to hers. His alien eyes never blinked. "*Calm Horizons* is aware of the decisions which have been made, and of their outcome."

"In that case"—she turned away because she didn't trust herself to conceal how she felt—"we'd better get going.

"Helm, this Amnioni will give you the coordinates. Getting there won't be easy, but you can do it. If you engage a little rotation, you'll have enough maneuvering thrust to point us in the right direction."

"Right, Captain." Helm spent a few seconds keying commands. Then he gestured Taverner to his board so that the Amnioni could enter the coordinates.

Taverner didn't delay. Apparently he saw no reason to thwart Sorus now. Releasing his grip on her console, he let himself drift in the direction of the helm station.

While his back was turned, Sorus met scan's look. Just for a moment the two women grinned at each other like idiots.

DAVIES

He came out of the darkness of anoxia and acceleration wondering why he was still alive.

Stupid. He was forever wondering why he was still alive. What was the matter with him? Didn't he ever learn? Wondering changed nothing; helped nothing. Only the fact mattered.

G had let go of him, and every bone and sinew in his body hurt, but he endured among the living.

No, g hadn't let go. He still weighed more than he should have. His pulse seemed to cut and scrape in his veins, as though his blood were clotted with broken glass. Mortality held him in his g-seat, leaning down pitilessly on all his pains. Someone had driven spikes through the cast into his arm; into his ribs. He wasn't sure that he could lift his head, or swallow. He was doing his best when he opened his eyes.

At first what he saw didn't make sense.

Through a migraine of phosphenes and dehydration, he recognized the bridge. That remained constant, at any rate. And the decompression klaxons were silent. He could breathe, as long as he didn't try to inhale deeply. To that extent, at least, *Trumpet* remained intact.

But the scan display in front of him seemed to indicate that she wasn't moving. Thrust said she was: the muted hull-roar of the drive said she was: g said she was. Scan said she wasn't.

The screens were big enough to see, but his eyes refused to focus on anything smaller: his board's indicators; the messages on his readouts. Simply lowering his head to get a better look at them hurt too much. He had no idea what was going on.

Respiration whispered around him, as if the air-scrubbers were gasping softly. That didn't make sense either. He'd never heard scrubbers produce such a sound. When pads were clogged, they sometimes emitted a low, aggrieved sigh, like an asthmatic moan. But never this choked clutch for breath.

He had to move his head; *had* to.

The pain of tipping his head forward brought tears to his eyes. That helped: when he'd blinked the dampness away, he was able to see more clearly.

His readouts answered his first question. *Trumpet* was running on automatic, and her failsafes had overridden helm. Too much rock in the way: Morn's preset instructions would have killed the ship. In self-defense the automatic systems held *Trumpet* stationary in the swarm, shifting her from side to side only when an asteroid threatened collision.

But she was still in reach of the black hole. Its hunger called to her constantly, urging her backward. She couldn't refuse unless she used thrust to counter the commanding tug of the gravity well. Fortunately her failsafes provided for that.

Thank God Morn had thought to activate them before she lost consciousness.

Where was the gap scout? Where in relation to *Soar* and the other ship?—to the singularity and the swarm? Davies hunted scan for information.

No sign of *Soar*; of any ships at all: that was good. And the black hole was precisely *there*. But— He gaped, and his heart stung, as he realized that *Trumpet* had covered less than five k since he'd blacked out. No wonder the black hole still gripped her.

Trumpet was a sitting target.

Scan insisted that there were no other ships within range of its instruments. But there *would* be, Davies thought—slowly, painfully, his mind obstructed by the wrong neurotransmitters—if the gap scout didn't move soon.

Or maybe he didn't need to worry about other ships. Maybe the black hole's event horizon was the only real danger. As the singularity fed, it grew. It was a small thing as such phenomena were measured. Before long it wouldn't be. Given enough time, it would grow large enough to devour the entire swarm.

Long before that, it would become too strong for *Trumpet* to resist.

At least now he knew why stones streamed constantly past the gap scout. They were diving into a ravenous maw of g.

But why couldn't scan tell him where she was?

Of course. Slow, he was too *slow*. His brain wasn't working worth shit. *Of course* scan couldn't identify the ship's position—except in relation to the black hole. There were no referents. Every identifiable object in the area had already been sucked down. And the surrounding swarm was still far too thick to permit any conceivable access to the starfield. This deep in the torrent of asteroids, even Greater and Lesser Massif-5 didn't register on the instruments.

Well, fine. In that case Davies would simply have to assume that *Trumpet*'s present orientation bore some resemblance to the heading Morn had chosen before she lost consciousness. The ship needed to go straight forward. He hadn't studied her helm. In fact, those functions hadn't been routed to his board. But his training in the Academy would enable him to cope. Somehow he could make *Trumpet* go where he pointed her. All he had to do was unclip his belts, carry his mass across the deck to the command station, secure himself there. When he was safely settled, he could figure out how to increase thrust until *Trumpet* finally pulled herself out of this gravity well.

But first he needed rest. Right now the effort of getting out of his g-seat was beyond him.

The sounds of battered, limping respiration continued, as if two or three people were dying on the bridge behind him; breathing their last— It didn't make sense. Scrubbers couldn't produce that kind of noise. If *Trumpet* were losing atmosphere in distant gasps, the decompression klaxons would have warned him.

He was altogether too slow. His thoughts seemed to struggle and stagger under their own weight: his head might have been full of cat. Something he'd forgotten— Had Morn finally gone to sickbay, drugged herself to protect the ship from her gap-sickness? And was he really her, cloyed with her drugs as well as her memories, stricken by her illness?

Was this what clarity felt like, when the universe spoke?

Somewhere nearby a panted exhalation became a small groan of pain.

Involuntarily, fearing to see what he'd forgotten, Davies turned his head.

Apparently he'd forgotten everything he truly cared about.

Morn sprawled in the command station g-seat. Trails of blood ran from her mouth across her cheeks in streaks drawn by g: she must have bitten her lips or tongue. Her breathing came in little gulps of distress, barely audible. Davies seemed to see her eyelids fluttering as if she were in the grip of a seizure.

Another faint groan made him think that she was recovering consciousness.

That wasn't the worst of it, however, oh, not the worst at all, if that had been the worst he might have been able to forgive himself for forgetting her. But as soon as the pain of turning his head cleared, he saw that her bleeding, her unconsciousness, her disturbed eyelids were trivial. There was other damage, worse—

Her chest twisted painfully on the edge of the seat back, as if she'd tried to squirm out of her restraints under hard g. And she was held in that tortured position by the impossible angle of her right arm.

No human limb could hang like *that* and be whole.

While *Trumpet* burned against the singularity's pull, Morn must have pushed her arm past the cushions until the force of *Trumpet*'s escape caught it; nearly ripped it off—

Without transition, as quick as a gap crossing, Davies Hyland became a different person. Endocrine extravagance transformed him in an instant. Noradrenaline vanquished pain: dopamine and serotonin sloughed off weight. He didn't waste time shouting her name, or panicking. Instead he slapped open his belt clips and pitched out of his g-seat.

He was half again too heavy. Under other circumstances, he would have been able to manage his effective mass; but not easily. Now he thought he could feel his ribs grinding together. Nevertheless he ignored the extra kg as if they didn't exist. He hit hard, but didn't feel the sting in his soles, or the jolt in his knees.

Trumpet's bridge had been designed to gimbal in heavy g, orienting the g-seats to protect their occupants as much as possible. But now the ship had attained a stable orientation. The deck was level under his boots.

Two strides reached the command station. Morn would be in agony as soon as she woke up. Simply looking at the deformed line of her arm made his joints ache. What could he do to help her? He was no medtech. Did he dare move her?

Yes: that was better than leaving her like this.

Carefully, quickly, he lifted her arm and shifted her toward the middle of the seat back.

A groan seemed to bubble past the blood on her lips like a drowned whimper. Her eyelids stopped fluttering: instead they squeezed tight as if she had to fight a wave of nausea. A weak cough leaked blood onto her chin. Then, slowly, she began to open her eyes.

Now he whispered fearfully, "Morn. Morn? Can you hear me?"

Did it work?

Intuitively he knew that she'd done this to herself on purpose. If she was filled with pain, she might have no room left for gap-sickness. And if it did take hold of her, she would be too crippled to obey it.

She lifted her eyes to his face. Her mouth shaped a word, although she made no sound.

Was she trying to say his name? No. When she tried again, she found enough breath to be heard.

"Angus."

He nearly cried out. Did she think he was his father? Was Angus all she cared about?

Then a worse thought struck him.

Shit, *Angus*! He'd forgotten *Angus*, too, forgotten both his parents, even though the two of them had just saved his life.

Angus had been outside the ship; had used his portable matter cannon to detonate the singularity grenade. The black hole must have sucked him down; must have snatched him off *Trumpet*'s side as lightly as a pebble. Even a cyborg's strength would have been far too puny to resist that g.

But Davies had heard more than one hoarse, dying sound. Like a wince, he lowered his face to the command station intercom, put his ear to the speaker.

Shards of pain twisted between his ribs as he bent over.

Faint as a whisper of static in the vacuum: respiration. From Angus' suit pickup came the low, hollow scrape of excruciated air, in and out—

Davies jerked up his head. "He's alive. Morn, he's alive. He's still outside," somehow Angus must have anchored himself in time, cleated his belts to hold him, "but I can hear him."

The muscles in Morn's cheeks tugged: she may have been attempting to smile. Almost inaudibly she murmured, "That's good. I can't do this again."

"Morn?" Davies bent over her, straining not to miss her words. "Morn?"

"When I'm in trouble," she said like a sigh, "the only thing I can think of is to hurt myself. Self-destruct— I need a better answer."

Her voice trailed away like the fall of her eyelids. Gently tension seemed to let go of her as if she'd dropped off to sleep.

He stared at her in dismay. Self-destruct? What the fuck are you talking about? Wake up, damn it! I need you!

Trumpet had to move; he had to move the ship. Already g had increased as the gravity well deepened and the failsafes brought up more thrust to counter it. Angus was still outside, *my God, still alive*, and *Soar* could be anywhere. *Free Lunch* had been sucked down, but *Soar* had been farther from the black hole; could have survived it. She might be closing for the kill right now.

Yet Morn was desperately hurt. Davies didn't have time to rouse her. And he didn't have the heart—

A new rush of urgency snatched him into motion.

With the heel of his palm, he slapped the command intercom, silencing Angus' faint respiration. A stab of his fingers keyed open a ship-wide channel.

"Mikka?" he shouted. "*Mikka?* Do you hear me? I need you."

He had his father's voice: his fear sounded like rage.

"And don't tell me you can't leave Ciro!" he snapped as if his anger was aimed at her. "Let him do his own suffering for a while! I *need* you. I'm alone here!"

He didn't know whether she would answer or not. He didn't give her a chance. Still on the same channel, he barked, "Vector? Vector, *move*! I can't do this many jobs at once. *I'm alone here!* If I don't get some help, it's all going to be *wasted*," everything Angus and Morn and the ship had endured would go for nothing.

"I hear you." Vector's voice sounded unnaturally loud over the hull-roar of thrust. Davies had turned the gain on the intercom too high. The geneticist's tone was tight with suppressed distress; all this g must have brutalized his sore joints. Nevertheless his reply was prompt; ready. "Tell me what you want. I'll do it."

Davies didn't hesitate. "Angus is outside!" he fired back. "He went out with his cannon—" The situation was too complicated to explain. "He shouldn't be alive. But he left his pickup open. I can hear him breathing.

"Put on a suit. Go get him—bring him in. But be careful! This g is trouble. And it's going to get worse. We're caught in a gravity well. We need more thrust to break loose. If you don't keep yourself anchored, we'll lose you."

We'll lose you both if you try to hold Angus yourself.

"I'm on my way," Vector replied. He might have been obeying an order to take his turn in the san. "Don't worry about me. I'll take every precaution there is. I'll bring him in somehow."

Without pausing he added, "I'll set my suit for this channel. That way I can still hear you. Can you talk to me? Tell me what's happened? How's Morn?"

Punching the toggle, Davies closed the intercom. "I haven't got *time*," he rasped to the bridge. "I need *help*."

Or he needed Divine inspiration, so that he could save the ship without taking time to study helm first.

The bulkheads answered with the muffled fire of *Trumpet*'s drive. God didn't say anything.

"I'm here," Mikka croaked from the head of the companionway. When the bridge gimballed, the stair automatically retracted itself to keep the space clear, but it came back into position as soon as g stabilized. "What's going on?"

She wobbled on the treads, hampered by too much weight. Her damaged forehead hadn't had time to heal, despite the best sickbay could do for her. And Ciro and g had hurt her more: Nick's treachery had attacked her at the core of her being. Even calling on Morn's memories, Davies had never seen her look so weak.

Yet she advanced down the steps, gripping the handrails on both sides to keep herself upright. Carrying her flesh like a burden which had grown too heavy, she reached the foot of the companionway and stopped, waiting for Davies to speak.

She was exhausted; nearly beaten. But he couldn't afford to care. *Trumpet* was no better off. Angus might well die before Vector could bring him in; might be hemorrhaging inside his suit, filling all its space with blood torn out of him by the black hole he'd created. And Morn was in too much pain to hang on to consciousness.

Mikka had done some of the navigating until Nick had taken over Angus. She'd already studied the board—

"Take helm," Davies ordered harshly. "Get us out of here. We're caught in the gravity well of a black hole. Don't ask me how that happened. I'll tell you later. Or you can read the log in your spare time.

"Morn needs sickbay bad. I'll get her there—then I'll come back. Don't worry about g. I'll handle it somehow." He had no idea how. *Trumpet* might double or triple her effective mass before she broke the singularity's grip. "Straight ahead," he went on, "until scan tells you where we are. Then try to find a way out of the swarm."

He didn't wait for Mikka's response. Grimly, dreading how much he would hurt her, he unclosed Morn's belts. In one motion, he leaned her forward, set his shoulder under her torso, and heaved her up from her g-seat; braced her by gripping one of her legs and her good arm. The pain in his ribs seemed to pierce his chest as he stepped clear of the command station so that Mikka could sit down.

She hadn't moved from the companionway. Her face was empty of questions: her attention had turned inward. Davies feared that she would refuse him. She would say that Ciro needed her too much, or that she was too worn-out to function. Groaning inside, he marshaled his strength to yell at her, curse or beg—

But he'd misread her immobility. She seemed to be thinking aloud as she murmured, "Or I can reconstruct our position from the log and the location of the black hole. Look at g vectors in relation to where the rocks used to be around us. I should be able to put us back on the same course Lab Center gave us."

Damn it. *Damn* it. Why hadn't he thought of that? What was *wrong* with him?

No. He didn't have time to waste on his own inadequacies. "Do it," he panted. "Otherwise we're finished."

Gasping under the pressure of so much weight, he stepped cautiously toward Mikka and the companionway.

She shifted out of his way; watched him reach the support of the rails before she moved to the command station.

The black hole and *Trumpet*'s thrust loaded him down with at least a hundred kg more than he was accustomed to carrying. His damaged ribs and bound arm throbbed with stress. The companionway looked frightfully high, impossible to climb.

But perhaps this was what he was good for; perhaps his conditioning in Morn's womb had prepared him to succeed now. His enhanced endocrine system made him stronger than he had any structural right to be.

Clamping Morn's limbs in the crooks of his arms, he grasped the rails and started upward.

Yes, he could do this. He could *do* it. If Mikka didn't add thrust too soon, he would be able to gain the head of the companionway. Then all he had to do was stagger along the passage until he came to sickbay.

That part would be dangerously easy. *Trumpet*'s orientation in the gravity well gave the passage a sharp downward slope.

Two steps. Five. Seven. Yes. The muscles of his thighs burned as if they were tearing, but they didn't hurt enough to stop him.

As soon as he achieved the last tread, *Trumpet*'s drive began to howl more deeply. At once Davies and Morn took on another twenty kg; thirty—

In an instant he changed his mind about carrying her. The passage looked as sheer as a cliff. Straining to handle her gently, he lowered her to the deck, then held her by her good arm and let her slide downward. At the extent of his reach, he followed her. By catching at handgrips and the corners of doorways, wedging his heels between the deck and wall, he kept their descent under control.

He saw Vector ahead of him, at the suit locker. Vector had almost finished struggling into his EVA suit. While Morn and Davies slid toward him, he sealed his helmet, closed the faceplate, activated the suit's systems. Then, anchored on a handgrip, he crouched near the wall to help Davies stop Morn at the sickbay door.

More g. Davies was barely strong enough to straighten his legs. How much did he weigh now? Twice what he should? More?

With Vector's assistance, he climbed to his feet at the door, levered Morn high enough so that he could lock his arms around her chest.

The external speaker on Vector's suit crackled. "I've never done this before," he said distantly. "I hope there's no hurry. I won't be able to reach Angus and bring him in quickly."

"Do what you can," Davies grunted. "Sickbay needs time to take care of Morn."

Now Vector didn't ask what had happened to her. G increased by the second: soon movement would become impossible. He keyed open the sickbay door for Davies, then turned away to heave himself up the handgrips toward the lift.

Davies staggered backward into sickbay, dragging Morn with him.

The lower wall of the room seemed to loom under him, as deep as the singularity's well. If he and Morn fell down there, he would never have the strength to raise her to the surgical table.

But if he hesitated, the danger would only get worse—

He gasped a hard breath, tensed his legs. A desperate lunge carried him across the gap between the door and the end of the table, missing by millimeters a plunge which might have broken his bones as well as more of Morn's. The impact of the table on his ribs snatched a cry from his clenched throat.

Fortunately his task became easier then. Lift her onto the table with her legs downward. Secure a g-sheath and restraints around her, leaving her shattered arm free. Settle her wrist, forearm, and upper arm firmly into passive clamps provided by the surgical apparatus. Key the cybernetic systems for automatic diagnosis and treatment; automatic g protection.

Done. The g-sheath and restraints held her. The sickbay equipment would take care of her as well as it could.

He'd stopped breathing effectively. The gravity well dragged more air out of him with each exhalation, let him inhale less. By now he knew that he wouldn't be able to regain the bridge. No matter what he'd said to Mikka, he couldn't leave this room until *Trumpet* won free of the black hole. The effort would kill him.

He didn't try to talk to her, tell her he was staying with Morn. The intercom was entirely out of reach. Instead he folded himself carefully to the deck, then released the table and slid to the lower wall. There he stretched out with his back against the bulkhead to endure the brutal seconds while Mikka Vasaczk fought to save the ship.

If Angus could still breathe, he'd already survived worse than this—much worse—without the benefit of a padded g-seat and belts; without so much as a wall at his back. But Davies didn't really believe that his father was alive. If Angus continued drawing in air and letting it out, that was only because his smashed bones and pulped flesh didn't have enough sense to die.

Three times his own weight squeezed Davies into the junction of the deck and wall. And the stress increased constantly. Soon he would be helpless to do anything except pass out.

But while he clung to consciousness he found that he couldn't prevent himself from grieving for both his parents. Or for himself.

Nearly an hour elapsed before Vector brought Angus in.

By that time g had ceased to be a factor. *Trumpet* was well away from the black hole, moving easily at last toward the fringes of the swarm.

Sib Mackern had been left for dead. His friends hadn't had any other choice.

Limping and sore, as if he'd been cudgeled from head to foot, Davies had returned to the bridge as soon as he could, resumed his place at the second's station. He was there, working scan and communications while Mikka picked *Trumpet*'s way among the rocks, when his intercom speaker snapped to life, and Vector announced, "I have him. We're in the airlock. As soon as it cycles, I'll take him to sickbay."

The former engineer sounded cruelly exhausted. An arthritic pain seemed to throb in the background of his voice. Still his tone suggested that he was proud of himself.

Davies was nearly exhausted as well; sore to the bone; drained of energy. More and more he felt like a little kid who might start to cry at any moment. What he wanted more than anything was to give responsibility for the ship to someone else. Return to watching over Morn and let the rest go. The need for revenge had lost its hold on him. He didn't think he could afford the effort. His mortality was too heavy for him.

He couldn't imagine feeling proud of anything he did.

Fearing the worst, he asked Vector wanly, "How is he?"

The unmistakable hiss of the airlock came across the intercom as atmosphere accumulated around Vector, transmitting vibrations to his helmet pickup.

"According to his suit indicators," he answered, "he's intact. Relatively. He's unconscious and dehydrated. I can see some bleeding. There may be other problems." No EVA suit had instruments to measure internal hemorrhaging, or the condition of vital organs. "It looks like all of his systems red-lined while he was out there.

"But his suit thinks he's going to be all right."

A sudden tightness closed Davies' throat. For a moment he felt sure he was going to weep.

But he'd already made too many mistakes; let too many essential details slip past him. He needed to stay in control. *Trumpet* was far from safe. *Soar* might still be alive; might still be hunting the gap scout. That UMCP cruiser, *Punisher*, was presumably somewhere in the VI system, tracking *Trumpet* for her own—or Warden Dios'—dangerous reasons. And the gap scout had already been attacked by one strange vessel. Where there was one, there could easily be more.

Trumpet wouldn't be out of immediate danger until she escaped the swarm and acquired enough velocity to go into tach.

Cursing to beat back his weakness, Davies rasped into his pickup, "Can you take him to sickbay? Morn's there. She's probably done by now." How much could he ask Vector to do? He didn't know. Roughly he added, "She should be in her cabin."

"Take him to sickbay?" Vector echoed. He sounded vague, as if he were falling asleep. "Take Morn to her cabin? In zero g? I think I can handle it."

Then he went on more strongly, "But I have to tell you, Davies, I'm tired of not knowing what's going on. Being outside in that much g was the hardest thing I've ever done. I didn't think I was ever going to reach Angus—or keep my grip on him when I did. And I didn't exactly relish the prospect of being sucked into a black hole. I'm not Deaner Beckmann." His tone hinted at a fleeting smile. "It bothered me that I didn't know why I had to do it. Whenever I think I'm about to end up dead, I can't help wanting to know why."

Slowly—she did everything slowly now that *Trumpet* was out of the well—Mikka tapped a toggle to open a ship-wide intercom channel.

"Tell him," she said to Davies flatly. "And tell Ciro. They both need to know."

She didn't mention her own needs. Maybe she'd gleaned everything she could absorb from the log. Or maybe in some basic way she'd temporarily ceased to exist for herself.

Instinctively Davies shied away from her demand. He'd made too many errors, forgotten too much, served the ship and her people too poorly. Now he feared that if he thought about all the things he couldn't forgive, his weakness might overwhelm him.

Nevertheless he knew that Mikka was right.

Precisely because he felt so weak, he had to act strong.

She watched him dully as he faced his pickup.

"None of this was my idea," he rasped, coercing himself with fierceness, "or Morn's. Angus set it up."

Remember that. Remember who kept us alive.

"We thought we were following *Soar* out of the swarm, but she managed to get behind us. Then we ran into *Free Lunch*." Davies had fired at her stupidly, without so much as focusing targ. "Morn told you about her. Angus wasn't sure how to fight her, so we headed back into the swarm. He wanted to deal with *Soar* first, before we had to face *Free Lunch* again.

"Angus didn't leave us any choice." Davies tried to make his meaning unmistakable. He hadn't saved *Trumpet* himself: everyone aboard would have died if their lives had depended on him. "He set the ship to play dead—I guess he thought he could lure *Soar* in. He programmed everything he wanted. Then he took that portable matter cannon of his and went outside.

"Before we could move, *Free Lunch* caught up with us. She started firing at *Soar*." Grimly Davies described what he and Morn had done; what he knew of Angus' actions. Then he grated, "It should have been impossible, but it worked. *Free Lunch* fell into the black hole. Maybe *Soar* did, too—I don't know. I'm assuming she's still around somewhere, trying to find us.

"Breaking out of the gravity well wasn't easy. We never had a chance to let Angus come back inside. G shattered Morn's arm." He had no intention of explaining that she'd caused her own injury. He didn't think he could bear to say that aloud. "And we couldn't go back for Sib." He swallowed once, fiercely. "By now he's dead. If the black hole or the fighting didn't kill him, he ran out of air."

Brave, terrified Sib Mackern deserved a better farewell; but Davies couldn't think of anything else to say.

"At the moment we're safe. Sort of. We're following our old course out of the swarm. We still haven't caught any sign of *Soar*. Maybe we'll know more when this rock starts to thin out, and scan can see farther."

He glanced at Mikka to see whether she was satisfied. But she wasn't looking at him. She sat in her g-seat with her head back and her good eye closed, resting briefly while she listened.

His readouts told him that the lift had reached the central passage. Soon Angus would be in sickbay. After that Davies could key his board to call up a display of Angus' condition from the sickbay systems. If he had the nerve— If he wanted to be reminded that no one was left to relieve him of responsibility.

He didn't try to answer that question. Instead he returned his attention to the intercom.

"In the meantime," he went on, "there are other things you should know." Now that he was done remembering his mistakes—at least temporarily—he could speak more easily. "I've been learning my way around communications, and I've found two more details Angus must have programmed before he went outside."

Decisions Angus had made without consulting anyone; not even Morn.

"One is that we're already broadcasting Vector's message. And I mean *broadcasting*. We're spraying it in all directions as loud as we can. Nobody can hear us yet. There's too much rock in the way, too much static. But as soon as we reach the fringes of the swarm, *some*body is going to receive this transmission. Once we're past the rocks, VI won't be able to avoid hearing us."

Not to mention every other ship in this quadrant of the Massif-5 system.

"Unfortunately that'll make us *very* easy to spot. We might as well shout our location at anybody who wants to find us."

Davies paused. Mikka blinked her eyes open, turned a look like a groan in his direction.

"That's all right," Vector put in. His helmet no longer constricted his voice. He was using the sickbay intercom. "The risk is worth it. We don't need much time to make sure Valdor hears that message. Then we've won.

It won't matter if *Soar* gets us. It won't even matter if *Calm Horizons* herself comes after us. VI will know about the immunity drug.

"Humankind will finally have a defense that works."

Davies nodded wearily, even though Vector couldn't see him. "In any case, there's no point in postponing transmission until we're out of trouble. Angus made sure of that."

Mikka lowered her wounded face into her hands as if she were afraid to hear what was coming.

"The other thing he did," Davies explained, "was activate a homing signal. A Class-1 UMCP homing signal, emergency trace-and-follow. It doesn't just tell where we are, it gives coordinates, course, and velocity. If we go into tach, it includes our gap drive parameters and settings." So that any UMCP vessel in pursuit would know where to reacquire the signal. "That must be how *Punisher* got close enough to reach us with a message. She knew exactly where we were.

"There's probably some way to turn it off," he finished, "but I haven't figured out how."

Deliberately he didn't say, If *Soar* catches us—or if *Calm Horizons* actually comes after us—maybe we'll have help. He didn't dare. Like Morn and Vector, he knew too much about UMCP corruption. He couldn't stifle his inherited respect for Min Donner, but he no longer trusted anything Warden Dios did.

If the UMCP director had really intended to free Angus, why had he first given Nick Angus' codes?

"Shit," Mikka breathed. "This is a mess. A fucking mess. Whose side are we on? What're we supposed to do? Angus rescues us from *Soar* and *Free Lunch*, I still don't understand how, and then he starts shouting so loud we can't hide from *anybody*. God, that datacore in his head must have made him crazy."

Davies reached out to silence the intercom, then stopped himself. "Vector," he asked, "is there anything you want to say while you have the chance? Anything else you want to know?

"Ciro?"

Vector made a tired sound which might have been intended as a chuckle. "Words fail me," he drawled. "I'm just glad I'm not trained for helm. Or targ. This is *your* problem. You'll handle it better than I would."

Ciro didn't reply. He may not have heard the intercom at all.

Thanks. Davies took a bitter breath, let it out slowly. Just what I wanted to hear.

"In that case," he muttered thinly, "you'd better brace yourself for another fight. Secure Angus in sickbay, Vector. Take Morn to her cabin, put her to bed. Then do the same yourself. No matter what we do, we aren't safe until we get away from Massif-5."

"Right." Davies' speaker emitted a small pop as Vector toggled the sickbay intercom.

Mikka kept the ship-wide channel open, however. As soon as Davies silenced his pickup, she leaned over hers.

"Ciro, did you hear all that? Are you all right? Ciro?"

Still Ciro didn't say anything.

Was he asleep? Unconscious?

Or was Vector wrong?

If Sorus Chatelaine's mutagen had become active—

Even now Mikka moved slowly. Fatigue and gloom weighted her movements as she unclipped her belts and floated up from the command station. "I need to check on him," she murmured as if she were talking to herself; as if no one else would care what she did. "If he's all right, he would have answered."

"Mikka!" Davies protested involuntarily. The thought of being left alone appalled him. He couldn't do everything himself; the burden was too much to bear. "I can't run helm!"

But the panic in his voice dismayed him. Despite his weakness, he swallowed as much distress as he could. "I haven't had time to learn," he said more quietly. "If *Soar* shows up while you're off the bridge, we won't stand a chance."

She didn't look at him. Squinting with anxiety or yearning, she studied the empty passage at the head of the companionway as if she were peering into a darkness as deep as the black hole *Trumpet* had left behind. Yet she didn't move away. Adrift above the command station, she stared one-eyed at the passage like a woman who hoped that the singularity's attraction might release some fatal truth, if only she waited for it long enough; wanted it enough.

Watching her, Davies thought his heart would stop. He'd come to the end of what he could do. No wonder Morn had chosen to go with Nick instead of turning herself over to Com-Mine Security. Her son would have done the same: her hunger for the artificial transcendence of her zone implant made sense to him. Like her, he didn't know how to live with his limits.

"Please, Mikka," he breathed. "Vector did the best he could. He said the antimutagen worked. I need you here."

So softly that he barely heard her, she answered, "You don't know what it's like. He isn't your brother. You don't know him the way I do.

"Vector cured him, but he's not all right. Sorus— She hurt him in places I can't reach."

Surrendering to the drag of her weariness, she sank back to the command g-seat. Her hand on the seat back settled her against the cushions. She closed the belts around her again. For a moment she bowed her head: she may have been praying. Then, burdened and slow, her movements clogged with loss, she lifted her hands to the board and began tapping keys like a woman who'd abandoned hope.

Places I can't reach.

Davies didn't think he would be able to put off weeping much longer.

Indications of battle reached *Trumpet* before she found the fringes of the swarm. Emissions on particular wavelengths leaked through the thinning barrier of stones: characteristic spikes of violence registered on the ship's sensors and sifters.

Matter cannon, the scan computer announced across one of Davies' readouts. Two sources, presumably blasting at each other. One delivered fire in concentrated barrages, pausing to recharge between them. The other blazed away less powerfully but more steadily, pouring out a nearly continuous stream of force.

One source—the one firing constantly—appeared closer to the swarm. The other lay more directly in line with *Trumpet*'s heading.

Davies routed everything scan gave him to the displays so that Mikka could follow it with him. But he didn't say anything. She didn't need advice or instructions. After her years with Nick, she knew far more about actual combat than he did.

In any case, he felt too weak to talk. *As far as I can tell, I'm Bryony Hyland's daughter. The one she used to have—before you sold your soul for a zone implant.* Driven by distress, he'd sneered at Morn; but he saw clearly now that he'd been dishonest with her—and with himself. If anyone had offered him a zone implant here, he would have accepted at once, despite all the time he'd spent watching her pay for her decisions.

Mikka herself was too weary to discuss the situation. Mutely they concentrated on their separate responsibilities.

First she slowed *Trumpet*'s pace to a walk. Then she began picking her course forward with extreme care, keeping the gap scout occluded by the largest asteroids she could find. From behind rocks charged with static, *Trumpet* could peek out toward the embattled ships while taking the smallest possible risk that either of them might catch a glimpse of her.

They could hear her already: that was unavoidable. If her scan could see their cannon firing, their dishes could certainly receive her transmissions. But her broadcast and the homing signal still reached outward by bouncing off quantities of stone. For that reason, the combatants might not be able to triangulate on her position.

As *Trumpet* eased past the horizon of each successive asteroid, Davies sharpened his efforts to learn everything he could about those ships.

The same radiant reflection which helped conceal the gap scout prevented him from determining their positions with any precision. Nevertheless the rough angles of the rocks did little to distort other kinds of information: thrust characteristics; energy profiles; emission signatures. Before *Trumpet* reached the last stones she could trust to cover her, stones several times her size, his computer gave him id.

As steadily as he could, he coded the display blips which approximated the locations of the combatants.

One was *Calm Horizons*. An Amnion "defensive" engaged in an act of war. The computer knew her too well to be mistaken.

From where she waited, she covered all *Trumpet*'s conceivable lines of escape.

The other must have been *Punisher*. Her signature matched that of the vessel *Trumpet* had passed when the gap scout had first emerged from forbidden space. If *Trumpet* had been sending out a Class-1 UMCP homing signal all this time, a UMCP cruiser would have had no difficulty following her here.

Scan suggested that *Punisher* was on a course which may have been intended to put her between *Calm Horizons* and *Trumpet*.

Davies couldn't imagine how either of them survived. They both poured out enough destruction to pulverize each other a dozen times over. However, his scan image wasn't yet exact enough to tell him what evasive actions they took—or what condition their sinks and shields were in.

Nevertheless for some reason *Calm Horizons* wasn't using her super-light proton cannon. Even surrounded by reflections and static, the gap scout's instruments could hardly fail to recognize that specific type of emission.

Probably the Amnioni kept her most powerful gun charged and ready so that she could be sure of killing *Trumpet*.

Suddenly Davies found that he couldn't swallow. His mouth was too dry. The pain of his damaged bones had become an incessant throbbing, like a knife in his side. Despite his best efforts to control them, his hands shook on his board.

Bryony Hyland's daughter. Before you sold your soul—

With a touch of her finger, Mikka keyed her intercom. For the first time in nearly two hours, she broke the silence.

"All right, Vector, Ciro—Angus and Morn, if you can hear me. This is it." Fatigue throbbed in her voice, but she seemed to ignore it by an act of will. She was nothing if not a fighter. "We're at the edge of the swarm. And we have two ships in our way. They're going at each other hard. Maybe they're fighting over us. The computer says one of them is UMCP cruiser *Punisher*. The other's our old friend *Calm Horizons*."

She scowled darkly. "At least now we know what we're worth. Apparently war isn't too high a price to pay."

Somehow Warden Dios or Hashi Lebwohl had brought this about. But was it what they wanted? Or had they simply made some terrible miscalculation?

"I can't be sure," Mikka growled, "but I think by now our broadcast is leaking out where it can be heard. It's a good bet both *Punisher* and *Calm Horizons* know what we're doing. Before long they won't be the only ones.

"That's the good news.

"The bad news is, we can't get past them. They have us covered. Unless we want to go all the way back through the swarm," back past the raging hunger of the black hole, "we're stuck here until one of them finishes the other off.

"I guess we'd better hope *Punisher* does the finishing. We still don't know what the damn cops want, but they aren't likely to kill us as fast as the Amnion will."

Tiredly, Mikka silenced the intercom. Without a glance at Davies, she went back to work, looking for ways to improve *Trumpet*'s position which wouldn't expose the gap scout to direct scan from either *Punisher* or *Calm Horizons*.

Shamed by her example, he wrestled for calm. *Bryony Hyland's daughter*, like hell. The woman who'd stayed at her post and died to save her ship would have cringed at the sight of him. There were worse things than zone implants; worse crimes than selling his soul. Being too weak to remember his parents was one of them; too weak to remember what he cared about, or why—

Angus and Morn had saved his life. It was his turn.

Angus had told him once, *You're spending too much time on the guns.*

Concentrate on our defenses. Weapons wouldn't save *Trumpet* now; she couldn't face down a warship in open space. No matter what Hashi Lebwohl had done for her, she didn't have that much firepower.

Davies let his hands shake. Trembling wouldn't kill him. He had more important things to worry about.

Deliberately he checked the dispersion field generator; ran every status and diagnostic check he could find. Then he turned to scan again, searching the discernible spectrum for information he might be able to use.

He nearly cried out when he caught sight of *Soar*.

Like *Calm Horizons*, she was too well-known; the computer couldn't be wrong about her.

She was scarcely forty k away—a trivial distance in space, but still considerable in the fringes of the swarm. In fact, it was possible that she hadn't spotted *Trumpet* yet. Plenty of rock jockeyed and ricocheted in the gap between them. Most of *Trumpet*'s data about her enemy came in by reflection—and there was nothing symmetrical about the way emissions bounced around the stones.

Soar appeared to be limping; maneuvering poorly. But her guns were charged—poised for use.

Shaking feverishly, Davies labeled her blip on the display so that Mikka could see it.

Her jaw sank as she looked at the screen. "Perfect," she muttered to herself. "Fucking perfect."

Even his bones shook. His brain itself seemed to tremble. Unsteadily he asked, "What do you want to do?"

The muscles at the corner of Mikka's jaw knotted. "Get her. Get her now. Before she fixes targ on us."

"We can't." *Bryony Hyland's daughter*. "Too many asteroids in the way." *If we can stand being that ashamed of ourselves*. "We don't have a clear line of fire."

Soar also had no clear line.

"And if we try," he went on urgently, fearfully, "*Calm Horizons*'ll see it. She'll know where we are. Just this much rock won't stop that proton cannon from reaching us."

Mikka turned a glare like a curse on him. "Then what can we do?"

His voice shook like his hands. "If *Calm Horizons* uses her matter cannon, I can keep her from hitting us once. We have a dispersion field—it breaks up that kind of blast. But we can't face a super-light proton beam. We'll have to run."

"Run *where?*" Mikka snapped back.

Davies had no idea. "Anywhere. Out past *Punisher*. Maybe she's on our side. Maybe she'll try to cover us."

"From a proton cannon?" Mikka rasped. "No chance. One good hit, and that gun'll smash both of us."

Nevertheless she bent to her console and began designing hypothetical trajectories, hunting for a viable route through the last rocks; a course which would allow *Trumpet* to emerge from the swarm as much as possible in *Punisher*'s shadow.

The gap scout truly could not fire at *Soar:* scan and targ agreed on that. Too many obstacles. The same stones which protected her also paralyzed her.

But *Soar* must have spotted her by now; *must* have. And Sorus Chatelaine worked for the Amnion. Even if reflection distorted the precision of her instruments, she could transmit what she knew of *Trumpet*'s position to *Calm Horizons*.

Then the Amnioni would be able to triangulate—

What was the lag? A second? Less? How much time did *Trumpet* have before *Soar* talked to *Calm Horizons*? Before the defensive acted on Sorus Chatelaine's information?

"That rock!" Davies croaked suddenly. "The biggest one!" He pointed frantically at the scan display. "Get behind it! Before *Calm Horizons* fires!"

Maybe Mikka understood him. Or maybe she'd already grasped the danger for herself. Hard and fast, she stabbed at the helm keys. Thrust kicked through the ship, roaring like a furnace, as Mikka scrambled for the occlusion of the largest remaining asteroid.

An instant later the Amnioni's proton cannon spoke.

During the space between one nanosecond and the next, the asteroid shrugged, staggered, and transformed itself to scree.

Debris tore at *Trumpet*'s shields like a barrage. When it passed, it left the gap scout exposed to open space; effectively naked in the face of another onslaught.

For a moment Davies couldn't comprehend why *Calm Horizons* didn't fire again immediately. Then he understood. If she turned her other guns away from *Punisher*, the cruiser would smash her. And she needed time to recharge her proton cannon.

A minute? Two?

Trumpet had that much longer to live.

SORUS

It could be done.

The helm first was good; one of the best. Even though the ship had lost a 30° arc of navigational thrust as well as one of her main tubes, he performed miracles with the jets she had left. And her surviving enemies were out of scan range; beyond knowledge. If either *Trumpet* or *Free Lunch* still lived, they weren't near enough to pose a threat. *Soar* would be able to reach the coordinates Milos Taverner had provided; take up the position *Calm Horizons* wanted.

Limping and sputtering, close to ruin, she moved tortuously through the long seethe of the stones like a cripple looking for death.

Sorus Chatelaine had her own ideas about that, but she kept them to herself; hid them in her heart and wrapped silence around them so that they wouldn't show.

Taverner stood in front of her, as uncompromising as a statue. For the time being, he'd finished talking to *Calm Horizons*. Instead of attending to his SCRT, he watched Sorus and the bridge: absorbing everything scan, data, and helm showed on the screens; noting every order Sorus gave. Nevertheless his fingers continued to tap the keys of his odd device as if he were recording a log of what was said and done. Maybe he was preparing the testimony he would present to the Amnion Mind/Union so that his actions could be judged.

Sorus snorted to herself. She was sure that she and her ship would be judged long before the Mind/Union learned what had happened here.

Once again she checked her maintenance status readouts. Some time ago one of the ship's lifts had moved—the one nearest the breached cargo bay. More stress damage? Probably. Like thruster tubes and scan vanes—like Sorus herself—lifts could malfunction or break under enough pressure.

Casually, dishonestly, she asked Taverner, "How does that thing work? It's hard for me to believe you're in instantaneous contact with *Calm Horizons*."

Intervening rock would have baffled any ordinary transmission. According to Taverner, however, his SCRT was far from ordinary. It sent messages back and forth, he'd claimed, *without measurable delay*. And he'd said it had a range of 2.71 light-years.

The way he looked at her suggested that he'd forgotten how to shrug. "It functions by means of crystalline resonance," he answered without inflection. "Do you doubt that I have described its capabilities accurately?"

She shook her head. "You aren't stupid enough to lie to me about it." Not under these conditions. "I'm just—amazed. I didn't know that kind of communication was possible." She may have been looking for an oblique reassurance that *Calm Horizons* was indeed "heavily engaged" by a UMCP cruiser.

To disguise her intentions, she added, "This whole job would have been easier if we'd put one of those boxes aboard *Trumpet*. Then we would have known where she was all the time. We could have forced that poor kid to tell us what she was doing, instead of expecting him to sabotage her."

She was morally certain that Ciro Vasaczk would have tried to carry out her orders, if he'd had the chance. Still she suspected that he'd been betrayed by his own distress. *Trumpet*'s people had noticed his terror and prevented him from doing what she'd instructed.

"That was not possible, Captain Chatelaine," Taverner replied. "Such devices are"—language failed him momentarily—"difficult to produce. *Calm Horizons* could not have supplied us with another, and this one could not be spared."

Apparently he'd taken her comments literally. Very little of his former humanity remained accessible to him.

She was counting on that.

"How're you doing, helm?" she inquired so that the Amnioni wouldn't say anything else. "Is it getting any easier?"

"Not bad, Captain," the man replied, stolid with concentration. "I wouldn't say it's getting easier, but I'm getting better at handling it."

"Do you need rest? I don't want to relieve you, but your second can probably cope if you want a break."

"I'm fine, Captain." He glanced up from his board long enough to meet her gaze, smile faintly. "This isn't easy. I wouldn't wish it on anyone else."

Sorus cocked an eyebrow. Some hint in his eyes, some echo in his voice, gave her the impression that he, too, understood, that she and the woman on scan weren't the only ones who'd begun to hope.

If targ understood as well—

Hiding grimly from Taverner's scrutiny, Sorus turned to scan. "Anything I should know about?"

"It's not clear yet, Captain." Like helm, scan kept her attention fixed on her board. "But we're close enough— I think I'm getting hints of a battle. Some of my readings don't look like static. If *Calm Horizons* and that UMCP warship are firing their matter cannon, maybe what I see are discontinuities leaking into the swarm.

"I'll know in another five minutes."

"*Calm Horizons* and the UMCP warship are firing," Taverner pronounced unnecessarily.

"In that case, targ," Sorus said quietly, "it's time to charge the guns."

The targ first nodded without speaking.

Five minutes. Less?

Yes, less.

"Captain," scan announced abruptly, "that's definitely battle emission. We're almost there. We should reach the fringe of the swarm in" —she tapped keys—"call it twenty minutes. We'll be able to see *Calm Horizons* and the cruiser from there."

If *Trumpet* was alive, maybe they would be able to see her as well.

Sorus touched her intercom; warned her people that they were going back into battle. Taverner wanted her to help *Calm Horizons* against the cruiser. And to help kill *Trumpet*. She intended to show him that she was ready to obey.

"Captain," communications called suddenly, "we're receiving a transmission!"

Memories of Succorso's attack tightened around Sorus' heart. "Source?" she demanded.

Succorso had outplayed her in the swarm. She hadn't forgotten that —and she hadn't forgiven him.

"Can't tell," the woman replied. "There's too much reflection. We're picking up the signal from three or four directions at once."

A transmission from an EVA suit wouldn't bounce. It would be too close—

Sorus let herself breathe for a moment before she asked, "What does it say? Is it coded?"

"For compression, not encryption," communications said. "There's a lot of data here." A moment later she tensed. "Captain, it's from Vector Shaheed! Aboard *Trumpet*."

Taverner turned away from Sorus as if he pivoted on oil, faced communications and the rest of the bridge. His fingers sped on the keys of his SCRT.

So the gap scout had escaped the black hole. Taverner was right. Under other circumstances, Sorus would have hated that. But now it pleased her.

It suited her hopes.

Studying a readout, communications summarized the transmission as her computer decoded it.

"He says he's developed the formula for a mutagen immunity drug." Involuntarily she glanced at Taverner; snatched her gaze back to her board. "My God, the formula's *here*! He *included* it. And a whole series of test designs to prove it works."

Swallowing hard, she concluded, "Captain, *Trumpet* must be trying to get this to VI."

"Triangulate," Milos ordered flatly. He moved to the communications station as if to ensure that he would be obeyed.

"I can't," communications snapped at him. "I already said there's too much reflection."

"Scan," Sorus put in, "is the swarm thin enough for that transmission to leak out?"

The scan first chewed her lip. "Hard to tell, Captain. Are they ahead of us? Behind us? Maybe—"

"This signal," Taverner intoned like a sentence of death, "can be received beyond the swarm. *Calm Horizons* has heard it."

Disaster. The ruin of everything the Amnion had risked by sending *Soar* after the gap scout; by committing *Calm Horizons* to an act of war.

From the communications station, he confronted Sorus again. "Captain Chatelaine, *Trumpet* must be stopped."

"Why?" she sneered. "We can't exactly erase that transmission. It's out there now. You ordered me not to kill her when we had the chance. This whole exercise has been wasted."

He didn't hesitate. *Calm Horizons* had already given him his answer.

"Gap drive implosion," he pronounced passionlessly, "emits electromagnetic static sufficient to disrupt all microwave coherence. The volume of space affected is limited only by the power and hysteresis settings of the drive imploded. Because the static crosses the gap, the area affected is many times greater than the distance a waveform travels in a comparable time.

"When *Trumpet* has been destroyed, *Calm Horizons* will implode her gap drive." If he felt any emotion, his alien voice was unable to show it. "This transmission will be effaced from the Massif-5 system."

Calm Horizons intended to commit suicide.

When she did, Sorus' hopes would die in a burst of inconceivable static.

"You would have been instructed to perform this function," Taverner remarked inflexibly. "Damage deprives *Soar* of any future use to the Amnion. However, your gap drive lacks the necessary power."

Then he repeated heavily, "*Trumpet* must be stopped."

If Sorus didn't act in time, she would lose her only chance.

She met his alien gaze. A harsh smile bared her teeth.

"You heard him, helm," she drawled. "We'd better reach the fringes fast. So we can see."

"Right, Captain," helm replied.

At once unsteady thrust multiplied through the ship, doubling and then tripling *Soar*'s velocity; nudging Sorus back into her g-seat.

"Scan," she continued, "this rock should be thinning out. *Find* that ship. She's still in the swarm somewhere. Otherwise her transmission wouldn't bounce. And if she tried to leave, she would already be dead."

Calm Horizons' super-light proton cannon would see to that.

"I'm on it, Captain," scan acknowledged. She faltered momentarily, then said, "But we've got so much damage— Some of our instruments don't work for shit. The rest aren't adequate. They weren't designed to function alone."

She was offering Sorus an excuse, in case *Soar*'s captain wanted to miss *Trumpet*.

But that wasn't what Sorus wanted. Not at all. On the contrary, she needed to know exactly where *Trumpet* was.

She needed to know immediately.

"Do your best," she ordered. "This is vital. If we don't spot that ship, we won't have anything to hope for."

Are you listening, Taverner? Do you understand?

You would have been instructed to perform this function.

She was sure that he was too alien to understand anything as human as what she had in mind.

"Forget it!" a raw voice barked behind her. "You've got *nothing* to hope for. You fuckers are all *finished!*"

Stung by surprise, *Soar*'s people wheeled their stations. The Amnioni jerked his attention away from Sorus.

Panic and recognition and a kind of cold, absolute rage took hold of her. She turned her head to look past the edge of her g-seat.

Nick Succorso stood in the entrance to the bridge.

Of course.

Scan gasped, "Christ!" No one else made a sound.

Succorso wore a battered, nearly ruined EVA suit, but he'd discarded the helmet. Above his bare teeth, his eyes seemed to cry out like small shrieks of madness. The scars Sorus had given him were as black as gangrene; slashes of rot eating fatally into his face. Despite the barely palpable g of *Soar*'s rotation, he appeared to wobble as if he could hardly stay on his feet.

In his hands he held the biggest laser rifle she'd ever seen. Its muzzle pointed straight at her head.

He may have been almost too weak to stand, but he held his rifle steady.

"You bitch," he rasped, "I'm going to burn your head off."

He looked like he wanted to scream; but his throat couldn't sustain the extremity of his vehemence. He broke into a fit of coughing. The black hole's g may have damaged his lungs.

Between spasms he forced out words.

"Then I'm going—

"—to cut your fucking heart out—

"—and eat it."

His aim still didn't waver.

He must have abandoned his attack on *Soar*'s proton cannon just in time to avoid being caught by the blast when Sorus jettisoned the gun. After that it was easy to guess what he'd done. Impossible to understand—but easy to guess.

He'd reached the relative protection of the breached cargo bay before *Soar* met *Trumpet;* fought *Free Lunch.* Even then he should have died. If nothing else, the energies of all that matter cannon fire should have fried his suit's systems. So he must have cut the airlock wiring and forced his way inside before the battle. Must have found some wall or bulkhead to support him while *Soar* was in the terrible grip of the singularity.

Then he'd worked his way to the bridge, moving slowly, cautiously; trusting that Sorus would be too busy to study her maintenance status readouts.

Cold fury kept her steady. Her people flung mute consternation and alarm at her from all sides, but she ignored them. Concealed from Succorso by the back of her g-seat, she unclipped her impact pistol from her belt, even though she knew she would never be able to raise her gun and fire at him fast enough to prevent him from killing her.

He retched for air.

"Did you think you could beat me?" he demanded. "I'm Nick Succorso. *I'm Nick Succorso!* You can't beat *me*! I could rip—"

Again coughing broke him into fragments.

"—your goddamn ship apart—

"—all by myself.

"I could do it in my *sleep*!"

Helm and targ stared at him as if they were afraid to take their eyes off his rifle. Scan faced Sorus with pleading in her gaze.

Sorus forgot nothing. She forgave nothing. "You're wrong, Succorso," she retorted. "You're asleep now—you're already dreaming." Rage held her hands and arms steady, but her voice shook. "Beating you is easy. It's putting up with you that's hard."

So that he wouldn't fire, she went on quickly, "There's something I should tell you. Before you kill me. I don't know why." She scowled darkly. "Honor among illegals? Or maybe it's just pity."

You fucking sonofabitch—

"You see Milos Taverner?"

—if you think—

"You see that strange box he's carrying?"

—I'm going to—

"It's a detonator."

—let you—

"He's put mutagens in the scrubbers. Mutagen mines. They're airborne. If you breathe, you're finished."

—stop me now—

"If you kill me, he'll set them off. He has to. He can't control the ship without me."

—you didn't learn anything when I cut you.

"Too bad you got rid of your helmet."

Exhaustion must have slowed his brain. He needed a moment to understand her.

Then his face seemed to break open. He wheeled toward the Amnioni with a howl in his throat, turned his rifle—

In that instant she whipped her hand and arm over the back of her g-seat and fired.

Force that could buckle plate steel and powder stone caught him in the center of his chest. He'd already begun to clench the firing stud of his rifle, but her fire kicked him backward, flung his arms up. His laser scored the ceiling for an instant: then he dropped it.

Blood spouted from the hole in his suit. He looked down at the wound. When he raised his head, his features were contorted with grief. A lifetime of hunger underlined his gaze.

Like an accusation, he breathed, "You did this. You did this to me."

Then he toppled.

"Morn—" he sighed as he fell. "God—"

After that he was gone. His blood settled slowly around him, staining his EVA suit.

"Good riddance," Sorus growled to herself. "I should have done that the last time I had the chance."

Around her, her people let out their shock and fear in gasps and curses.

"Captain Chatelaine—" A moment of humanness seemed to overtake Milos Taverner. He had to clear his throat before he could say, "That was well done." Then he added, "It will not be forgotten."

She grimaced her disgust. "It's history. Nothing's changed." Other issues were more important. Raising her head, she told the bridge, "We have work to do. Let's get on it."

She forgot nothing. She forgave nothing.

In a flurry of whispers and keys, her people obeyed. Taverner didn't comment when she put her pistol back in her lap.

Still slowly, despite the best helm could do for her, *Soar* slipped forward.

Sorus resisted an impulse to hold her breath.

Succorso didn't matter to her. He was gone; trivial. Behind her his corpse dripped its last blood into his suit. She cared about other things.

Death or victory were only minutes away; but she was no longer sure that she could tell the difference between them. Maybe there was no difference. Or maybe it didn't matter. Years of excruciating subservience had brought her to this.

Despite the cost, however, her heart was high. Violence and joy seemed to swell in her veins. At last she'd conspired with her doom to bring *Soar* to the edge of her personal abyss. Death or victory. She would be happy with either one.

"Captain," scan reported, "*Calm Horizons* and that cruiser are hitting each other hard. They're *frying* space out there."

Fine. Sorus nodded. Let them.

If Taverner hadn't been watching her, she would have grinned fiercely.

"Swarm's thinning, Captain." The scan first sweated on her keys. "Scan range improving by the second."

Muttering over her board, communications observed, "Shaheed's message must be set for automatic broadcast. It repeats constantly. And it's *loud*. That little ship has one hell of a powerful transmitter."

Sorus nodded again. Fine. Let her.

Death or victory.

"Can you triangulate yet?" she asked.

"I'm trying," communications returned. "Give me two more minutes. I'll find her as soon as I can calculate the reflection vectors."

Taverner turned away from Sorus. "*Calm Horizons* also seeks to triangulate," he stated. "Your coordinates and hers will identify *Trumpet*'s location."

Releasing his grip on the command station, he drifted to communications. Anchoring himself there, he instructed the woman to display everything she could glean about *Trumpet*'s broadcast.

The communications first looked quickly at Sorus.

"Fine," Sorus said aloud. "Let him."

As soon as the data appeared, he entered it on his SCRT.

"Better slow down, helm," Sorus warned while Taverner was too busy to contradict her. "We need to stay in the fringes. That's our cover. If we overshoot it, *Trumpet* might be able to hit us before we spot her."

Or the cruiser might.

"But make sure *Calm Horizons* can see us," she went on. "We don't want her confused about where we are or what we're doing."

Helm nodded. He was working too hard to speak.

A moment passed before Sorus realized that she, too, was nodding. Her head bobbed up and down as if she couldn't stop.

"Ready, targ?" she asked.

"Ready as I'm likely to get, Captain," the man replied, "considering the damage." Considering that Succorso had cost *Soar* her best gun. "Matter cannon charged. Torpedoes primed. Lasers on-line."

Sorus swallowed an impulse to repeat, Fine. Fine.

One k at a time, *Soar* eased into position. Helm did his job perfectly. When she settled to wait and watch, she had a clear view of *Calm Horizons*, but caught only glimpses of the cruiser.

One by one communications identified the reflection vectors for Vector Shaheed's broadcast. They converged on one of the screens, guiding scan—

"Got her!" scan cried suddenly. "That's *Trumpet*. No mistake."

A blip appeared on the screen in front of Sorus.

Like *Soar, Trumpet* waited in the fringes of the swarm, where she could still use a few big asteroids to occlude her from *Calm Horizons*. Was the gap scout also concealing herself from the cruiser? Sorus couldn't tell: the scan image wasn't precise enough to make that detail clear.

"Open fire," Taverner commanded immediately.

"Can't," scan and targ retorted at the same time.

"Too much rock in the way," targ explained. "We don't have a clear line on her."

"Of course," scan followed, "that also means she doesn't have a clear line on us."

The Amnioni didn't argue. The displays made it obvious that scan and targ were telling the truth. Rapidly he tapped new data into his SCRT.

Sorus found that she was nodding again. She had the impression that she'd been holding her breath for some time.

That was important. Nod. Hold her breath. Keep herself under control. Until *Calm Horizons* knew *Trumpet*'s position exactly—until the big defensive attacked the gap scout—any action would be premature; fatal.

Trumpet had set herself behind a substantial piece of rock, obviously hoping to block *Calm Horizons*' fire. The asteroid was four times the size of the gap scout. Was it big enough to protect the ship from a super-light proton blast? Just one?

Yes.

Good.

Sorus wondered how long she would have to hold her breath.

Then she knew.

The defensive's proton gun blazed. Without transition the asteroid shattered, hailing shards like shrapnel at the gap scout.

Trumpet's shields held. She survived.

But now she had no cover. As soon as *Calm Horizons* recharged her cannon, *Trumpet* was finished.

"Captain!" scan called, "the cruiser's increased her rate of fire. Matter cannon, lasers, torpedoes—she's throwing everything she has at *Calm Horizons!*"

Trying to defend *Trumpet*.

Fine.

Now.

Sorus let herself breathe.

"Oh, Milos," she murmured sweetly. "Milos Taverner, you lump of Amnion shit. I have something for you."

Her tone must have touched a nerve in the human residue of his mind; an atavistic instinct for panic. Despite his growing inflexibility, he turned sharply, nearly flung himself around to face her. His fingers danced on his SCRT.

In one motion Sorus swept up her impact pistol and fired straight at his face.

His skull exploded like a smashed melon. Gray brain and greenish blood splashed past the communications station, hit the screens, spread like ruin across the displays. Carried by the blow, he tumbled backward; crumpled against the screens; rebounded drifting in zero g over the bridge stations. More blood formed a streaming green corona around his carcass until it made contact with his shipsuit and skin. Then it stuck to him, prevented from spreading outward by surface tension.

Got you, Sorus panted, you God damn, treacherous, murdering son of a *bitch*!

Her people stared at her. Data and targ looked shocked. Communications seemed to fear that some of Taverner's blood might have touched her. But scan's face shone with savage glee. Helm grinned as if he wanted to start cheering.

In an instant of pressure on the firing stud of her handgun, Sorus had changed everything.

"Now," she announced to the bridge. "This is our chance." She sounded wonderfully calm. "Everything we need to get away from the fucking Amnion is on *Calm Horizons*. All we have to do is help that cruiser beat her. It doesn't matter how many charges the cops are holding against us. If we help them beat an Amnion defensive in human space, we're heroes. At the very least they'll let us salvage anything we need.

"We have until *Calm Horizons* finishes charging her proton cannon. Maybe a minute. Let's not waste it."

Calm Horizons absorbed the cruiser's onslaught too easily. The defensive must have cross-linked her sinks so that she could use them all to bleed off force from the point of impact.

In that case, she was vulnerable on this side.

"Targ," Sorus ordered clearly, "I want you to hit that Amnion bastard. Hit her with everything we've got.

"Hit her *now*."

The man gaped at Sorus for a few seconds. His eyes were full of terror and death.

But then he gulped, "*Yes*, Captain," and his hands sprang at his board.

Yes.

Victory or death.

A moment later Sorus Chatelaine's only hope spread sizzling echoes through the hull as *Soar* opened fire.

MIN

Helpless in one of the support personnel g-seats, Min Donner watched *Punisher* fight her way toward an intersection with the line of fire between the encroaching Amnion defensive and that part of the asteroid swarm where the cruiser's sensors had spotted a kinetic reflection anomaly.

If *Punisher* could reach that intersection in time—if she could put herself between the big defensive and the place where *Trumpet* was most likely to emerge from the rocks—she might be able to give the gap scout enough covering fire to escape.

She still had a long way to go. Twenty-five minutes, according to estimates posted on one of the displays. Too slow. The alien had silenced her proton cannon. Obviously she expected to acquire a new target almost at once. Certainly not twenty-five minutes from now.

Yet even Min Donner, with all her fierceness, her instinct for extreme actions, knew *Punisher* couldn't go any faster. Patrice on helm had to work his board like a madman simply to gain this much velocity without sacrificing the evasive maneuvers which frustrated the Amnioni's cannon—or the rotational thrust which enabled targ to maintain a steady assault. Min feared that if his burdens were increased one iota, he might crack.

Secretly she believed that she herself might have already broken if she were in his place.

The limitations which slowed *Punisher*—which might cause her to fail—were human ones. No ship could outperform the people who ran her.

At the best of times, Min had an uneasy relationship with mortality.

Now she positively hated it. Humankind needed a better defense than the one *Punisher* had provided so far.

Apparently Dolph Ubikwe felt otherwise. If his faults and failings bothered him, he didn't show it. Preternaturally secure in his g-seat, he rode the thrashing cruiser as if nothing could trouble him. His orders were cheerful: his manner, almost merry. At intervals he produced soft, subterranean sounds like tuned groans, as if he were humming to himself.

He might have been a tension sink, absorbing strain and apprehension and bleeding them away so that the people around him could concentrate.

"News, Porson," he rumbled equably as *Punisher* strained ahead. "I want news. I get bored if I'm not inundated with information. Where is *Trumpet*?"

"I can't see her yet, Captain," the scan officer admitted apologetically. "All these vectors—the computer has to collate too many new coordinates with too many different instruments. We're giving it fits. Half my readouts show error alerts.

"Sorry, Captain."

Captain Ubikwe grumbled or hummed. His fingers tapped the edge of his console. "Then what does that damn defensive see?" he countered rhetorically. "How does she know so much more than we do? So what if she has better scan? We've had time to catch up. If she can locate *Trumpet*, why can't we?"

Maybe, Min refused to say aloud, somebody aboard *Trumpet* is talking to that Amnioni. Maybe they've already given her their position. Maybe Nick bloody Succorso is even more treasonous than I thought.

That probably wasn't true. *Punisher* would almost certainly hear any message *Trumpet* sent. No tight-beam transmission could get through all that rock: only a general broadcast would bounce around enough to leak out of the swarm.

Despite the cruiser's distance from the region of the kinetic reflection anomaly, she was fractionally closer to the outer asteroids than the alien was. If anything, she should be able to hear better than her enemy—

Matter cannon fire echoed like scorching in the hull. The sinks gave off a keen, palpable whine, as if they were crying. G kicked the ship from side to side, up and down, around in circles. Spacesickness tugged at the lining of Min's stomach, despite her experience and training.

Out of the confusion, Cray barked, "Captain, I'm picking up a transmission!"

Oh, shit.

Dolph cocked his head. "VI? I hope it's good news. I could use some."

"No, Captain," Cray gulped as she studied her readouts. "Down there."

He opened his mouth lugubriously. "What, from the swarm?"

"Aye, Captain."

He made a show of swallowing his astonishment. "Well, don't keep me in suspense. Who's sending it?"

Cray gaped at her board for a couple of seconds, then wheeled her station to face his.

"Captain, it's from Vector Shaheed." Her voice was hoarse from overuse. "Aboard *Trumpet*."

Dolph steepled his fingers, pursed his mouth. "Maybe," he mused, "that's how our friend out there knows where she is. We'd better look into this.

"What does Dr. Shaheed have to say for himself?"

Cray bent to her readouts again. "He isn't talking to the Amnioni," she reported. "Or he says he isn't. He claims this is a general broadcast. For anyone who can hear him.

"Captain"—she struggled to clear her throat—"he says he's developed a mutagen immunity drug. He says he's been working on it ever since Intertech shut down their research. Now he's succeeded. Then—" Cray's voice failed momentarily. "Then he gives a formula."

A *formula*? Christ! Min knew how the communications officer felt. She had difficulty containing her own amazement.

A mutagen immunity drug, *the* drug, the one Hashi had developed from Vector Shaheed's research. The one Hashi had supplied to Nick Succorso so that Succorso could play Hashi's games with the Amnion.

Trumpet was broadcasting the *formula*?

Cray hadn't paused. As soon as she mastered herself, she explained, "That's just the first part of the message. But all the rest is test designs. To help whoever hears him prove his formula is effective."

Min should have been filled with dismay. Hadn't Warden agreed to suppress Intertech's research for a reason? Hadn't he told her that his survival as the UMCP director depended on his complicity with Holt Fasner? General broadcast! Surely this was a disaster?

But what she felt wasn't dismay: it was an acute, visceral sense of pride. God, this was wonderful! A mutagen immunity formula on *general broadcast*. If Vector Shaheed had thought of this and carried it out all on his own—

No, she didn't believe that. *Trumpet* was too small: with Angus to help him, Nick Succorso could too easily control everyone around him.

There was only one person aboard who might have persuaded Nick or Angus to permit this; only one who'd been trained in the same ethics and responsibility Min herself served—

"After that it all repeats," Cray finished. "Continuous broadcast. I guess *Trumpet* is planning to beam it out as long as she can."

A grin stretched Captain Ubikwe's fleshy mouth. He may actually have been amused.

"Well, we can count on one thing, anyway," he remarked. "Our friend as sure as shit doesn't want to hear *that*.

"My congratulations, Director Donner," he drawled over his shoulder. "When you told me *Trumpet* was headed for a bootleg lab so Dr. Shaheed could do this, I thought you were guessing. Remind me to be more respectful."

Min ignored him; hardly heard him. Her head churned with inferences and concern.

God, had Warden planned for *this*, too? Or were *Trumpet* and all her people completely out of control?

Morn Hyland was aboard. Warden had planned for that. But did he know what she'd become? Did he know what months of zone implant addiction, months of Thermopyle's and Succorso's brutality, had made of her?

Did he know that in spite of everything she was still a cop?

How well did even Hashi Lebwohl understand Nick Succorso? Or his own creation, Angus Thermopyle?

The minute anyone around Massif-5 picked up *Trumpet*'s message, the Amnioni was effectively beaten; checkmated. Even that vessel couldn't go to war with the whole system.

But she could still kill *Trumpet*.

And no one aboard the gap scout deserved to die; not scant minutes after they'd achieved this incredible victory.

"Captain Ubikwe." Min's voice was husky with emotion, but she didn't care. "We aren't fast enough. We need more speed."

He glanced back at her. Humor and darkness glinted in his eyes. "Maybe if you and I get out and push, Director Donner," he commented sardonically, "we can save a couple of minutes."

Before she could retort, however, he turned away. Speaking to the rest of the bridge, he went on more sternly, "I don't think a little extra speed is going to help us. Even if we were at our best, we wouldn't be able to get where we need to go fast enough. But Director Donner is right. *Trumpet* has earned anything we can do for her.

"That Amnioni knows something we don't. Otherwise we would still be dodging proton beams. It's time to get ready.

"Engage laser tracking," he told Glessen on targ. "Program torpedoes. And see if you can find a way to pack more charge into the matter cannon. Brace yourself to fire everything on my order. If we want to cover *Trumpet* and survive the experience, we'd better be serious about it.

"Try to triangulate, Cray," he continued. "Calculate reflection vectors or something. And give Porson anything you get. It would be particularly useful if we could locate that gap scout.

"As for you, Sergei—" Dolph chewed his lower lip for a moment, thinking hard. Then he said, "When I give targ the order, I want you to stop evasive action. That'll make Glessen's job easier. And if we want our friend to concentrate on us, we might as well give her the best target we can."

His people obeyed as if he hadn't just commanded suicide.

He was doing as much as he could: Min knew that. She approved, despite the risk. And yet her whole body burned like her hands to *go faster;* fast enough to fend off *Trumpet*'s doom.

Morn Hyland was a *cop;* a UMCPED ensign. In the performance of her duties, she'd given humankind a staggering gift: an effective defense against the Amnion.

Min Donner couldn't bear the thought of letting her be killed.

"Help me out, Porson," Dolph rumbled. "Where is *Trumpet*? I'll take guesswork if you don't have real data."

"Something—" Porson muttered over his readouts. "Just hints—"

A moment later, however, he said more strongly, "I don't know, Captain. That looks like two ships."

Blips in tentative colors appeared on the scan schematic which showed the relative positions of *Punisher*, the Amnioni, and the seething margin of the swarm.

"*Two?*" Captain Ubikwe demanded.

The scan officer nodded. "But I can't be sure. Unless I'm seeing ghosts, they're keeping themselves occluded.

"One of them must be *Trumpet*. The emission match is pretty close. I just can't tell which one she is."

Dolph flung a look at Min, but she shook her head. If one was *Trumpet*, the other might be the ship which had followed her out of forbidden space. Or the vessel might be Hashi Lebwohl's mercenary. She had no way of knowing.

Her nausea increased. She needed work, activity; something to occupy her mind so that she could forget the distress in her gut. That other ship was a threat. Whoever she was, she would attack *Trumpet* as soon as she got the chance.

"Are they together?" Captain Ubikwe asked Porson.

"From our point of view, Captain, they might as well be. But they're still in the fringes. Using the stones for cover. Stationary, it looks like. Down there that much distance is considerable. There may be enough rock in the way to keep them from scanning each other."

Then the scan officer flinched as he saw new data scrolling down his readouts. "Captain, that other ship— She could be the one we saw coming in from forbidden space. Before we left the Com-Mine belt. Her signature is close, but it doesn't quite match. Could be damage. If she's half-crippled, she might look like that."

Not *Free Lunch*.

Another Amnioni? An illegal working for the Amnion?

God, how had either of them found *Trumpet*?

Dolph's tone took on an edge. "Be ready, Glessen," he warned. "Our friend is going to fire. When we see which target she picks, we'll know which of those two ships is *Trumpet*."

"I've already got her, Captain!" Cray put in excitedly. She assigned a label to one of the blips on the scan display. It indicated that *Trumpet* was the nearer of the two ships—nearer by an insignificant thirty or forty k. "That broadcast can't be coming from the other ship," she explained. "The reflection vectors are wrong."

"Good." He grinned his approval. "Porson," he went on at once, "I can't tell by that schematic. Is *Trumpet* occluded from our friend?"

"Looks like it, Captain," Porson answered.

"Good again. Now—"

Before he could finish, emission numbers along one of the screens flared in new directions. At the same instant the scan display showed a detonation among the rocks of the swarm; a concussion as vehement as a bomb. Hard radiation and brisance globed outward like the effects of a thermonuclear explosion.

The blast wiped *Trumpet*'s blip off the screen as if the gap scout had ceased to exist.

Afire with alarm, Min strained against her belts; fought *Punisher*'s wrenching stagger so that she could see the numbers clearly, understand what they meant.

"Proton cannon!" Porson cried. "The defensive fired! Direct hit! *Trumpet* is—"

Gone. Smashed. No mere gap scout could survive a direct hit by a super-light proton cannon.

But an instant later the scan officer yelled, "No! She's there, I see her! The defensive hit rock!"

Then he called urgently, "Captain, that was *Trumpet*'s cover! She's wide open!"

"Now, Glessen!" Dolph ordered; loud and sharp as breaking granite. "*Everything!*"

Immediately the targ officer leaned his palms onto his board as if he were pushing all his keys at once.

At the same time the cruiser's stumbling rush stabilized as Patrice simplified her maneuvers; pulled her onto a direct heading toward her goal.

Lasers wailed into the dark in coherent streams. *Punisher* lurched as flights of torpedoes blasted from their cradles. The hull-burn of the matter cannon sharpened like screaming as Glessen fed every possible joule of charge to the guns. With every force and weapon she possessed, *Punisher* hammered at the Amnioni, striving at the outer limit of her strength to attack the big defensive so hard that the alien would have no choice except to deal with her, try to beat her, before firing on *Trumpet* again.

It couldn't work. *Punisher* was too far away; lacked the sheer might she needed to coerce reactions from the Amnioni. The defensive had already shown her capacity to withstand continuous matter cannon fire. Lasers could be deflected by glazed surfaces, stymied by shields—or ripped completely apart by the chaotic energies unleashed when matter cannon bursts struck particle sinks. And torpedoes were too slow; limited by thrust to space-normal speeds.

The best *Punisher* could do wouldn't stop the Amnioni.

And *Trumpet* had no more cover. She didn't have time to run. Even at full burn, she couldn't acquire enough velocity to go into tach. Her image on scan shone hot with emissions as her drive roared, hurling her into motion on a line past *Punisher* toward open space; blazing desperately for speed. But she was too late; inevitably too slow: the alien's targ would track her with ease.

As soon as the defensive recharged her proton gun—

Then, without warning, new numbers blazed on the screens: new force vectors streaked the vacuum.

"Jesus!" Porson shouted. "The other ship! The one from forbidden space. She's firing!

"She's firing at the defensive!"

Impossible, it was all impossible, the other ship was an enemy. Yet Min saw the truth on the screens faster than Porson could say it aloud. From out of the swarm the unidentified vessel delivered a massive barrage at the Amnioni.

If the alien warship had cross-linked her sinks in order to handle *Punisher*'s attack, this new onslaught would catch her unprotected; virtually defenseless—

"*More*, Glessen!" Dolph roared like a thruster tube through the din. "Don't let up!"

Punisher's unremitting assault on one side; the stranger's blast on the other—

"She's hit!" Porson called. "She's hurt! The defensive is hurt! We're overloading her sinks! We're starting to get through!"

One hundred eighteen seconds to recharge the proton cannon. Min saw a countdown on the displays; held her breath. Could *Punisher* and the other ship damage the Amnioni fast enough to prevent another blast?

No. The time was nearly gone.

Perched on a torch of thrust, the gap scout scrambled out of the swarm, accelerating at a killing rate. But her escape window would close in eight seconds.

"Do it, you bastard!" Captain Ubikwe raged at the defensive.

Five.

"Save yourself!"

Two. One.

The alien's super-light proton cannon spoke again.

A coruscating flare of emissions bloomed on *Punisher*'s scan as *Trumpet*'s unexpected ally broke open and fell into oblivion. In milliseconds her hulls cracked wide, spuming atmosphere to feed the static of the swarm; her drive imploded, its energies driven in on themselves; released power crackled across the rocks. Bodies and hopes too small to be discerned at this range were flash-burned to powder. A heartbeat later all that remained of her was the residue of destruction.

The Amnioni had saved herself. That made sense. She was hurt; lurching with pain. If she'd fired at the gap scout instead—a moving target rather than a stationary one—she might have missed. Then she might not have lived long enough to know whether *Trumpet* was dead.

And the gap scout's broadcast would reach VI.

But now the small ship had another hundred-eighteen-second window.

It sufficed. Min knew that before Bydell's calculations confirmed it. At this rate of acceleration, *Trumpet* could survive. She would have enough velocity to engage her gap drive effectively in another eighty seconds. And her automatic helm controls were more than adequate to carry her safely out of the Massif-5 system, even if all her people were unconscious.

"Well, *that's* a relief," Captain Ubikwe murmured almost softly. "I must admit, I was starting to worry."

Yet he didn't delay. The Amnioni's proton cannon might be turned on *Punisher* next—especially now that the cruiser was in a better position to cover *Trumpet*.

"Sergei," he instructed promptly, "I think this might be a good time to resume evasive action. Just because our friend is hurt doesn't mean she can't hit us."

No. With an effort, Min straightened herself in her g-seat. No. The defensive had known where *Trumpet* would emerge from the swarm. She might know where *Trumpet* was headed now. And she might have other allies—allies she didn't expect. Hashi's mercenary, *Free Lunch*, remained unaccounted for. That ship might be somewhere in the vicinity, waiting for her chance to strike.

Punisher still had work to do.

"I think, Captain Ubikwe," Min countered, "this might be a good time to get the hell out of here."

He wheeled his station to face her. He may have been about to protest, Get out of here? And leave an Amnion warship running loose in human space? But she didn't give him time to speak.

"*Trumpet* needs us," she pronounced, summoning her full authority. "What you call 'our friend' could decide to go in pursuit. She'll have to do it from a standing start, but she might try it anyway.

"And we haven't seen *Free Lunch* yet. If she's watching all this, she knows *Trumpet*'s alive. She can still try to fulfill her contract.

"This is our chance to get ahead of them both."

Their chance to make sure humankind didn't lose what the gap scout's people had to give.

Fortunately Dolph understood her. He didn't require a time-consuming explanation.

"All right." He nodded decisively. "We'll let VI's gunboats have that defensive. If she sticks around long enough for them to find her.

"Bring us about, Sergei," he ordered. "Let's see if we can catch *Trumpet* before she produces any more surprises."

Patrice didn't hesitate. "Aye, Captain."

Roughly he threw *Punisher* into a turn so hard that Min's vision went gray at the edges, and her heart seemed to falter against her ribs. Nevertheless she kept watching the screens until she saw *Trumpet*'s blip wink out in a characteristic burst of gap emission. The gap scout had gone into tach.

Ten minutes of brutal g and matter cannon fire passed before Cray announced that *Trumpet* had left a Class-1 UMCP homing signal trace behind her.

This is the end of *Chaos and Order*.
The story concludes in
The Gap Into Ruin *This Day All Gods Die*.
